This book is dedicated to my kid brother, Kinley, at the age of four the first to appreciate my stories.

To my twin sister, Wendy, who couldn't understand any of them.

And to my daughter, Helen, a beautiful story herself.

All three gone now, may they rest in peace.

To my lovely family, I say this…the next books are dedicated to you.

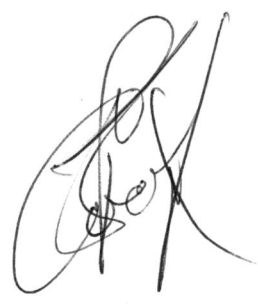

The Gateway

Book One of The Search

Philip J Cook

Published in 2011 by YouWriteOn Publishing

First Edition

British Library C.I.P.

A CIP catalogue record for this title is available from the British Library.

Part One

LIMBO

And his God Spoke.
'Find the key, Zorzecai, and you will have your life returned to you, vastly more powerful than you have ever enjoyed in the past.
Me?
I will have my revenge!
To gain our aims you must follow the plan and kill the boy for he has means to kill me.
Kill the boy and all who follow him.
One is near and is no threat, the others draw close.
To kill them you must let my minions free in the world.
To free my minions you must open the gates.
Any gate is the path for the key.'

One

Just before full light on their fourth morning at sea, the old wizard woke very abruptly when Aidan's blankets dragged across his face. They, and the boy, fell from the bunk above.

'What in God's name are you up to now you...you stupid boy, have you been at my brandy again? I've warned you!' Lord Tragen had spent his entire life waking up irritable and was too old and set in his ways to change his habits, even if he'd thought he needed to.

But then, throwing the blankets aside his stomach flipped—the ship had heeled right over alarmingly and Aidan was looking like a child's rag doll thrown in the corner.

'I haven't touched your bloody brandy, we couldn't find it,' came the muffled answer from the depths of the bedding covering his head.

'You wha-at!'

'I was only joking! Ouch my elbow, ah my head,' complaining and rubbing both unnecessarily harshly Aidan was hoping to cover his gaffe as he surfaced.

He and his best friend, Anders, had been severely punished the last time they had sampled Tragen's cache. It had taken them days to find the case of Gilian even though Aidan had employed a new form of magic to locate it. But both had blamed the wizard for not telling them of its almost lethal potency for they had fallen over in a drunken stupor before their liege lord.

Tragen, infuriated, had whinged at the shame of the two boys vomiting over the Prince of Mantovar's boots. But Aidan suspected that his mentor had been more upset because his spell of illusion had failed to hide the twenty bottles from his apprentice.

Aidan yawning and peering about in the gloom took in his topsy-turvy world. 'Hey, the ship's not supposed to do this, is it?'

The aged wizard glared through sleep-filled eyes. 'Get up quick, boy; of course it's not.'

Tragen swung his long legs over the edge of his bunk and struggled into his second-best green robe. Aidan, trying to extricate his own robe from amongst his tangled blankets, was getting nowhere fast. Tragen, exasperated, pulled the brown garment free of the jumble and threw it at him.

'Come on boy, we're needed now, not tomorrow.' He made for the door grabbing his staff and pushing it securely through his rope belt, the large knuckle at the top settling into its safe haven in the crook of the wizard's neck and shoulder…its normal resting place when not being used. The stave, only five feet long, seemed to gather strength when it was in contact with its master's skin.

Aidan, muttering imprecations against the ship, followed him. Struggling to don his robe and at the same time keep his balance on the heaving deck he stumbled against the bulkhead and again banged the same elbow.

'Ow! Master, don't go so fast will you,' and, as he fell again, it suddenly came to him that this was a very dangerous situation. 'Hey,' he called, very scared, 'are we sinking?'

'Stupid boy, how in God's name am I supposed to know when we're down here?'

The wizard – his long white hair and waist-length white beard all awry – forced himself forward to the crazily tilted doorway ahead of him. He stepped over the storm sill and pushed his way through holding the door ajar for Aidan to come after.

Turning for'ard they stumbled along the short, dark passage to the hatchway ahead of them and, climbing the ladder first, Tragen pushed up the heavy cover. Immediately a great gust of wind wrenched it from his grasp and it crashed to the deck almost smashing its hinges. A gale rushed through nearly blowing them both off the ladder, and a wash of seawater cascaded down over their heads. Tragen, quickly wiping his face with his hand and bending his head against the deluge, grasped the coaming tightly and poked his head up into the nightmarish storm and looked around the upper deck. They had surfaced in the waist of the huge five-masted warship.

Tragen blanched, the quarterdeck – aft of the hatchway – seemed a terribly long distance away in that gale. The wind was blowing the Grim well over to larboard, the rails on that side swamped continually by enormous grey waves. Tragen turned and looked for'ard to the mainmast and saw the outer end of the main yardarm dipping in and out of the heavy seas, its enormous sail trailing half in the water. The bo'sun and the few sailors visible in the atrocious conditions were scrambling all over the mains'l lines wielding axes to cut free the canvas. Others were doing the same at the foremast, but there it proved fatal for one man—he fell into the torrent and was swept along the hull.

Aidan stared at the body floating face down in the violent spume, the man's tarred topknot sticking up incongruously from the top of the otherwise bald, tattooed head.

Tragen held his breath when the boy raised his hand and pointed into the sky above the drowned man.

'What is it?' he asked.

'He was lost, so I showed him the way.'

The old wizard breathed deeply to disperse the lump in his throat, he could never get used to the way Aidan communicated with the dead—he'd never ever come across anyone before with the same inexplicable ability.

'Come on, my boy,' he smiled nervously as he heaved the hatch closed, 'hang on to my belt. Let's find the captain.'

They waited for a wave that was not quite so threatening and fought their way aft. Climbing the ladder onto the quarterdeck, his long wet robe sticking to his body and Aidan dragging heavily on his belt, Tragen eventually found his friend, one of two huge men in the darkness ahead of them.

Hugo Locklear, master of the Grim, the largest sailing ship in the known world, and its chief helmsman, Talbot, were desperately grappling one of the wheels of the two-wheel steering chain controlling the rudder.

Tragen and Aidan groped their way to the helm. With Aidan's hands still clinging to his belt, Tragen grabbed the second wheel to add his weight to that of the seamen.

Locklear, whose long black hair and full beard were dripping like a river, greeted them with a quick grimace. 'Welcome!'

'When did this start?' the wizard asked.

'Less than half an hour ago,' the captain replied, leaning across to shout into Tragen's ear. 'A normal blow at first, or so I thought, but only the Gods' know what happened then. The wind veered suddenly and came at us straight out of the east and we nearly broached. I had given the order to furl the sails when something went wrong on the main and fore, the sheets tangled, I've never known that happen before,' he paused, breathing deeply. 'I have also never known a wind increase as this has done. If we don't get that mains'l free soon, we won't be able to hold her, we have to turn her head on. Did you see how they were doing?' With his very broad shoulders now bunching with the severe strain, Locklear was living up to his nickname of "the Bear".

9

'I did, the sail has almost been cut free but it's trailing in the water, pulling us over.'

'Damn, we need that sail we have no other.'

The wizard, as tall as his friend, despite his great age was remarkably strong and his hold never wavered on the wheel. Aidan, standing at his side holding on for dear life, was only a young man fifteen years old. He was short and lean, dark and wiry, his own particular strengths more psychological than physical. Aidan inclined his head towards Locklear but could barely hear the captain's next words over the clamour of the storm.

'Tragen, I'm worried. The stress on the helm is unbelievable I'm afraid it'll fail and we'll lose the rudder. If that happens we'll broach and we'll all be lost. Is there any way you can help?'

The wizard wiped water from his eyes and stared at the pillar between the wheels for long moments. Making a decision he pushed his arm through the spokes and placed his hand on the central hub. 'I can feel it, Hugo,' he shouted in his friend's ear, 'the chains are almost at breaking point. I'll keep my hand here and direct power into the helm to strengthen it. But we have a problem…no spell created in a tempest of this ferocity will last for long I'll need to continually renew it. This I can do but I won't be able to give you aid on the wheel.'

'Master, be careful, if the wheel slips it'll take your arm off,' Aidan warned.

'Boy, I'll make sure that doesn't happen,' said Locklear. 'You make your way to the bo'sun and inform him that my orders are to save the sail. He is only to abandon it if the ship heels over farther. Tell him to send another man up here immediately to help at the helm and I will try and give him another hour. We need that sail after this storm, boy, emphasize that.'

Aidan's stomach clenched, mortally afraid he nearly lost control of his bladder, the thought of crossing the decks to the mainmast on his own in this weather turned his legs to jelly. He licked his lips nervously and glanced at Tragen, he couldn't refuse, could never allow his master to see his cowardice.

The wizard returned Aidan's gaze, his fear showing in his surprisingly young, grey eyes. He debated going himself and leaving Aidan here to strengthen the helm, but knew he could not. The boy was simply not strong enough to sustain the spell for any length of time.

'Do you understand why I cannot go instead of you?'

Aidan nodded and smiled faintly. 'Aye, I know...you're too old,' the reply automatic, he was forever poking fun of Tragen's age. 'I'd better find you at this wheel when I return. I don't want you doing anything heroic without me here to help.'

Trembling with fear, Aidan released his grasp on Tragen's belt and dropped to the deck, he slid across the boards to the larboard rail of the quarterdeck before the next wave swamped them.

Aidan descended into the waist banging his ankle painfully on the bottom step of the ladder when he slipped. Gripping tightly with one hand he bent down and rubbed the soreness away, cursing all the while. Straightening, he glanced along the ship, quaking at the melee that met his eyes at the mast he swallowed bile rising in his gullet. He studied the starboard rail above him, tension starting a headache, he slid and slithered his way up to it. Clinging desperately to the slick timber he dragged himself for'ard, almost blinded by the torrential rain stinging his face.

The sky was nearly as black as night although it was only getting on towards mid-morning. It wasn't long, though, before he was in dire straits, his arms and his shoulders aching and his feet frantically scrabbling for a purchase on the heaving wet boards. He tried to ignore the thunder crashing above the wailing of the wind, the reverberations echoing in his head, the distraction threatening his progress, slowing him down.

He was terrified of sliding into the sea almost directly below him, his headway unavoidably sluggish and erratic. He yelped with the pain of instantly bloody fingers where rapidly forming blisters burst. In the swiftly lowering light he glimpsed the fore-hatch just for'ard of the mainmast. Coming up level with it he released his grip on the rail and slid down to relative safety.

He lay for a while gasping against the wooden coaming, easing the soreness in his arms and shoulders, recovering his strength as he sucked the broken skin on his hands. He moaned and swore under his breath using language that Anders would have been proud of.

He sat up and looked aft at the chaos surrounding the mast. Jason, bo'sun's mate and ship's minstrel was lying along the larboard yardarm with his legs in the ocean, using an axe to hack through the iron hard ropes. Others were securing lines flying loose in the gale and yet more were tugging free heavy wet canvas where it had become snagged.

11

Aidan, wiping the rain from his eyes, searched for the bo'sun quickly and espied the man at the foot of the mast. His shout failing to attract his attention in the screeching wind, he waved his arms in an effort to draw the man's eye and again failed.

But he did attract the unwelcome attention of Leash. The tall, dark-haired sailor standing the other side of the bo'sun saw the boy gesticulating and, recognizing Aidan, he watched him through lidded eyes, saying nothing. But inwardly he gloated. Four days at sea and finally an opportunity had arisen to kill the boy.

Between Aidan and his destination was a short open space with a clear drop to the ocean racing away below. Aidan sought for a way to get across the gap and glimpsed a rope hanging free from the main shrouds. He bided his time until a very strong gust brought the line to him and, clutching it desperately, he held it tight against his chest while he plucked up courage to leave the safety of the hatchway.

Leash perceived immediately the boy's intention; he turned his head and scrutinized those working around him. None were looking his way, all frantically busy. His eyes flashed red and he smiled at the prospect of dealing a mortal blow to his enemy, he raised his axe.

With his heart in his mouth Aidan tugged the line to ensure it was secure. Satisfied, he lunged for the mast tearing the hem of his robe on the hatch bars at the same time. But moments after his feet left the deck he felt the rope running loose above him and he was slipping towards the ocean and oblivion. Closing his eyes he waited for the water to engulf him knowing there was no way he would regain the surface alive if he went under.

Leash rejoiced, the boy's dying would devastate the wizard and he had hacked at the other end of the rope. Smirking, he watched the boy plummeting to his death.

But Aidan was lucky. From the corner of his eye Trumper, the bo'sun, had glimpsed the line spring taut and then run free. Peering quickly through the dimness he glimpsed a body hurtling towards and then past him. He made a grab for the boy and pulled him into his arms.

Aidan opened his terrified eyes, blinked and swore profusely at the same time thanking all the Gods, and especially the bo'sun as he clung to him like a limpet.

'Lad, what are you doing here?' Trumper shouted disentangling himself with great difficulty from the boy's embrace, neither of them noticing the abject disappointment on Leash's face.

12

'I have orders for you,' panted Aidan, hardly believing he was still alive. Then, as he heard the snap of a line giving way and the rush of canvas across the deck he repeated Locklear's orders quickly.

Morgan Trumper, a stocky man with a red face and an extremely loud voice, pushed Aidan nearer to the mast so the boy could hold himself safe and then turned to Leash, the ship's second helmsman.

'Move it, Leash. Go like the devils of hell are after you, the captain needs you on your job.'

Bellowing, he ordered those men working nearby to secure the sail as it fell free. Quailing, they set to with the backbreaking job of dragging half the sail from the ocean. But it wasn't long before they realized the job was too much even for their combined strength.

'We can't do it Bo'sun, the sail is saturated, it's too heavy,' shouted Jason.

'We've no choice, get your backs into it,' Trumper ordered, his own back breaking with the strain.

But then Aidan had an idea and leaning over he gripped an edge of the sail and chanted. And as the chant strengthened droplets of water appeared on the surface of the canvas and rolled away leaving the fabric beneath as dry as a sunburned deck.

Trumper, Jason and the others looked on astounded until Aidan shouted. 'Go on drag it now, its lighter I've used a water-repellent spell, but it won't last long in this rain.'

Trumper grinned. 'Come on, you horrible lot, or are you going to deprive a young lad of his glory.'

With that the seamen accomplished the almost impossible task whilst avoiding swinging pulley blocks heavy enough to kill. As the last of the lines parted, the sail's vast bulk was finally hauled inboard and the yardarm lifted from the water.

However, the Grim still heeled over abeam although by not nearly as much.

Trumper turned to Aidan. The bo'sun had, of course, seen the boy many times around the ship, usually in the company of the cabin boy when, nine times out of ten, mischief was usually the outcome of their reckless behaviour. He had on several occasions lost his temper with both of them, promising a severe beating if they didn't behave.

'Aidan,' he shouted over the gale, 'you've surprised me. I've always thought you a festering carbuncle on the hull of this ship. But struggling here as you have and then helping us drag the sail from the sea has proved me wrong about you. Anyone who can exhibit that sort of bravery and think as quickly as you did can count me a friend.'

Aidan amazed, stared at him with eyes wide in disbelief. 'Well, I don't know about bravery, Bo'sun, but if the captain ever wants me to do anything like this again he can go jump in the bilges—I'll be hiding.' And Aidan trembled as he clung closer than an abscess to the teak mast.

Trumper laughed deeply. 'You'll do boy, but take a bit of advice—never let the captain hear you voicing that sentiment, it smells of mutiny and he'll clap you in the brig before you take another breath. But the Grim owes you. Now go, and on your way change your clothing, robes are not for storms. I don't wish to repay the debt by pulling you out of the sea today. But tell me first, that was a very unusual spell for this weather. Why didn't you just heat the canvas and boil the water off?'

Aidan stared for a moment at the man who had often threatened to use the cat-o'-nine-tails on him, and he decided not to come out with another smart retort. 'I'm not supposed to use those spells without permission,' and he mumbled quietly. 'I might have used too much.'

'What?'

'I might have burned the sail,' he shouted sheepishly.

On the way to his cabin he resumed his moaning and groaning, the pain in his back and legs almost taking his mind from the violence of the storm.

On the quarterdeck, the four men straining at the wheel instantly felt their task ease as the ship righted. They sensed the rudder and keel resume their proper places, once again fully immersed in the ocean.

Tragen looked to the man alongside him. Leash had arrived eventually, but steadying the helm had not seemed to get any easier with his help. He could not actually see the man malingering but he suspected it, the seaman's sullenness not endearing him at all to the wizard.

Tragen frowned; he had seen Leash somewhere else before coming on this voyage but just couldn't place where. Leash was an enigma, a man who gave the appearance of being a landsman perfectly at home at sea. And yet he had no friends, no close acquaintances among the crew. He was a seaman alone amidst the two hundred or so sailors and two hundred marines that formed the complement of the

Grim. Even so, Tragen felt drawn to the man, fascinated as a fly is mesmerized by the spider that has trapped it.

When the old wizard looked away, Leash, his lithe frame dripping water, his unruly brown hair plastered to his face, glanced at him with complete and utter loathing. He took a swift peek at the wizard's staff held snugly in the sorcerer's belt. Shuddering uncontrollably, Leash remembered the power of that stave having been a witness to its devastating effects years before—and he was petrified of being in its presence. His lack of effort was not because of total indolence; his fear totally consumed him, denying thought for anything else.

'Are we right now Tragen? Is it safe to remove your arm?

'Aye, my friend,' and Tragen drew his arm from between the spokes and gripped the wheel alongside Leash.

'Now my boys we turn head to windward and we do it very cautiously,' roared Locklear. 'Wait for my word and then a last effort from you all, please!'

The wind had not ceased howling since the storm's onset, it setting everyone's teeth on edge. The thunder continued to roll and crash and the lightning to flash, robbing every one of their sight the moment it left the heavens. With ears ringing, the rain beating on men and decks both, the captain and his three companions fought to bring the wheel up inch by slow inch, turning the bows into the wind. A painstaking task, it seemed to take forever but with muscles bulging, backs and legs straining, an hour later they had brought the ship around.

The monstrous waves that had previously inundated the ship from abeam threatening annihilation, now rolled beneath the keel from bows to stern, giving a more normal motion to the vessel. The very high waves still broke over the bows and water continued to flow through the scuppers like rivers back into the ocean, but the crew now breathed a little easier as the danger of imminent sinking receded.

Hopper, the ship's first mate, brought men with him to the quarterdeck and they relieved the exhausted men at the helm. Talbot immediately dropped to the deck and sat with his back against the starboard rail his head bowed taking deep breaths. Leash slid down just along from him watching his arch enemy, his eyes again flashing strangely red until he'd regained control of his nerves.

Tragen gazed at the chaotic state of the ship and groaning he stretched his weary back. His hands clutching the rail, his knees bending in time with the heaving deck, he peered at the mains'l now lying in a heap at the foot of the mainmast—and promptly remembered Aidan.

'Where's my boy got to Hopper, have you seen him?' Tragen asked agitatedly of the Grim's second in command, grabbing his elbow and interrupting the mate's reporting to his captain on the unhappy state of the ship.

Wearily Hopper glanced from his captain. 'Your boy?   I haven't seen Aidan at all today.'

Tragen paled. 'But you must have passed him as you came up here; he was with the bo'sun at the mainmast. You were working at the foremast weren't you?'

'Aye, Milord, I was and I spoke with Trumper on my way here. I didn't see any sign of Aidan.'

Seriously worried, Tragen fought his way back to the for'ard rail and searched the ship ahead of him in the darkness.

'I'll never reach him in this weather,' Tragen muttered, knowing he had no other option but to attempt it.

Jamming his body into the larboard corner of the quarterdeck, he removed his staff from his belt and held it in front of him in both hands. The stave tapering to a needle sharp barb at its base – a spike that was used for more purposes than just magic – he braced firmly on the deck. The large knuckle of indeterminate form at the top of the staff – moulded by the heat of his hands – he placed beneath his chin.

Leash watching him, tensed, his mouth involuntarily twisting into a snarl as his eyes once more glared red. He was scared witless at the magician invoking the power in his staff.

Tragen calmed himself, endeavouring to ignore the wind blowing at his robe, tugging viciously at his hips and legs, striving to make him fall. He closed his eyes, opened his mind and delved the ether in search of Aidan's young mind.

The mindmeld was a very old tool of the magician, possibly the oldest, and it could not be acquired as lore could be learned. Some in the wizarding world, those who could not communicate with their minds, contented themselves by becoming adepts in disciplines that did not require them to converse silently.

But Aidan had the aptitude and had used it frequently to survive as an orphan of the streets in his hometown of Miskim. Tragen, discovering him there, had taken the urchin in hand. And while attempting to instil in him the correct moral virtues of a decent

16

young wizard, and at the same time teaching him the different methods of controlling magic, he had discovered another overwhelming talent in the boy.

Correct behaviour incumbent on a young aristocrat – a station in life awarded to all wizards – was still a long way from realization in the hyper-active young man. But Aidan's special talent begged forgiveness for his misdemeanours. And, of course, the threat of Tragen's retribution quite often curtailed the youngster's antics.

Tragen suffered a severe battering by the storm as he mindmelded for his apprentice. The screeching of the wind invading his thoughts, the biting rain in his face and the violent motion of the ship inevitably distracted him and ensured his failure. He could not maintain his concentration in the midst of nature's tirade.

He opened his eyes and looked ahead hoping for a glimpse of Aidan in the darkness, despair creeping up on him unawares at no sign of him. He closed his eyes for a second attempt, steadied himself, and calling up more power from his staff he again probed the airways.

And this time he connected—with something totally unforeseen. Tragen rocked on his feet. Opening his eyes he came back to himself feeling a terrible premonition take hold. He lifted his chin from the knuckle of the staff and full of trepidation he turned and stared white-faced at Locklear.

'My friend, what ails you?' Locklear asked, startled.

'We need to talk and talk now.' He steered the big man to the rear of the quarterdeck and sheltering below the overhanging poop, he whispered. 'Let us go to your cabin, this is for your ears alone.'

'Tragen, I cannot possibly leave my quarterdeck in this storm!'

'You must, Hugo, you must come with me,' whispered the wizard vehemently.

'I will not leave my quarterdeck in bad weather, Tragen.'

'Hugo,' he drew himself up to his full height, 'Hugo, someone evil is attempting to ensnare the Grim! We must talk.'

Locklear, startled, stared intently at the friend he'd implicitly trusted all his life.

'Hopper, remain here until I return. I won't be long,' he said, vexed by Tragen's stricken face.

'Aye, aye sir…I'll set the lifelines now.'

Locklear nodded his agreement, and he and the wizard withdrew, making their way down the aft companionway to the master's cabin abaft and below the quarterdeck.

Leash, relaxing now that the wizard's staff was leaving his immediate vicinity, watched them departing. He smiled slyly, his bloodshot eyes returning to normal, his snarl disappearing. Seeing the wizard troubled made him very happy.

The fact that the very powerful wizard was obviously deeply distressed in the midst of the worst storm he had ever encountered, worried Leash not at all.

Two

Aidan was fed up to the back teeth. He was cold, drenched to the skin, exhausted and he ached from head to toe. He had spent all morning in darkness being hammered by the storm, with occasional sightings of a horrendous sea below him trying its damnedest to drown him. And, although his errand had been completed, he was still very frightened.

He missed the reassuring presence of Tragen and yearned to get back to him, he'd always felt safe when the old wizard was near. When danger threatened, or insecurity and depression set in, Aidan always made a bee-line for his mentor and stuck to him like glue. He needed Tragen. He knew in his bones that nothing bad would happen to him with the sorcerer close by.

The relentless, brutal motion of the ship continued to cause him harm. Besides the knocks bruising every bone in his body, the sound of the wind moaning through the rigging inflicted a very odd light-headedness and his soaking wet, woollen robe chafed his legs and neck. Though the ship was no longer leaning right over, there was still a corkscrewing of the vessel and he felt sick every time he looked up at the mastheads swaying across the sky. The ship had not yet been turned into the wind and he prayed for it fervently.

'Come on, Master, turn this bloody thing quick or I'm going to throw up everywhere.' He often talked to himself when he was scared and he was always anxious when alone. 'I know, I know, I'm not a baby, I shouldn't whine like this, but if you had my stomach you'd feel the same.'

He rested in the lee of casks that had somehow not broken free of their lashings. And as he stared out over the rail at the high grey water racing along the hull his earliest memories came flooding back. He'd heard that drowning men saw their life rushing past their eyes just before they succumbed and crossed over. Did this mean he was about to die? He smiled determinedly—there was no way he was going to die yet, not without knowing that Tragen was safe.

A sudden dousing by a heavy grey wave recalled him to the Grim and his immediate danger, forcing him to put his recollections to the back of his mind. He struggled to his feet again and reached the after hatchway, waiting for another very menacing gust of wind to disperse before raising the cover. Crouching, he flung his leg over the coaming, stepping onto the top rung of the ladder he brought in his other leg quickly. He lowered his hunched body into shelter, slamming closed the hatch above him, shutting out much of the noise and the little light that remained behind the ever-darkening clouds.

He started down the ladder rapidly in the blackness and abruptly halted as he stepped on something soft. The hand, jerked from beneath his foot, was accompanied by one almighty yell. Aidan panicked and because his hands were cold, wet and blistered and he was feeling very alone, he lost his grip. He fell, landing on the body of the owner of the hand who bawled for a second time.

Aidan banged his head once again. 'Ow! No more, I've had enough,' he exclaimed, holding his head in his hands. 'Who in hell are you!' he shouted into the darkness. 'You've no right to be on that bloody ladder when I'm coming down. Didn't you see me opening the hatch?'

'No, I didn't, all right! Not until it was too late! You clumsy idiot, how was I to know you'd come down as I'm climbing up? It's dark down here I can't see a thing! The first I know the wind is trying to blow me off the ladder and then some fool standing on my fingers. You came down too fast for me to do anything! Couldn't you have looked first...get off me!' He pushed Aidan roughly to one side, resulting in another bashed elbow for the wizard's apprentice.

'Okay, Anders, okay. Calm down, I can't see anything either.' Aidan said, relieved at recognizing the voice of his best friend, Hugo Locklear's cabin boy and nephew.

He and Anders had become virtually inseparable since their first meeting, ten years before, when they had played with a model boat. The only time that they were apart now was when the occasional voyage on a real boat interfered with their lives. This was one of the few cruises they'd ever shared.

Anders was big with long blond hair. A lot taller and broader than Aidan, he was also more prudent. Aidan was impetuous and a risk taker, although Tragen called his behaviour crass stupidity. Nevertheless, the young wizard was a natural leader, daring, with a sense of humour that was sometimes beyond his friend's reckoning. But his status as a wizard's apprentice accorded him a certain respect in Anders' eyes, though this deference did not stretch to being landed on, in the pitch dark, on a ship rolling like mad on the seas.

'Aidan? Where've you been, I've been looking everywhere for you?'

'Didn't you think to look up top? Ooh! I'm hurting all over,' he moaned.

'Where the hell do you think I was going when you so kindly trod on me?' Anders snapped, clutching his own fingers tightly to try and stop the pain.

'All right...all right, forget it! I'm sorry, let's get to my cabin I have to change out of this robe before going back up on the quarterdeck.' Aidan rose gingerly from the floor and leaning against the bulkhead waited for Anders to regain his feet.

'Where's your lantern, Anders?'

'Are you mad? How the hell could I carry a lantern with the ship dancing about like this? It's safer without one; you want me responsible for starting a fire in this weather? Don't forget these timbers are impregnated with tar.

'Okay...okay! Let's get to the cabin,' Aidan said, more cheerful now that he had company, 'we'll find a lantern there somewhere.'

'What were you doing coming in that way if you were on the quarterdeck, that's the wrong end?'

'I was at the helm with Tragen when the Bear ordered me to the bo'sun at the mainmast. I had to leave Tragen up there. I hope he's all right, I haven't seen him for ages.'

'Who, the Bear or Tragen?' asked Anders, knowing who Aidan meant but unable to resist teasing him. Aidan only ever worried about Tragen.

Aidan chose to ignore him and as they arrived at the door of his cabin they heard loud female voices from farther along the passage. And Aidan recalled the other passengers.

'Hell, I forgot about them and I wouldn't mind betting Tragen has as well. Come on, hurry up, when I've changed we'd better see if they need us.'

'They're all right, I've just left them. They're the ones who sent me to the Bear...they wanted to know what was happening. I was hoping to find you first'

'Oh yeah! And what were you doing down here with them?' asked Aidan, smirking in the darkness. 'Which young lady were you more concerned about?'

'It wasn't like that,' said Anders blushing, thankful he couldn't be seen. 'I have strict orders, if anything seems untoward and the captain isn't around, I am to place myself at their disposal. You know that, so stop messing about!'

Laughing, Aidan pushed his door open and they both entered an even blacker hole. 'Help me search for the lantern, I want to get my britches on instead of this robe, it's rubbing me raw. We'll go along anyway and see what all that noise is about.'

Anders eventually found the lantern tipped on its side on the bottom bunk. He lifted it and shook the well. 'There's only a drop of oil left in it, the rest has leaked into the blankets. Oh well, all we need now is a flame to light the thing.'

'Hang on I can light it,' Aidan said as he put all thoughts of the girls to the back of his mind.

'Whoa, are you sure? We can't afford an accident in here,' Anders, all of a sudden, was very nervous.

'Hey, show a bit of faith, I've made fire hundreds of times, haven't I? Now, hold it still man, I don't want to burn you.'

'How can I hold it still with this ship jumping around?'

Nevertheless, Anders held the lantern chest high between them. Only the groaning of ship's timbers undergoing enormous stress, and the muted wailing of the storm was audible at first. Then a moment later a low murmur grew which shut out all external noise. Aidan gently sang the chant.

Anders liked this spell; it always gave him a pleasantly warm feeling starting in the pit of his stomach. It made him think of summers spent in the meadows along the river bank outside the castle of Mantovar. He pictured his family and without warning homesickness was a heavy lump in his chest. He loved being the cabin boy on the Grim and was very fond of his uncle, Hugo Locklear, but he did miss his father and mother and even missed quarrelling with his brothers.

The ship lurched and threw his shoulder against the top bunk, jarring him.

'Keep still, Anders,' warned Aidan, biting his bottom lip.

'Sorry!' Anders broke into a cold sweat, he'd seen too many of the young wizard's spells go awry.

Gradually the darkness lightened and as visibility increased so Anders breathed again. Fascinated, he saw Aidan standing in front of him with his left arm outstretched, in the palm of his hand a small flame flickered. Anders glanced at his friend's face and watched his lips moving. Witnessing Aidan make magic always gave Anders goose pimples, and such was the case now.

'Come on, open the glass, I can't hold this forever.'

Anders complied and the wick ignited, giving a bright white light. Aidan withdrew his hand preparing to extinguish the small flame. They were both completely unready for what happened next.

It was this very moment the four men on the quarterdeck turned the ship into the wind. It couldn't have come at a worse time. Aidan stumbled forwards and Anders instinctively pushed him away from the lantern to keep it safe.

The wizard's apprentice scrabbled frantically to grab hold of the top bunk, missed and, falling after it, he dropped the flame on the bed beneath. The spilled oil ignited. Aidan rolled from the flames and landed on the floor. Anders, moving abnormally fast for him, dropped the lantern on the deck, and grabbed Aidan's blankets from where they had fallen earlier that morning in the corner of the cabin. He threw them onto the blaze and dropping on top of them, he smothered the flames. Luckily, the lantern remained upright, but it slid rather inconveniently against Aidan's leg and he gave another agonizing moan as the hot glass burnt his shin—and there was another scream from along the passage.

'What the hell's happening to me today? Why did I get out of bed?' Aidan groaned as he handed the lantern up to Anders. 'Oh aye, that's right I had no choice did I? I fell out of bed because this bloody ship decided to fall over. And what's that racket all about?'

Aidan stood up and surveyed the carnage around him. The bottom bunk now had a dirty great hole burned in it; wisps of smoke were floating about in the air, acrid and stinging. There was a pile of smouldering blankets alongside Anders who was striving to control his shattered nerves. He was sitting on the edge of the bunk with his eyebrows and hair singed and his face and clothes covered in smuts. Aidan laughed and looked down at himself and saw the self-same smuts covering his own drenched and torn robe.

'I might as well throw this away,' he said, pulling bits of soot off his chest. And then the full significance of what he was seeing hit him fair and square between the eyes. 'Oh, my God, when Tragen sees his bed I'm dead!'

There was another scream, an angry female voice complaining her words at this distance indistinct. They stared at each other a moment and then scrambled up and rushed for the door, colliding in the doorway, they made for the cabins aft and all the noise. Anders held his lantern aloft at the entrance to Princess Augusta's cabin.

You could tell at a glance this was a rich person's berth. The room was relatively spacious, had only one cot and something unheard of in the lesser cabins, its own bathing facilities on a dresser in the far corner. On normal days, the berth would catch the daylight and cooling sea-breezes through the open porthole. Now, though, the cabin was dark and very wet.

Two girls in their middle teens were struggling to close the porthole, and at the same time trying to avoid the foaming water washing through it.

Aidan burst out laughing at the black-haired girl, her arms at full stretch, groping to find the clips and at the same time bending her head away in a vain attempt to avoid the inundation.

'Pull it harder will you? It's nearly closed.' Augusta shouted in temper.

'I'm pulling as hard as I can, it's your clip…you've jammed it. Why you opened it I'll never know,' Beatrix retorted, blowing her blonde hair out of her mouth.

'I didn't know half the ocean would pour in, did I? Release yours a bit for me to shift mine, you silly girl, how can I move the damned clip if you're holding it tight?' It was then she heard Aidan laughing behind her and turning, Princess Augusta glared at the two scruffy boys standing in her doorway.

Anders caught the baleful glint in her eye and gave Aidan a hefty nudge in his side to silence him.

'Not you again?' Augusta said icily. The mutual animosity of the heir to the principality of Mantovar and the apprentice wizard reared its ugly head once again. 'Well churl? What are you finding so amusing?'

Aidan kneading the ache from his side ceased laughing. His prince's daughter usually vented her spleen in his direction with the result that nine times out of ten he ended up being reprimanded for upsetting her. But seeing water dripping from the end of her nose reminded him of the nosebleed he'd once inflicted on her and he had a twinge of conscience.

'I apologize, Highness; I've had a bad day. Here let us shut it for you.'

He and Anders strode into the cabin and Beatrix moved away from the open porthole, glad to be out of the direct line of the water. The two boys managed the clips easily although Aidan got another soaking; not that it mattered he'd had the sea thrown at him all day.

Aidan turned to Augusta wondering if she'd thank him this time, not that she ever had in the past. He stood just in from the doorway staring at her, waiting for any sign of gratitude.

'Well churl! Why are you standing there? You may go now,' her eyes flashed angrily.

Anders' lantern, held up by Beatrix, illumined not only the cabin, but also the scowl on Aidan's face.

'All right, Anders, thank you for helping me to close the lady's porthole, very kind of you,' he said sarcastically. 'I think we should go now.'

'Thank you, Miss,' Anders said, taking the lantern from Beattie's hand, accidentally touching her fingers as he did so.

Beatrix replied softly, her eyes lowered as her face reddened. 'Thank you for your help, Master Anders.'

Anders paused, her unusual reaction startling him. He didn't know that over the years Beatrix's thoughts had turned many times to the handsome, tall, blond boy who hung around with the young wizard. He nodded and touched his forelock and wondered why the object of his daydreams was blushing. He glanced at Aidan and pulled him away, turning they made to leave the room.

As they did, a short, fat lady came bursting through exclaiming at the top of her voice. 'What is amiss? What is all this noise? Why is this boat never still? Ah! What are these boys doing in here?' The scandalized lady, not stopping for breath went on shouting. 'Get out, get out, you should not...'

And saying this, she caught her toes in the torn hem of Aidan's robe and fell forward, taking the apprentice down with her. All heard a mighty crack as the lady's ankle snapped. Screaming in Aidan's ear, she promptly fainted.

Everyone stopped breathing; time stood still, no-one made a sound; they looked at each other, stunned. Aidan was the first to recover and he gently removed himself from beneath the heavy woman whilst almost spitting invectives.

'I have now had enough! Don't look at me like that, Anders, it was not my fault. She was the one who came barging in not looking where she was going. She fell on me, remember?'

Augusta shouted her hands akimbo. 'Lady Cornelia, my lady-in-waiting, has more right in here than either of you two!'

'We were helping you close your bloody porthole, or have you forgotten?' Aidan snapped thoroughly incensed, not caring a damn that the girl was his liege lord's daughter.

'Please, everyone, let us see to her hurt and argue later, can we?' Beatrix pleaded as she knelt beside the unconscious woman.

'I think I heard a bone break,' Anders said, going down on his knees beside his princess' companion. 'Can you lift her gown for Aidan to check, Miss?'

'Lift her gown!' Augusta exclaimed her sensibilities shocked. 'Most certainly not; indeed not, that is an outrageous suggestion!'

'Highness, we will not need to lift it high. Look you can see her foot is at a very odd angle,' beseeched Anders.

Augusta paused; her mouth closed, lips stretched thin her eyes travelling to the lady's ankle. Reluctantly agreeing with the cabin boy's diagnosis, she glared at Aidan.

'You...look away. It is enough for one male to see her ankle and as you're the one that broke it I don't...'

Aidan curled his lip, sneering. 'Look...you...' but before he could continue with a remark that would have definitely resulted in serious punishment, Lady Cornelia groaned as Beatrix slid the hem of the big woman's gown partway up her shin to expose the wound.

Aidan turned his back on his princess thereby showing his utter contempt for her and knelt to examine the fracture.

'Do not touch her boy, do you wish to do her more damage?' Augusta ordered.

Aidan, his temper at boiling point, for once had the sense to bite off the earthy retort he had in mind. He looked up at her.

'I am a wizard's apprentice, and I am skilled in healing. I may not have the airs and graces that you deem so important, but I can begin the restorative process in all injuries. That I deem far more important! I need to keep her sedated now until my master gets here to help me, asleep she will at least be unaware of her pain. So please, for once in your life, SHUT UP!'

Augusta, utterly shocked at being spoken to in that manner, complied without thinking twice.

Aidan turned to his friend who was equally dumbstruck. 'Anders, find Lord Tragen and tell him I need his help right away, he's probably still on the quarterdeck. Tell him I'm keeping her sedated until he gets here.'

Anders ran, bouncing off the walls along the very dark passage to the captain's companionway.

The undoubted authority in Aidan's voice, lingering in the cabin, coerced Augusta into remaining silent. She watched him sitting on the floor cradling the injured woman's head in his arms. Aidan put his hand on Cornelia's forehead and closed his eyes. Singing his chant and stroking with his fingers above her eyes, the lady slipped into a deep, painless sleep.

Augusta and Beatrix looked at each other both unable to comprehend the transformation in the boy who had plagued them for so long. In all the years of their childhood they had never actually seen the apprentice heal. Though they'd heard stories of his talent bandied about the castle they'd never really believed any of them. Augusta had always thought him a perishing nuisance, a thumping headache. But if she was honest with herself, she never avoided his company and on times actually sought it—usually to bait him.

'If you'll excuse me, Highness, I'll get something to keep her warm, she's lying in cold water.' Beatrix moved across and retrieved the thick blanket folded at the foot of Augusta's cot.

Augusta, her feelings in turmoil, all at once recognized that she was feeling guilty, a sentiment that she never usually acknowledged. Her thoughts tumbled through her head confusing her even more. Her impatience, her anger, always so near the surface ready to erupt at the slightest provocation, she knew there was no need half the time for her to be so irritable. Her manner was deplorable. And yet she couldn't stop, so she bit her lip looking for excuses, thoughts running wild in her head.

'It has to be this seasickness, I...I can't help it. And now...oh God, poor Cornelia! I do hope this boy knows what he is doing.'

Three

Tragen was in the captain's cabin with Hugo Locklear. Ignoring the disarray caused by the storm and, walking either side of the after-jigger mast which pierced the centre of the cabin, they stood facing each other across the large desk overlooked by the sloping window in the stern gallery. A window that now showed in the lightning flashes, a very angry sea as waves tore away aft and disappeared leaving the ship to ride the violence.

Locklear, who looked even larger in the confines of his own cabin, studied his friend for a moment before breaking the silence.

'I cannot leave the quarterdeck for long. Now speak of what you know. Who is trying to take the Grim? He leaned towards the wizard, his huge hands on the desk before him.

Tragen wondered if he'd be believed, in the relative peace of the cabin he almost doubted it himself. He sighed, and stumbling as the ship abruptly keeled over and just as swiftly righted itself again, upended a chair that had fallen nearby.

'You are not going to like this, Hugo…we have been found,' he said sitting down.

'Found? I didn't know we were hiding,' as Tragen looked fixedly at his hands, Locklear went on. 'Come man. What ails you that you trouble to tell me? I must return to my quarterdeck, no responsible captain leaves his command in rough weather.'

'This storm is not a normal storm…'

'I am aware of that,' he interrupted, perplexed, not understanding the wizard's reticence. 'I have been at sea a long time now and have never encountered one such as this. This storm seems to have a mind of its own, as if it's deliberately attacking us. Your statement implies I am correct'

'Yes, Hugo, I am convinced we are under attack.'

'Then tell me who threatens us. What do you know, man?'

'Did you see me looking to mindmeld with Aidan? It went nowhere at my first attempt; the storm's ferocity ensured my failure,' he rubbed his eyes. 'But on the second attempt I utilized more power in my staff and…and I seemed to meld with the storm, an occurrence I have never heard of before.' He stared at his friend, helplessly. 'In the storm I discovered someone else.' He looked down at his hands in his lap; they were trembling ever so slightly, another unique occurrence.

'Who…who did you discover?'

28

'I do not know who, but I know what I felt. I heard laughter, Hugo. Felt his malevolence, his malign glee and I do not know whence it came. All I know is that he was delighted he had found us and I knew that the storm, and I mean the whole purpose of the storm, was to ensnare us.'

The captain stared at the wizard for a moment and then looked around for his own chair, replacing it before his desk he sat down. 'Do you know why he wants us?'

'No, I was afraid to keep in contact for long in case he, or they, discovered me listening.'

'Is that a good thing? That they do not know you're here.'

'My instincts told me then, as they tell me now, whoever they are should not become aware of my presence.'

Locklear, who always combed his beard with his fingers when he was seriously worried, did so now. He stared at his friend.

'How powerful are they? It has to be someone who can wield an extremely potent force, if what you fear is true. Have you any idea who may be looking for us?'

'Oh, by all the Gods, Hugo,' and he rubbed his weary eyes again, 'ideas? I have several...all of them frightening. 'You are correct, the power needed to create this storm rule out a great many. But of those that remain the first that springs to mind is the Magus, Margrave Brenin of the Guild of the Brethren of Wisdom and his deputy the Landgrave, Drudwynn. If it's they then the storm will become even more powerful the closer we get to shore. The magus is the most formidable sorcerer in the world I could never beat him alone. But, as in all magic, the more potent the spell the more energy it takes to cast and consequently the more exhausted will the conjurors become. And for this tempest, I cannot for the life of me imagine that they can possibly maintain the barrage for long.'

'How long is long?'

'How long is a piece of twine, Hugo? I don't know. It must be taking tremendous resources to cast the spell this far from shore that is why I suspect more than one behind it. We are at the edge of the storm so we must almost be at the limit of their range. But even ten...twenty spell-casters must rest eventually.'

'I suppose so. But what is their purpose? Unless of course...' and Hugo's eyes opened wide, 'it is Princess Augusta they're after.'

'It's the only possible reason that comes to mind Hugo. Her father's many enemies may very well recruit the Guild, and the Guild has its own reasons for not wanting her at home.'

'You mentioned other possibilities?'

'Those scare me even more, Hugo.'

'Go on...enlighten me.'

'There are always the dwellers in the Ringwold.'

'Dear God, from the stories I've heard of those we do not want to get entangled with them,' Hugo shuddered. 'But I thought they were demons not spell-casters? And they are well over a thousand...maybe two thousand leagues away, surely too far to affect us here?'

'True, the Ringwold is way up in the frozen north. But whatever or whoever resides in that bleak spot is powerful beyond measure. I have not heard of them being active in the outside world for thousands of years and more, yet...whether they can influence events after all this time I'm not sure. But it's inconceivable they can reach us here and I know of no reason that they would want Augusta. No...only the Gods are omnipotent, Hugo.'

'Could it be them?' he asked, his voice trembling just at the thought of those fickle beings hunting them.

'The Gods you mean? I do not believe they would bother themselves with the politics of mere mortals they are too busy fighting amongst themselves. At least I do not want to believe it.'

'Do you rule them out? You seem unsure.'

'I rule out no-one in this. That terrible laughter really was inhuman.'

Both men silently took refuge in their own thoughts as they examined the consequences of each scenario, any of which would mean the end of the Grim and its occupants. If it was the infernal Ringwold, it meant the end of civilization as they knew it—demons would run amok in the world. If it was the Gods, then their souls were forfeit as well. Terrible though it was it seemed the least evil were the very powerful black sorcerers of the Guild of Brethren.

'What do you suggest we do? If I understand you correctly, moving towards home will bring us closer to the Guild and the nearer we get the more severe the storm will become. It must be obvious we cannot sustain much more damage. Heaving-to in this weather will be very dangerous but not impossible; and if we stay here it cannot be for long we all have to rest.' Hugo stroked his beard and again tapped his chin. 'The holds have been partially flooded, we have sustained sprung boards and the wells are filling. We desperately need to pump the bilges. Can you help us in this?'

'Whatever magic I use now to repair the ship will result in extreme fatigue for me, Hugo. I will need to rest often and for longer periods each time. And I am afraid that I may be incapacitated at the very moment need of my help would be critical. No, my friend, I had better hold off until there is dire need—I must remain the last resort.'

Locklear stared at the wizard, acknowledging the sense of his argument. 'We can always run before the storm, I suppose, but that will take us farther from home and into uncharted waters; not taking into account, of course, that turning the ship in weather such as this will be an absolute nightmare.'

Tragen gazing at his friend went through the options in his mind. 'Let us go for the easiest until we know more. Let us wait them out until the morning. Whoever has created this storm may well be exhausted by then and if there is a lull we can take appropriate action at that time.'

'All right, we'll heave-to, I'll...' Hugo halted at the sound of hammering on the door. 'Enter,' he shouted.

Anders, distinctly dishevelled, opened the door and peered around the jamb. 'Excuse me sir, I have an urgent message for Lord Tragen.'

Screwing his eyes in puzzlement at the state of the usually clean Anders, he nodded. 'Then by all means, deliver it.'

The cabin boy, breathing deeply to steady his nerves, entered and stood before the old sorcerer and couldn't help but notice a small cyst on the end of Tragen's nose. For a moment Anders thought it looked like a nose growing on a nose and he nearly burst out laughing, recovering quickly he delivered Aidan's request for help.

'I'm sorry, Milord, but Aidan needs...needs you,' all at once he stuttered to a halt. Tragen always got very irritated when Aidan was involved in an accident, even if it wasn't his fault. And what's more he usually got dragged into it, suffering the same penalty as his friend.

'Aidan is all right, isn't he?' The wizard asked jumping up from his chair and grasping the cabin boy's shoulders, concern etching deep lines in his brow.

'Yes, he's fine, Milord, but he wants you to attend on the Lady Cornelia in Princess Augusta's cabin.' Panicking at having Tragen stare at him so closely, he went on, a tremor in his voice. 'He said to tell you it is definitely her ankle and he is keeping her…sedated, I think is the word he used, sir.'

'What is definitely her ankle young man? What has happened?'

'Oh, I'm sorry, Milord, she…' and he gulped, 'she tripped over Aidan and fell down and broke it, sir.'

'My God, that boy is going to be the death of me yet,' he said to no-one in particular, as he moved to leave. 'Why, on the God's earth, did I choose an apprentice so very accident prone?'

Halting at the door, Anders following behind nearly bumping into him, Tragen turned to the ship's master. 'You will take the necessary action, as we agreed?

'Aye man, it seems to be the most sensible option at present.'

Still agitated, Anders followed the tall, thin wizard as he made his way to Augusta's cabin. The companionway down to the main passenger cabins was very dark but Tragen didn't seem to have any trouble negotiating the passage. Anders glimpsed the captain behind them making his way to the quarterdeck. His uncle was not a very happy man, the Bear was weary and definitely out of sorts, as if he had something on his mind other than the storm.

When Locklear reached the quarterdeck, Talbot was back on duty at the wheel accompanied this time by Nkosi, a huge black seaman from the Dark Continent way to the south of Drakka. Hopper was at the forward quarterdeck rail peering at the bows through the gale, trying to make out the details with the aid of the intermittent lightning strikes.

Hugo strode over and shouted over the top of the screaming wind. 'How goes it Hopper, are we coping?'

'Aye, aye sir, we are for now.'

'Are we making any sort of headway?'

'No, sir, and the storm is getting worse.'

'All right, we'll heave-to, see if the storm eases, set sea anchors and then get some rest, I'll remain here now.'

Hopper touched his forelock and set off to find Trumper.

Hugo looked about him. Had the wind increased? His first mate was positive, Locklear tended to agree with him but now he had other things preying on his mind. He sighed, those problems he put to the back of his mind there were more pressing matters to deal with first. He stared into the clouds through the teeming rain concentrating on the nuances of the storm. It was getting even darker, but was that because it was getting on for nightfall, or was there some other dark reason?

He had to be careful now; they had been battling this storm since before dawn. Exhaustion was setting in. This was the time when trivial errors had a habit of turning into major setbacks, especially when the only means of communication was by touch or signing. He was going to have to send men to rest, which meant that those remaining on duty would need to exert themselves even more. Hugo well knew the effect that the constant buffeting would have— confusion would set in, minds stupefy and minor injuries become major. In the following days and nights movement would become instinctual. And survival would depend on whatever nourishment could be doled out by Dolly, the ship's cook, hopefully something hot during lulls in the storm.

Hugo's thoughts returned to Tragen's tidings. How were they to discover the identity of the creator of this storm? Confronting someone who could command nature's violence was not a prospect that instilled much confidence of success. No. they'd have to flee, find a safer haven before they even thought of retaliating. He shuddered at the thought of turning about in this weather; it would be a diabolical task.

The Grim was Locklear's life, the only ship in the world able to bear five masts. Veterans of the sea maintained that a ship bearing more than four was intrinsically unsafe, but Locklear had proved them all wrong. His skills had brought the Grim through ferocious seas many times in the past. From the very first day plans of the ship had been proposed, he had been involved in the design. His experience had been invaluable and he had overseen the building of her from the hour the massive keel had first been laid. The Grim was his baby; he knew her moods and her capabilities. If the storm's intensity remained at this level, the ship would be fine, but if the weather deteriorated even more?

But if the worst came to the worst, the safety of Augusta was paramount; boats would need to be prepared with extra provisions stowed. Locklear combed his beard again as he strode his quarterdeck staring up at the topgallants bare of their sails. The thought of his princess on a small boat in these seas terrified him.

Meanwhile, Tragen had reached his destination with a distinctly worried Anders in tow. The nearer they came to Augusta's cabin, the closer they were to that of Aidan's. And in the passageway there was a distinct smell and bitter taste of old smoke, which had not yet dispersed because of the tightly closed hatches. Tragen sniffed ominously as he hurried.

The old wizard peered into the gloomy cabin and studied the almost silent scene. Beatrix was sitting against the bulkhead at the head of Augusta's cot, one hand in her lap the other keeping the cot – suspended from the deckhead by ropes in each corner – from nudging Aidan's back. Tragen smiled quickly at the young girl, he noticing her blonde wavy hair had kept its bounce despite being wet. Augusta was sitting in the only chair at the other end, nearest the door. She was also using one hand to fend off the swinging bed, her index finger on her other hand stuck in the corner of her mouth. Both girls looked the worse for wear, soaking wet from their earlier fight with the porthole, their gowns a mess. They were staring at Aidan, wonderment on their faces, concern for the lady-in-waiting clouding their eyes.

Aidan was still sitting on the deck, his head bent over the recumbent body of Lady Cornelia, her foot protruding from beneath the blanket. The boy was stroking her forehead rhythmically and gently and his brown eyes were closed. He was chanting the lullaby of sleep, quietly and melodiously, his whole attention centred on the unconscious woman.

Tragen stared intently at the wound. Blood was seeping slowly from a break in the white skin where the ragged edge of a bone could just be seen poking through the surface of her fleshy limb. Aidan continued his chant without a break even though he sensed the presence of his master.

Ignoring everyone else, including Anders standing in the doorway watching avidly, Tragen spoke gently. 'You are doing well, my boy, she is not suffering.'

Aidan opened his eyes and, staring at his mentor, he slowly ceased his singing. 'The fractures are bad, very bad,' he continued his tender stroking of Cornelia's forehead.

'Can you see all the injury?'

'Yes, there's more than one splinter, she...'

Augusta, shaken out of her torpor by Aidan's answer, interrupted. 'What do you mean, Lord Tragen? How can he possibly see more than one?' She swallowed quickly as she looked at the foot. 'I can see but one bone protruding.'

'Highness, my young apprentice has a unique talent,' and he smiled at Aidan. 'He is a most extraordinary healer. He can sense the impairment beneath the flesh of a maimed body and detect its maladies, not only by touch and smell, but also with sight. I, on the other hand, am but an ordinary mender of bodies. It's the gift of common sense he lacks!'

'Master!' Aidan replied taking umbrage.

'I'm sorry, my boy, my great age does make me flippant on times. Haven't you noticed?' he grinned.

'You mean to say that he can see the bones inside her leg?' Augusta asked, astonished, not understanding their banter she was becoming more anxious.

The wizard gazed at Augusta. 'I do, and if you will forgive us, Highness, we must now decide on a course of action,' he turned once more to Aidan. 'What do you suggest?'

'Well, she also has the sickness of the old in her bones to complicate matters.'

'And her weight will not help, hey?'

'No. It is difficult to see the actual breaks through so much flesh.'

'You wish us to change places, I sing the song of sleep and you repair the fractures?'

They did not speak as they changed ends. Tragen knelt at Cornelia's head as Aidan slid out and replaced his master at her feet.

'The "old" sickness is very deep-seated; I will need to deal with that as I repair the bones.' Meeting Tragen's smiling eyes he grinned in response. 'I'll need someone to help while I manipulate the bones.' He looked around at his audience. 'You'll do, Anders. Sit beside me and do as I say.'

Anders nodded, very nervous and it showed.

'Don't worry; you won't hurt her as long as you listen to me.'

'Beatrix take that blanket off the cot and fold it, please,' Aidan looked at the jittery girl and smiled. 'Now place it under her leg as we raise it.'

And while Tragen chanted the song of sleep in a somewhat deeper voice than his pupil, Aidan set to work. He took his time. All his movements slow and well considered before actually being carried out, contending with the lurching floor as he did so. There was silence from all except Tragen chanting, Anders obeying his every command, Augusta and Beatrix totally absorbed in his every action. As Aidan

35

worked, the bone disappeared below the surface and back into place, the ruptured tissue closing.

Time seemed to pass very slowly as Tragen continued to sing, taking great pride in his apprentice. Even after ten years of watching Aidan at work, he was still astounded at the boy's power.

Aidan glanced up at the girl sitting on the chair beside him. 'I need strips for binding and something to use as splints.'

Augusta jumped up with alacrity and searched the room taking care not to stumble near those on the floor. She tore a cotton sheet into long lengths for him as Beatrix came back from her cabin with slats of wood. Aidan gently wrapped the bindings and the splints in place.

'Done, now we lay her in bed for the healing to continue,' Aidan sighed with relief.

'It will be very difficult to carry her to her cabin; you'll never get her through the door. You had best place her in my cot here,' Augusta ordered, immediately standing to rearrange the bedding.

'But where will you sleep?' Beatrix, immediately alarmed, enquired.

'I will take Cornelia's bed and share the cabin with you while she recovers.'

Beatrix paled; the thought of her mistress in the same cabin unnerved her she was a lot like Aidan…a veritable affliction.

Tragen, using magic, helped the two boys lift the heavy woman and they settled her into Augusta's cot, the ropes in each corner creaking audibly as they took the strain.

'Well done, my boy,' said Tragen, beaming. But abruptly his face lost its look of pride and he peered closely at both boys, a very stern expression on his face.

'Now, Highness, we will leave you and your companion to disrobe Lady Cornelia and make her comfortable while I and these two repair to my own cabin for a long discussion on the whys and wherefores of accidents.'

With a bow, he departed through the door and the boys followed very reluctantly, remembering what Tragen would find at his destination.

'One of you bring the lantern,' the wizard called over his shoulder.

Augusta wondered where her seasickness had gone. And if she but knew it, Aidan and Anders did not wonder why all of a sudden they felt sick

Four

On the quarterdeck it was so dark Locklear could barely see the ocean skimming aft down both sides of the ship. The storm raged as the Grim creaked and groaned, riding the turbulence with ever increasing difficulty.

'What do you think are the chances of setting a stormsail in this wind, Bo'sun?' Locklear asked, peering up at the black sky looking for non-existent stars.

'It would last precisely as long as the men climbing the mast to set it, Cap'n, and besides, I don't believe we'd be able to manoeuvre using it.' The bo'sun, another veteran of Locklear's command, was allowed a certain liberty in his manner and never shirked in voicing criticism of what he thought of as inept seamanship. He did not look a happy man as the rain poured down his face.

'In other words you do not recommend it?' Locklear was an unusual captain he often asked for advice, sometimes taking it.

'I do not, sir, at least not until morning when we can see a bit better.'

'Do you honestly believe visibility will be restored to us at daybreak?' He sighed and braced himself against the quarterdeck rail. 'We will wait, Mr Trumper. If, as I suspect, we are being driven astern, then it will be safer to remain with bare poles.'

Locklear strode to his chair and lifted himself into the high, wet seat, his home in bad weather and rested wearily, again stroking his beard worriedly. If Tragen was correct then this storm was the least of their worries.

Tragen stood in the passage at his cabin door looking in at Aidan futilely attempting to hide the wreckage.

'There has been a fire here, what do you know of it?'

'Only a small fire, we put it out straight away.' Aidan replied hurriedly, his voice trembling.

The wizard stared icily and repeated the question in a tone that brooked no nonsense. 'What do you know of this fire?'

'It was an accident, Master, honest! When the ship turned I fell and dropped the flame.'

Aidan knew that lying would only result in a more severe punishment. And punished he would be unless he could talk his way out of it. Tragen could read him like a book.

'It's all right, Milord, I'll sleep on the floor and you can have my bunk until I get it repaired.'

And Aidan knew instantly that his mouth had got him in trouble again; he only ever called Tragen "Milord" when he had done something he knew beforehand he should not have.

Tragen stared at the dark boy standing in front of him, a boy seeming to grow faster now he'd reached his middle teens—a boy full of immense power but so often lacking in common sense, anger deepened his voice. 'I thank you for giving up your bed, boy; in that you have no choice. Now tell me of this naked flame.'

Aidan bowed his head even further, desperately searching for an answer that would, at the very least, call down a more lenient punishment than seemed likely at present.

'I'm sorry, but we had to light a lantern somehow,' he glanced up at his mentor, failing to detect clemency in the young/old eyes. 'I know I'm not supposed to use that particular spell in an enclosed space. I know you've always told me it is highly dangerous in a small room. I'm sorry,' he repeated.

His battered body aching, weary to his bones, his spirit hiding somewhere near his feet, he knew of no way to persuade the wizard. Tragen's retribution could be terrible if anyone's life was ever put at risk by thoughtless use of magic and he had just endangered the whole ship's company.

Anders' heart bled at seeing his friend in so much trouble. 'My Lord it was my fault. I stumbled and fell against him that's why he dropped the flame. I was holding the lantern…I couldn't…I…' scared, his voice trailed away, he also had experience of being at the wrong end of Tragen's temper.

The irate wizard glared at him. 'So, you are both at fault, as if I hadn't guessed!' his voice rising, he continued. 'Aidan has strict orders never to use that spell onboard this ship,' he shouted, shaking his finger in Anders' face, 'and you are aware of it. Do you both realize how lucky you were at being able to extinguish the flame? A fire on a ship at sea usually means a burned out ship and its passengers and crew, if not dead, at the very least adrift in small boats. Would you like to be in a small boat on these seas?' He glowered at the culprits, his grey eyes narrowing. 'Now, whilst both of you are cleaning this cabin and later, when you undertake your punishment, think about those consequences, think deeply because this is the last time that I will suffer your stupidity.'

He gazed heavily at Aidan as he moved to leave and unexpectedly noticed the burn mark on the boy's bowed neck. Disconcerted, he entered the cabin and bent his head to take a closer look.

'What is this on your neck, my boy?'

Aidan looked up quickly, surprised at the enquiry and seeing the concern in Tragen's face he again lowered his head and stared at his feet, hope flaring as a glimmer of a plan came to him. For all his rhetoric Tragen could be merciful on occasion, so much so that he could be inveigled into forgoing painful outcomes. He'd been in serious trouble before and got away with it, all it needed was a bit of cunning.

He raised his hand to his neck and gently touched the burn. 'I have burns on my legs as well...and I think I've grazed my back because I was sliding all over the deck when I was sent to the bo'sun,' he whimpered quietly and sniffed. 'It's the reason we needed light, we couldn't see a thing. The burns were hurting me so much I desperately needed to dry myself and...and Mr Trumper had ordered me to change into britches.' He sniffled again. 'Anders came to help me, Master, when he found me weeping at the foot of the hatchway because I'd fallen off the ladder.' He peeked out of the corner of his eye at Anders standing to one side, his jaw dropping to his feet. 'I fell because I was dizzy and I...I don't know, I had a sudden weakness in my arms.'

'Oh, Aidan, Aidan, why did you not say earlier, come, do you wish my help?' Tragen led him to one end of the burned bed and made the boy sit while he examined the wound in the light of the lantern that Anders was holding.

'I'll be all right,' Aidan groaned meaningfully. 'If you could just find me the salve, Anders will help me get my clothes. But if you could hold off your punishment until the balm takes effect...please,' he sighed.

Scrutinizing the charred flesh on his apprentice he retrieved the jar of unguent from his store. 'I think these burns, accompanied by the cleaning you have to do, will be enough punishment for now.' He frowned, and as he stood to leave, he added, showing that he had not been completely taken in.

'My rules may seem silly on times, Aidan, but they do have a sensible purpose. Learn to follow them or you will encounter more severe hurts than mere friction burns.' At the door, he turned to both boys. 'If you need me I will be with the captain.'

Anders stared incredulously at Aidan. 'Weeping! It was me nearly weeping when you fell on top of me!'

Aidan stood up, looked at his friend mournfully for a moment and then said slyly, a twinkle in his eyes. 'Worked didn't it? No punishment.'

'You little...' and then Anders laughed. 'Get a move on, look for your britches,' and he added out of the blue, 'I wonder if we should go and see if those two need our help before we tidy up?'

'For God's sake, Anders, after we've cleaned the cabin,' he said desperately. 'I can get away with flummoxing Tragen once but I'll never do it twice in the same day.' He proceeded to disrobe. 'My britches and braes are in that trunk, pass them over and you can apply this balm to my neck, it's hurting me something awful,' he complained with some fervour.

In Beattie's cabin not all was happy. They had struggled to undress a very heavy Lady Cornelia, so that she could rest easier and she was now swaddled in Augusta's bedclothes, sleeping fast. It was then they had discovered that Augusta had no dry attire to change into, the water pouring through the porthole had doused Augusta's wardrobe.

'Come Beattie, we must search for clothing in your cabin.'

'Highness, I have nothing that you could possibly wear.'

'Nonsense, you usually have use of my cast-offs, do you not?' Augusta spoke very pompously when she thought obstacles were being placed in her way.

'Yes, but I was told that baggage space was at a premium and very little would be allocated to me. Most of the storage room has been taken up by Lady Cornelia.'

'Umph! I can't see me donning her clothes, can you?' Augusta smiled broadly at the thought of even attempting to wear her lady-in-waiting's capacious garments.

Crossing from Augusta's cabin, they espied Tragen at the end of the passage. 'What do you make of our wizard?

'What do you mean?'

'Do you like him?'

'To be honest I find him frightening sometimes. When he gazes at me with that faraway look I get goose pimples up my arms.' And with that Beattie automatically rubbed her hands up and down her forearms.

'What! Even that time my father had him teaching us to lip-read, which was a complete waste of time I could never get the hang of it.'

'You couldn't, no, I found it easy enough,' Beatrix smirked, she did like having one up on her mistress, it didn't happen often. 'Strangely enough, though, I like him as well—he makes me feel safe.'

'Yes, I agree,' Augusta said ignoring the jibe. 'He's also a very attractive man, is he not?'

'Highness!' said Beatrix shocked and then recovering her composure, she smiled. 'I have never given the idea much thought. He is very old, after all, like a kindly grandfather.'

'Mm...I suppose you're right. Come on, we'll search your baggage.' And as she entered her companion's domain she stumbled over a trunk that had been placed to one side of the door.

'Damn, my ankle!' she moaned, sitting on the bottom bunk rubbing its soreness away.

'Shall I get Aidan, Highness?' Beatrix asked impishly. 'I'm sure he wouldn't mind healing that.' She dodged when Augusta threw a pillow at her.

For a time they fruitlessly searched Beattie's clothing. Augusta refusing point blank to appear in her old clothes, they subsequently turned their attention to Lady Cornelia's wardrobe with the same result, everything too large, an impossibility to wear.

It was at this point that Anders arrived at the door with Aidan following. The apprentice wizard, smelling of sweet unguent, was now wearing a thigh length shirt outside his calf length britches, both tied at the waist with a rope belt, he was barefoot as usual.

'Do you need any help, Highness?' Aidan enquired, his tousled head poking around the bulk of his friend, not really expecting an answer. They were utterly perplexed at the garments dumped everywhere.

Beatrix looked up in a thoroughly bad mood, she hated doing a job that was pointless and finding suitable clothes for Augusta in Cornelia's wardrobe was the height of futility. For a pretty girl she now had a bright red face under her long blonde hair and she was sweating profusely, this cabin being smaller than her mistress' was also hotter.

'Go away! We are trying to find dry clothes for Princess Augusta. How can you possibly assist us?'

'Well, we could always lend you some of ours if you're desperate, you know.' Aidan said laughing, and Beatrix snorted in disgust.

Augusta straightened and dropping a huge bodice on the bed, looked at him thoughtfully. 'Now, that's an idea, Beattie!'

All three gazed at her in sudden consternation.

'What do you mean? You can't possibly wear boys' clothes! I mean, the only lady on board this ship wearing britches!' Beatrix admonished and then seeing the look on Augusta's face she added as an afterthought. 'You'll be showing your ankles, it would be scandalous.' Very agitated she'd often found herself in trouble when her mistress ignored convention, which Augusta did when it suited her.

'If we wish to go on deck though, britches are far more suitable than a gown!'

'Who wants to go up there in this weather?' Beatrix, thoroughly appalled at the idea, continued. 'Highness, you cannot be serious, please. It would appear very strange you in britches and me in a gown. You would seem to be my maid!'

'Yes, I suppose you're right; we could not possibly have people thinking that.'

Vastly relieved, Beatrix, her shyness with Anders all but forgotten in her anxiety, once more turned to the boys and shooed them away.

'You may now leave; we do not require your presence any longer.'

'Wait,' interrupted Augusta. 'I said it would look strange if I was wearing boys' clothes…on my own!'

'What do you mean? Oh no! Highness, please I beg you; you cannot do this to me—to us,' Beatrix put her hands to her mouth in desperation, all blood draining from her face as she realized what her mistress intended.

'She can't do what to you?' Anders said, very concerned at the mad panic in Beattie's face. And then he comprehended and his expression mirrored hers. Aidan's big mouth was about to get them in trouble, again.

Beatrix sat on the floor abruptly, still with her hands to her mouth, shaking her head.

Augusta standing over her turned to Aidan. 'Do you think that the two of us match you in size? I do, so I will take up your suggestion. Please bring me some of your clothing, Beatrix and I will be delighted to wear the same as you.'

Aidan stared, his mouth agape. 'I wasn't being serious! You can't be seen wearing britches and…and shirts, either of you, it…it would not be decent and…besides, Tragen would kill me!'

'I will handle the wizard, boy, do not argue with me,' Augusta, speaking imperiously, was getting impatient with Aidan again. Forgetting the healing he had just performed on her lady-in-waiting, she was reverting to the opinion she had held for ten years, that he was an insolent layabout. 'Now hurry before I catch a chill…or would you have your master blame you for that as well?'

Aidan departed his brain in a fog as he made his way back to his cabin. That bloody girl, he thought, he'd had enough of her she was getting right up his nose all over again. Just because she was a princess didn't give her the right to drop him in it. Retrieving spare britches and shirts from his baggage, he stopped short…would they need braes? He grabbed two of the male undergarments.

Muttering under his breath he returned to find a soundly distraught Beatrix still sitting on the floor her head in her hands so shocked she couldn't even weep. He handed everything to Augusta.

'Wait outside for us, both of you; we may need your advice,' she ordered, Beatrix wailed.

'Be quiet Beattie, think of it as an adventure,' she admonished, slamming the door, leaving the boys in darkness in the corridor.

Aidan was mortified; all he could see in the mists before his eyes was Tragen's livid face. There was no way out of it, the blame was all his. He must have lost his senses. To actually suggest that the prince's daughter dress as he did, after all he knew what she was like! She's probably doing it to get back at me for some imagined slight, he thought. But where was her sense? It was a joke, for God's sake! A joke! Not only would she look ludicrous, she would also be indecent. Showing her ankles was very unseemly for a young royal, not that he cared about that, but Tragen would. The wizard was a stickler for correct protocol and often berated Aidan when he didn't follow it.

And he would have to shoulder the responsibility. His unguarded humour had set the whole idea in motion. What was wrong with the girl? She'd always been pig-headed, but how could she possibly think he'd been serious? Was she stupid? Didn't she have any perception of how she'd appear to the crew? He knew he shouldn't have come on this voyage; he'd had plenty of work to do at home. But he'd needed a rest, recuperation after breaking his arm. So when Tragen had mentioned that he was to escort Augusta home from Drakka where she'd spent a time being educated at the emperor's court, he'd jumped at it. But they had obviously never taught her common sense, he mused.

That was one of the two reasons for this voyage—to bring her home, even though her schooling was not quite finished.

The other, to ascertain the rumour of a new-fangled weapon, a bombard, a strange device that used something called "villainous saltpetre", had yet to be fulfilled. Apparently, the thing was deep in the south somewhere in the Dark Continent, or maybe in the east, no-one was quite sure. Nkosi thought he knew where it could be found but they had no time to go searching.

The Prince and Princess of Mantovar needed their daughter at home as soon as possible, and no-one on the Grim knew the reason for the haste, except possibly Tragen who was Prince Bertrand's chief advisor.

Oh, my God, he thought, if Tragen doesn't murder me, the prince surely will. Aidan was mortally afraid of his liege lord after their last run in. It had happened when one of Aidan's conjurations had gone "slightly" awry; at least that's what the apprentice had claimed at the time. The resultant flight of the prince across the courtyard in front of all and sundry, a very humiliating experience for the monarch, had been the result of a growth spell created by the young wizard practising on an insect. The chrysalis had matured into a very beautiful butterfly. Unfortunately, it had not stopped growing until it had reached a monstrous size and had taken a fancy to the prince. Bertrand, understandably, wanted to lynch the culprit. Aidan had hidden for a week while his liege lord calmed down.

His morose thoughts were interrupted when Augusta called them back in to the cabin. She and Beatrix were now wearing britches and shirts and she dumped the braes on Aidan, stating, with a disapproving frown, that females had their own underwear, thank you! Blushing, he thrust them out of sight behind the water barrel standing at the door.

Beatrix mesmerized, not believing what was happening, was picking at her shirt in an unconscious effort to straighten it as she would tidy a loose bodice.

Anders, grinning all over his face despite his concern for Beattie, couldn't help offering his opinion. 'Very fetching!' and he added tongue in cheek. 'You appear on deck in this weather dressed in those shirts and no-one will possibly mistake you for young men.'

Augusta rounded on him, furious. 'And what is the purpose of that remark, churl. I do not want to be mistaken for a man, thank you. And why are you laughing?'

'You mistake me,' his grin growing even wider. 'It's just that girls are a bit different to us and wet shirts not only cling where they touch, they also become transparent! I think I'd better get you tunics to wear over the top of those.' He laughed uproariously and went off to his sleeping quarters in the captain's cabin to find suitable modesty enhancing garments.

Augusta and Beatrix screeched, their arms coming across their chests instantly, and for the second time that day, Augusta was speechless whilst Beattie's face again turned red, this time with embarrassment.

Anders' words had not registered with Aidan; he was too worried about the consequences to him personally to care about anything else. He tried once more to dissuade Augusta.

'Please, can't you see the problems this decision will make? Can't you make other arrangements? It shouldn't take long for me to dry your clothes, or…perhaps I could search the baggage in the holds?'

'Don't be silly boy,' she persisted, her mind made up. 'It's pointless drying our clothes they'll be encrusted with salt from the seawater. Anyway, how are you going to dry our clothes in this weather or retrieve anything from the hold? No, these will be fine, I'm getting used to them already,' she tugged at her britches and looked down at them admiringly. 'I understand now how you males seem so easy in your movements around the ship. This raiment is very comfortable and is eminently suitable for sailing. When the boy returns with the tunics you will take us to the quarterdeck, I wish to see the situation there for myself.'

Aidan paced the small cabin, wringing his hands, desperately thinking of other arguments to use, the two girls having to move out of his way constantly to avoid being knocked over.

'Sit down, will you,' Augusta ordered, exasperated, 'there is no way I am going to change my mind, whatever you say.'

He ceased his pacing and stretched out on the bottom bunk. A moment later he jumped up banging his head on the bed above. 'Ow! I know! I could create a cleaning spell, they'll be all right then,' he said, rubbing his forehead.

Anders returned at that moment carrying the tunics; he had also taken the opportunity to change into dry clothes. 'No way, you can't cast those spells down here…Tragen will string us up, this time!'

Aidan gave in, not gracefully though, muttering constantly under his breath his fear grew as he desperately searched for a means to make Augusta reconsider.

While Anders was remonstrating with Aidan the girls took the opportunity to don their tunics. They were overly large; Anders was a lot bigger than his three companions but the garments more than sufficed. Beatrix felt a little easier with the brown tunic draped to her knees. But Augusta, a natural extrovert, felt far more devil-may-care and danced a little jig around the cabin.

'Aidan, lead the way,' she ordered cheerfully, relishing her new-found freedom, giggling she grasped Beattie's hand to follow the boys along the passageway aft.

When they arrived at the foot of the captain's companionway Aidan desperately attempted to assert the authority of an apprentice magician. 'I'll climb first and see what's happening. If the captain is too busy we'll go away and come back another time.'

'Since when were you given the right to make my decisions, churl?' Augusta sneered at him over the sound of the wind outside. 'I will see Master Locklear this instant; now either get out of my way or move ahead forthwith,' she could never allow a scruffy young tearaway to dictate her actions!

Aidan bit his tongue, there were so many things he wanted to call this horrible girl and they were all guaranteed to get him life imprisonment or worse. His temper was rising, she was really playing on his nerves. I know she's a noblewoman and all that, he thought, but she's no need to talk to me like a slave, I've even gone out of my way to help her! Nevertheless, muttering under his breath, he opened the door on to the quarterdeck and peered through.

At first, he could see nothing in the darkness, but then in a flash of lightning he saw his master talking to the captain. He carefully groped his way to the larboard rail, and bowing his head against the rain…and his retribution, he awaited his downfall.

Five

But instead of hearing a roar of disapproval, Aidan heard a howl of laughter.

Puzzled, he turned round very tense, and was startled to see that it was Locklear bellowing with laughter and what's more Tragen was grinning broadly, his white teeth shining brilliantly in the gloom.

Locklear looked at Tragen through his tears. 'What on the Gods' ocean have we here, my friend? Was this your idea?'

'Nay, Hugo, not me. I would never have thought of hiding her like this.'

'Neither would I and damme if it isn't perfect for this weather as well.' Locklear, with his back to the wind looked at Augusta and dried his eyes with his hands. 'Why are you dressed thus?'

'As you say, Captain, it's perfect for this weather.' She was taken aback at being laughed at, but knew if she objected it would probably add to their merriment. Her father never allowed her to put on airs and graces with his closest confidantes and these two were his oldest friends.

'This boy gave me the idea,' she indicated Aidan who was trying to make himself invisible behind her. 'I couldn't help but notice earlier that he was struggling to get around wearing a robe. He was experiencing the same problems that Beatrix and I were having wearing a gown. But why mention hid...' and she ran for the rail and vomited over the side.

Moaning, she wiped her mouth clean on her sleeve. When she finished retching, she blinked the tears from her eyes and continued staring over the rail, holding her stomach. She had completely forgotten what she was about to ask.

Tragen and Hugo stared in astonishment as Anders and Beatrix immediately groped their way to her side and helped support her as she retched again.

'Oh, I don't feel well,' moaned Augusta, one hand on her belly the other holding her head ignoring the dribbles from the corner of her mouth. 'I thought the sickness had left me...ooh!'

Aidan thought it was justice after what she had put him through all day. He was feeling pretty bloody-minded where she was concerned. But pity for her condition gradually seeped to the surface. He wouldn't allow an animal to suffer the malady of the sea let alone a human being—if you could call the arrogant prig a human, he mused.

Mind you, he should be used to her manner; she'd always treated him with the "holier than thou" attitude. But he, himself, was prone to suffer the sickness of the sea at the beginning of each voyage and it sometimes took days for him to get used to the motion of the ship. He glanced at Beatrix and Anders standing either side of her, making sympathetic noises, and he made up his mind.

Aidan put his hand on Augusta's arm and uttered the worst words he possibly could have in his attempt to comfort her. 'You shouldn't look up at the masts, they'll always make you dizzy if you're not used to the sea.'

'You stupid boy,' she snapped. 'How can I not see them when I look along the deck? They're waving around in front of me!' She waved her arm around in front of his face in mock imitation of the masts. 'Beattie, remove me from here before I really lose my temper with him,' she turned to her companion for solace.

'Do something, Aidan,' Anders enjoined. 'You can stop the sickness.'

'No, he's not touching me,' Augusta broke in. 'He's nothing but a loathsome brute, I'd rather…' and she leant over the rail and vomited again, or at least tried to; there was nothing in her stomach to come up.

Beatrix looked at Aidan with equal abhorrence. 'Let Anders and me help you below to our cabin, Highness, you'll feel better there.'

Augusta moaned again as she hung on to the rail in the gloom, 'I just want to die…I want to die! I'll never come up here ever again. Why did the sickness leave me and then return?'

Tragen came across. 'Highness, I am not in a position to help you at present, healing uses a great deal of energy and I must conserve my strength for the morning. But if you allow him, Aidan can relieve you of this malady.'

Tragen stared at his apprentice as Augusta lay groaning in her companion's arms. 'Well, Aidan, are you going to turn your back on her?'

'Master, you know I'd never do that! I'd already decided to help her despite her insults.'

'Of course, my boy, and I sincerely apologize for suggesting it.' Tragen accepted his rebuke knowing that it was deserved. 'I have other things on my mind, at the moment; it was thoughtless of me, I'm sorry. But please heal her quickly, it is unsafe here.'

'All right, I will, but I'm not happy about it. I am not a stupid boy…or a loathsome brute.'

'Well, let us hope that one day, and may it be soon, she will come to understand your virtues.'

It then struck Aidan what Tragen had given as a reason for not healing her himself. 'Why have you got to save your strength for the morning? What are you up to?'

'Later, Aidan,' and he smiled to take the sting out of his words, 'your master does not have to be "up to" anything that you need know of.' He pointed at the stricken girl. 'Well?'

'All right,' he said, not satisfied with the answer. 'Highness, whether you like it or not, this stupid boy is going to heal you. Now, stand up straight and shut up!'

For the second time that day, she hearkened instinctively to the authority in his voice, greatly surprising herself that she allowed him, again, to speak to her in such a manner. Looking up at him, he was a little taller than she, Augusta found herself unavoidably staring into his dark eyes as he placed his hands either side of her head.

'Why my head when I am sick to my stomach?' she asked sarcastically, at the same time not understanding her reaction to both his order and his eyes.

'Leave her be, it is obvious you know nothing of this sickness.' Beatrix ordered, at the same time attempting to pull his hands from her mistress' head.

'No, Beattie, stop. I don't understand it either but I've seen him heal many times. He does know what he's doing, honestly,' said Anders, taking full advantage of the situation he put his arms around the girl to restrain her, and smiled. 'Just watch, it is truly amazing what he does.'

Beatrix stared up into Anders' face and was persuaded, against her better judgement, by his encouraging smile and the comfort of his arms around her. She stepped back a little from Aidan and Augusta, Anders supporting her on the heaving deck, and followed the proceedings nervously.

'It's motion sickness that's making you ill, girl; and motion sickness is an imbalance in your brain, very easy to fix,' said Aidan, staring into her eyes.

Augusta had no option but to return his gaze, and she had the strangest feeling she was losing herself in his eyes, the sparkles in his brown irises very alluring. Then she noticed that his hands were becoming warm, almost hot at her temples, and her head and belly were responding to that warmth. How long she stood in front of him she didn't know, all she wanted was the comfort of his hands, and to fall into his eyes. The sickness and dizziness left her gradually, as if by magic and then, of course, she realized Aidan's form of healing was magic.

'Are you well now, Highness?' Beatrix asked eventually, studying Augusta very closely, still not trusting Aidan, but somewhat confused at the look on her mistress' face.

Augusta smiled as she stared at the young wizard's face mere inches from her own. And she suddenly realized that everyone was staring at them.

Aidan reluctantly lowered his hands, for some reason he didn't want to release her—something more than the healing of her malady had just occurred. He turned to leave.

Augusta grabbed his arm before he moved too far and with her feelings in disarray she knew she had to say something. Swallowing, she waited a moment plucking up courage.

'Will you please forgive me, Aidan; I will never call you a stupid boy again.' It seemed that the animosity between them had also disappeared, at least for a while. She waited with bated breath for his answer, knowing that his acceptance of her apology meant a great deal to her.

It was now his turn to feel guilty. He had been around the aristocracy long enough to realize a little of what it cost her to utter those words in front of everyone, and he found himself admiring her courage.

'Don't mention it, Highness,' and he smiled broadly, his eyes twinkling.

Tragen went to ruffle his hair but at once thought better of it. That is one thing a young man growing up does not require in front of his friends – especially lady friends – he thought. Instead, his eyes glowed again with enormous pride.

Beatrix, her arm around her mistress, was nonplussed. Her loyalty to Augusta was in no doubt, but she was sorely tempted to distrust her mistress' sanity. Noblewomen did not apologize to those of a lower class, they had no need to. In her surprise at Augusta's words she'd completely forgotten her own mother's teaching and would have been severely castigated for thinking such a thing.

Anders stood by slightly bemused his arms still around Beatrix; he did not understand what had happened between his best friend and the princess. But something good had arisen from the encounter. He wondered if it was the beginning of friendship. He hoped so; he so much wanted to keep close to Beatrix.

Meanwhile the storm still beat at them, the wind howling as Tragen and Locklear resumed their conversation. At the helm was Talbot, accompanied by Leash looking very unhappy.

Leash had seen that the boy had accomplished something out of the ordinary and wondered if the young wizard could help him. But he knew he could never allow a wizard into his mind—it would be the end. So he watched, he waited and he schemed knowing another chance to get at the boy was inevitable. Harming the apprentice was the only way to hurt Tragen.

And Leash wanted revenge for all the years of torment and loneliness.

Augusta, Beatrix, Aidan and Anders stared at the towering grey waves threatening the Grim, their thoughts elsewhere.

The princess more cognizant now that she no longer suffered seasickness was still confused her emotions in turmoil. Aidan had affected her in ways she could not understand. His eyes, the touch of his hands and his smile at the end accompanying his forgiveness—she wanted more.

Anders thoughts drifted away from Beattie although his arms were still around her. He was not going to release her unless he had to. There was a great majesty about the huge waves washing along the Grim, its spume lifting in the wind to form an unimaginable array of shapes. Despite having been born in a castle far inland, the cabin boy had always wanted to go to sea, ever since he'd been taken down to the estuary of the River Mantovar as a very young child to meet Hugo Locklear, his father's oldest brother. The ocean held an almost supernatural fascination for him—he could see things below the surface of the moving water that no other could. He didn't know why. He and Aidan had discussed it on more than one occasion, and it had been mooted that perhaps it was because he was the seventh son of a seventh son. But whatever it was it seemed that Anders had a gift for perceiving the obscure that not even the young wizard had.

Beatrix, though, was becoming more scared by the minute even though Anders was holding her safe. The violence of the storm was overwhelming her, she liked order, craved it. But this disorder was beating at her sensibilities, its chaos and its gloom frightening her; she had never liked the dark.

'Highness, should we not return to our cabin now? Lord Tragen says it's not very safe up here and…and I'm inclined to agree with him,' she said with fervour.

'You'll be all right with us,' interposed Anders, laughing. 'We won't allow the sea to take you, at least not yet,' and he removed his arm from around her waist. Turning her slightly so that he could see her face he put his arm around her shoulders, ostensibly to comfort her, the real reason because he needed to be near her.

'Don't make jokes like that, the sea nearly did have me this morning,' said Aidan morosely, shuddering at the remembrance.

Augusta looked at Aidan, still baffled by him, bewitched by his rapidly changing moods. 'You cannot leave it in the air like that. Tell us. What happened, did you nearly fall overboard?'

So he told them of his errand to the bo'sun at the mainmast, of his precarious journey clinging to the rails and the finding of the rope within his reach. He recounted how he had felt when he realized the line was not secure and that it had run free as he hugged it. And then he told them of the bo'sun saving his life in the nick of time.

Beattie's hands were at her mouth, tales of danger and of heroes overcoming impossible odds, captivated her. But Anders was subdued; he had not heard the full story of his friend's experiences that morning. Was it only this morning? So much had happened in the meantime.

Augusta looked for'ard along the ship to the mainmast, and found the salvaged sail at its foot. Looking at its immensity she wished that she'd had the power to pull it from the ocean without Aidan having to place himself in danger.

'I'm glad you survived, Aidan.' She looked at him, willing him to believe her, and then determined to extirpate the serious turn in the conversation added. 'If you had drowned who would I shout at?'

'Hey, hang about, what was it that Tragen said earlier…he had to conserve his strength for the morning?' Aidan looked at his soaking wet companions. 'Does anyone know what he was on about?'

'Ask him,' said Anders when no-one spoke up. 'Go on,' he urged when the young wizard hesitated.

'Hey, Master, what were you on about just now?' Aidan called out. 'What did you mean when you said…hey, wait a minute,' and without warning he stopped and looked Tragen up and down. 'Your robe isn't wet, are you using a water-repellent spell?'

'I am,' and before Aidan could ask, he said. 'No, you're not using the spell in this storm, I conjured this earlier. I would not have if I'd known that I needed to save my strength. But it's too late to go back and undo what has been done; it would take even more energy.'

Tragen said this in such a serious tone that his apprentice became very apprehensive and thought better of mentioning that he'd used that particular spell to help Trumper salvage the sail.

'That's what I wanted to ask. Why do you need to save your strength?'

'The captain and I have been discussing the affect the weather has on the Grim,' he paused and grasped the larboard rail, steadying himself as the Grim slid down the back of a huge wave. 'We have concluded that the longer we endure this tempest at its present ferocity, the more serious will be the damage the ship will suffer. The only option left to us is to turn away, remove ourselves from this vicinity.'

'But shouldn't we continue on this heading to get home?' Anders asked.

Beatrix interrupted, squeezing his hand. 'Haven't you noticed, Anders? The ship has no wake, we are not moving forward at all.'

'You're right; we do have to turn the ship, don't we?' Anders asked.

'Aye lad, we do, and I will need Aidan's help.' He combed the rain from his beard with his long fingers and continued. 'It is late now, so we have made the decision to wait until morning before attempting the manoeuvre. You realize, of course, that turning about in these seas could very likely lead to us capsizing, and that will happen if we fail.'

He turned to his young apprentice. 'It will require an extraordinary spell to suffice and consequently an extraordinary amount of energy. I will have to be fully rested and that is why I will be retiring to my bunk before long, or rather, to your bunk,' he said, smiling gravely. 'I will need your support, my boy, but you need only conjure small magic. Nevertheless, after today's trauma you are exhausted and are equally in need of sleep. As your bunk is damaged, the captain has agreed that Anders will give up his berth to you for tonight. He will sleep on the floor alongside you.'

'What spell will you cast?' Aidan asked, puzzled.

'We will discuss our actions in the morning. For now, as I said, it is late. Find nourishment as best you can all four of you. I am sorry,

Highness,' Tragen turned to Augusta, 'but in this crisis you must inevitably help yourself. I am afraid that your companion will not be able to fulfil her usual duties. We must not forget that Lady Cornelia needs your care as well. Now, if you will all leave the quarterdeck to the captain...' and he raised an arm to usher them away.

It was as they were passing the helm that it happened. They were following in line, Aidan bringing up the rear, Anders leading and already at the companionway beneath the poop. With their heads bowed against the wind, eyes squinting against the rain and groping their way across the deck, Leash saw his chance. As Aidan drew abreast of him, Leash gave a surreptitious look around, saw no eyes on him and stepped back, colliding hard with the young apprentice.

Aidan, losing his balance, went skidding across the deck. Reflex made him grab Augusta in front of him. Taking her with him, he slammed against the starboard rail—releasing her, he toppled over.

All there was below him was certain death.

He screamed, so did Beatrix on seeing him go over. Augusta, coming up against the rail, was winded. Seeing him slide down the outside of the hull she instinctively lunged for his belt and somehow found enough strength to hold him long enough for Aidan to scrabble for a hold and take his own weight. Anders flew at the both of them and tried to drag him back up whilst Beatrix clung on to Aidan's belt with Augusta.

Hugo reached them just in front of Tragen and, grasping the boy, he hauled him like a sack of feathers, to safety.

Aidan was trembling so much that he held Tragen in a vice. 'How did that happen, my boy? By the Gods I thought we'd lost you then.' He stroked Aidan's head as he returned the hug, his eyes glistening.

'I...I don't know, one minute I'm...'

'All right, calm yourself, take your time you're safe now.' And Tragen continued to hold him tight until Aidan recovered his composure.

Augusta, Beatrix and Anders gathered around, all in various degrees of shock. They looked at each other, the aftermath giving them a sickness in the stomach nothing at all to do with the sea. They gradually relaxed, the tension leaving them, not quite understanding or realizing yet, that all four had acted intuitively as a team.

Leash seethed his face thunder as he looked on from his station at the wheel. Livid at failing for the second time that day, the boy's death now became an obsession. He made up his mind there and then that a means would be found to end the boy's life. The wizard must suffer—he had to! Leash, frustrated, was almost in tears.

The princess of the empire of Drakka and her girlhood companion, the ship's cabin boy and the apprentice wizard; two pairs of friends when they awoke this morning, now fast becoming a foursome, left the quarterdeck on Tragen's orders. Not that Aidan needed much telling. They groped their way along the dark passage stumbling on the jumping deck until reaching Beattie's cabin they all collapsed in silence savouring the safety of the four timber walls.

Aidan did not feel very well at all. His was not the physique to withstand prolonged physical trauma. He had suffered almost continuous strain since awaking that morning, trapped in his blankets on the deck of his cabin. He sat on the bottom bunk with his head in his hands, looking very haggard, his shoulder-length black hair plastered to his skull and face.

Augusta gazed at him with mixed feelings. She just did not know what to make of him. For years she had seen him running around the castle, in her opinion causing disruption, being insolent and not caring one jot that she was a princess. The first time today that she had spoken with him seemed to confirm her earlier held beliefs—he had been making fun of her. Then, although being reprimanded by her for his insolence, he had healed her beloved lady in waiting, exhibiting a caring skill beyond anything she had ever encountered in her life. Ready to forgive his impudence because of that, he had again irritated her with his effrontery; an attitude that no-one else ever subjected her to. And because of that, she had taken great pleasure in seeing him sweat, afraid to meet his master. And how does he repay her for her reprehensible behaviour? He heals her of seasickness. He completely exasperated her.

And then he had frightened her. Her heart in her mouth she had seen him fall towards his death and, in that moment, knew his dying would have devastated her. She had grabbed him wondering now how she had found the strength to hold him. Gazing at him he reminded her of a lost and forlorn orphan begging for comfort. A soaking wet orphan sitting on her bed.

'Get off!' she shouted. 'You're ringing wet…soaking my bed, Aidan!'

He jumped at the sound of her querulous voice. 'What? Oh, I'm sorry, I didn't realize.'

He slid to the floor and rested his back against the bunk instead. He looked up at Augusta and noticed her sopping tunic and britches, her black hair a tangled mess, strands straying across her face. And all of a sudden matters became too much for him and he laughed uncontrollably, his mirth turning quickly to hysteria. He had nearly been killed twice today, had been battered black and blue, nearly drowned on numerous occasions, and this girl was worrying about him soaking her bedclothes!

Beatrix, her sympathetic nature closer to the surface than the others and unable to hold a grudge for longer than five minutes, was the first to his aid. Anders was too surprised to move, and Augusta too confused at the abruptness of the shocking change in him. The royal companion sat beside him on the floor and put her arm around him, cradling his head on her shoulder.

'Sh, Aidan…you're safe now…you're with friends.'

And Aidan sobbed copiously; he couldn't help it, he was a boy whose emotions were akin to the girl's holding him. Like Beatrix he couldn't hide his feelings. His distress brought tears to the eyes of both the girls and nearly to those of Anders standing over them.

Augusta felt the overwhelming need to offer her share of comfort but wasn't sure how. She knelt on the floor the other side of Aidan and hesitantly squeezed his shoulder.

Being consoled by female friends was a new experience for Aidan. He had never had close companions before, other than Anders…never girls. Eventually his tears ceased and he lifted his head and wiped his red eyes.

'I'm sorry,' he sniffed, 'I'm being stupid.'

'No you're not, Aidan,' said Augusta quietly, 'you're being very sensible, getting it out of your system will make you feel better. God knows, I would have broken long before now and I've been trained not to show my emotions.'

Beatrix looked askance at this.

Augusta had never cared enough to hide her feelings before and she had never seen a boy weep and hadn't even been sure if they could. But seeing Aidan cry, and showing him her concern, had somehow removed the last vestiges of any ill-feeling between them.

'Hey, now who's calling who stupid?' Augusta asked.

Aidan sighed, and looked up at them all. 'I'm absolutely bloody starving. Have you any food?' he asked, and then he grinned sheepishly.

Beatrix laughed as she gave him a quick hug. 'You're not supposed to swear in front of ladies, but as it happens we do have bread, cheese and the last of the red apples,' and she rose to get them.

'Oh hell, I think we need to change our clothes again,' said Anders, wringing water from his tunic.

'After we eat, Anders, we'll hang them up overnight to dry. No...I don't mean to use magic so take that look off your face!' The expression on his friend's face had been enough to put spells right out of Aidan's mind.

'Yes,' interposed Augusta, 'we'll do the same after we've checked on poor Cornelia. How long will she sleep Aidan?'

'Until the afternoon and hopefully longer; the more she sleeps the shorter the healing process. And before we go to sleep, my big friend,' he turned to look at Anders, 'I'll need you to spread more unguent on my burns.'

Later that night, Tragen slept in Aidan's bunk and Aidan slept in Anders' berth; Lady Cornelia in Augusta's cot and Augusta in Cornelia's bunk bed; Beatrix slept in her own.

It did not sleep, it liked the dark hours and it watched the filthy, bound man being hauled across the cold, stone-flagged floor towards it. The two holding the prisoner upright with their arms in his armpits, his feet dragging behind, walked with bowed heads and white cowls raised. All was silence until they thrust the captive into the cage and slammed it closed. The mesh banged hard against his nose, breaking it and this stirred his consciousness, the prisoner opened his eyes...and screamed in its face.

It hissed its laughter.

Aidan, fast asleep, heard him—and saw him. 'Please, why are you laughing? Please stop laughing he is in great pain!'

Only Anders had the most uncomfortable rest, not just because he slept on the hard floor alongside his friend—he heard Aidan talking in his sleep.

Six

Tragen – his long white hair and beard brushed immaculately – woke Aidan the next morning, the second morning of the storm. Stepping over Anders in the narrow berth, a very small room hidden behind a heavy curtain in the captain's cabin, he accidentally disturbed the cabin boy.

Anders, despite lack of sleep, awoke highly animated. He never missed Aidan creating magic whether it was with or without permission. Tragen, having given up years before in his attempts to separate the boys – the two could never understand that they could not do everything together – assented to Anders accompanying them to his cabin to hear Aidan's instructions.

Augusta, bleary-eyed, opened the door into the dark passageway and bumped into them on her way to check the condition of her lady-in-waiting. Augusta was once again wearing the same shirt and britches from the night before, although soiled and crumpled they were, nevertheless, very comfortable if a little smelly. With her shoulder length, black hair brushed and tied back at the nape in nautical fashion and barefoot, she was the very epitome of a young sailor.

'Where are you going, Milord?' she asked pompously.

'Just along to my cabin, Highness.'

'Oh, you're going to give Aidan his instructions, aren't you?' Augusta asked excitedly, her pomposity vanishing instantly.

'I am, Highness.' Tragen sighed. He had managed to creep past her cabin without disturbing her on his way to fetch the boys, but he would have had to be very lucky to evade her on the return.

'Can you wait just a moment while I see if Lady Cornelia requires anything? I would love to see at first-hand how wizards work.' She added as an afterthought, just to please the magician. 'I promise not to interfere in any way, Milord.'

The wizard raised one eyebrow disbelievingly. 'You will have to hurry, the captain is to join us and he cannot be away from his quarterdeck for too long.'

Her incapacitated lady in waiting was still sleeping fast, her vast bosom rising and falling rhythmically as she lay on her back snoring, the high sides of the violently swinging cot keeping her safe from falling to the deck. As Aidan followed his mentor into their shared accommodation, Augusta ran from her cabin and grabbed

Beatrix, who was trying to extricate Augusta's blankets from beneath the bunk, how they had ended up under there was a mystery that Beatrix would never comprehend.

'Come on, quickly, they are deciding on what magic they will use,' Augusta ordered.

Beatrix, electrified, seized their still damp tunics from the previous night; donning them they reached the doorway of Aidan's cabin, just ahead of the burly figure of Locklear.

'If you will excuse me, Highness, I believe, in this case, that I should enter before you,' Hugo said, rather brusquely.

Augusta turned and her eyes widened at the obvious fatigue in the man's face. He was wet from top to toe and looked as if he had been up all night, which he had. Hugo Locklear never slept in bad weather. She immediately moved to allow the stressed man access to the small room and crowded after him into the little space left at the door.

Tragen looked up from his chair below the porthole. 'I'm sorry, Hugo, but there will be no privacy to discuss these matters.'

'They will know soon enough, my friend. So…you have rested?'

'Aye, little enough I fear, I have been thrown about on my bed most of the night, I hate the top bunk, but it will have to suffice. The storm, is it any worse?'

'Wizard, can you not feel it beneath your feet?' his weariness making him irascible. 'The wind has increased enormously; we are no longer hove-to we are being driven astern, it is only the sea-anchors that are holding us steady. If we do not turn about soon it will be too late—the Grim will have turned turtle.' He rubbed the exhaustion from his eyes with his huge knuckles. 'Whatever action you have to take, do it now. I have every available man, sailor and marine, bailing and pumping and repairing sprung boards constantly. We have to ease the strain on the hull immediately and the only possible way is to run before this wind.'

'Very well, Hugo, as we have no other option,' he turned to his apprentice. Aidan was standing there feeling very guilty; it was his accident that had deprived his master of a good night's sleep.

'We do not have much time to accomplish the deed, my boy, so listen carefully. I will attempt a shield enchantment to calm the seas forward of the ship and curtail the worst of the wind. The spell will of necessity be one of the most powerful I have ever conjured and it will sorely tax me.'

He paused and studied his apprentice worriedly, Aidan still seemed traumatized. The actions of the day before had exacted their toll on his slight body, and sleep had not restored his vigour. His face was drawn and his dark eyes sunk deeply beneath his eyebrows. His body, though, was a lot stronger than its lack of weight implied. Tragen sighed; he needed his apprentice's strength this morning, for if they failed the penalties would be dire for all.

Tragen resumed, 'I, of course, will use my staff, but great concentration and power will be required to form the shield. As such I will not be able to create the light needed for the captain to know when to turn the ship. You will have to stand with me and cast that particular spell. You must ensure the light is of sufficient strength, not only to show him the shield in front of us, he must also see the surface of the ocean. Do you understand, Aidan?'

'I do,' and he inhaled deeply. 'But where will we stand so that he'll see us? I know the obvious place is in the bows, but standing there will be too dangerous, won't it?'

'Alas, Aidan, we must place ourselves in grave peril—it has to be in the bows we stand. However,' and he turned to the ship's master, 'we will need ropes to tether ourselves to the foremast and sailors to aid us in this. Hugo, how many men can you spare?'

Locklear stared at his friend, his face more drained than ever. 'I am afraid, Tragen, I can spare no-one to help you. If I remove even one from their present duties the ship will founder.'

'By the Gods, Hugo, you have four hundred men aboard this ship—we must have help! We have to be fully engrossed on the enchantments…we may need to be physically held in place.'

'I know the Grim's complement, Tragen; I don't need you to tell me.' He tugged at his beard angrily and sighed. 'I'm sorry; I know what you are going to say. If you are unable to cast the spells necessary for us to turn, the ship will come to grief anyway. I say this, my old friend; if I take any men from pumping, bailing and patching the hull, we will sink as we turn. Tragen, you and Aidan must manage on your own.'

'We can help,' Anders interrupted, shocked at hearing his uncle quarrel with the wizard.

Tragen and Hugo gazed in consternation.

Anders continued. 'I know it will be dangerous, Milord, I have been at sea long enough to know what can happen to us there. But none of us can stand to one side while Aidan and you risk your lives for us,' he licked lips that had suddenly dried. 'We're all in danger, Milord, and we're the only ones who are free to help you although you may think we're too young. I promise you we'll obey you in whatever way you...'

'Please, Milord,' urged Augusta, as Anders ran out of words. 'We are the only help you can get. I assure you, we will follow your orders without question.'

It was Beattie's quiet remarks though, that swung Tragen, helping him make the decision. 'We have the right to help save the ship, Milord. We cannot stand aside and do nothing...you do not have the right to deny our aid.'

'What say you, Hugo? I believe the young lady is correct, hey! And Aidan and I will be in desperate need; can you supply us with the necessary ropes?'

'Aye, man,' he said, reluctantly agreeing. 'The bo'sun is working at the sail locker beneath the foc's'le he'll pass them to you. But beware Tragen, if the prince ever discovers that we intentionally placed his daughter in grave peril...'

'Don't worry on that score, Captain Locklear. I am in grave danger anyway,' interrupted Augusta, 'and that is what I will tell him if needs be. He will agree that it is my duty to help in any way I can.'

'Very well, I will return to my post on the quarterdeck now. I wish you good fortune; you carry the prayers of us all. Aidan,' he turned to the boy standing silently by, 'please keep in mind—I will need the light to be as bright as possible for as long as it takes us to turn about.' Saying that, he departed with one long and intense look at them all, it was as if he was trying to implant their images on his memory.

Before Locklear had reached his companionway, Tragen addressed the four youths in no uncertain terms. 'I must emphasize this point although you have already promised. You have no option but to obey me instantly whatever the command, all our lives may depend on it. Do you understand?'

He put his hand on Aidan's shoulder to reassure the haggard apprentice wizard. 'We will tether ourselves on long lines to the foremast. Once the bows are safe you and I will move as far forward as possible. That is where the main power of the conjuration will be created. There you will stand to one side of me and conjure your light. Remember—raise the illumination high enough to enable those on the quarterdeck to see as much as possible. While you are at that endeavour, I will invoke the shield with my staff. Beware my movements, for as the ship turns I will turn the opposite way and increase the strength of the spell to cover the increasing aspect of the ship facing the storm. The greatest danger will arise when the Grim is beam on to the wind, should we fail at that point then the ship will broach.'

He smiled encouragingly at his young apprentice, whilst the others, beginning to understand now what they had let themselves in for, grew more apprehensive.

'I do not expect to fail; we know each other too well for there to be any misunderstanding between us. But if events do not go as planned, do not attempt to mindmeld with me. It may prove fatal to distract me at that moment. Do you understand, Aidan?'

'Aye,' he nodded.

Tragen turned and spoke to the others. 'It will be your tasks to ensure our safety as best you can. As there are three of you, Anders being the biggest will ward me on his own, you two ladies together, will protect Aidan. But I must stress, you are to take great care of your own safety as well. Do not under any circumstances place yourselves in a position of extreme risk just to rescue us. And in this you will obey me,' he ordered.

They nodded silently. Augusta made to question Tragen, but seeing the steely glint in his eyes she recalled what Beatrix had said the day before. Unexpectedly afraid of him, she changed her mind and stilled her tongue.

Tragen and Aidan led the way from the cabin. The old wizard tucked his long staff into his belt and quickly climbed up to the hatch, Aidan already on the bottom rungs before he reached the top. Tragen removed the bolt and recalling that the last time he'd lifted the cover he'd nearly lost it, took especial care this time. But even then the wind caught it and almost blew it out of his hands.

The fury of the tempest assailed them immediately. The wind no longer howled but screamed its rage and the rain stung bitingly. The waves swooped by horrendously high and frighteningly fast, a wall of iron-grey hard water. White spume formed an almost continual sheet as it was blown from crest to crest way above their heads. And the crackling of the lightning distorted their sight, the horizon, when they could see it, just feet away.

Aidan and Anders closed the hatch and then, clinging to the lifeline that stretched fore and aft, they all moved forward passing the mains'l still piled at the foot of the mainmast. Resting a moment to catch their breath they continued on past the redundant galley pipe to the foc's'le steps either side of the foremast. They clutched desperately at the slippery line, expecting at any moment to be blown, or washed, overboard.

Trumper looked round at their arrival his face expressing his surprise at seeing the youngsters; nevertheless he reached inside the sail locker doors and retrieved ropes for them all. The bo'sun, his normally ruddy face now ashen, stared apprehensively at the party struggling slowly up the steps on to the forecastle.

Tragen, bareheaded, his beard blowing back over his shoulders, tied one end of his rope around his waist and, gauging the length as best he could, he secured the other end to the foremast, leaving enough play for him to reach the bowsprit. He waited for the others to do the same.

They were battered in mind and body when they reached the small bow deck and found the conditions absolutely appalling. Standing in waist-high water on occasions, the bows almost continually underwater, the incessant clamour beating at their ears, they found it impossible to rest even for a moment. The wizard stood with his back pressed against the foremast his eyes closed, his legs braced on the heaving deck, and he raised his staff vertically in front of him and faced directly into the wind. Beatrix and Augusta hugged the foc's'le rail squinting through eyes impossible to open wide while Aidan joined Anders in holding Tragen steady.

They all watched the old wizard, only his lips moving in the gloom and it was a long time before any change was detected…an easing of the pressure on their ears followed by a lessening of the wind tugging at them. Then a low rhythmic cadence rose above the gale, and as the mantra increased in strength, the beat of the rain and the wash of the waves across the bows gradually declined and amazingly ceased altogether.

The youngsters stared about them at the dream world in which they abruptly found themselves. All around the tempest raged as before, the crests of the waves too high to see, the rain sweeping past in sheets, but none of it had any impact in their close vicinity. They stood as if in a dry hole in the ocean, the deck at their feet, clear of waves for the first time in two days. They waited; preparing to carry out the tasks allotted them, the vista unbelievable, all their senses dumbfounded.

Tragen walked forwards toward the bowsprit as Anders carefully paid out the rope tied to the wizard's waist. Aidan accompanied his master and both stepped into the bows of the beleaguered ship. All was black before them, the enchanted shield, invisible to the naked eye, also hid the lightning flashes ahead of the ship. And then Aidan conjured his light.

The wizard's apprentice sang out loud and clear and full of confidence. At once, a brilliant white light formed and grew ever larger in the boy's outstretched hands. An incandescent ball of light, blindingly beautiful in its brilliance, smelling powerfully of lavender, and the bow of the ship was lit up as if it was noon in August.

Tragen glanced at his apprentice and again wondered fleetingly, as he had done many times in the past, why Aidan's spells always gave off the aroma of the bluish-purple flowers.

Augusta gasped and blinked, blinded by the brightness of the light. Recovering quickly she and Beatrix watched with astonishment as Aidan seemingly grew larger and they gripped his line even firmer.

Anders though did not take his eyes from Tragen when the magician's voice grew louder and deeper in tone, as Aidan's softer tones gelled with his.

Locklear, high up on his quarterdeck, sighed when he saw the light come up, the sight of the bows and the sea just ahead, an enormous relief. Hopper immediately ordered the sea-anchors raised and as men readied a stormsail the Grim appeared to breathe its appreciation, its happiness, at being relieved of the tremendous pressure of the storm.

Locklear shouted to the four men now on the helm. 'Prepare yourselves my beauties, we are about to find out if you are seamen or landlubbers.'

Talbot smiled grimly and grasped the wheel even tighter as did Nkosi and Bertram, two of the others. The fourth man, Leash, his mind full of schemes to ensure the demise of the apprentice wizard, wished ill on them all, though he was very careful to hide his thoughts from his fellows. It did not seem to register with him that if Tragen and Aidan failed then his own death was assured—or maybe it wasn't, he wasn't sure if he'd be allowed to die.

In the bow the light increased, its brilliance reflecting off the air forward of them. Tragen's shield became visible, a haze similar to that of a current of warm air, shimmering before them.

The wizard raised his staff and held the pointed base in his fists. Holding the stave aloft on outstretched arms, Tragen quickly glanced at Aidan alongside him and winked.

Aidan laughed, thoroughly enjoying himself; he was at ease performing magic with his "father" and he couldn't be happier.

The wizard resumed his chant, his total concentration ensuring the growth of the shield. Gripping his staff even tighter, he sang louder still and lowered the knuckle at the top of the rod until he was pointing it directly ahead of him. The knuckle glowed a deep carmine, and the shield advanced further forward and grew ever more until it formed a barrier, dense and unyielding, across the expanse of ocean and sky before them.

The ship commenced its turn slowly as if waking from a daze, nearly toppling Anders, Augusta and Beatrix, all struggling to maintain their foothold on the sloping deck. They watched the unearthly spectacle taking place in front of the wizard, a sight so implausible that their brains refused to take it in.

Tragen, stood rigidly in the bow, as if he was an extension of the boards of the foc's'le, a part of the substance of the ship. His single-minded attention focused on the enchantment, the energy he was using in holding the staff at arm's length not worrying him at all.

Aidan, in creating a spell of a vastly lower class, was far more relaxed and he took the time to look around the ship. He studied the seas below the bows, felt the lightness of the breeze, witnessed the small ripples playing on the surface of the ocean and scanned the anxious faces of his friends. He smiled at them all before returning to attend his master. Aidan's strength was only needed to hold the light aloft and to ensure the illumination was sufficient for the captain's needs. But, on examining his master closely, he became concerned at the exhaustion he could see building in the wizard, a fatigue that was not apparent to anyone else. This was the most powerful spell Tragen had ever conjured and however much the wizard had prepared, there was bound to be a serious depletion in his stamina and repercussions on his health.

The ship came about slowly to larboard, and Tragen turned the other way to continue facing east directly into the wind. At the same time, he held his staff level and began waving it from side to side so that the edges of the shield widened to conceal the body of the Grim.

It seemed forever before the turn reached its most critical stage, the point at which the vessel lay broadside to the wind. Tragen was now staring directly over the starboard side of the ship, the storm gnashing at the borders of the spell. Tragen's face was a bath of sweat although his voice remained strong and Aidan's light remained steady and bright in the palms of his hands, his feet like his master's, seemingly stuck to the deck.

Augusta, Beatrix and Anders were beginning to relax, their attention waning, when Tragen all of a sudden cried out and staggered back. He fell to his knees releasing the staff to fall alongside him. Immediately the shield shook and began to fade.

Aidan, although every bone in his body had warned him to expect something to go wrong, stared in disbelief for moments. He turned quickly for his helpers, and knowing his instincts to be correct, beckoned to Augusta.

'Quick, come here.'

And Augusta accustomed now to obeying his orders walked forward and stood alongside him not knowing what to expect as she stared at Tragen on his knees.

'Don't be afraid, Augusta,' using her name for the first time without either realizing it. 'Hold up your hands like me.'

And she raised her hands in front of her. He stared deeply into her green eyes, his own conveying his trust and placed the ball of enchanted light into her hands.

'There is no need for fear, Augusta; you have magic, just hold the light. Hold it high for the captain; it will not harm you. Tragen needs me he is in great danger.'

Augusta, shaking like a leaf, raised the light with no second thoughts all her previous misgivings about him forgotten forever. She lifted the light high and wondered—what magic? And what was the strange feeling in her chest, was it the magic or was it Aidan?

Aidan shouted at Anders and Beatrix. 'Protect Augusta! Keep well away from my master and me.'

The cabin boy and the lady's companion stared at each other, bewildered and fearful. They did not know what had happened to the wizard, or how Augusta could have the magic to hold the light, but both remembered Tragen's admonishment not to distract him if there was trouble. They watched their friend approach the wizard, and then

Aidan's last words registered with Beatrix. She was appalled; how did he have the gall to call her mistress by her chosen name, not even she did that?

Aidan reached the old man, kneeling, holding his head in his hands his staff forgotten for the moment lying on the deck against his foot, its runes pulsating brightly. He stood behind his mentor; staring down at him intently he placed his hands over Tragen's.

'*Master, what's wrong?*' and receiving no answer he continued even more forcefully. '*Come back, Master.*' Again there was no response, Aidan put his forehead to the top of the wizard's head and repeated the mindmeld. '*Master, come back, please*' he begged.

Ignoring the express instructions given him earlier, he searched frantically for his master's consciousness and unintentionally spoke aloud. 'I have to find you, Master, forgive me for my disobedience...I...I don't know how else to help you.'

Anders started forward acutely worried, he'd never seen his friend in this much of a panic before. But Beatrix held him back, her faith in Aidan beyond question.

'Leave him be Anders, he knows what he's doing—trust him,' she using similar words to those used by Anders the day before.

They stood at the rail afraid to take their eyes from Tragen and Aidan. But the storm began encroaching on the ship again as the shield weakened, small waves appearing, the wind rising blowing straight into their faces.

'Quickly, Aidan,' shouted Augusta, in alarm, taking her eyes from the ball of light in her hands. 'We're going to broach.'

Aidan glanced up at her and ceased his mindmeld. With a heavy sickness deep in the pit of his stomach, he stared around, at a complete loss; despairing, he had no idea how to contact his master.

'Heal him, Aidan,' shouted Beatrix intuitively.

At his wits' end he latched on to her suggestion; he again turned to the wizard and gripped his master's hands even tighter. Shutting out all outside influences, totally engrossed in his task, he achieved success almost immediately. Tragen, waking from the trance shook Aidan's hands from his head.

'What happened?' Aidan asked shaking with relief. 'We lost each other and I...I was so scared.'

Tragen felt the wind in his hair and swiftly realizing their predicament, grabbed his staff. 'Later! I need your energy my boy mine is all but spent. Assist me, hold my staff with me.'

Shock pierced Aidan. He had never even touched the staff before. In fact, it had been hammered into him over the years that it was sacrosanct; he was never to as much as place a fingernail on it. He looked at his mentor, frightened witless.

'You want me,' and he swallowed audibly, 'to actually touch your staff?'

Tragen stared at Aidan quickly comprehending his fear. 'Aye, my boy, you have incredible power...you have the strength to wield this staff with me. Haven't I just felt the immense energy in your hands? Your healing power is more than enough to sustain you; my staff cannot hurt you now.'

Tragen, with Aidan standing close, held the base of the staff horizontally in their hands and the knuckle once again faced the tempest. The shield strengthened instantly, the ocean calmed and the shimmering of the enchantment was again lit up at the bows as Augusta once more held the light aloft.

Locklear who had nearly given up hope when he saw Tragen fall, gazed on the ocean once more, a gentle swell on its surface. He at once renewed his efforts and those of his crew at the helm. The long ship came about slowly but surely, and with its stern facing the wind at last, the stormsail bellying full, the great vessel flew from its tormentor. The crew fell to the deck wherever they were stationed, gasping for breath, the tension of the last hours leaving them trembling. They had no strength for cheering.

Tragen held the shield in place until the ship was safely on its way...to where was debatable. He eventually lowered the staff and Aidan reluctantly relinquished his hold. Gradually the shield dissipated, the tempest resuming its attack on the ship, but this time at its stern. The occupants of the bows, now sheltered a little by the upper structure of the ship, collapsed exhausted to the deck, all that is except Augusta. Tragen, his head down inhaling deeply and hoarsely was drained beyond measure. Aidan, his bones trembling to their core because of the magic he'd encountered in the staff, now understood how much he didn't know of the art. Anders and Beatrix, glad it was all over, sitting shoulder to shoulder, holding hands their backs against the rail, sodden to the skin taking comfort from each other's nearness, neither daring to acknowledge it.

And Augusta, her long black hair sticking wildly to her face and neck, standing with the light in her hands, mesmerized by the magic and wanting more.

Aidan lifted his head and smiled up at her. His prince's daughter, much his age and much his height…slim and very attractive, her looks registering somewhere in his subconscious, her emerald eyes reflecting the wonder he often felt when conjuring spells.

'Augusta,' he said quietly, disturbing her reverie. 'I had better extinguish the light now.'

She looked down at him. 'How come you passed this to me? I have always thought only those with a talent for the magic arts could sustain a spell,' she was completely enthralled. 'I have never made magic in my whole life!'

Aidan rose to stand in front of her. 'You are right. But then I remembered when I fell on the quarterdeck yesterday, you caught me by my belt and held me. Your strength was far greater than it should have been, no girl should have been able to halt my slide into the sea. And then I saw it in your eyes—magic! That's why I passed the spell to you,' he smiled wearily. 'How you have magic now I don't know, but I suppose we'll find out…in time.'

'I really have magic?'

At his nod she gave a great beaming grin and stared at the ball of light in her hands. 'I adore magic, Aidan!'

He laughed. 'So do I…so do I,' and Aidan, making small intricate finger movements, extinguished the light, but only in her hands.

Her eyes continued to shine brilliantly.

'You will show me more?' She asked eagerly, grasping his hands and ignoring everyone else, 'please, Aidan.'

Tragen interrupted. 'Be careful, my boy, magic in a woman has ensnared many a wizard.' He paused to catch his breath, raking his long white hair from his face. 'I am confident though, that you will discover how she comes to the ability.'

He turned his head to include Augusta. 'Wizards and Adepts are always born with their skills—always! I have never known magic precipitously appear in someone who has never been able to display such ability previously.'

Hesitating, he again spoke, solely to his apprentice. 'When you come to teach her make sure you start with the small conjurations, and remember—no showing off! Be vigilant, and above all, show her infinite care. I do not know if her father would wish her to know our craft. No wizard has ever gained a throne so this may have untold consequences for Mantovar. Your training of her may have to cease when we return home. Until her father decides, her skill must be kept secret and yet she must be taught to control it. But the ability to pass on knowledge is another lesson an apprentice has to learn...it may as well start here.'

'Yes! And you can carry on calling me by my chosen name,' said Augusta, beaming at him, grinning simply for the reason that she felt absurdly happy, even though they and the Grim were still in grave danger, battered and threatened by an unearthly tempest from hell.

Seven

'My God, Tragen, when I saw you fall my heart stopped. What happened?' Locklear asked worry over the last hours had etched deep lines in his face. Both men were taking their ease in the captain's cabin sharing a bottle of his best Gilian brandy, a present off Tragen. The wizard, exhausted, and pulling at his beard, needed his bed more but he could not go to sleep without sharing the ominous knowledge he alone had discovered.

'Ah, Hugo, again I heard it and this time I nearly succumbed. If not for Aidan and his healing of my mind, I…I would have been lost.'

He leaned his back against the hard, brown leather of the chair, crossed his long legs at his ankles and propped his elbows on the ornate arms. With a mug in one hand and the other holding his staff to his body as if afraid he'd lose it, he continued, knowing he had no answers yet.

'Laughter, Hugo…the same laughter and this time like a fool I forgot everything and went searching for it.'

'And did you find it?' Locklear alarmed, leant forward across his desk.

Tragen was again looking his centuries-old age. 'I confirmed my fears,' and he stared into his mug, gently swirling the deep amber liquid. Distracted momentarily by the light reflecting off its richness, he understood why Aidan and Anders had yielded to its potency. 'Oh Hugo, I touched its mind, and the horror I sensed there seemed to steal my wits. It drew me to it.'

'So, whatever it is, now knows of you?'

'That's the strangest thing I do not believe it does. I felt no change as I perceived its mind, if a mind it was…it may just have been its emotions. The laughter altered not even one iota, which it would have if it had known I was there. No, it continued its manic merriment.' Tragen swallowed another mouthful of the Gilian and allowed the warmth to sustain him as it found its way to his stomach.

The fleeting silence his remarks brought to the cabin, making him anxious, he gulped the rest of his brandy and clutched the empty mug in his tired hand.

Locklear sat up straight, staring at the wizard. 'Did you glean any more of its purpose?' He stretched across and replenished the wizard's empty mug.

Tragen shook his head. 'All I sense is its single-minded malevolence with us as the object of its hate.'

Locklear turned sideways in his chair and peered out the gallery window at the storm, the huge waves towering above the stern obliterating what little light there was. He stroked his full black beard and sighed.

'Well, with luck, my friend, we will soon be free of this tempest. Whoever, or whatever, is behind this cannot keep it going for much longer. And the greater the distance between us and this evil thing the better we'll feel.' Looking again at the wizard, he said. 'But just in case there are other unforeseen events, I think it best if we continue to keep the lady hidden.'

Tragen nodded. 'It would be ideal if she remained masquerading as a young member of the crew, as she is now.'

'Should we tell her of our fears?'

'I do not believe there is need to, Hugo…at least not yet, there is no need to frighten her. There is a friendship developing between her and the others. I say we leave it progress normally for now. And besides,' lifting his mug to be refilled for a third time and taking another larger swallow of brandy, he continued, 'she seems quite taken with wearing britches.' He chuckled, lifting the sombre mood briefly. 'But Lady Cornelia should be informed of the whole situation, I know her personally and her reputation is formidable. She is a very determined lady and has the full support of Augusta's mother in whatever action she deems necessary for the protection and upbringing of her charge. Cornelia will not be very happy at seeing Augusta improperly dressed and running around with servants. She will have grave doubts for the girl's safety and will order her to resume her normal attire, and her proper station in life…unless we can persuade her otherwise, of course.'

'But, Highness, it is not seemly. He is nothing but a young scoundrel…you, yourself have always said so! We don't even know anything of his family, if he has any. How can you possibly allow him to be so familiar? Not even I call you by your name and I've grown up with you! Lady Cornelia will never approve, neither will your father, and your mother will be shamed.'

'You are nagging me, Beattie, desist. I have made my decision. Aidan will use my name and if it makes you feel better I give you permission as well. Cornelia will not criticize me for long,' and she smiled, conceit written all over her face. 'You know I can twist her around my little finger.'

'You think so,' Beatrix said looking sidelong at her, could she dare use her name?

'And talking of being familiar, what is going on between you and Anders?'

'I don't know what you mean,' said Beatrix, blushing like mad.

'No? I've seen you holding hands. But never mind that, Cornelia will have to realize that when Aidan comes to the end of his training he will gain his peerage and he'll be deemed a suitable friend by everyone...so why wait! Besides, he did heal her and she'll be very grateful for that, won't she?'

'But the completion of his schooling is a long time off yet and...and what will she say of these clothes?' Trying another tack, Beatrix was becoming truly desperate, whatever she said her mistress appeared to be heading for trouble. 'You can't tell me she will approve of us wearing britches and going barefoot. And these clothes are not even clean now,' she wrinkled her nose in disgust.

'Then we must ensure that nothing else is available,' Augusta countered determinedly, and saying this, a wicked grin stretched her mouth wide.

'Oh no! What are you thinking of now?' Beattie's stomach lurched; she had plenty of experience of this particular look.

She and Augusta had known each other since birth; both had been born on the same day, fifteen years before in the huge Castle of Mantovar. Beattie's mother, Lady Dotrice, besides being the princess' favourite lady-in-waiting along with Lady Cornelia, was also her closest confidante and friend. And the two girls had literally grown up together, usually sleeping in the same nursery. It had always been an accepted fact that when Augusta went south into Drakka to further her education, Beatrix would accompany her as her companion and share her lessons. But this look on Augusta's face always boded ill for them both; she had a knack for instigating wild schemes which usually had an outcome quite unexpected.

There had been one remarkable experience a while back and the outcome of that was still a mystery. She and Beatrix lived under strict orders never to leave the confines of the castle unless accompanied by an armed escort, but the year before leaving for Drakka a carnival had arrived in the town. Excitement had gripped everyone and the whole town and castle erupted with delight. Augusta and Beatrix couldn't wait to experience the sights and sounds of the shows and dressed as peasant girls had for the first time sneaked past the castle guards. Relishing the freedom from bodyguards, the two young girls dawdled in the marketplace of the town sampling the wares from several of the local trades' people.

But as the morning progressed eventually they arrived at the meadow where the troubadours had set up camp. They were utterly captivated. The travellers had pitched their myriad stalls and tents in a haphazard fashion throughout the large field. A kaleidoscope of colours greeted them reds, yellows, greens, browns, you name it there was a splash of the colour somewhere in the meadow. The two girls spent hours wandering through, tasting the goods on a variety of stalls, staring wide-eyed at the performers inside and outside of brightly striped tents.

In due course, they had found themselves outside a small white tent, on the edge of the encampment. A very pretty, middle-aged woman was sitting alone in its doorway, but everyone was walking past her, ignoring her as if she was invisible. It was her dazzling smile more than anything that intrigued them. It was very unusual in a peasant to have pure white teeth for they usually had mouths full of broken, black or yellow teeth, very often none at all. The lovely smile, along with her long black tresses and the lingering smell of lavender attracted the two girls and they went over to talk to her and discovered she was a seer. But what she told the girls was such a lot of nonsense that they soon left her and returned home to find the castle in an uproar. Their absence at luncheon had been noticed and a search had been mounted for them, Prince Bertrand and his wife frantic, worrying for their safety. Their punishment had lasted a month.

But when the troubadours performed at the castle in front of Augusta's parents later that week, the girls questioned the travellers about the woman, but not one knew of her. In fact, they denied all knowledge of travelling with a seer. One even smiled indulgently, explaining that a white tent would never be used by any member of the carnival—the colour never attracted customers. The girls were mystified and despite searching amongst the crowds they failed to find any sign of her.

They had wanted to ask her to explain further about what she meant when she said they would aid a son to find his father. Her disappearance had been very puzzling.

'You will be carrying wash-water to Cornelia in a moment,' Augusta said, interrupting Beattie's thoughts. 'When we are attending her you will have an accident and tip the water over the clothes in my wardrobe that are not already ruined by the sea.'

'There will not be sufficient in that bowl to soil all those, that's not going to work.'

'Then let's see if the boys can help. Kindly go and fetch them, and hurry, I do believe I hear Cornelia stirring,' she said, imperiously waving her companion out the door.

Beatrix obeyed reluctantly, muttering beneath her breath.

Anders, who was nearer, opened the door when she knocked and was unceremoniously pushed into the room when she rushed in, the door rebounding loudly against the bulkhead.

'What the hell...' he asked, falling promptly onto the burned bed. Aidan startled, looked round, a wet shirt in his hands.

'You must help me...now! My mistress is demanding your aid for a mischief that will only succeed in causing terrible trouble. I can feel it! You have to stop her, come quickly and DO NOT DO as she asks!'

The two boys stared at each other in amazement. Beatrix ran out and down the passage, Anders raced after her. Aidan flung his shirt on the floor and promptly fell over it. Cursing, he rose, and rubbing his knee he followed, catching up with the two of them as they arrived in Beattie's cabin.

Augusta, only just managing to avoid the swinging overhead lantern, was pacing the short distance within, her eyes almost closed and her index finger in the corner of her mouth. Beatrix watched as the plot developed in her mistress' mind. The plan almost visible behind her flashing eyes when she opened them wide to stare at the new arrivals.

'Highness, what is it now?' Aidan asked, worried.

'Right, Aidan...yes!' She stopped her pacing and stared at the apprentice wizard. 'I want you to ruin the rest of my clothes,' and seeing the shock on his face, added. 'I don't mean for good, just for a few days, until Cornelia gets used to me wearing britches.

'Why? I mean, why on earth do you still want to wear our clothes?' Anders asked.

'You obviously don't know what it's like to wear a gown onboard a ship, do you?'

'Of course I don't,' replied Anders, very indignant.

'Mind you, he wouldn't tell you if he did,' smirked Aidan.

'Shut it! You're the one who wears a robe, not me.' Anders retorted.

'Quiet, the pair of you! Take it from me…it is very uncomfortable in this weather. And climbing ladders is an abomination.'

'Well, as a temporary measure we could soak them again, I suppose. We can use this bowl of water, it might help for a little while,' Aidan said dubiously, stirring the contents of the large washbowl rather vigorously with his hand.

'No, we've thought of that. Beattie says there's not enough and she's probably correct. No, you'll have to think of something else,' Augusta said, smacking Aidan's hand to stop his splashing.

The relief on Anders' face was short-lived when he realized that Aidan was contemplating the use of magic. Aidan's face, on the other hand, was gleaming at the prospect.

'And I gave you permission to call me Augusta, didn't I?'

'You did, yes Highn…Augusta.'

'Good! Now then, little wizard…how will you do it?'

Flummoxed, Aidan paused, scratching his head. 'Hang about; I have to think it through, first. I can't just conjure any old spell for a job like this; it takes a lot of thinking about.'

'You haven't got long, Cornelia seems to be waking. I'm sure this will only need a little spell,' she said impatiently, standing over Aidan who was now stretched out on the bottom bunk, his hands behind his head.

Anders burst in desperately. 'Highness, he has express orders from Lord Tragen that he isn't to cast spells in confined spaces.'

'He only means warming spells!' And at Augusta's enquiring look, and ignoring the yelp of fear from Beatrix, Aidan went on. 'Tragen has the stupid idea I have accidents with spells involving heat. Anders will tell you that it was his fault last time when I burned the bunk. Now where are your clothes, Highness…sorry…Augusta?'

Just then, there was an anxious cry from the cabin over the way. Lady Cornelia had awoken to find herself ensconced in her mistress's cot, with her ankle swathed in linen.

'Augusta,' she shouted, 'Augusta where are you? What am I doing here?'

76

'Quickly Beattie, go and calm her. Tell her I'll be right along.' As she ran out, shaking her head and muttering that all hell was about to break loose, Augusta turned to Anders.

'You, grab that bowl, pretend it has water in it for washing Lady Cornelia and take it in to Beattie. Aidan have you had any more thoughts? He shook his head. 'Come on hurry up I have to go in and see her she's not going to wait much longer.'

'Well, she can hardly get out of bed to come and get you!'

'Aha! I know that,' she said sarcastically. 'But she's going to smell a rat if I don't get in there before long.'

'That's it!'

'What?'

'A spell of fragrance should do it,' he pondered. 'Yes, I can cast an enchantment to make your gowns smell,' and he grinned evilly at her, 'smell absolutely foul.'

'Yes!' she laughed. 'Yes that should do it. That's a wonderful idea. I should have thought of that myself.'

Aidan preened, rubbing his fingernails on his chest. 'You need a smart mind like mine for that.'

'Huh,' she said disparagingly, 'don't push it. Wait, nothing can go wrong, can it?' She gave him a worried look remembering the wizard's restrictions on heat spells.

'Don't panic, of course nothing will go wrong. Now where did you say these clothes were?'

'They're hanging in the chest next to my cot.'

'Awkward, I'll have to create the spell alongside her. You'll have to distract her.' He looked at her confidently. 'But first things first, you have to get me in there.'

'That's easy, I'll tell her you are there to help remove my wardrobe to this cabin. And once I inform Cornelia how you healed her, she'll want to convey her gratitude personally and will not suspect a thing.' Grinning, she pulled him by the hand from the bottom bunk and into the passage.

'Whoa!' he shouted bumping the doorjamb as he went through. At the door of Cornelia's cabin Aidan stopped, abruptly jerking Augusta to a halt he held her hand tight. 'You are not to tell her that I healed her.'

'Why ever not?' Augusta asked puzzled, brushing her black hair out of her eyes.

'Never mind why…I don't want you to, Okay? Promise me, now, or I won't help you…I mean it.' Aidan was adamant, a tremor in his voice.

'All right, if that is what you wish,' she said frowning, not understanding his strange attitude. 'But she'll find out anyway.'

'Aye, but not when I'm around…okay?' and he released her hand.

When Augusta and Aidan entered, Beatrix was washing Cornelia's face using a facecloth dipped into the bowl held steady in Anders' strong hands. She was that flustered, she hadn't noticed the water was dirty. Beatrix and Anders glanced at each other nervously wondering what madcap scheme had been dreamed up.

Cornelia looked up when Augusta appeared in the cabin. 'I'm sorry, Highness, for being in your bed. I…I don't know what has happened to me. Please, if you can obtain assistance for me, I will remove myself immediately.'

'Nonsense, Cornelia, it is me who is moving out. Aidan here has kindly consented to help me in moving my wardrobe into Beattie's cabin. I will use your bed until you are fully healed.'

Without warning the purple-faced lady-in-waiting screamed. 'Augusta…Augusta, what are you wearing? Oh, my God, your father will flay me alive!' And the large lady made as if to rise and then, as the cot swung wildly and she grabbed hold of its sides to avoid falling out, she noticed that she was not wearing any outer garments. 'Agh!' she said with a strangled shout. 'Get these boys out of here, I cannot be seen like this,' and she drew the blankets up to her neck.

'Come, come, Cornelia,' she said comfortingly, patting the lady's podgy hand. 'Please, do not fret, you will make yourself ill. My own clothes have been ruined by the storm. These are the only suitable clothes we could find and as you see Beatrix refused to allow me to wear such clothing alone.'

Beatrix stared at Augusta, disbelief playing on her face, biting her bottom lip to stop herself blaring out the truth.

'Suitable?' Cornelia said, noticing Beattie's clothes for the first time, the further shock making her tremble. 'Oh Augusta, can we not find other raiment for you?'

Aidan, taking advantage of the lady's distraction opened the chest door and peered inside. 'Oh boy,' he muttered, 'this is going to be simple.' Manically he glanced around, caught Anders' eye, and winked.

Anders knew the wink, and he mouthed desperately, 'No, don't,' and grabbed Beattie's hand.

Aidan ignored him and once again turned to the open wardrobe.

Beatrix returning Anders' frantic grip, followed his gaze, both of them forced to watch as Aidan commenced his incantation. The song was very low and quiet, hardly discernible half a foot away. They watched his hands, his fingers describing intricate patterns inside the doors. And in less than a moment he had finished. He looked around at the others a look of pure innocence on his face and awaited gleefully the result of his spell-casting.

Cornelia continued imploring her charge. 'Perhaps there is more dignified wear in my own wardrobe or in Beattie's. Please, Augusta, you must search.'

'We both have and if these boys had not come to our rescue we may have had to remain in wet clothes for days. I might well have caught a chill.'

'Yes, my dear Cornelia in that she is correct.' Tragen interjected at the door, seeming to appear from nowhere to give his totally unexpected support. 'Forgive me, Highness, but I need a word with your lady-in-waiting and...' his voice trailed away as he looked around the cabin sniffing, the pimple on the end of his long nose quivering.

'Agh! What is that smell?' Lady Cornelia exclaimed, holding her blankets tightly over her small nose, her face ashen. 'I am going to be ill!'

A stench had gradually arisen in the room, a smell like no other. Aidan looked around, his hands to his face. 'God, it smells like rotten meat, like something's died. It's coming from this chest. What on earth is in here?'

Augusta screamed convincingly. 'Quickly, my gowns are in there, they'll be ruined.'

Aidan grabbed a few. 'Too late, Augusta,' he said, not thinking, 'they already are.'

'Agh!' for the third time Lady Cornelia nearly strangled. 'He called her by her name! Punish him, Lord Tragen...punish him severely. Get out of here you evil boy!'

Aidan, not realizing his mistake, made to apologize even though he was only following orders...anything for a quiet life. Then an even worse odour overwhelmed the stench of rotting meat. Beatrix, Augusta and Anders, along with Lady Cornelia, started gagging.

Augusta, her hands up to her mouth, stared at Aidan and unmistakeably her look said enough was enough.

Aidan was in a quandary, he couldn't tell her that he had finished the spell without divulging her part in the deceit, besides he didn't know what had gone wrong, although this new sickly aroma seemed familiar.

Panicking, Aidan grabbed Anders and pulled him towards the door, flight appearing the appropriate action. Unfortunately, being so close to the appallingly sweet and obnoxious tang on Aidan caused Anders' stomach to rebel. He vomited into the bowl he was holding. Aidan, taken completely by surprise, accidentally jogged the bowl and spilled its contents over Cornelia's bedclothes.

Lady Cornelia screamed somewhat hoarsely, she was now losing her voice. Luckily, the contents landed on her abdomen and not on her injured ankle.

Augusta jumping clear of the spray collided with Beatrix who, rushing to help Anders crashed into Tragen at the door.

Utter pandemonium reigned for minutes before the wizard shouted and restored a modicum of peace and order.

'Aidan, you are reeking,' stated Tragen, again wrinkling his nose in disgust.

And before his mentor could continue, the irate apprentice interrupted. 'I know, I know,' he shouted, 'it's this bloody balm on my neck and legs! I didn't know that would be affected as well, did I?' and then he cringed as Tragen, raising an eyebrow, stared at him.

Aidan wilted.

'I am going to teach you, my boy, if it's the last thing I do!' He raised his hand in the air and made small rippling movements with his fingers, enunciating at the same time a countering spell. The stench of rotting cadaver and foul balm vanished from the cabin and a cool refreshing breeze blew through, clearing the heads of both Cornelia and Tragen.

Augusta, her plan a dismal failure, made an unconscious decision that was to have far reaching consequences for her, resulting in a cementing of a friendship began the day before. Instinctively, she knew that Aidan could not be allowed to shoulder the blame alone, but before she could utter a word, her lady-in-waiting spoke.

'My Lord Tragen, I do not know what is going on here, but I would appreciate it if you could relieve me of this…vileness on my bed.'

'Of course,' and his fingers glided through the air and the obnoxious mess rolled up into a ball and disappeared. 'If I may take up some of your time in a moment, I hope to alleviate a little of your ignorance of these past few hours.'

He stared at all four culprits, for he knew that to a greater or lesser degree they were all at fault. 'I should leave now if I was you…and Aidan,' he grabbed his apprentice's shoulder as he rushed past, 'you will all wait for me in the ladies' cabin.' And glaring at her severely, he bowed to Augusta as she scurried after them.

'Thank you, Tragen,' vastly relieved at now having clean bedding again, Cornelia smiled weakly. 'Please, be seated and tell me all, since I opened my eyes I have been subjected to bewildering behaviour. Start with my ankle if you will, I recall falling, but nothing else.'

He sat in the vacant chair, his exhaustion cherishing the brief silence, and went through the events of the last twenty-four hours. As he did, the lady, from reclining comfortably as he commenced his tale, at the end was sitting bolt upright, even more agitated and bemused. He began with her accidental trip on Aidan's robe, and the subsequent healing of her fractured ankle.

Here she stopped him. 'You mean that boy has the gift, Tragen? And there was me thinking he was trouble through and through.'

'Far from it, Cornelia,' Tragen's pride in his boy, obvious in his tone, 'he has a truly wondrous power of healing—his is an extraordinary gift. He can actually see a malady within a body and, whereas I heal from the outside in, he heals from the inside out. A method that is far superior to mine,' he paused, regarding her for a moment, wondering if further comment was needed.

'As for his mischief-making, his causing of trouble, you would say. I believe it to derive from the goodness in his heart.' He held up his hands before she could speak. 'I know it may seem malicious, but I assure you it is not. He just happens to be very accident prone, and it is he who usually ends up being the injured party.' Tragen stroked his beard, thinking back over the years, and the loneliness in his life before Aidan had come along. He continued with a little of the boy's background.

81

'He is a young boy whose life used to consist of surviving in the gutters for that is where he was when I met him first. Now, he is an honest young man learning a different form of survival, a way to live amongst decent people.' He rubbed his weary eyes. 'I do not mean to excuse his bad behaviour but I am convinced his purpose in spell-casting here had a sound reason…at least to those four it would seem sound. He is growing up and like all adolescents he makes mistakes. I ask you to forgive every one of them for I suspect the involvement of Augusta as the primary force in this latest prank.'

Lady Cornelia closed her eyes, considering the wizard's words for a moment. 'Very well, but I have no choice anyway I have to forgive him, do I not? After all, I would be in a great deal of pain right now,' she sighed and lay back against her pillows. 'You know I have the sickness of the old in my bones, Tragen, and I am prone to fractures.' She looked up, tears in her eyes, despair in her quiet voice, meeting his sympathetic gaze. 'This…' and she pointed at her bound ankle, 'could have happened at any time, and will occur, unfortunately many times in the future.'

Tragen smiled, knowing his next words were going to utterly astound her. 'You did have the sickness of the old, Cornelia. My Aidan has set the healing process in place for that illness as well as for your fractured ankle.'

She stared at him, stunned, the truth of his words taking her breath. 'You are telling me that I no longer need fear breaking my bones? I need no longer be afraid of trips and falls and…and open doors?'

He nodded his assent.

Loud sobs bubbled from the very depths of her being, her body shaking violently, her face in her hands. Tragen leant over and grasped her hands, bringing them from her tear wracked face, comforting her with his presence.

'My God, I have lived with the fear of it most of my life. No other healer has been able to help me, even you tried once.' She paused, thinking back over the pain filled, ever so careful, years.

'My mother died quite young, you know; she accidentally banged her head in a doorway.' Using the blanket, she dried the tears rolling down her face and, breathing deeply, she composed herself before continuing. 'It was only a small tap, nothing really, but because she had the malady the bang fractured her skull. We could not find a healer in time. It was then my father told me of the "old" sickness and that I was expected to come down with it. He was right!'

She leant forward to emphasize her next words. 'You will not punish that boy...I mean it. You are not to even think of it. To heal me of that horrible, terrible illness,' she shuddered. 'I must reward him.'

'He would not accept one. In fact he would be seriously offended if you were to offer him anything. Be advised by me...never speak your gratitude, he hates being thanked.'

'He hates it? Well...he needs money, does he not? He is not from a rich family, is he? Is there any way I can endow him without his knowledge?'

Tragen shook his weary head and managed to stifle the yawn that had been coming on him in the last few moments. 'I do not know his family but he has all he needs from me. If he wishes more, he knows to ask and he will get it. There is no need to provide anything.' He smiled his thoughts fully on his boy...his love for his adopted son. 'He is a very unusual young man, Cornelia.'

'Yes,' she nodded, tears again glistening in her eyes. 'You are fond of him, I see.'

'Yes, very much so, he is the son I never had, and I am enormously proud of him.'

'So you should be. Tell me, the boy could be famous and command untold influence. Why have I never heard of him?'

'He demands secrecy from all those he heals. I expect him to extract that promise from you, ere long. You see, he sees his power of healing as a bounden duty. It is his nature to heal—anyone or anything; he also heals the maladies in animals. Even the ability he has for creating magic is based on healing, not as mine...on the mind. But there are two conditions when he cannot or will not heal.'

'What are those?' Intrigued, she wanted to know everything about the young wizard who had given her hope for a normal future.

'The first are those maladies affecting people whose time is at an end.'

'What does that mean? I don't understand.'

Tragen peered at her, he was very tired now, the energy expended creating the shield wall had been phenomenal, and the alcohol he had just consumed with Locklear was not helping him to stay awake. His eyes were drooping and he still hadn't broached the subject that was his purpose in coming to her.

83

'He can see and communicate with the dead, just as easily as you or I speak with each other. He knows when a person is going to die because he can see the aura of death surrounding them. If he meets someone who is dying and they are in pain, you know what he does? He eases their passing by removing that pain and he does not leave them to die alone…he remains with them, comforting them, until they have passed over safely. Is that not remarkable?'

'The second condition you mentioned, what is that?' she asked astonished.

'Ah! To me it is the strangest thing of all about him, even stranger than when I actually witness him in contact with the ghosts of those who have gone on. He will not heal himself or allow another healer to use magic to cure his maladies.' Tragen, a puzzled look on his face, shrugged his weary shoulders. 'He believes it to be improper and grossly selfish. The gift is for others he says, not for himself. That is why he uses that balm you smelled earlier. He has burns on his body and will not let me treat him with magic.'

'My God, Tragen, that boy is truly special!'

'He is also very modest and would never acknowledge that he is different to his peers. That is why there is such a close friendship between him and Anders. Anders, bless him, accepts Aidan as an ordinary boy and yet respects his abilities. As I said earlier, Aidan actually gets very upset if anyone expresses their gratitude. And if you persisted he would probably never talk to you again, he would be highly embarrassed.' He grimaced. 'I do not pretend to understand his reasoning; his outlook on life and death unnerves me quite often. But like I said, he truly does have a heart of gold and the mistakes he makes in growing up are the same as those of any other young man his age.'

This time Tragen could not withhold the yawn. 'I'm sorry, Cornelia, but now I must talk of another matter…the reason I came to see you this evening.'

'What is it, my friend? I apologize I see that you are weary, be quick then and tell me.'

'We need to hide Augusta,' he said, more abruptly than he intended, extreme exhaustion his excuse.

'What!' Cornelia lost all colour and gasped. 'Why?' she said, clasping her hands across her chest.

'It seems that we have been found by someone whose intent is malicious,' Tragen paused again. 'This tempest is not normal; it appears to have been created by a force that has been searching for us.' As he examined her face, he wondered if she would be able to understand. 'I do not know the identity of the hunter, or why he is hunting us. As for where he is at this time, I have no idea. I can only assume he is now far behind us as the gale now blows from the stern. How far, we should have an idea in the morning. If the storm lessens by then, I believe we can safely assume that we have succeeded in escaping.'

'And if the weather does not improve?'

He scratched his beard. 'We will cross that bridge when we come to it.'

'You believe whoever it is, is after Augusta?'

'If she is taken it will have untold consequences for Mantovar. And I honestly cannot see a power as mighty as this being used just to steal your jewellery.'

'I agree, but how can we possibly hide her on this vessel…it may be a huge ship, but for this purpose it's far too small?'

He smiled at her. 'I think she is already doing it for us. Who would dream of finding Mantovar's female heir dressed as a common sailor? She is running around the ship in company with three other youths of the same age. If, God forbid, we are taken, she will blend in quite nicely as part of the crew.'

Lady Cornelia lay back on her pillow, her lips pursed, silent for a moment thinking of the consequences. 'The rest of the crew will they not know who she is? After all, everyone knows that your purpose for being on this voyage was to bring the heir home. How will you deal with that?'

Tragen breathed a sigh of relief, this woman was no fool. 'I have thought of a plan Cornelia. What say you, if you assume her place? I know,' and he raised his hands again to halt her interjection, 'what you are about to say. You are a lot older; you could not possibly be mistaken for her. But think a moment. We have only been at sea for five days and for two of those we have suffered this storm. The first three days Augusta spent in her cabin suffering seasickness, am I correct?' Cornelia nodded. 'So, very few on board have actually seen her. If you stay in here, in this cabin, everyone else will assume that she is still ill and no-one will be surprised, this storm has made even seasoned sailors sick to their stomach. Stay here until we deem it safe, and we swear all who have seen her, to secrecy. Then there should be no problem, and Augusta can masquerade as your companion along with Beatrix.

'Waited on…by my charge! Now that would be a novelty,' Cornelia chuckled. 'She must change her name; we cannot have her called Augusta if the Princess Augusta is ill in bed,' she said as Tragen rose to leave.

'I am sincerely relieved to have your cooperation in this Cornelia. Let us hope these precautions are a waste of time.'

The wizard stepped across the narrow passageway and found all four youths waiting silently in Beattie's cabin. The lantern, still swinging overhead, shone light on four very agitated countenances.

'It was not Aidan's fault, it was mine,' said Augusta, jumping to her feet immediately he came through the door. 'If anyone is to be punished it should be me, it was my idea.'

Aidan hunching his shoulders even more knew it was pointless her taking the blame; he was the one who had conjured the spell. How could he have been such an idiot not to realize that everything nearby would be affected. His unguent was still emitting a sickly sweet odour but nowhere near as bad as it was, at least Anders was no longer gagging.

Anders, staring at his hands in his lap, was sitting on the floor at Beattie's feet; she sat bedraggled and biting her bottom lip. She was feeling decidedly nervous as she peered up at the wizard and she unconsciously shifted closer to Anders, her leg now pressed against his arm.

'Very well, Highness, I can well believe it was your idea.' Tragen appeared to consider his next move although he knew that Aidan would be next to open his mouth.

'Come off it, you know full well it's my fault. There's no need to punish these others. The blame is mine; none of them were actively involved.' Aidan said utterly dejected, he was about to receive his worst punishment to date and was dreading it.

'No, we knew you were going to do something, so if one is punished all should be punished.' Beatrix said surprising herself. She was now emulating her mistress in being protective of him and not understanding why, instinctively knowing though that it was right.

Anders nodded his blond head, agreeing with her, as far as he was concerned Beatrix could never be wrong.

'Don't listen to them, I ordered them to aid me in this and now I am ordering you to exact punishment only on me,' said Augusta.

'My dear lady, your father gave me this mission to bring you home. At the same time he ordered me to do as I thought best to keep you safe from harm. I consider your orders to these three in that context. Ordering an invocation in a confined space is dangerous—you were therefore in peril. Aidan knows this as does Anders. Beatrix as your companion should have known it; she's been around magic long enough. Therefore you will all be disciplined, whether you dispute it or not. Highness, from this moment Lady Cornelia and I have decided that she will assume your identity until we reach home.'

'What! How dare you, wizard?' She spluttered, aghast at his words, the others staring at her, mouths agape. Aidan had never before heard anyone use that tone of voice to his master.

'I dare, madam, as the person with overall responsibility for your welfare.' He continued before she could catch her breath. 'Lady Cornelia will remain in your cabin until such time as we deem fit. You will take up the task of her companion and will fetch and carry for her.'

'I will not!' Augusta shouted, her green eyes blazing, hands on hips.

'You will, Your Royal Highness,' the wizard using her formal title to stress the seriousness of his threat, 'or I will inform your father on our return that not only did you disobey my instructions, you actively put yourself in danger. Do you understand?'

Augusta quailed; the thought of news of this escapade reaching the Prince of Mantovar terrified her, he was a very loving father, but also a very strict disciplinarian. It wouldn't be the first time he had punished her for disobeying the orders of his people. Her shoulders slumped, and nodding, she acquiesced grudgingly.

'You, Beatrix, will have to teach her the duties of a companion and maid.' A horrified feeling came over Beatrix at the thought of instructing her mistress on how to scrub the cabin floor. 'And I am warning the pair of you,' he looked from one to the other of the silent girls, 'you are to put your heart and soul into the deception. You are to be convincing at all times, whether it be in public or privately here in your cabin. Beatrix, do not be afraid to quarrel with your mistress over this, it is very important that the deception is believed. As for your attire, ladies, you will continue as you are in these clothes.'

'But, Milord, I have proper clothing she can wear,' said Beatrix, interrupting.

Tragen pretended not to see the well-aimed kick from Augusta. 'Ah, yes! Your name, Highness,' he said, as Beatrix grimaced.

'What about it,' confused, Augusta could not now take her eyes from his face, dreading his next words, although the strange order to continue wearing Aidan's clothing came as a pleasant surprise.

'You must have another name. Yes…we'll call you Mabel, I think,' Tragen now had a twinkle in his eye which Aidan, not quite believing these strange orders, was the only one to see.

Aidan and Anders both burst out laughing at the horror on Augusta's face.

'You cannot be serious, Milord. Please, I absolutely abhor that name,' Augusta said, her consternation bringing her very close to tears.

'Beatrix,' he asked, ignoring the desperation in his princess, 'how many servants in the castle do you know with the name Mabel?'

Meekly, Beatrix replied. 'Quite a few, Milord.'

'Very good, then I am correct, it is a very apt name. From this moment, all of us will address you as Mabel. Do you agree?'

Augusta glared at her friends, daring them to laugh. Aidan, of course, could not help himself and he did again, uproariously. The thought of calling this sometimes very snooty girl by the common name of Mabel, was hilarious.

'You may find it amusing, Aidan, but I have not yet come to your punishment,' said Tragen, instantly silencing the young wizard.

'Now, Anders, what am I to do with you. Not only did you know beforehand that Aidan was going to cast a spell, when that spell went wrong you vomited all over the poor lady ill in bed!'

'Milord, it was an accident I couldn't help it.' The cabin boy, incensed at the injustice of the complaint, for the first time in his life voiced an objection to a statement made by the wizard.

'If the spell had not been cast, you would not have had an accident and Lady Cornelia would not have had a lap full of the contents of your stomach. You, from this day, besides having your present duties for the captain, will also have the duty of care of both Beatrix and Mabel,' Augusta winced but said nothing. 'You are to accompany them whenever they leave this cabin and are to aid them if required, but you are not to replace Mabel in her duties.'

Anders was utterly confused it occurred to him that he was already doing just that. He sat mute, staring at the wizard and again he couldn't help noticing the pimple on the end of Tragen's nose. It was getting larger.

'And now, Aidan,' Tragen pulled at his beard. 'You seem not to understand that spells must not be cast in small rooms. You are obviously competent at casting the spells of flame, fragrance and light. But think about it, the only spell you cast that did not have grave consequences was that of light which took place out of doors. The other two resulted in accidents. Do you agree?'

'Yes, I understand, but I'm going to have to create spells indoors sometimes.'

'Not for practical jokes, my boy! Now it will be your task, along with Anders, to keep Mabel safe from harm. You will carry on teaching her rudimentary magic and report to me each week on her progress.' Augusta perked up at this. 'You are not to instruct her in high magic but you may reveal as much of the history of the art as you think appropriate. You understand?'

Aidan nodded waiting for the axe to fall.

'It is late now, you are all to partake of your supper and retire. Aidan, you will again sleep in Anders' berth but this time you will have the floor and he the bed.' As he reached the door, he wished them a goodnight and left four very perplexed teenagers to mull over his punishments.

That same night Anders was again woken by Aidan talking in his sleep.

The man continued to scream long after the spear entered his eye. It took its time, eking out the man's agony for as long as possible.

'Master,' a voice uttered from behind, 'you sent for me.'

It withdrew the spear and turned to look on its minion. 'We have a wizard in our net!'

'You are sure? The storm has ensnared an enchanted one?' the servile one asked excitedly, wringing his hands.

'Yes! I have espied him in the scry using his staff. The stave holds immense power. It may even be enough!' It hissed its sibilant jubilation. 'Our time is near at hand...O Lord,' he intoned raising his arms in supplication. 'O Lord, a wizard comes! You will be free!'

'What do you mean "a wizard"? There is more than one coming for you,' Aidan said, threateningly, before falling quiet for the rest of the night.

Anders lay awake for hours afterward—confused and scared.

Eight

The following morning started badly with Beatrix teaching Augusta the rudiments of bed-making. Augusta, of course, didn't want to know and attempted rebellion. Beatrix, though, was having none of it.

'This is the easiest task of all,' she explained, losing patience. 'If you cannot make a bed, how will you do the rest of the chores? Lord Tragen will definitely speak with your father when we get home.'

That argument seemed to settle it and Augusta set to with a will for about two minutes before complaining.

'How am I to survive without having breakfast first? You know I can never wake up unless I have a cup of tea before I rise!'

The boys arrived in the middle of the heated exchange the shouting audible from one end of the dark passageway to the other.

The storm had noticeably decreased in intensity, the motion of the ship not as violent. Augusta and Beatrix were now finding it easier to keep their feet on a deck not jumping about so much. The waves, though, were still running high and the ship continued to dip and climb, very alarmingly on times. The crew spent most of their time controlling the level of flooding by manning the pumps every hour of the day and night and the replacing and repair of sprung boards was never ending.

As soon as they had awoken, Anders from his bed on the floor – he had been cajoled mercilessly into giving up his berth again – had questioned his friend.

'What were you dreaming about, Aidan?' he asked, pretending nonchalance.

'Oh…what? I don't know, why?'

'You were talking in your sleep again, something about wizards going somewhere. You sounded very strange, as if you were threatening someone.'

'Was I? Don't know what you're on about, come on I'm starving let's go to the galley.'

'I've got to tidy the Bear's cabin first, you can help.'

Five minutes of frantic activity, resulting in charts and clothes deposited in some very unusual locations, and the two boys were racing each other down companionways and ladders to "Dolly's" kingdom—the galley, one deck below the passengers, and forward of the mainmast.

Anders, not happy with his friend's answer, still fretted, this was his second sleepless night and fatigue was telling on him, increasing his anxiety. He couldn't recall Aidan ever having nightmares before. Standing in a line behind Bertram, pots in hand, Anders' thoughts were elsewhere. Aidan's dreams were not normal, something untoward was happening, something that was likely to have nasty consequences.

The ship's cook, Dolphin, had been named by his mother, a very dominant wife of a very quiet fisherman. She had loved the big mammals of the sea and had nearly called her son Walrus. Dolly's father would have preferred him called that, after all Wally was a lot better than Dolly. But he was one of those strange men who loved a violent woman and he had acquiesced, for when his wife was drunk she was usually aggressive with both her fists and her tongue.

Dolly was short and bald, with an enormous belly. He was also a very hard man, growing up on the docks with the attendant blessings of that name he had to be. Nevertheless he was famous throughout the fleet for two things—his knife-fighting skills and being the only ships' cook who hated fish.

Dolly came from a small fishing community in southern Mantovar, one of many villages that supplied the large inland towns with the harvest of the sea…and Mantovar with sailors for its navy. His father dearly loved his son and had not wanted him to leave home, but Dolly found he could not remain after the tragic death of his mother.

He brought with him to the Grim a culinary skill not often seen in ships' cooks, and he prided himself on supplying hot food and drink in almost any weather. The Grim, being the largest vessel afloat, had the area around the stove protected by magic, no coals could fall on nearby decking to cause a fire. But in this storm, Dolly had not wanted to tempt fate. Spells did fail on times, especially the ones that needed renewing each year as this one did. So, over the last two days he had only been able to supply cold meats and hard ships' biscuit, a miserable fare to sustain life in atrocious conditions. This morning, though, he made up for it with a hot burgoo, a porridge made of oatmeal, sugar, butter and salted water. This, along with very sweet tea, was heaven on earth to men who had survived unspeakable strain.

Having eaten to bursting point in the galley, the boys gathered caddies of piping hot tea and pots of the burgoo and toted them through dark passageways up to the girls and Lady Cornelia.

While Augusta/Mabel and Beatrix carried breakfast in to Lady Cornelia, the boys made themselves at home in Beattie's cabin. Aidan stretched out in what had become his usual place on the bottom bunk after pulling the blankets straight, Augusta had again failed to carry out the task properly. And Anders picked his favourite spot on the floor, stretching out his long legs before him, his back against an old wooden chest, his shoulders in contact with a woollen blanket folded on its lid.

'I can't understand it Anders, this is no punishment nothing's changed. We were watching over the girls already and ...' the girls returned with a clatter that stopped him in mid-sentence. 'All right, Mabel, why so noisy?' Aidan baited, mischievously.

'I am going to throw a boot at you if you call me that horrible name again, little wizard.'

Anders joined in. 'Well, we must call you something. Hey! How about a boy's name then, she could pass as one dressed like that, couldn't she?'

'Aye, come to think of it she looks like Bertie Smallpen...you know, Anders, the kitchen hand back at the castle, hey, that name suits her! All we need shout then is "Beattie and Bertie behave yourselves or you'll get a battered bottom"!' The two boys collapsed in hysterics.

'Very funny...ha, ha...remind us to laugh won't you. For your information you are to call me Nellie, Cornelia allowed me to choose another.' Sitting down on the end of the bunk pushing Aidan's bare feet out of the way, none of them wore any footwear, she tucked into her burgoo.

'I have a cousin Mabel,' Augusta grimaced between mouthfuls, 'a short, skinny, spotty, horrible girl. There are things I could tell you about her that would make your hair curl,' she shuddered.

'Oh, go on then, I'm all ears,' said Aidan.

'I can't in mixed company.'

'Why not?' Aidan asked, his ears flapping.

'It would not be genteel and proper,' replied Augusta, flummoxed.

'Oh, come on...since when do maids have to be genteel and proper? Beattie isn't,' Aidan winked at Anders.

'You say that again and I'll throw more than a boot at you,' said Beatrix, nearly choking on her food.

'You were saying, when we came in, that you didn't understand Tragen. What was that all about?' Augusta asked, changing

93

the subject rapidly she accidentally slurped her food as the ship rapidly dropped down a sharp incline.

'If I made a noise like that, you'd call me a pig,' complained Aidan.

'Shut up and tell us,' said Beatrix, exasperated. And then, realizing what she had said, added. 'And don't dare tell me you can't shut up and speak the same time.'

'I wasn't going to. You're getting as bad as Nellie.' Aidan settled himself more comfortably on the bed as they carried on eating. 'No, he's up to something is Tragen and if I know my master, he'll leave it too late to tell me.'

'What do you mean by that?' Beatrix asked. 'Why should he tell you, anyway?'

'Because whatever he's hiding affects us, and he thinks we're kids. I'm fifteen not five...well at least I think I am.'

Augusta looked at him quizzically. 'Don't you know your age?'

Aidan glared at her and refused to answer.

'What makes you think he's hiding anything?' Anders asked, breaking the icy silence.

'Yeah, come on little wizard...tell us,' enjoined Augusta, sarcastically, 'I'm sure we'd all benefit from your inside knowledge.'

Aidan, ignoring her sarcasm, put his arms behind his head and nodded to himself. 'Do any of you call what he gave us last night, a punishment?' He looked around waiting for an answer, and as none was forthcoming, he went on. 'Because I don't, he gave us what we wanted and pretended to lecture us. Now why is that?'

'You may not call it a punishment, you won't have to teach Augusta how to be a maid,' disgruntled, Beatrix answered.

'Hey, I won't be that bad,' said Augusta, indignantly. 'The hardest part will be answering to Nellie.'

'Oh yes, Highness, and when it comes to the laundry, are you prepared to get wet to your elbows?' Beatrix retorted.

'I am, and don't call me Highness!' Augusta said, accepting the fact that the task of protecting her from her father's anger would mostly fall on her companion. But at the same time, she was appalled at the thought of scrubbing smelly clothes.

'Whoa ladies, no more quarrelling, we're all in the same boat here. I agree with Aidan, I don't feel I've been punished. It's very strange, it seems as if Tragen seeing us together, means to keep us together, and I for one would like to know why.' For Anders, normally reticent, this was quite a speech and Aidan was so surprised he rose on one elbow and stared at his friend. 'Don't stare at me so, I'm agreeing with you.'

'All right, don't you two start, arguing will get us nowhere. What we need is a strategy to find out what he and Cornelia are up to,' said Augusta, pursing her lips. 'All of you…think!'

'Hey, that's a good joke, Anders,' Aidan chortled.

'What is?' Anders asked.

'We are all in the same boat!'

'Oh…yeah, I didn't realize,' he laughed and turned to Augusta. 'Why include Lady Cornelia?'

'Because last night we left her and Tragen talking, and they were together a long time, which means they were not just passing the time of day. No,' she finished eating and, placed her bowl on the floor. 'I know my lady-in-waiting…they were plotting.'

'Perhaps he was romancing her,' Aidan said, impishly.

'Don't be silly, Lord Tragen's not her type,' said Beatrix dismissing his suggestion as absurd. 'I agree with Nellie.'

'OK then, boys and girls, how do we find out?' Aidan asked, lying back on the pillow.

'Simple! You work on them. You question your master, Aidan and Hig…oh heck, Al…Nellie, you interrogate Lady Cornelia. You two know them best, you know their little ways.' Beatrix rose from the floor as she said this and started gathering their dirty breakfast dishes. And at the same time trying to get her mouth around what she should be calling her mistress.

'I see a small problem there.' Aidan got up from the bed and swung his feet to the floor. 'Unfortunately, Tragen knows me as well. He'll be expecting me to try and worm it out of him and he's going to clam up.'

'The same with Cornelia,' said Augusta. 'I will never get her to reveal anything; she can be quite a cow on times.'

'Augusta!' Beatrix, scandalized at her mistress' swearing, nearly dropped the dishes.

Aidan, though, glanced at Anders and smiled—he liked her choice of words.

'But we have to try. We'll all work on them, starting now,' and Augusta pulled Beatrix with her as she moved to the door. 'We have to clean her cabin, do we not, my friend? Cornelia here we come,' and they marched out, Augusta grinning and Beatrix slightly bemused at her mistress acknowledging her a friend at last.

'Aidan, shift yourself, you can help me in the Bear's cabin again…it's still a mess, and if it stays that way much longer I'll be skinned alive,' and Anders dragged Aidan from the bed.

'That's a contradiction in terms, if you don't mind me saying so, Anders. We'll see you later,' shouted Aidan to the girls disappearing into Cornelia's cabin.

'What's a contradiction in terms?'

'Well, you implied, "the Bear will skin us" whereas it's usually us skinning…'

Lady Cornelia called from inside her cabin, interrupting Aidan's explanation. 'Is that the young wizard? Come here young man, I wish to see you.'

Aidan, apprehensive after the debacle the day before, stepped through the door followed by Anders equally nervous. But Aidan did not walk forward into the body of the cabin. He unexpectedly stepped to one side immediately he crossed the threshold, and this movement took Anders completely by surprise. The cabin boy found himself manoeuvred into the forefront in the prime position to bear the brunt of whatever followed. The young wizard had learned over the years that aristocratic ladies were not to be trifled with—they usually ended up shouting at him. So, just in case, he was determined to remain nearest the door to enable a quick escape.

Anders, taking his first good look at the pale woman, was struck by the fact that she appeared to be no older than thirty or thirty-five – he'd expected her to be older – but oh boy, was she fat! Then, when she uttered her next words, he suddenly knew what was about to happen and he prepared to cover Aidan's exit.

Lady Cornelia, sitting up in her cot wrapped in a brightly coloured shawl, beckoned Aidan closer. She wanted an uninterrupted look at the boy who had just turned her life around.

'So, you are the lad that healed my ankle, are you?'

'I've started the healing process, Milady, that's all I do…it will still take time to heal fully,' Aidan nervously answered, his stomach churning as he waited for it.

'Yes, so Lord Tragen informed me. Is it…is it true you have also commenced the healing of the "old" sickness in my bones?' Cornelia stared at him, holding her breath, not daring to believe it, yet desperately not wanting to hear a denial.

Aidan nodded, feeling more uncomfortable—he'd completely forgotten about the gratitude, until now.

'My God, boy, do you realize how I have suffered with that illness?'

'Yes, Milady, I've come across it before.'

She stared at him, her eyes brimming. 'Oh, my boy…thank you…thank you, M…'

'Please, Milady, there's no need to thank me, I couldn't leave you in pain,' Aidan, frantic, shuffled to the door all his thoughts bent on escape, 'excuse me, I'm needed in the captain's cabin.' Aidan barged past Anders and ran quickly and noisily up the corridor.

Augusta and Beatrix stared after the fleeing boy, shocked, not knowing what to make of his unexpected exit.

Lady Cornelia sat with her hands to her face weeping with both gratitude for his healing and guilt for thanking him—her acknowledgement so obviously causing him distress.

Anders, finding his voice, spoke to them quietly and forcefully. 'He can't abide being thanked, ladies, he hates it and I won't say sorry for him running away. I'll tell you though that healing is as normal to him as breathing…he heals without a second thought. He could never stand by and see anyone suffer, Milady.'

Cornelia, drying her eyes, sighed and gazed at Anders. 'Lord Tragen told me much the same last night, I should have heeded him. Please tell Aidan I will not mention it again and that I hope he'll forgive me. Tell him…no…ask him for me, ask him to come and see me later.'

Anders nodded and bowed, leaving the cabin he chased after Aidan.

'Well!' Augusta said, looking at Beatrix and Cornelia. 'How very puzzling…that boy…I don't know, he never fails to surprise me!'

'Yes, Nellie,' and with that name Cornelia regained the upper hand. 'This cabin is a mess with all your comings and goings,' her eyes swollen with suppressed tears, 'I suggest you tidy it, right away.'

And the lady-in-waiting, having a lot on her mind, lay back comfortably in Augusta's cot and supervised both girls while she daydreamed of walking in the forest at home without fear of stumbling and breaking bones. She so loved the Great Forest and all it succoured.

Anders caught up with Aidan. The apprentice was slamming around the cabin replacing papers and pens that had fallen to the floor, picking up chairs that had tipped over and generally putting things to right…but doing it very noisily.

Anders had always known to leave him well alone when he was in this mood, he'd come out of it by himself and not before. It still perplexed Anders though…why should Aidan take on so every time someone wanted to thank him, it was natural to show gratitude, wasn't it? After all, the woman had suffered a terrible illness for most of her life. And now that Aidan had healed her, she could, perhaps for the first time be hopeful of her future. He peeked out of the corner of his eye at his friend wandering the room messing desultorily with things that no longer needed tidying.

Aidan eventually ceased his pacing and aimless rummaging around. He stood in the stern gallery staring out through the small panes in the window, his thumbs hooked in his belt.

He brooded. He had encountered the same old problem again and still didn't know how to deal with it. He knew he was at fault reacting as he had, but he just couldn't help it. Being thanked brought on guilt—a gut wrenching shame. He didn't deserve gratitude, if people realized how he felt they'd shun him. It would devastate him if he lost the love of Tragen and Anders as he surely would if they discovered his secret. He sighed and rubbed his face, staring through the window with sightless eyes. The simple fact was he took an inordinate amount of pleasure in the act of healing. Too much pleasure, he thought. It was almost as if he enjoyed seeing people hurting. The sheer enjoyment that gripped him when he destroyed the disease or watched the broken bone knitting together was overwhelming. There was no other word to describe the aftermath of any act of healing—guilt. He needed to hide the knowledge that sick people made him happy.

He turned from the window, and waited for his best friend to finish checking the Bear's clothing. Anders was meticulous in ensuring his captain was clad appropriately.

'Let's go up top, Anders…I could do with some air.'

Anders replaced the last of Locklear's clothes, bowing his head a moment he realized that this time he couldn't leave it alone, not yet. Circumstances had changed over the last couple of days; their circle of friendship had now doubled in size, for one thing. An increase that Anders welcomed with open arms and given time to think on it so would Aidan. They were all at a loss to understand the young wizard's attitude and this could only lead to unrest and doubt amongst the four of them. He couldn't allow this unpleasant feeling to remain, it would grow and fester—the newly formed friendship of the four would not survive the strain.

'Aidan, we have to talk and I said talk, not shout at each other.'

Aidan waited, shoulders slumped. 'Go on then, say what you have to say.'

'The lady meant well. In your heart, you know it. I don't understand why you take on so at people thanking you, it's a natural reaction after all.'

'Have you finished,' he said, moving towards the quarterdeck door.

'No, I haven't,' he continued even more strongly and his friend stopped, his hand on the door latch. 'People are always going to be beholden to you. You're going to have to get used to their thanks or you'll make your own life a living hell. People need to show gratitude, need to thank you it's…it's part of the healing process for God's sake. Either accept that as a fact or cease healing.'

Aidan glanced up, his eyes glistening. 'I can't stop healing, you know that.'

'Aye, I know,' he said exasperated, 'then why do you feel as you do?'

And Aidan nearly told him. But he knew he could never divulge his shameful secret, not to him, he thought too much of Anders to burden him with it. He didn't want to lose his best friend, but he also accepted the truth in his friend's words. His life was already hell because of the guilt.

'I can't tell you why,' he sighed deeply, tears glistening, almost falling from his eyes. He blinked. 'I'll make you a promise, though,' and he looked up at the concern in his big friend's face. 'I'll try to change…I'll do my damnedest to cope when they thank me, I won't succeed all the time, but I will try.'

'Come on, let's wheedle the truth out of Tragen,' Anders said, understanding his friend more than Aidan would ever know.

On the quarterdeck the storm was still raging, not as intense as at its height but the rain still fell in sheets stinging their faces. The wind continued to blow ferociously, its sound deafening. The seas though were not so rough, visibility had improved and the horizon had moved further away from the ship. And if Aidan was not deceived, the air seemed a lot warmer.

Tragen was at the rear standing on a box and staring over the poop deck, past the after-jigger mast and out over the stern at the storm blowing now from the northeast, a pensive look on his face as he scratched his beard. Leash was at the wheel accompanied by Nkosi, it was still taking two men to hold the vessel on a good heading. The small stormsail stretched taut above and behind them, the wind singing through the lines. Trumper, the sword scar below his left eye livid in the rain, was reporting to the captain. And behind him, just climbing the steps up from the waist was Hopper, a very worried frown on his face.

As Aidan and Anders reached the larboard rail, they overheard the last of the bo'sun's report.

'Aye, if this temperature increases much more the humidity will sprout the weevils. I must spread it before long for the air to get at it.'

'What's he talking about, Anders?' Aidan whispered.

'He's on about the mainsail. At present it's bundled up, soaking wet on the deck. You've noticed the heat?' Aidan nodded. 'Well the warm air and stagnant water in its folds will breed worms that will eat the canvas. It must be spread out, even in this wet weather, to stop the weevil growing.'

'Very well, Bo'sun, do your best,' ordered Locklear. 'You and the men fought hard enough to salvage it…it would be outrageous to lose it now.' The bo'sun touched his forelock and departed the quarterdeck.

'Hopper, how goes it?' Locklear grasped his mate's arm to drag him beneath the overhang of the poop deck, not that it provided much shelter.

'I've checked the holds and talked it over with Dolly; we have enough provisions to last possibly a week if we ration. It will be basic provender and the passengers will have to manage the same as us,' he sighed. 'What really worries us is the fresh-water, many barrels have been spoiled. We estimate we have enough drinking water to last four, perhaps five days. We need provisioning desperately.'

Locklear ran his fingers through his heavy, black beard. 'If I'm correct, Hopper, this change in temperature signifies we are being driven south into the tropics. That fact, coupled with the storm blowing from the east means, at this speed, we are leaving home far behind. Undoubtedly we are lost well into the Deep.' He paused and looked up at the darkened sky. 'If we have been pushed south and west from the coast of Drakka we should raise the Griffin Islands eventually, do you agree?'

'Aye...or the Siren, if we've been blown too far south!'

Locklear glanced at him sharply. 'We don't want to come too close to that. I saw it once on the horizon—that was too near, the noise was appalling, that beneath it was worse. Wait a minute...between us and that is Blackfire Island. There are plenty of trees there!' and he smiled.

'Aye, and fresh water, but no food worth mentioning.' Hopper grimaced; talk of the Siren always knotted his guts he'd once seen a ship disappear in its depths. That vessel had just left Blackfire. Anxious, he stared out over the dark ocean, silent for a moment. 'You've visited Griffin haven't you, Cap'n? What did you make of them? I was there only a short time.'

'I never made landfall, I was chasing pirates at the time,' he pulled at his beard. 'We will need to be vigilant, Hopper. Some of those islands are extremely dangerous, in more ways than one.'

Locklear glanced at Anders and Aidan. 'I do not want you spreading false stories amongst the crew, some of the islands are perilous, aye...but then again, from what I've seen, a lot are not.'

He turned back to Hopper. 'I'll make a decision on our destination later, when we know our position. Drakka may be nearer. But if I decide Griffin is our destination and the first island we reach appears safe we'll take the chance and send ashore a provisioning party.' He stared up at the rainclouds, disgruntled, 'It will be useless setting tarpaulins to catch some of this rainwater, the waves are still too high, the spume will only contaminate it. As for food, well, if this storm ever ceases we can live on fish, just don't tell Dolly yet. I just hope Tragen is right and we have reached the limit of their range. Thank you, Hopper,' and Hugo tapped his arm in gratitude. 'See to it please, and I'd be obliged if you will take command for an hour, I need to go below.' He turned to leave.

At that moment there was a harsher gust of wind and a sharp crack from above their heads. Looking up, a tear appeared in the stormsail and immediately the bows swung to leeward as headway was lost. Tragen reacted instinctively; raising his staff he pointed the knuckle at the gash. Uttering a very loud and strident incantation a light shot from the staff and travelled along the rip, sealing the canvas as good as new.

'Thank you, my friend,' said Hugo, vastly relieved.

Tragen resumed his examination astern as Hugo went below.

Aidan looked at Anders and nodded him away out of earshot of the mate. 'Did you hear that Anders? Locklear said "reached the limit of their range", who are they? That's what their hiding,' he whispered.

'Oh, come off it, he meant out of range of the storm…nothing else.' Anders was busy speculating on what the consequences would have been if Tragen hadn't been on the quarterdeck as the sail tore. Could Aidan have repaired it? Would Aidan have even thought of it?

'Then why would he need Tragen's advice? The Bear's the sailor, not Tragen, so why had he spoken to him about it.'

'Oh boy, you really are clutching at straws.'

Aidan grabbed his arm. 'What's the Siren?'

'It's a giant whirlpool—come too near it and we'll get dragged in. I've heard it wanders.'

Aidan swallowed and looked around nervously.

Leash watched the boys from beneath hooded eyes. As soon as Aidan had arrived on deck, Leash's mind had gone into overdrive. He would have to be careful; he couldn't attempt the same attack as last time. The boy was not an idiot he would be bound to cotton on that his near fatal scrapes were deliberate. It wouldn't take him long to realize that the second helmsman was always around when he had a brush with death. Leash watched and he waited.

Because of his infection his hearing was enhanced to a greater degree than was normal and, despite the phenomenal noise of the storm, he had heard everything that Hopper had reported. And the news worried him.

He'd not wanted to sail on this voyage or on any other; he'd been quite content on land. But, having slipped up the last time on shore and nearly been caught, he'd had no choice; going to sea had been the safest option although it carried its own risks. The sea had been a refuge many times in his life and strangely enough he'd discovered a hidden talent. He found he was a very good helmsman and had taken to the work like a duck to water.

But to satiate his need with immunity required solid earth beneath his feet—it was so much easier to hide. Nonetheless, he had been forced to flee to sea again to escape the consequences of his last episode. Too many people were after his blood and a nice soft voyage to Drakka had seemed a godsend. So he had signed up with alacrity knowing that a few weeks away from Mantovar would cool the chase.

But one of the first people he had bumped into onboard was the instigator of his isolation, his acute loneliness, the reason his infection was getting the upper hand—the one man he hated above all others, Tragen. The wizard was the one person in the world who scared him senseless, the man who had interrupted him and spoiled their pleasure many years ago—him and his damned staff. But Leash's luck had held.

The wizard had not recognized him.

Not surprising really, it had been very dark at the time of their last encounter. God, he had been fortunate to get away. If the wizard had not stumbled, the full blast from his staff would have killed him. As it was the trip had upset Tragen's aim. Some of the power had collided with a nearby wall punching a large hole in it through which he'd fled; the rest of the staff's energy had ended up elsewhere doing all the damage. He didn't want to think about where it had finally landed. He had run for his life.

He loathed the wizard and all those connected with him, his hatred consuming him. He wanted to hurt the magician, kill him if it was feasible, but he was very afraid to be anywhere near the old man. Tragen was far too powerful a magician. And the infection within Leash knew that if it was possible to die, then the wizard would be the one to kill him. The apprentice though was a different matter. All right, he thought, the sod had eluded him twice; he would not the third time.

But above all, Leash wanted to survive this voyage and the thought of going without water and food unnerved him. He could get hold of drinking water easily enough today, hiding it was the problem. He watched Aidan as the boy went across to the wizard. Then he smiled. Two birds with one stone, and Leash almost laughed aloud.

'Master, excuse me but I must ask you something,' said Aidan, politely.

His voice immediately placed Tragen on his guard, the boy would never learn, he thought. 'Well, what is it?'

Anders stood alongside them both listening to every word.

'I was wondering how much longer you expected this storm to last now that we're at the limit of their range.'

Anders stared at Aidan dumbfounded. He had not expected his friend to be quite so blatant.

'This storm will run its course, my boy,' Tragen answered, pausing only slightly, choosing to ignore most of the question.

'Yes, but we've now reached their limit. Can't you give us any idea of how far we'll have to sail to get completely away from them... whoever they are?'

'Limit, Aidan?' and the wizard gave him a very puzzled look, again ignoring the second question. 'I do not understand what you mean. I have no yardstick to measure the storm. Now may I ask you a question in return?'

'Of course, but...'

'No buts, Aidan. Tell me, I gave you a task last evening and that task included watching over the two young ladies, did it not?'

'Yes we know that, but...'

'No buts...get to it. Obey me, now...or else!'

Anders grabbed Aidan before he could say anything else and pushed him into the companionway.

Below in the passageway Aidan was exultant. 'I knew it! He's definitely hiding something. Did you see the way he reacted?'

'Reacted? He went nuts!'

'Yes, and that's the proof there's something going on! He very rarely loses his temper with me. He knows I'm not afraid of him when he shouts at me. He only scares me when he bollocks me quietly. Come on, let's see if the girls have any news,' and whistling a sea shanty he proceeded to the girl's cabin, bouncing off the bulkheads as he hurried along in the dark.

Nine

The door of the small cabin was ajar and the sounds of a further altercation reached them along the dark passage. Beatrix was instructing Augusta again on the correct way to make a bed, Aidan having left it ruffled.

'It seems a lot of bother tucking the blankets in; when I go to bed I'll only pull them out again.'

'Augusta, you have to pass as a maid, so you will do the job as a maid should; that's what the wizard told us. If you wish to argue the matter, go and see him, if you don't then you will do as I say and make the bed as it should be, all right?' Beatrix shouted. Red in the face, her temper flaring, she seemed to spend a lot of time lately with her face crimson.

'I am not a maid and neither are you!'

'I am a maid on this voyage since Meggy was taken ill and couldn't come with us. And, of course, you said there was no need to find another maid we wouldn't need one; we wouldn't be long sailing home. So I have to carry out a maid's duties!'

'Well I didn't know we'd encounter this storm! So, go and tell the wizard!'

'I wouldn't go and see Tragen yet, if I were you,' Anders interrupted Augusta before she could get up too much steam, 'he's just been shouting at Aidan.'

'Did you get anything out of him?' Augusta asked, dropping the blanket on the bed. Beatrix grunted and threw her arms up in disgust. 'We couldn't get anything out of Cornelia. She used the excuse that she was in a lot of pain and could we leave her sleep.'

'Pain? She shouldn't be in any pain, I saw to that. She must have been expecting you to question her,' said Aidan, frowning. 'Well, we succeeded a bit. Tragen and the Bear admitted we were running from someone,' Aidan replied smugly.

'No they didn't, Aidan. The Bear said we had reached the limit of the storm, nothing else.' Anders argued.

'He said we'd reached the limit of their range, not the storm,' retorted Aidan.

'Who's the Bear?' asked Beatrix.

'Oh, that's my uncle's nickname, we all call him that. Well he looks like one, doesn't he?' Anders added.

'It's very strange,' baffled, Augusta sucked at her index finger in the corner of her mouth.

'It's not,' Anders said, 'the captain's huge like a bear and covered in hair.'

'Aye, he is as well,' Augusta laughed, 'no, I didn't mean that. Reaching the limit of their range implies that we are fleeing someone, or something.'

'He was talking about the storm,' stated Anders, emphatically.

'No, Anders,' Beatrix stopped what she was doing, and turned to him. 'I do believe they may have a point. If we were fleeing just the storm then they'd just say "its range" or something like, oh…I don't know, perhaps "running from the storm". No, "the limit of their range" means something else entirely. Are you sure he said "their", Aidan?'

'Aye, I'm positive.'

Anders gave in, he'd never dispute anything with Beatrix whatever she said was gospel. They stared at each other, none of them knowing quite what to think. Anders went over to the bunk and helped Beatrix to finish tidying the beds. Aidan sat on the floor this time with his back against the chest, while Augusta sat on the chair her finger again in the corner of her mouth.

Anders straightened from tucking the final corner of the blanket under the mattress. 'If you are correct, and I'm not saying you are mind,' he glanced fleetingly at Beatrix to let her know that he wasn't actually disagreeing with her views, 'then fleeing from someone means we are being hunted. So, have any of you any idea who could be after us and why? Don't forget we are now leagues upon leagues from home, well off course.'

'It also means that whoever is doing the chasing is phenomenally powerful to get at us out here,' mused Aidan, listening to the storm battering the Grim.

'You mean that serious magic is being used?' Augusta asked, rising from her chair. She paced the little bit of floor space left free by the others, as Aidan nodded. He watched her, it registering with him that she was becoming more adept at keeping her sea legs on the bucking deck; illogically he thought it must be the britches she was wearing.

'I know this may sound silly,' interrupted Beatrix, peering through her tousled, long blonde hair. 'But you could all be wrong.' And she shouted above their voices when they all started talking at once. 'Wait, think about this. What if they are not chasing us, but whoever it is maybe…I don't know, maybe he's cunning and is luring us to him?'

'Nah,' said Aidan, 'if that was the case then the storm would get stronger the closer we got to him. The storm is getting weaker now.'

'But if his purpose was to sink us then I would agree with you, the storm would get worse. If it had another aim though, like capturing us maybe, the weather would ease to lull us into a false sense of security,' said Beatrix. 'It's just a thought,' she added, not quite giving up on her idea.

'Right, we'll keep that in mind,' said Augusta, not giving much credence to the idea. 'Now listen, we have to think on three things.' Holding up three fingers, she enumerated. 'The first is who is after us; the second is why he is chasing us and thirdly when we have figured out those two things, what do we do about it.'

'And fourthly, what we all seem to have forgotten…why has Lord Tragen not imposed a proper punishment on us?' Beatrix reminded, staring at them all, a knowing look on her face.

Anders abruptly sat down on the bunk, his face ashen. 'Aidan, do you remember what Tragen said, before your accident on the quarterdeck yesterday? I mean, when he laughed on seeing these two wearing our clothes?' He gripped his friend's shoulder tightly to emphasize his point.

'Yeah, he said they were suitable clothes for this weather. Ouch, you're hurting me,' and he shook off the cabin boy's hand. 'What are you on about?'

'Think man…he also said,' and here Anders paused to add stress to his next words, poking his finger in Aidan's chest. 'He also said, when the Bear asked him if it was his idea about these clothes,' and he waited all attention now on him, 'he said "he would never have thought of hiding her like this". Now my little wizard what do you make of that?' As he spoke, the shock on his face was replaced with a very superior look.

'Yes, he did! I remember now, I was going to ask him about it, but I was sick instead,' said Augusta.

'Yes, and last night when he gave me orders to ensure Augusta behaved, he told me, us, the deception has to work she has to appear a maid even when we are alone, it was very important that she did! Oh, my God, what is going on?' Beatrix asked her hands at her face.

White-faced, Beatrix turned to her mistress. 'It can only mean that you are in danger, Highness. But why would they want to hide you, on this ship, out here?'

Scared, Augusta answered. 'I am my father's heir, of course. Somehow some enemy has discovered me on this voyage,' ashen, she stared at her friends as she bit her lower lip. 'There is something I have not told you. My father sent Lord Tragen to bring me home early, for a purpose that my father would not even tell the wizard. And it has to be something extremely serious for he trusts Tragen above all others. The emperor was not pleased at me leaving early, I can tell you. Tragen carries a missive from him to my father and I know it's not very pleasant. Perhaps this is it, there are people hunting me.'

Aidan rose from the deck and started pacing the small room. 'If we are right, then Tragen and the captain need her to masquerade as one of us. And for that, they need our help. So, stop calling her Highness both of you, you may well be risking her life. We have to find out more.'

Aidan halted and leant against the end of the bunk. 'Augusta, you need to work some more on Lady Cornelia. I think she's the weaker of the two.'

'You don't know her…she's not weak at all.'

Silent again, thinking desperately now, no-one doubted that Anders had come up with the reason for Tragen's and Cornelia's long discussion the night before—and their strange behaviour since.

'Then change over,' Beatrix said.

'What do you mean?' Aidan asked.

'You, Aidan, you question Lady Cornelia, and you,' wondering if she'd ever get used to calling her mistress by name, 'Augusta, tackle Tragen.' She explained her reasoning as she sat on the bed. 'Well, Tragen doesn't know Augusta as much as he knows you, Aidan, and Lady Cornelia has only just met you. So, who knows what they'll divulge. They won't be on their guard with either of you.'

'That's good thinking, Beattie,' smiled Anders, looking at the girl who was now always in his thoughts. 'I do believe you have the makings of a good spy.'

Beatrix blushed; she swore she could hear admiration in his voice.

Leash, meanwhile, was busily stealing salted beef and ships biscuit from the provisions bins held in the forward hold. He had filled the small sack he carried and figured that he had enough to last him two weeks with care. He had settled on a strategy. At first, he'd eat the same as everyone else but, if the rations were too small, he would supplement his appetite with this hoard. He was afraid to take a greater amount in case the missing food was noticed. He did not want the theft discovered yet.

His plan was still in its infancy. If he waited until everyone was starving then arranged for a secret hoard of food to be found in the boy's possession, there would be anger, great anger. But he had yet to hide his own cache; he would collect a second sack of food later. He moved from the main hold under cover of the storm, taking his stash with him. Patience was now required before he could steal more.

Later that afternoon the four very crestfallen conspirators were back in Beattie's cabin discussing their next plan of action.

Following Beattie's stratagem, Augusta and Beatrix had climbed to the quarterdeck accompanied by Anders. The cabin boy had informed the girls they could not go alone; Tragen had already challenged Aidan for leaving them on their own this morning.

When they reached the quarterdeck, the wizard was nowhere to be seen. Hopper, who was in command at that time, informed them that Tragen had gone to rest in his cabin. He had not yet fully recovered from the exertions of creating the shield spell the day before, and he had left orders that he was not to be disturbed. Especially by any of "you lot" the mate had added.

Augusta had blown at that. 'What does he mean "you lot". He may very well be a wizard but that does not give him permission to be impertinent! Come "you lot" I am going to wake him.'

Anders was appalled. 'You can't. He'll get nasty. Aidan says he's always horrible when he wakes.'

'I don't care; he can't talk about me like that. I am his princess, for God's sake! My father will put him in the cages for this.'

'Not out here he won't, Augusta,' stated Beatrix peremptorily. 'And if you threatened him with it how do you propose to get him to divulge the information we need?'

Augusta paused, shaking her fists in futility. 'But it's not fair, Beattie!'

'I know, Augusta,' she put her arm around Augusta's shoulder to comfort her. Augusta – accepting the gesture with no thoughts of correcting her companion's impudent behaviour, which she would have previous to this voyage – stood at the bulwark, dejected.

'We'd better go back to the cabin and hope Aidan has more success,' said Anders, catching hold of Beattie's hand and leading them below.

But Aidan did no better. As soon as they returned to the cabin and informed him of their failure he left and knocked on Cornelia's door. Putting behind him all the embarrassment he had felt the last time he'd been in the lady's company, he pulled his shirt straight and retied his belt in the hope of making a good impression. He had, of course, forgotten what Augusta had said. This lady was no fool and, unbeknown to him, she had been briefed by Tragen on the future possible actions of their charges. Her subterfuge started as soon as he entered.

'Ah, Aidan, good afternoon, I am very happy to see you again. You have forgiven me? You are well?' And before he could answer, she added without pausing for breath. 'Of course you are, a fine strapping lad like you,' and she straightened her blankets on the bed, her bound foot poking from beneath the covers, not yet ready for any weight to be placed on it.

'I have called in to see if you require anything, Milady.' Aidan beamed at her, getting ready to settle in the chair alongside her, preparing his opening gambit.

The poor boy never had a chance.

'Oh, I'm so glad, Aidan. Before you sit I'd be much obliged if you could obtain a fresh pot of tea for me, would you be so kind? Not the magicked brew, I find that very…um…dry, don't you?'

And Aidan did oblige at the same time wondering how anyone could find a drink "dry". After the tea, fetched from the galley, she required her specially baked biscuits, also from the galley. And then it was a lighter shawl from her old cabin, unfortunately after much searching by all four friends, he fetched the wrong one and had to go back and find another. Aidan was worn out running back and forth. And just when he thought she had everything she needed and he had sat down ready to begin his interrogation, she asked him if he didn't mind leaving her to rest as she was quite worn out with his visit.

And that was the end of that highly unsuccessful bit of intrigue. He rejoined his friends who had been watching his running around with increasing bewilderment.

'Don't you ask,' he moaned, 'don't you dare ask me how it went.' He stretched out on the bottom bunk with a groan. 'That bloody woman never stopped wanting. Every time I went to sit down and talk to her, she needed something else.'

Beatrix grinned at him, her blue eyes glinting with mischief. 'Now you know what it's like to be a servant. Most of the time it's "I want this" or "I want that", and always when you could do with a rest.' She sneaked a look at her mistress, waiting for Augusta's reaction. Well, if I have to teach her my duties perhaps she'll realize and remember what it's like when we're back ashore, she thought.

'I do not behave as bad as that Beattie,' and then she had second thoughts, 'do I?'

Beatrix laughed and relented. 'No, not all the time,' and then she halted mid-sentence as a thought occurred. 'You know...Lady Cornelia never behaves such as she just has...never!'

'What do you mean?' Aidan asked, frowning.

'She is always very careful not to abuse her position.'

'Could this be a part of what they were plotting?' Anders suggested, peering around at everyone.

'What are you getting at?' Aidan asked, sitting up.

'Tragen is dodging us in his cabin and Lady Cornelia is stonewalling you. I think Tragen and Cornelia knew you'd swap over and try to question them. It stinks. We've got no further with gathering information, have we?' Anders stared at them, his eyes large, awaiting their agreement.

'Oh, I don't know any more. I'm fed up; let's leave it until the morning I'm getting a headache. You're probably right though, Tragen loves scheming.'

And Aidan sat back down on the deck not realizing that scheming is what the four of them had been doing since breakfast.

'Okay, but we can't sit here staring at four walls, we've got to do something or I'll go mad. I know, we'll play cards, Beattie, can you find them?' Dispirited, Augusta sat back in her chair.

And that's what they did. All four of them until Aidan threw his cards to the deck in a fit of pique an hour later. 'This is ludicrous Augusta. You've won every game you've played me!'

'Ah, a poor loser, are you? It's not my fault if you play obvious cards so...obviously,' jeered Augusta.

'I never make obvious moves, never...ask Anders. I am usually very, very good at this game. I can't understand your luck at all. It seems as if you know every card in my hand and exactly which card I'm going to play next.'

'Well, you are rather careless hiding them. And you can't blame me if I look, that's your fault.' Augusta smirked.

'I didn't show you my cards. But come to think of it, you did have extraordinary luck.' Aidan retorted, examining the backs of the cards, really getting worked up.

'You horrid boy, are you accusing me of cheating? How you...' Augusta was furious.

'How could she have seen your cards, she's sat opposite you?' Beatrix said attempting conciliation, she turned to Augusta. 'And the same goes for you, Augusta, there's no need to wind him up by telling him he's careless in showing his cards to you.'

'But I could see them, every single one. And I have not marked the backs, Aidan,' she said angrily, throwing her cards across the cabin at him. 'Okay! I'm not lying! They were there in my head—as plain as the nose on your face.'

Her three friends stared at her.

Aidan stared the hardest.

'Don't look at me like that, Aidan, you're frightening me,' upset, Augusta folded her arms across her chest.

'How plain were they? In your head I mean,' questioned Aidan, a very strange light in his eyes.

'How plain is plain, dolt! I saw your cards, every little spot and every little stain...is that plain enough for you?' Augusta shouted in his face, close to tears.

Aidan and Augusta locked eyes. *'Did Anders tell you what cards I held?'*

'No!'

'Did Beattie?'

'No, Aidan, stop it, Anders never said a word to me,' Augusta's eyes were brimming. 'And neither did Beattie.'

Anders jumped in seriously worried and confused. 'What are you saying Augusta, I never said a word about what? And...and what wouldn't Beattie tell you?'

'You heard him...he just accused you of telling me what was in his hand, you and Beattie.' Augusta was distraught; she had never been accused of cheating in her life. And over the last couple of days she'd come to love having these three as her friends, she had never been so close to people before. She didn't want to lose them over a

112

silly game of cards. But how could she get it across to them that she definitely saw Aidan's cards, and without cheating.

'I'm sorry, Augusta, but I never heard Aidan accuse Anders, or me, of anything,' said Beatrix.

Aidan interrupted. 'No, you didn't hear me but she did,' they looked at him quickly and saw him beaming.

'Come off it, will you! You never said I helped her and…why are you grinning like that?' Anders, exasperated, threw his cards to the deck.

Augusta, desperate now, grabbed hold of Beattie's hand for support and Beatrix turned on Aidan. 'Cease this tormenting, Aidan…enough is enough. You are truly upsetting everyone. I have never known Augusta to cheat, ever.'

Aidan laughed. 'You know Augusta…you really are a wonder!'

'For Gods' sake Aidan, stop this messing around; stop teasing her it's getting nasty! Leave her be!' Anders grasped the wizard's shirt and shouted at him.

'Ah, I'm sorry, you've got me wrong,' he continued grinning idiotically. 'Augusta really is a marvel—she saw my cards because I did show them to her. I have no doubt of that now. After all she just proved it by answering my accusations.'

'What accusations?' Anders shouted angrily. 'And stop that silly smirking, will you?'

Aidan burst out laughing and grabbed Augusta's hands in both of his own. He gazed into her emerald eyes the way she liked. 'You really do not understand what you have done, do you?'

Completely baffled now she returned his gaze, and again she felt as if she was submerging in his eyes, a very pleasant feeling that she did not understand. Quietly she asked him. 'Please…please, you're really scaring me. What have I done?'

'Not only do you have magic in you, you just joined me in a mindmeld,' stated Aidan, unable to stop grinning.

And then all hell broke loose again as there was an almighty crash from on deck and the ship heeled over.

Locklear had been back in command all afternoon on the quarterdeck, the weather improving with every passing hour. The thunder and lightning had ceased, the rain diminishing to a light drizzle and the bows were now visible from the captain's chair.

Locklear was immensely relieved as he studied the long deep swell; it seemed now that the worst was over, the storm receding aft lifting the spirits of everyone aboard.

A thin column of smoke constantly dribbled from the galley pipe forward, indicating that Dolly was cooking, following a normal routine again. When the crew had rested, Locklear intended breaking out the fishing gear. He just hoped it wasn't mackerel in these waters; he would have the devil's own job to persuade his ship's cook to even touch it.

Hugo pondered on how far they were from home as he sat back in his chair contemplating the dark clouds overhead. It was still impossible to take sightings but hopefully the stars would be visible sometime this coming night, he wondered if he'd recognize them. He knew though that they had been blown well to the southwest of their course and were now into the tropics, the air temperature was increasing quickly as was that of the sea.

Hopper joined him at his chair after completing an inspection of the hull. 'We seem to be holding our own, Captain. The pumps are keeping the water levels steady although the men are exhausted. We've rigged a chain pump in the forward hold and have abandoned the hand pump. There are no signs of any new boards springing a leak at the moment but we desperately need a beach to repair those that have. We've shored up the bulkhead in the sail locker but there is a lot of water seeping into the main cargo hold.' He paused to dry his eyes. 'I have ordered the salvageable provender moved to a drier location aft of the mizzen and have placed Leash in charge of stacking some of it in the passageway outside the passenger cabins.'

'Very well, Hopper.' Hugo looked around his vessel studying the damage. 'I wish Tragen had the necessary strength to repair the Grim, it would solve so many problems.'

'Why hasn't he?'

'He is afraid it would weaken him at a crucial moment. He is an old man and there is just too much to be done. He would need sleep for an unconscionable amount of time and, according to sod's law, he'd be out of it at the very time we'd need him most.' He brooded for a moment. 'All right let's move from this place a little quicker, I've had enough, we can put on more canvas to speed us on our way…wherever that may be.'

'Aye, aye sir,' said Hopper, and he shouted for Trumper to get the duty watch aloft.

And it was as if the storm had waited for this moment.

As the mainsail unfurled on the main yardarm, an enormous gust of wind blew again from abeam. A blast like a battering ram hit the ship and caught the sail. The ship heeled over sharply and the mainmast groaning under the unexpected weight of wind and canvas, cracked.

And before anything could be done, the mainmast snapped at man height above the deck and fell overboard dragging rigging, shrouds, sail and men with it. The wreckage encroached on the mizzen mast resulting in that also succumbing to the inordinate pressure and it snapped at the same height.

Bedlam reigned for those first moments as Trumper and the men on deck swarmed over the wreckage of both masts with axes. Lines were chopped free and men jumped clear as the masts slid overboard and this time the mainsail they had fought so hard to retain went with them. And as the last line was severed, not only did the ship come up but the wind ceased its almighty blow.

Unnerved the crew peered about them. Gales and storms were not supposed to have the sole intent of destroying you. But every man onboard was convinced that the only purpose of that gust of air had been to do just that.

Tragen arrived on the quarterdeck in the aftermath of the wind and watched the skies intently for any other adverse signs. Aidan and his friends watched Tragen's every move. Something was very wrong here, and they all knew it.

Locklear standing at the forward rail turned to acknowledge Tragen when the wizard moved up alongside him. The four young friends, stationed along the starboard rail, watched the activity on the lower deck, everyone that is, except Aidan.

He took his chance and a very troubled Tragen felt Aidan's mindmeld. *'Master, that was their final blow...their last chance at Augusta, wasn't it?'*

'Yes, I hope so, my boy,' and he turned to Aidan and raised his eyebrows. *'I thought I wouldn't be able to hide it from you for long.'*

'Or me, Lord Tragen,' Augusta interposed.

'Good God, she's mindmelding!' Tragen said staring at her he was utterly astonished.

'Yes, I am. Now do you not think I have the right to know who's hunting me?'

Tragen stared at Augusta and Aidan, lost for words, he was completely nonplussed. He nudged his friend Locklear. 'It appears Hugo that we have been discovered in our subterfuge.'

Hugo startled, sat up in his chair. 'What do you mean?'

Looking pensive Tragen added. 'These four...it is the four of you who suspect, Aidan?' At his assent Tragen continued still not taking in that Augusta could mindmeld. 'These four are not as ignorant as we assumed. They have realized that we are being chased by this storm.'

'No, Master, we have realized that we are being chased by someone behind this storm.' Aidan stared, daring him to contradict his statement.

'Before I tell all of you of what we surmise, I will need to think about this last calamity. I must ask for your patience and your forgiveness, Highness,' he said to Augusta. 'I promise I will divulge everything we know, and think we know, tomorrow. Hopefully, you will also be able to explain how you have come upon the art of mindmeld.'

'Mindmeld! What's this?' Hugo asked, frowning.

'It seems we all have secrets to impart, Hugo.' Tragen stared at the youngsters, a rueful smile on his face. 'I suggest you look in on poor Lady Cornelia before you retire. She must now be frantic with worry about this latest attack of the storm.'

As they moved to go below, the unhappy captain called down to Trumper. 'Bo'sun, enquire how many men died, please.'

'There's no need, Captain,' Aidan looked at Locklear, a very haggard looking bear now. 'There were three...I watched them pass over,' he smiled strangely and gazed up at the sky. 'They're fine now.'

Incredulous, Locklear stared after the boy as he and his friends entered the companionway to return below.

Later that night, Augusta and Beatrix lay in their bunks mulling over the events of the past days. 'What do you think of Aidan, Beattie, do you like him?'

'Oh yes, of course I do, he's quite remarkable isn't he? A lot different to what we always thought he was.' Beatrix smiled her mind elsewhere. She couldn't get Anders out of her thoughts, and didn't want to. She knew now that she was seriously in love with the tall, blond cabin boy, but how to tell him she had no idea.

Augusta turned over to go to sleep. 'I don't know about being a lot different...he's still an insolent pig, sometimes,' she smiled. 'What do you think he meant by saying that those three men who died were all right?'

'I'm not sure. All I know is there is something distinctly odd about him, sometimes.'

'Odd, but nice,' she replied, smiling radiantly.

Even later that night Anders was roused very abruptly from his dreams of Beatrix.

It lowered its arms and thrust the dagger slowly into the prisoner's belly, blood spurting all over it amidst the captive's renewed screaming. But this time the terrible, agonizing noise did not last for too long. The man quietened as his life bled away to fall into the fog billowing up from the rock basin below. It laughed loudly and gleefully whilst its minion cowered behind, terrified in case it noticed that he was afraid—for fear is what it sought.

Aidan screamed, crying out hoarsely. 'Red...God...God...God, everywhere red! Stop, please stop, please...please...you're h-u-rting h-i-m!'

Aidan did not wake. Anders did not sleep.

Ten

'What's wrong, Anders, you look terrible?' Beatrix asked, her concern for him unconsciously making her grip his hand harder. They were both in her cabin sitting on the bottom bunk waiting for the other two to bring breakfast. Anders' face was very drawn, his scruffy clothes even scruffier and he could hardly keep his eyes open. 'You look as if you've been up all night.'

'I have...I think,' and he sighed deeply. 'I haven't slept much at all,' staring at her through bleary, red eyes, he went on. 'Aidan is worrying me silly...I don't know what's going on...what's happening to him, but he's scaring me bonkers.' He sat on the edge of the bunk and stared at her hand in his, taking strength from the coolness of it.

'Why...what's he done this time?'

Anders looked down at her, admiring her pretty face for a moment, and combed his long hair with the fingers of his other hand, not even contemplating releasing her delicate fingers. His hair was lighter than hers, reflecting the morning light pouring through the porthole. He was desperately anxious and seeing the concern on her face discovered the need to speak of it. Aidan's nightmares were even more frightening now, and although his friend could not recall their content, they were having a malign effect on him. Aidan, always lean, was looking even thinner, his face paler, the black bags beneath his eyes even more pronounced. Anders sighed; maybe Beatrix would understand and know what to do.

He took a deep breath. 'Aidan has been talking in his sleep for the last three nights, saying things that puzzled me at first...now they scare me.'

'Go on,' she urged, when he paused showing no signs of continuing, 'tell me.'

'Well,' and he took another deep breath, 'the first night he woke me, he was talking about someone laughing.'

'That doesn't seem very much,' she frowned.

'No, but I got the impression it was not pleasant laughter,' he squeezed her hand. 'Then night before last, he woke me sounding as if he was threatening somebody. He was shouting about wizards coming somewhere. I don't know where and honestly, the way he spoke sent shivers up my back.'

'And last night...what happened last night?' She was afraid to ask seeing Anders tremble, she grasped his hand even tighter in both of hers. 'Come on tell me, it can't be that bad, can it...I mean it was only a dream, wasn't it?'

'I don't know,' he swallowed. 'He screamed...long and loud. It's a wonder no-one else heard him; the Bear must have been on deck. He said...he said something about everywhere being red and someone was hurting him.'

'What was red? Who was hurting him?'

He shook his head. 'I don't know, but it frightened him as well as me.'

'Have you asked him about these dreams?'

'Aye, all I get is a look that says I'm an idiot. He doesn't remember a thing, so he says...or perhaps he doesn't want to.'

Silent, anxiety creasing both their faces, she stared down at their hands intertwined in her lap and then quickly realized she was alone in her cabin, holding the hands of the very personable young man she was besotted with.

She jumped up nervously, their grip lingering until she started pacing the small cabin. 'Do you think we should tell Lord Tragen? After all, if these aren't dreams they could very well be portents, they sound like it.'

'They do? I don't know...let's wait, pick our time and both of us tackle Aidan, hey?'

Beatrix nodded as she heard Aidan and Augusta come down the passageway, the sounds of their laughter preceding them.

It had been Augusta's first ever visit to a ship's galley and she had been beguiled by Dolphin. She found it a strange name for a funny little man and she had nearly burst out laughing in front of him when Aidan called him "Dolly", Aidan kicked her just in time. He had then informed her of Dolly's prowess with a knife and that no man ever ridiculed the cook and survived without being cut. She wasn't sure whether to believe him or not but looking at the man wielding the ladle she had been fascinated by his enormous belly. It seemed to have a life of its own as it danced about above his rope belt its loops holding assorted knives.

While they had waited their turn, Augusta – pretending to be a maid – peered around into the steamy, hot atmosphere, the closeness of the crew assailing her nose with a variety of not very pleasant smells. The men were at their ease and savouring both the hot food and their brief respite before returning to duty. Now that two masts had been lost, the ship needed an even closer watch kept; no-one would be getting much rest until landfall was made. And they would only rest then once repairs had been made.

As Augusta and Aidan were leaving the galley with the burgoo and tea, Leash watched them from behind a pillar. He was sitting on the deck close to the stove, alone even amongst the crowd. He was sweating because of the radiant heat—he didn't mind, it was the cold he hated. He stared expressionless but was smiling inside. They were to hump stores from the forward hold that morning; or rather, the men he would be supervising would do the toting while he watched. He had already made sure that bails and casks had been stowed right outside the wizards' cabin. The opportunity for his plan had presented itself earlier than he expected. All he had to do now was obtain the second sack of food and his scheme would be up and running. There would be no problem planting the evidence.

As Aidan and Augusta negotiated the dark passageway, now obstructed with boxes and sacks, the ship rolled down a steep sea and Aidan banged his shin against a protruding corner.

'Bloody hell, if I get another bruise I'll be black and blue all over!' he complained.

'Don't you know you're not supposed to swear in front of ladies, little wizard,' laughed Augusta, repeating her companion's words.

'I didn't know there were any ladies present, Nellie,' he retorted rubbing his leg vigorously.

'Watch it, boy!' she threatened, 'or I'll kick your other leg, you won't notice the difference then.' She laughed and they entered what had now become her cabin as well as Beattie's. The first thing that struck her was the silence, the second, the strained expressions on the faces of Beatrix and Anders.

'What's wrong with you two?' But before either could answer, Lady Cornelia having been woken by the noise from the passage, shouted through for her breakfast.

'Ooh! She has no patience that woman…she must get it from you, Augusta,' said Aidan teasing her.

'I'm never like that…Beattie, tell him.'

Beatrix didn't answer but gave a telling look. 'I'll take her breakfast in while you share ours out.'

'Beattie, I'm not like that…' she shouted bad-temperedly, the boys grinned as Augusta shared out the porridge mumbling all the while. When Beatrix returned, Augusta sat on her bed and stared at Aidan.

'When are you going to start teaching me?'

'What? Oh yes, magic…I haven't forgotten, I've been a little preoccupied lately, what with one thing and another,' he replied, nearly choking as his food went down the wrong way. Augusta slapped his back.

'Ouch! Don't hit so hard, will you?'

'I didn't…big baby!'

'You are not teaching her here,' interrupted Anders, unnerved. 'Tragen said you're not to do magic in small rooms, remember?'

'Okay, I'm not going to…so stop nagging me!' He looked at his friend and grimaced. 'For some reason I don't feel up to it today, anyway.'

'Why is that?' Beatrix asked, looking pointedly at Anders. 'You don't appear well; aren't you sleeping?'

'I didn't last night, I had a…wait a minute, have you been talking, Anders?'

'I mentioned it, yeah. I'm worried about you. After all it's not every night I have to listen to my best friend's nightmares—just the last three!' Anders stared at Aidan daring him to deny it; he turned and smiled quickly at Beatrix glad that she had brought it out into the open.

'What are you lot talking about?' Augusta asked her spoon balanced precariously half way to her mouth.

Beatrix answered. 'He's been having dreams…horrible dreams.'

Augusta looked at Aidan a mixture of concern and curiosity on her face. It was then she noticed the drawn, pale look he had about him, the black bags under his eyes looking as if they'd been painted with kohl. Not concentrating on holding her bowl she slopped a little onto the floor as the ship climbed up and over the crest of another high wave. She settled herself in a more comfortable, and safer for everyone, position.

'Are you having nightmares?'

'Well I don't know about the other nights, but I'm beginning to remember something from last night.' He paused and rubbed his suddenly sweaty hands on his britches. 'It was scary. Don't ask me what…I don't know myself yet. All I know is, I didn't like it,' and he stopped speaking, lying back in his usual position on the bottom bunk.

'So, you may have been dreaming the other nights and don't remember.' Augusta turned to Anders. 'Tell me about these dreams.'

'Night terrors, more like it!' And he did, explaining at the same time that they were getting worse each night. 'I think Beattie had it right, just now. She said that these may be portents not dreams.'

'Portents! You mean he's seeing things in the future?' Augusta asked, now fascinated, intrigued and more than a little troubled. She and Beatrix had met a seer once before and come away confused and worried. She turned to look at Aidan on the bed, his arms behind his head. 'Are you…are you seeing the future?'

He thought for a moment and, bringing his arms forward, he rubbed his eyes. 'No, I don't think it is…the future I mean.' He stared at them blearily and then looked at his feet stretched out before him. 'I have the feeling that whatever it is, it's happening as I see it.'

They stared at him uncomprehending. Aidan continued. 'It's like a mindmeld Augusta. When you join with me or Tragen it's in the present…you are seeing and hearing events that are happening at the instant we join.' He grabbed her hand. 'When you become more experienced at mindmelding you will get this special feeling. I can't describe it…it's a knowing in your head, an acceptance of what the other person understands.' He squeezed her hand. 'And that's the feeling I'm getting, I can't recall what the dream was, but I can remember the sensation. I was mindmelding with someone—someone who frightens the life out of me.'

They stared at him in silence, all three apprehensive.

'I thought you couldn't mindmeld with someone unless they allowed it.' Anders said, breaking into their thoughts. 'And if you have, whoever it is will know of you now.'

'Not necessarily.' A voice said from the door. Unknowingly Tragen, walking in his usual silent manner, had come to the door and overheard their discussion.

Moving into the cabin accompanied by Lady Cornelia supported on his arm, Tragen repeated. 'Not necessarily,' and he added, 'I believe the same has happened to me. Now, Aidan, if you will kindly get up from there, and you Augusta move over, Lady Cornelia can sit on the end of the bed.'

The lady-in-waiting struggled over to what had once been her bed, and lowering her heavy bulk to sit, she turned to Aidan. 'Well, my young wizard, my ankle has healed, but I am still a little shaky. I could not stay abed any longer those four walls are playing on my nerves, besides, I would only get crotchety and end up making your lives a misery.'

'Crotchety, Cornelia...never let anyone dare say that!' Augusta said, tongue in cheek. 'You are looking a lot better now, though.'

'Yes, but I'm afraid you cannot have your cabin returned just yet, my dear. We all feel you have to stay in hiding, at the very least until we reach land.'

Augusta looked up at the wizard standing alongside her. 'My Lord Tragen, can you tell us now all you know...or think you know, as you promised?' She raised her eyebrows quizzically, reminding everyone present that she was the heir apparent to Mantovar. It was then that Locklear appeared in the doorway looking rested after his long ordeal on deck.

'Hugo, my friend, it seems that Aidan has been having the same experiences as me. He has mindmelded with the same being, I believe, in his dreams.'

Locklear opened his eyes wide in surprise and gazed at Aidan. 'Does this mean he is known?'

'Not necessarily.' The wizard repeated for a third time. Stroking his beard, he continued. 'I suppose I had better try and explain the fundamentals of mindmelding, but it is extremely difficult to understand for those who are unaccustomed to the art. But I believe now, as Aidan does, that anyone can use the skill if it is awakened in them.'

He turned to his boy. 'You know more of the intricacies of the human brain and use plain words better than me...you explain.'

Aidan looked up at the wizard and smiled weakly. 'Very well, Master. Your brain, Milady,' he spoke to Lady Cornelia, 'contains many compartments...like this ship. Many of the compartments are used all the time and remain open, like the galley and that bit of your brain that controls your speech or your sight.' He stared at his friends, not knowing how to simplify matters so that the uninitiated could understand. This was something that had taken him years of training to come to terms with. 'Some compartments are only opened now and then; access to the bilges is an example of those, as is the ability to read. But, there are other compartments that are hidden...dark places that only the rats know.'

He looked up as Beatrix gave a small shriek, and he smiled reassuringly. 'No, Beattie, don't be afraid, perhaps I'm not explaining things properly…rats also need warm, comfortable spaces in which to sleep and rear their young.'

'Are there rats on this ship, Captain?' asked Augusta, interrupting Aidan's flow, shivering at the thought of the brown rodents creeping around her cabin while she was sleeping.

'There are rats on every ship, Highness. But rest easy, they live very low down in the ship…in the bilges as Aidan says,' replied Locklear.

'The secret places in your brain are much the same…warm and comfortable,' Aidan continued. 'Although there are other compartments not so nice, but we can speak of those some other time.'

He gazed around at his listeners, their ears seeming to flap; he warmed to his subject. 'There are many lovely spaces as well that most people don't know about. Wizards and healers are born with these already opened, and that is why they have magical abilities. All people have the same abilities but can't use the special ones…the magical ones, because the doors to those particular compartments are closed and always will be. At least I always thought they'd be,' he glanced at Augusta and wondered…how on earth does she have the ability now?

'Is that what's happened to me, Aidan? Is that why I can mindmeld and do magic now?' Augusta asked him, reading his glance if not his mind.

'It must be,' he shrugged his shoulders. 'Some part of your brain that was previously inaccessible is now no longer blocked and your magical abilities have been freed. Why, I don't know.'

Beatrix noticed that whenever Aidan spoke of magic, his voice changed and the manner and tone of his speech sounded more mature, as it was now. He sounded years older than he was. Is that what magic does to you, she wondered—make you old before your time.

'And now I must break the code of wizardry,' Tragen spoke as Aidan finished. 'I have to share a secret with you and I ask that you do not divulge it to anyone. It is a fallacy spread by wizards over the centuries that you cannot mindmeld with someone who is not willing,' he grimaced. 'Not true! Wizards have hidden this ability for obvious reasons…it comes in very handy if you can be in your enemy's mind with him completely unaware of it,' he looked at Locklear. 'But those wizards of an impeccable nature, those who follow the white arts, never invade the minds of people without their permission, unless they feel threatened for some reason. And we never enter the minds of our friends unbidden. However, there are rogues in any profession, magicians are not unique—we have our dark side, practitioners of the black elements.' This last comment he stated very firmly, catching the eye of everyone present.

'But we can and do infiltrate the minds of enemies without them being aware of our presence. And we can do this at any time...awake or sleeping.' He breathed deeply before continuing. 'I believe this is what Aidan and I have been doing. Me, when I am awake, Aidan when sleeping. And we have been mindmelding with the same person.'

Aidan stilled at the words, his mouth dry, he had not known for sure that he was mindmelding and didn't know, of course, that Tragen had been doing the same. The listeners were stunned; knowing their minds were open to any wizard, at any time, and not being able to do anything about it came as a great shock.

Augusta, blushing, turned to Aidan. 'You have not been in my mind without me knowing, have you?'

'No, of course not, you are my friend. Why?' Aidan asked puzzled, not noticing the colour in her face.

'Nothing, nothing,' she said and turned away. God, she thought to herself, I do have to be careful.

Tragen went on with what he was saying. 'There is only one way of detecting another's presence in your mind,' and this captured their attention again. 'Your sensations can be felt! When you are as one in a mindmeld, you experience the emotions of each other. Therefore, it is very important for us to remember to suppress our feelings when we mindmeld so that the other does not sense us. Only with practise can this be achieved,' and he looked at Augusta. 'Take this time to learn with Aidan. You must attain the ability to enter your foe's mind and at the same time protect your own from all. You are our liege lord's daughter, our princess...it would not do to have Mantovar's state secrets divulged to your enemies,' he said gravely.

Beatrix stared with wide eyes, frightened for her mistress she had not realized how vulnerable Augusta was. She moved closer to Anders, entwining her fingers in his, she felt safer being near him.

'You still haven't told us why you're hiding Augusta,' said Aidan.

'This boy does not forget anything,' said Cornelia, smiling.

'Only when to wash behind his ears,' Tragen said laughing, the mirth increasing when Aidan automatically put his fingers to his ears to check and then went red as everyone looked at him.

'Master, enough,' he said, 'tell us.'

Tragen became serious again. 'On that first day of the storm I mindmelded searching for you, Aidan, for you did not reappear from your errand at the mainmast. That was when I made the initial contact. I failed to find you and instead I heard terrible laughter and felt its evil. That same night, Anders heard you mention laughter in your sleep, and he did not like it. Correct, Anders?' the cabin boy nodded and Tragen moved on. 'The second day, when I was casting the shield spell, I felt it again. And that time the feeling of malice in the laughter was so great it took me over and I collapsed. I, and the captain, knew at that time that someone was hunting us, and that night you dreamed of wizards going somewhere. But your mindmeld last night of seeing red and it hurting you worries me. I do not know how it fits in. But the captain, Lady Cornelia and I all agree on one thing. Whoever created this storm is chasing the Grim, and the only motive we can think of is because Augusta is onboard.'

'The storm has abated now and should disappear within the next few hours,' said Locklear, who had remained silent until now. 'We seem to have reached the limits of the storm and are now running out of the range of the devil. Hopefully, we can now look forward to a period of calm before we turn for home and possibly meet it again. But if we do encounter this storm or this being again, at least we will now be prepared...and Princess Augusta will be well hidden.' He summed up. 'My first priority is to make landfall so we can carry out repairs to the hull and the masts. If we meet this tempest again before these repairs are completed, the Grim is unlikely to survive.' Locklear turned to leave but halted with his foot over the storm sill when his friend stopped him.

'A moment, my friend,' said Tragen, 'before you go, I must emphasize to our young friends here the need to keep Augusta's identity secret, her life may very well depend on you. If we do meet this being in the future we do not want any of the crew knowing who she is. The less who know the safer she will be. So enjoy your freedom, Nellie, while you may and remember the lessons that my young apprentice will teach.' He moved to leave with Locklear, and as he put out his arm to help Lady Cornelia to rise, Beatrix spoke.

'Wait!' she shouted, and she reddened when everyone looked at her. Nervously, she said quietly, 'I'm sorry, but I think there is something you may have missed.' She gripped Anders' hand for support; she had never spoken in such a manner to such people of high

126

station before and wondered if they'd believe that a mere companion could possibly have anything of importance to relay. 'I mean...oh I told these earlier,' and she indicated her friends, 'they dismissed it then, but I don't think we can ignore the possibility any longer,' she said in a rush, looking down now at her feet and clinging to Anders.

'What is it, Beatrix? Come, don't be nervous,' Tragen smiled at her, 'believe it or not, we are all friends here.'

She looked up at him, this old, very stately man. The thought of him naming her a friend nearly struck her silent. Then feeling Anders squeeze her hand, she continued. 'I don't think this "being" you believe is chasing us,' with a voice gaining more confidence as she spoke, 'is behind us...I think he's in front of us.'

Tragen looked at her puzzled. 'What makes you say that?'

'In his mindmeld with the creature, Aidan said that there was not "a wizard coming" but there were "wizards coming". Don't you understand,' she said exasperated, '"coming" he said, not "going"!' And at their still puzzled looks, she continued. 'That storm you assume was created in Mantovar, could it not have been conjured here...on this side of the storm? May not the creator's intention be to lure us to him, to stop us getting home to Mantovar? And what about Aidan's third vision, he said everything was "red and hurting", not necessarily hurting him, it may have meant someone else was hurting and...and he saw it, and...and that is what is waiting for us!' She finished abruptly and held her breath waiting for their reaction, every bone in her body telling her it was true.

They were going towards the danger not away from it.

Tragen stared silently. Locklear ran his fingers through his black beard, tugging hard, his mouth pursed tightly. Cornelia sitting back down on the bed clasped her hands together and gazed into space thinking of the ramifications. Augusta was scared and wished she could hold Aidan's hand as Beatrix was holding Anders'.

Aidan felt her fear. *'Don't be frightened, Augusta, we're all here, we'll look after you,'* he mindmelded comfortingly.

'Oh, Aidan, she's right isn't she?'

'It never occurred to me but I do believe Beatrix may be correct,' Tragen broke into their mindmeld and into the heavy silence in the cabin.

Beatrix breathed easier and smiled nervously up at Anders holding her tight, now she would not have to worry on her own.

127

'It seems we have a lot more thinking to do, Hugo, Cornelia,' and he turned to include the lady-in-waiting. 'Although I do not think we should panic quite yet. Yes, if young Beatrix has it right then whoever is behind the storm has very cleverly hoodwinked us.'

'And if that's the case the cessation of the tempest has lulled us into a false sense of security,' added Locklear.

'And what's more important,' Tragen paused a moment tugging his beard while he thought, 'it means that I have been discovered. Aidan heard this being talk of a wizard coming and then Aidan threatened him with more than one,' he paused. 'It means that I have been identified and it has sought fit to hide the fact from me. Nevertheless, this being has yet to discover Aidan's presence. Why did he not detect my boy if we both mindmelded with the same creature? That is a puzzle! Anders, you must keep a close watch on Aidan tonight and every night, if anything about him worries you inform me immediately whatever time it is. You are to interrupt me whatever I am doing.'

As each and everyone looked from one to the other, Cornelia said. 'We must leave each other to our own thoughts and meet again, Tragen. As you say, we do not need to panic yet, and we ought not to make any unreasoned countermoves. If he is enticing us to him, then we must be very careful when we sight land for that may very well be the place this evil being is at.' She struggled to her feet. 'Come let us leave it at that for now. And as for you, young Beatrix,' she smiled, 'I can't see you remaining just a lady's companion for much longer.'

And that really did flummox young Beatrix.

After their meeting, the four went up on deck to clear their heads. They avoided the quarterdeck and went up forward on to the foc's'le. The storm had subsided, the drizzle had stopped and, although the sun had not yet reappeared, it was warm. Tomorrow promised to be a clear day.

The ship's superstructure was in a chaotic state with broken rigging needing securing and shrouds in great need of repair. It was going to be a mammoth job to splice the necessary lines and both broken masts were in a very sorry state, sharp slithers poking to the skies from the tops of the stumps. However, sails could fly on the foremast, jigger and after-jigger and the captain had already ordered them set. Despite the ship's obvious handicap, the vessel was proceeding at a fair speed, despite the difficulty in controlling the steering. Where the ship was going they were still not sure, the overcast denying them their position.

The four friends settled in the bows staring out to sea. Quiet for the moment, their thoughts on what had transpired in their discussion.

Beatrix, although relieved at having persuaded her companions to her way of thinking, was very troubled at the danger her mistress now found herself in and along with her, of course, all of them were now in serious peril. Moreover, what had Lady Cornelia meant with her parting comment? Beatrix had been trained from a very early age to be a lady's companion. Her mother was the princess' favourite lady-in-waiting and both had grown very close their friendship lasting years. Beatrix was very proud to carry out the same duties for Augusta, although up until these last few days, their relationship had not seemed to be as strong. Beatrix smiled; their friendship had certainly blossomed on this voyage. She continued to contemplate the direction her life had taken recently, her thoughts leading her everywhere, most of them frightening and looking at Anders her heart skipped a beat, her feelings made even less sense where he was concerned.

Anders was a worried young man standing at the rail close to Beatrix. What were they getting into? Aidan's visions scared him; mindmelding with an evil being took some believing. And Aidan's actual sightings, of the Gods knew what, really frightened him. He peered around at his friends, silent with their own thoughts. A lump came to his throat, so many friends. He'd only ever been close to Aidan, and like Aidan he'd never had female friends and now, as he glanced at Beatrix, it seemed that he had more than a friend. He hoped so. He smiled. What would his six older brothers say to that? Being the youngest in his family had its advantages; his mother always spoiled him. But it had its disadvantages as well, especially when you were fifteen years younger than the next brother. He'd always had to fight for his father's attentions, and been made to feel slightly inferior to all of them; tolerated was the word. But here he was now, an equal, friends with royalty and wizards; and in love with Beatrix. It must be love, he thought, otherwise he wouldn't have enormous butterflies in his stomach every time he looked at her. We have to be very, very cautious; I want nothing to harm any of us, he thought. Moving closer to Beatrix and rubbing shoulders with her, they both studied the ocean, each very conscious of the nearness of the other.

Augusta, usually carefree, was now thinking very seriously of what was ahead. All her life she had known that she had enemies and that they would love to deny her Mantovar, some would feel it their duty to kill her. She was used to being in danger and used to having bodyguards. Her parents, and her teachers, had always drummed it into her that she had to be very circumspect when choosing her friends. They should always be from "proper" families, those very loyal to her father. She knew that her future husband would be chosen for her from that clique, probably within the next year. Then her heart flipped, was that the reason for her early recall home? Had her parents decided already? The thought of that made her very miserable. Up until this voyage she had not had second thoughts about being married to someone she didn't know, it was her duty. But now, and she looked at her friends, she shuddered at all thoughts of betrothal to a stranger. She sighed and stared over the rail at a dolphin swimming nearby. Look at me now, the only real friends I have ever had are these three – a lady's companion, a cabin boy and a wizard's apprentice – hardly members of a "proper" family, except for Beatrix of course. These three would be more loyal to her and far better friends than any members of the aristocracy of Mantovar, or those of Drakka. She felt safe with these despite the unknown enemy chasing her. And then she smiled, she was now a wizard, she had the ability to mindmeld and do magic. She would be the first ever monarch to practise the magic arts, could she also be the first ever monarch to choose her own husband? Then another thought made her anxious; would a wizard be allowed the throne, someone had tried once before and failed.

Aidan on the other hand was nervous. A responsibility unlooked for had fallen on his young shoulders. He had to teach a member of the monarchy the intricacies of mindmelding and of magic. He was under no illusion as to the complications of this course of action. The prince would be astonished that his daughter had the ability; suspicious as to how she had acquired the art and mistrustful of this young apprentice teaching her how to use it. He would not like his daughter falling under the influence of a wizard even though his best friend was one. There were many in the principality, and indeed the empire, dubious of the powers held by these mysterious people. Wizards, and in some cases Adepts, although welcomed in many places, were always treated with extreme caution. Indeed, in the case of the Guild of the Brethren of Wisdom, a mysterious sect of black sorcerers based in the south of Drakka, fear was the ruling factor— ordinary people avoided them like the plague. He looked around at his companions and marvelled. He had only ever had one friend before –

Anders – but now he had three. He smiled, regardless of all that was ahead he was happier than he had ever been before in his young life.

Leash watched them from his position at the helm. He also was happy. He had hidden the contraband sack of food in the wizard's cabin. Looking back it had been so easy. His task of toting provisions from the forward hold and stacking them in the dry, in the passenger corridor, had given him the opportunity. When Tragen and the others had been in the maid's cabin that morning, he had stolen the food from that in the passageway. He had then secreted it under the boy's clothing in the trunk behind the door of the wizard's cabin. He had not even had to rush, there had been nobody around to see him enter or leave the berth. Now, when everyone was starving, as they all would be in the next week or so, he would arrange for its discovery. He smiled, it would be the end of the boy – the crew would be hard-pressed not to lynch him – and the wizard would be gutted. Leash only had to wait.

Eleven

That night Anders lay awake on a palliasse on the floor, anxious, staring at the bulkhead above him waiting for the next vision, or portent, or nightmare whatever to strike Aidan. He lay listening to every board creak alongside his head, jumping every time Aidan snored. But exhaustion won in the end and in the small hours his young body succumbed to the need for sleep.

Aidan lay on the bed tossing and turning. He was tense and very afraid of contacting their enemy in his sleep. Debating with himself, he preferred to be aware of the unknown foe whilst awake; he'd have more control perhaps. Giving in to temptation he attempted to mindmeld, searching him out, a very dangerous strategy he could so easily be discovered—and he knew in his heart of hearts that he needed to keep his presence a secret. The enemy knowing of one wizard would take protective measures to nullify Tragen's abilities. If the enemy succeeded in disabling Tragen then having another wizard nearby could seriously upset his plans. But, of course, there was now a third wizard on board and her safety was paramount—she had to be kept hidden at all costs. Aidan was restless far into the small hours, eventually falling asleep as dawn was breaking. He had no visions that night but his lack of sleep still meant he woke exhausted when Anders rose next morning.

Anders left Aidan in bed and went to fetch Locklear's breakfast and washing water. On returning, he found the apprentice had not risen. 'Not getting up today?'

'Did I dream? Did you hear me say anything, anything at all?'

'No, all I heard was you snoring.' He paused and gazed at his friend. 'Come on, me and the girls have got us all breakfast so move quickly or it'll get cold. Mind you it was going cold anyway; Dolly was showing us his knife juggling tricks. That man is a true artist throwing the blades around, he showed us this trick with a misericorde that was really amazing. He frightened the life out of Leash, he threw one at him and it nearly parted his hair when it stuck in the pillar behind him. Everyone laughed, except Leash of course, he snarled and stormed off.'

'What's a misericorde?'

'Oh, a small dagger used to finish off your opponent.' Aidan stared at his friend mystified, and then his look changed to horror as Anders concluded. 'It's thrust into the neck to sever the windpipe.'

'Please, no more!' Aidan shuddered. 'Leash, he's the one who was near me when I fell the other day on the quarterdeck. Come to think of it he never made a move to help me, did he?'

'Nah,' said Anders, 'he's a very strange man; I don't think he has any friends at all.'

Aidan sat very pensive. 'You know there's something about that man that's not quite right. Have you noticed his eyes? He's always staring into space as if he's seeing someone else and I've heard him talking to himself a lot.'

'Maybe he's just very lonely,' said Anders, after all he was also guilty of just that lately, thinking of Beatrix. 'He's a loner sure enough. Now, come on shift, let's see what the girls have planned for us today.'

What they had planned was lesson time, Aidan being the teacher, Augusta his pupil and the other two eavesdropping.

Strolling up on deck they encountered the sun for the first time in days. No rain or drizzle, bright sunlight, calm seas and a warm breeze greeting them as they settled themselves amidships at the foot of the demolished mainmast. Trumper had been busy and his work had thwarted their attempt to settle on the foc's'le. The bo'sun had spread several canvases across the deck and was preparing to sew them together to make a larger sail to replace the mainsail. Not that they wanted to be anywhere near the canvas—it was mouldy and smelled abominably having been submerged in the sail locker for days. As it was, a team of sailors were washing it down, sloshing buckets of seawater everywhere.

It wasn't long before Aidan stretched out in his usual position, flat on his back with his head resting on Augusta's lap, she didn't seem to mind. Anders and Beatrix were also in their favourite position, seated together automatically reaching for each other's hand. The four savoured the balmy weather and were silent for a while just soaking up the sun. They listened to the shrill voices of a family of dolphins swimming alongside, their sleek shiny bodies glistening as they leapt and dived amongst the shoal of herring that was providing them with nourishment.

They weren't allowed to remain at peace for long, though; a flurry of activity disturbed them as a party of sailors flung a small net over the side to catch the remaining fish before they disappeared down the throats of the large mammals. The net went into the water twice more before the shoal took the hint and fled, along with the dolphins.

'Frigging fish! I suppose that's all we'll live off for weeks now,' moaned Dolly.

Aidan looked around, noticing the ship's cook for the first time. With a very forlorn look on his face Dolly stared over the side as each heavy load was swung inboard using a temporary davit.

On the quarterdeck, Locklear and Tragen also watched the fishing, so did Leash at the wheel, seething. His mind a turmoil, he'd just heard Locklear thank the Gods for this fresh food. Leash's plans fell apart; hiding contraband food in the wizard's cabin had been a pure waste of time. He was going to have to think of something else—maybe secrete fresh water?

'Catching enough fish to supplement the rations is a godsend, Tragen,' said Locklear. 'If we can make landfall within the next week, and if the shoals are as plentiful as this, we will have no fear of starving.' He clapped Tragen on the shoulders, wearing the first smile on his face for days. 'The only concern I have now is that the drinking water will not last.'

'My friend, you can be very dense on times. Your best friend is a wizard, is he not? One of the easiest spells to conjure is that of extracting the moisture from the very air we breathe. And just as easy is the conjuration to summon fish,' he watched comprehension dawning in Locklear's eyes.

'You mean I worry for naught?' said Locklear.

'Aye, my friend,' and the wizard laughed. 'There is no water or food shortage, I and my staff will see to that. Even Aidan can conjure the water, only at a slower pace as he has not yet his own staff. And he is quite adept at summoning fish, although he does tend to find the wrong kind. No, my friend, what we have to worry about is our destination.'

The ship shuddered as Leash's hands convulsed on the wheel.

'Careful helmsman, keep your mind on your job,' chided the captain as he turned to the wizard. 'Come; let us go to my cabin. We can discuss our course as we take refreshment. I'll send for Hopper.'

'Dolly, how come you hate fish so much?' Aidan asked as the others sat idly by listening. Aidan stood beside the short, fat man and joined him in staring out over the clear blue ocean the dolphins barely in sight at the horizon.

Dolly glanced at the young boy and wondered if he could trust him. Dolly's natural caginess when talking to wizards seemed to lift with this boy, this young one had never posed a threat. Yet Dolly knew that wizards should be avoided until needed, at least the ones he'd met previously. But Aidan had an open face, no guile in his manner and moreover his reputation for healing was the best. Dolly sighed, realizing he needed to talk, wanting to tell someone his secret. He had bottled it up for years and it was eating him up inside. This young healer and his friends had always shown him kindness; never ridiculed him...did they have a sympathetic ear? There was only one way to find out and perhaps speaking of the tragedy would help ease his pain.

He said very seriously, tears started welling in his eyes. 'My ma...she was et by a fish, years ago.'

The four friends stared at the cook disbelieving their hearing but as the import of his words sunk in Beatrix had to kick Anders to stop him laughing out loud. Augusta stood; biting her lip to stop smiling she went and stood the other side of the little man.

'What do you mean, Dolly...et, I mean eaten...by a real fish?' Augusta asked.

'Aye, o' course it were real!' he paused. 'It were a whale as big as our ship what did eat her. I saw it when I were little. I saw it gobble her up and...and ever since, every time I handle a fish, every time I get ready to gut it I expect to find bits o' me ma inside.' And the little cook stared into Augusta's face the tears now brimming in his eyes. 'I never told anyone afore,' he said, his voice cracking. 'They all think I'm barmy cos I don't like fish,' and he rubbed his eyes with his rough red hands, 'an' I don' wan' them to know, alrigh'.'

'Okay, we won't let on,' said Aidan, having great difficulty in keeping a straight face. 'But how did it happen?'

Dolly gazed around at them through watery eyes, and he sniffed. 'I blame me da...it were his fault he...he shouldn't have asked her how many candles she'd bought that week.'

'Candles,' said Anders, his mouth agape. 'What's it to do with candles?'

'Well it were coming on to night and he needed a light to cook by in the galley. He taught me all I know about cooking, did me dada, see. So he stuck his head up through the hatchway and asked me ma how many candles she'd bought cos he wanted to light an extra one.

Well that did it…me ma did her nut.' He turned his head for a moment and spat phlegm over the side.

Beatrix trying not to grimace at the cook's gross behaviour couldn't help but ask. 'What has that got to do with your ma…I mean your mother being eaten by a fish?'

'Ah, she were drunk on account of feeling a bit guilty, see, and she were in a bad mood cos of it. She shouted at me da and asked him what he meant by that remark. Well me da was truly flummoxed at that. Cos what he didn't know, but as everyone else did…me ma was getting more than candles off the candlemaker. If you know what I mean,' and he winked.

'Go on Dolly, what happened next?' Augusta asked intrigued and puzzled at the same time…what else did candlemakers sell. The others were no longer laughing either, all totally immersed in the emerging story.

'There was me da, his head sticking up out of the hatchway…a perfect target, so me ma musta thought. She picked up a belaying pin alongside her and took a huge swing at his head,' as he said this Dolly started weeping again. 'Me da saw the pin coming and ducked…and that's when it happened. Me ma couldn't stop her swing and she lost her balance, slipped and fell overboard.' He put his hands over his face and continued, bereft. 'There was this enormous great whale swimming alongside us, and…and she fell straight into its mouth.' He sniffed and looked up at the four friends. 'We never saw her again.'

Aidan looked at him, astounded at the thought of someone having the extraordinary bad fortune to fall to such an unbelievable death. And he was bewildered at how Dolly thought it was his father's fault.

'I'm sorry Dolly but I don't understand…how was your father to blame?'

'He shouldn't have ducked! Her swing would have stopped if he hadn't dropped his head. Instead…' and he burst into tears again.

Augusta and Beatrix put their arms around his shoulders, comforting him and at the same time trying not to look at each other in case they burst into laughter. The boys turned away desperately attempting to keep silent but turned back sharply when Augusta spoke.

'Dolly, we're so sorry. I tell you what…we'll help you. We'll gut the fish and you can cook them, all right?'

The ship's cook looked at her with a glimmer in his eyes, and then stared around at the others. 'Would you really...I could manage if you did that.'

Aidan, Anders and Beatrix were aghast but it was already too late to get out of it.

'Augusta what are you saying. That's a horrible, stinking job. It's backbreaking and we'll smell for days and days,' Aidan complained.

'Oh, she replied, *'I never thought of that. Still, we'll manage...the poor man!'* She continued loudly so all could hear. 'We don't mind Dolly, we understand how you feel. You just tell us when you want us to start and we'll be there.'

'Good,' he said, and pulling himself together, he smiled. 'You had better start right away. The fish will need cleaning as soon as possible or they'll go off, I have to salt them before they go into the bins...come on.'

And before the friends knew it, they were up to their armpits in fish guts, everyone else keeping their distance, and sharks swimming alongside making a feast of the entrails.

Tragen and Hopper, sitting opposite Locklear in his cabin, were imbibing Locklear's best Gilian. The stern gallery window was open and a cooling sea breeze played amongst the captain's papers, riffling them gently, not enough to blow them to the floor.

'Hugo, do you have any idea now of where we are?' Tragen asked, relaxing for the first time in days.

'Aye, man,' replied Hugo, his deep-set eyes twinkling, as he sipped the brandy. 'Ah, that's good!' He rolled it around his mouth anticipating the warm feeling he would get as it trickled slowly down his throat to hit his stomach. 'Hopper and I took sightings of the stars as soon as they appeared last night. We confirmed our position at noon, today. We are a very long way off course somewhere to the south and west of Drakka. Aye, my friend,' he said to the dismayed Tragen. 'We are now far further from home than when we set out.'

Hopper broke in. 'And in answer to your next question we have estimated we are now about four weeks normal sailing from where the storm first hit us. And if we can turn about and make it back to that point we would still have another three weeks to the river into Mantovar.'

'By the Gods,' Tragen pulled at his beard. 'Seven weeks from home and we still have to make landfall first to affect repairs. I never thought the storm would have driven us at such a speed.'

'Neither did I, 'said the captain, 'but Hopper and I are agreed on our position. It confirms what we thought at the outset…our unknown antagonist must be very powerful indeed. We have pulled the charts, such as they are for this area, and we have several options before us.'

Hugo rose from his chair carrying his brandy and walked to the chart table, the others followed. A large, mostly blank parchment, held open at each corner by various objects from Hugo's desk, lay on the table. Their destination, the river mouth in Mantovar, was inked in at the top right hand corner easily recognizable. A little way south of there a heavy line was drawn, its direction southwest. The line started at a point just off the coast of Drakka in the east where a large cross indicating the point at which they'd encountered the storm had also been inked in. There were islands situated in the bottom left hand corner and midway to the north, opposite the coast of Mantovar another smaller set of islands, these looked to be at an equal distance from Mantovar as the Grim was now. Taking all the space at the top of the chart was the land of the frozen desert, a vast area dwarfing Mantovar and Drakka. All three men bent over the map taking in its lack of detail.

'This is the course we have been blown along,' said Hugo, running his finger along the line south-westwards from the storm. 'To the east of us lies the southern coast of Drakka, to the north of Drakka is Mantovar. Between us and home is the storm.' He looked up at his companions. 'We obviously cannot attempt Mantovar in the ship's present state.'

'These islands ahead of us, Hugo, what are they?' asked Tragen.

'They are the Griffin Islands…Hopper knows them better than me.'

'I've only been there once, Milord, for a period of a few weeks, the ship I was on stopped in for repairs.' Hopper grimaced and went on, not very happily. 'Another name for them is the Mysterious Isles and they are not called that for nothing. There are about forty or fifty islands scattered over about a thousand leagues. The vast majority of the islands are too small for people to live on but there are other, larger islands that are inhabited, some by very strange people. There are fisher folk on most of the islands, of course, and some of the larger are home to farmers and also to ironworkers. The largest island, Griffin, is huge and has its own iron mines and foundries. Surplus ore and raw iron is exported to markets all over the world.

'There is a monastery on Sanctity, the next largest island. The monks from there used to travel all over the isles, they were the local healers, but for some reason they ceased their travelling and I never knew why,' Hopper frowned. 'There is talk of islands disappearing and then reappearing. I could not get to the bottom of that tale and I must admit I did not heed the stories much; they seemed to be used as a threat to get children to behave. But people do disappear on Griffin and each time there is a link to green devils. Who they are I've no idea...it's probably just a local superstition.'

'Green devils? I wonder if they mean the Green People,' interrupted Tragen, scratching his head. 'I can't, for the life of me, remember anything much about them, except that they were supposedly the guardians of nature and that they disappeared from the face of the earth along with the elves.'

'Are any islands wooded, Hopper?' asked Locklear.

'There are woods with trees suitable to supply many masts. They are all on Sanctity.'

'Good, good,' Locklear's eyes gleamed, 'if we agree on the Griffin Islands as our destination then we'll head for Sanctity as soon as possible.'

'How about these islands to the north,' Tragen prodded the point on the map to the west of Mantovar, 'are these the Onyx isles?'

Hugo nodded. 'Those we both know, eh Hopper?'

'Aye, the isles of plenty...plenty of wine and women. The Pleasure Isles some name them.'

'Home to brigands, a nastier, more terrible set of pirates you could not meet anywhere else in the world.' Locklear straightened his back and paced the floor a moment before returning to stare at the chart. 'I have fought them many times, they are a relentless foe. The worst of them are led by Captain Jos Osvaldo in his ship the Lobos. They do not surrender...ever, but they will to the Grim—one day. Once they are engaged in conflict, it is a battle to the death...the death of the ship. The victims, whatever's left of them, are overpowered and taken into slavery and the ship disappears, sunk or taken for purposes of their own, its name changed. We have battled him many times and he has always found us too strong, but it doesn't stop him wanting the

Grim.' He looked at Tragen. 'That is the last place we should make for in this condition, and with Augusta aboard.'

'Where then, return to Drakka and await the storm's ending?'

'How do we know it hasn't ended already? How do we know that it's not awaiting our next move home?' The ship's master was troubled. 'Besides, Drakka is as far away as Mantovar. No, Tragen, we gain nothing by returning there.'

'Unless we were to take Augusta home on the overland trek up the Great Northern Road,' said Tragen, 'it is an option that is also open to us.'

'Aye, but that would mean passing through the Drikander and the inhabitants of that forest have no love for the emperor. Besides it wouldn't solve the problem of getting the Grim to Mantovar, and I will not leave my ship behind,' stated Locklear in no uncertain terms.

'Where then? You've ruled out Mantovar and Drakka, you say the Onyx Isles are too dangerous for Augusta. I rule out the frozen wastes of the north...'

'Why do that, Milord? If we proceed from Griffin straight north to the frozen desert, we avoid the brigands and the storm. We can sail southwards from there following the coast and enter the river from the north. I know it will take us months once we have our masts, but it seems the safer route to me,' Hopper said, staring curiously at the wizard.

Tragen stared out of the cabin window at the ship's white wake, it was a pleasing sight after the black violence of the previous days...a pity his thoughts weren't so pleasant. Should I tell them all of it, he reflected. The frozen desert frightened him to death, not because of what it was, but because of what was hidden there.

On the shores of the cold north lived the greatest warriors in the known world. They were giants, an ancient people, older than the elves and dragons and green people. The giants and their families followed the more peaceful occupations of whalers and seal hunters, but they never forgot their primary purpose, they patrolled the rugged terrain from one end of the coast to the other, continuously. Working out of harbours that froze solid in winter the Giants were a people that thrived in isolation, making contact with the outside world only to trade for grain and metal goods. They did not welcome strangers in their homeland and were truly savage when riled.

The giants, though, did not scare the wizard; they weren't the reason for his anxiety. He could handle them easily enough after all the wizards had placed them there originally, though it was so long ago most wizards had forgotten it.

However, leagues inland in the midst of the glaciers and broken ice plateaux, was a place he could not handle. He shuddered remembering the legends. Legends he knew to be true.

He turned from the window and looked at the two seamen for a moment. 'No, my friends, the cold north holds something that no mortal man should even acknowledge exists let alone approach. It is the habitat of the Ringwold.'

Hopper sucked in his breath. 'They are a tale of nightmares surely…stories to frighten children. Are you saying that they really exist?' he said, incredulously.

'Ah, my friends, it seems that I must confirm your worst fears concerning wizards.' At their quizzical looks he continued. 'Wizards have always been highly secretive and this makes us doubly suspicious in your eyes,' he paused a moment to collect his thoughts.

'I must tell of a responsibility that wizards took upon themselves without thought of consulting others. An action that we deemed so vital to protect the earth that we dared not trust anyone else, except for the elves as we needed the dragons. We arrogantly thought ourselves to be so superior there was no need to inform those of lesser abilities…a belief that has, inevitably, led to our downfall. No-one trusts us now.' He went and sat in his seat at Hugo's desk.

'Exasperated mothers, to quell the noise made by their offspring, have often used the Ringwold as a deterrent. I don't know why this is so, I have never been able to understand how frightening a child to death will bring that loving child comfort. The tales are horrendous of course, bogeymen, witches, trolls and demons, "they will all come and eat you up if you don't go to sleep". By the Gods, how can anyone sleep if they know of those vile creatures?'

Tragen sat in his chair and with his elbows resting on the arms he placed his fingertips together and pursed his lips in thought. 'Legends are born from facts that have become distorted over the centuries, and if no new concepts emerge then old ideas become even more coloured. This suited us wizards we used it to ensure your safety.' He stared at his friends' consternation.

'We had to find a means to ensure that mortals stayed away from the interior of the icy wastes. Aeons ago we asked volunteers to live on the shores of the desert. These volunteers would live by hunting and fishing the great mammals that abounded there. The main objective of these people however, was to turn all others away...deter any who wished to journey inland. The only ones to come forward were the giants, unsurprising really as they love the sea and are impervious to the cold. Apparently this strategy has succeeded so well that the volunteers have now become indigenous to that part of the world. They have settled in so deeply that their purpose of deterrence has become ingrained. No-one can get past them.'

'Aye, that's true enough,' said Locklear, 'I know men that have tried...they barely escaped with their lives.' He gazed at the troubled wizard. 'All right, you have told us that we should not go there. I know something of what's up there, or at least dark rumours of the place, enough to frighten me silly, can you tell us more? Can you tell us of the Ringwold inhabitants?'

'I wish I could but I cannot. Wait!' and he waved his hands to silence both his companions. 'Please let me explain before shouting me down...I am talking of thousands of years ago. The sorcerers of that time knew the Ringwold intimately.' He blanched at how well the wizards did know it. It had been the Black Sorcerers that had created the place; the White Sorcerers – with the help of dragons – had enclosed it. He could never tell these the whole truth.

'We have known for what seems forever that the details of these inhabitants were too horrible to document and so the lore was handed down by word of mouth, wizard to wizard. We know now that was also a mistake. The time has now been so long that even we wizards have forgotten the salient facts.

'Except for one unassailable truth—if the Ringwold ever comes south then the world as we know it ends.'

Tragen stood and stared long and hard at both of his comrades. 'We must never think of going north to the wastes. If you do, then I will do all in my considerable power to stop you.'

Hugo stared up at him silently; he had never heard that tone from the wizard in all their years together. 'Then you believe all these nightmare figures of trolls and bogeymen, goblins and ghouls, to be true, my friend?'

'Not as stated in threats by irate mothers, no...but they are based on indisputable fact. Whatever is in the Ringwold is devastating for mankind.'

'But surely,' Hopper interrupted, 'we need not go that far north. I'm not on about making landfall; I'm talking about following the coastline.'

'We do not know for sure the origin of this storm. If it stems from the Ringwold then it would be likely they would detect us. We may even be forced to land. We cannot risk it!' Tragen, his stare implacable, silenced them both.

'Then that makes the decision easier, I suppose,' and at their looks Locklear continued. 'There is only one option...the Griffin Islands. Let us hope and pray that young Beatrix is wrong and that whoever created that storm is not before us. What else can you tell us of the islands, Hopper?'

'Before I do, you haven't mentioned Blackfire, that's only five days sailing due south of here.'

'I would rather not go anywhere near the Siren with only three masts. If we were rigged as we should be I'd take a chance. But, of course, if we were there'd be no need for us to venture there, and as you said earlier there's no appreciable food supply on the island. The Griffin islands are our best bet, their roughly the same distance, they have food, water and masts. We'll leave Blackfire as a last resort.' Locklear sighed, tugging at his beard he stared out the open window.

'Tell us of the islands, Hopper,' Tragen asked breaking the silence.

'The only one I landed on was Griffin. It has an enclosed deep-water harbour, very busy, mainly used by the large ocean-going vessels carrying iron-ore and coke. But it also has a very healthy trade in other goods, usually those from farther west; they also trade in fertilizer and some say slaves from the south, the Dark Continent, I believe...not that I ever saw any of those poor people. But like all successful ports it has a cross-section of people, a fair share of them on the seedier side of life. There are two clans on that island and for some reason they, if not in actual open warfare, carry out a clandestine violence—they detest each other and people do die.'

'Do they have any military?' Locklear asked.

'Not as such, armed militia certainly and a small, highly professional navy is needed to protect against the brigands from the north and to support their customs service...smuggling is rife. The Portolans, the clan in the south, have full control over both the militia and the navy and they have a giant of a man leading them. The Montetors of the north have their own forces, from what I could gather at the time, more covert than overt.'

'Do we have cause to worry, if we ask for aid?' Tragen asked.

'I believe not, Milord. But circumstances can change in ten years.'

'Then we will play it by ear,' and with that Locklear took up the flagon of brandy and poured them all a new and larger mug of the amber nectar.

Tragen mulled over these new concerns, and then his mind recalled the worries that Beatrix had voiced. Was she correct? Was the perpetrator on Griffin or perhaps on Sanctity or any other of the smaller islands? If she was right—he had no idea how to proceed.

Twelve

'Oh, my poor fingers!' groaned Aidan, holding his sore hands in the air before him, shaking them slowly in an attempt to cool the inflammation. It was dusk and they all sat in a state of utter misery in the girls' cabin.

'Augusta, you have a big mouth,' he said, as she sat dejected on the end of her bed.

'Don't blame her, we all went along with it,' said Anders, nursing his own hurting hands. 'I have never smelled so bad,' he grumbled, sniffing his clothes.

'Oh, I don't know…I've had to share your berth these last few nights,' said Aidan laughing.

Anders, forgetting his hands a moment, threw a cushion at him and then moaned in pain as he broke another blister. Even he had found the chore exacting. Being used to manual labour, he thought, did not mean you were used to gripping a knife for hours on end, and gutting fish was not an easy job. Poor Augusta was in a dreadful state…blisters as big as apples on her palms, her fingers red and aching. The only other one to cope reasonably well was Beatrix; her hands were a lot harder than those of her mistress.

The chore had been so mind-numbingly disgusting that they had not realized that they had paired off until later. Beatrix and Anders had shared the task, the labour coming as no shock to them. Being ignored by Augusta and Aidan was an added bonus, their young love grew as they became even closer and they found it quite easy to forget the presence of the other two.

At first she had struggled, Augusta not even knowing how to hold a knife, until Dolly had taken pity on her enough to show her how to use it. Then, as Augusta assisted Aidan, they both fell into mindmelding almost by accident. At first, it had been hard going, Augusta finding it increasingly challenging to concentrate on seeking his mind and at the same time cut a fish. Aidan's lack of patience didn't help—he had great difficulty keeping his temper. Nevertheless, as time went on the easier mindmelding became because of their desperation to be distracted from the appalling stench. By the time they had cleaned the last fish, mindmelding had become almost second nature for Augusta. But being taught to hide her emotions enough to remain undetectable in Aidan's head was a dilemma that she thought she'd never overcome. But Aidan had assured her that the ability would come with time and practise; he had also found it a formidable task when Tragen had first begun his training many years before.

One pleasurable side effect of their dabbling was the fact that they discovered a mutual sense of fun – what others would call irresponsibility – throwing fish heads at each other was not everyone's idea of enjoyment, especially when a fish's entrails ended up down someone else's collar! But they did forget almost entirely that Anders and Beatrix were stood at the table with them.

'Aidan, can you do something about these, they're very bad?' Beatrix asked, examining Augusta's sore fingers.

Aidan ceased his moaning and kneeling before Augusta he cradled both her hands in his. He grinned up at her.

'Relax now and watch closely, you'll actually see the blisters dry up. In a couple of hours the dead skin will wear away.'

Holding back her tears she stared at the white blisters on top of white blisters, hardly able to stretch her fingers out straight. Watching silently – butterflies jumping in her stomach at the thought of more magic – she could see nothing unusual happening to begin with but as his chanting, at first very low, increased in momentum, the fluid within the blisters darkened. And within moments the pustules had dried forming hard calluses, her fingers lost their crumpled whiteness and returned to a normal colour and the pain disappeared.

'*Thank you,*' she mindmelded as she flexed her hands, wonder replacing the glistening in her eyes.

Aidan flinched at her thanks but said nothing and he turned to Beatrix. 'Your turn next young lady…let me have your hands.'

Beatrix raised them for him to hold. 'Yours are worse than mine, you should be healing your own first,' she said as his chanting began.

'It's all right Tragen has a salve me and Anders can use.'

'Why don't you heal Anders and yourself? Wouldn't it be easier and faster if you did?' Augusta asked as he finished with Beattie's hands.

Aidan looked at her in horror and, without speaking a word, strode out of the cabin to retrieve the balm from the store in his locker.

Augusta, mystified, turned to Anders. 'Now what have I said?'

'Don't you remember?' Anders replied. 'Aidan won't heal himself.'

'Oh hell, I'd forgotten.'

'Augusta your language! You're sounding more like Aidan every day.' Beatrix turned to Anders still holding his hands out before him being very careful not to hurt them more. 'Why didn't he heal you, then? Why have you to use the salve?' She ceased her rummaging around to stare at the boy she couldn't bear being apart from. She was tidying as usual, unable to rest in the middle of a mess.

'Ah well, Aidan and I have an agreement of a sort. If he doesn't heal himself he's not to heal me—unless it's life threatening, of course.' Anders looked at them and grimaced. 'Don't say that's a stupid vow or ask me to change my mind, Aidan and I have been friends for a lot of years, now. I've seen him sustain cuts and bruises loads of times; he even broke his leg once in a fall off a horse. That time his leg was bound up for a couple of months before it healed on its own, Tragen was frantic worrying about him. He's only now recovering from a broken arm. I decided long ago that I wouldn't allow him to heal me unless he heals himself.'

'Then he'll never heal me again,' said Augusta determinedly, wondering at the same time if she'd stick to it.

'Or me,' added Beatrix, keeping her fingers crossed in case she ever had to keep her promise.

'You may not have the choice, ladies,' said Aidan, overhearing the last as he returned with a pot of unguent. And as the girls started to protest he broke in on them. 'I'm not listening—leave it alone!'

He walked over to Anders and they both rubbed the sweet-smelling, yellow salve into their hands from the open pot between them. An abnormal silence settled in the cabin the girls, not for the first time, contemplating Aidan's very strange attitude where healing was concerned.

Tragen appeared at the door on his way to Lady Cornelia. He spent a lot of time keeping her company these days as she could not leave the cabin waiting for her "old" sickness to finish its course of healing and, of course, to remain hidden from the crew. Both were happy with each other's friendship and relieved that her masquerade as Lady Augusta appeared so successful. No-one, as yet, had questioned the fact that their princess was still suffering seasickness.

He looked in at them puzzled over the lack of noise. 'Hello, what have we here? Taking a well-earned breather from your chores I see.'

Receiving dirty looks he thought better than to wait for any retort. 'Aidan, we have a job to do tomorrow,' and four pairs of ears perked up. 'Yes…we are going to replenish the drinking water; barrels are being checked as we speak. The captain has been worrying because the remainder of what we have will last only a few days more and that's with rationing. So be ready in the morning and be well rested the incantation may have to last quite a while.' With one last look he escaped swiftly before any questions were voiced.

Augusta and Beatrix gazed excitedly at Aidan, the atmosphere changing instantly.

'Go on, tell us what you and he are going to do…how do you extract water, and from what?' Augusta asked.

'Oh, it's dead easy that spell,' Aidan replied, looking around smugly. 'Tragen will either use his staff to create the spell and I'll keep it going using my hands, or I'll create it and he'll keep it going,' he paused, staring down at his fingers stretched out before him, evidence of their activities in the afternoon showing beneath his fingernails. He'd have to scrub them, he thought, before helping his master or the fish debris would contaminate the clean water.

Augusta punched him on his shoulder. 'Come on, tell us the rest. Where does the water come from and what exactly have you to do. And why haven't you got your staff yet?'

'Ouch, that hurt,' he said, rubbing his shoulder, 'slow down and give me a chance.'

He waited until he could see suspense killing them before resuming. 'Okay, Tragen will stand somewhere on deck and hold his staff out in front of him. He'll chant the spell and water droplets will appear in the air. The droplets will form a cascade and he'll pour it into the water barrels. Dead simple,' he said, 'once the water is falling into the barrels I'll take over as the power of the staff won't be needed any longer. I'll make sure the flow doesn't stop until all the barrels are full. Just like magic,' he said smiling, rubbing his dirty fingernails against his shirt.

'Aye, but don't forget,' added Anders, 'the longer you have to keep the spell going, the more tired you're going to get. So I suggest we all get to sleep before long.'

'Wait a moment,' interrupted Beatrix, who was now sitting on the floor her attention as fervent as that of Augusta. 'You haven't told us why you haven't got a staff. I've noticed Tragen's—it's very beautiful. Why won't he give you a staff or at least allow you to use his?'

'It's a long story, I'll tell you in the morning.'

'No way, you tell us now, or we won't be able to sleep,' ordered Augusta. 'You are not going anywhere yet.'

Aidan looked at his three friends and thought of Tragen's bewilderingly magical staff, recalling the dream he had nurtured now for almost ten years. For all of that time he had watched his master use the fabled wizard's staff and had felt a hunger as acute as starvation to have his own.

'Okay, listen up,' he smiled and settled himself comfortably on the floor alongside Beatrix. Augusta curled up on her bed not taking her eyes off him. Anders, having heard the story many times before, sat the other side of Beatrix.

And as the story progressed Aidan brought to life his love of magic for them all to see. Augusta's eyes gleamed.

He began with the teachings of Tragen's old master, Herman, a wizard so old at the time of his demise that no one could remember who had been on the throne when he'd been birthed. Tragen had been devastated for months, and still talked of Herman as if he was still alive. Aidan, smiling at his master's stories of his mentor, wanted to tell him that Herman's spirit was still alive and well—on the other side of death. But he knew his master wasn't yet ready to understand that.

The sorcerer Herman had shown great patience when teaching Tragen the intricacies of constructing his own staff. Indeed, Tragen was showing the same patience over these intervening years in instructing Aidan.

The methods needed to create a staff required an extraordinary physical energy, and a prodigious mental strength. Both could only be acquired over years of an exhausting apprenticeship, a traineeship that sometimes lasted a lifetime. Each apprentice was taught that he and only he knew when to make his staff. The staff signified the end of the traineeship, the time when he must leave his master—although making the staff was not the end of learning. No wizard was the same and no wizard's staff was the same.

The staff that became a wizard's life companion was unique and colossally powerful. For not only was the staff a corporeal object it was also sentient; it held a part of its maker's soul.

Memories of its forming flitted through it constantly—memories of its mother trees, and of the soil in which the trees grew. Recollections of the forests and woods and groves; and of the sunlight they stretched towards and the moonlight under which they rested. The staff remembered the life that dwelled in the mother trees, the sap that gave it life, the insects crawling beneath the bark, the birds nesting in the branches and seeds grown to fly away in the wind to grow other trees. The staff recalled the winds and the rains, the droughts and the famines.

It also retained memories of its maker.

Aidan without warning stopped and looked up at his friends. 'Am I boring you?'

'No, get on with it,' they chanted in unison.

Each wizard chanted a mantra as he searched for the mother tree's location and when discovered each tree answered. The wizard sang his request of the tree; he sang as he made the incision taking no more and no less of the timber than was required, removing the sliver in one cut. He chanted his gratitude as he wrapped the piece to preserve it until the other woods were found.

Many different woods were required, the number dictated by the woods themselves. In Tragen's staff had been melded woods from three trees found many leagues apart. Tragen had travelled to far Birkton to find the Tree of Horns growing high in the snow-capped Scissor Mountains. Chanting the spell whilst removing the paring had taken days, infinite care had been employed. Then there were the searches for the other two woods, Bellwood from Arken, and Spotsbush, which he had found eventually, after months of searching, not far from where he lived in Mantovar. It had been the red stained, yellow Spotsbush which had let Tragen know it was the last required.

The actual melding of the three woods into one indestructible stave had been a long process, intricate and totally astounding. Forming the knuckle at the top with just the heat of his hands had exhausted him more than anything else had as once the process of configuring its shape had started it could not be halted. He had persevered, undergoing a loving task with no time for food, only water sipped as he sang. Then he had the task of moulding the taper at the base of the staff—a taper that ended in a point so hard and keen no mortal means could ever blunt it. Tragen was skin and bone at the end of the staff's creation—skin and bone and ecstatic.

The runes he had etched with the power of his mind and his fingers. He had learned the purpose of each rune before his decision to embed them in his staff. Each rune had added its strength to the immense power of the staff. Aidan told them that Tragen had still not completed his collection of the magic symbols. But now they took longer to carve, earlier symbols had to be driven deeper into the staff to make room for subsequent runes to be carved, sometimes one on top of another.

Aidan told of the staff memorizing the sound of its maker's voice…the different cadences and rhythms as Tragen chanted. It learned the smell of its maker's body, the taste of his sweat and the feel of its maker's skin as he caressed the woods. It felt the love pouring into it and accompanying that love all the memories of its maker. The staff had become a spiritual being as it absorbed its maker's entity. And it shared the wizard's life not as a tool but as a partner.

It was an immensely powerful object and only Tragen could use it. No other wizard would even attempt to touch another's staff as the unique force contained within, could send another into oblivion. Occasionally a wizard would allow a loved one, and only a loved one, to hold the staff as it would recognize its maker's love bestowed on another. This was why Tragen had allowed Aidan to hold his staff during his spell-casting of the shield. Tragen and Aidan loved each other as father and son, and Tragen's staff, recognizing this, had allowed Aidan to add his strength to that of his master.

Aidan concluded. 'Now do you understand why I can't use Tragen's staff? He can give it to me to hold, or I can fetch it for him, but if I attempted to create a spell with it the power would kill me.' The others nodded spellbound with his tale.

'Wait a minute, Adept Hospitaller Andrew once let me carry his staff…he doesn't love me or me him. How was that then?' asked Augusta.

'Adepts are not full wizards, their staffs are not as powerful,' Aidan answered. 'But saying that, adepts must give permission or you'll end up with a very nasty burn.'

'When will you be ready for your staff?' Beatrix asked a few minutes later, staring wide-eyed at the nearly wizard, her friend.

'I have no idea. It may be years yet, after all I don't reach the age of manhood until next year…I think,' he added as an afterthought.

'Do you know how many woods you'll need, because when you go searching I want to accompany you?' said Anders. 'I want to watch you make your staff if I can.'

'Aye, course you can, but you'd find it boring, though…I wouldn't have time to talk to you when I'm actually making it. As for the number of woods, I won't know until I've found the first, because the first will send me to another, and so on.'

'Could you stop at one wood?' Beatrix asked utterly enthralled.

'There's a legend that says a staff made from the wood of a certain tree would be the most powerful in the world. No other staff would survive in a contest of wills. That wood is from the Tree of Paradise, which is a legend itself; no one has ever discovered the site of one.' They sat silently, completely mesmerized by the story.

'How come you don't know your age, Aidan,' asked Augusta out of the blue.

'That's another long story that will definitely keep for another day. I believe it's now time for us to leave, I'm knackered.'

As Aidan and Anders left, Beatrix shouted after them smiling as she did so. 'You are not supposed to swear in front of ladies. And do not say we are not ladies!' Laughing she closed the door as the boys departed along the passageway to Anders' berth.

'I cannot wait for the morning, Beattie. I wonder if he'll allow me to help,' she hunched her shoulders, a calculating look in her eyes. 'Well, he is supposed to teach me magic, isn't he? I wonder if I'll ever get to make a staff.

Beatrix said nothing, feeling very nervous all of a sudden.

Leash had just finished his duty at the helm and was lying in his 'pit' as sailors called their cot. As he was the last man to be recruited to the Grim, in the sailors' quarters below the foc's'le he should have had to sleep in a hammock. But using a hammock was onerous when you were tired, it entailed having to sling it before going to sleep and having to bundle it up, unsling it and stow it away on rising. But being a bully helped him in achieving comfort. He had throttled nearly to death the small occupant previously allocated the cot and that man now kept well away from the surly helmsman, slinging a hammock the other side of the crew's quarters. Not one of the two or three present at the time had the courage to report his violence.

Leash was still seething over his plans coming to naught. His hatred of the wizard was growing if that was possible. Every time he failed to hurt the boy, Leash loathed him the more. He often saw the wizard's boy walking about the ship but the boy was never alone, at least one of the brats serving the prince's daughter always accompanied him. If he could manage to catch the apprentice on his own then it would be no problem to throw him overboard after making sure he could not call for help. Lying back in his bed and staring at the deckhead above him he thought about the several ways in which he could kill the boy—and anticipated immense pleasure in the actual act

152

of slaying him. But because the boy had had the luck to survive his previous murderous attempts Leash began to hate the young wizard as much as he hated the old.

There was one distinct advantage in going after the boy, though, besides the boy's size and age. Aidan had no staff. Leash was mortally afraid of Tragen's staff. It had ruined his life, taken all his hope, his means of remaining safe – all that was precious – and that he could never forgive.

Leash lay on his bed tossing and turning. There had to be a way of getting the boy alone. He closed his eyes and turned over to sleep, settling to dream the same dream that he had every night—the one that made him feel safe—but she was not happy with him.

Anders had given in to his friend's nagging and again given up his cot on the grounds that Aidan would probably have nightmares again through lack of sleep. The cabin boy had claimed blackmail but didn't want him returning to his own berth, he'd not be able to keep an eye on him there.

Aidan, of course, didn't want to return for his own reasons. Firstly, he had the knack of always being able to persuade Anders to fetch and carry for him. Anders, not realizing this, had stated many times that Aidan could charm the hind legs off a donkey but he would never fall for his tricks. Secondly, Aidan would have had to sleep on a bed with a hole in the middle of it, and last but not least—Tragen rattled the walls with his snoring.

Lying on his back Anders asked. 'You did mean it didn't you? You will take me when you search for your staff, won't you?'

Aidan peered down at his friend. 'Aye, I meant it. But what if we're not friends when it's time for me to leave?'

'Don't be silly,' scoffed Anders, 'we'll always be friends.' And he turned on his side—Aidan did irritate him on times.

A little while later Anders unable to sleep looked up at Aidan. 'Hey, are you awake?'

'No.'

'If I ask you something I don't want you saying anything to her … OK?'

Aidan turned over and stared down at his friend. 'All right, you can bring her as well.'

'You know then?'

'What, that you're nuts on Beattie? I think everyone knows.'

'Oh, God, you don't think she's aware of it, do you?' Anders asked, fear knotting his belly.

'I expect so. Now go to sleep!'

God, Anders thought if she does, how am I going to face her in the morning?

But little did either of them know that Anders would be the first to discover the Tree of Paradise and when he did, Aidan and he would both be in a very strange association.

Thirteen

On the quarterdeck, Locklear paced slowly. It was a beautiful evening, the skies clear, an abundance of stars beginning to show, the moon waxing. A gentle breeze was blowing just enough for the Grim to make headway. Cruising weather Locklear thought as he looked over his ship, a ship silent except for the occasional creak of a board or a wave lapping the hull. The storm was now far behind them and he mused on its aftermath, studying the splintered ends of the broken masts reflecting the moonlight he hoped for luck in finding replacements. Only certain types of trees would suffice and the mainmast alone was made from five trees of differing lengths, the mizzen used four. But Locklear took heart from what Hopper had said earlier, there were plenty of trees on Sanctity, he prayed there'd be no trouble acquiring them. With the weather now settled, on the morrow after Tragen had filled the water barrels, he would have Trumper rig a jury mast to increase speed.

Below, in Cornelia's cabin, Tragen was again keeping the lady company, drinking tea that he had conjured from empty air. It still tasted fresher than tea from the galley, he thought, and Cornelia seemed to be enjoying it. The porthole was open and the light evening breeze stirred the air.

'You truly believe that Augusta has been given the gifts of wizardry?' Cornelia asked, worriedly.

'I do.'

'Well, I honestly don't know what her mother and father will think of that. How could it possibly have happened?'

Tragen shrugged and settled himself more comfortably in a chair that he had also conjured from thin air as there had only been one in the cabin.

'It is a complete mystery to me. It has never been known before for a wizard's abilities to suddenly appear like this—I'm completely baffled. I just hope that Aidan doesn't go overboard in his teaching of the art. They both appear to have the same sense of, how shall I put it…delicacy in handling sensitive matters?'

'I agree, Tragen, they are both rapscallions,' she chuckled. 'So we make for the Griffin Islands,' said Cornelia, holding a flower-patterned mug of tea in her hands.

'We have no choice I'm afraid. You know of the Onyx Isles, we could never come near there with you and Augusta aboard. The ship would founder if we attempted to return through the storm. I have already made it clear to Hugo that I will foil any attempt to head straight north to reach the frozen wastes and follow the coast around to Mantovar. Without masts we would find it increasingly difficult to make the voyage to Drakka and it would be pointless, anyway, as we would in all probability encounter the storm again on leaving.' He shrugged his shoulders and sighed. 'I only hope we recognize the enemy when we meet him in Griffin.'

'You believe Beatrix to be correct in her assumption then?'

'Yes, unfortunately,' he paused and sipped his tea. 'I am very glad that young lady accompanies us for I admit I knew that the storm had been created to stop us entering Mantovar but it had not occurred to me that the storm's purpose was also to entice us to his lair.'

'She is a very able young woman, that one. Mind you, the princess speaks very highly of her mother. In fact Dotrice is suspected of being the princess's chief advisor…in an unofficial capacity of course.'

'Along with you!'

Cornelia blushed and changed the subject. 'Have you estimated how long it will be before we reach home?'

'No, at this time I have absolutely no idea, and that worries me. I have to find some way of informing the prince of what has transpired and that for now his daughter is safe and well.' Tragen stretched his back, taking care that he did not spill his tea. 'I could attempt to use a gull, of course, when one appears. However, they are not very dependable as they do not like flying more than ten or fifteen leagues from their nests, and we are hundreds of leagues from home. I think I will have to seek my young apprentice's advice.'

'You heed a lot of his advice?' Cornelia enquired smiling fondly; the more she knew of the boy the more she was falling under his spell.

'Yes,' and he laughed, 'at least some of his advice. In many respects, he is a normal, mischievous, lovable rascal with a heart greater than any I have ever known! However, he has an odd knowledge of the spirit world far more than I will ever know. Perhaps that is why he is of the opinion that it is his bounden duty to heal anyone suffering and I do mean anyone. I believe he would heal the hurts of his enemies without them asking.'

He rose from his chair. 'Well we have plenty to think on tonight, Cornelia, and I shall leave you now. Sleep well, Milady,' he said as he left.

'Goodnight to you, my friend,' Cornelia uttered quietly as Tragen closed the door behind him.

In Anders' cabin, the two boys lay sleeping, silent except for the slight nasal noises Anders was making as he slept on his back. It was another night without a vision.

The next morning was glorious. A scorcher of a day in the offing as the sun crept up the sky. There was very little cloud cover, just feathers of high cirrus floating in the azure sky, the smell of ozone permeating the light breeze invigorating the senses. The Grim was carrying all possible sail on its three remaining masts and the ship glided slowly but purposefully south-westwards on the long swell of the Great Deep.

Collecting breakfast from the galley, Dolly informed Aidan and Anders in no uncertain terms that he was depending on them to ensure the galley barrels were full of 'proper' drinking water. What the cook meant by "proper" was anyone's guess, but it would make a change to cook with water devoid of stench. He also gave Anders a long throwing knife called an anelace, and told him to practise with it. In answer to Beattie's quizzical look, Anders told her he had a natural talent for the weapon, so Dolly said.

There was an air of suppressed excitement onboard. Magic was well known throughout the empire but no one ever saw it often. This morning the Grim was preparing to witness another conjuration, the third in less than a week. This spell was not to be as spectacular as the shield enchantment, and not many people had seen the repairing of the stormsail but judging by the number of people already on deck, a lot more would watch this spectacle.

Leash again took his post at the helm, relieving Talbot at the end of his morning watch. The second helmsman still scheming, his eyes red-rimmed, was determined that before the week was out the boy would be dead one way or another. He was holding together with great difficulty, wilder and riskier scenarios running through his head he could not take his eyes from Aidan. Caution was needed now, if he lost control of himself then his secret would be divulged and he would be a dead man in Purgatory, the wizard would see to that. But there was something about the boy, something was niggling in the back of his mind. The more he stared at the apprentice the more Aidan reminded him of someone, but of whom he couldn't recall.

'Nellie' and Beatrix had carried out their duties for 'Princess Augusta' and left her consuming her inevitable pot of tea, musing at the way Augusta was settling in to her role as a companion and maid. Augusta was enjoying every minute of her new distractions despite the fact that she was worrying about the chore promised for later that day. Beatrix had earmarked it as their laundry day. She wanted to wash their clothes – their very dirty clothes – in suds, in a tub on deck. Aidan had promised to supervise her endeavours and only laugh occasionally. Augusta cursed. Meanwhile Anders was attempting to cajole Beatrix into doing his mountain of washing and was not succeeding at all well, but he was full of hope.

The girls, impatient for Tragen to arrive, were rebuffed by Aidan refusing to wake the wizard.

'No way, Tragen is evil in the mornings. We'll let him come around all by himself, thank you,' he said, 'and stop throwing that knife around, you're making me nervous.'

'Don't be daft, little wizard. Dolly told me to practise the techniques he showed me…that man is really something with a knife,' said Anders admiringly. Squinting through his blue eyes, he took another aim at the barrel at the foot of the mainmast, and carried on throwing the narrow bladed anelace.

'Take care, Anders, you said last night that you won't allow Aidan to heal you so please do not take out your eye, or mine,' said Augusta, flinching.

'Well, I think he's pretty good with it,' said Beatrix, though she did tend to lean away from him.

Just then, Trumper arrived. 'Mind it you lot, you're standing right in the place we're stacking the casks.' With that, half a dozen men trundled up rolling the water barrels, wooden, metal-hooped vessels of various sizes, colours and odours. One of the middling sized ones Beatrix recognized as always standing in the passageway outside her cabin door. She used it often and had noticed earlier that day that the residue in the bottom was beginning to pong.

They leant against the rail staring out to sea comfortable with their friendship. They were able to remain silent in each other's company without feeling anxiety having no need to make small talk. The morning drifted by as they do at sea in the tropics, quietly and slowly, tension seeping away as they watched the gently swelling ocean. The day gradually got warmer, the breeze soothing their nerves and lulling their senses, the storm already receding into their subconscious.

'We're having a party tonight, Dolly's providing his special pies and Jason and some others are going to sing,' Anders said, interrupting their thoughts, but not the sound of the occasional thud of the dagger as it sank into the timber of the broken mainmast.

'Oh, I've never attended an entertainment onboard a ship before,' said Augusta.

'Neither have I,' added Beatrix. 'What are Dolly's "special" pies?'

'Ah well, no-one seems to know and no-one has the courage to ask him, but he's been seen messing about with rotten apples and old pork,' answered Anders.

'Ugh!' both girls said in unison.

'Jason…isn't he that tall, blond, good-looking fellow?' asked Augusta.

'Oh, I don't know about good-looking,' replied Aidan feeling slightly peeved. 'He's a fair singer though and Anders and me, we're going to dance.'

Augusta laughed. 'Dance! I can't imagine you two dancing a minuet around the deck.'

Anders nearly choked. 'A minuet! We don't dance all stiff with our noses in the air like you do, we do proper dancing…like the hornpipe.'

Augusta, slightly abashed at her gaffe, recovered quickly and glancing mischievously at Beatrix said. 'I've heard of that…isn't that the one where you do a lot of jumping on the spot waving your arms in the air?'

Anders was speechless, he was proud of his dancing. 'Jumping…jumping, I'll have you know…' Just then, there was a flurry of activity from the quarterdeck and the captain came into the waist accompanied at last by Tragen.

'Well, ladies and gentlemen,' Tragen said, as if announcing an entertainment in front of gentry. 'Welcome to one and all.' He bowed with an elaborate flourish, the voluminous sleeves of his green robe flapping like a chicken held up by its legs, he grinned at all who caught his eye. Tragen may be an old aristocrat but he loved acting the troubadour, thought Aidan, joining his teacher at the stump of the mainmast.

'Ah, Aidan, you are ready?' Tragen asked, waving his arms and continuing to play to his audience.

'Oh, yes, Master. I await your bidding,' and Aidan, aping his mentor and bowing with an equally graceful flourish, beamed at all those around and about.

The crew were in high good humour, happily talking loudly, clapping hands, whistling and cheering in appreciation. And the mood lasted until each and every barrel was full of good, fresh drinking water. For a long time the crew had been battling the fiercest tempest they were ever likely to meet and they were worn out, recovering from a nightmare. Despair had been commonplace amongst them for the long days and nights of the storm and now they had to look forward to even longer days and nights of hard, gruelling work sailing a five-masted ship with only three poles.

They needed light entertainment now to raise their morale. Tragen knew this, as did Locklear, and the wizard was fully prepared to perform outlandishly in order to fulfil their needs.

Aidan, of course, knew his master was in one of his playful moods and he was prepared to follow Tragen's lead—up to a point! He recalled the last occasion his master had been this jolly—he had ended up the butt of Tragen's jokes. This time he was going to get his own back, in front of everyone, and he grinned.

'Form a circle my friends,' Tragen commanded. And after much shuffling and juggling for position a circle he got, though a somewhat erratic one. Tragen, his dark green robe signifying he was a master wizard, stood in the centre his hand on Aidan's shoulder. Silently he looked around at his audience and awaited their full attention.

'Look at Aidan, Augusta! Look at him, that boy is shaming us; look at the state of his clothes! We must wash them later, we just have to,' Beatrix whispered as Augusta paled, Anders smiled he'd got out of doing his laundry.

Augusta shut her eyes, pain on her face. 'They're boys, Beattie, boys...they're always dirty they're supposed to be. Sh! Let's watch.'

Tragen continued. 'A cask if you please! Thank you my good man,' and he stepped aside as Jason rolled the first barrel into place and upended it in front of the two performers.

'Wonderful, wonderful,' said the wizard, prodding Jason in the nether regions with his staff as the unfortunate sailor turned his back. The crew roared.

Jason rubbed his backside ruefully and jostled his mates as he settled again to watch the goings-on.

Tragen entered into his full patter. 'Now, here you see an empty cask,' and he pointed with his staff. 'But, gentlemen, you know and I know that an empty cask is no good to any man—unless, of course, you're drowning,' and he winked. 'So…we had better fill it. Aidan, kindly give us a tinkle, please,' he ordered.

'I beg your pardon,' Aidan couldn't help it, he blushed, he was going to have to bear the brunt again he knew it. The crew fell about.

'I could do with a tinkle myself,' a voice shouted out from the back.

Tragen looked towards the voice and intoned. 'Beware all ye who require tinkles, for once this miracle of enchantment begins, a fair torrent may flow…and not just into this barrel.'

'By the Gods, out of my way I need the heads,' Nkosi panicking shoved through his laughing mates and ran from the circle.

Augusta looking puzzled turned to Anders. 'What is the matter with that man, and whose head does he need?'

Beatrix leant across, and grinning, whispered into her ear. 'The heads is a sailor's term for latrine.'

'Oh,' she paused, still looking puzzled. 'Then why did the men laugh when Tragen asked Aidan for a tinkle?'

Beatrix stared at her, saying nothing. Anders nearly bit his tongue trying to stifle his laughter.

Augusta was nonplussed until comprehension swiftly dawned on her. Shocked, she put her hands to her scarlet face and turned back to watch the two clowns at the stump of the mast.

'Come on, my lad. Have you forgotten how to tinkle?' Tragen asked.

Aidan looked at him and if looks could kill Tragen was dead a thousand times. Just wait master, just wait! The apprentice raised his right arm and moved his fingers and wrist in a disjointed pattern. As he did the air in front of him thickened and darkened. Everyone ceased laughing and gazed at the boy, watching his every move. Aidan continued his gyrations and moved his hand over the empty cask. The air grew even thicker and Aidan commenced his singing.

Augusta watching him recognized the excitement and the love of magic shining in his eyes and heard it in his voice; he had a lovely voice, she could listen to it for hours. The magic gripped her. Ever since she had held the light she had felt such a yearning, it was agonizing to watch magic and yet not have the knowledge to use it safely. She needed to be part of this and was determined that things would be different at the next show, whether Tragen liked it or not, next time she was going to take part.

Aidan continued to sing and the audience, not quite knowing what to expect, eagerly watched his every move.

Anders, who had seen this spell often, was still intrigued at the interplay between his friend and his friend's master. Grinning, he saw it was not going to go quite the way Aidan expected and, what's more, it would not go quite the way Tragen imagined either and he gleefully awaited the outcome.

Augusta sat spellbound; she had never experienced anything like this. The visiting magicians to the Court of Mantovar never performed their arts in a jocular manner, they were far too serious. She gripped Beattie's hand, not taking her eyes from the spectacle, loving every minute of her friend's antics—she was so very proud of him.

Tragen, his long white beard trailing below his waist, stood tall alongside his shorter protégé and watched as Aidan's enchantment released a spot of water no bigger than a raindrop, from the air in front of him. The first drop of water was followed by a second and then a third, the flow akin to rainwater dripping from the eaves of a roof at the end of a short shower.

Tragen looked around at his enthralled audience, spreading his arms wide he turned to his apprentice. 'Is that the greatest tinkle you can manage, Aidan? Strain boy…strain!' Laughter erupted again.

Aidan looked up at him, and grimacing he sang louder relishing his revenge. The flow of water now increased to a steady, if slow, trickle.

'Well, gentlemen, there you see a boy's tinkle,' the wizard smiled. 'Now I will show you a man's,' and lifting his staff he pointed the knuckle at the stream of water gently falling from thin air. Tragen broke into a song that was very similar to Aidan's, but far stronger and deeper. And it had the desired effect. The gentle stream transformed into a veritable inundation as a ray of light shot from the staff and hit the flow. The waterspout poured into the cask, filling it to overflowing within minutes. The crew watched silently, completely bewitched. All of a sudden laughter erupted at the slight problem unforeseen by both the old wizard and the young.

When the water first cascaded into the barrel, Aidan had been rather slow in moving out of the way. The first outpouring drenched him to the skin.

'Oh, bloody hell, Master, be careful will you,' shouted the soaking wet apprentice.

'Tch, tch, Aidan, you should not swear in front of ladies,' shouted Augusta before she could stop herself.

Aidan made up his mind it was now or never, his turn for some fun now. 'Master, we need more casks quickly. Shall I stop the water while we change barrels or shall I divert the flow instead?'

Tragen, loving the situation he had created, shouted over the roar of the spouting water, not thinking for a moment of the consequences. 'Divert of course, Aidan, divert it, there's no need to stop it there are plenty of barrels yet.'

Anders watched an evil gleam appear on Aidan's face, looking at the girls nervously, he warned. 'Watch out you two, he's up to something,'

Augusta and Beatrix, surprised, glanced at Anders quickly and then studied Aidan as the apprentice took over the chanting. The tempo of the song changed to a slower, lighter sound.

Tragen walked in a circle around his apprentice, bowing to his audience and every now and then dancing a little jig his back to Aidan, completely oblivious to what was happening behind him.

The stream of water, ceasing to pour into the full cask, curled upwards as Aidan sang. The spout of water formed a u-shape in mid-air. Utterly bemused some noticed a strange, manic gleam on Aidan's face and they wondered. Fidgeting nervously, the noise diminishing, they glanced at each other instinctively knowing that something untoward was happening.

Tragen, not detecting any difference in their manner, carried on acknowledging their reducing applause.

The end of the waterspout quickly reached a level with the outpouring from the air and then recommenced following the laws of gravity. The heavy gush of water again fell.

Tragen turned at that moment finally becoming aware of the strange behaviour of his audience, frowning he stared at Aidan,

And the water fell—smack bang on the top of Tragen's head.

There was appalled silence, men watching astounded as the water, pouring on the wizard like a river, soaked him to the skin.

Beatrix, mortified, grabbed Anders' hand. Aidan had really done it this time, there was no way he was going to talk himself out of this.

Augusta stared at Aidan pouring the water over his master. His face was a picture as he stood with his arm outstretched grinning delightedly at the dumbfounded wizard. The young apprentice was wreaking his sweet revenge with manic delight. For a moment Augusta did nothing as she looked from a soaking wet apprentice to a soaking wet wizard. Then, unable to maintain self-control over the complete absurdity of what she was witnessing, she laughed and it bubbled from her. Standing up, she lost her balance and slipped on the water sweeping across the deck. She fell to the floor and slid along the boards coming up against Tragen's legs, knocking him to the deck alongside her.

Locklear chuckled loudly and deeply until Aidan, with the devil fully entrenched, pointed his curled fingers at the captain and saturated him with the deluge. And then there was absolute pandemonium as Aidan, spinning in a circle the spout of water following him, aimed the water into the audience and commenced drowning everyone in sight.

Fourteen

Later that same afternoon Trumper and his team commenced work on jury-rigging the mainmast. From a jumble of spars and ropes piled alongside it, a somewhat narrower and flimsier upright was lashed to the stump of the mainmast.

At the same time, Augusta found herself up to her armpits in suds, scrubbing in a large tub, the clothes of herself, Beatrix and Lady Cornelia—a very new experience for her. Grumbling continually she kept an eye on Beatrix kneeling alongside her who was also washing clothes...for those of the boys, the captain and Tragen. As Anders and Aidan had explained, the blisters on their hands inflicted by gutting the fish the day before, at Augusta's insistence they reminded her, had still not healed.

They stood to one side at the rail keeping the girls company, occasionally giving uncalled for advice when Augusta got in a knot. At one point Augusta and Beatrix, losing their temper, had ordered the boys to clear off but Aidan had explained that Tragen would do his nut if they disappeared and left the girls alone—they had to perform their duty of care. Anders was again practising knife-juggling techniques while Aidan was whittling away at a length of wood, the girls not realizing that the boys were gripping their knives in hands that showed no signs of soreness.

But they were not the only ones catching up with their laundry. Lines were slung all over the ship and clothes were hanging to dry giving the impression that the ship was festooned in multi-coloured banners. Even sailors who disliked soap and water for personal cleansing had to follow Locklear's orders when he told them he'd had enough of their clothes stinking.

That is everyone except Leash, he, being on duty at the helm had missed the fun in the morning. Not that he cared; he didn't much like fun. Nevertheless, he was optimistic a chance was bound to come about at the forthcoming festivities. He stared at Aidan. Smiling slyly, he savoured the different methods he could use on the boy, bludgeoning, drowning—strangling would be nice, he would be able to feel the life leaving the boy's body. He liked that idea. But then he smiled wondering for a moment if, perhaps, he could employ his infection's method. Looking at Aidan, he yearned to use it but knew it would be too risky—decapitation would jog Tragen's memory. If that

165

happened, then Leash was a dead man walking, but then he grimaced, he was that already.

Tragen walked past the girls scrubbing diligently and noticed his green robe in Beattie's tub. He stopped by the two boys enjoying themselves at the rail.

'Why are they washing our clothes, my boy?'

Aidan and Anders raised their hands for the wizard's inspection, the lesions from the day before hardly visible.

'We have to keep these blisters dry to aid the healing, Master, so Beattie and Al…Nellie offered to do ours.'

'Offered…nagged into it, you mean!' Augusta said, very disgruntled.

'Oh come, you know they can't do it with their hands in that state. Besides, it gives you practise,' said Beatrix, wiping suds from her nose.

'Practise…practise! What do I need practise for? I'm not doing this when we get home, ever.'

'When we agreed that you were to masquerade as a maid, I never meant for you to carry out each and every task of a domestic if there's no need.'

'Milord, there is every need for clean clothes,' Beatrix said, scandalized.

Aidan, preparing for flight, grabbed Anders' arm making him drop the knife he was about to launch at the mast. 'The Bear is calling you.'

'Watch out! I could…' Anders started to say as Tragen halted them with his staff raised across their path.

'Aidan, I wish you to help the young ladies accomplish this task,' he ordered, 'or shall I ban you from this evening's frivolities?' Tragen wondered if this boy would ever carry out mischief successfully and he struggled to keep a straight face.

'He can't, Milord, his…' Beatrix stopped as Tragen put his finger to his mouth to silence her.

'Well, Aidan?' Tragen waited.

'You said I wasn't to do magic onboard,' he said, looking everywhere but at the girls.

'You know full well that I said "in enclosed spaces".'

Aidan caved in. 'All right…stand away from the tubs you two.' And they looked on bewildered, water dripping from their arms and dirty suds clinging to their shirts and britches, their faces bright red from the exertion of scrubbing clothes for the last hour. Aidan lifted both his hands over the tubs and intoning a chant, curled his fingers and moved his wrists in another complicated series of gestures.

The clothes in the tubs took on a life of their own and leapt from the water perfectly clean. And, as Aidan directed them with his hands, they draped themselves over the line alongside the wet clothes already drying in the sun. Aidan then turned his attention to the mound of dirty clothes dumped on the deck between the tubs and these dipped in the water on their way to the drying line…also as clean as a whistle.

'Thank you Aidan, I'll leave you to it now,' said Tragen, walking away grinning. 'Should we call a truce, Aidan?'

Aidan watched his mentor's shoulders shaking with suppressed mirth. He laughed and turned back to the girls, it was only then he realized his dilemma.

'Now ladies, he only did that to have his own back on me for soaking him.' The grin fell from his face as the girls grabbed him. 'Don't take it to heart, will you, I mean…'

For the second time that day, Aidan was drenched. The girls dumped him into the nearest tub of foul-smelling water.

They left their cabins and, climbing up to the waist at sunset, joined the throng of resting seamen already congregating and vying for a place near the musicians. Forming a circle, with the main hatch at the centre, the crew left an area around it for the dancing, usually exuberant when performed by relaxing, drunken sailors and marines at sea. Sitting in pride of place on the hatch cover and being feted as the principal entertainer of the evening, was Jason and his fiddle, alongside him was a small man almost hidden by a large drum. A third man, Bartholomew, a tall, gangly, red-faced sailor was striking up a tune on his reed pipe. And one particularly sozzled sailor, his long pigtail swinging behind him, was already giving an impromptu rendition of a very bawdy sea shanty whilst swigging from a large tankard.

Several rum and ale casks were in place, as was a makeshift table groaning with pies. Dolly standing guard alongside the results of his labour, had every reason to be proud of his skills, the smell making saliva flow in many a mouth.

The weather could not have been more conducive for reducing tension, the evening warm with a slight breeze carrying the scent of

167

the sea, a clear sky and a rising full moon a myriad stars twinkling in the heavens.

A league or so from the ship the first blue whales seen for over a week were making their presence felt. Their voices were a welcome sound and the spouts from their blow holes a magnificent sight, except to Dolly of course who studiously kept his back to them.

Aidan and Anders flanked both the girls, all four sitting with their backs against the starboard rail. Augusta and Beatrix breathed a sigh of relief; at one point they thought they were going to miss the party. Earlier that afternoon they had been subjected to a long and tedious lecture given by Lady Cornelia. She not wanting them to attend, knowing exactly what sailors were like when drunk. But having been told by Tragen that it would look extremely odd to the crew if the maids did not attend, and that he'd be there to keep an eye on them anyway, the lady-in-waiting gave in grudgingly.

'There, I told you he was the good-looking one didn't I?' Augusta said, nodding towards the minstrel tuning his fiddle.

'Oh, yes, he is too,' replied Beatrix not taking much notice, twitching in an effort to get comfortable on the hard deck, 'we should have brought cushions.'

'You two must be blind,' said Aidan. 'I've seen better looking whales. Look there's one over there,' and Aidan pointed over the rail directly behind Dolly.

'Oh don't, he'll only think you're laughing at him,' said Beatrix.

'Sh! you lot, the Bear's going to say something,' said Anders.

The captain, accompanied by Hopper and Tragen, stepped to the forefront of the quarterdeck and looked down at the crew milling about in the waist.

'Before the party begins men of the Grim, I want to inform you of our present situation and my decisions on our future.' Hugo Locklear was a giant of a man towering above them. 'But first I must offer my sincerest thanks to you all for your courage and extraordinary exertions over these past days. If it was not for your excellent seamanship, your stamina and your trust, the Grim would have been lost and us along with it. I am immensely proud of you all and I give you a toast,' the captain and his two companions held up a mug of spirits to the men and then supped deep.

Locklear continued, his beard wet from spilled brandy, he wiped it quickly with his hand. 'Unfortunately, we lost four of our shipmates in fighting the storm, and although I have been assured that they are safe in Paradise,' here he glanced at Aidan before going on, 'we will still miss them amongst us. So stand and bow your heads in remembrance and ask your Gods to care for them.'

Locklear resumed his speech a moment later. 'The tempest was the worst I have ever endured in all of my forty years at sea. There was a reason for it being so severe,' he paused and pulled at his beard. 'It was not a natural storm but one created by malign beings.' He paused again, his crew quizzical, unable to grasp the meaning of his words. 'Aye, you may look puzzled. I was until Lord Tragen explained that sorcery was behind the storm. We do not know its origin or its purpose, but we have come through its onslaught relatively safely. However, we have sustained critical damage which must be rectified sooner rather than later.'

Aidan and Anders glanced at each other both surprised that magic had been mentioned, though the suspected purpose behind the storm had not been. Aidan was of the opinion that if the attempt to capture Augusta was ever voiced in public then that would very likely bring on the outcome they dreaded. He continued to stare up at the captain, on pins awaiting his next words.

'It is only fair that I tell you of the sorcery as I wish to retain your trust in the times ahead.' Locklear pulled at his beard and took another sup from his mug. 'The storm has blown us about four weeks off course and we are at present approaching the Griffin Islands. Some of you may have heard of these isles, others have not. Suffice it to say that wherever we make landfall we must all be on our guard. The enemy may be behind us, or he may very well be on the island at which we provision. Whatever the future holds, one thing is certain we need to make repairs to our hull and step new masts. Without these tasks being completed we will not survive our journey home. And let me assure all of you,' Locklear raised his voice and slammed his fist on the rail before him. 'It is my intention to get home and take you all with me. I calculate that we are seven weeks from Mantovar and a couple of days from Griffin. The quicker repairs are made, the earlier we will reach home and our loved ones.

'Men of the Grim enjoy yourselves this evening you have earned it, and for those of you worried that we will run out of grog, calm yourselves. Lord Tragen has assured me that he can cast a spell that will produce everlasting supplies of rum. And he has also promised he will not let his apprentice anywhere near it.' Anders joined in the laughter and thumped Aidan's back.

'Captain,' a voice from near the bows shouted, 'I wouldn't mind being drowned in grog.'

'Aye, and from what I've heard,' Locklear replied recognizing the voice, 'drowning is what you need, Nobber.' Once again, there was uproar, except from Leash standing at the starboard rail glaring at the back of Aidan's head.

A few hours later in the midst of the merriment, Anders decided to show the two girls how to dance. Unfortunately, he and Aidan had been supping ale almost continuously since the party started and it showed. 'Come on, little wizard,' Anders slurred quite happily, rising from the deck where he had been sitting, as always, alongside Beatrix. He grabbed Aidan and pulled the smaller boy to his feet.

'Not now, Anders, you're drunk and I'm...hic...tired, I'll sit here watching you...hic...and point out the good details of your performance...hic...if there are any,' he smiled drunkenly, holding on to Augusta's shoulder to keep upright.

'I can dance better than you, boy, drunk or not, come on.'

Aidan and Anders tottered into the centre and calling to Bartholomew to set up a reel, both boys stood patiently in the centre of the deck, arms crossed at shoulder height staring at each other. The crew gradually quietened and prepared to watch the boys' performance; both had a reputation for dancing the hornpipe second to none and very often engaged in a contest of skills. Bets were already being laid to see who would stick the pace and remain standing at the end.

Augusta and Beatrix watched enthralled for despite being the worse for drink both boys danced expertly. And as Bartholomew increased the tempo on his reed pipe so the boys skipped and stamped their bare feet faster and louder.

Beatrix couldn't help but show her pride for Anders and urged him on, but looking around at the crew cheering and placing even bigger bets, she noticed Leash staring very strangely at Aidan from his place at the larboard rail.

Leash had been drinking non-stop since he'd finished his stint at the helm and he'd grown surlier as the evening wore on. Though nowhere near drunk – alcohol had no effect on him – his patience was coming to an end. All evening he'd been waiting for Aidan to walk off alone and it had not happened, the boy had even gone to the heads accompanied by the captain's brat. It seemed he'd have to reconcile himself to the fact that he was not going to get a chance at the boy this night.

Beatrix, a cold shiver running up her back, nudged Augusta, nearly slopping her ale down her front.

'Careful, Beattie, for God's sake I'm enjoying this,' she said unable to hide the slur in her voice.

'Look at that man over there by that rack of belaying pins, the helmsman, I don't like the way he's staring at Aidan,' Beatrix said, ignoring Augusta's warning.

Augusta followed her gaze and at that moment Aidan finally gave up the contest and fell to the deck, the ale had got the better of him, Anders' supporters cheering wildly as they collected their winnings. Leash, his manic black eyes even blacker, sneered and Augusta, suddenly afraid and not knowing why, wanted to hurt the helmsman to protect Aidan. She stared at the belaying pins alongside him and wished that she could hit him with one, like Dolly's mother had wished to do to her husband. Feeling guilty for wishing to commit violence for no discernible reason, she turned quickly away and went to help Aidan stand. The next thing she heard was an outraged shout from behind her, someone had really hit Leash with one of the pins. Nobber, just before he fell down drunk, had insisted that the pin had swung through the air on its own—like magic.

Augusta thought no more about it, she and Beatrix went on enjoying themselves up until Aidan vomited over their legs. Utterly disgusted, the girls ordered the boys to bed. And such was the level of inebriation, the boys did not dream of arguing.

Aidan dreamed of laughter again.

And Anders awoke when Aidan screamed. He leapt from bed and did the only thing he could think of—he clasped the distraught boy to his chest. Aidan struggled violently, his hysteria only calming when Anders would not relinquish his hold.

He opened his terrified eyes. 'Go get Tragen…quick!'

Anders ran through the captain's cabin, shouting an explanation to Locklear he left the Grim's master to keep watch over Aidan. He raced down the passageway bellowing for the wizard, waking Augusta and Beatrix as he did so. The girls were not long flinging on their clothes and racing to Aidan.

171

Tragen pushed past Locklear to Aidan's side and sat on the bed with him. There was a slick sheen of sweat covering the boy's face and neck and he stroked his boy's brow, reassuring him.

'Oh, my boy, my boy, what was it, hey? Are you feeling better now? Tell me what happened. I'm sorry; I have to ask now while it's still fresh in your mind.' Tragen beside himself with worry gripped Aidan in an embrace near to choking him.

Aidan was in a very sorry state. He had a hangover worse than any in his past; his skull felt as if it was home to an anvil being hammered by a very energetic blacksmith, and coupled with it he had recollections of a terrible dream, a nightmare he could not unravel.

'Nothing at all that makes much sense. Ah…my head is pounding,' he replied, pushing his head into Tragen's shoulder. 'Anders, get me some water, will you?'

Aidan pushed himself upright, taking the water he swallowed deeply. Refreshed, his head still felt as though drums were pounding between his ears.

'You're right, I have to tell you now before I forget,' he paused, and the others leant forward in the doorway to hear his low voice.

'Someone or something was hanging from…I don't know, I couldn't quite make out what it was,' Aidan shuddered. 'A man was standing before it with a spear in his hands, there were red chains, and…and the man appeared to be dressed in a red robe, and…and he was laughing. And then…' Aidan stopped and looked into the mug in his hands and tears rolled down his face unable to speak of the incident, the revolting sight he'd witnessed.

'Take your time, my boy; take as long as you need. I'm here…here with your friends. You're safe now,' and as Tragen said this he remembered that this was the second time he'd said these words in the last few days. What was happening to Aidan—why him? 'Come, drink some more, you'll feel better.'

'As the man dressed in red laughed, the thing hanging there…screamed, and it could not stop screaming.'

The apprentice passed the mug to the wizard and lay back down on his bed. 'It scared me, scared me silly. I didn't know what to do, what to think, I couldn't do anything. All I could do was stand there, watching. For a moment I almost appeared to be the man in red, and…' Aidan trembled violently for a moment. 'He was evil, Master, truly evil he didn't seem human...I felt sick!' He shuddered again. 'God! I...I can't remember any more.'

'Rest, my boy, rest, Anders will you stay with him for a while?'

'I will never leave him, Milord, he knows that.'

As Tragen rose from the bedside Aidan spoke again, his voice muffled in his pillow. 'Master, there was one other thing,' and Tragen turned to him. 'As the man was laughing, he said...he kept saying "wait for the wizard, wait for the wizard"!' Aidan lifted his head and stared at Tragen with despairing eyes. 'You are in grave danger, Master,' he turned over and faced the wall and Anders moved to his side determined to stay awake the rest of the night.

Tragen joined Hugo, Augusta and Beatrix – drying her eyes on the sleeves of her shirt – around the captain's desk.

'Drinks, we all need a drink,' said Locklear and he brought assorted mugs and a carafe of wine from his bedside table. He poured for all as he spoke. 'I know the time seems wrong for this. It's either very early in the morning or very late at night; however, I have never needed one so badly.'

'Milord, have you any explanation?' Augusta asked softly, staring into the untouched mug of heady, red wine.

All three stared at him awaiting his reply. Tragen gazed out of the stern gallery, seeing very little except the occasional lonely star, the moon now obscured by clouds, evidence there'd be rain before long.

The wizard sighed and turned from his musings at the window. 'The thing hanging and screaming could only be a man, I suppose...'

'Or a woman,' interrupted Beatrix.

'Yes, or a woman,' agreed Tragen. 'Whoever it was, he or she was being tortured, hence the spear and the chains.'

'Why were they red chains, though?' Augusta asked him, the use of torture not coming as too much of a surprise. She had heard that her father used it in his dungeons, but never having come into actual contact with it she had never really given it much thought. He was the lawmaker and protector of Mantovar; she was his daughter and had never been asked whether or not she condoned its use.

'The chains were covered in blood,' said Beatrix, almost in a whisper, shocked to her very marrow. 'Aidan actually witnessed a torturer at work.'

Augusta blanched. The full implication of what the practise entailed, sinking in. No, she thought, my father could never do that to anyone...could he? Augusta nearly retched.

Locklear broke the silence. 'The man with the chains, Tragen, was he wearing a red robe or was it red because of the blood?'

'I won't even pretend to know the answer to that, my friend,' he paused and resumed pulling at his beard. 'A red robe may denote the wearer is a wizard, but I know of monks that wear the same colour. But if it was red because of the blood then there must have been an inordinate amount to have coloured him completely. What did my boy overhear "wait for the wizard" was it not?' Locklear and Augusta nodded and he continued, Beatrix sitting silently staring into space. 'Now Aidan believes me to be in grave danger, have we got it wrong? Could it possibly be me this being is hunting? My boy is convinced it's me. This man does not even seem to know of Augusta.'

'He has not mentioned her which does not mean he is ignorant of her. On that point we must keep an open mind.' Locklear replied, he stood and took his own turn in the gallery. 'If it is you he's after how does he know of you? Or is he seeking any wizard, and if it is any wizard then why not Aidan as well?'

'He hasn't detected Aidan has he, Milord?' Beatrix asked anxiously.

'No, I don't think he has. But why hasn't he is the question...why not?' he pondered.

'Could it be because you are the more powerful wizard?' Locklear asked.

'I am more powerful than Aidan that is true, but only in magic based on the mind which is the usual form magic takes. Aidan's magic is unique—I know of no other practitioner of his art. His magic stems from healing and in that he is far, far more powerful than I am. No, there has to be another explanation he has remained undetected. And there must also be another reason that he is not receiving these visions every night. We must think on it.'

They all thought of nothing else as they lay in their beds attempting sleep for the remainder of the night left them. All were denied their rest, of course, except Aidan who, because he lay with his face to the bulkhead, soon fell asleep and aped his master, snoring loud enough to keep the fish awake.

When they finally admitted defeat and rose from bed not long after sunrise, Augusta and Beatrix went in to update Lady Cornelia. As the three, very sad and concerned ladies considered impossible options, Tragen joined them.

'Have you come to any sort of conclusion?' Cornelia enquired sadly.

'I am still mulling over consequences of certain actions, Cornelia. There is only one decision to be made at this time though, and it has priority over everything—we have to discover some way of informing Mantovar of all that has happened.'

'Will the prince be able to send us aid all the way out here?' Cornelia asked.

'I will certainly request that in the message I send him. Unfortunately, I have a further problem in pursuing that aim, I must seek Aidan's aid as exhausted as he is, but my boy can be somewhat unpredictable in what he delivers.'

'What on earth do you mean?' Augusta bristled, coming to Aidan's defence.

'Yes, how can you possibly say that? Are you saying you can't depend on him?' Beatrix retorted.

'Cease ladies. Let me explain, please,' and he smiled at each of the three in turn, taking immense pleasure in Aidan's friends.

'Aidan has a certain knack with animals and birds. He has a greater affinity with them than I do, it may be because he can heal them, I don't know. Whatever, my boy is more adept with dealing with fauna than I will ever be. The trouble is, when he calls for a specific animal another is quite likely to appear,' Tragen chuckled and went on to clarify.

'There was a very memorable occasion, two summers ago; we needed a sheepdog to bring in a flock of lambs from a hillside being plagued by a wolf. The shepherd had been injured by this particular animal but had managed to chase it away. Aidan and I were staying overnight at the local inn after a long journey on the border of the Great Forest, and it being a warm evening and the tavern room very hot and restful, we were imbibing a little alcoholic beverage…just to cool us down, you understand. Well, more than a little of it if I remember correctly,' Tragen paused, smiling sheepishly.

'Well, this shepherd rushed into the inn and asked for our help. We could not refuse, so Aidan and I helped each other rise from the table…we were very tired, you know,' the wizard said, winking. 'We stood at the bar of the tavern and, Aidan being better with animals than me, I allowed him the conjuration. Poor boy, poor me, I should have remembered.' Tragen couldn't stop grinning; the event had been so ludicrous and, as it turned out, highly dangerous.

'What...' said Cornelia, 'what happened?'

'Aidan created the necessary enchantment for the calling of an animal which entailed picturing the required creature in his mind. The one problem being, and what I should have realized is, that when you're drunk, a dog and a wolf have a similar appearance.'

'Oh, oh!' Augusta interrupted, laughing. 'I get it; a wolf appeared instead of a sheepdog, is that it?'

'You are perfectly correct, my dear. A wolf did appear...a very large wolf...a very large and very wild wolf. The same wolf in fact which had savaged the shepherd on the hillside. It appeared right in front of us, in amongst the tables in the middle of the tavern. There was utter pandemonium,' Tragen halted, a silly grin on his face.

'Go on...what happened next?' Beatrix asked, not quite believing her ears.

'The whole village turned up eventually, as we were extricating ourselves from a haywain parked outside the broken window of the main room of the inn. There seemed to be a lot of men sitting in trees as I recall, and there was not a window left whole in any wall of that tavern. We were unceremoniously marched out of the village, which was a bit silly as we'd offered to repair the damage free of charge as drunk as we were—we usually ask for a small fee for that kind of work. But for some reason they did not want to trust us again. We never did find out what happened to those lambs...or that wolf.'

'Lord Tragen,' Cornelia said, after she managed to stop laughing. 'You jest surely, that was not a true occurrence, was it?'

'Unfortunately, every word was the truth. Now do you see the problem? If I allow Aidan to call a creature, I do not have any idea what animal may turn up. As I have no patience with animals if I attempt the calling ninety-nine times out of a hundred the one I summon will also be impatient. It will undoubtedly be totally unsuitable, highly dangerous, and everything will turn into a disaster.' Tragen tugged hard at his beard.

'Then we must rely on Aidan, shall I see if he's awake, Milord?' Beatrix asked, her eyes red, this time with tears of laughter.

'Aye, young Beatrix, ask him if he is well enough to join us on the quarterdeck.

Fifteen

Aidan was sitting in a chair in Locklear's cabin his head in his hands nursing a pounding headache, when Beatrix and Augusta arrived. He had breakfasted a little on his usual burgoo and Dolly had sent up some of his sweet biscuits because he had heard of the boy's trauma. But Aidan couldn't hide the ravages of the night, he still looked haggard and worn out.

'What now, can't they leave him be for five minutes?' Anders asked angrily. 'He needs time to get over this.'

Augusta and Beatrix swiftly realized that Aidan was not the only one suffering from lack of sleep. Anders had hardly closed his eyes whilst keeping vigil.

'It's all right, Anders, I'm fine now. I could do with a breath of fresh air and so could you, come on,' and Aidan, rising slowly to his feet, pulled Anders along with him.

'What does he want, do you know?' Aidan asked.

'I'd rather he told you!' Beatrix replied smiling nervously.

Augusta said nothing and commenced chewing her lower lip to bits.

Tragen studied his apprentice's face for the first few moments of him arriving on the quarterdeck and, although worried by what he saw, smiled his welcome.

'You have recovered a little, I see,' Tragen said, unable to keep the lie and the concern from his voice.

'He has not rested enough, Milord,' Anders interrupted, still angry.

'Enough, Anders, please? I'm all right; I can't stay in bed all day.' Aidan playfully punched Anders' shoulder and turned to Tragen. 'What's up?'

Tragen nervously tugged at his beard. Aidan loved calling on the animals of this world, he found it exciting. And, of course, quite often it was—but not in the way that either of them expected.

'Um…Aidan…I need to send a message to the prince, with some immediacy now. We have to apprise him of our situation and ask for his aid.' Tragen swallowed and paused for a moment with fingers crossed beneath the folds of his robe. 'We need a bird. What do you think?'

'Ah,' Aidan, his headache instantly disappearing, gazed wide-eyed at his master. 'What sort of bird?'

'Obviously one that can fly a long way, it's no good calling a bird that's going to fall into the ocean halfway home!' said Tragen, visibly agitated.

'A seabird then,' and Aidan, looking around the horizon with his hands on his hips, ignored his master's sarcasm. 'This is going to take some calling, there's absolutely nothing in sight. Still…something is bound to turn up.'

'Aidan, please be careful. We do not need any unwanted creatures appearing.'

'Master, you're always the same…have faith in me,' Aidan admonished. 'Don't forget you taught me this, you'll only have yourself to blame if things go wrong.'

'I know, I know…may the Gods give me strength,' and the wizard stepped quickly to the rear to shelter beneath the overhanging poop deck. Locklear followed hurriedly seeing the strangled look on Tragen's face.

'Talbot secure the helm and get back here with me,' ordered Locklear, he didn't want his chief helmsman hurt. And as Talbot complied Anders, thinking the same as his master, grabbed Beatrix. They both followed until all except Augusta were in comparative safety behind the apprentice.

Augusta remained with Aidan at the front of the quarterdeck. She couldn't understand why everyone was showing so little trust and was determined to show her loyalty by not leaving his side.

Aidan hadn't taken a blind bit of notice of anyone moving away and he continued to stare around the empty ocean. 'We must have a bird that lives off the open sea, not one of the coastal birds. How about a gannet, Master…they're big and strong?'

'Whatever you say, Aidan,' Tragen said, now crossing his toes in his sandals.

Aidan smiled at Augusta as he raised his arms, his fingers spread wide. He closed his eyes and then emitted an ear splitting screech. Augusta jumped in surprise, and closing her eyes in pain, clapped her hands to her ears as did everyone else in earshot. Aidan continued to screech, his voice seeming to stretch over the horizon so powerful was the tone. And then when they all thought they could bear the noise no longer he ceased.

Aidan opened his eyes and stared forward searching the skies ahead and to either side. 'Damn, nothing yet. I'll give it a couple of minutes and then try again.'

But a couple of moments later he frowned. 'That's strange; it's gone a bit dark hasn't it?' They all opened their eyes to see what he was talking about and stared forward, a shadow seemed to be hanging over the quarterdeck.

Augusta, standing in front of Aidan, and facing him when he started his call, opened her eyes and glanced over his shoulder towards the stern. She immediately fumbled for Aidan's arm as her body spasmed, her eyes popped in her head and her mouth fell open. The others hiding beneath the poop stared at her, completely baffled by the look of utter panic on her face.

'Ow, Augusta, you're hurting me, stop squeezing,' Aidan said, and then he noticed her face. 'Hey, what's wrong, Augusta...why are you staring like that?'

'*Because she sees me, human.*'

'What the hell! Who's mindmelding?' Aidan said swinging around looking at everyone behind him still hiding beneath the poop deck.

'What do you mean? Nobody's mindmelding,' said Tragen. Seriously worried now, he knew that the expected contrariness of Aidan's spell-casting had occurred again. Something had gone awry with the calling.

'*I am not mindmelding, human...only you can hear me.*'

'What the...' Aidan looked around frantic. Where was the source of this voice, it was near he knew—he could feel it, like something breathing heavily on his neck, he shivered. He looked at the girl beside him. 'Augusta, do you know...' and he stopped.

Augusta was standing as rigid as a pole, not moving at all, mouth open, eyes still popping wide and staring—upwards.

'Augusta what's the matter, what can you see?' He turned and followed her gaze...and the breath on his neck was explained. He was utterly lost for words.

'*I repeat...she sees me, human.*'

Resting on the poop deck, directly above the heads of the people sheltering beneath, was the biggest bird he had ever seen in his life. Its body was a lot longer than two tall men and it was extremely fat. It had brilliantly white plumage and appeared to have very long wings folded tight to its body. With black patches at the end of its wings and tail, flesh coloured legs and feet, and small black eyes it stared unblinkingly straight at him over a long, hooked, pink beak.

'Oh boy…oh boy…oh boy,' Aidan said astounded, returning the bird's gaze.

'*Is that all you can say, human?*'

'What is it Aidan?' Anders asked, venturing forth gingerly to look up on to the poop. It took a few seconds for it to sink in what he was seeing. 'By the Gods, it can't be…it's something out of a story!'

'*Tell him I am no story,*' ordered the bird.

'He said to tell you he's no story, Anders,' said Aidan, his voice returning accompanied by a look of pure rapture.

Anders looked at his friend bewildered. 'What do you mean he said…can you speak with him?'

'Aye, I hear him,' and he beckoned everyone from the rear of the quarterdeck. 'Come and have a look,' he cried, ecstatic he bounced up and down on his toes.

Tragen, Locklear and Talbot looked up and found their faces on a level with the bird's massive webbed feet. Beatrix ran to Augusta just recovering her senses.

'What is it?' Augusta asked.

'It's a Great Albatross,' replied Anders, awestruck at the sight.

'*Tell him I am no Great Albatross, human…I am a Giant Albatross…a Wandering Albatross. There are not many of us left,*' the bird added.

'Anders, he says he is a giant wandering albatross…'

'*No human, I am not a giant wandering albatross…I am a Wandering Albatross of the Giant Albatross family! Oh, never mind! Just tell me why you called me,*' he was getting ratty.

'I'm sorry, albatross; I thought I was calling a gannet to carry a message home.' All on the quarterdeck were watching and, although listening to a one-sided conversation, somehow still managed to follow what was being said.

Tragen interrupted as Aidan finished speaking. 'Ask it if it will carry the message, Aidan.'

'*It…it! Who is that old human calling "it"? Tell him I am male, human, or he'll feel my beak,*' said the albatross.

Aidan laughed. 'Ooh, Master, don't call him an "it", he is a male bird, and a very angry male bird.'

Tragen looked from Aidan to the albatross. He was now completely mesmerized at the turn events had taken. 'All right, Aidan. Master Albatross I humbly apologize.' He bowed low to the bird whilst his companions looked on amazed.

The albatross grunted. *'Where is the destination of this message?'*

'We wish you to take it to Mantovar, to the prince, if you wouldn't mind,' said Aidan.

'And what do I get in return?' The albatross asked staring into the apprentice's eyes.

Aidan, puzzled, squinted against the sun. 'What do you get in return…what is it you want?'

'I want a voice,' the albatross stated without any hesitation. *'You have the power to give me the ability to speak, I see it in you.'*

Aidan was struck dumb again and his mouth fell open.

'What does he want, Aidan?' Tragen asked staring at him. 'Tell me.'

Aidan turned to his master, ecstasy alight in his eyes. 'Watch this all of you,' he said, peering around to include everyone. 'Captain, please lift me on to the poop I have to touch our new friend.' Locklear gasped. 'It's all right, he won't hurt me.' Locklear bent down and Aidan stepped into his hands to be hoisted and deposited at the feet of the giant albatross.

Standing so close Aidan could smell the sea in the albatross' newly preened feathers, almost taste the fish on the bird's breath and admire the razor-edged beak that was lowered to a level with the boy's mouth. The Giant Albatross of the Wandering Albatross family bent its head to get a closer look at Aidan. They stared intently into each other's eyes. Unlike most animals this bird did not treat a direct stare as offensive—at least, not from Aidan.

As the apprentice stepped closer to touch the bird, the albatross warned. *'Mind my feet they are not made to be stood on.'*

'Okay, Master Albatross, let's see what I can do,' and Aidan placed both his hands around the throat of the giant bird, his fingers stretching to encompass the short temples either side of the bird's head. Aidan smiled into the small black eyes of the albatross towering over him. Six sets of eyes stared up from below, Beatrix emitting a nervous whimper in the strained silence.

They seemed to stand still forever, the black eyes of the bird gazing into the brown eyes of the boy, its long neck in the boy's hands. Aidan returning the stare and grinning wide as he sang a very weird sounding chant. Augusta described it later as a sort of sea-weedy, plopping noise. A tremor worked its way through the bird from the tip of its beak to the end of its tail via the curled up webbed toes. And all

181

of a sudden a small lump sprouted in the neck between Aidan's hands—a prominent Adam's apple had formed. The albatross opened its beak and yawning wide he nearly knocked Aidan on the head.

'Thank you,' he said loud and clear.

His words reached those in the waist, the deck now full of the crew, all of them drawn to this phenomenal bird. A talking bird! No-one would ever believe them back home.

Aidan jumped into the air shaking his arm, giving a loud cheer—and promptly came back to earth landing on the bird's foot. The bird screamed, his feathers sticking up all over as if they'd been combed the wrong way. He opened his wings and flew straight up, the backdraft knocking Aidan to the deck. He circled once, bringing his webbed foot up close to his underbelly, his toes curling in pain.

'Ah! You stupid bloody boy...agh...my foot!' And the bird promptly landed in the ocean alongside the ship and waggled his bruised limb in the water. 'Ooh, that's better,' the bird sighed, closing his eyes, his feathers settling once again.

To say that all who watched were stunned was an understatement. Everyone watched the albatross floating on the sea, its vast wingspan, at least forty feet of it, spread wide and resting on the surface of the ocean.

Aidan was the first to recover. Rising from the deck he rushed to the side of the ship. 'I'm sorry, honest, it was an accident.' The bird ignored him as it busily soothed its aching toes.

The others ran to the rail and peered over at the giant bird, their senses in turmoil. 'Aidan, that bird swore exactly as you do,' said Augusta, looking up at him. 'Why does he curse like you?'

'Because he gave me my voice, little girl,' said the bird.

'Who are you calling a little girl, you...' shouted Augusta taking umbrage, she hated being called little.

'All right, don't you dare start arguing, he's only just learned to speak,' said Beatrix. 'Have you a name, Master Albatross?' She asked formally, the only way she could think of to talk to a bird.

'I have,' the albatross replied, 'but your tongue could never say it. You will have to give me a human name,' his voice uncannily similar to Aidan's.

At that chaos reigned all over the ship. Locklear, uncharacteristically allowing excitement to have the upper hand, shouted names at Talbot. Talbot shouted names at Anders, the girls shouted names to everyone, the crew shouting enough to drown out

182

everyone's suggestions. Tragen, stared at his boy, they were the only quiet ones in amongst the furore.

'Well, Aidan, you've excelled yourself this time, haven't you?' He smiled as he helped Aidan down from the poop.

'He's lovely, Master, just look at him!' Aidan was enraptured. 'He can fly anywhere, and he's strong enough to fly for weeks.'

'Yes, but will he carry our message to the prince?'

'Of course he will. I've given him what he's always wanted. He can speak! Oh yes, he'll do anything we want.'

'As long as you don't stand on my toes again, little wizard,' shouted the albatross. His hearing was very acute, even managing to hear their conversation above all the hubbub, which he found very strange, for an albatross his hearing had always been poor. 'Now give me a name…you all have one, I want one.'

The commotion died on the quarterdeck and five faces looked at the two wizards expectantly. There was still bedlam in the waist as the crew, taking heed of the bird's request, again volunteered names, unfortunately some were rather indecent and those men received a look of utter contempt from the albatross.

'Why not let the ladies name him, Aidan?' Tragen suggested.

'Yeah, well…okay. Augusta you saw him first, got any ideas?'

Augusta stared at the albatross. 'You are truly a magnificent albatross,' she told him as she curtsied.

'Thank you, I agree, there has never been another like me,' he paused, his expression sad. 'I dwarf all other albatrosses.'

'Then you must have a name that suits your stature in the avian world. Give me a moment, please.' Augusta studied the bird as she sucked her finger in the corner of her mouth. He seemed very depressed at his size, perhaps he was bullied for being so big, she thought. Well she wouldn't name him anything to do with being a giant. He'd said there were not many of his kind, could she use that? No, she decided—he was the first albatross able to speak; he was then definitely a first amongst his kind.

'I have it…Ryn! You will be known as Ryn, which means leader.'

'I accept…now tell me yours,' ordered Ryn

Augusta glanced quickly at Aidan and Tragen and said. 'I am called Nellie.'

'That is not your true name, but if that is what you wish me to call you then I will.' Ryn gazed at her.

'I don't know what you mean,' said Augusta hurriedly.

'Well little wizard, I know your true name is Aidan, tell me of this message.' Ryn chose to ignore her.

'My master, Lord Tragen, can tell you more,' and Aidan indicated the wizard.

'I have written it on parchment, Ryn,' and he showed the bird the smallish roll in his hand. 'Can I attach it to you in any way?'

'You may hang it around my neck, Lord Tragen, and then Aidan can show me my destination.'

'Show you, how?' Tragen asked puzzled, descending the ladder into the waist so that he could reach the bird.

'I can enter Aidan's mind, so he must picture my route that I may see it through his eyes,' answered Ryn, swimming closer to the ship to accept Tragen's missive.

The wizard having made a large loop in the twine tied around the parchment, bent over the rail and dropped the loop over the beak and head so that it slipped down the stretched neck of the bird. When it had settled comfortably against his chest, Ryn ruffled his feathers quickly and the missive disappeared, hidden among the pure white down, he then swam a little farther out from the boat so that he could see Aidan up on the quarterdeck.

'Are you ready, Ryn,' asked Aidan, and at the bird's nod, Aidan closed his eyes and visualized the stars in the sky above Mantovar, the river into Mantovar and the route upriver to the castle.

'I have it, little wizard, now picture the prince,' he ordered.

Aidan searched for his princess. '*Mindmeld with me Augusta, you have a clearer image of your father than I do,*' and he held her hand to maximize contact.

'*So that's her real name, why don't you use it?*'

'*That is a long and secret story...too long for now,*' Aidan replied

'*Very well, I like hearing secrets, tell me when I return.*'

'*You are coming back then?*' Augusta asked.

'*Yes, but how come you understand me when I am in Aidan's mind?*' Ryn was puzzled, something more had happened than being given a voice—there were side-effects of the boy's magic that he couldn't figure out.

'*When we mindmeld Aidan and I become one mind...because you are in his, so you are in mine,*' answered Augusta.

'I go now—I am confused,' said the Wandering Albatross of the Giant Albatross family as he flexed his wings causing an enormous ripple on the surface of the water. 'I will see you again in a few weeks.'

And before anyone could say goodbye, he gave two flaps of his enormous wings to gain height and he was airborne, his wings locked in place to enable him to ride the thermals with no strain on his body and soon he was soaring above the three remaining masts and flying northeast.

That evening the ship continued to cruise south-westwards in ideal weather conditions, and Augusta commenced her lessons in serious magic. Both she and Aidan were sitting on the poop deck facing aft, their backs resting against the after-jigger. Augusta, her full attention directed on Aidan, listened eagerly as he went through the rudiments of the art.

'Remember, magic is formed of the mind, along with chanting and hand movements. Sometimes all three are required, on occasion maybe just one or two…depending on the type of spell, the difficulty in creating the spell and the strength of the spell-caster,' he instructed as they sat side by side cross-legged. 'The more powerful you are at conjuring dictates how much energy you use—the stronger you are the better. Don't forget, the more complex the spell is, the greater the energy needed and the more tired you'll become at the end of it. You understand?'

'Yes,' she answered, 'but you said magic is of the mind, yet I've overheard Tragen say that your magic comes from healing…why is mine different to yours?'

'I don't know…can you heal?' Aidan asked.

'Don't be silly, you know I can't.'

'Right, then we'll assume your magic is the same as everyone else's—based on the mind. Shall we continue or are you going to keep interrupting?'

'One more thing,' she said nudging him with her elbow, 'you said that spell-casting burnt up energy, yet you didn't rest much after creating the spell for drinking-water yesterday, did you? And you seemed a long time creating that one.'

'A lot of that was theatricals it just seemed longer than it actually was. But I am used to magic and can control my energy usage…besides it was a simple spell. Hopefully by the end of today

185

you'll be able to conjure water from the air. Wait,' he said as she went to interrupt, 'not yet, at the end of the day, I said.

'Okay, ready?' She nodded excitedly and he continued. 'Right, look around you at the sea…and I mean look at all the parts of it.' As she did, Aidan studied her face checking her concentration and suddenly realized that she was a very pretty girl and not half as horrible as she used to be—in fact he liked her a lot. She turned her head to him and caught him staring.

'What is it?'

'Nothing,' and he looked away embarrassed. And then his heart turned over, he'd have to watch his thoughts, if she mindmelded at an inappropriate moment…' '*Close your eyes…now, show me the ocean,*' he mindmelded.

And returning his mindmeld, she showed him her interpretation of the sea.

'*A bit blurry isn't it?*'

'*Well, I suppose it is, a bit.*'

'*Okay, open your eyes.* You must visualize to the best of all your senses, not just sight but smell, taste, touch and sound. Look at the ocean again,' Aidan said, 'and describe it to me.'

She braced herself and tried again. And with his questioning she looked harder at what was before her eyes, until she could describe not only the size of the individual waves, but the speed and colour of each individual ripple, the occasional flurry of foam. She described the height of each peak and the depth of each trough. She even managed to describe the density, taste, and smell of each wavelet, and even the noise of the waves lapping against the sides of the ship. It took her over an hour to complete her examination, dusk was falling rapidly.

'By the Gods, I didn't realize what I was seeing.'

'Or feeling…you must acquire this habit. You cannot create efficient magic about something you cannot visualize properly. Tragen is always saying that to me. He says that's the reason my spells sometimes go wrong—they're not wrong at all, they go in an unexpected direction that's all. He doesn't know what he's talking about sometimes, I think it's because he's getting old.'

He looked at her, and settling into his role of teacher helped calm his nerves after their shattering of the night before. And he found that he didn't want this lesson to end, not just because he was afraid to fall asleep, but he was also thoroughly enjoying her company. He was beginning to understand why Anders wished to be alone with Beatrix.

He glanced around and saw his other two friends standing hand in hand in the foc's'le, oblivious to the stares of passing crewmen.

'Stand up and stretch your arms out in front of you. Good,' he said as Augusta complied, and he rose with her to stand shoulder to shoulder. 'Now spread your fingers wide, and wiggle them.'

'Like this?' And she waved her hands around at the same time.

'No…careful, you must always think of what you're going to do before you do it!'

'What do you mean?'

'Well,' he wondered if she'd remember, 'I once made a girl's nose bleed accidentally. She'd upset me and I stuck my finger up to her while I was thinking nasty thoughts. Her nose bled off and on for days…so I heard later.'

'Ooh, that happened to me once, years ago. I remember going out in the carriage with my father and…it was you! You made my nose bleed…with magic?'

'I'm sorry, it really was an accident and I've never done anything like it since,' he stared into her eyes as green as the ocean, he liked her eyes. 'Do you forgive me?'

'Tell me first how I upset you.'

'Well…it was my first day in the castle,' he said remembering the occasion vividly. 'You were so…so magnificent in that carriage, so beautiful, so much like a dream. I'd never seen anything like you in my life. My mother used to tell me stories of beautiful princesses and their caring, wonderful ways. You captivated me. I'd have done anything just for you to notice me,' he smiled ruefully. 'And then when you did, what did you do? You stuck your tongue out at me and shattered the dream. You were still beautiful but…well you still are, but back then I thought you were horrible.'

She returned his stare; he'd called her beautiful and meant it. She felt herself sinking into his eyes and then as the ship lurched slightly, enough to break eye contact, it brought them both back from they knew not where.

'You mean you can hurt as well as heal?'

'Aye, but do you forgive me?' For some reason her answer was very important.

'Of course I do, but you must also forgive me. I was a thoughtless, spoilt brat then.'

He laughed the relief palpable. 'I thought you still were.'

'Aidan!' And she nudged him even harder as they both laughed. 'Let's get back to the magic, okay?'

'All right, Highness,' and he bowed to her as his laugh subsided. 'Now examine the ocean again. You see the ripples?' She nodded and he went on speaking slowly and quietly, his concentration completely on her. 'Now, we'll start with the smallest part of the surface…move your fingers to copy the motion of the small ripples between the waves. That's it…now keep your fingers going and also move your hands to copy the bigger ripples and now your wrists to follow the waves.'

With her fingers, hands and wrists in motion, she glanced at Aidan and saw he was smiling, and she smiled in return, making him happy was all she wanted to do.

'Ooh, this feels strange.'

'Strange as in horrible…or strange as in nice?'

She laughed out loud. 'This is lovely.'

'Good, now this time the ocean as a whole, sway your arms to copy the motion of the swell and remember, keep in mind these sensations when your eyes are closed. Now, recall the vibrations of the ocean, not only in your arms but also in your whole body and in your mind. When you are satisfied that you can call up these feelings again, I want you to close your eyes. This time, you will visualize the ocean as it is not as you think it is, and we will explore the sea in our minds. Okay?'

She nodded, her total being absorbed in the task. And then she closed her eyes and Aidan entered her mind to share her enlightened perception. And he was pleased at what he found.

'*Very good, Augusta,*' he mindmelded, '*now keep these feelings. Whoa, slow down keep the pace. If you move faster than the present speed of the ocean, then you will cause the sea to move faster, and we've had enough of storms to last a lifetime. Now look towards the horizon ahead of you. Do you have the same impressions of the ocean there as here?*'

'*Yes, I have never seen the horizon so clear before.*'

'*In magic most things become clearer. Now you are going to look over the horizon.*'

She did not hesitate. She was now facing aft with her arms outstretched waving in front of her and her wrists, hands and fingers making intricate movements in the air. Augusta found it fascinating and felt she was soaring in the skies much as the albatross this afternoon. And thinking of Ryn her mind found him, flying high and straight, his huge wings spread wide and, unlike other birds, his wings not flapping as he rode the air currents. He flew directly away from her.

'*Do you see him?*' She asked, awestruck.

'*Aye, practise and you'll be able to follow him for longer. Now leave him and turn your head. I want you to look around.*'

First, she looked to her right and saw nothing but the ocean, she turned and looked left and espied a small squall far off. Then turning her whole body and staring forward of the bows she found a small island.

'*Aidan!*'

'*I know, keep looking,*' and Aidan cast around for Tragen. '*Master, can you see the island Augusta has found?*'

'*Yes, come away both of you. I'll be with you shortly...I'll bring the captain.*'

Aidan and Augusta waited, Augusta ecstatic that her first real foray into magic had been so successful. She was so happy in fact that sitting alongside him she put her arm through his and held it tight until Tragen called them down onto the quarterdeck.

'How far away is the island? I estimate a day. Do you agree?'

'Probably...at the earliest we'll reach it at lunchtime tomorrow, but we'll see it well before then, possibly not long after sunrise.'

'Can you see any details of the place, Tragen?' Hugo asked.

'None yet, my friend, we are too far away.' Turning to Augusta, he added, his satisfaction evident. 'Well done, Highness,' and he smiled, 'the more you practise, the more you will see. We will now leave it until the morning when I hope we will discover more. I want you to stay away from the island until then, we do not wish to alert anyone, unknowingly.'

At dawn the following morning, Aidan and his friends arrived on deck to find most of the crew already taking advantage of every observation point, some even straddling the bowsprit. All were facing forward, peering ahead of the bows. Arranging themselves comfortably on the poop deck and sitting with their feet swinging over the forward edge, they found that Tragen and Locklear were standing directly below and just forward of them.

On the horizon ahead was a vertical column of high white cloud in the otherwise clear blue sky. Anders explained that this cloud hovered over a land mass in the midst of the ocean. He added that before long they could expect turbulence in the sea in front of the island as they approached it.

'What do you think we'll find there?' Augusta asked.

'Nothing much, I fear. It's not a very large island. It's probably home to turtles and small rodents, probably terns and gulls are nesting there.'

Just before noon seagulls were flying overhead and details of the island, now only ten or twelve leagues away, were discernible below the hanging cloud. Mid-afternoon saw them in the midst of the turbulence. The ship's heading was changed to sail south of the island.

'Well there's nothing much there wizard, unless you fancy turtle for dinner,' said Locklear.

'I have never acquired a taste for that particular mammal, but their eggs are something else,' Tragen salivated at the thought.

Locklear laughed. 'We cannot waste this light by tarrying here, my friend. We must wait and see what our new acquaintances will offer us.'

'If we are welcome,' said Tragen.

As the island passed on the starboard side, they could see it more clearly. It appeared to be a low hump in the middle of the ocean, a small hill bearing low scrub, prickly pears and the occasional short, sunflower trees. Turtles were slowly plodding across the small white beach, gulls and smaller birds screeching above them.

Rounding the island a vast panorama of other islands appeared, all as smudges on the horizon except for one. Closer to the Grim a huge land mass stretching for leagues across the bows of the ship, grew out of the sea about a day's sailing away.

'Hopper,' shouted the captain across the quarterdeck 'is that Sanctity?'

'No, that is Griffin, sir; Sanctity is many leagues further west again.'

Aidan turned and searched for sign of Sanctity and found instead a darkening of the sea in that direction. 'What is that on the water, Captain?'

'I don't know; have you any idea, Hopper?'

'I can't make it out, sir.'

'How about you, Tragen,' Locklear asked.

Tragen peered west for what seemed ages. 'It's all right; it's just a large patch of seaweed floating on the surface…wait a minute! That's strange…it's just disappeared.'

'It's just dropped below the surface, Milord,' interrupted Anders squinting through narrowed eyes.

'What do you mean?' asked Locklear.

'What I said…it's still there only you can't see it.'

'How can you see it, then,' Hopper asked, mystified.

'I've always been able to see things that others can't.'

'Well, never mind. Are the militia on Griffin likely to bother us, Hopper?' Locklear asked.

'I don't believe so, but perhaps I should explain a bit more about the enmity between the two clans. The Montetors and the Portolans have been at loggerheads for years and I believe we should do all in our power to avoid their quarrel, we don't want them turning on us,' replied Hopper staring at the vast island. 'We'll need to be constantly aware of the ill-feeling between them, it erupts into violence quite often or it did when I was here years ago.'

'Their quarrel, Hopper…can you tell us the reason for it?' Tragen asked beckoning both the captain and mate to the relative privacy beneath the poop. Unfortunately, this area happened to be directly beneath the four friends now hanging over the edge listening intently.

'Not the reason, no, but both clans have an arrangement of sorts. Open warfare had not yet been declared then as both sides knew that neither could survive without the other. I have heard rumours of the islands over these last years and nothing seems to have changed. The dispute manifests itself in small misdemeanours, a series of tit-for-tat incidents.'

'How do you mean?' Locklear asked.

'Well,' Hopper continued, 'a particularly nasty incident occurred when I was here. A Montetor drove a wagon of iron ore over the legs of a Portolan dockworker who was calculating the weight of the ore deposited in a ship's hold. The following day that Montetor driver fell into the harbour off the pier and was crushed between the ship and the wharf.'

'Of course, both clans insisted that both events were accidents. But I was told later that the dockworker had molested the daughter of the ironworker,' Hopper took a breather.

'Then justice was served,' added the captain.

'Not quite,' said Hopper grimacing. 'The ironworker is reputed to have assaulted the wife of the dockworker a few months previously. And so it goes on, and has done for what must be fifteen or twenty years now. I was here about ten or twelve years ago, and the feud had been running a few years then.'

Hopper paused and stared at his companions. 'The death of the crushed ironworker was blamed on an itinerant drunken beggar fast asleep some way along the pier. He awoke as the Montetor man screamed and he crawled over to the edge of the wharf to search out the noise. The Portolans found him looking, accused him of attempting to rob the ironworker, and strung him up on the jetty before he could be questioned by anyone else. There is a permanent gibbet on the wharf which serves as a reminder to all. The Portolans are the law on the docks as the Montetors are the law in the hills.'

'So we have to make certain we are never present at any unpleasantness between these people,' stated Tragen. 'Hugo, no-one must be allowed to wander alone on this island.'

'I agree,' replied the captain. 'You eavesdroppers above...do you understand?'

Anders jumped in surprise. 'Aye, aye sir!'

'But, Captain, why are we stopping here, the mate has already said there are no suitable trees to supply a new mast?' Augusta asked, prodding Anders in the side to move him over. Her elbow was becoming a lethal weapon.

'Highness, we need a variety of other things, metal fastenings, candles, ropes, canvas, food and many other supplies, including fresh drinking water. I do not wish to be drenched again by sorcerers' apprentices.'

Locklear moved off smiling to himself, he was getting used to seeing these four young people together—it was as if they were meant to be.

192

Sixteen

Leash overheard everything, with eyes glinting and his brain churning, he saw many possibilities in using the feud. Having failed to kill the boy on the ship he would slay him somewhere on the island. There was always more opportunity to arrange an "accident" ashore. It was common knowledge that docks were notoriously dangerous places, and if he played it right the Montetors and Portolans would be blamed.

Leash knew youngsters, knew they were insatiably curious and loved exploring new places. If the town was large enough, isolating Aidan would be child's play. All he had to do was follow them, and wait.

He only wished he could somehow let the wizard know the reason for the boy's death...seeing Tragen demented with self-loathing and grief would be a memory sweet beyond measure. And then Leash blinked tears away—it would never erase his own loneliness. He went to his bunk that night happy. Chuckling, he climbed into his cot, his fellow crewmates keeping well away from him.

But as he fell into his happy dream expecting relief from misery, he detected an air of disquiet—she disapproved.

The following morning was a replay of the morning before. Not a spare space anywhere along the rails, everyone wishing to examine the island, and the closer they came to it the more heavily was it inspected.

Griffin was an enormous island stretching for many leagues east and west, a reef on the south side enclosing the harbour, protected the large town behind it. The hinterland, only glimpsed at this distance, was immense. The Grim approached the island from the south and the shoreline filled the horizon ahead. It had twin peaks, one twice as high as the other. A veritable forest of short growth trees covering the foothills of the higher of the mountains with thinner growth towards the summit; the other mountain was bare rock.

The deep valley between them was occasionally hidden by sporadic black and grey smoke with the odd flash of bright light amidst the fumes. These were the sites of the many foundries belonging to the Montetors. The mantle of pollution would be hiding a rabbit warren of red dust-laden houses, the inhabitants equally as grimed.

Hopper pointed out some of the sights of the town. It sprawled over high cliffs in the west where a huge house had been built overlooking the ocean; this was the home of the harbourmaster, his manorhouse. Spreading eastwards, the town continued around and over a large promontory on which a beacon was maintained. Below the beacon the evidence for its existence was plainly seen...a frothing, foaming mass of water breaking over large rocks encroaching far into the sea.

The harbour was wide and deep, a broad looping lagoon. Many jetties protruded into the harbour from a common wharf, myriad vessels of all shapes and sizes tied up alongside. But the western end below the manorhouse was kept for their navy—warships, large and small were moored there, although there were not many.

Waterfront warehouses, most long, black and ugly stretched the length of the wharf, but as one sailor was overheard to say, iron and coke were not a pretty sight. The wharf was strong and sturdy, cargo piled neatly at intervals waiting to be loaded for export to other exotic destinations. Even more stockpiles of goods were being landed from ships, the whole dockyard one hive of activity.

To the west of Griffin Town, a couple of leagues down the coast, a fishing village plied its trade. Small fishing boats sailing to and from the jetty jutting into the small bay in front of it. Seabirds in abundance were swooping over the village pilfering the seething catches at the slightest lapse in vigilance. Gulls screeching and the occasional lonely petrel overflying the Grim added a certain magic to the exotic spectacle. A single fishing boat beating its way home, passed close to the Grim, its fishermen ceasing work to give a wave and stare open-mouthed at the huge, damaged ship.

The morning wore on and Beatrix rejoined Augusta and Aidan on the poop, she had been below to tend to Lady Cornelia. As she lowered herself to sit alongside Aidan, Anders returned from his duties in the captain's cabin and he slumped down heavily beside her.

'How much longer before we dock do you think, Anders?' Augusta asked, bending forward to peer at him around Aidan and Beatrix.

'A couple of hours that's all, this opposing current is slowing us up a bit.'

'Argh!' Augusta abruptly screamed, leaping to her feet and staring at her tunic. 'Those bloody birds have had me!'

'Augusta, please, your cursing is getting as bad as Aidan's,' Beatrix chided and at the same time wrinkled her nose in disgust at the sight on her mistress' tunic.

'You'd swear as well if it happened to you. Stop laughing,' she shouted at the boys as she aimed a kick at Aidan who was closest.

'Ah well, they do say it's lucky for a bird to crap on you,' Aidan laughed quickly rolling out of the way.

'Lucky! I'll give you lucky you come near me. Ooh...Beattie, help me clean this will you?' Augusta implored.

'You know what Dolly calls seagulls? No?' Anders, receiving puzzled looks for an answer, continued. 'He calls them airborne rats...nothing but scavenging, crapping...'

'All right...all right, no need to give any more details, we get the picture,' said Beatrix, stopping him in mid flow. 'Come on, Augusta, let's go to the cabin and clean it off.'

'We can't be long; I don't want to miss anything.'

Aidan stopped giggling as the girls proceeded past him. 'Hey, wait a minute. Clean it here...with magic!'

Augusta almost convulsed—spinning around she stared at him. Even the idea of her using magic caught at her soul. Her eyes wide and bright she stalked back to the young wizard.

'Sh...show me,' she stuttered losing control. 'Please, Aidan,' she begged.

He smiled. 'Okay, calm down and sit down. You don't need to close your eyes for this. You know what the fabric beneath the crap looks like.' They all stared intently as he continued. 'Now with your hand just above it, move it in a circular motion as if you are actually washing the filth with a cloth. That's it.'

As Augusta moved her hand she could see the mess rolling into a small pellet—a small tight ball!

'Now...flick it away,' ordered Aidan.

And she did, leaving the fabric of her tunic cleaner than it was before, she had also removed the grime beneath the crap. Augusta laughed. 'I did it...look!' She held the cloth out towards Beatrix and Anders for their inspection. 'Oh, I could have killed that bird.'

Aidan paled, the smile wiped from his face. 'Don't say things like that, Augusta. Never threaten to kill.'

Augusta looked up, startled. 'Why on earth not?'

'You are learning to be a wizard...wizards can kill by just wishing it.'

Augusta paled. 'You mean I can actually kill a bird just by wishing it?'

'More or less…but you can also kill people.'

'By the Gods, I never realized that. Can you do it, Aidan? I mean…can you kill?' Augusta asked, intrigued and also frightened.

'I've killed in the past, yes, but only animals for food, and then just enough to eat. I've never killed more than necessary.'

'And people?' Beatrix persisted, unable to hide her ghoulish nature, the macabre fascinated her.

'Never! I could never harm another's soul and neither should you.'

'But surely that's nonsense, Aidan. You have to kill your enemies, don't you?' Augusta asked, troubled greatly by what she was hearing. 'My father has had to do it many times. What is wrong with that? He's been protecting Mantovar.'

'Augusta, when a man passes over, his soul goes on to Paradise where it rests for a while before being called to live another life. But souls as well as bodies can die! When you kill, you inflict damage on your own soul, you weaken it. And if you kill often, then your soul's chance of an afterlife is gradually chipped away until it has not the strength to survive. It enters Oblivion then where hopefully it will die…if not a worse fate…' and he shuddered, unable to complete his thoughts. 'Killing people is always wrong!'

'But what if it's your life in danger, Aidan? I mean, what if it's you or them. You have to kill them before they kill you, don't you?' Beatrix asked tensely, her arm through Anders', clinging to him tightly. 'Otherwise, if you give up and not fight back, surely that's a form of suicide, isn't it? And I've always been taught that suicide is wrong.'

Aidan stared at her his facial muscles twitching; his eyes had a far away, unfathomable look. 'I haven't worked that one out yet…I haven't got all the answers. All I know is I cannot knowingly kill anyone.'

They were struck silent at that, their thoughts their own as they pondered on Aidan's strange outlook on life and death.

'Aidan, what is worse than dying in Oblivion?' Augusta asked.

Aidan replied, fear filling his voice. 'Many things, but enough for now, I'll tell you some other time.'

'But…' Augusta was interrupted by a shout from down in the waist of the Grim.

'Captain, can we allow the bumboat alongside, sir?'

'Aye, aye, watch he doesn't scrape the paintwork, Trumper,' shouted Locklear, smiling pensively. He also had overheard Aidan and had no idea what to make of it all.

The men on the deck below laughed and jeered as they eagerly watched the boat full of local produce come alongside, the two men in the boat shouting up to those on the enormous ship offering fresh melons and limes for sale.

Anders was grateful for a distraction from the dark mood into which Aidan's words had plunged him. He jumped up and led the two girls in a race down the ladder to the starboard side of the waist.

Aidan, bringing up the rear, followed a little slower, trying to shake off the depression, and the fear, brought on by Augusta's final question.

As the Grim limped through the entrance in the reef and advanced into the sheltered harbour in front of Griffin Town in the middle of the very hot afternoon, the hubbub of the harbour hit them like a blow in the face. Bellowing sailors, the creak of timbers, the flapping of unfurled canvas and the bawling of orders on the dock, assaulted the ears. And above it all, they savoured the numberless other sounds and exotic, spicy smells floating across to them from the town. Excitement gripped the four friends anxious to get ashore to explore an island none of them had ever heard of before this voyage.

An ornate barge oared by six men in uniform left the quayside and, wending its way between the warships, came out to meet them. Standing in the bows looking very grim, was a short fat man wearing a very large brimmed, floppy hat presumably to protect his face from the sun. This, Hopper informed Locklear waiting on his quarterdeck, was the harbourmaster, Seneschal Lodovico Portolan. Standing alongside him also graven faced was a very tall man, both men wearing a very plain blue uniform.

As the harbourmaster's barge drew alongside, the rope ladder was lowered for the party to climb aboard. On orders from Trumper, all men were told to show the utmost respect. It was anticipated that this short, fat man climbing the ladder, would inevitably result in a very comical display of seamanship.

Trumper rounded on the crew as they awaited the spectacle. 'Woe betide any man who laughs, sniggers or even smiles at the harbourmaster. Be warned, this man is dangerous, he has the power of

197

life and death in this port—and he exercises it ruthlessly and often.' Trumper turned back to the rail ready to help the harbourmaster come aboard as Hopper arrived at his elbow to escort the seneschal to the quarterdeck.

Lodovico Portolan, despite his bulk, did not seem in the least bit perturbed by the rope ladder. For a man of his size and shape he exhibited a nimbleness that could have put many a sailor to shame. Climbing over the rail to the sounds of the bo'sun's call, he straightened his long, plain blue, immaculate coat embroidered with a multi-coloured coat-of-arms – a griffin rearing on hind legs in a crown above two stylized peaks – on his left breast.

Even though he was grossly overweight he did not appear to sweat more than usual. He had a handsome, clean-shaven face with eyes sunk deep above dark bags giving the appearance of being a worried man suffering from lack of sleep. But his manner denied this as he stared around at the crew now standing at attention. He smiled thinly, he knew that he had surprised and disappointed them…robbing them of their merriment.

Following him over the rail was his companion, a giant of a man, again immaculately uniformed in blue and carrying an enormous straight sword at his waist. This man, like the seneschal, wore no jewellery; neither man gave the impression of needing any show of frippery. The crew needed no urging to remain silent—they stared at two strangers who were harder than any men they had ever seen on any waterfront.

Touching his forelock Hopper stepped forward and greeted the harbour's tyrant. 'Welcome aboard the Grim, Seneschal Portolan. The master, Captain Hugo Locklear, is on the quarterdeck and awaits your pleasure.'

The seneschal stared at Hopper, coldly assessing the second in command of the ship, finding him formidable. 'You are the first mate?' he asked, his words carrying just a smidgeon of sweet wine fumes, he had indulged a glass of red Cornia at lunch.

'I am, sir, if you will kindly follow me, please.' Hopper turned and led the way aft along the waist.

The harbourmaster slowly glanced around the upper deck, noting the damage. Accompanied by his very tall companion, he strode after Hopper, not sparing a look for the four youngsters lounging at the foot of the quarterdeck steps. The tall man did though, and his look seemed to pierce their very souls. Not much passed by this man, thought Anders.

Aidan, astonished, turned to the others as the three men climbed on to the quarterdeck. 'Bloody hell, did you see the size of that man? He must be seven foot if an inch! What do you reckon, Anders, his bodyguard?'

'Aye, he must be. Did you notice his shoulders? They're wider than the Bear's! We have to watch ourselves here...this port is not a happy place, methinks.'

'The harbourmaster reminds me a bit of the Abbot of Sentinel,' said Augusta, chewing her index finger.

'Does he?' Aidan asked, surprised

'He has the same cold, calculating look,' she shuddered, 'yes, most everyone I know is wary of the abbot—they all stay well away from him if they can,' whispered Augusta as she joined the others in listening to the conversation just above their heads. 'That big man was a handsome devil, wasn't he Beattie?' And at Aidan's scowl she poked her tongue out and laughed.

'Good afternoon, Seneschal Portolan. I am honoured and very glad to meet you,' said Locklear cheerfully shaking the fat hand. 'Let me introduce my friend, Lord Tragen,' and he waved his arm in the wizard's direction.

For a moment, there was a flicker of consternation or perhaps speculation, in the eyes of the harbourmaster. 'A wizard...we have not seen any of your brethren in this part of the world for many a long year, Milord.'

'No, Seneschal, and my niece and I did not expect to be here now, unfortunately the storm...' said Tragen shrugging, he glanced at Locklear. If there were no wizards on Griffin could the torturer be a monk, perhaps on Sanctity?

'Yes...the ship has suffered, you have a great deal of damage, Captain,' The seneschal said, turning away from the wizard at last, making the point of not introducing the tall man standing quietly at his shoulder. 'You have stopped in for repairs, I take it. We can supply most things usually but we are awaiting deliveries from all points. We have other ships expected, of course, some are overdue by weeks. Perhaps the same storm has delayed them...or the brigands of Onyx, of course.'

Aidan and his friends listened to every word and when Tragen mentioned his niece, Anders was shushed into silence before he could ask.

Hopper, standing to one side keeping a surreptitious eye on the tall bodyguard, was unsurprised at this mention of delays. It was the usual opening gambit in negotiations for the seneschal's payment. The mate had already figured out what this would be. Lodovico Portolan liked wine, good wine, and there was bound to be a shortage of Mantovar's excellent beverage on this island, if memory served him.

Because of the island realm's distance from the eastern continent trade was very inconsistent between them. But the smuggling of wine, brandy and tobacco from many parts of the world was a thriving industry on Griffin Island even though the penalty, if caught, was always death. The Portolans demanded their taxes be collected promptly on all imports into the south of the island. And the Montetors extracted the same revenue on trade crossing the border into the north, or by whatever was brought ashore in the small inlets dotted around the northern end of the island. The Montetors, unlike the Portolans, did not enjoy the amenities of a deep water harbour, but both clans shared the facilities of the south for trade.

Tragen had a hoard of the grape juice from the temperate regions of Drakka, a very popular and rare vintage, very expensive. The wizard's pained expression was frank evidence of his reluctance to part with even one bottle…Hopper smiled.

'Nevertheless, Seneschal, we can surely help you in your endeavours to assist us,' said Locklear. A seaman arrived just then with a carafe and the best silver goblets of the very wine Hopper had in mind.

Taking a sip the seneschal's eyes lit up. 'Ha! Drakka…Enzore region I believe. The Enzoreans are true masters of their craft,' he smacked his lips in appreciation. 'What I wouldn't do for a bottle of this,' he smiled for the first time, though the smile did not reach his eyes.

'Oh, I'm sure we could spare more than one bottle for your table, Seneschal,' said Hugo, Tragen wilted. The harbourmaster's smile grew broader, and he wandered to the forward rail to assess the visible damage and to speculate on the unseen.

'We can discuss the supplies you will require over dinner, Captain. Please be my guest ashore tonight. I will send a carriage for you and your two passengers. I hope your niece will accompany you,

200

Lord Tragen,' Seneschal Portolan asked glancing at the wizard. 'It is not often that my son and I entertain. Now, I must take my leave…until later, gentlemen.' He swallowed the remains of his wine and handed the goblet back. Nodding his head curtly to Locklear and Tragen, he left the quarterdeck followed closely by his giant of a retainer. The tall man's eyes continually roved over the ship, not missing a thing, assessing the crew as he disembarked.

At the foot of the steps, the four friends waited silently until they heard the bo'sun's pipe and saw the harbourmaster step over the rail and descend, just as nimbly, to the awaiting barge. And then they made a mad scramble up onto the quarterdeck, Aidan anxious to tackle Tragen about his 'niece'.

'*Say nothing, yet…wait,*' Tragen mindmelded, anticipating the questions. '*Join us in the captain's cabin, we have plans to make.*'

'Hugo, let us indulge ourselves with what little of my wine remains. If you wouldn't mind I need a word in your cabin.' Hugo glanced quickly at the departing barge and, followed by the youngsters, he and Tragen went below.

Hopper strode to the starboard rail and watched the harbourmaster heading for the wharf. His son's health must have improved, he thought; it was unusual for the seneschal to receive guests with his son present. At least, years ago it would have been strange. Circumstances must have changed over the last twelve years, how old had the boy been then…three, perhaps four years old? Hopper recalled the stories of the poor mother's death, dying in that manner and nearly taking her son with her. A bad business, mused Hopper— tragic. Had the boy recovered? Hopper paced the boards and stared at the very busy wharf across a narrowing gap of water. There were a large number of the dockworkers staring up at the Grim, none of them ever having seen a five-masted ship let alone one that had sustained such severe damage and still made port. The captain had proved all the doubters wrong…this ship could sail in any weather, but there again Hugo Locklear was an exceptional seaman.

Tragen, greatly disturbed, silently studied Aidan and his friends. The wizard sat in the chair to one side of Hugo's desk, Hugo in his usual chair behind with his back to the stern gallery. The four youngsters, having found available perches around the largest cabin onboard, made the room appear overcrowded. Anders took it upon himself to open the windows in the stern gallery. Fresh air, even if it was imbued with the slight smell of brimstone drifting on the breeze, made their meeting place far more amenable.

Tragen stared deep into his wine goblet for a moment before saying anything. 'Lady Cornelia will now masquerade as my niece whilst we are here. We could not possibly keep her hidden from the seneschal…too many people know there is a woman of importance in that cabin, and when the dockworkers come aboard to facilitate repairs, the harbourmaster will wonder…'

'Aye, Tragen,' replied Hugo, 'but the crew believe it is their princess. How do you propose to get around that?'

'They must be exhorted to remain silent where she is concerned…they must not speak of her to anyone!'

'I do not trust that Leash,' Beatrix said.

'Why not?' Tragen asked.

'He always seems to be hanging around us,' and she hunched her shoulders, 'he watches us, especially Aidan,' she finished lamely, not quite sure of her feelings.

'He's a very good helmsman, Tragen,' said Hugo, dismissing her opinion.

'Nevertheless, Beatrix has already proved she has remarkable mental insight. We shall all keep an eye on him, Beatrix,' Tragen assured her, he believing in women's intuition even if Locklear did not. 'Now the arrangements for this evening…we will be expected to have our own servant accompany us, Hugo. You agree, Augusta?'

'Yes, of course, we must stand behind you whilst you are seated at dinner and see to your needs.' She perked up a little at the thought of going ashore and acting as companion to her lady-in-waiting, overhearing the talk at the table.

'We dare not allow Augusta to act as maid to Lady Cornelia, Tragen. However hard she'll try she will never pass it off for a whole evening, the Portolan's servants will soon discover she is an impostor.' Hugo stated flatly.

'He is right, Highness,' forestalling Augusta's objection. 'Think about it for a moment. If one of their servants says anything to disparage Lady Cornelia, or a little scullery maid speaks to you in a manner that you think is inappropriate, you will not be able to stop yourself. You will react in a way that will ensure they realize you are no ordinary maid. And that we cannot have. We cannot risk this harbourmaster and his family discovering your identity. No, you must stay here and Beatrix will go as my niece's body servant. Anders will accompany his master and also double up as my servant…'

Aidan spoke up indignantly. 'I'm your servant, I should accompany you!'

'You are not a servant—you are my apprentice. When it comes to performing a servant's duties at table you will encounter the same problems as Augusta and not be able to hide your magical abilities. We are all agreed that we should also keep you hidden as well.

'Seneschal Portolan is a very shrewd man and for some reason desires the company of a wizard at dinner. It is not normal for a man in his position to ask an unknown sea captain to partake of his hospitality. He believes himself, rightly or wrongly, to be above such people. But he could not invite me and my niece alone. He would be insulting Hugo needlessly and he hopes to make a lot of money out of repairing this ship.

'The seneschal needs me for some unknown purpose and until I know what that is, I do not want him to know there is a second wizard onboard—or even a third,' he glanced at Augusta. 'Besides, I need you to remain here with Augusta. Under no circumstances is she to be left alone in these waters. There have never been any diplomatic ties between Griffin and Mantovar, therefore I do not have any idea how the seneschal will react if he knows the heir to Mantovar is in his country. Any problems and both of you can mindmeld with me; the distance should not be too great. You understand, my boy?'

'Aye, I suppose,' Aidan said, deflated, his disappointment obvious. 'But you take care, there is something else happening here I don't understand.'

'What is that?'

'I'm not certain, but it's something to do with the storm…I need to think on it. But his manservant, the giant, he is not what he seems, either.'

Tragen disturbed at Aidan's words reached over and ruffled his hair forgetting for a moment that Aidan's contemporaries were watching. 'If you need to discuss the matter of the storm come to me immediately. As for the giant, I marked him well, my boy, and I agree. Hopper has already informed us that the man is the commander of the seneschal's militia. He will need careful watching. I must go now and inform my niece to ready herself. I expect she'll be very happy to get out of her prison for a few hours.'

203

Seventeen

At dusk, Aidan and Augusta stood at the head of the brow watching the invited guests descend to the wharf.

Several ships had been forced to move and berth at the shorter jetties to make room for the giant ship. This had taken time and the hours had been utilized to bring up a whole flotilla of small boats to push the Grim alongside the wharf. There had been no shortage of help from the dockworkers—all it seemed wished to have hands on in securing the biggest ship they would ever see in their lives.

A closed carriage pulled by four powerful, jet black horses their long manes curled with red ribbons, had drawn up on the quayside at precisely the time the first dog watch ended at six o'clock. The coachman climbed down and held the door ajar for Tragen to assist his niece to climb the steps.

Lady Cornelia, her broken ankle healed completely, and still not quite believing that the 'old sickness' in her bones had also disappeared, was determined to enjoy the rigours of being conveyed in a horse drawn vehicle—an experience that previously would have resulted in a shattered spine. She fairly loped into the carriage, grinning widely, although being a very large woman she slumped heavily onto the seat, the leaf springs groaning as she did. Tragen glanced quickly back up at Aidan and Augusta and winked reassuringly.

Locklear paused and shook Hopper's hand before climbing the few steps onto the brow. 'Beware of all not of the Grim and keep a double watch posted until I return. No stranger is to come aboard unless they have my written permission.' Glancing at Augusta standing nearby, he continued. 'You know whose safety is paramount. If it comes to a choice…you know which one to make.'

'Sir, if I may keep you a moment. When I was here before it was common knowledge that the seneschal never entertained in company with his son. In fact he never ever introduced his boy to anyone. The seneschal's wife died giving him birth and something about that time has been hidden, her death was unusual—maybe even unnatural. I cannot think of any reason that the subject should crop up in conversation, but if it does…beware.'

Locklear paused for a moment, thinking on his words. 'Are you saying that there was something strange about the boy, that he was deliberately hidden from sight?'

'Aye, sir,' the mate nodded.

'Thank you, Hopper; I will heed your advice.' Locklear descended the brow as the bo'sun's mate shrilled the captain's salute on his pipe.

Hopper, Aidan and Augusta watched in silence as the carriage sped into motion, the coat of arms on the door shining bright, the captain ensconced inside with the wizard and the lady-in-waiting. The two servants, Anders and Beatrix, riding up on the hind seat waved across to them as the coach disappeared around a corner of a long, black warehouse.

'This is going to be the worst part, Aidan,' Augusta looked at her companion with mixed emotions, 'waiting.'

Subdued, he stared at her. 'Everyone is worried for your safety, Augusta, everyone. How can you bear to live the way you do knowing that people wish you harm?'

Augusta shrugged. 'I grew up with it…I'm used to it,' and she added, 'I try never to think on it. You've learned to live with the fact that wizards are never trusted, haven't you? So, come on, cheer up and teach me some more magic.'

She put her arm through his and dragged him to the poop deck to await the return of their friends. She was determined to take full advantage of this opportunity of being alone with him, to find out a little more of his life—and perhaps his family.

The carriage wound through narrow backstreets over the cobblestones between warehouses, shoddy dockworkers' homes and even grubbier taverns. Beatrix couldn't help but compare the quality of the many buildings. The warehouses seemed well cared for, but the houses and the inns this near the waterfront, were definitely not. The slum dwellings, some three and four storeys high, tumbled against each other, each needing the support of the next to remain upright. Each roof of the wooden dwellings leant precariously toward its neighbour across the street blocking out overhead sunlight, giving rise to suspicious shadowed niches and sordid alleys. And yet most had washing lines strung from eave to eave across the road.

But the deeper into the town they travelled, so the buildings improved and they discovered a seemliness that displayed an exotic affluence. The occasional house painted in bright cheerful colours, others with sturdy frontages. And, although smelling sometimes overwhelmingly at intersections, the sewers were covered, the drains disappearing below ground.

The town behind the docks was far larger than it appeared from the sea and was far more prosperous away from the seafront. Long, wide thoroughfares crossed each other at odd intervals, giving glimpses of richer homes and cleaner shops. The coach rattled on its way passing through large open squares home to ornamental fountains and small trees, some having benches for the local residents to take their ease.

Anders, who had found it strange that four horses had been needed to pull the coach, discovered the reason before long. The carriage progressed along the first of many steep winding roads through the richer end of the town, leading to the plateau above. Here the style of dwellings changed from one house to the next, no two the same, showing a difference in cultures, denizens from many other countries had settled in Griffin Town. Some had small gardens planted with dogs tooth violets, nicotiana and orange calendula, with roses climbing the whitewashed fronts, dazzling in daylight.

Beatrix sitting on the swaying seat above and behind the passengers was looking forward to bringing Aidan and Augusta with them on the morrow. It was going to be fun exploring the town, all four together. But the exotica she espied in the shop windows would require a large purse, excitement already making her stomach churn. She glanced out of the corner of her eye at Anders. Would he accept a gift?

From her vantage point she watched as the townspeople went about their business, not all the inhabitants were poor dockworkers. Beatrix identified professional people wearing silk stockings and wide brimmed hats, married women wearing bonnets carrying parasols and rush baskets in their hands, and well-dressed children running about between the coaches and street stalls as youngsters did everywhere. The overall impression was of the well-to-do businessman in the western end of the town, with the poverty stricken dockworker mainly in the east, and in between the hard-working artisans upon which every commercial venture relied.

'Much like towns in Mantovar,' said Anders.

'Yes, smells different though,' replied Beatrix, 'but, have you noticed, not many people are smiling?'

'They do seem a bit anxious, don't they?'

The horses eventually reached the crest of the last slope and picked up speed across the headland above the harbour. The view out over the sea was magnificent even at dusk. The lights of the town sparkled, their brilliance mingling with the lights displayed on the many ships and boats at anchor, alongside the jetties and out in the bay. The beacon, though, outshone all from the eastern headland directly across the lagoon from their destination.

The home of Seneschal Portolan and his family was set in a large country estate, a high timber fence running for leagues around fields and woods. The wheels of the coach hummed along on the well-kept scarlet maple- and white poplar-lined avenue leading to the home estate. Uniformed sentries, standing at several vantage points along the winding driveway, watched the visitors' progress. These were hard men, well-armed with swords, crossbows and even large cudgels.

The home estate stood behind ten-foot high stone walls which abutted onto dense woods growing at the rear of the house. Through the woods ran a high fence patrolled at intervals by militiamen. The iron-gated entrance in the south wall opened onto a circular drive leading up to the main building, a large three-storey structure built of blocks of grey stone. Several chimneys stood proudly in line along its roof, one or two spouting black smoke almost invisible in the growing dusk. The front of the house boasted three lines of windows all fitted with glass and showing light. A narrow road led around to the rear of the house, presumably to the stables and servants quarters. A covered portico at the front led up a flight of steps to a set of heavy mahogany double-doors, and these were swung open to greet the visitors as the carriage drew to a halt.

A footman ran to open the carriage door and to unfold the steps for the passengers to descend. Anders and Beatrix were motioned down by the coachman and they stood at the rear awaiting further orders. Both were a little nervous, Anders more so as he had never attended a function such as this before. But Beatrix used his lack of experience as an excuse to hold his hand—Anders didn't mind.

Three people walked through the high doors to welcome their guests. Seneschal Portolan, although hatless, was resplendent in full uniform sporting a red cummerbund stretched very tightly across his ample waist.

Standing alongside him was a young, overweight boy with shoulder length brown hair. Taller than the harbourmaster, he looked about the same age as Anders and Beatrix. He was wearing tight dark-blue trousers to the knee, long white socks disappearing into black shoes with silver buckles, a white shirt ruffled at the neck and frilled at the wrists. Over all, he wore a coat of black watered silk again embroidered with the Griffin coat of arms. The whole magnificent effect somewhat marred by the vacant expression on the boy's face. His blue eyes stared straight ahead, seeing nothing.

The third person, a woman standing behind the boy giving the impression that she was the boy's bodyguard – which in reality she was – looked to be in her forties, small and motherly. Dressed a little dowdier than her companions she had an air of authority that the visitors only understood later.

Locklear, resplendent in his dark-blue Mantovarian uniform, minus his sword, etiquette barring guests from wearing arms in their host's home, descended the coach first followed by Tragen wearing a green robe, his staff in hand. The wizard turned back to the carriage to assist Lady Cornelia as she alighted. She was dressed in the height of fashion, a long green and white gown with a diamond necklace at her throat.

The seneschal stepped forward extending his hand to the wizard. 'Welcome, Lord Tragen, to my home,' he said, looking around the wizard, unable to take his eyes from Cornelia. 'This must be your lovely niece,' he said, strangely tense as he turned to her. Taking her hand he bowed over it.

'This is indeed my niece, Seneschal,' Tragen was somewhat surprised by the affect the lady-in-waiting seemed to have on the harbourmaster. 'Allow me to introduce Lady Cornelia.'

'It is years since this house welcomed such a beautiful lady, I am honoured.' He turned to Locklear, reluctantly releasing his hold on Cornelia's hand. 'Ah, Captain Locklear you also are welcome of course. Please allow me to introduce my son, Thaddeus.'

Cornelia, nearly losing her composure with the unexpected compliment, joined Tragen and Locklear in staring at the young boy. Tragen made to shake his hand—to have it completely ignored; the boy continued looking ahead as if he saw no-one in front of him.

'Unfortunately, Lord Tragen, Thaddeus has a medical problem. He has been unwell since his birth and is in constant need of care. This is supplied by me and his nurse, Mistress Barbat,' he indicated the third member of the welcoming party. 'Nevertheless, Thaddeus always joins me for dinner and I see no reason to exclude him this evening.'

The harbourmaster gazed at his guests, his hard eyes daring them to contest his decision.

'Of course he must,' Cornelia replied. 'It is an honour for us to meet him, and what an apt name to give him. You know its meaning of course, Uncle?' Tragen shook his head. 'It means "gift of the Gods" does it not, Seneschal Portolan? A lovely name, for a lovely young man,' and the large woman strode to the boy's side and took his arm in hers. There was no reaction at all from Thaddeus as he automatically accompanied Cornelia indoors.

Lodovico Portolan watched bemused, his response a picture of unremitting pleasure; totally bemused he was unable to cease smiling, his eyes softened as he followed Cornelia whose whole attention was now taken up by the boy.

All six moved into the main entrance hall of the house and ascended the dark oak-lined main staircase winding up from the left immediately behind the front doors.

Beatrix and Anders, of course, were not allowed to follow them up the main stairs and instead were taken to the right, through a side door into the kitchen. A small boy sat to the side of the fire turning a spit, roasting the huge joint of lamb suspended in the oval basket, fat dripping and spitting in the flames. The smell made Anders' mouth water and he earned a nudge from Beatrix as he licked his lips in appreciation. The cook/housekeeper, a miserable looking woman with a perpetual scowl on her face, led them on through another door recessed in the corner, into the servants' hall. Here they were told in no uncertain terms that they were to help carry the hot food up the side stairs directly into the banqueting hall.

Beatrix was surprised, as the servants of guests they also should have been treated as guests in the servants' hall. Nevertheless, she was used to seeing deplorable treatment of servants in big houses and she took it in her stride. She smiled at Anders encouragingly before he was tempted to complain.

'Tragen was right,' Anders whispered as they carried the hot soup tureens up the narrow stairs. 'I could never see Augusta putting up with being spoken to like that!'

'Quiet on the stairs!' the cook shouted from below.

Anders poked his tongue out and made a face nearly making Beatrix drop the tureen as she struggled not to laugh.

'That man you mentioned before, the Abbot of Sentinel, tell me about him,' asked Aidan, 'I only ever saw him now and then, and that was at a distance.'

Augusta shivered and settled herself more comfortably alongside him in their favourite place on the poop deck, the lights on the after-jigger shining down on them. Hopper was below on the quarterdeck, standing at the forward rail, his head continually turning, both to watch the activities on land and the business of the ship. The crew had been refused shore leave until the captain returned with more knowledge of the situation in the port. They went about their duties glancing occasionally up at the quarterdeck or over on the quayside, sharing the mate's apprehension.

'He's head of the monastery on Sentinel,' replied Augusta quietly, 'you know that island in the estuary of the river Mantovar. He's a tyrant. He rules the monks with a rod of iron; they aren't even allowed to talk with anyone outside the order. Abbot Cumbria's eyes are much the same as Seneschal Portolan's...cold and calculating,' she paused and bit at her bottom lip. 'The abbot's tall and very thin, he's bald, his cheekbones are almost sharp and they protrude alarmingly and he sneers all the time. But it's his eyes...they really are horrible.' She shuddered and leant a little nearer Aidan, nudging his shoulder. 'Perhaps I do Seneschal Portolan a disservice by likening his cold eyes to the abbot's. The seneschal is clearly a hard man but I don't think he's cruel; Cumbria is—he is brutal. I've managed to avoid him most of my life, only meeting him once or twice a year when my duties forced me.'

Aidan put his arm around her comforting, her distress obvious. 'Where did he come from?'

'No-one is quite sure, some say from Drakka, others from the east...I mean from the far side of the Scissor Mountains. One man I know said he was from Enzore in the southern mountains bordering Qula, but I don't think he's from there, everyone I've ever met from Enzore has been pleasant...Cumbria is certainly not. One or two whisper that he's from the north, but they won't say how far north.' She trembled again and Aidan held her closer.

'If he's that terrifying why did your father appoint him,' Aidan asked, puzzled.

'I don't know,' Augusta shrugged and turned her face to look at him and as she did her hair brushed his mouth.

They both swiftly became aware of how close she was being held and they separated a little, embarrassed. Aidan removed his arm from her shoulders and clasped his hands in his lap to halt the small tremor in his fingers. He had butterflies in his stomach, his feelings in turmoil he stared up at the headland, his master's destination. Augusta smiled to herself, she well knew the effect she was having on him, and then she realized he was having the same effect on her.

'The Abbot of Sentinel very rarely comes to the castle; he spends his time at the monastery when he's not travelling. When he does attend on my father it is always at night. The little I've met him makes me want to scream, those eyes of his…when he stares at me my skin crawls. I don't want to cross him.' Augusta sucked her finger in the corner of her mouth for a moment and then continued. 'You know something I don't think my father knows where the abbot is from. He turned up about twenty years ago, I believe, and has led the monks ever since.' She fell silent.

'Now it's your turn,' she said, changing the subject, she didn't want to think of the abbot any more. 'Tell me of your family,' and she nudged him playfully, 'and why you don't know your age.'

Aidan looked at her, her sparkling green eyes enticing; he smiled apprehensively, would she think less of him? It was no good lying to her she'd see through him straight away and anyway he didn't want to be untruthful. All her friends were of the aristocracy and would say what she wanted to hear, he didn't want such an obsequious relationship. But it was only the accident of having magical ability that would elevate him to the peerage when he finished his training—or when Tragen died. He shivered; he didn't want to even think on that. But he had still come from abject poverty and if Tragen hadn't found him he would probably still be living in the gutter. Would she think any the less of him if he told her? He knew her opinion of him mattered a great deal.

Thinking of the wizard he closed his eyes and thought back to the day he had first met his mentor. He'd been one small member of a gang of orphaned roughs in the large town of Miskim, a border settlement way to the north of Castle Mantovar. It had grown up on the edge of the Great Forest, in the foothills of the Scissor Mountains, the eastern border of the princedom. The market town was frequented by travellers from all points of the compass, by mountain men and plainsmen as well as the local farmers and drovers.

Occasionally a lone mystic ended up in the town after journeying many hundreds of leagues, not one of them knowing the reason for their visit, eventually leaving the town sometimes weeks later, confused and somehow bereft.

Aidan had lived on his wits and his unusual abilities. He'd no clear idea then how long his life had consisted of stealing from stallholders, running from irate innkeepers and sleeping rough in smelly hovels. Not that any so-called "victim" wished to punish him, for he had healing hands even though he was accident prone. People thanked the God, Tarria, for any encounter with him—once they'd cleaned up his mess.

But it had been a year after his mother died when Tragen caught him.

Aidan smiled. He remembered his mother as a warm, comfortable feeling, her long black hair smelling of lavender, always falling across his face when she cuddled him. Although he could no longer picture her face in his mind the fact did not seem to bother him. She had met her end after leaving him playing in the small lean-to they shared adjacent to The Scourge, an ancient tavern, across the road from the Moot Hall. His mother had been an enchantress of small ability, a hedge-witch usually employed to charm warts and other minor, unsightly disfigurements. She had gone to ply her trade in the local market and had never returned. His father he had never known although he vaguely remembered a light-haired man.

His life had changed dramatically when the old wizard caught him red-handed using magic to make a large, florid-faced man look the other way so that he could steal one of the newly baked pies off the stall in front of one of the only two bakeries in the town.

He didn't know he'd used magic. All he did was wave his hands about and sing and, lo and behold, he appeared invisible to the stallholder—or so he thought.

But he was still visible to the wizard. Tragen had seized him, and instead of turning him over to the village watchmen – who unknown to Tragen would have released him anyway it being an unspoken agreement in the town that the boy should always be kept fed and clothed – he had purchased two of the large and very hot meat pies, one for himself and one for the small boy.

But he had been cautious. As young as he was then, he had learned to run from strangers, especially strange men. But he was also insatiably curious and very hungry. He had never seen a wizard before let alone actually converse with one. And the man did look very funny in his long green robe and strange pointed hat, its brim ragged and flopping down around his face. With a long white beard that he had to keep flinging over his shoulder whilst eating – a ludicrous habit that had fascinated him and even now ten years later still brought a smile to his face – he and the old man had sat together on a bench in a corner of the main square. He had listened to the wizard's proposal as the succulent, thick gravy dripped down his chin, ending up splattering his already dirty, ragged clothes. And after a long discussion, and another pie, he'd agreed to apprentice to the wizard.

He was too young to realize what he was getting into, of course. He had never heard of apprenticeships and did not understand what they entailed. But at the promise of regular food and a warm bed, he thought he'd give it a try. Why not, if he didn't like it he could always leave.

But the watchmen had been called by concerned citizens and they would not allow him to leave until Tragen had satisfied them of his motives...fact that had surprised the wizard no end. There were many damp eyes watching the boy walk the road south.

'Aidan? What is it?' Augusta asked.

He breathed deeply and told her all of it.

His words shocked her, she'd had no idea. She stared at him, coming to understand now why he was so different to other boys she'd met.

'Tell me more of your mother?'

Aidan smiled; he always did when he thought of her. 'My mother was lovely...and warm and kind and always smelled of flowers,' he paused, staring into space.

'Go on...can you tell me what happened to her or would you rather not talk of it?' Augusta asked apprehensively, staring at his face she realized how very handsome he was even though he needed a shave.

'It's all right, it's just I don't know...I think she was murdered.'

'Murdered! Good God, Aidan,' and she put her arm through his and held him tight. 'How? I mean...I don't want to know,' she squeezed his arm against her and held his hand. 'Your father, do you know anything of him?'

'Only what my mother told me. For some reason she always cried when she talked about him. I remember that because I asked her once why she was always sad when I asked about him. She told me he was ill and that it was her fault. I asked her where he was, because if he was ill he should be in bed. She said he had to stay away from us because of the nature of the disease, I never understood that at the time. But I've thought it over many times since, and it could only have been some sort of highly infectious ailment, you know, like the plague,' he paused as she squeezed his arm again, comforting him. 'She loved him very much, though, everyone used to tell me they were joined at the hip…I'm not sure what they meant by that.' Why was he telling her all this? He'd never told anyone before.

'Why was it her fault that he was ill?'

'I've no idea,' Aidan stared off into space. 'But she said something else which makes me think it may not have been the plague.'

'What was that?'

'Something very strange…she said his illness made him forget me.'

Augusta was shocked, staring at him she didn't know what to think. 'What ailment makes you forget your son?'

'I don't know. Anyway, I went to live with Tragen, when I was five, I think.'

'So, little wizard, you come of age next year the same as me.'

'I suppose so, what difference it'll make, though, I don't know. Tragen allows me to make most decisions that affect me, already. It's only where magic is concerned that he treats me like a kid.'

'You love him, don't you?'

'Of course I do…he's my dada, not that one back in Miskim.'

'Do you think he's dead?'

'He has to be. I know there were plague victims dropping dead about then. We used to come across their bodies when we were hiding from the watchmen.'

She shivered at that and changed the subject again. 'Tell me about the storm. It must have been a very powerful wizard to create it. Why couldn't Tragen counteract it with his own spell of calming?'

'He wanted to, I think, but he realized the storm was far too great. So he decided to use a different spell…the shield. But he had to use his staff to aid him, and even that wasn't enough. It could not protect him fully as you saw when he fell; neither could it calm the storm sufficiently. To create a tempest that vast, several wizards must have combined the power of their staffs. Tragen and his staff alone

214

were not enough to beat them. And…and the more I think on it…' he paused, frowning, 'the more I think on it convinces me that he should not have been able to block the storm as he did.'

'What do you mean?'

'It's almost as if he was allowed to succeed—and that's what I meant to tell Tragen before he left.'

Augusta scared even more by this knowledge, held on to Aidan's hand tighter as they watched the sun go down.

For some reason he could not understand, Aidan was very happy then…just sitting there, arm in arm, her hand in his.

Eighteen

The banqueting hall was impressive, large, high-ceilinged and airy. Heavy oak panelling predominated on each wall, its darkness alleviated by two large, four-paned sash windows overlooking the drive. Twice as long as it was wide, the room held three tables, two running parallel to the long walls, each able to seat at least forty people. The third, placed across the heads of the other two, stood on a raised dais so that the occupants could see and be seen by everyone present.

The long mahogany head table groaned under the weight of food of all descriptions. Bowls of fresh oranges, pineapples and bananas evenly spaced along the surface accompanied at intervals with freshly segmented melons, yellow and green. Platters of newly baked manchet bread, cheese trenchers and bowls of nuts added to the rich aroma of roast mutton, beef and chicken. All was lit by two elaborate glass candelabra suspended from the ceiling on silver chains, the light reflecting off the solid silver tableware.

Portraits of Portolans past and present, hung along the walls, the faces with stern expressions except for the only painting of a female suspended directly above the fireplace in the long wall opposite the windows. The sunshine streaming through the glass during the day, would serve to emphasize the very happy scene that must have delighted artist, model and onlooker. The lady depicted was a very fat woman, with deep laughter lines around her eyes, dressed in a long green gown and wearing a large pendant in the shape of a griffin, on her chest. She was sitting upright in an armchair, her hands in her lap, smiling affectionately at someone who must have been looking over the artist's shoulder. In the place of honour behind the head table, hung a portrait of a man who bore a striking resemblance to the seneschal although it was of a much thinner man.

When Beatrix and Anders entered at the back of the room with their heavy tureens, the steward was pouring wine into silver goblets. Seneschal Portolan sat in a high backed chair in the centre of the high table, to his right sat Lady Cornelia, on his left, Lord Tragen, and on the other side of the wizard sat Captain Locklear. But the seneschal's eyes were concentrated to his right watching Cornelia helping Mistress Barbat to settle Thaddeus between them.

Cornelia, proving now why the Princess of Mantovar trusted her so completely with the upbringing of her daughter, was talking animatedly with the nurse. She had the true aristocrat's innate ability of putting people at their ease and Mistress Barbat, very happy and surprised to have Cornelia's aid, showed that she in no way resented the additional care given her charge.

The seneschal and the wizard were fascinated. Portolan with the fact that this very attractive stranger seemed so comfortable with his mentally abnormal son, a boy that he spent all his waking hours – and a lot of the hours of darkness – protecting from the world. And Tragen by how Lady Cornelia, without realizing it, had utterly beguiled their host. The wizard hoped it boded well for the future.

Dinner progressed with small talk, Seneschal Portolan continually distracted by Cornelia taking her turn at feeding his son and in keeping his chin clean of spilled food. And what was more important to Lodovico Portolan, and did more than anything else to unreservedly charm him, Cornelia did not ignore Thaddeus, did not treat him as a dummy but talked to him as if nothing was amiss.

Tragen asked the harbourmaster during a lull in the conversation about the gentleman in the portrait behind him.

'He is my brother, Paul…The Portolan, leader of our clan.'

'Will I have the pleasure of meeting him while I'm here?'

'I shouldn't think so, he is away at present, and not expected home for some weeks,' he answered, dabbing his mouth with his napkin. The hard look lifted by Cornelia's treatment of his son returned, his glacial eyes seemingly intent on unpleasant memories.

'And the lady in that portrait, who is she?' Cornelia indicated the painting above the fireplace.

'She is my wife, or rather was,' he continued, staring at the painting his eyes softening. 'She died of head injuries a few moments before giving birth to Thaddeus. Unfortunately, I am told by wizards,' and he looked at Tragen, 'that nothing can be done for him. He was birthed by the physician having to take him directly from his mother's womb shortly after her death. Wizards tell me that although Thaddeus is physically well, only his body came forth…not his soul. Thus he is as you see him.'

'By the Gods…never!' Cornelia said, shocked to her very core. 'I do not believe it.' She looked at Thaddeus and cupping his chin in her hand, she stared into his eyes. 'If he had no soul he would be totally wicked, this boy is not evil…never evil,' and tears welled in her eyes as she stroked his face.

The seneschal, surprised at her vehemence, stared at her for a moment. 'Nonetheless,' and he sighed, the despair of years in that murmur, 'that is what I have been informed. Do you concur with your colleagues, Lord Tragen?' He placed his napkin beside his plate, attempting to keep the anguish, and the hope, out of his voice and not quite succeeding.

'I could not possibly say without examining him. Will you allow me time alone with him, maybe tomorrow?' Tragen now realized why the presence of a wizard was so important to the man.

'Yes, of course. I will send my coach for you in the morning,' Lodovico Portolan composed himself and supped his wine. 'And now, Captain Locklear, I am remiss, tell me of this storm.'

Locklear glanced at Tragen wondering whether to divulge the knowledge of malign sorcerers being the cause. Tragen, understanding the look, imperceptibly shook his head. Locklear, beckoning Anders to refill his goblet, paused for a moment to collect his thoughts and to put them in the right order. Staring at his host he spoke in terms understood by seafarers all over the world. He told of the intensity of the tempest and their consequent battle to survive. He described the height of the waves, the strength of the winds and the lack of visibility leading to loss of position. Locklear, a born storyteller when imbibing good liquor – they were drinking Tragen's gift – went on for over an hour. He brought to life the terror and peril of those days, and he finished with the description of Tragen's shield spell which had saved them. He did not mention Aidan.

'And your immediate requirements, what are they?' The seneschal asked coolly as he used his small, razor-sharp, food knife usually kept in his belt when not eating, to cut a sliver of mutton, before dipping the roast meat into a small salver of pungent sauce.

'A dry-dock, if you have one?' At the seneschal's nod, he went on. 'We also require timber and caulking, ropes and canvas as well as food and water. And, we desperately need new masts.' Locklear sat back in his chair and again beckoned Anders to replenish his goblet.

'The dry-dock is going to be a bit of a squeeze. When we built it we did not envisage a ship as large as yours having need of it. But, with care it should suffice. Nevertheless, it is going to be a devil of a job to move it into place, my dock-master is going to have his work cut out,' he smiled wryly.

'We can supply everything except masts,' the seneschal nibbled a small wedge of cheese and continued. 'We have no trees

218

suitable on Griffin thanks to the Montetors tearing down the forests for their mines. Our masts have to be imported, now. You can always sail to the Onyx Isles for them, of course, a journey of some weeks I'm afraid. Should you have luck and fine weather, you might make it easily, otherwise…' and he shrugged his shoulders. 'But I think you should wait here while we send for them,' he glanced at Cornelia, a strange intensity in his eyes, 'they should only take a few months to arrive. I'm sure you know the reputation of those islands, Milord, I wouldn't be happy with the thought of your niece coming within a hundred leagues of those brigands.'

'I agree with you, Seneschal, Hugo has told me a great deal of those barbarians. But it is time that we're short of, we need to get home without any further delay,' answered Tragen.

'Then I don't know what you should do…you need masts, Onyx has them in abundance.'

'Can't we obtain new masts on Sanctity, that island is only days away, after all?' Locklear enquired, wondering why their host had not mentioned his neighbour.

Shocked silence greeted this request. Mistress Barbat gasped and put her hand to her neck as if she was suffering a constriction. The footman standing next to Anders nearly dropped the platter he was holding.

'I am sorry, Captain, but no-one is allowed to visit Sanctity without permission of the brethren who live there. And they never give consent to strangers.'

The seneschal, visibly shaken, abruptly placed his napkin on the table, the hard man's voice now barely disguising fear. 'It is late I'm afraid and I must see my son to bed. Lord Tragen I will see you in the morning. Captain, I will send an aide to you, he will assist you with the dockworkers.'

Rising from the table, he turned to Cornelia. 'My Lady, you must forgive and excuse me. Would you care to accompany your uncle in the morning? It would give me great pleasure if you would, and then maybe Thaddeus and I can show you our home.'

'Of course, I'd be delighted, Seneschal, and I thank you for a wonderful evening.' Cornelia smiled, careful not to show her astonishment at such an end to the conviviality.

Back in the coach long before they expected to be, Locklear turned to Tragen. 'Well, my friend, I did not expect that reaction.'

'No, he was terrified of something and I know not what. Could it be this torturer of Aidan's visions? It would certainly account for his fear. Perhaps Cornelia and I can ferret out an explanation from the nurse tomorrow,' he closed his eyes and leant back against the seat. 'Cornelia, you had a remarkable effect on the seneschal, did you not?'

'Did I? I didn't notice I was too busy with that poor boy—no soul indeed!' She stared at her feet, a slight colouring in her face, not admitting that the man had had quite an effect on her. 'Have you a possible diagnosis of the boy's problems?'

'Again we'll have to wait until morning. I don't hold out much hope, though, if the boy's brain is damaged, or again if the boy truly has no soul, then I know of no cure. But, of course, there's always Aidan...who knows? It does explain Portolan's worn appearance, though, the boy's condition must call for many a sleepless night.'

Above them on the hind seat, Anders and Beatrix listened to every word, knowing they would be closely questioned on their return. They looked at each other, gripping each other's hands tightly, neither wishing to acknowledge their growing trepidation. What on earth was on Sanctity? And how could anyone be born without a soul?

As soon as they arrived back aboard the Grim Locklear gave instructions for the morrow. He had come to the decision to lighten the ship to facilitate entry into the cramped dock. The ship needed to float higher on the water and, to enable this, the holds would be emptied, an immense operation that could take all day. Not many ports had a dry-dock the purpose of which, besides being a place to build new ships, was also to enable the hulls of older ships to be repaired or careened without the ship having to be heaved on to its side. In the dock, the ship would be propped upright in a cradle with the keel on supports. With the water pumped out of the dock there would be less abnormal stress on the hull and work on that part of the ship usually submerged, could be carried out swiftly and efficiently.

Locklear moved off with Hopper and Trumper to discuss the complex arrangements. It would be the first time that the Grim's hull had ever undergone repair to such a great extent and the opportunity to careen would also be taken. The three men wished to prepare for all eventualities.

Tragen, espying Aidan called him over, inevitably Augusta, Beatrix and Anders followed. The four were inseparable now and the wizard smiled...at least a part of his plan was working.

220

'Aidan, we have a strange ailment to diagnose and I want you to mull it over before Cornelia and I leave in the morning to return to the harbourmaster's home…'

'Can I come?' Aidan asked eagerly.

'Not yet, we still need to keep you and Augusta concealed, but if I do not succeed in discovering a cure, a way must be found for you to examine the boy.'

'What boy?'

'Wait, and stop interrupting, we have had a long night,' he paused. 'Tell me; is it possible for a baby to be born without a soul?'

'Bloody hell…what a question!'

'Well,' Tragen gave one of his mean looks which boded ill for his apprentice if he did not reply quickly.

He hurriedly answered. 'Of course not, whatever gave you that idea?'

'Never mind,' Tragen said. 'I expect your friends will tell you. When they have, I will appreciate your advice. Now goodnight to you all,' and he moved off escorting Lady Cornelia to her cabin.

'When you retire please do it silently, I do not want to be disturbed I have a lot to ponder on.' Cornelia said as she arrived at the door to step below. But she impulsively turned to Aidan and this time she implored. 'Please, Aidan, think on it well. It is imperative you come up with a diagnosis and a cure, the boy is suffering terribly and perhaps his father more so. Goodnight.'

'You two,' Augusta ordered Beatrix and Anders, waving her finger at them, 'to our cabin immediately. We want to know everything and I mean everything.'

'What! You really mean that the seneschal fancies Lady Cornelia?' Aidan asked, stifling a laugh.

Augusta poked him in the shoulder. 'And why not? Cornelia is a lovely person, warm and sincere and she is no idiot like some I could mention. And, what's more, the concern she expresses inclines me to think that she may have taken a shine to the seneschal…she definitely has to his son.'

Beatrix and Anders had been closely questioned for nearly an hour. A very harrowing experience, Augusta and Aidan taking turns at battering them.

'The seneschal's wife looked very much the same as Lady Cornelia…you know, big and fat and he talked of her with great affection,' Anders said.

'Please, Lady Cornelia's love life is not the most important thing here, the boy is and whatever is on Sanctity.' Beatrix said, highlighting the immediate problems.

'Sorry, Beattie, you're right. His mother died just before giving birth, eh! I wonder what the cause of her head injury was. He never said?' Aidan asked. The two shook their heads.

'Have you any idea what could be wrong with him?' Augusta asked.

'Not really, I'd only be guessing. I've seen babies born in the same circumstances before…you know from a dead mother. And they've always been brain damaged because they couldn't start breathing in time. They're murder to heal. It sometimes takes weeks because I'd have to heal each symptom in turn. And they have symptoms like drooling, slurred speech, and quite often, they are unable to use their limbs or raise their heads. Moreover, the healing has to be in a particular order, different in each victim. If I heal one thing in the wrong order then it may reappear later as another unhealed symptom affects it.' He paused and the others, not interrupting, watched as he pondered the situation.

'No,' Aidan continued, 'I can't understand this illness. He is physically well, but does not talk, do anything for himself except swallow and he acknowledges no-one. I can't diagnose this without seeing him.'

'And Sanctity? What troubled Seneschal Portolan about that place? Has anyone any ideas?' Beatrix asked.

'You're sure he was frightened?' Augusta asked.

'He was shocked rigid when he mentioned the island, and so were the others in the room,' said Beatrix.

'Aye,' added Anders, 'no-one wanted to know. The manservant standing beside me wouldn't even look my way!'

'So it seems likely that Beattie's assertion was right, that the storm was used to entice us here,' said Aidan worriedly. 'Whoever, or whatever, is on Sanctity that scares the harbourmaster so much could very well be the creator of the storm.' He looked around at everyone gravely. 'He could be the torturer I saw. When we reach Sanctity, none of us is to be alone at any time. We look out for each other, all right!'

That night Aidan and Anders talked well into the night, Aidan continuing to pump Anders of all that he'd heard at the Portolan's. But despite the cabin boy's unusual ability to perceive the deceptions behind people's facades, Anders could not discover the reason for the harbourmaster's fear.

Eventually Aidan gave up and both boys settled to sleep. It took them a long time and, unknown to each other, for more or less the same reason. Aidan recalling his time alone with Augusta, his arm around her shoulder on the poop deck earlier that evening. And Anders smiling idiotically as he dreamt of Beatrix—he could still feel Beattie's fingers entwined in his.

Nineteen

In hindsight people said it was an accident waiting to happen—that it should have been foreseen was without question.

The crew were hard at work emptying the forward cargo hold when Anders and Aidan came on deck the following morning. This hold, being the closest to the bows was the one that had suffered the most damage, boards had sprung in several places allowing water to pour in, ruining a substantial amount of the cargo. Although pumping had kept the water level manageable, wooden packing cases and canvas wrapped bails were still standing in water. A hoist had been rigged directly above the hold and men were removing the very heavy containers. Using slings, these loads were lifted on to the deck prior to transferring them to the dock using the derrick on the wharf. Leash was sat on the coaming supervising the two men below and the team above.

The two boys approached to watch the unusual activity and heard the shout from below that a crate on the hoist had burst open. The contents, which seemed to belong to the captain, were spilling out.

Leash called a halt leaving the crate suspended in its sling about twenty feet above the floor of the hold. Ever the one to take advantage of an opportunity to put Aidan in danger, he said. 'You, cabin boy, you and your friend better get down there and sort something out before the captain loses his belongings.'

'I'll have to see what's up, salvage what I can, wait here for me I'll go and have a look,' said Anders, making his way to the ladder into the hold.

'Hang on, I'm with you,' and Aidan trooped after him, both boys still bleary from their late night. If they hadn't been they may have had second thoughts.

Leash's eyes, gleaming as he watched the boys descend into the chaos below, wondered if this could be it—could this be the chance for which he'd been praying? Could this be turned into an opportunity to kill the apprentice? Glancing at the very insecure load on the hoist, he smiled, every nerve tingling in his body. On tenterhooks, every muscle humming with tension, he studied every man within sight on deck. Satisfied that his team were taking advantage of the stoppage to skive, he again stared at Aidan.

All he needed was good timing and a bit of luck.

Anders arrived on the floor of the hold and sloshed about thigh deep in the cold water, Aidan a little way behind. Both boys looked up at the broken crate swinging gently above them. The iron straps girding the crate had pulled through the rotten timbers, opening gaps for canvas wrapped bundles to fall through.

'Some of these are the Bear's journals, some his spare clothes…God, there's even a few charts here,' said Anders, 'quick, pick them up before the water destroys them.'

Wading around in the dim light, the two boys wandered back and forth beneath the overhanging crate not realizing the danger created by the very unstable load.

Leash, bending over the hatch coaming watching them, bided his time his eyes burning into Aidan's back. Every muscle in his body was at breaking point with the stress, this time he was going to succeed—he could feel victory in his bones, and he relished the agony that was about to befall his enemy.

Revenge was going to be so sweet, all these years of loneliness and despair, of unutterable grief—all caused by the wanton actions of an old man. Before he'd come along life had seemed, if not exactly normal, at least safe and loving. Oh, he'd loved—deeply and passionately and had been loved equally in return. But now he was condemned to eternal damnation, everlasting abandonment and isolation. If only the old wizard had waited—just a few more moments! But it was no good looking back "if" was a big word, a big, useless word. His life now was full of danger, being discovered a perpetual risk. The wizard had doomed him to a hopeless, demonic existence.

No-one else was taking any notice of what was happening in the hold, those men on deck not holding the rope were taking a breather, they didn't care about the hold-up, it was Leash's job to control the hoist. The man in the hold who had shouted earlier had his back to the boys and with his mate was busy inspecting another crate in the far corner, preparing it for lifting.

The two boys continued their salvage operation, clambering amongst the cargo, struggling in the brackish water. Leash had to be very careful now; Aidan and Anders were wearing identical shirts and britches—their difference in size indistinct from up on deck. But this didn't worry Leash; he had not taken his eyes off Aidan for more than half a second the whole time. From the moment Aidan stepped over the coaming and descended the ladder, to watching him retrieve the sodden possessions, Leash, obsessed with retribution, awaited his chance.

But self-preservation was also very important to Leash. If what he was about to do was witnessed by another! He had to check where his team were and what they were doing before he could take advantage of the situation. He hurriedly glanced around; the nearest men on deck had no line of sight into the hold. He looked up into the rigging; the only men aloft were working on the jigger mast further aft, again he was unobserved. He sighed as mania – and something else – glinted in his eyes, he was satisfied he could do the deed and no-one the wiser.

But in the moments his eyes were off the boys, Aidan and Anders had changed places.

'All right, you lot,' Leash ordered the men on the end of the rope, 'secure the line while they recover the captain's property.'

Leash held his hand near the rope as if he was preparing to steady the load while the men tied it to the rail. But, as the second helmsman knew, the rope was bound to swing a little, and when it did Leash feigned his grasp on the rope.

Afterwards witnesses, even those who were very wary of him, swore on oath that Leash's intentions were to halt the movement. But in actual fact, by grasping the rope, Leash caused the load to rock even more—the broken crate shook in the sling and it fell apart.

The contents and the crate fell directly on top of Anders. An iron strap struck the cabin boy across the temple knocking him senseless, and as he fell to the floor his head slid below the water. Debris rained down on him, crushing his body, holding him submerged.

There was pandemonium from above as Leash ordered men below to assist, and in the hold mayhem as Aidan and the two sailors working in amongst the cargo, rushed to Anders' aid.

Aidan managed to get to him first, and kneeling amongst the wreckage he plunged his hands below the surface and raised his friend's face clear of the putrid water. Placing his hands either side of Anders' head, at his temples, he held his friend's face clear.

Frantic shouts and pounding feet on the deck brought Augusta and Beatrix from their cabin. As they arrived on deck, Trumper shouted up to Locklear on the quarterdeck that one of the boys had been seriously injured. Augusta and Beatrix raced to the hold and, desperate to ascertain the circumstances, pushed crew members out of their way and peered over the coaming into the murkiness below.

'Who is it? What's happened?' Augusta shouted. 'Will someone please tell me…please?' She was afraid, mortally afraid that something had happened to Aidan, an icy lump formed in her chest, she could hardly breathe. The fact that her friend Anders could possibly be in danger never even crossed her mind.

Beatrix, pushing around Augusta, grabbed hold of Jason, the ship's minstrel making his way down the ladder to help. 'Jason, who is it, tell me please, it's not Anders is it? Please tell me it's not, I…' her voice getting shriller by the minute. She, like Augusta, never thought of the other.

The veteran sailor looked up at her, his face grim, he breathed deeply afraid to tell her. 'Aye, Miss, it be young Anders,' and the panic in her face spread, her body trembling from head to foot. 'A crate fell on him, his body is…his body is beneath the full weight of it, and he's been knocked unconscious. But the wizard's boy has saved him from drowning,' he paused and put his hand over hers. 'Be brave, Miss,' he said quietly, and releasing her, he descended the ladder.

'No!' She screamed. 'No! I have to see him, out of my way.' She charged roughly past another man who was about to climb down. Taking his place, she was quickly followed by Augusta, feeling relieved that Aidan was not the victim and desperate because Anders was.

And as they descended the ladder, Tragen and Locklear arrived both wasting no time in following the girls.

The scene in the hold was a nightmare. Lanterns hung from the deckhead or were held in swaying hands, shedding a wavering light on the two boys in amongst the wooden crates and canvas bails.

Aidan was sitting up to his chest in the water, cradling Anders' head and shoulders, the boy still unconscious. Water was occasionally lapping at the lower part of Anders' face, swilling around his mouth whilst men struggled to remove the debris holding his body trapped. Blood, seeping from the cut on his forehead where the strap had hit him, was dripping down over closed eyes.

Beatrix knelt to one side of the boy she adored, and took on the task of mopping the blood from his head with her kerchief, at the same time gripping his hand tightly. With tears running down her face, Augusta, kneeling the other side of him, kneaded Anders' other hand trying to bring warmth into freezing fingers.

'Heal him, Aidan, please heal him,' Beatrix kept repeating over and over, the litany almost hypnotic, tears streaming from her red eyes.

'Can you, Aidan?' Augusta asked, as desperate as her companion. 'You healed Cornelia; you must be able to do the same for Anders,' and when he didn't answer, she shouted, despairing. 'Come on, do something please, don't just sit there.'

'Leave him be, girl,' said Tragen standing over her. 'That is what he is doing. Look at Aidan's eyes, he's not with us…he's with Anders.'

Silently they watched while Aidan, ignoring all around him, concentrating his whole being on his best friend, palpated Anders' temples, his lips moving soundlessly. After moments that seemed like hours, the apprentice wizard inhaled sharply and looked up at the people surrounding him. 'His skull has been fractured and there was bleeding into his brain, it's sorted now,' he smiled hesitatingly at Beatrix. 'I've stopped the bleeding and his head has started to heal,' he stared at his stricken friend, her grief and misery almost making the tears flow in his own eyes. 'Next, we have to be very careful not to move him until I have checked for crush damage to his chest and abdomen,' his smile encouraging. 'Beattie, he's feeling a lot easier now, honestly.'

'Remove those timbers gently, boys. We do not want any more accidents to befall him,' ordered Locklear, the normally impassive man allowing his emotions to get the better of him. 'I have had the care of my cabin boy, for three years now…I do not want another in his place, yet.' This was the nearest he had ever come to expressing fond feelings for his nephew.

'Hey, Aidan, did he nearly say that he liked me, then,'

*'Aye, I think he means he loves you, you idiot, so don't…*bloody hell you're mindmelding!' Aidan exclaimed out loud, utterly shocked. 'Master, did you hear him?'

'Yes, I can't believe it,' Tragen said, astonished.

'Hey, don't ignore me, you two. Can you hear me, Augusta?'

'Yes, Anders. Yes! Oh, Anders, how are you feeling?'

'Can Beattie hear me?'

'Can you, Beattie?' Augusta turned to her.

'Can I what?'

'You can't hear Anders mindmelding, can you?' Aidan asked.

'Is that what he's doing? But he can't mindmeld, he's never been able to,' and then she realized what it meant. 'Oh, my God! Ask him if he's all right, I have to know…please,' she begged, roughly drying her eyes on her wet sleeve.

'You ask him, he can hear you even if you can't hear his answer.' Aidan looking at her, knowing how desperately she needed to hear him, suffered with her.

'Tell her I'm feeling a lot better now with that weight off my chest…hell, I could hardly breathe.'

'Are you in pain?' Augusta asked aloud, so that Beatrix could hear.

'Not so much now. Go on, tell Beattie, I don't want her to cry anymore,' said Anders.

'He's recovering now, Beattie, he's giving us orders again,' and at the doubtful look in her face, Aidan added. 'Really, he's in a lot less pain. I'm only keeping him unconscious so that he doesn't move before I say it's okay. I'm going to have a look at his chest now and then check the rest of him, once I've done that we'll take him on deck, all right?'

'He's going to live…truly?' Beatrix asked, tears continuing to fall unashamedly.

'Aye, now leave me alone for a while so I can get on with it.' Aidan again placed his arms around Anders' chest, spreading his fingers to cover as much of Anders' rib cage as possible.

An hour later, Aidan had examined all of Anders' injuries and had caused the healing to commence in each. Locklear arranged for a board to be placed alongside and Anders was lifted gently and strapped to this. Extreme care was taken in hoisting him to the upper deck where he was lowered to the boards alongside the broken mainmast where there was ample room for everyone to crowd around.

Beatrix and Augusta again sat either side of the prone boy holding his hands. Both girls, red eyed from their weeping, now feeling a lot happier with Anders at last in daylight and in the dry. Everyone waited for Aidan's next move, no-one wanting to leave the cabin boy until he had woken.

And, as the moments passed in silence, Augusta realized that Aidan was not doing anything, making no attempt to bring Anders around. She looked up at the boy who had worked so hard to save the life of his best friend—and saw tears streaming down his ashen face.

'What is it, Aidan?' Augusta asked softly, very puzzled. Getting no answer from him, she repeated her question. But this time she sensed something she knew she didn't want to hear. 'Please,

Aidan, please you're frightening me again,' and everyone turned to look at him. 'Aidan what is it? What's wrong?' She stood up and moved closer to him. But when she put her arm around his shoulders he shuddered and nearly fell. He leant against her shoulder for a moment and his trembling made her shake.

'*I want you to wake me, Aidan. I must speak to Beattie, and I want the Bear,*' Anders implored. '*I know what's happening to me, Aidan, and I must speak to them now…you know I don't have long.*'

'What is he talking about?' Tragen asked softly, foreboding in his mind.

Aidan stared at his master and his friends, catching Locklear's eye he knew he was about to devastate all those close to Anders. Locklear, the man who looked on his nephew as the son he never had, Beatrix who was clearly very much in love with him, and Augusta, their princess, who had also come to love him as a very close friend. And Tragen—who loved Anders simply because he was Aidan's closest friend.

Aidan's voice broke. 'Master, why are the Gods so cruel?'

Tragen stared at his boy, realizing at last the dreadful outcome. 'We do not know their purposes, my boy,' he answered softly. He placed his palm to Aidan's face and stroked gently, feeling the beginnings of adolescent bristles. 'Although strange purposes they have without a doubt…some we will come to understand, many we will not,' he continued gently.

'*Hurry, Aidan, tell them and wake me,*' ordered Anders.

Aidan tore himself from their arms and knelt beside Anders. Placing both his hands over the eyes of the comatose boy he chanted under his breath and Anders awoke.

Aidan, resting back on his haunches, watched as Beatrix, bewildered, smiled through fresh tears. 'You're going to be fine, Anders,' she said, cupping his face in her hands and sniffing. 'Aidan has healed you, now. Everything's going to be fine…rest now. Oh, Anders, my love, I was so worried; I thought you were going to die, but you're going to be all right now,' and crying, she leant forward and hugged him.

'Sh! Beattie, no more tears…please.' Anders said, holding her tight and caressing her back while looking up at Aidan. 'And you, Aidan…cease your weeping. You know I'll be safe.'

'Aye, so you will be.' Aidan's voice broke again. 'But I won't be with you,' he moaned and didn't attempt to hide the tremble wracking his body. Utterly distraught he stared down at his friend, unwilling to take his eyes off Anders' face.

Tragen knelt alongside him and again put his arm around Aidan to comfort him, the wizard understanding and despairing at his boy's abject grief.

'What do you mean?' Augusta asked a dreadful premonition taking root she also fell to her knees alongside them and reached over to grasp Anders' hand.

Anders took his eyes from Beatrix for a moment and smiled at his prince's daughter, a friendly aristocrat...one that saw him and, unlike the others of her class, did not look through him, a friend that he loved dearly. And then he gazed up at the man who he looked upon as a second father, perhaps an even better father than his first—his uncle, the man he had most admired in all of his very short life.

Hugo returned his gaze, mortified he also suspected the dreadful outcome.

'Uncle Hugo,' Anders said, taking his hand from Augusta's and holding it up to grasp Locklear's.

Locklear, not wanting to believe what he was seeing and hearing, knelt alongside Augusta, tears welling in the big man's eyes. 'Ah, Anders, it's come to this, eh! I'm sorry, my boy, so sorry. We have not had enough time together, have we? I wish there was more.'

'But the time we have had has been magic. I've loved every bit of it, I would not have missed it for anything,' he paused to take a breath and to hold back on his own tears. 'I am the luckiest boy ever, to have had a captain such as you. I do love you, Uncle, never forget that!'

'And I, Anders, I love you...I'll miss you so much,' Locklear fought his tears unsuccessfully.

'What is going on?' Beatrix shouted desperately, her face ravished she had no more tears to shed. 'Anders, Aidan has healed you. Why are you talking as if he hasn't? Stop it! Stop it, now!'

Anders stared into her eyes and grasped her hand even tighter as he brought it to his lips. 'My dear, Beattie...I love you...there,' he smiled up at her, 'I actually found the courage to say it.'

'Anders...my dear, dear Anders, I love you too, you know that please stop this talk, you're scaring me!' Beatrix begged.

The prone boy inhaled deeply and stared into her eyes. 'My Beattie, you are right, Aidan healed me. He did all that he possibly could, and eventually I would have been as good as new, but...' he gulped as he looked at the only girl he had ever loved. 'He could not prolong my life Beattie—my time has come.'

'No, Anders,' she giggled hysterically. 'No, Anders, you're being silly, stop it, stop talking like this...we have years yet, we're only young, please...I mean...'

'Beattie, my only love,' and he cradled her face in his hands, interrupting her protestations. 'Beattie, what will be, will be. I'm sorry. Aidan is not a God however much he wishes it at this time. No, my love, please...promise me...promise me that you will not grieve for too long.' He stroked her face, losing himself in her eyes. 'Thank the Gods I've had the time to tell you I love you,' and he kissed her, putting all his pent up emotion in that, their first kiss.

The others looked on silently, in appalling misery.

'Aidan, there really is nothing to fear, is there?' Anders asked apprehensively; fear taking momentary hold he glanced quickly at his friend.

'Nothing at all, Anders, you will be welcomed into Paradise with open arms,' Aidan replied, still unable to halt his weeping or keep his voice from shaking. 'I thought we'd always be together, Anders,' he said, giving in to his despair.

'Aidan, remember the first day we met? You asked me how long we'd be friends.' Aidan nodded, unable to speak.

'Ask me again, Aidan.'

Aidan stared at him not caring who heard him crying. 'Anders...Anders, how long...how long are we going to be friends?'

'Forever, Aidan!' And with that Anders pulled Beatrix to him, held her tightly in his arms and for the second time kissed her.

And breathed his last.

Twenty

Later that afternoon Augusta and Beatrix sat with Aidan while he stitched Anders into the burial shroud. The stretch of old canvas and the heavy boulder to be sewn in at the feet – to ensure the body sank to the bed of the ocean – had been supplied by Trumper who also told him to place the last stitch through Anders' nose. When Aidan had looked at him in horror he had gone on to say it was tradition, to confirm that the body was dead—the pain of the large needle piercing the nose would surely awaken anyone. Aidan, realizing that old Trumper meant well, forgave and promptly forgot the barbaric instruction.

But he couldn't get Anders' last words out of his mind and he thought again on the promise they'd just reaffirmed. The oath they'd sworn on that day ten years before when he'd first come across Augusta and Beatrix—and Anders playing with a small boat.

He'd had no idea how he and the wizard had travelled the distance between Miskim and Mantovar in so short a time, magic probably, but being young it hadn't overly concerned him. It had been the day following his arrival at the castle a week later, that he'd met those who would have such an impact on his life.

He'd risen early from the floor beside his bed that morning. Only ever having slept on a palliasse and then on anything he could find, he'd found the mattress on his new bed too soft, so he'd discarded it in favour of the hard boards. He'd donned the new britches and shirt he had placed on the only chair in the room the previous night. But as for the new sandals he took one look at them and had left them under his bed preferring to go barefoot.

Leaving his chamber he'd tip-toed quietly into the large sitting room. Finding it empty he'd glanced about quickly and walked across the floor to the door of the wizard's chamber. Opening it gingerly he peeped into the second bedroom of the lodgings that he was about to share with the wizard for the Gods knew how long. He'd found Tragen in a large four-poster bed its canopy made of some heavy, brightly dyed fabric, ruffling in time with his snoring. The immensity of the high mattress had amazed him and he'd stared goggle-eyed at it for moments before closing the door.

Turning back he had inspected his new surroundings—the table bearing books and parchments that the evening before the old wizard had informed him he'd be taught to read. The deep straw-filled leather chairs he'd relax in although he couldn't imagine ever doing such a thing, the long-piled carpet on the floor, the wizard obviously liking his comfort. He'd walked across to the heavy oak door and opening it had peered into the wide and quiet corridor.

He'd glanced back at the wizard's chamber wondering if he should tell the wizard he was off out, but thought better of it. There was no need to wake him to seek permission to go wandering the castle that was now his home. He'd been warned there were certain rooms and corridors that he was not allowed to enter. Those were the royal quarters and the government halls and so he'd set off for the castle kitchens. He'd noticed them and the large woman reigning supreme over her staff the night before and instinctively knew that if he ingratiated himself with the cook he'd never want for anything.

Emerging eventually into the courtyard he'd found the castle's owner on his great white steed, and his retinue which included a small open carriage conveying two little girls. He had stood at the roadside for a time watching them ride past; he'd been a total stranger to such finery, then. He wasn't now of course, these days he was at home with the aristocracy and peasant alike. But at that time everything he saw and heard astounded him.

He was in a different world.

He'd stared brazenly at the very pretty girls, Beatrix with long blonde hair tied in a plait down her back, Augusta with shoulder length black tresses hanging loose. He'd been mesmerized, never having seen such visions of innocence. The young ladies seemed so magical in their white lace dresses, they were fairy princesses and heroines in a story told him by his mother at bedtime.

Augusta had caught his eye and, although she was used to being stared at, she didn't usually take much notice of who did the staring. But for some reason this boy's look was different. She'd guessed who he was having heard her father and the wizard the night before discussing Tragen's "find". But when she'd caught his eye she'd felt a very peculiar attraction and this unnerved her and so the devil had gripped her and she'd poked out her tongue at him.

Aidan had been so surprised he automatically stuck his finger up in a very rude gesture. Then, realizing that there could be nasty consequences, he had ducked behind a haywain travelling the other way. But being naturally inquisitive, as all boys are at that age, he followed a little way down the slope until his very short legs grew weary trying to keep pace with the procession.

As the falconry party moved on towards the ferry with the little black-haired girl holding what appeared to be a blood-stained kerchief to her nose, he had fallen back out of sight. It had been a few years later he'd realized that he was responsible for causing the bleed; he still suffered pangs of conscience, albeit small ones for Augusta had irritated him something chronic over the years!

It was then he had espied the perfect lair. A late-flowering oleander, its white blooms very bright in the sun, had taken root at the foot of a long grassy slope leading down from a small postern door set into the eastern wall of the huge castle. The large shrub had grown wild about twenty yards from the banks of a gurgling brook, a tiny tributary of the main river on which the town and castle of Mantovar stood.

Throwing away the stump of an apple he had taken from the castle kitchens at the behest of Mistress Chloe, the cook, he had settled down amidst the branches to watch the busy world go by. Very little sound reached him from the rambling town. Only the occasional clash of swords and pikestaffs drifted on the breeze as knights and men-at-arms trained in the castle yard. Further east across the busy river, a peregrine falcon was flitting high and low in the clear azure sky. The Prince of Mantovar was out flying his favourite bird near the Great Forest.

He had been hiding in the bush for about half an hour when the big blond boy arrived and stretched out face down at the slow moving stream.

Aidan had raised his head slightly to see what the other was doing, inadvertently shaking a small branch as he did so. He remembered holding his breath in case the other heard. He relaxed as the big boy carried on humming to himself, he'd moved silently or so he'd thought. But the big boy had big ears.

'You can come out now, if you want to,' the big boy had said out of the blue, not taking his eyes from the water. Getting no reply, he'd turned his head to peer between the blooms, screwing up his eyes against the sun. 'I saw you arrive yesterday morning with Lord Tragen…he's a friend of my father's. You don't have to be afraid of me.'

Aidan had bristled at the suggestion of fear after all he'd survived amongst a gang of much bigger boys for the last year. 'I'm not afraid of you,' he said bravely, 'how did you know I was in here?'

The big boy glanced around quickly again and then returned his attention to the water. 'A family of field mice live under there, and they always come out when I play here. They haven't come out today so they must be hiding from something, and then I heard you moving.'

'Yeah, all right, but how did you know it was me?' Aidan had persisted.

'You smell differently from the rest of us.'

'I don't smell. I had a bath last night!' He had taken offence at that.

'Exactly! Anyway, that's a daft place to hide, that bush is poisonous. Are you coming out now? I don't much like talking to twigs and leaves.'

He'd climbed out from between the branches, snagging his new britches and went over to the brook warily. He sniffed, smelling the horse dung clinging to the boy.

'What are you doing?' he asked, wrinkling his nose and watching a small model of a boat floating on the surface.

'I'm sailing the high seas!'

'Don't be silly, the sea is hundreds of leagues from here, isn't it?'

'Ah, I know that, you know that, but my ship doesn't,' and he pushed the ship along the surface with one hand while he used his other hand to make small ripples on the surface of the weed strewn water.

'That's a good ship, that is. Can I have a go?' The small boy asked eagerly, overcoming his nervousness.

The big boy paused and looked up at him. 'How old are you?'

'Five, I think,' answered the small boy.

'All right, as we're the same age,' and he pushed the ship towards Aidan now squatting alongside him. 'If you were older I wouldn't have let you.'

'Why's that?'

'Big boys break things for spite. I want to keep my ship until I go to work on a real one.'

They'd been silent for a while, happy just pushing the ship back and forth between them, the sun glinting on its small greenish-brown sail made from a small oak leaf. A gentle breeze ruffled something sticking out of the big boy's pocket.

'What's that?' Aidan asked, pointing at the parchment nearly falling from its place in the seat of the boy's britches.

'This? Oh, that's a puzzle my mother sets me every now and then.' He withdrew it and flattened it out on the grass, displaying a charcoal drawing. 'She calls it a labyrinth,' he replaced it in his pocket.

'What's a labyrinth?'

'It's a maze…a mixed-up path. She says it'll teach me to watch where I'm going. Are we going to be friends?'

'I don't know. I've never had a friend.'

'Right, then we'll be friends. I don't have a real friend either, only my brothers and they don't count. My name is Anders, what's yours?'

'I'm Aidan,' and then, after a long pause, he asked hesitantly. 'How long are we going to be friends?'

Anders, perplexed, looked at him. 'Forever, of course!'

That promise hadn't half got them both into trouble—and out of it!

The last few hours had been a total nightmare. Beatrix had to be torn from Anders' arms utterly bereft. Locklear had stalked off like thunder to his cabin…no-one had the courage to see how he fared. Augusta, fighting her own grief and failing had said a light had gone from her life, and had taken charge of Beatrix—both girls sitting silently arm in arm watching Aidan.

Cornelia came down from the quarterdeck from where she had witnessed the awful scene. Taking Tragen aside she had informed him she had sent the harbourmaster's coach away with their apologies, the bereavement too much of a shock.

'Ah, Cornelia, you did right I had forgotten we were due there this morning. We must ask the seneschal if we may borrow a barge to take Anders out beyond the reef to bury him,' he gazed at his boy. 'Come let us see to it now. I'm afraid I cannot linger here another moment,' and taking her arm, both Cornelia and Tragen, his eyes glistening, moved off leaving the youngsters to share their grief alone.

Leash was in the galley in his usual place beside the stove, sweat running down his face. He was in a terrible, black rage. He had been questioned by Hopper and Trumper for hours and had been forced to act full of remorse and even to weep. But all the time, inside, he raged. He hated Aidan now just as much as he loathed Tragen.

He wondered at the boy's phenomenal luck—couldn't the boy be killed? Was there an unknown spell protecting him? Were the Gods guarding him? It certainly felt as if there was a guardian angel looking after him. Leash's infection was getting worried. Leash now had a serious problem; he had to kill the apprentice very quickly before Aidan questioned the coincidence of the helmsman always being nearby at the time of his near fatal accidents. If Aidan didn't realize his involvement then those damn maids would—perhaps they also should have accidents? Thinking on three killings brought a smile to Leash's infection. Oh, it would be sweet, it thought, so sweet.

At his stove Dolly saw Leash smile and it sent a shiver down his back. He felt an overwhelming urge to ease the misericorde in his belt.

Hugo slumped in his chair staring out of his gallery window, not seeing anything as memories came flooding back to haunt him. He had never had any children. His wife had died giving birth to his stillborn son thirty years before and he had vowed never to love again...he could not handle the grief. And yet, looking back at their very short time together, Anders had grown close. The cabin boy had been his youngest brother's youngest son—how was he going to tell Anders' father that he had failed to keep him safe. How was he going to tell the boy's mother? Aidan was right—the Gods were very cruel.

Tragen walked into the cabin, disturbing Hugo's morose thoughts. 'Come, my friend, drink this,' and Tragen passed him a full mug of brandy, the same brandy that he had been hiding from Aidan and Anders. 'And if you don't mind I'll join you,' he settled into the seat opposite his friend, sighing he held his beard away so that it didn't jam down the side of the chair.

Hugo turned around, gazing at his friend through tears. 'You know, Tragen, I have not wept since my dear wife passed away. Who would have thought...' and he turned back to stare out of the stern gallery window. 'I thought the seventh son of a seventh son was supposed to be special—you realize that Anders was such a one?'

'Aye, Hugo, and Anders was special, a lovely lad with a heart of gold, we will all miss him terribly. It is not wrong to weep, Hugo. You loved your nephew as a son, so you should weep as a father

238

weeps. You would not be human if you did not. So weep, my friend, it will help. The harbourmaster has sent word to Cornelia that we may borrow his barge tomorrow to take Anders beyond the reef. So, tonight we talk of Anders…we drink…and we talk of him some more. In the morning we say our goodbyes.'

In the waist of the Grim, Aidan sat silently at his friend's uncovered head, the shroud pulled back from Anders' face. Augusta and Beatrix sat with their arms around each other, Augusta not trying to comfort the distraught girl, but attempting to obtain comfort for herself. The crew left them alone only Dolly bringing them burgoo and a pitcher of water. It was hours before they drank the water…they didn't touch the porridge.

The three friends maintained their vigil throughout the night, determined not to leave Anders alone, and resolved not to cover his face until the last possible moment. Sometime in the night, Aidan moved to sit between the two girls and he clasped them in his arms and the three dozed against the stump of the mainmast.

It was while they were sleeping that Dolly placed a blanket around them, not for the warmth it was a sultry night, but because Dolly wanted to show he also grieved for Anders.

And as Dolly left them sleeping at the mast he removed from his belt his misericorde and placed it deep within the shroud covering Anders.

'Take some protection, my boy, there be demons everywhere.'

The following morning dawned as it always did in these climes, sunny, warm and as the morning progressed, the humidity rising. It was mid-morning when the barge, black with gold trimmings, arrived off the larboard side rowed by its crew of six. It was handed over to Hopper by the very tall man who had accompanied the seneschal on his visit two days before.

'Good morning, Lord Tragen, my name is Janne, my rank, Marshal, and I am commander of the harbourmaster's security forces. Seneschal Portolan sends his condolences and is happy to have you use his barge, although he wishes it could be in circumstances that are more pleasurable. He requests that you and the Lady Cornelia visit him as soon as you think fit.'

'Thank you, Marshal, my niece and I will gladly convey our thanks to him personally, hopefully tomorrow if not the day after.'

Tragen studied the huge man, dressed in a dark-blue uniform. Janne stood well over seven feet tall and had a physique to match, very broad shoulders and long, muscular arms, the huge haft of his immensely long sword fitting comfortably into hands the size of shovels. His most compelling feature though, was his eyes—deepest black and well experienced in hiding his thoughts.

Marshal Janne looked round at the crew standing at the rails and at those in the shrouds, all of them subdued as they waited for Anders' body to leave the Grim on his last journey. Taken slightly aback at the sight of the three friends with the canvas-draped body he turned to Tragen. 'He was popular, this boy?'

'Very…he was Captain Locklear's nephew,' replied Tragen.

'But unlike Thaddeus this boy could talk and had friends. Captain Locklear is more fortunate than Seneschal Portolan,' said Janne, an edge of bitterness in his tone. 'You wish my men to row the barge, Milord?'

Tragen glanced quickly up at the big man, taken unawares by Janne's plain-spoken comments. There was clearly more than security in the relationship between the harbourmaster and this man. 'If you don't mind, Marshal, I think the Grim's crew are forming a queue to man it. As I said earlier, Anders was a very popular shipmate and will be sorely missed by all aboard.'

Janne nodded. 'Those three with the body…particular friends were they?'

Tragen wondered what this big man was searching for, why this talk of popularity and friends? And what was his relationship with the harbourmaster if he could speak of the son like this.

'The four were inseparable they are grieving mightily,' he paused at a sudden thought. 'Thaddeus has no friends at all?'

'None, Milord, he cannot communicate in any way.'

'I have an idea. What would the seneschal say if I brought these three with me when next I visit? They will need a distraction in their grief and, who knows, a relationship may develop if we allow them to meet Thaddeus.' It would also be a perfect opportunity, he thought, for Aidan to surreptitiously examine the boy and hopefully diagnose the problem without Portolan discovering that Aidan and Augusta were wizards.

Janne stared at Aidan and the two girls for moments before answering. 'We have tried many things in the past, Lord Tragen, but allowing him time with his peers is not one of them. Forgive my asking, but are they trustworthy? They will not make fun of him?'

'Never! Besides, the boy Aidan has assisted me many times in healing and may notice something that I miss. You need have no worries for Thaddeus' well-being,' he studied the concern etched on the marshal's face and his curiosity got the better of him. 'Am I right in thinking that you also are very fond of Thaddeus?'

Janne stared into space for many moments before answering. 'I have assisted Seneschal Portolan in the rearing of his son since the day Thaddeus was born...yes, I also look on him as my son,' he paused. 'Very well, I will ask the harbourmaster on my return. In the meantime I will remain here while you bury your dead and then return the barge to its berth.' Janne moved off and, all of a sudden changing his mind turned back to Tragen. 'You mean this boy Aidan is a healer?'

'I did not say that,' and Tragen could see the momentary hope die in his eyes. 'Nonetheless, he has helped me many, many times in my healing and he has a certain knack for diagnosis. Let us await the outcome of their meeting before giving up hope, don't forget I, myself, have not yet made an examination.'

Janne, his eyes steely, nodded and walked off to give the burial party privacy and leave to carry out their sombre duties.

Aidan stood at the rail with his arms around Augusta and Beatrix watching Jason, Nkosi, Talbot and Dolly lift Anders on the board upon which he had been brought from the hold. Anders' face had still not been covered but needle and thread was sticking in the shroud at his shoulder ready for the task. The vast majority of the crew stood around the deck and some helped transfer Anders to the barge, laying him across the middle thwarts. Jason, Nkosi along with Talbot and Dolly and two other crewmen took the oars, sitting either side of the body. Locklear and Tragen stood in the prow and Aidan, Augusta and Beatrix sat in the stern at their friend's head.

The journey through the reef was calm and dignified but the short time taken to reach the chosen burial site had a detrimental effect on Beatrix. She could not take her eyes off Anders, his handsome face very pale under the morning sun, his blond hair blowing in the breeze, and her thoughts turned to what could have been. They had loved each other frantically for the short time of this voyage, although she believed she had always loved him, and still did. As the barge bobbed gently on the calm surface of the sea she fantasized on the life they

241

could have had together. Perhaps a farm…he'd loved horses, had learned a lot from his father, maybe a property by the sea…he so loved the ocean. And lots of children, Anders would have made a loving father and husband. And suddenly her loss grew too much for her to bear and she fell into a deep trance unnoticed by anyone.

Out beyond the reef they waited for Aidan to place the final stitches in the shroud. But before doing so, Aidan kissed his friend's forehead and was quickly followed by Augusta. Beatrix sat immobile; dry-eyed, she stared blankly at her dreams, grieving too much to weep as the others were doing.

'Beattie,' asked Augusta. 'Beatrix, do you wish to kiss him a last time?' Beatrix displayed no reaction and Augusta looked at Aidan anxiously. 'Do something she's in shock, she'll never forgive us if we don't wake her to make her goodbyes.'

Aidan, distraught with his own grief, searched Beattie's eyes; he was holding the needle in his hand. He laid the needle down on Anders' chest and leant across to her. Holding her head between his hands, he massaged her temples and delving into her head felt the depth of her extreme loss.

'Beattie, my friend, please don't get lost in despair, Anders wouldn't want that,' and he continued to gently palpate her temples as tears streamed down his face. 'Dear Beattie, you have friends here, friends who love you. Come back to us…please!' And he touched her forehead with his and began to sing, his voice both beautiful and terrible.

He sang a dirge that he remembered from his deep past. The dirge that had been sung at his mother's burial years before. And singing it brought him relief as the tears continued to pour down his face. Augusta joined them in their embrace; putting her arms around both Aidan and Beatrix she lowered her head against theirs. Beatrix shuddered, sobbing at last and her tears mingled with those of her friends, the tears of friendship and love falling on Anders' face. The hardened crewmen watching gave in to their own tears, as did Tragen and Locklear.

'Come, Beattie, kiss Anders before I cover him,' Aidan said, finishing the song for the dead. Beatrix stirred and lowering her head, she kissed Anders gently, imparting her love with her embrace. She pulled the shroud over his face and nodded at Aidan to complete the sewing.

The sound of the gentle splash as Anders entered the sea would remain with them until their dying day.

Back on board the Grim, Augusta and Beatrix went immediately to their cabin and slept in their clothes throughout the remainder of the afternoon and most of the night, watched over by Cornelia.

Aidan slept in his own cabin that he shared with Tragen. He also did not remove his clothes before getting into the top bunk. 'Master,' he said just before dropping off to sleep. 'I think you'd better repair your bed now. I can't go back to Anders' room...ever.'

'Very well, my boy,' and he took up his staff, pointed the knuckle at the hole burned into the middle of his bed, chanted, and the damage disappeared.

On deck the work continued to empty the fore-hold, Leash back in charge. He was still in a foul mood but people put it down to remorse at being responsible for the death of the cabin boy. At least those who didn't know him put that as the reason. A few others were very doubtful and kept their distance.

It started with a mumbling, and that is what woke Tragen. The wizard, in his nightgown and his hair mussed, lay on his back staring upwards at the bottom of the bunk on which Aidan was tossing and turning making incoherent noises. Tragen listened, in a quandary, not knowing whether to wake the worn out boy.

And then Aidan screamed long and loud and Tragen leapt from his bed.

He clasped Aidan to his chest while the boy continued screaming and thrashing about, breaking into a cold sweat his eyes starting from his head. Augusta, Beatrix and Cornelia arrived at the door as Aidan fell into a coma, the silence almost deafening—everyone staring in fear.

Aidan's neck stretched long and vulnerable, his head lolling back over Tragen's arm, his eyes staring blankly into space, his breath hardly detectable. For the first time in his long, long life Tragen was at a loss, he had no idea how to cope with this situation.

Augusta approached the bed and lifted Aidan's head into a more natural and comfortable position, placing it against the shoulder of his master.

Cornelia, gazing at Tragen, realized that the wizard was incapable of making any decisions.

243

'He is not dead, Lord Tragen,' said Beatrix quietly, breaking the silence she went to Aidan and stroked his brow. 'He will come around, Milord; the Gods would not let me lose another friend in so short a time.'

'Tragen what has happened?' Hugo shouted bursting in on them and then, stopping in his tracks, he saw the boy. 'By the Gods, what is happening on my ship?'

Tragen shook himself from his stupor. 'I don't know, Hugo, but something terrible has happened to him. He has had another vision, this one seems almost fatal...his mind wanders,' he stared at Aidan. 'I must do something now that I promised him I would never do.' And he kissed Aidan's head. 'I must heal him.'

'No!' Augusta and Beatrix shouted together.

'I must or I will lose him.'

'You will lose him forever, Milord, if you heal him,' said Augusta.

'He will never forgive you. You will be going against everything he believes in,' Beatrix added, 'I don't think he'd be able to live with it.'

'Then what do I do? Do I leave him to die? I cannot do that,' Tragen's eyes glistened. 'I cannot let him die without trying something to bring him back.'

'He is alive, Tragen, take heart from that and thank the Gods the contact with whatever now seems to have ended,' said Cornelia. 'Why not wait a while, see what he is like in a few hours? Hopefully he will rouse on his own. But I do believe the girls are correct—it would be the end of him if you healed him. Come, let him lie and we will take turns watching over him.' They lay Aidan to rest gently on his pillow.

'I will sit with him first,' said Tragen, trembling.

'No, my friend, you have suffered enough for one night,' said Hugo, 'it is now my turn to watch over you.'

Augusta and Beatrix stayed with their friend long after dawn broke.

Every colour under the sun and moon, all shades, bright and dim, in motion and still...shapes, tall and short, fat and thin, square and round, some with clearly defined borders others wavering and melting into its neighbour, the ensemble moving and pulsing and living as one. It was a panorama stretching ever higher and extending endlessly wide. The whole was a pageant that smelled of every scent imaginable, some sweet, some sour, others clean, yet some that were foul and it was emitting a demanding hum—a disharmony of voices muttering and animals baying.

He stared at the wall of colours for a long time not understanding at first, and then as dawn breaks to reveal a blue sky so his mind opened and he realized he was staring at the full panoply of Life.

And then he looked down.

His feet trod shorn grass, each blade the same length and shape as the one next to it, all bright green and shimmering with dew—an unnatural growth yet strangely comforting. He turned around slowly, his bare feet feeling velvet, his toes curling in the softness. Keeping his eyes on the grass he discovered small multi-coloured daisies, a vast profusion dotting the landscape, the aroma heavenly.

He lifted his eyes and peered ahead. Far in the distance was a pinpoint of light, bright in the extreme—hurting his eyes, blinding him yet he was not afraid. He looked at the ground nearer to him and blinked the soreness away. He was on the brow of a hill, one of many separated by denes and shallow basins.

He looked up the slope to his right and met an endless expanse of what was at his feet, a calming vista he breathed easily for the first time.

He turned and gazed down the slope to his left and his heart lurched for he felt dismay—utter desolation. At the base of the hill many, many leagues away was a sprawling darkness, a fog, a pulsating cloud of fear hovering, returning his stare, inviting his interest and his dread. Terror crept up on him, ice gripped his brain and horror constricted his throat. Struggling to breathe, he fell to his knees, the act tearing his eyes away from the obscenity…and his fear fled, normality returning and restarting the pumping of his heart.

The clarion call of the wall of colours behind him reclaimed his gaze and standing again, he stared for aeons at the scenes before him attempting to decipher the bewildering maelstrom of Life. He was entirely fascinated and yearned to be a part of the living picture, a wanting that could not be without finding the means to enter.

He walked away from the wall and tramped unhurriedly over the hills towards the light. He averted his gaze from the darkness at his left and the empty vista to his right, keeping his head lowered he was not blinded by the intense brilliance ahead. He searched for the way into the wall of colours in the ground he trod knowing instinctively that leaving Life behind was the only way of obtaining the knowledge to regain it.

He walked for hours over the cushioned grass, across the brows of many high and low untroubled hills and down into a myriad contented vales.

He did not thirst or hunger and did not remember either sensation. Fatigue was a feeling forgotten. The sun didn't exist here unless you desired it, neither did the moon nor the stars—was it ever night time here, he wondered? The warm breeze blew gently through his unkempt, black hair, he'd always liked that…so had his friend. They loved the smell of fresh flowers as well, clematis and honeysuckle especially and they grew in abundance in the fields all around here. A large stretch of yellow and red impatiens over to his right rapidly changed form and he was looking at different coloured heathers. He wasn't fussed on heather, but his friend loved the smell of erica.

He halted at the top of a higher than usual hill and inspected the scene at his feet. The grassy slope below reminded him a little of home, but the river was missing at the bottom and the castle at the top. His eyes were drawn relentlessly to the darkness at his left and, as he stared, fear again lanced through him making him double up holding his belly. He trembled and turned away, he needed to obliterate it from his senses—it shouldn't be here. In his world should be comfort and love—not fear and hate. He walked the brow of the high hill refusing to descend to the darkness, though it repeatedly called to him its voice almost hypnotic.

He looked to his right at the hills rolling away to the distant horizon. A huge albatross flew overhead, he paused, a memory niggling in the back of his head.

On he went over the short grass, an everlasting meadow beneath his feet, until an orchard appeared…apple trees, pear trees and sumptuous red cherry surrounding him on all sides, his friend's favourite fruits. Who was his friend?

And there, standing resplendent in the middle of the orchard dwarfing all others was a very tall tree, slim and elegant its branches arranged symmetrically and shining brightly in the sunlight, one of a kind it stood proud yet not boastful. It exuded life—and love. Did it beckon him? No, he thought, I am not yet ready and on he went enjoying peace and tranquillity and—loss?

He walked on down a slope, closing his eyes he relished the warmth, the softness beneath his feet and the comfort radiating in the air around him.

Until a feeling of absolute terror seized him, and trembling, he broke into a cold sweat.

He opened his eyes and discovered that the slope had betrayed him—had brought him to the border of the fog, almost near enough to stretch out his arm and touch the mist.

He fell to his knees, moaning in horror, his eyes inexorably drawn to examine the interior of the dark cloud, he shuddered the stench was appalling. There were shapes within and as he looked so the indistinct silhouettes seemed to beckon him, their cries of welcome discordant shrieks.

Amongst them he heard a lone voice calling sweetly, reassuringly, telling him there was no need to worry, no need for anxiety.

'Come,' it called in his head, 'come home!'

And then it was joined by others. He fell to all fours and started crawling towards the voices. His mind, completely focused on the mesmerizing cadences, he was oblivious to all around him. But when his hand touched the first traces of the mist he heard another shouting stridently in his ear and he halted.

'No, Aidan, don't go in there—that way is Death.'

From the depths of the recesses of his mind he recalled the second voice, but couldn't place it.

'Come, my friend,' the unknown first voice interrupted, 'come, peace and comfort awaits you.'

'No, Aidan, do not listen! It lies. Aidan, Aidan! I cannot come for you. I daren't go near the Darkness, it would take me. But you are stronger. Purgatory lies that way, turn away your real friends are waiting for you out here!'

Aidan stood up, his foot almost within the fog. 'Anders? Is that really you?'

'Yes, Aidan, come away, that place is evil!'

'Your friend is mistaken, Aidan. This is a place of tranquillity where you no longer need to be alone, or be afraid. Your father is on his way—your mother also. Come—be ready to welcome them, be a family again.'

Tears streamed down his face, the voice offered all he needed and he stepped forward slowly unable to make up his mind. But he'd be leaving Anders behind! Why couldn't he have his family and Anders—and Tragen? And then he remembered Augusta and Beattie.

'Come, my friend, they will all join you in time,' coaxed the first voice.

And then the stench was enveloped by the smell of lavender and he heard a woman's voice.

'My darling, turn away…return to us!'

Aidan shuddered and turned away from the dark mist.

Trembling, he walked back up the slope and strolled for what seemed like hours more and this time his ramble took him into another vale, a shallow basin larger than any before with a single magnificent oak tree growing at a crossroads in his path. One branch of the track descended into the blackness behind him, another over the empty hills ahead. A third travelled on his right to the wall of colours, a fourth on his left into the shimmering, hurtful light in the distance.

Sitting with his back to the tree and staring his way was Anders, smiling a welcome.

'Thank God you listened to me! Well, don't just stand there, come and join me,' Anders said, indicating a spot beside him.

Aidan sat silently for a while, the comfort he felt from the tree against his spine irresistible. He closed his eyes savouring the peace. A little while later he stirred and inspected his friend from top to toe.

'You're dead, Anders…how do you feel?'

'I feel as I want to feel…sometimes happy, sometimes sad, sometimes I'm hungry, more often not. How do you feel?'

'Confused, this isn't Paradise is it?'

'No, this is Limbo…my Limbo. It's a strange place…a wandering place of lost souls.'

'Ah, no wonder the grass looks as if it's been mown and your favourite fruits are the only ones I've seen,' he smiled. Anders' Limbo reminded him very much of home and then he thought of the implications of his friend's other words. 'Are there many souls lost here?'

'Not in my Limbo…I expect there are in other Limbos.'

'How many Limbos are there?'

'As many as there are lost souls.'

'Are they all like this?'

'No…everyone's Limbo is different except for this oak tree— this crossroads is the same in them all.'

Aidan frowned, his confusion was growing. 'Do lost souls remain in Limbo?'

'Aye, until either they discover the way into the light...or they are tempted into the Darkness below—as you nearly were. It can take an eternity to find your way out of here,' said Anders, sucking a blade of grass.

The two friends silently contemplated their surroundings. 'I thought you'd have passed over easily enough. What are you still doing here? Are you lost?'

'No,' he sighed. 'I did go through the Light.'

'What happened? What's it like?'

'Well, you were right! I was welcomed by everyone and everything. There was no longer any wanting in my life—it was there before me, everything I ever needed. And yet I never needed anything. Peace—I was home, really home!'

'Then what are you doing here?'

'I was sent back to wait for you.'

'Oh, then you are going to take me through? But the light hurts me.'

'I'm not here to help you into Paradise...only the dead pass through. You are not dead yet that is why the light harms you.'

'I'm not dead? But I'm here,' said Aidan, bewildered.

'The Darkness...that is what brought you here. The Darkness and its minions are abroad in Life and it brought you here through your visions of the evil you have encountered.'

'I recognized your voice just in time but who was the woman?'

'What woman?'

'There was a woman smelling of lavender—she also called to me.'

Anders threw away the chewed stalk and a knife, a misericorde, appeared in his hand along with a short stick—he commenced whittling. 'I have no idea, I only heard me. But I do know of another woman, perhaps she is the same, although I don't remember any particular smell about her...but, of course, there may have been.

'Aidan, you have to go back into Life and fight the Darkness—that is what I've been told to tell you.'

'Who told you?'

Anders shrugged his shoulders. 'I don't know who she is. She appeared in the Light one day, and informed me that I was to give you the message.'

'What do you mean "one day"…you've only been dead a couple of days?'

'Time runs strangely here, Aidan, sometimes it flows fast…sometimes slow. It can even move backwards if you wish it. But there is something else I have been ordered to do, as well.'

'Aye?'

'I must remain here in Limbo to watch over you and help when you need me.'

'What…to fight the Darkness? Why?'

'Because it's creeping up the slopes here as well.'

Aidan couldn't help it he shuddered at the horror of that fog. He gazed at his friend, perplexed. 'How are you going to help me if I'm alive and you're dead?'

'I don't know.'

Aidan laughed. 'You don't seem to know a lot. You haven't changed!'

'Watch it! I'm still bigger than you. I can still rub your nose in the dirt,' he smiled, taking the menace from his words.

Aidan and Anders looked into each other's eyes and suddenly hugged each other. 'I've missed you, Anders.'

'What did I tell you, Aidan?' Anders said, rubbing his eyes. 'I said we'd be friends forever didn't I. Well we are…a little thing like death makes no difference to that promise. Remember it when you go back.'

'And how do I get back?'

'Easy…listen for our friends calling you. But before you go,' Anders ceased shaving slivers from the stick and stared at the knife, not seeing it. 'Tell Beattie that she was my first love and I will always love her. Tell her also that I will not mind when she finds someone else. I know she'll keep a little bit of me in her heart, although she'll love another.'

'Hey, that's a bit heavy this time of the morning isn't it?'

Anders laughed. 'Aye, my friend and remember this—if any of you need me at any time, just call.'

'And how will you talk to the others…you're dead!'

'With the magic you passed to me.'

'How did I do that? I thought it was only mindmelding I'd given you,' Aidan smiled, he was happy now…he still had his friend.

'I don't know but I now have magic whereas I didn't before. It makes Life a lot easier to understand when I read the Wall—that, and all those puzzles my Mum gave me as well! You've also passed on magic to Beattie. All four of us are wizards now!'

'I don't understand.'

'All four of us and one other are to battle the Darkness. Now close your eyes relax and listen. Augusta, Beattie and Tragen are calling you,' and he held Aidan's hand.

Aidan entered the wall of colours and woke in his own bed with those he loved watching over him.

Would they believe his tidings? And would Tragen believe that he had also seen the Tree of Paradise?

Part Two

THE GATEWAY

And his God spoke.
'I felt his presence, Zorzecai.
As near to me as the other.
He is no threat at this time but he will be.
Open the first gate.
Release my minions to kill those who follow him.
Find the key.
Bring it to me and all you desire will be.
Kill the boy.'

Twenty-one

Aidan lay without moving, eyes open drinking in the sight of those he loved. He stared at the three faces, one lined with great age, his grey eyes hidden and his long white hair awry, his very long beard held in his hand. The second, a lovely face framed by shoulder length wavy black hair, her magical emerald eyes unseen. And the third, long blonde hair tied back at the nape nautical fashion, her pretty face home to eyes that changed colour reflecting her frame of mind, flashing dark when in a temper, pale blue when at peace, again concealed behind long blonde eyelashes.

All three faces were straining with the effort of calling to him even though they had no conception at all of where he'd be.

Lord Tragen, the centuries-old wizard he looked on as his father, the one who'd taught him all he knew of controlling magic, often unmanageable in Aidan's hands. Aidan smiled, anticipating the reaction he would get when he told him he had seen the Tree of Paradise.

Aidan moved his eyes ever so gently to bring them to rest on Augusta. Princess of Mantovar, his liege lord's heir and his friend—and the one they sought to protect above all others. Was her safety now their chief priority? Hadn't it shifted now they knew of the Darkness? Augusta the plague of his early childhood, the snooty girl who always got up his nose, or had until he found she always gave him butterflies in his stomach whenever he looked at her. The first one he'd passed his gifts of magic on to.

And then there was Beatrix sitting next to her, Augusta's companion and friend from birth, the prim and proper young lady who abhorred his cursing yet adored being in his company. The one who tried to bring order out of the chaos that always erupted around him, the one utterly in love with Anders dead two days. How would she receive his last message?

Aidan closed his eyes and thought of Anders his first friend. Was he still sitting alone beneath the oak tree in Paradise or was he now at the wall of colours watching Life from his place in Death? Anders in Limbo—would these three believe the unbelievable? He didn't even know himself if he accepted Limbo as true, that place all must pass through on their way to everlasting peace in Paradise—or eternal damnation in Purgatory. What had Anders called it—a place of wandering, a place of lost souls? He wondered what Anders' thoughts

255

were as he wandered his Limbo. Was he happy? He would definitely spend a lot of his time in that vast orchard, the one with the strange tree, he was manic for cherries. The two of them had spent many a happy hour delighting in seeing how far they could spit the pips, not caring if anyone got in the way. There had been one memorable occasion … Aidan giggled involuntarily aloud and opened his eyes again.

Augusta heard him, startled she looked over at him tears glistening on her cheeks. 'Aidan,' she gasped her voice breaking. 'Aidan, are you all right?'

'Aye, course I am. Come here!' And he wrapped his arms around them all in turn as everyone talked at once.

'Beatrix can you fetch the others, please,' Tragen asked. He stroked Aidan's hair and stared transfixed at his boy looking for signs of illness but only finding wonderment in his face.

A clattering in the passage soon announced the arrival of Locklear and Lady Cornelia.

'Before you all lay into him with questions he is drinking this tea,' ordered Cornelia, taking charge of Aidan. 'Come, my boy,' she smiled, 'all of it, it's hot and sustaining. I've added a little something to bring colour to your cheeks.'

Aidan smiled his thanks, he could taste the rum. He had grown to like her a lot over these last weeks even though he was afraid of her sharp tongue. When she shouted he ran.

But then he couldn't help staring at Beatrix as he drank. He was anxious. It was all very well entering the afterlife and coming back, but to return with a message was awkward in the extreme. It was bound to upset her. Could she accept it for what it was a last communication from the boy she loved? He'd be mortified if he exacerbated her hurt. But however he delivered it, the message and the fact that he had met Anders, was going to come as a tremendous shock.

'Anders, I could kill you sometimes.'

'You can't, I'm already dead,' said Anders.

'Ha, ha! Very funny, Anders!' Aidan answered instinctively aloud, forgetting everyone would hear.

'What?' Beatrix asked. 'Why did you say that?'

They stared at him mystified, except for Tragen. He knew, had heard Aidan speak with the dead before, it always unnerving him, never becoming accustomed to it, never quite believing it.

Aidan contemplated his next words. '*I didn't want to tell her as abruptly as this,*' he said, communicating with the dead was different to mindmelding so the others never heard his words.

'*Too late, you're going to have to tell her now.*'

'Aidan, please, what is going on?' Beatrix asked nervously.

'You are speaking with him, aren't you, Aidan?' Tragen asked.

Stunned, Augusta, Beatrix and Locklear stared back and forth between the wizard and his apprentice. Cornelia, knowing of Aidan's ability, put her arm around Beattie's shoulder.

'Beattie,' Aidan said, handing the mug to Augusta he grasped Beattie's hands in his and locked his eyes to hers. 'I have a gift that would be shocking to most people if they knew of it,' he paused. 'You know I can see the dead, but there's something else as well—I can speak with them.' He held her hands tighter as she froze. 'There is no need to be frightened,' he smiled. 'I love the ability as much as I love healing and magic,' he paused and gripped her hands even tighter. 'I have a message from Anders for you,' he watched as tears welled in her very red eyes.

'Go on,' she said.

And to her surprise, hearing his words she felt relief. 'I doubt I'll ever find anyone else. Tell him, Aidan...tell him I'll never stop loving him.'

'No need for me to say it, he's watching over you, he can hear you. If you ever need him, just speak his name, he'll answer.'

Aidan settled back on his pillow, unexpectedly weary as he thought of the task set them by a mysterious woman in Paradise.

'Listen, all of you, this is going to take a bit of believing! This seizure or vision, whatever you want to call it, sent my soul wandering. I can't tell you how it happened, but I do know why and where. It sent me into Limbo,' he paused before stating baldly. 'I crossed over into the afterlife.' He studied the scared faces before him.

'In Limbo I found Anders waiting for me. Some power, a woman he said, had sent him out of Paradise to warn me—warn us. There is a Darkness, a black cloud of evil in Limbo that threatens all Life here and Paradise there. Anders doesn't know why or how this Darkness affects us, only that it is our task to fight it. And it is imperative we win.'

Aidan stopped for a moment and looked at Tragen. 'Master, our battle will be so crucial that Anders has been told he must remain in Limbo to assist us in any way he can, for as long as needs be.'

The wizard found his voice first, uttering his confusion. 'You mean, you died and came back to life?'

'No, I didn't die, but I did go there and it was you three mindmelding brought me back.'

Tragen swallowed bile, his stomach could not quite handle this knowledge—it frightened him silly. He'd never known of an occurrence such as this in all his long life. 'This Darkness, can you tell us any more of it?'

'I saw it close up. It tried to trap me—take me to Purgatory, but Anders and someone else called me away,' he shuddered. 'If they hadn't I wouldn't have come back.'

There was appalled silence until Beattie spoke. 'Someone else, you said besides Anders—who was it?'

'I don't really know but... but she did call me "darling". I don't know if it was my mum, I didn't recognize her voice, but after all this time I wouldn't know it if I did hear it,' his eyes glistened.

'The Darkness, my boy, can you describe it?' Tragen asked gently.

'It's a black cloud...smog. I saw figures...shapes inside it, I don't know what they were they sort of merged into each other. But whatever it is Anders and I think the torturer we mindmeld with is part of it,' he shivered. 'When I stared at it, it seemed to draw me...take my soul, I was absolutely terrified.'

He quickly yawned. 'I'm sorry, I feel as if I haven't slept for a month.'

'How do you know I can mindmeld?' Beatrix asked out of the blue.

'Anders told me. He said I was the one responsible for passing on magic to Augusta and I've also passed on magic to you and him. I've no idea how I did it though.'

'Dear God! I have magic!' Beattie's eyes opened that wide they nearly popped out of her head.

'We know how you did it,' Augusta said smiling, 'we worked it out when we were watching over you.'

'How? Tell me.'

'They can tell you later you are too exhausted. We will leave you now,' said Cornelia. 'Sleep well, and remember we are all here if you need us,' and turning to the others she continued, 'I believe we can all do with some sleep.'

'Wait, there is more. There are to be five of us not just us three and Anders. The Lady told him there is to be another one, she didn't say who.'

'Another wizard? Is it me?' Tragen asked.

'If it is you, why didn't she say? She told Anders of us three. Anyway, we don't even know if this other one will be a wizard.'

'This is getting more confusing by the minute let us sleep on it,' Cornelia said, 'who knows something may come to mind.'

'Master,' Aidan said as Tragen reached the door, 'when I was wandering lost I saw the Tree of Paradise,' and he beamed at the shock on Tragen's face. 'Don't worry, I'm not leaving you yet although it called me—I told it I wasn't ready.'

Back in their cabin, Cornelia asked the girls what Aidan had meant.

'Each wizard makes his own staff, usually from the wood of several trees, but only when he is ready to leave his master. The wood of the Tree of Paradise will make the most powerful staff in the world. Trouble is, nobody knows where to find it,' Augusta explained.

'Except Aidan now knows,' interjected Beatrix.

'I don't know, perhaps not. He saw it but I don't think he knew exactly where it was, he was lost remember,' said Augusta, wrinkling her brow. She was frowning a lot lately, she would have to stop she thought, or she'd end up with age lines on her forehead well before her time.

'How are you feeling now, Beatrix,' asked Cornelia, gently, 'it must have felt strange having a message from the afterlife?'

Beatrix smiled radiantly. 'Strange? Yes, it was, but what a dear, dear message. I feel better now I know he's watching over me,' and she suddenly burst into tears, giving the lie to her statement. 'I just wish I could hold him.'

Cornelia left Augusta comforting her friend and joined Tragen and Locklear in the captain's cabin.

'Your boy is truly surprising, Tragen. The girls have just told me of this tree he's seen. Is it really as powerful as they say?'

'No wizard will ever stand against a staff made from the Tree of Paradise. Legend says it can only be wielded by the most powerful of sorcerers.'

'Then why did he not take it when he had the chance?' Locklear asked.

'Perhaps he had not the opportunity. All he said was that he had seen it—not that he had access to it. And Aidan knows he isn't ready yet, that he must develop more of his own skills before attempting to make his own staff. But if it truly was the Tree of Paradise calling him, then Aidan is destined to become a wizard such as we have never encountered.' And if that's the case we'll need to hide that knowledge from the magus, Margrave Brenin. Tragen sat shaking his head wondering whether his boy really could be the one of fable. 'His apprenticeship is not yet completed, he has much more to learn and that makes him vulnerable,' he paused, tugging at his beard he went on anxiously. 'But it is the Darkness that worries me more at the moment.'

'If this Darkness is threatening the afterlife it must be tremendously powerful, how can we possibly fight it?' Cornelia mused.

The wizard looking uncharacteristically dejected, 'Well it seems that someone else must appear before we can begin the battle.'

'Then you believe you are not the fifth?' Cornelia asked.

'Well I was not named by this Lady in Paradise whereas the four youngsters were. Dear God, I have no ideas any more, I am too tired to think straight,' he grimaced. 'Perhaps we should follow the example of the youngsters and sleep on it.'

'Yes,' Cornelia sighed, matters were becoming more bewildering by the minute. 'I agree and I also believe we must meet with the seneschal before too long otherwise he will feel slighted, I suggest this evening if we are rested.'

'Go, both of you,' said Locklear. 'I must complete my preparations for entering the dock in the morning. I was hoping to make the move today but Hopper tells me we will not be ready for this afternoon's high tide. While you sleep I will send for the seneschal's coach. Something terrible has got its hands on my ship. If it's the torturer and we discover he's a servant of the Darkness, then when— and I mean when we come up against him, he cannot be allowed to succeed.'

Later that afternoon, after a few hours of well needed rest, Aidan, Augusta and Beatrix, waited at the brow for Tragen and Cornelia before they all disembarked for the manor.

Aidan had eaten a phenomenally large lunch, his excuse being that his abnormal sojourn in the afterlife had given him an abnormal appetite. Augusta, of course, huffed and puffed and called him a pig. At that Aidan held his nose and waved a finger in the air as he had done years before when he'd made her nose bleed, though he was careful not to use the middle finger this time. Augusta instantly stuck her tongue out at him and then aped his gesture and as they tried to out-stare each other, they both burst into laughter. Beatrix, looking at them, wondered if they'd lost their senses.

But Aidan's dark mood of the last days had lifted a little and instead of grieving deeply he was now infinitely more cheerful, although he still suffered attacks of anxiety every time he recalled the terror of the Darkness. And however much he thought on it, he was still baffled at how he had been able to cross over into death and come back—and equally puzzled at how he had passed on his gifts of magic to his friends.

Aidan stood at the starboard rail looking ashore at the seneschal's coach waiting on the jetty. Marshal Janne was standing motionless alongside his magnificent jet-black destrier, the warhorse's white blaze shining brilliantly in the still hot sun of late afternoon, its coat glistening. It was a mount that was huge in height and girth, as it needed to be to carry its owner. And like Janne it seemed to stand at attention not moving a muscle. A long sword, its black cruciform hilt ending in a golden pommel, hung at the marshal's side and an arbalest, was slung between his shoulder blades. The commander of the seneschal's security would be riding as escort to the coach party and he intended no harm befall his charges.

'What is it like to die?' Augusta asked out of the blue. 'How did you feel?'

Startled, Aidan looked at her. 'I don't know, I didn't die, I told you that.'

'I know, I heard but I don't understand…you passed over, yet you saw Anders and he's dead!'

'Aye, I passed over and I sat with him below the oak tree and we talked…how can I explain it? To die my soul would have to separate from my body—completely. But it didn't, part of it stayed in my body and sort of anchored the rest, tethered it on the end of a long line, my lifeline. The greater part of my soul travelled over into the afterlife, aye, but because of that little bit stuck here in my body, I didn't die. Okay?'

'I suppose I'll understand one day.'

'Right, now you tell me how I passed on magic to you…you said you'd worked it out.'

'Yes, we solved it when you were unconscious,' Beatrix answered. 'We were talking in whispers, I don't know why because we wanted you to wake up, but anyway we just sort of drifted into it. We were mindmelding for ages before we realized we were talking and not moving our lips. It came as quite a shock.'

Augusta interrupted. 'We went over everything we could think of and then we discovered the common factor,' she paused, also grinning broadly. 'Do you remember healing me of seasickness?'

He nodded, his eyes drifting from one girl to the other.

'You placed your hands at my temples. You did the same for Anders when you held his head above the water. And yesterday when Beattie was in a trance in the barge…'

'I held her head in my hands and massaged her temples,' he grinned. 'Bloody hell, bloody…'

'Did you mean it, Aidan, have you passed on magic to me?' Beattie interrupted begging the answer she wanted.

'Well, Anders said I have.'

Beatrix whooped loudly and grinning she flung her arms around him, hugging him tightly.

'You will have to investigate on our return, Aidan,' said Tragen, coming up behind them with Cornelia. 'I have never known of a wizard passing on magic to those who have never previously shown the ability, it warrants explaining!'

'We know why, though, don't we? We have a small group of people here who can now communicate secretly with each other and who also share extraordinary skills.' Cornelia gazed at Aidan, Augusta and Beatrix, her face full of trepidation. 'These three, with Anders, have been brought together to fight the menace…along with another. But why these, Tragen, why were these chosen—and by whom?' she asked, fear in her voice. 'It is imperative we find the answer to both questions. But now I think we have kept Seneschal Portolan waiting much longer than is seemly. Shall we go?'

Tragen and Cornelia sat opposite each other in the carriage on the plush red leather seats, contemplating their forthcoming meeting with the formidable man who was governor of the island in his brother's absence.

Cornelia's thoughts were full of the boy Thaddeus and what could be done for him. But at the edges of her mind pleasant thoughts of the boy's father intruded. Men had not played a great role in her life; her size and the 'old' sickness had impeded any romance. She had come to terms with the fact that she was not attractive to men, indeed had planned a future for herself which precluded a partner, but the seneschal's wife had been much the same size as she was now, hadn't she? Tosh, she thought, she was being very silly.

Tragen on the other hand was debating with himself the problem of obtaining information about the island of Sanctity, the mention of which had frightened Lodovico Portolan so much. He had to know what to expect before making any definite decisions on whether to sail to there. If the mysterious torturer was anywhere in the Griffin Islands then that would probably be the place and if it was, then measures to safeguard them all had to be taken. But, if there was danger on Sanctity, he desperately needed knowledge of those that resided there. Was the "man in red" of Aidan's visions, a monk? His thoughts turned to the nurse, could she possibly help? If she knew anything would she divulge it? So many questions, too few answers, but he daren't rely on speculation. The need for accurate information outweighed the need for healing the seneschal's boy, although neither Aidan nor Cornelia would ever agree with that.

Beatrix had a momentary pang of despair when Augusta and Aidan joined her on the hind seat. Knowing that Anders was watching over her did not entirely wipe away the misery of his absence before her eyes.

Augusta and Aidan, happy to be off the ship for a few hours were excited to at last be seeing an island they had never expected to visit. Neither of them gave much thought to Thaddeus, Aidan because it was pointless making assumptions before even seeing the boy, and Augusta because she was very apprehensive. She now had to act the part of a servant among other servants. Could she carry it off? She had one big advantage though over anyone else attempting such a deception. If she was about to err or speak in a manner not normally used by a maid, then Beatrix and Aidan would mindmeld instructions. But Augusta didn't hold out much hope, she knew she was short-tempered and intolerant of fools. Would her friends react in time to avert a disaster?

The coach rattled through the town at a faster pace than previously, mainly because the townspeople, seeing Janne escorting the vehicle, melted away into doorways. The children, of course, did not, but they did cease playing and stood at the roadside on tip-toe trying to see who was in the carriage, only resuming their games when the coach had turned the next corner.

'Hey, you two, I've just had a thought,' said Aidan quietly so that the coachman in front wouldn't hear.

'Is it a sensible one?' Augusta asked sarcastically.

'Funnee! I was just thinking, now that I've passed on magic and mindmelding to you two and Anders I wonder if I could pass it on to anyone else. What do you think?'

'Ooh! You're going to have to be very careful, little wizard, aren't you?' Augusta said abruptly, her nerves getting the better of her.

'You've also forgotten someone else's head that you held,' said Beatrix brooding over Anders' death.

'Who?' Aidan asked, 'I can't think of anyone else.'

'No? Then how about a big bird you gave a voice?'

'Bloody hell, Ryn! I wonder...' and he grinned at Augusta. 'Boy, will your father be surprised.'

Passing through the iron gates on to the driveway leading to the house, Aidan and the girls espied Seneschal Portolan, his son and Mistress Barbat again awaiting their guests at the high double doors beneath the portico. On this visit neither the hosts nor the guests were dressed formally, although Tragen was still attired in his green robe, he didn't seem to own any other colour, or any other style of garment.

Tragen and Cornelia were warmly welcomed and taken through the banqueting hall into the family's parlour behind; there they were joined by Janne. This room was much less formal with easy chairs and a sofa lining three walls, the fourth taken up by a smaller dining table placed beneath a large picture window. The Portolan family spent most of their time in this room, Mistress Barbat's embroidery basket lying open on a heavy side table, adding to the informal atmosphere. Again, a portrait of the late Mistress Portolan was hanging on a wall.

Tragen walked over to the window and gazed out over green lawns and an ornamental fountain depicting children playing beneath a waterfall.

'An unusual fountain, Seneschal, but why are the children green?' Tragen asked, turning to his host.

'Please, here in this room we are friends, all on first name terms. I do not usually allow formality in my parlour, I am Lodovico, Mistress Barbat is Alessa and Janne is Marcus. And to answer your question, green is the colour of the first inhabitants of these islands according to our folk tales.'

'Green people? Strange…I haven't heard of them in centuries and yet this is the second time I've thought of them in recent weeks. They died out with the elves and dragons I believe,' said Tragen, smiling and wondering what the seneschal meant by "usually". 'So you had these mythical people on Griffin as well.'

'As well?' Lodovico asked sitting on his chair and indicating for Tragen to be seated.

'Yes, Lodovico, there is a fountain similar to this one, I think, in Abferkarn is there not, Tragen. It's of green men and women anyway…very old, no-one knows who sculpted it,' said Cornelia, 'and, come to think of it, there were also elves living in or near that city at one time.'

'Abferkarn?' Where is that?' The seneschal asked curiously.

'Oh, I'm sorry, Abferkarn is the ancient capital city of our empire…of Drakka,' she smiled, 'and the fountain is hidden away in small woodlands used for recreation by the local people.'

'Ah, that fits in with our history…the Green People were foresters. Our fables tell us their disappearance was because of a prophecy, no-one knows the substance of that prophecy, or if it's true of course. But, please, I am remiss; let us partake of a beverage. Which would you prefer Cornelia, a cold fruit drink or my favourite at this time of day…tea, hot and sweet?'

Cornelia smiled, despite his hard demeanour, she did like this man.

Below in the servants' hall, the atmosphere was not so amicable. Mistress Lacey, the cook/housekeeper, was not an easy woman to like in fact she seemed to spend most of her time being obnoxious. In her eyes servants were lazy and unreliable, needing to be supervised continually. Cleaning vegetables, or clearing away and washing dirty pans and dishes were about all they were good for, was her verdict.

Augusta was getting seriously annoyed, having bitten her tongue three times in as many minutes. Aidan thought the whole situation hilarious and was thoroughly enjoying the spectacle. But Augusta was really getting uptight, her face turning purple, her hands trembling as her temper rose. Beatrix, though, knew her mistress and was on pins waiting for her to blow—all hell would break loose then. There was no getting away from it, Beatrix thought, Augusta not having been brought up to fetch and carry would never succeed in this sham.

Leash, having watched the coach leave for the manor, felt an almost irresistible urge to fly at Aidan and his friends, an action that would certainly have ended in his death.

He turned away from the wharf when the coach disappeared around the corner of a warehouse and walked along a narrow alley to search behind the waterfront. He was looking for somewhere dark, not necessarily quiet but a place catering for the dregs of the docks.

He discovered the "King Prawn" in a back alley a couple of streets behind the harbour, the broken weather-worn sign swinging lop-sided from one bracket. The windows of the two storey building looking on to the street had not been cleaned for years, although the grime had been smeared on the inside of the glass in places to enable customers to peer out. The only solid bit of the whole frontage was the door, wide open at this time of the evening. A smell of boiled cabbage wafted through into the street accompanied by the stale taste of rotgut ale. Inside the long, gloomy taproom was a bar consisting of a couple of heavy planks laid across the top of two large, empty kegs. Roughly repaired shelves behind the barman contained an array of pewter mugs, none too clean and all chipped. Rickety tables which appeared to be survivors of a war zone were littered randomly in the middle of the sodden, straw covered floor, and at the rear of the dark room were alcoves, each holding a small table with a short bench round three sides.

Smoke pervaded the atmosphere, most of it tobacco, but there were other exotic smells familiar to Leash. A pungent tang assailed his nostrils one he had no problem in recognizing. The drug lypyn weed – banned on the Grim because it rotted the brain – was very popular with the down and outs of the docks. Lypyn's sweet, cloying fragrance reminded Leash of fresh blood, but the hallucinogenic drug took men from this world into a place of dreams and wonder, where everyone was a friend, even your enemy. He smiled, find the source of the fragrance and he would discover all he wanted to know.

He had money, by the look of this place enough to buy the tavern two or three times over. All he had to do was find the customer with only half his brain cells amongst the dirt poor dockworkers in the crowded room, flash a little money, obtain some lypyn, ale for himself and with luck a plan to kill all three youngsters would be forthcoming.

He moved deeper into the room his feet squelching on the old straw, disturbing the lice that loved the humidity. He threw a coin amongst the slops on the bar and pointed at the jug of ale in the barman's hands. The landlord's sullen expression lifting at sight of real cash grabbed a mug from the shelf behind him and hurriedly poured the light amber ale. Taking the drink, Leash's eyes roamed the dim room while behind him the barman surreptitiously bit the coin to test its authenticity. Leash made his way slowly amongst the tables and headed for the alcoves at the back, pausing now and then, sniffing covertly. It wasn't long before he discovered the source of the reek despite the overwhelming stench of boiled cabbage, sour ale and urine.

The blood smell drew him to an alcove in the corner adjoining the kitchen. Two old men were sharing one mug of ale and a pipe of lypyn. Sitting on the bench facing the centre of the room, they leant with elbows on the wet table, grinning foolishly at all and sundry.

Leash well knew the look of lypyn stupor, he moved into the alcove calling to the barman to bring over two fresh mugs of the acerbic ale. It didn't take long for Leash to realize these men were not going to be much help. But they did point him at the Montetor.

Twenty-two

Beatrix looked askance. *'No, Augusta, not like that,'* she mindmelded as she and Aidan cleaned turnips and cabbage. *'You do not clean potatoes in that fashion. Scrub them vigorously with the brush.'*

'Bloody hell, Aidan, you've got to help me, please,' Augusta begged, ignoring Beattie's scandalized stare at her swearing again. *'Use magic on these before the old witch comes back, if she shouts at me much more I'm going to flatten her.'*

Aidan, reacting without thinking, waved his hands. He chanted almost inaudibly, and the surface of each of the tubers was pristine not an eye to be seen and in the pan ready for boiling.

'You've done it now! Both of you are in deep trouble,' said Beatrix.

'Why, they're clean, aren't they?' Augusta asked.

'That woman is superstitious; I've seen her crossing her fingers and such. No potato in the world has ever been scrubbed that clean, the first thing she'll think of is magic. And we are supposed to be hiding the fact we are wizards. Tragen will not be best pleased.'

'Oh God, she's right. Quick change them back, I'll just have to persevere with the witch.'

Aidan smiled nervously. *'It's not as easy as that. Undoing magic takes a lot of time and a great deal of concentration...it's very difficult chanting a spell backwards. If it's not done exactly right...'*

'What?' Augusta and Beatrix asked together, both all of a sudden very apprehensive.

'Well, sometimes a new spell is created...and...and something else happens.'

'Oh God, you be careful, very, very careful. I may be his prince's daughter but that will not stop Tragen punishing me—and you.'

'And me for not stopping you,' added Beatrix desperately, visions of potatoes dancing around on spidery legs singing bawdy songs at the tops of their voices, was running through her head.

'Okay...wait let me think.' They were in the small curtilage, the room adjoining the kitchen where fruit and vegetables were prepared for the family's dinner.

'Where's the old bag now?' Aidan asked, wringing his hands.

Beatrix looked at him. *'She's in the garden talking with someone,'* she paused. *'Aidan, you are not instilling me with much confidence.'*

'Don't worry I've got it, now. Augusta, tip them back in the bowl and stand back.'

'What are you going to do?' Beatrix asked panic-stricken.

Aidan took a deep breath, raised his hands and commenced his chanting. Besides the backward spell having an absurd grinding sound nothing appeared to happen to the tubers in the bowl.

'Well, come on...do something,' said Augusta impatiently. *'She'll be back any minute.'*

'Wait', he said, *'the skins are growing back.'*

And they did, looking exactly as they had previously...with one problem. The skins were as hard as iron, Augusta couldn't even mark the outer layer let alone scrub the skin away.

'Oh my God, you've done it again. She's going to kill us,' Augusta said desperately.

'What do you mean me? You're the one who asked me to do it.'

'I didn't expect you to make a total mess of it, did I?'

'Stop it you two, arguing isn't helping,' shouted Beatrix.

'Let me try something else,' he said.

'No...no way, enough's enough,' said Beatrix, 'God knows what else will happen. No, they look all right; we'll tell her...you will tell her Aidan, that they're too old to clean.'

'Me! Why should I tell her?'

'Because you mucked it up...look out here she comes.'

Marcus Janne sat with the nurse on the heavy, flower patterned sofa. They were speaking quietly to each other whilst keeping an unobtrusive eye on the wizard, their body language radiating tension, Thaddeus sitting silently between them. Cornelia sat the other side of the room with Tragen, their host pouring the tea.

'Has Captain Locklear everything ready to enter dry-dock?' The seneschal asked as he handed Cornelia her cup.

'Hopefully, he intends moving the Grim into the dock at high tide tomorrow morning,' replied Tragen

'Good,' he answered distractedly. 'And you Cornelia, you are well after the bereavement? I must offer my condolences, I'm afraid I never took much notice of the boy the other night. It was remiss of me.'

'Not at all, Lodovico, after all he was a servant not a guest, you were not expected to acknowledge him,' she replied, spooning sugar into her cup from the bowl that he held for her.

'Nevertheless!' He paused a moment still holding the sugar bowl before the lady-in-waiting, although she'd clearly finished with it. Distracted by his worry for his son he was unable to conceal his admiration for Cornelia and she blushed. Startled by her reaction he cleared his throat with embarrassment and he turned to the wizard. 'I gather your servant took it particularly badly, Tragen.'

'He did, as did his other friends…but they seem to be coping with their grief phenomenally well,' Tragen replied.

'Marcus told me of your idea. As you appreciate, Thaddeus being the way he is has led to a certain over-protection on our part. Thaddeus is never alone, one of we three is always with him. You know your boy and these two maids well, Tragen?'

'I do, and Cornelia will agree with me, they are utterly trustworthy.'

'A dangerous statement to be made of mere servants,' said the seneschal, lifting his eyebrows quizzically.

'Lodovico, I will trust these three with my life and with that of Thaddeus' believe me,' said Cornelia.

He sighed and peered closely at Tragen. 'I am a desperate man, so I will take your word for it, but as you have not yet examined him yourself it may not be necessary.'

'Marcus, please, seat Thaddeus with me at the table,' Tragen asked.

They sat – facing each other – on high backed chairs beside the table, the tall wizard, his long white hair and immensely long beard brushed immaculately and the tall, overweight, young man sitting with his hands clasped in his lap, staring straight ahead, not seeing anyone.

Tragen leant forward and cupped the newly shaved chin in his hand and gazed into the young, blue eyes for long minutes attempting to see behind the orbs and ascertain the state of his brain. Releasing him, Tragen placed his hands either side of the young man's head crushing his blond curls, and then on his chest.

'It is strange,' Tragen said, not taking his eyes away. 'I can feel his heart and his lungs I can feel the blood coursing through his body. All his physical attributes are normal.'

Lodovico, Marcus, Alessa and Cornelia waited with bated breath.

'The boy's brain has a certain activity, all that is necessary to control his bodily functions, but...but there is something missing.' Tragen ran his fingers through his long beard as he contemplated what was before him. The boy doesn't seem to be here, he thought. Could Aidan be wrong and a life can be born without a soul? He looked at the seneschal. 'I need my boy, Lodovico.'

The seneschal, his jowls quivering, despaired. This wizard is just like the rest; he doesn't know what is wrong but will not admit it. How is a young servant going to succeed where other, more learned people cannot? He sighed as Marcus and Alessa returned his disappointed gaze.

'Very well, Alessa, if you will.'

Mistress Barbat rose to her feet and as she did so Janne squeezed her hand affectionately, his hold lingering. 'Shall I bring the two maids as well?'

'You might as well, we can't leave any stone unturned, who knows, hey?' The seneschal patted her arm perfunctorily as she passed him.

The relationships are explained—Janne and the nurse, they are a couple. Cornelia was relieved, she had wondered if it had been the nurse and the seneschal. She, despite her heart lifting, stared despondently across the room at the two sitting quietly at the table waiting. She was very afraid for Thaddeus.

There was pandemonium downstairs. Mistress Lacey had already called Augusta a stupid girl for not being able to clean a potato, and Aidan an idiot boy for saying the potatoes were too old. But as Mistress Barbat walked through the door into the hall, the cook had just begun shouting at Beatrix, accusing her of being a lazy good for nothing.

That, of course, did it for Beatrix. Augusta and Aidan stood dumbfounded, as Beatrix snapped.

'And you are a stupid, bloody old cow. You could never hold down a proper cook's job in a proper household. We are servants to your master's guests and as such should be treated as guests in the servants' hall, if you can't understand that then ask a real housekeeper...we are not scullery maids!'

'Well said, Beattie!' Augusta said, not bothering to hide her smile.

Aidan beamed openly, not a care in the world, his next very happy moment would be when Beatrix realized she had cursed—he couldn't wait.

The seneschal's domestics standing nearby were also smiling, highly delighted at the woman's discomfiture. Mistress Lacey, her chin dropping to her feet turned purple with rage, being an unmitigated bully whose authority had never been questioned she was speechless with shock. No-one had ever had the courage to stand up to her before let alone verbally abuse her. The young maid's stature grew tenfold amongst the downtrodden staff.

But before the cook could retaliate the nurse stepped into the middle of the melee. Mistress Barbat's unique position in the household ensured she was treated as a member of the family. She was entitled to the respect and veneration given to all the Portolans and because of this all sound ceased immediately in the servants' hall and everyone stood in her presence.

Frowning, Alessa Barbat beckoned to Aidan, Augusta and Beattie. 'Come with me, Lord Tragen requires your presence.'

They followed her obediently as she led the way up the back stairs, Augusta still astonished at her friend's reaction. Beatrix beginning to tremble with the shock of her tirade was unable to understand where she had found the audacity to speak as she had. She hoped Aidan had not noticed her language, but seeing the glee on his face she knew he had—how could she possibly reprimand him again? She hung her head in shame.

Reaching the top landing, the nurse turned to them before opening the door. 'I do not know the reason for the altercation with the cook, but please remember these are the family's private rooms and you will show respect at all times,' and she led them through into the parlour.

The wizard looked up. 'Ah, Aidan, come here please,'

Augusta and Beatrix hurried over to Cornelia, and each girl grasped a hand of the lady-in-waiting, all three watching avidly.

'Meet Thaddeus, my boy, he is the son of our host.'

Aidan glanced at the harbourmaster and smiled cautiously as Seneschal Portolan nodded his head, his hard eyes inscrutable. Aidan paused a moment to compose himself before looking at the boy on the chair. He had been in many circumstances like this before with parents of patients watching his every move. And though he had become accustomed to the stress, he still didn't like what the outcome could be if the desired healing didn't materialize. He had seen people injure themselves in their grief. Standing alongside his mentor, he anticipated the euphoria of healing as he prepared to diagnose the problem. He was in his element as he stooped and gazed into the eyes of the silent boy.

'Master, may I sit there?'

Aidan wriggled on the chair a moment to get more comfortable ignoring everyone else in the room. He examined the boy's outward appearance first, satisfied with what he saw he then studied the boy's face and eventually peered closely into Thaddeus' eyes. There was no reaction at all from Thaddeus at the change of face before him.

'*What have you learned, Master?*' Aidan frowning asked a minute later, he was baffled, he'd never seen an illness such as this. Augusta and Beatrix overheard his mindmeld.

'*All his physical abilities appear normal, he breathes, eats and drinks all as instinct dictates. It is in his head that the lack of something exists. Are you sure no-one is born without a soul?*'

'*Aye, I'm positive. Leave me be a little, I want to look deeper,*' Aidan placed his hands on Thaddeus' temples and looked behind the eyes.

'*Be careful, Aidan, don't forget that is how you gave us the gift of mindmeld,*' said Augusta.

'*And magic,*' added Beatrix, still unbelieving of it.

'What is happening, Tragen?' The seneschal asked in the seemingly never ending silence of the room. All he could see was the boy Aidan staring at Thaddeus whilst holding his head, the only movement being Aidan's hands massaging Thaddeus' temples.

'Aidan is attempting to search for your son's mind…not an easy process.'

'How can he do that? You told Marcus your boy is not a healer.'

'Ah, I may have misled you, but I assure you it was with the best of intentions,' Tragen wondered if his explanation would be plausible. 'I did not realize the severity of the problem and as you did not know my boy I was afraid that you might not allow him to examine Thaddeus. I ask Aidan to heal only the most difficult of maladies—he has a special gift. He is no ordinary healer; he has the

273

ability to peer into your body and your mind. He heals from the inside…if he can diagnose the illness.'

'He will not hurt my son?' he asked anxiously, suspicion in his tone.

Cornelia answered. 'Lodovico, I trust him implicitly, I assure you he'd never harm Thaddeus,' she smiled reassuringly. 'Aidan has just healed me of the "old" sickness.'

'The bones disease, you mean?' Alessa asked disbelievingly.

'Yes, my dear, and for that alone I would defy anyone who does not place his trust in Aidan.'

'Master,' said Aidan puzzled, effectively silencing the conversation he had inadvertently interrupted. 'I cannot see him. It's as if he's not there. No wonder others say he has no soul, even I am unaware of it—and that's impossible.' Aidan had spoken aloud unintentionally.

'Are you confirming that my son has no soul?' asked Lodovico Portolan despairing.

'No, Seneschal, of course he has a soul…I just can't find it yet.' Aidan continued to massage Thaddeus' temples.

'*Aidan, you are going to give him mindmelding for sure,*' warned Beatrix.

'*Perhaps that's what he needs for me to get through to him,*' and Aidan moved closer, now sitting almost nose to nose with the unresponsive boy.

The silence in the room increased the tension to breaking point and the seneschal fidgeted in his seat, seeing nothing changing he thought the worst. 'He is not going to help, is he, Tragen?'

'Lodovico, patience, we have only just started. Your boy is ill and has been for a long time. Whatever troubles him is deep-seated and may take a long time to discover. But I swear to you, Aidan will find the cause of this problem.'

Aidan quickly sat up straight and removed his hands, speaking aloud he said. 'Master, I don't believe this.'

'What?' Tragen asked, the astonishment in Aidan's voice surprising him.

'He is lost!'

Portolan frightened, jumped up from his chair, groaning his anguish. Mistress Barbat buried her face in Janne's shoulder, himself ashen.

Cornelia put her hands to her mouth. 'Aidan, there is no hope at all?'

Aidan turned from Thaddeus, a strange wonder lighting up his face turning quickly to puzzlement as he saw the reaction of the adults in the room. 'What…'

Augusta broke in. 'You said he's lost…what does that mean?'

Only then did he realize the false interpretation of his words and the devastation they had caused.

'Oh no, please, you misunderstand me, I'm sorry,' and he beamed. 'Thaddeus is lost in Limbo—I have found his lifeline.'

'By the Gods, Tragen, what does that mean?' Portolan said utterly distraught.

'It means, Lodovico, that Aidan has found your son's soul, or at least knows where it is to be found,' said Cornelia.

The seneschal collapsed back into his chair utterly lost for words. Mistress Barbat leapt to her feet and ran across the room. Standing protectively behind Thaddeus, she hugged him tightly.

'What can you do? I don't understand…what is Limbo?' Janne asked, as confused as his friend.

'Limbo is the place we must all pass through in the afterlife to reach Paradise,' said Aidan. 'As for what can be done I must know how he got there.'

'What were the circumstances of his birth, Lodovico?' Tragen asked. 'I believe his mother died of head wounds, what was the nature of those wounds?'

The seneschal, pursing his lips, remained silent a look of pure torment on his face as he stared at Alessa Barbat.

'You have to tell them, Lodovico. If there is any chance this boy can help our Thaddeus, you must tell them everything,' Alessa implored.

Portolan stared at the young man who had just made such a fantastic diagnosis. 'What has his mother's death to do with this…this Limbo? You talk of the afterlife; does that mean my son is dead?'

'Thaddeus is not dead…he is physically well; it is his mind, his soul, that is somewhere else, Seneschal. And believe me I know that a life adrift in Limbo is in very serious danger. We have to bring him back, but to do that I must know how he got there. His mother's injuries, what were they?'

'You must speak, Lodo, you have no choice,' said Janne.

275

'What has his mother's death to do with Thaddeus?' The seneschal repeated not taking his eyes from Aidan.

'Maybe nothing—maybe everything,' said Aidan. 'Something unnatural happened in his birth…tell me.'

Portolan took a deep breath and screwed his eyes shut, pain in every line of his face. Everyone stared at him, waiting. 'My wife, she…she did not have an injury to her head. It is a story we put around to cover up the shameful facts,' he opened his eyes, breathing deeply he continued. 'Bettina, my wife that I loved dearly…was mad.' Portolan, tears streaming down his cheeks now, went on. 'She died screaming and shouting, and in her last breath the physician took Thaddeus from her womb. My son without a soul.'

There was horrified silence.

Aidan stared penetratingly at the seneschal. 'Why do you say mad, I don't see any madness in your son? If his mother was mad I'd see some of it in Thaddeus but there's nothing anywhere. What was she shouting? Tell me, Seneschal, what did she say?'

Portolan could not answer; he sat with his hands over his face.

Mistress Barbat looking over Thaddeus' head spoke. 'It was nonsense, terrible, terrible nonsense. I…we will never ever forget it. We had to hold her down, she kept wanting to get up as if she was getting ready to fight someone, and then…then she would scream in pain and grit her teeth. The next minute she'd shout at us, "take him, take him quickly before they get him" and then she would scream some more,' Alessa's voice trembled. 'A moment later she'd appear to shout at someone else, saying things such as "you're not having him, he's ours, you're not having him leave us alone",' the nurse wept and rocked as she hugged Thaddeus. '"Take him Lodo", she'd say, "take him quickly", and then she'd scream again. Oh, she screamed! I can still hear her,' and she buried her head in Thaddeus' hair.

Aidan knelt before the seneschal and took both his hands in his.

'Seneschal, I want you to listen to me. Your wife was not mad you…you heard your wife being murdered!'

It was dusk and Leash was roaming the streets, searching the taverns, shops and stalls that he had not previously visited. He was looking for the Montetors, one in particular.

Leash gloated. It was going to be easy to use the cover of the feud to kill Aidan and the girls. The distrust and dislike, sometimes flaring into open hatred, shared by most Montetors and Portolans was a tangible emotion, felt by all who visited Griffin.

Life hadn't always been like it, prior to the feud Portolan and Montetor had intermarried quite often, the clans got on well and trade was engaged in to everyone's mutual benefit. But now, reciprocal loathing quite often led to violence when north met south and Leash was planning murder, with their help.

The two lypyn-soaked old men had spoken of the Montetor leader at length. They had variously described Bazyli Montetor as tall and short, black hair and definitely blond hair, soft spoken and harshly voiced. Only on one point did they find agreement—Bazyli's face. The Montetor sported a scar running from his hairline straight down the right side of his nose. On the way, the sword cut had removed the eye, and the end of the lesion pulled up the corner of his mouth into a perpetual sneer. His remaining eye was black and cold, frightening to Montetors and Portolans alike.

The two old men said Bazyli would kill you as soon as look at you, but there again so would Leash, this did not worry him at all. If Leash could gain the Montetor's assistance Aidan would be dead within the week, and Bazyli was amply placed to render the necessary aid.

The Montetor was always on the lookout for likely captives to add to the Montetor Quota. But despite repeated questioning the men would not divulge the Quota's purpose, and this made Leash curious. It was almost impossible to hide anything when under the influence of lypyn, indeed, mention of the Quota seemed to sober them and they clammed up.

Leash had no idea how he was going to arrange the abduction and eventual killing of Aidan, but the maids would have to disappear as well. They were intelligent and watchful, and were always in the company of the boy. Leash only had to slip up once and they would have him…or the wizard would.

He walked for hours through the dark streets and alleys peering in doors and windows as he went, keeping his ears open for any squabble, he might find his prey somewhere in the vicinity of any fracas. It was nearly midnight and Leash had decided to return to the Grim when he turned down a particularly smelly lane. He emerged on to a brightly lit thoroughfare, a league or so from the waterfront. Halfway up on the north side was an inn of the better sort and outside talking to a woman was the ironmaster.

Leash smiled, he was a happy man that night. All he had to do was keep track of the movements of the three youngsters and inform the Montetor. There would be a contact working on the quay, notify him and Bazyli would do the rest.

But Leash had been adamant, he wanted to watch them taken and he wanted to watch them die and Bazyli had promised both. Leash smiled and turned over in his cot, closing his eyes he drifted into his safe dream, he'd ignore her contrariness this night.

Portolan was shocked beyond belief, drained of all colour he stared at Aidan.

'Murdered? But how? There were only we three, and the physician present, none of us killed her.'

Janne and Alessa stared at the young wizard in horror; his ordinary appearance somehow accentuating the eeriness of his words, they were staggered. And as they continued to listen to him, his explanation of death and Limbo sounded even more fantastic, could it ever be true? But the terror he evinced when speaking of the Darkness could never have been a fabrication, and this frightened them even more. Standing behind Thaddeus, Alessa suddenly felt the need for comfort and she held out her hand for Marcus, her other arm clasping Thaddeus even closer to her chest. The big man rushed over and put his arm around her, his face ashen he caressed the blond curls on Thaddeus' head.

Janne remembered the birth all too well; it still gave him many a sleepless night. He had been walking the boards outside Bettina's bedchamber that night and he had heard the screams and shouts through the thick oaken door. He and Lodovico Portolan were long-time friends, Marcus supporting him as best man at his wedding. He had been the obvious one to call on when matters were getting out of hand. He recalled the horrendous sight that had greeted him when he entered the room. Bettina's face had turned purple as she shouted, her large body shining with abnormal sweat as she thrashed about on the bed. Listening to Aidan, it explained her colour, her violence; Bettina had been raging, struggling, fighting for her son's life. If only they had known, but then even if they had, could they have done anything? The devastation of that night had never left him and now that he knew what she had gone through, what she had been doing when he had been restraining her, he felt even more ravaged.

But ever since the birth his and Alessa's romance had been side-lined as both dedicated their lives to caring for the traumatized boy. And in doing just that, not only had the two grown even closer, they had come to love Thaddeus as their own.

'Seneschal, your wife was no more insane than any of us here. I know, I have experienced the same terror and ended up stranded in Limbo. No-one in this life killed her. What she saw was something evil, a demon trying to take your son's soul and she fought, and died, to save him. At the very moment of her death Thaddeus' soul was forced into Limbo and there he remains. It was probably the last desperate act of your wife to save his soul from the devil that was murdering her. Or it may have been the last act of the demon to put Thaddeus in extreme danger; maybe it thought it would have a better chance to seize his soul if it was in the afterlife already. Whatever the reason, mortal danger exists where he is; we must find and return Thaddeus' soul to his body.'

'Bettina saved our Thaddeus,' said Alessa, smiling up at Marcus through her tears.

'Aye, she did, she was one hell of a fighter—she had to be to beat the demon. It failed to take Thaddeus' soul,' replied Aidan smiling from one to the other, 'or hers.'

'How do you know that it failed with Bettina?' Janne spoke still holding the nurse very tightly.

'I'd have felt it in Thaddeus' soul…part of both parents' souls are always passed on to their children, as my parents passed theirs on to me. That is why I believe a child instinctively knows its parents or a parent its child. Even though they may not have seen each other since the birth, there is an attraction a sort of knowing of each other though they may not recognize the feeling.'

'Can we search for Thaddeus,' asked Augusta, 'the three of us?'

'Wait…please wait my head is spinning,' said Lodovico. 'Explain this Limbo again and this…this Darkness?'

Aidan rose from his knees and resumed his seat in front of Thaddeus. Taking a sip of water from a goblet on the table, he turned and looked at the seneschal.

'I was lost there, in Limbo. My Master, Beatrix and Al…Nellie,' Aidan just managed to stop himself using her right name, 'called me back.' Aidan sighed; this was difficult enough to understand without the emotional shock of the last hour.

'When you die your soul enters Limbo, it's a kind of halfway house. For some souls dying comes as a hell of a shock and they need to get their bearings, some souls are so confused they don't even know they're dead! I know you have absolutely no idea of what I'm talking about, but please persevere with me; hopefully I can make it clearer. Once a soul knows where it is then it has a choice to make. It can enter Paradise immediately by travelling through the Light, or it can linger in Limbo, for eternity if it wants, but that's a dead end,'

Augusta couldn't help it; she failed to stifle a giggle. The thought of a dead person walking round in a dead end forever struck her as hilarious.

Aidan glanced at her quickly and continued his explanation. 'Sorry, I mean the soul goes nowhere. But hanging about in Limbo is boring and this leaves the soul at risk of being taken into Purgatory, which I think is the evil within the Darkness,' he paused and sipped from his mug, everyone hanging on his words including Tragen

'Am I going too fast for you, Seneschal?'

'No, young man, I don't think so, but it's going to take me one hell of a while to assimilate all this. But my Thaddeus, are you sure you've found his soul?'

'I'm sure! He's lost in Limbo and very definitely alive! But it is the Darkness, or whatever's within it that killed your wife and tried to kill Thaddeus. That same Darkness threatens us in Life, and also terrorizes Limbo and all who are lost there. It's like a lodestone for a soul. What exactly this evil is we don't know. So far only three of us have seen it, Anders, me, and I assume Thaddeus.'

'Anders…your friend that just died?' Janne asked quietly. 'Did the Darkness kill him?'

'No, Anders' death was an accident. But later he showed me the Darkness in his Limbo and he warned me of it.'

At the incredulous look on Lodovico's face, Tragen interrupted. 'Aidan can communicate with the dead, my friend. It is another of his extraordinary gifts.'

'I cannot take this in, I'm sorry, I need time. All these years I have thought…my wife was not mad…my boy's soul is lost, Alessa…Marcus…' Portolan looked at them in confusion. But then he breathed deeply, composing himself he turned back to Aidan.

'Young man, you do not know what you have done for me. I now have hope for the first time in years,' he paused. 'You find my son, bring him home and if there is anything you need you have but to ask it of me. And while you're about it, find out all you can of this Darkness so that I may kill it,' the seneschal's voice sent a chill down everyone's spine.

Alessa clung to Thaddeus, both her arms now around his shoulders, hands clenched over his chest. 'Aidan, how will you him?' she asked, her face caressing the top of Thaddeus' head, her eyes red and swollen.

'I'll search in Limbo, with the aid of Nellie, Beattie and our friend Anders. It means that we'll all have to stay here with Thaddeus. We'll need to form some sort of relationship with him, for though his soul is not present to recognize us, his feelings will be. And through his feelings hopefully, we can reach his soul.'

Tragen and Cornelia returned to the Grim leaving behind the three youngsters ensconced in rooms not far from Lodovico Portolan's chambers.

From the first moment he had left his wet nurse, Thaddeus had slept in the truckle bed alongside his father. The boy was protected through long nights by an ever watchful Lodovico.

Cornelia and Tragen, sated and tired, joined Locklear in his cabin. Sitting down in the familiar surroundings, Tragen sighed with relief.

'Where are the others, Tragen?' Hugo asked, perturbed as Hopper joined them from his post on the quarterdeck.

'They are willing guests of the seneschal, my friend, and will be for a few days yet, no need to worry. At the very least we will have peace and quiet while they're away,' he smiled.

'You look pleased with yourself, wizard, tell all,' he ordered as Hopper poured them brandy from Locklear's seemingly endless supply.

'With luck, I believe we now have the opportunity to learn all we can of Sanctity,' the wizard stroked his beard. 'That is if Aidan, Augusta and Beatrix can find Portolan's son.'

'What on earth do you mean?'

Tragen and Cornelia told them. It took well over an hour, constantly interrupted by questions from both seamen; even then they made only a cursory attempt to explain Limbo for Hopper's benefit.

'A most unusual evening,' said Hopper.

'The Darkness killed Mistress Portolan fifteen years ago. How is it only now we've heard of it?' Locklear asked.

'Probably because we are very near Sanctity, Hugo, for I am convinced, as is Tragen, that is where the answer to our problems lie,' said Cornelia. 'And if we are right, then surely Aidan is in even graver danger. And something else,' Cornelia turned to Tragen, 'it's an almighty coincidence that Aidan has the vision which sends him into Limbo, the night before discovering a boy is lost there. It's almost as if someone is guiding us—or at least him. That Lady in the Light probably and if it is her then the Gods are manipulating us all.'

'His visions are becoming increasingly more perilous, true, and yes I agree it is very strange we discover at this time the unusual circumstances surrounding Thaddeus. But why should the Gods be guiding us, we are mere mortals. But if that is the case, and they need Aidan and his friends, what is their purpose? Is it aid they require or are the youngsters to be sacrificed at their whim? Why should Aidan have these visions and not me? This evil being, this torturer in red, this demon knows of me, not him!'

'Is Limbo all he saw in his last vision? I mean, did he ascertain much of the Darkness...or Paradise?' Hugo asked.

'I don't know, and I'm afraid to ask. As crazy as it sounds this was no vision, Aidan travelled into the afterlife and back. Why, we know of...how, we do not!'

'Could it be something that we are doing?' Hopper asked, looking around at the others. 'After all, the mindmelding skill in the youngsters was passed on by the common factor of your boy's hands, Milord.'

Tragen mused over the mate's words. 'You know, you may have a point. Is there a trigger?'

'Something occurs to me. Is there only one servant of the Darkness?' Hugo asked, tugging at his beard. 'If there are more they must have killed many others in these intervening years.'

No-one had an answer to that.

Twenty-three

In the middle of the following morning Aidan, Augusta and Beatrix were sitting in the Portolan family's summerhouse with Thaddeus. Built against the backdrop of the woods at the rear of the lawn behind the main house the pine retreat, all three walls formed of hand-carved trellis work, was bedecked in rambling roses of all colours. It was a fine-looking, peaceful place designed by Bettina Portolan just after her marriage and maintained by the household in loving memory of the very popular mistress.

Thaddeus sat bolt upright in the brown wicker chair at the small circular table, his back to the rear wall where earlier the two girls had placed him between them. Aidan sat opposite, lolling with his feet up on a spare chair whilst Augusta sat with her elbows resting on the table, her hands cupping her chin and staring out over the manicured garden. Beatrix pouring fresh lemonade wondered if she should lift the drink to Thaddeus' mouth, he hadn't taken any notice of the tumbler she'd placed before him. Nervously she held the drink to his lips and without any urging from her he automatically drank and didn't stop until she replaced the tumbler on the table.

Portolan, Janne and Alessa Barbat, for the first time in fifteen years were without the stricken boy in their charge and each was confused—the seneschal remarked later that it felt as if a living limb had somehow got lost. The nurse continually discovered excuses to pass and linger at the back windows overlooking the summerhouse. Portolan unexpectedly found an opportunity to organize a clean-up of the drains and gutters at the back of the house and Marcus Janne, after his usual morning inspection of the Griffin militia, decided that urgent paperwork could not be deferred any longer. His office was a small room on the corner of the third floor; his window commanding a view of the woods, with the summerhouse just visible if he craned his neck.

Hope swelled their chests, excitement wriggled in their stomachs, but common sense prevailed in the heads of the three adults wandering lost within the house and grounds. Was Aidan right in his diagnosis? The conclusions reached by him seemed so unbelievable. How did he know so much of death? Could these three youngsters and a dead boy's spirit possibly find Thaddeus' soul?

But their anxiety was nothing compared to the rage that filled the heart of the seneschal. All these years of believing that Bettina had died a mad woman! How could he have possibly thought it? God, he'd lived and loved her for so long, his childhood sweetheart, he knew her body and soul. Surely he should have guessed that there was another reason for her distress. But now, after all these years to be told that he had witnessed her fight for their son's survival. The shame of watching his wife die violently at the hands of a demon, even though he knew it not, brought on enormous guilt. By the Gods, he promised, whatever it was he'd destroy the Darkness.

'Well, what is your plan of action, little wizard?' asked Augusta grumpily, her hand in front of her mouth, yawning widely.

'What's up with you?' Aidan asked.

'Oh, I don't know, do I? It's that bed, it was bloody uncomfortable. Every time I turned over I nearly fell out.'

Aidan laughed. 'What did you expect? You've slept in a bed that moves for the last few weeks…it's going to take time to get used to one that stays still.'

'You're language is getting worse, Augusta, you're sounding more like Aidan every day. I don't know what your father'll make of it,' Beatrix tutted disapprovingly.

'You are nagging again, my father will never find out unless you tell him.'

'The rate you're picking it up you'll be telling him yourself!'

'Shush, the pair of you, you're giving me a headache,' said Aidan, cleaning a fingernail with a small stick. 'Hey,' and all of a sudden he sat up straight, his feet on the floor, grinning widely, 'didn't I hear you cursing yesterday?'

'That was an accident! I was provoked and anyway, it was your fault!' Beatrix was scarlet.

'My fault! How do…'

'Ugh! Stop doing that, that's disgusting,' said Augusta pulling a face, interrupting the start of another argument. 'Clean your nails elsewhere, pig!'

'Oh God, I'm bored! Can't we do something instead of just sitting here doing nothing,' asked Beatrix.

'We are doing something; we're creating a bond between the four of us. Our different feelings and emotions will learn to identify each other's. If we're going to contact Thaddeus by mindmelding, he has to recognize us and this is the only possible way.'

'What did you say?' Beatrix asked.

'Gone deaf, all of a sudden, have you?'

'Don't start…no, you said "the four of us", I wonder?'

'What?' asked Augusta.

'Could he be the fifth one we've been told of?' she asked staring at Thaddeus closely.

'God knows! If he is, it's a hell of a coincidence us meeting him now. Well, if we are going to succeed in contacting him wouldn't it be better if we all held his hands?' asked Augusta.

'I'm not holding his hand…he's a boy! I'll hold your hand, though, while you're holding his.'

'Not with dirty fingernails, you won't,' said Augusta, grimacing.

'They're clean now, look. And besides there's something else, one other thing,' he glanced nervously at Beatrix. 'I need to know if I've passed something else on to you.'

'What?' Augusta asked.

'Speaking with the spirits, I want to see if you two can do it. But to test it we'll have to contact Anders. How do you feel about that, Beattie?'

Beatrix beamed. 'I had a long talk with him during the night…it was lovely. Honestly,' she said as the others stared at her, startled.

'I'm not on about you dreaming of him,' said Aidan.

'*She knows that, urchin,*' interrupted Anders.

'*Oh, Anders is that really you?*' Augusta asked, bursting into tears.

'*Don't cry, Augusta, please? And that answers your question, Aidan,*' he said. '*We're going to be talking together a lot over these next weeks, Augusta, so dry your eyes and smile! Hallo Beattie.*'

'*Hallo, Anders…*'

'*Okay, now we know, enough of the greetings. Meet Thaddeus, you can see him can't you?*' Aidan asked all business-like.

'*Hey, don't speak to Anders like that, or I'll clout you,*' said Augusta, at the same time struggling to come to terms with the gifts that Aidan had passed to her. Nothing was going to surprise her anymore!

'*What was wrong…?*'

'*All right, enough you two, don't start again we're trying to contact Thaddeus not fight amongst ourselves,*' ordered Beatrix.

'*Do you think you might have given mindmelding to Thaddeus?*' Anders asked.

'I don't know...I did everything I can remember doing with you three. I held his head, I rubbed his temples and I stared into his eyes. I'm just hoping it's travelled along the lifeline to his soul.'

'Can you see this line he's on about, Anders?' Augusta asked, drying her eyes.

'Yes, it's shimmering in this light...it's very thin though as if it's been stretched to almost breaking point. It just goes off forever into the distance.

'It's not going to break is it?' Beatrix asked.

'Nah, not yet, but it has to be fragile after fifteen years, though.'

'But you said souls linger in Limbo for eternity sometimes,' said Aidan.

'Aye, but that's when they're dead. This boy isn't dead—yet.'

'So...what do you suggest, Aidan?' Beatrix asked anxiously, not liking Anders' use of the word "yet".

'Anders, can you follow his lifeline?'

'I can try, but I'll probably come across tangles in the path...you know when his soul has travelled into other Limbos and back again. It may be murder to unravel the trail.'

'Well, you'll have to try. Meantime we'll carry on trying to mindmeld with him.'

'OK, I'll give it a go. I'll get back to you straight away if I find anything,' he said not sounding hopeful. *'S'long, Beattie.'*

'Goodbye, Anders, take care please,' Beatrix said quietly, her eyes glistening despite her resolve not to cry.

They were deep underground in a vast, roughly circular, cold, stone arena illuminated by candles in sconces spaced more or less evenly in niches around the walls. Surrounding them were raised tiers of cold, stone seats numbering upwards of five hundred. The ceiling was so high it seemed almost non-existent in the darkness far above.

Just visible to the naked eye were chains strung across the room at a height of three floors, and from the centre of these chains, an iron cage was suspended. The cage itself consisted of two equal halves opening on hinges along its length—the length of a tall man. There were other chains hanging down alongside and these were used to raise and lower the device, the chains and the bars of the cage itself were stained a dirty brown.

Directly below the cage was a large cloud of ice-cold vapour, black it absorbed all light appearing darker than the blackest coal. The whole churning mass was contained within the perimeter of an almost circular basin, its edges of naked grey rock bearing the glistening chisel marks of having been recently hewn from the living bedrock.

A little to one side of the smoking, vaporous fog and resting on a raised dais, was a waist high altar of granite. On the upper surface of the altar was a scooped out hollow. Running through the bottom of the void was a channel, shallow at the top end very deep at the other it flowed beneath a two-foot high, black stone, two-horned pyramid before leading into the boiling mass of freezing, reeking fumes.

At the north end of the room was a wide archway, an iron grille erected across its entrance and through which a corridor led off into deep recesses. At the south end was a doorway, now closed. On the western side of the room, a chest high, granite font stood on a podium, the contents of the font emitting a green light.

Standing at the font staring into the scrying vapours was a very tall figure wearing a black robe, the cowl raised. Standing behind on the floor of the arena, was a middle-aged man dressed in a white robe, the cowl around his shoulders. He was also tall, and lean, his head shorn of all hair, although black stubble showed at his nape.

The black-robed figure spoke without turning from the scry. 'You are ready?'

'I am, the ship is manned and I can leave whenever you give the word,' he trembled in his sandals; the sibilant hiss of his master always unnerved him.

'Take this pendant; place it around your neck for now. If you have to remove it for any reason remember—keep it about your person, always,' the figure, without turning, held out a neck chain. Hanging from it was a small, black, two-horned pyramid similar to that on the altar. 'Wear it always and the wizard cannot enter your mind or anyone else's whilst in its vicinity.' What was not voiced was the fact that the talisman would also render the white-robed man's mind unreadable to his master.

The monk shuddered as he took the proffered necklace gingerly from the claw-like hand. Hanging it around his neck he couldn't help but notice that it reminded him of a bell without a clapper. He frowned, he'd seen one once before but had forgotten where. He hid it beneath his robe the silent bell resting in the middle of his chest felt like a lump of ice.

The black-robed figure continued. 'Contrive an opportunity to submerge the artefact in the wizard's drink. It will remove all his powers for a time. The longer it is immersed, the longer he will be without his magic. But be cautious, immerse the stone for too long and you will deprive him of his abilities forever. I need him to regain them when I have him here on the eve of Midsummer.'

The white-robed man shivered again as he fingered the unearthly relic. He wondered if the power in the stone would affect him in any detrimental manner. He looked up at his master's back…how long was too long? He was too afraid to ask.

'It will take more than a week to repair their ship. Remember, I must have the wizard alive and carrying his staff. With his death, your ambition will be realized and my part in this mission will be complete. This place will never be favoured by me again. Make sure your request appears genuine; otherwise, he will suspect ulterior motives.'

The black-robed figure sniggered, sending another chill down the spine of the monk. 'I see him; the fool is using his staff to aid the crew. He has no idea it attracted the storm and that using it opens the only way for me to oversee his actions,' a hiss followed these words. 'Everything falls into place…go, Brother Dyfrig,' and the black-robed figure warned coldly. 'Do not fail me.'

The Grim, because of its gigantic size, caused almost impossible problems in moving it into dry-dock. Heavy, thick hawsers were secured to all points amidships and paid out to so many launches that from the cliffs above they looked like leaves strewn across the water by some violent tornado.

It took all morning, the multitude of small boats pushing and pulling, the men cussing and nursing the occasional careless injury. But once the Grim was lined up with the gates, the hawsers leading from the bows were wound around the huge capstans at the far end of the dock, and horses were used to turn the vast spindles.   The whole operation was precarious and time consuming. In the early evening the dock gates were closed and Tragen invoked the power of his staff to increase the rate of the pumps and veritable jets of water poured over the doors into the lagoon.

By mid-morning of the following day, the dock was empty of water, initial inspection begun and the wizard was at Aidan's bedside, holding his comatose apprentice in his arms.

As the Grim was manoeuvring in the harbour, Aidan, Augusta and Beatrix were again sitting in the summerhouse with Thaddeus, all four again holding hands after what seemed like hours to Augusta, and the girls were again bored to tears. Tedium set in rapidly as the expectation of quick results soon dissolved.

'Aidan, this is getting us nowhere. We've been mindmelding for him for hours and nothing's happening...there's no reaction at all,' said Augusta, fidgeting in her seat. *'Ooh! My back is aching sitting here; can't we walk about a bit? We can still hold hands.'*

'Augusta, have patience; reaching for Thaddeus could take days. I don't like sitting here anymore than you do,' Aidan said, though he felt no inclination to stir himself, it was cool in the shade and his eyes were drooping. Despite the hard chair, it was pleasant resting there with his feet up holding Augusta's hand.

'Patience! Since when did you have any patience, little wizard?'

'Here we go again,' said Beatrix interrupting the flow. When Augusta was in this mood her tirades could go on forever. *'She's right, Aidan, we can reach for him just as well, walking about the grounds.'*

Aidan gave in grudgingly. The two girls strolled either side of Thaddeus holding his hands comfortably and as they walked through the gardens along pathways bordered with fragrant orchids and white and red helleborine, across the well cultivated lawn and into the fringes of the woods behind the house, Aidan explained in more detail what he thought was required.

And as they roved, so Seneschal Portolan popped up occasionally in their path, or they'd come across the nurse sitting on a bench or Marshal Janne standing with a sentry posted not too far distant.

They ambled along in silence for, of course, they were mindmelding.

'We have to feel for him with our emotions, visualize him as he should be, think what he must be thinking,' instructed Aidan.

'Well that's easy enough, isn't it?' Augusta said sarcastically. *'How in hell do we do all that?'*

'How can I see him as he should be if I don't know how he feels, let alone know what he's thinking?' Beatrix said, baffled.

'Our feelings and his feelings will come together somehow, the more we are with him. As for seeing him...look at him, look into his eyes try and see behind them and imagine what he sees looking out. I know it's going to be hard, I know it sounds impossible but we have to try,' he paused and kicked at a small stone in his path. *'And as for*

what he's thinking? He's lost out there somewhere. Imagine if you were in the same predicament,' and as if he could read the future, as if he had a premonition, he added, *'Don't forget he has never known life in this world. But what if he can see it, I mean, what if he can see the life he should have and can't get here because he's trapped. I don't know about you, I'd probably go nuts. But if he is aware of this life and can see that we are trying to contact him, surely he will do his damnedest to get through to us, hey?'*

Augusta looked at Thaddeus and lifted his hand in hers. *'Do you reckon he'd like holding hands with me and Beattie?'*

'Better than holding my hand,' Aidan said laughing.

They continued their ramble through the short undergrowth, Thaddeus instinctively stepping over stones and roots, around trees and through the occasional bramble bush, quite safe in his meandering. An ability that intrigued Aidan, Thaddeus' physical perceptions had in no way been denied him.

Augusta ceased her absurd inclination of blowing at all and sundry as she walked around sweet birch, southern nettle, beech and fir trees. A habit that Aidan again pondered on as she very rarely exhibited it away from the trees and bushes.

'Beattie, look at him...he's very good-looking, isn't he?' said Augusta out of the blue.

'I don't think so,' interjected Aidan, *'he looks a bit girlish to me.'*

'You're only saying that because he's more handsome than you,' Augusta said waspishly.

'No I'm not...look at him he's a bit fat as well. He'll need to work that off when we find him.'

'A very good idea, you're best yet, little wizard! We could all do with some proper exercise after being holed up on that ship for weeks. You could do with building up, you're too thin,' snapped Beatrix.

'No I'm not, I'm...svelte!'

'You're skinny!'

'Not as skinny as you!'

'Hey! I think he's listening to you two quarrelling!' Augusta said.

'We are not quarrelling; we are having a difference of opinion!' Beatrix said.

'Look at Thaddeus' eyes—they're brighter. I'm sure he's there, listening to us.'

Aidan and Beatrix stared into the boy's blue eyes sparkling in the sunshine.

You're imagining things, I see no difference,' said Aidan, dismissively.

'Neither do I,' Beatrix agreed.

Augusta stared again and shrugged her shoulders. *'I'm positive he was there—his eyes were different. There was definitely something, they moved a little as you two argued,'* she said disappointed.

'Aidan, I've had a thought,' said Beatrix.

'Well that's new,' he replied, having his own back.

'When we were talking just then, we were ignoring Thaddeus. What if that's what we should be doing?'

'What! Ignore him?' Aidan said.

'No, that's not what I meant, now listen. When we spoke we were being ourselves, I mean we were not striving for him as we have been all morning. If Augusta is right, perhaps he would find it easier to get through to us if we carried on as we normally would.'

'Quarrelling, you mean!'

'Shut it,' Augusta said.

Late that afternoon Leash was hiding behind a young elm tree in the same woods behind the manor, watching his prey, he'd been following them for most of the day. Now Aidan and his three companions were walking along the path to the low kitchen door in the corner of the back wall of the house.

Leash had found it relatively easy to enter the grounds having avoided the security patrols with a self-confidence that came with experience. Wending his way through the darkening woods, climbing the fence with alacrity, his path illuminated by the newly lit lamps in every window of the large house, his brain seethed with possibilities.

For once the wizard had done him a favour using his staff. With the pumps flowing magically his presence on the Grim was no longer needed and he had jumped at the chance to accomplish two very urgent tasks.

The first, to establish his connection with the Montetor spy, a task carried out with a nod of his head to a dockworker he had seen the night before in the company of Bazyli Montetor. The second had been a little more difficult, but working near the wizard that afternoon, he had overheard Tragen say that he would be visiting Aidan on the morrow to "ascertain any progress with the seneschal's son". Leash had smiled; in one sentence, he had discovered the whereabouts of the three youngsters, a problem that had been vexing him since he'd risen that morning and found them missing.

Peering round the elm at the two girls arm in arm with a boy he did not know, but assumed to be the seneschal's son, he studied Aidan and wondered why he was waving his arms about as if he was talking animatedly. Leash could not hear a thing. He studied the strange boy walking between the two girls, would he be a problem? But he decided that he didn't care, if the boy happened to get in the way it would be hard luck on him and his father.

The seneschal sent a coach for Tragen in the early hours of the following morning with the news that Aidan had succumbed to another visitation according to Augusta and Beatrix this, the worst yet.

The apprentice had been screaming "leave me alone...go away, get from me"! He had repeated this over and over, the words recalling memories of Bettina Portolan's death. The seneschal was mortally afraid, re-living the moments of his wife's death in the boy's delirium he knew that if Aidan was to die, there would be no hope for Thaddeus. Lodovico Portolan watching the boy thrashing about on the bed and hearing his desperate pleas, now believed every word that Aidan had said about demons and Limbo and the Darkness. And he prayed as he'd never prayed before.

When Tragen arrived, he discovered the two distraught girls with their arms around Aidan; he had ceased his ranting and lapsed into unconsciousness. Augusta and Beatrix were weeping copiously, utterly helpless.

It was not like the last time. This time Aidan knew where he was immediately—he was in the Darkness and he was terrified.

The physical sensations were easily recognizable; they battered hard at his brain, overwhelming his senses. A dark mist swirling before his eyes ranging in differing shades of grey and black, its density constantly changing. Visibility, sometimes restricted to a handbreadth from his face, at other times stretching away from him but not far, disclosing horrors he had yet to recognize but knew he didn't want to see.

The stench of decay permeating the very cold air was overpowering, the smells redolent of blood and faeces and above all, rank fear. His breath rose before his face adding to the dark cloud, the acrid taste of the black atmosphere drying his lips forcing him to swallow…and retch. The bitter touch of the fog on his skin bringing forth goose-pimples, its clamminess and its unnaturalness, making him sweat and shiver uncontrollably.

The clamour unnerved him most, its stridency making him flinch repeatedly. He peered around searching through his upraised arms, crouched as if he was warding off an attack. The background noises of discordant screeching and occasional thuds and bumps were the least of his nightmare, those just hurt his ears. It was the sounds amidst the cacophony that he could distinguish and recognize, that frightened him silly. Violence threatened and promised, screams and weeping and the abhorrent, obscene, very loud laughter

He was utterly shocked, unable to think clearly his mind completely encompassed by the horrors, he never thought to move. As his eyes grew accustomed to the murkiness, he began to make out shapes moving erratically through the fog and he screamed.

'Leave me alone…go away, get from me!'

He dribbled down his chin, too afraid to put one foot in front of the other, he remained rooted to the spot, hunched over almost double, only turning his head to search for escape. The figures came nearer and he could see they were people though they were maimed into misshapen parodies of human bodies. Many had limbs missing or broken and often just hanging loose as if partially torn from joints by the Gods knew what. Gradually awareness grew of what the moaning meant and he gibbered in fear, nearly wetting himself. People wandered through the mists, mewling in dreadful agony their grotesque injuries untreated. Despite his senses telling him not to, he looked down when he felt something against his foot. It was a severed head, its eyes open, its mouth wide in silent agony—it blinked.

He fled in unparalleled terror, his eyes starting from his head, his panicked path leading him deeper into the Darkness, deeper into the unfathomable waste. He seemed to run for hours in his madness, for his mind had crossed the threshold of sanity into craziness, his only aim to escape the horrendous sights. But he could not and this fact penetrated his brain infinitesimally slowly and eventually he stopped and looked around again.

His new location seemed exactly like the first. Wherever he moved in the Darkness, it remained the same. And little by little he came to understand that there was no point in walking anywhere. His reason disappeared completely when he witnessed two horribly mutilated bodies biting lumps out of each other.

Hours later he wondered why no-one had yet attacked him. Comprehension dawned slowly and with it semblances of rationality returned—perhaps they couldn't see him. He began to think; if they couldn't, they may also be unable to feel him. If they couldn't do either then they wouldn't be able to hurt him. He stared at the figures, panic taking hold at the thought of testing his theory.

He lifted his arm and held it out to his side, waiting with bated breath for someone to come along and touch him knowing that if any did he'd have to flee like the wind. He trembled as a figure with the nominal features of a woman with a badly mauled face came near. Unable to watch her approach close, scared to death that she'd feel the encounter with his arm, he closed his eyes and tensed ready to run. After minutes that felt like forever to his horrified brain he realized that he had felt nothing and he opened his eyes a moment later to find the woman had wandered off. Had she touched him before going? He didn't know, he hadn't experienced even the brush of her body against his fingers.

Biting his lip until he tasted his own blood, he kept his eyes open at the next encounter. He watched as the cruelly stooped figure of an old man wandered through his arm leaving no sensation whatever.

He shivered with partial relief. He had proved they could not feel him, but he had no sensation of touching them either.

Now the hardest part, he cringed inwardly, could they see him? He waited again, panic just below the surface, what would he do if they did see him? The next man to wander into his vicinity had one arm; he was carrying the other in his hand. Aidan tensed – sweat running down his back despite it being bitterly cold – taking his heart in both hands he stepped to the side until he was directly in the man's path. As the crippled man walked forward, Aidan walked backwards in front of him and stared into the man's sunken eye sockets and discovered the maimed creature before him lacked an eye.

Unexpectedly Aidan began to weep and groan. He had discovered their terrible existence. This man was a soul, a dead soul in torment, trapped, wandering aimlessly in the black fog of the evil Darkness.

He fell to his knees and the man walked through him. Crossing his arms over his chest he lowered his head and rocked back and fore, keening uncontrollably. He was a young man whose whole life had been built on healing and here he could see hurt unimaginable. The harm, the agony of these souls overwhelmed him. He could not help them. He needed to feel them physically in order to heal, and he wanted so much to end their suffering. He was lost in a world that was anathema to him. This was an existence of pure detestation and desperation—no soul could ever survive this terror.

And he realized that the sick did not give him pleasure, there was no need to feel shame at people's gratitude.

Aidan wept until no more tears would form. Utterly bereft, he rose and roamed as the souls roamed. He stared down at his feet, moving through the souls this time not bothering to turn aside, what was the point?

Despair beyond measure was all he knew and eventually he dropped to the ground and curled up on his side, hugging his knees.

'Lord Tragen, we must do something, this coma is very deep he is almost not breathing. He is frightening me,' said Augusta, staring at the distraught wizard.

'What do you suggest? Do you want me to heal him? Even if I could, which I doubt, you said yourself he would then be lost to us forever. Can't you contact Anders, he may know?'

'We have been trying,' said Beatrix. 'But we sent him searching for Thaddeus. We think he's too far away to hear us calling.'

Augusta and Beatrix glanced at each other. 'We've been thinking, Milord,' said Augusta. 'Although you have immense power in your staff we know you cannot speak with the dead as we can. So,' she continued hesitatingly, 'how about using your staff to send our minds into Limbo to search for him? You may be able to send us closer to Anders.'

Tragen stiffened and suddenly paled. Holding his staff before him he moaned in agony as he stared at it.

'Milord, what ails you?' Beatrix asked rushing to him. Augusta, Portolan and Janne stared at him perplexed, none having heard such a cry of despair before.

Tragen gazed at his staff and then down at his boy. 'Augusta…Highness, you have just discovered the reason for his visions, his journeys.'

'I have?'

'My staff! Every time I have used my staff in these last weeks, Aidan has received a vision the same night.' Utterly desolate he added. 'I and my staff have sent my boy's mind into mortal danger.'

Anders was baffled. He had been following Thaddeus' lifeline all over Limbo and now Aidan's lifeline had abruptly appeared, both running alongside each other down the slope and into the Darkness. Anders was afraid, he could not enter the Darkness and return, all souls of the dead remained in its clutches forever. He would have to wait for Aidan to emerge, and possibly Thaddeus, if he could. Thaddeus' lifeline, not as bright as Aidan's, looked as if it had been in the entryway to Purgatory for years. They couldn't wait years. Whatever he was here to help Aidan accomplish had to be done now, not at some time in the far future. If Thaddeus' soul could survive in there for ages, it didn't automatically mean that Aidan's would. If either of them got within reach of Purgatory then either or both souls would die and be lost forever.

I need help, he thought staring into the gloom in the distance, afraid to go any nearer, knowing it would take him. He turned and ran to the wall of colours.

Leash sat in the servant's hall drinking the harsh black coffee of Griffin with Mistress Lacey. He had been seconded to escort Lady Cornelia for no self-respecting lady ever travelled without a bodyguard in foreign ports.

Entering the house they had learned that Aidan's health was now a cause of great concern and Cornelia hurried upstairs to the sickroom.

Leash suffered a pang of unease, why he wasn't sure but it surprised him, for one moment it was as if he cared about the boy's safety. But recovering quickly and putting the strange notion out of his mind he smiled, he and he alone wished to be responsible for the demise of the wizard's apprentice. And as the lady rushed away, Leash smiled at Mistress Lacey and set out to gain as much knowledge as he could of the workings of the estate.

Cornelia, rushing into Aidan's bedchamber, found Tragen being comforted by Augusta and Beatrix. Janne and Portolan, standing just inside the door, glanced at each other at a loss for words, neither understood the wizard's words.

'What is it, Tragen?' She said breathlessly, anxiety etching deep lines in her fleshy brow. 'What has happened?' Receiving no answer she turned her attention to the seneschal. 'Will you enlighten me, Lodovico?'

'I'm not sure if I am able, Cornelia,' he said, staring at her a deep frown lidding his eyes. 'There seems to be more than one mystery here. Firstly, Tragen states that it is his staff which is responsible for Aidan's trauma. Secondly, the spirit of Anders has gone missing in Limbo, presumably searching for my son. And now your maid Nellie appears not to be a maid at all but someone of authority named Augusta.' He stared at Cornelia questioningly. 'Perhaps you should enlighten me?'

Cornelia returned his stare, her mind working overtime. Was it too early to divulge their purpose? She straightened her ample back as she sat in a chair after moving it to the foot of Aidan's bed.

'Lodovico, we have kept a few matters hidden from you, not because we don't trust you but because we didn't know you.' She looked at Tragen; he lifted his head to the sound of her voice, and at his nod, she continued.

'Augusta is indeed someone of consequence...she is the daughter and heir of the Prince of Mantovar, and as such has many enemies. I am her lady-in-waiting charged, along with Lord Tragen, to care for and to protect her.'

'You are not Lord Tragen's niece?'

'No, Lodovico, we adopted that strategy because we wished to hide Augusta's identity. You understand our motive?'

'I do,' her answer seemed to please him, 'please continue.'

'We believe a servant of the Darkness created the storm to entice us here.'

'Oh...and why should the Darkness or whatever wish you here on Griffin?'

'We do not believe our final destination is Griffin,' Tragen interrupted, sighing, and watching for the seneschal's reaction he went on. 'Whoever he is wants us on Sanctity.'

Portolan instinctively shuddered. Janne drew in a short sharp breath through his teeth, the violent reactions of both men although expected, still surprised the Mantovarians.

'Seneschal Portolan,' said Augusta, 'perhaps you should tell us about Sanctity?'

'Later, if I think you need to know, Highness,' he grimaced. 'Now, I think someone should tell me all that has transpired in these last weeks.'

Tragen rubbed his eyes tiredly. The passengers of the Grim proceeded to relate the tale, including Aidan's role in saving Tragen's life. They held nothing back, knowing that being truthful was the only means of obtaining the seneschal's aid.

'If you and Marcus do not mind, Lodovico, please continue our subterfuge, Augusta is still the maid Nellie,' Tragen said, finishing the long tale.

'Of course! As for Sanctity, I have no evidence to suggest the Darkness is on that island—although there is a great evil there,' he rose from his chair and moved to the window. 'I have not been near Sanctity for nearly twenty years. The reason is my business and you will have to trust me. If I find it has a bearing on matters here then I will inform you.' He sighed as he allowed his eyes to rove over the dense wood at the back of the house. 'Our first priority is to regain Aidan's soul and return it to his body,' he grimaced hating the next words he must utter. 'The search for my son and his hunter, Anders, must wait. Even if the hunt is successful, nothing can be achieved without Aidan. As I understand it, you Tragen, can no longer use your staff, am I correct?'

'You are, yes…using the power may send him deeper into Limbo, into greater danger.'

'Then it is up to the young ladies,' said Portolan, staring at Augusta and Beatrix.

Aidan was cold, bone numbingly cold and it was this that brought him to his senses. His instincts informed his brain that he had to move to keep warm. Slowly he picked himself up from the ground and hesitatingly he put one foot in front of the other. The motion brought awareness creeping back and he quickened his pace. The faster he walked the warmer he became and with that warmth came consciousness of his surroundings.

Sorrow engulfed him as he roamed amongst these mutilated souls. Never mind what they looked like or sounded like or what they did to each other, they were lost souls trapped in the Darkness, imprisoned by evil, and he was deeply saddened. In time his own protective instinct became his saviour. He ignored their deformities. He became deaf to the shrieks and screams and raucous calling. The stench went unnoticed as he met their eyes and recognized the unutterable torment living there, and gradually the need to escape re-entered his mind.

His heart cried out, he had to escape to return and rescue them.

He continued walking, his eyes staring at the unchanging ground before his feet, the sameness of the sights before his eyes, his ears hearing the abject, hopeless anguish of souls tormented beyond belief.

Searching for a means to break free, he listened for his friends; for he knew they would be calling him.

All he had to do was find a way out of this horror, and then he could come back.

Twenty-four

Anders shouted, *'Beattie, Augusta, shut up…listen to me!'*
    'I have an idea, wha…' Beatrix halted in mid-sentence. *'Anders is that you?'*

'Who else would it be? Now listen, I need you and Augusta to help me. Why in hell is Aidan here?'

'What is it Beatrix? What were you saying?' Cornelia asked puzzled when the girl ceased speaking.

'Anders is back, Cornelia…sh! A moment,' said Augusta excited. *'Aidan's gone missing; we think it was caused by Tragen's staff. Hasn't it sent him into Limbo again? Isn't he with you?'*

'No, he's in the Darkness with Thaddeus I think. What do you mean Tragen's staff sent him here?'

'What do you mean…you think?' Augusta retorted.

'What I said! I was following Thaddeus' lifeline up until it disappeared into the Darkness. I'm standing there scratching my head, wondering what the hell to do next when Aidan's lifeline appears and runs alongside Thaddeus'. I can't enter the Darkness and survive, no dead soul can. I need you and Beattie here to help me get them out.'

'And how are we going to get into Limbo to aid you?' Beatrix asked, impatiently. *'We've already thought of using magic to get there, but we don't know how to use it and we daren't use Tragen's staff.'*

'I'll help you, tell Tragen to get Thaddeus in the same room,' said Anders. *'All four of you must hold hands it will be easier to track Aidan and Thaddeus and keep you safe. When you're ready I'll pull you through the wall.'*

'Seneschal, please bring Thaddeus here,' said Augusta, a tremor in her voice, the thought of what they were about to do, and where they were about to go, seriously frightening her. 'We need to hold hands, the four of us. For some reason Aidan and Thaddeus are in the Darkness together and…and Anders needs our help to bring them out. Anders is going to take us into Limbo to search for them.'

'Dear God…Janne move,' shouted Portolan, panicking. But even before Augusta had finished her words, the security commander was running down the corridor.

'I think we'd better lie down, we have no idea how long we'll be away,' said Augusta, looking at Cornelia and attempting to smile bravely, her stomach in a turmoil. Would she find out now what it was like to die, or was Aidan right, her lifeline would remain anchored in her body? But to actually enter the afterlife! And then, God, she realized Anders had not mentioned helping them to return!

A little while later, there were four truckle beds standing side by side, a little space between each. All were occupied with the prone figures of Aidan, Augusta, Beatrix and Thaddeus, each holding hands with their neighbour. With Tragen, Cornelia, Portolan, Janne and Alessa Barbat watching over them, Anders pushed his forearms into the wall of colours and dragged the souls of Augusta and Beatrix through into Death.

'Hey!' Augusta said, moments later, 'this Limbo is exactly as Aidan described it...will you two put each other down,' she said impatiently. After the initial shock of the translation from life into death, both girls having no idea what to expect, Beatrix had fled into Anders' open arms as soon as she'd seen him. They were hugging each other desperately, unmindful of Augusta's presence. 'I thought everyone's Limbo was different, Anders.'

'I'm sorry, but she can be such a cow on times. Oh, Anders, I've wanted to see you so very, very much, I've missed you so much it hurts,' Beatrix said, her eyes full she hugged him again.

'Hey, who's a cow?' Augusta said. Grabbing Anders herself when they came out of their clinch, she hugged him if not with quite as much fervour. 'Why is this Limbo the same?' she asked, releasing him finally.

'Because you are in mine.'

'Oh,' Augusta said, 'then what does my Limbo look like?'

'You haven't got one yet...you're not dead, Augusta.'

'Oh, Anders,' Beatrix said, bursting into tears.

'Hey, come on now, no more, please, Beattie?' He asked gently, putting his arms around her she buried her face in his neck. 'We have no time, we must run, come on,' and with Augusta's hand in his right, and Beattie's hand in his left, they flew over the hills and vales away from Life and towards the Darkness.

Anders, Augusta and Beatrix reached the brow of the vale where Anders had met Aidan on his previous visit. At the bottom of the slope was the large oak tree at the fork in the path.

'What's that tree doing there?' Augusta asked.

'Oh, it's the place where people opt to stay or go on...or just rest a while,' answered Anders.

'Go on? To Paradise, you mean?' Beatrix asked puzzled.

'Aye, everyone has a choice, but that's a long story, I'll tell you when we have more time.'

'Ooh! That light ahead hurts! What is it?' Augusta asked, turning her head away.

'It is the entrance hall; from there you enter your Paradise.'

'What do you mean?' Beatrix asked.

'Everyone has a certain control over their own Paradise, each of us has our own likes and dislikes and you wouldn't want something you hated in your Paradise, would you? But some things are beyond your control, placed in your Paradise by the higher beings, to test the level of your understanding of Life.'

'So it's not always lovely in Paradise?' Augusta asked.

'I don't know. I wasn't there very long before I was told to come back and wait.'

'The one who sent you back…who was she?' Beatrix asked, gripping his hand tighter all at once she was feeling very sad. She gazed at the boy she loved and knew their fate was inevitable; she was going to lose Anders to that light.

'I don't know. All I know is she was a being from a higher plane and we of the lower can't see them through their light. We obey their instructions, though, or we won't gain improvement.'

'I'm confused, what improvement?' Beatrix asked, swallowing convulsively; she was going to have to prepare herself for another parting from him, perhaps the final one.

'It's the whole purpose of life. We return to earth to learn specific lessons decided by the higher beings. Depending on how we do, dictates how we improve and rise to a higher level of existence in Paradise. There are many levels there and each soul strives to reach the highest.'

'Why?' Augusta asked.

'God, you're full of questions I haven't the time to answer. I don't know why we strive, not for sure anyway, but I think the ultimate plane is perfection.'

'God, I'm glad I'm not dead yet, then, being perfect is boring,' said Augusta, biting her bottom lip and peering through half-closed eyelids.

'Hang on, where do the Gods fit in, then? I thought they ruled Paradise,' Beatrix asked thoroughly confused. 'Don't forget it's the Gods quarrelling that have got us in this mess.'

Anders sighed. How could he possibly explain it in simple terms when he wasn't even sure himself? 'Look, Beattie, there are two sorts of Gods as far as we know, the good and the evil. Both survive because of us. I mean, the good ones save souls, the bad ones kill…the good Gods rule in Paradise, the bad in Purgatory. But, they encroach on each other's' territories. There's no hard and fast rule with any of them.'

'Then what happens if all our souls are saved or all our souls are killed? How will the Gods survive then, surely the good Gods need souls to be threatened so they can save them? And the bad Gods need souls saved so that they can kill them. Because if one side wins then the Gods will die out they'll have nothing to survive on.' Beatrix gazed at her friends. 'And if that's the case they're idiots and we're all losers, why bother to fight?'

'Because we're human and have the right to live, here in the afterlife and in Life,' Anders replied. 'Most of the Gods are incapable of feeling, they are unable to love so don't honestly care about us, all they want is power. And the more souls they gain means the greater their power. Can we leave it there for now we have a job to do and it must be done quickly?'

Augusta, trembling in fear, stared up at the oak tree towering above them, its dark knobbly bark and deep green leaves displaying a vitality rarely seen in its natural habitat in Life. She was terrified of Anders' explanation and Beattie's conclusion. But as she gazed at the tree it seemed to calm her and she turned her gaze to the two shimmering lifelines of the souls of Aidan and Thaddeus. The lines, floating in the air low to the ground veered left, Aidan's coming from behind them from the wall of colours, the other, Thaddeus', coming at them from the right. Both led down the long slope towards the Darkness glimpsed in the distance. Augusta hugged herself, even more terrified at the sight.

'Anders, do we really have to go down there?'

'Aye, just don't ask me what to do when we get there. Your guess is going to be as good as mine. But I must warn you, the Darkness has an unbelievable attraction for the souls of the dead. You must stop me entering! I will never return.'

Anders clasped both girls' hands again and they ran for hours down the slope, the terror of the Darkness growing in them the nearer they approached. They ran like the wind, there was no fatigue in Limbo, no hunger or thirst either and no real perception of time. But there was enormous danger and they were racing towards it as if their lives depended on it.

Aidan had been walking for hours, extreme weariness creeping up on him. So tired was he, that as he approached the large shape before him expecting to walk through it as usual, he didn't notice it was different until it split into two figures. He walked past the first which looked to be a normal woman, it surprising him so much he looked behind unable to take his eyes from her as she walked on. But then, because he wasn't looking where he was going, he bumped so hard into the second that he cried out in pain and stumbled backwards, nearly falling.

Petrified, he lifted his arms before his face waiting to fend off an attack. This soul was a solid being—different. And differences in this world were unexpected and therefore more frightening. The figure before him slowly came closer and Aidan, his senses gradually quieting, detecting no threat of violence, was able to distinguish its features. Tall, overweight, with blond hair, it was a young man much Aidan's age, and he was standing with blue eyes as wide as bright lights staring at Aidan through the dense fog.

Aidan slowly relaxed and lowered his arms though still wary. Staring into the young man's eyes, he realized he could be seen and with mixed emotions of shock and hope, he whispered. 'Who are you?'

'You are alive!' The boy exclaimed, amazed he approached even closer; his face now inches from Aidan's.

Aidan returned the boy's gaze, shocked rigid, he recognized him and for a moment thought his madness had returned.

'Mum...mother it's the boy I saw in the wall! I told you someone was looking for me,' and the strange boy smiled and held out his hand. Aidan grasped it, and feeling solid, warm flesh he almost cried out with relief.

Aidan turned and looked at the other figure, the one he'd passed. She was a large woman, her form not as distinct as the boy's her outline blurring and pulsating continuously. She was not a solid being and she appeared the same as all the other figures he had come across in the mist. Then he realized that this woman was dead, but unhurt in a world of pain, and what's more she also could see him!

Her eyes were shining. 'Thank the Gods, at last!'

Aidan, stunned, stared from one to the other completely lost for words. 'Thaddeus?' he said, disbelieving his own eyes and ears.

'Yes,' and turning to the woman, he said, 'this is my mother. I hope you can help me take her from this vile place.'

'I don't understand,' said Aidan. 'How are you here, I left you at home? How did you manage to find your mother and…and how can she see me?'

'My body you left behind in Life,' Thaddeus said, sadly, 'do you understand?'

Aidan stared at him, the Darkness had dulled his brain, and comprehension dawned slowly. He understood he was now speaking with the lost soul of the boy that Anders' was searching Limbo for.

'Aye, I understand. My God, what you must be going through in here! It pains me terrible…' and tears again came to his eyes, he was unable to cease weeping in this place. 'I don't exactly know what's happened, how you arrived in this unspeakable horror, but I do know your father wants you home, needs you desperately! And you, Mistress Portolan, I explained to your husband that you saved Thaddeus. I wasn't wrong when I said that, I know I wasn't! So how are you both in here, now?'

'That is my fault,' answered Thaddeus. 'My mother rescued me from the demon that was trying to kill me at my birth, although it resulted in her death and my isolation. From that day she has cared for me, denying the Light that called her, the refuge she sorely needs.' He strode to his mother's side and put his arm around her. 'She reared me from a baby as she would have in Life, even though she was dead and I wasn't.' He stopped and put his hand to his mother's face and caressed it lovingly. 'When I accidentally wandered into here, she followed me even though she knew she could never return. And in here we have watched out for each other ever since.'

'You must take him with you when you leave. He must have his life with his father,' Bettina said, desperately. 'Whatever my son says he must not stay with me, he will die in here. That demon is of this Darkness and still searches for his soul and if he succeeds then both of us will be condemned to enter Purgatory. And I can't have that my…my Thaddeus must live!'

'How can you see and hear me, how can you touch Thaddeus?' Aidan asked.

Bettina stared at him. 'What is your name?' And on being told, she continued with the story of their very strange and terrible existence.

'The day I discovered Thaddeus had walked into this evil place, my heart stopped, I could not leave him alone. I love him so much…he is my life. I had to find him and keep him safe. I entered the Darkness voluntarily, that is what makes me different. Our love protects us both, his sanity and mine, and our souls. Although the others here can see me, they cannot harm me though they try. I am stronger than they are because I made a choice, they, poor souls had no option. The Darkness trapped them against their will though they fought to get away. They failed. I, on the other hand, walked in to find Thaddeus.' She sighed and glanced from Aidan to her son. 'Now you must leave, Thaddeus, you have a life to live, I do not.'

'I can't go and leave you in this place, Mum. I would be abandoning you to hell, I could never live with that, you wouldn't expect me to and you know it. No, perhaps Aidan knows a way to get us all out.'

'Me?' Aidan said. 'I don't even know how to get myself out.'

'Oh, I can help you there,' said Thaddeus. 'I often leave to watch the wall. I find a safe haven for my mother and I go to watch my father. My mother never runs off she knows I would search for her forever. When I return I tell her of all I see and hear,' he paused. 'I will take you to the border so you can step into Limbo, but I will not leave her,' he reiterated vehemently.

Hours later Aidan lay prone in the Darkness between Thaddeus and Bettina Portolan. 'Do not move a muscle, Aidan, do not speak until I say,' Thaddeus whispered in his ear.

Aidan heeded his words as a deeper coldness crept into his mind, a chill to numb his very soul. They waited and gradually heard a sibilant hissing over the sounds of soft steps. Aidan raised his head slightly above his arms and peered in front of him through the gloom, the hissing tugging at his memory. He saw nothing at first except the feet of lost souls rushing past and then the quiet steps were almost upon him. He espied the hem of a dark robe sweeping along the ground and abject terror took hold of him. Thaddeus flung himself over Aidan and used his weight to hold the boy still, his face in the ground to stifle his screams, preventing his rising and fleeing within the swirling mists.

The figure halted almost within touching distance, a moment later it walked on a little and stopped again, turning it stared in Aidan's direction. The coldness, the evil, pulsed from it and enveloped Aidan in horror. At the very moment that Aidan's struggles to shake off Thaddeus nearly succeeded, the figure sniffed several times as if searching and then turned about and continued on its way. It disappeared deeper into the murkiness, the surrounding temperature rising immediately to just below freezing.

Aidan's chest heaved, gasping for the fetid air of the Darkness. Lying on his back, recovering his wits slowly, his breathing fell back to almost normal. 'What in hell's name was that?'

'Hell's name is right. That was a herdsman. There are many of them here and they all work for the One, they are the evil collectors of Purgatory. If it had discovered you we would have been lost, once they set eyes on you there is no escape. You can never break away and you follow without even realizing that you are following, the last vestige of your sanity disappears and you are finally lost to Purgatory. Even these poor mad souls have learned to run away though they do not know the reason. The herdsmen appear at random and take anyone they meet. And in Purgatory, the poor souls recover their sanity, the worst thing that could ever happen to them.'

'Why? I'd have thought that recovering their minds would make their existence easier,' said Aidan, rising from the ground.

'Ah, but then they relive their suffering and torment for aeons, unable to go mad to forget. And their cries and pain feed the One,' Bettina said, her white face even paler as she contemplated her future. 'So, we hide.'

'Who is the One?'

'The One who wields the Darkness. Come, we are near the border you must leave,' said Thaddeus, 'there are other demons besides herdsmen here and they do not distinguish between those who have died and those that yet live.'

'You mean there are others still alive in this dreadful place?'

'Oh, yes! Many, but we don't meet them often. The Darkness is immense,' answered Bettina Portolan.

Aidan, still quivering, followed the seneschal's dead wife and her living son. They hurried through the billowing, desolate fog, following a path unclear to the young wizard. Sometime later a deformed soul with the vague outline of a man, grasped the large, overweight Bettina Portolan, she, with a practised motion, tossed the figure away, breaking his arm in the process. She looked at the outrage on Aidan's face.

'They cannot harm Thaddeus, but they can maim me. Over the years I have had to learn to protect myself from physical injury, as for my mind, Thaddeus' soul protects that. Do not worry about that man, eventually his arm will mend, no soul dies within the Darkness, it is trapped in a never-ending cycle of maiming and renewal. This is the way we exist here and that is why you both must leave,' staring at her son, she added determinedly. 'You must take Thaddeus with you, he cannot live much longer here I can feel him fading.'

And then Aidan saw a lightening of the mist before him.

'We are nearing Limbo,' Anders turned to the apprentice wizard. 'I'm sorry, we may not have known each other for very long, nevertheless, I will miss you. But you understand why I can't leave my mother alone in here?'

Bettina wept when Aidan nodded his head. 'Aye, I…whoa!' he said, he felt a tugging and was dragged forward as Thaddeus fell over at his feet.

'Stop!' Thaddeus screamed. 'Stop, I will not go!'

Aidan lunged out of the Darkness and across the border into Limbo, and discovered his friends had decided on the only action they could possibly take. In desperation they were tugging at the lifelines of both souls.

'Wait! Pull us out when I say.' Aidan shouted, and he disappeared back into the Darkness. 'My friends have grabbed our lifelines and are pulling us through,' he told them.

'No!' Thaddeus shouted, desperately, rising from the ground. 'My mother will run.'

'Hang on, trust me, I want to try something,' and he stared at Bettina Portolan. 'Mistress, you told me that Thaddeus' soul protects your mind, didn't you?' She nodded and he went on. 'But your mind is your soul, isn't it?' And she nodded again, frowning, not understanding the purpose of his questioning. 'Right, Thaddeus read my mind.'

'What?'

'Close your eyes and stare at me.'

'How can I look at you with my eyes shut?'

'Do it!' Thaddeus looked at Aidan as if he thought the boy had gone mad, and then shrugged his shoulders and complied.

'You know my face…now picture me.'

And following Aidan's instructions Thaddeus mindmelded.

'Can you understand me…can you see what I wish to try?'

'Yes, I can, but how…'

'I gave you mindmelding I must have given you magic as well.'

'Don't be daft!' Startled he spoke aloud.

'What is going on, Thaddeus?' Mistress Portolan asked.

Aidan smiled at them both. 'Now let's see what two souls using magic, can do.'

And again, following the apprentice's orders, Thaddeus joined Aidan in wrapping their arms about Bettina Portolan, enclosing the soul of the dead woman in their magical embrace. And at Aidan's shout, Augusta, Beatrix and Anders pulled all three through into Limbo.

'Aidan, Aidan!' Augusta screamed and she jumped on him, bearing him to the ground. 'Don't you dare frighten me like that again, don't you dare,' she said, and tears rolled down her face as she hugged and repeatedly kissed his face.

Anders and Beatrix stared at Thaddeus and Mistress Bettina Portolan. They both knew instantly who the lady was. Even after all these years Bettina was still the spitting image of her portrait hanging on the wall in the family parlour. And Thaddeus' soul was an exact replica of his blond, overweight body back in Life.

Aidan reluctantly extricated himself from Augusta's tight embrace, he'd thoroughly enjoyed feeling her lips on his face, and he stood up bringing her with him. He grinned. 'Am I glad to see your ugly faces!'

He flinched as Augusta punched his shoulder, clinging to him, unwilling to release him in case he disappeared again.

Ryn perched on the top of the North Tower staring down at the two humans standing before him below the battlements. The breathless one was the man-at-arms, his pike by his side, who had run away on the arrival of the albatross at Castle Mantovar. He had returned a few minutes later with this cruel-faced, white-garbed stranger.

'My, my, aren't you a big bird! And you can talk so this fool tells me,' the white robed man, tall and lean, his very thin face sneering, glanced at the soldier standing to attention his back against the parapet. 'At least you had better be able to talk or this man will attempt to emulate your skills of flying from the walls,' he smiled cruelly. 'What is it you want?'

Ryn waited, distracted by the arrival of two archers through the small doorway which led below. They stood beside the man-at-arms, full quivers of arrows at their belt, longbows in their hands staring amazed at the huge bird.

'*Do you see the bird, Master?*' The white-garbed man was astounded, although he did not allow his astonishment to show on his face. His shaved head showing signs of sunburn, he mindmelded to an unseen being.

'*I do...ask him again,*' ordered a sibilant hiss which filled Ryn full of dread.

Ryn, his feathers ruffling on his broad back, was suddenly very afraid; he had never heard such menace in a voice before. Who is this other one, he wondered? It didn't sound quite human. He instinctively knew that it could never be the prince, that nice young girl's father would never frighten him like this. Where was he? It certainly wasn't this white-robed man leering up at him. Ryn stared unblinking, and felt it better not to let this one know of his own ability to mindmeld. And then it occurred to him—how could he mindmeld?

'I repeat bird, what is it you want here?' The man was growing impatient; resting his hands on his hips he craned his neck back, his head level with Ryn's feet.

'The human who calls himself the Prince of Mantovar, I have a message for him.'

The two archers jumped in surprise when the bird spoke, one instinctively retrieving an arrow from his quiver ready to nock it to his bow. Ryn glanced at him seriously worried now; he had met hostile bowmen before on ships plying the Deep.

'What is the message?'

'One I must deliver personally to the prince,' answered Ryn nervously.

'He is busy and cannot get here now. I will pass on the message to him.'

'Only he may receive the missive, I was so ordered,' said Ryn, his fear growing, not liking this situation at all.

'*Ask him who sends it,*' the cold voice hissed again.

'If you are not prepared to tell me the contents of the message, then at least you can say who it is from,' stated the white robed man. Turning to the archer with the arrow in his hand, he indicated he should prepare to let fly the missile. 'So, bird, who is it that sent you?'

'A wizard, and if I cannot pass this on to the prince at this time, then I will return when he is present.'

'If you do not give me the message now,' he smiled evilly, 'you will not be able to return.'

'Disable him…do not kill!' said the voice.

Ryn flapped his wings and squawked loudly, the noise and the backdraft of his enormous wings beat at the soldiers knocking them to the ground as he rose into the air. Recovering quickly an archer let fly, the arrow missing Ryn's heart, pierced his wing bruising the bone and removing several of his secondary feathers. Ryn screamed in agony, reflexively folding his wing he dropped through the air. Moments later he recovered his wits and again spread his wings, flapped once and made for the safety of the forest, the wind causing further pain as it passed through the hole punched by the arrow. Glancing behind him, Ryn was startled to see the white-garbed man throw the archer from the top of the tower. The man at arms and the second archer had disappeared, presumably through the doorway down into the castle.

The albatross flew over the Great Forest until the pain in his injured wing became too much to bear. Fortunately, he espied a large clearing a long way inside the forest, leagues from its border with the town. He circled to inspect the ground before landing and came to rest unable to fold his wing; it had become very stiff during the flight. He groaned with relief as he rested the outstretched damaged limb cushioning it on the tall grass.

He studied the old trees around him searching for sign of pursuit. Not finding any he relaxed and waiting for the pain to subside his thoughts returned to the prince. He couldn't understand what had happened. He had failed abysmally to deliver the message through no fault of his own. He had to find another way to get it delivered, he was honour bound not to give up.

Settling into the softness of the grass, he shuddered at his near escape from death. His thoughts turned momentarily to his family. What would they say if he'd been killed because of his voice? They had thought him strange when he had first communicated his desire. None had ever felt as he had, in fact they had despised him for wanting such a human trait. Those who had ostracized him jealous of his gargantuan size now found another reason to scorn him. And for a species well used to being lonely, he'd felt even more isolated and unloved.

The pain in his wing set his thoughts to examining the strange yearning afresh. It was something that came to him in a dream—he was supposed to speak, and he was supposed to be huge. In his fantasies he was a legend! One of a kind he had a purpose in life that was more than just being avian. And then all of a sudden he realized why he'd answered Aidan's call—the boy had also been in his dream!

Shortly after departing the Grim he had encountered the vicious storm that had nearly been the end of the great ship and he'd been forced to fly north around it. Expecting his flight to take far longer than it had, he now wondered at the rate he'd flown. He'd found air currents that had sped him on his way far in excess of their normal speed. But he'd still been weary at the end of his long journey and had been glad to see the huge castle.

He thanked his lucky stars he had heard the order to wound him, enabling him to flee instantly, but what was he to do now? He was hurt and didn't know how to heal his wound. The boy would know of course, but how was he to return to the Grim? And return he had to, if only to inform the boy of his not so happy welcome in Mantovar. He ruffled the feathers on his chest and felt the tubular package holding the message hidden safely. He sighed; he would endeavour to find another means to deliver it.

'So that's why you landed,' a shrill, small voice said in front of Ryn. It came from dense undergrowth below a tall elm tree. 'I watched you come down and wondered. I hoped you were a dragon at first, but we haven't seen those for thousands of years.'

Ryn peered through the bushes in the direction of the voice and failed to see the owner. He squatted, perfectly still in the tall grass of the clearing, his nerves all on edge. He didn't detect a threat in the words, but there again he hadn't thought there was a risk at the castle either, until it was too late.

Ryn had been in this clearing for most of the afternoon now and was waiting for nightfall to wend his way home. He didn't know how he was going to survive the flight across the ocean, the thermals usually kept him in the air without the need to flap his wings. But the air currents would seep through the hole in his wing and have an adverse effect on his buoyancy. He would need to rest on the waves every few leagues. He often slept on the waves, and salt water was good for open wounds anyway, he thought, he just hoped that no shark would come across him while he slept. He was depressed; it was going to take weeks unless he was fortunate enough to relocate those almost magical thermals that got him here so fast, he hoped he wouldn't hit bad weather. The pain from his wound, reducing to a deep throb, he had attempted sleep but succeeded only in dozing until the voice roused him.

'Aren't you going to speak to me?' the small voice asked again.

'You know I can speak?'

'Of course, all creatures of magic can speak.'

'I am not magic,' stated Ryn, lifting his head to the full stretch of his long neck. 'I am a Giant Albatross of the Wandering Albatross family.'

'And magical, I can see it in you. Whoever gave you your voice, gave you magic as well.'

'What!' Is that how I reached here in a few days rather than the weeks it should have taken, he wondered. 'Are you going to come out of there?' The bird asked very confused. 'Tell me…how can you see I am magic?'

There was a flurry from deep inside a dewberry bush and much shaking of leaves and then what looked like a very small boy appeared. Not an ordinary boy, he was knee high to a human, had pointy ears and was green. He wore a brown tunic much as humans did and dark yellow britches, his shoes were black and curled upwards at the toes. Slung across his back was a small crossbow and hanging from his waist a quiver full of dangerous looking bolts, a leather purse bounced against his other hip. The colour of his garb made him extremely difficult to see against the backdrop of the forest.

'All creatures of magic have an aura about them. Can't you see mine?'

'No,' said Ryn, finding his voice.

'Then you must be new to magic!'

'Who are you?' Ryn asked startled, he had never seen anyone so small, except a human child, but this was no human.

'My name is Shadramintamablinski; I am an elf of the forest. What is your name?'

'Dear God, that's a mouthful elf. What do they call you for short?'

'That is short, my full name is…'

'Whoa, say no more, I shall call you Shadra, my name is Ryn. Tell me of you, I thought elves had died away with the dragons.'

'We learned to hide from the world it has not been kind to us, and it seems that it has not been kind to you either. That is the wound of an arrow, is it not? Does it hurt?'

'Of course it bloody hurts,' said Ryn, startled, 'that's a stupid question,' and he added sarcastically, suffering a twinge from the inflamed wound, 'or do arrow wounds not hurt elves?'

'All right, all right! Calm down, keep your feathers on and maybe I'll help.'

'Maybe?'

'Well you have to ask, you know, it's only polite after all.'

Ryn looked down at him ready to swear again, but seeing the very small features staring up, he decided not to peck at him.

'Can you help me, elf?'

'Say please.'

'I'll bloody please you in a minute, get on with it, will you,' shouted Ryn, exasperated.

'Ooh, no patience, eh! All you foreigners are the same. Wait a minute.'

The elf opened his purse and rummaged around. He pulled from it a bag which grew in size as he removed it from the confines of the purse. This bag he placed on the ground alongside him. Ryn could see it contained food. The elf then proceeded to pull other articles from the small purse, a frying pan, a long knife. Ryn jumped at the sight.

'Don't worry, bird, I won't need this to aid you,' and he waved the knife around in the air as if he was sparring with a sword, until he accidentally dropped it, as luck would have it, handle downwards on Ryn's toe.

'Bloody hell!' Ryn said hopping around, 'you and Aidan…both clumsy idiots!'

'Hey! I'm sorry…accidents do happen you know,' and he continued hunting through the purse.

Ryn was flabbergasted he couldn't understand how such a small bag could hold so many things.

'Who's Aidan?'

'The wizard who gave me my voice.'

'Ah, there you are,' the elf said holding up a small green bottle he had removed from a black pouch. 'All right, bend down a bit.'

Ryn settled down on the grass and pushed his chest even further into the ground to lower his wing. The elf stretched out his arm, leant across, and poured a stream of thick, colourless liquid onto

314

the edges of the inflamed hole and the surrounding feathers. Ryn moaned with relief as the liquid touched the wound, the pain easing dramatically, and at Shadra's bidding, he manipulated his wing until he could fold it to his side.

'There that should do it. It'll take a while yet for the hole to close and your feathers to grow over it. Flex your wing every now and then to stop it getting stiff and I'll put some more on in the morning.'

'Thank you, Shadramintamablinski,' said Ryn gratefully. 'Are you going to stay with me overnight, then?'

'Longer than that, I think we may have need of each other,' and the elf beamed and gave Ryn a friendly tap on his wing. Unfortunately, the damaged wing, and when Ryn screamed he did say sorry.

Twenty-five

The man was twitching, the constant tic making rapid ripples run in his abnormally strengthened facial muscles. His face spasmed and the white sclera pulsed red around the pitch-black, oval irises of his unnaturally wide eyes. His hair hung lank, sweat dripping from the ends to join the sweat oozing from every pore on his body. His skin was yellow and stank of the sewers and his fangs had enlarged until they protruded between his lips. He was unable to form fists for his fingers had elongated and the nails had turned black and doubled in length, the whole resembling talons.

He shuffled through the back alleys of Griffin on legs enhanced for speed, nothing could catch him or escape his pursuit.

The Wanting was on him with a vengeance and he was not going to shake it off this time. The demon's need was great and would have to be slaked to quieten it otherwise he'd be discovered. It had been weeks now since the last resurgence had obtained mastery over him. Sometimes he could last months before being forced to concede defeat but more often now, as he grew older, the demon found it easier to gain control. Its existence within him demanded its lifeblood and however hard he fought against it, he always succumbed in the end.

There was a time, in the early years of the infestation, that the demon could be kept at bay, but he'd had help then and her support had allowed him to live a fairly normal life. But her assistance was now ethereal and very difficult to reach. The demon was gaining strength as her power to aid him waned; now it fully possessed him more or less whenever it wanted.

It was always a very risky business but once quenched the Wanting, and the demon's presence, would diminish for a while leaving him a guilt-ridden respite. Often he wished to kill himself, end the vileness his life had become, but the demon would not allow that. Every time his thoughts turned to suicide the demon rose in fury and subjected him to such pain that it drove him momentarily insane. And so his miserable, lonely existence continued with no end in sight.

But the last time he had satisfied the Wanting he had been forced to flee in a panic, leaving a bloodbath behind him as he escaped. What was he going to do this time? In terms of his survival this island was very small; he'd need to leave it as quickly as possible for he could not remain hidden here for long.

He flung his arms across his chest hugging himself tightly in an effort to halt the trembling and to quieten the moaning rising to his lips. He tried to shake it off by walking faster, but as dusk fell he failed and a low howling tore free from his lips and he bit his tongue in an effort to stop it. He tasted his salty, hot blood and the demon licked his lips in pleasure and gloated—it anticipated the sweet fire of another's blood trickling down his throat.

There was no stopping him now; the need overwhelmed him, the possession total. He no longer worried that news of the deed would spread like wildfire.

The young boy, no more than eight or nine years of age, left the side door of the taproom carrying his father's jug of ale. It was a ritual. His father finished his work on the docks at dusk and arrived home as his mother warmed the pottage on the side of the fire. While this heated, his father bathed in the backyard and Jack collected the ale from the Jug and Bottle in the next street. Jack's father savoured his ale fresh with his broth and Jack always sat at the table with him watching the foam dribbling down his father's ginger beard.

Jack turned into the long, dark alleyway between the houses, two minutes more and he would be home and listening to his father's day on the docks. Jack was excited more than usual, he wanted to hear about the strange, huge ship that had been manoeuvred into dry-dock the day before. His father had promised to try and get him permission to go aboard.

He never saw the big hands that engulfed his face, stifling all sound from his mouth. The man banged the boy's head against the wall rendering him bloody and unconscious but not dead, he wanted the boy alive and kicking—fresh! He looked up and down the alley, what little sound he had made had drawn no-one's attention. He picked up the boy and slung him under his arm. Keeping out of the moonlight, he made his way down to the docks, kicking the spilled jug of ale into the gutter at the side of the alley as he went.

It was half an hour later Jack's father found the jug; there was no sign of his son. And it took him a further hour to rouse his neighbours to search for him.

It was too late for Jack of course. The man had found the perfect answer to the problem of the murder being discovered. There was a coal sump below the boards of the wharf and this is where he dumped the body. In the slurry it would not be found for weeks.

The demon's needs had been satisfied by nearly ripping Jack's head from his small shoulders in his eagerness to lap every drop of the still living boy's blood. The man cleaned himself up, there had been a surprising amount of blood.

His body returned to normal, the man paid a short visit to the Jug and Bottle where he was asked by several searchers if he had noticed a little boy wandering about.

'You're the girl I saw in my mother's garden, holding my hand,' said Thaddeus, peering closely at Augusta, the wonder lighting his face couldn't hide the puzzlement. 'You are not dead so how come you to be here?'

'See,' Augusta said smugly glancing at Aidan and Beattie, 'you wouldn't believe me would you…neither of you. I told you he was there in his eyes.' She in turn stared at the two strangers who had unexpectedly appeared so fantastically from the Darkness. 'I'm Augusta,' and she introduced the others.

'You were the other girl holding my hand, you stopped them arguing. They made me laugh, but,' and he turned back to Aidan, 'why wouldn't I want to hold your hand?'

Aidan coloured and Augusta laughed out loud. 'It's all right Thaddeus, when we get you home he'll tell you all about it. Oh, but we are so very, very glad to find you, though I must admit I never expected you to be with your mother. Mistress Portolan,' and she held out her hand to the large woman, 'I am very happy to meet you.'

'And I, to meet you! You do not realize what you have done for my son and me,' almost echoing her husband's words earlier as the tears flowed down her ample cheeks. She glanced around at the others and then it struck her that she didn't recognize her surroundings. 'This is not my Limbo…whose is this?'

'Oh, it's Anders',' Beatrix turned to him and discovered that he was not with them. He had moved to one side staring transfixed at the Darkness, a glazed glint in his eyes. 'Anders…Anders, what is it?'

He ignored her.

'Anders!' Beatrix called again and went over and put her arm through his. 'Come, Anders,' and she shook with dread as she followed his gaze, staring herself at the billowing blackness. 'Come away from here, Anders my love, it is not healthy staring at that.'

He moaned and took a step forward pulling Beatrix with him. And as he took another step he groaned even louder, his dread transmitting itself to the girl. And then he took a quicker step and another, dragging Beatrix closer to the mists.

'Quick! Stop him...grab him; pull him away the Darkness is taking him!' Bettina Portolan screamed at her companions. 'The Darkness is summoning him!'

Thaddeus and Aidan reached the struggling pair just before Augusta; halting him they turned his sight from the black swirling fog. Anders fell to his knees and curled his fingers in the soft, velvety grass of his Limbo.

'Dear God, get me away from here! I can't control its attraction this close,' he moaned from deep within his stomach, retching. 'Get me back to the tree...I'll be safe there.'

They hurriedly trudged back up the slope, almost running to regain the crossroads, the terror of the Darkness receding behind them, but not the trepidation. They were to fight the mists according to Anders, but how do you fight something that has no solid substance, an enemy that will take control of you as soon as you come near it.

They reached the tree and all except Mistress Portolan fell to the grass and sat with their backs to the enormous trunk. As they touched its rough bark their fear fled and if a ghost could have colour then it returned to Anders' face.

Bettina Portolan stared up through the magnificent, vibrant foliage of the huge tree and smiled. 'This oak I remember. It was here she came to me all those years ago.'

'Who, Mum?' Thaddeus rose and stood before the woman who had been his saviour for fifteen years. The woman he loved beyond measure who had returned that love over and over, sacrificing her life and her death to nurture him—his mother, who he knew instinctively he was about to lose forever. 'Who came to you, Mum?'

She pulled him in to her embrace. 'My dear Thaddeus, my dear, dear boy,' and then she released him to stand facing her and she stroked his blond curls. 'There is something I have never told you. At the time of her appearance you were a new born baby and I'd just driven off a demon...the demon who wanted to take you into the Darkness. Ah, my Thaddeus, why it wanted you I still do not know for sure. But meeting these I now know that the lady was right in what she told me,' she paused a moment to regain her composure.

'When I first died and passed into my Limbo I had been forced to bring your soul with me or the demon would have killed you and you would have been lost forever in the Darkness. I didn't know then where I had got the strength to beat it. I was walking here with you in my arms—I knew then that you were special, the son your father and I always wanted,' she smiled and kissed his forehead. 'But I didn't realize how special you were until I reached this tree and found her waiting for me.'

'Who, Mum?' he repeated quietly holding her hands to his face, staring into her glistening eyes.

'I don't know who she was; I couldn't see her face because she was in a very bright light. But she told me that she had aided me in your rescue for you were to fulfil a task, a very special task and that I was to remain with you to care for you until you were rescued. She also told me that you wouldn't be alone to carry out the task, you would join with four friends.' Bettina Portolan looked at the others sitting on the ground at the foot of the tree.

'He is to help us fight the Darkness, then,' said Aidan sounding very depressed, 'he's the fifth, we did wonder. Do you know how to beat it Thaddeus...do you Mistress Portolan?'

'I'm afraid not. But Thaddeus does know the Darkness intimately. Dear God, my boy,' and she hugged him tightly, 'perhaps that was why you wandered into the mists...to discover all you could of it.'

'Whoa, Mum, that implies that I was directed there on purpose. I don't like the sound of that.'

'No, Thaddeus, you are right,' she shuddered knowing though that her words were truth. 'There must be another reason,' she added not wishing to frighten him further. 'But, now, my Thaddeus you are safe, thank all the Gods,' and tears flowed once more. 'Come, my friends, allow me to thank you.' And she embraced Augusta, Beatrix and Anders in turn, coming to Aidan last. 'And you, Aidan, can you complete my happiness and give Thaddeus his life with his father?'

'Aye, Mistress, and you? I can't take the dead back with me, what will you do now? Will you go on?'

She glanced over Aidan's shoulder into the distance and saw a glimmering that did not hurt her eyes. She turned to her son and hugged him tightly. 'My Thaddeus, I love you so much,' she caressed her son's face. 'But my task has ended I can go on through the Light, it calls me now that you are safe, you understand?'

Thaddeus, his eyes brimming, nodded. 'We have had a strange life, Mum,' and smiling through his tears, he went on. 'I can live happily with Dada now that you are safe,' and in a last desperate, aching leave-taking, he cried. 'I will never, ever forget you. I love you Mum!'

With a last lingering embrace and a kiss, she released her son into the care of his new friends. Smiling her gratitude, she allowed the Light to take her, her last words lingering in the air.

'Thaddeus, tell your father I will always love him and that he'll be happy with Cornelia…tell him it is time for him to let me go. Give my love to Alessa and Marcus, tell them to marry…tell them I shall be grateful forever.'

They watched until she disappeared, even though the Light hurt four pairs of eyes, the fifth yearned to follow.

'God, it's just occurred to me,' said Anders, 'the Lady who appeared to Mistress Portolan has to be the same Lady that sent me here.' Anders shouted after her. 'Tell the Lady it may take more than us to beat the Darkness! If she's got any more ideas…'

'Aye, and now we know it's definitely a war between the Gods we are mixed up in,' Aidan replied, sick at heart.

Anders stared at Beatrix for a moment and out of the blue realized his feelings for her were changing. Watching Mistress Portolan enter Paradise had brought him to understand her destination, her future existence, was also his and he needed to be there desperately. He turned from the Light and stared towards the wall of colours, to Life. He now knew that love and needing someone changed irrevocably in the afterlife other aspirations became more important. He'd heard it called going-on, a natural progression; he'd never understood it before. He was accepting the fact that he and Beatrix would part forever.

The bright Light in the distance abruptly blinked brighter as it accepted the soul of Bettina Portolan—fifteen years late.

It was early the following morning before a change was noticed in the four recumbent bodies in Aidan's bedchamber.

Since his arrival at Aidan's bedside the morning before, Tragen had refused to leave his boy's side. Except for a call of nature, the wizard had sat in the room finding it extremely difficult to come to terms with the fact that he had been the unwitting cause of his boy's frenzied suffering. Guilt was eating him up and he didn't know how to cope with it. He vowed he would never use his staff again until he knew the reason for its odd behaviour. He was not going to put Aidan in jeopardy another time.

Cornelia and Alessa found it equally difficult to remain still so spent their time caring for the needs of the menfolk, and overseeing the four youngsters. Whispering to each other in their concern a special friendship was fostered.

Janne was unable to get to grips with the very strange circumstances. Being a man of action he was incapable of watching the four supine youngsters whose souls had supposedly vacated their bodies. The very tall man left the room on several occasions to attend to affairs of security. Always returning in a rush when hope washed over him, or when despair bled his soul.

The seneschal was another who never left the room. Lodovico did not touch his food; he just stared at his son and the three lying with him. His mind was in turmoil. Looking at his son's companions, a forlorn hope in his heart one moment, anguish the next, he realized this was the only chance of ever finding Thaddeus' soul. He was not a religious man, never had been, but he prayed now, constantly. He needed his son as much as he needed the sun to rise in the morning.

And always in the back of his mind was the knowledge, the pledge that he was going to go into battle against the Darkness with all the strength in his body and in his mind. The method was beyond him at present, but he had never before been so certain about anything in his life.

The first to stir was Augusta, opening her eyes a few moments before Beatrix. Disorientated, it took both girls a couple of seconds before realizing they were back. Cornelia, at the first flicker of their eyes, fell to her knees between the girls and grasping their hands, she smiled.

'Welcome back,' and then she noticed the forlorn look on Beattie's face and her heart turned over. 'What ails you, Beattie?'

'Oh, Milady, I had to say goodbye to Anders again.'

Augusta sat up on the bed holding her head. She had been warned that practising magic would have a detrimental effect on her health and now she had a migraine.

Tragen grasped Aidan and lifted him in his embrace, but when the boy did not respond he turned a grief-stricken face to Augusta. 'Where is Aidan? Couldn't you find him?'

'Patience, Milord, patience, he is saying farewell to Anders that's all,' said Augusta and with that Aidan stirred.

'By the Gods, I'm glad to be back. I don't ever want to see the Darkness again, let alone enter it,' he said, gripping Tragen tightly. 'It was worse than any nightmare imaginable, Master, a terrible place,' and he trembled in every muscle of his body. 'We cannot let it win, Master, never!'

'I'm so sorry my boy. It seems that I am the perpetrator of all your ills. I and my staff are responsible for sending your soul wandering.'

'Your staff? What…'

Seneschal Portolan interrupted. 'My Thaddeus,' desolation making his voice falter, 'you did not find him?' Janne held Alessa tightly, her shoulders drooping with lost hope.

Aidan, Augusta her headache forgotten and Beatrix rose from their beds in a rush, Portolan's query reminding them instantly of what they had left behind.

'Seneschal, lift Thaddeus and hold him in your arms,' Aidan said, kneeling at Thaddeus' head. 'Go on, your son needs you.'

Lodovico stared with a desperate wonder at his son lying on the truckle bed. The only sound in the room was Thaddeus' shallow breathing, the only movement Thaddeus' chest expanding and deflating. Janne and Alessa Barbat, held their breath, they watched the seneschal raise his son gently and clasp him to his chest.

Aidan placed his hands on Thaddeus' head and spread his fingers. 'Slowly Thaddeus, slowly…remember what I said. Become accustomed to your body first, feel your arms, your legs.'

Lodovico's bearing stiffened listening to Aidan, not believing what he was hearing, he dared to hope but was afraid to move in case he broke the spell. Was Thaddeus' soul at last taking possession of his body? He would not let despair overwhelm him, but how could it not if the wizard's boy and his friends had failed. He hugged his son, willing his boy to open his eyes, willing his boy to speak, praying his boy did not die.

'Feel your heart beating, Thaddeus,' Aidan continued softly, 'taste the air…breathe in its sweetness…feel your father's embrace.'

And Thaddeus smiled and snuggled in closer to his father. Inhaling, he savoured the smell and the touch of his father, feeling the strength in his father's arms. And he returned his father's embrace, grasping his father even more tightly than he was being held.

'Hold me, Dada,' and Thaddeus opened his eyes and smiled for the first time into his father's face. 'I love you, Dada—don't you ever let me go.'

'What I can't understand is why your staff never had this effect on me before we encountered the storm,' said Aidan. He and Tragen strolled in the gardens of the seneschal's estate, accompanied by Augusta and Beatrix walking with Cornelia just behind.

It had taken but a moment for the passengers of the Grim to leave the Portolan family alone to wallow in a meeting none had remotely expected even a day before. Emotions were running very high in that bedchamber and the presence of the visitors was an encumbrance.

Indeed feelings were at fever pitch amongst the five in the grounds as the young wizards recounted the unbelievable events in the afterlife. Aidan's description of the Darkness horrified them.

Walking the well laid paths of the flower gardens, the many different hues and fragrances, the peace and tranquillity, gradually eased their minds. Relaxation was itself a medicine and a curative for the terrors, the brain seeking forgetfulness as a means to rid the mind of the horrors.

And Aidan, assessing the problem of his master's staff, was startled when Beatrix, who had been deceptively quiet until then, said. 'There is something else as well, that is puzzling,' she looked at Tragen. 'Originally, he had sight of a torturer in red who we assume to be on Sanctity and is awaiting the arrival of a wizard, again presumably you, Milord. But these last ones have thrown him into another world.'

'Where you were all able to follow, where you all had sight of this "Darkness" you are meant to defeat,' said Cornelia.

'Could it be that the torturer is able to manipulate the Darkness?' Beatrix added.

'Or is the Darkness manipulating him? Again your companion is showing a depth of foresight unusual in one so young, Augusta,' Tragen said, smiling as Beatrix blushed. 'On the one hand here in Life, we have a man who may very well be an agent of the Darkness, a torturer who needs me for some reason. And in the afterlife we have an entity that holds terrors that endanger our very souls.'

'This mysterious Lady that Anders and Mistress Portolan met, could she be warning us first of our peril in this life, and then secondly of the dangers facing everyone in Limbo?' Augusta asked.

'We don't know for certain if it is she that is warning us,' Cornelia broke in, 'a mysterious woman telling us of a task preordained for five young wizards. The torturer and the Lady cannot possibly be in cohorts yet are they enemies? We have definite knowledge now of two others involved, beside the man on Sanctity—the Lady obviously from Paradise and "The One" using the Darkness,' Cornelia frowned. 'The latter implies that the Darkness is a vast weapon wielded by some unknown, extremely powerful being. And the former indicates that there is someone in Paradise who opposes the One, another being so powerful that she can order the deceased to return and remain in Limbo to aid the living. I cannot believe that the visions and the journeys have been the result of the machinations of the same person. And how does your staff fit into the scenario, Tragen, no-one else can control its power can they?'

He stared at Cornelia; her words conjured so many unanswered questions. 'No, Cornelia, only I.'

'Then there can be no question, Tragen, these youngsters are correct in their conclusion, they are pawns in the quarrels of the Gods,' and she grimaced, 'their oft quoted forays into madness.'

'I agree, Cornelia, but what are we to do to aid these? I have absolutely no idea except that the sooner we discover what is on Sanctity, the better. Maybe we can do something to eradicate the menace in this life—the dangers facing all in the afterlife we cannot do anything about at present. Nevertheless, I cannot use my staff again until we discern the reason it is sending Aidan travelling, next time it may send him either deeper into the Darkness or into the clutches of the torturer. I am not risking the loss of my apprentice for any reason,' and he ruffled Aidan's hair affectionately.

'Tragen,' Cornelia asked, 'isn't there also a risk of this torturer on Sanctity discovering Aidan and,' she paused, 'Augusta and Beattie, if any of them use magic?'

'What do you think, Aidan?' Tragen asked, staring at his apprentice who was fast coming to the end of his apprenticeship. 'Will Sanctity detect you?'

'I don't think so; as long as we use low magic then we'll be hidden by your staff's power.'

'Tragen, there is something of hope here I believe. The Lady in the Light stated that five would battle the Darkness. They have now come together, maybe that fact augurs well for the future…the plan of one God at least seems to be falling into place!'

'Aye, but which of all the Gods is playing with us?' Aidan asked.

'Ah, Aidan, that is the question we must all find an answer for as quickly as possible. Hopefully, we will discover their identities before we encounter even greater danger,' the wizard tugged rhythmically at his beard.

'And this mysterious Lady is she the God or the God's messenger?' Beatrix asked of no-one in particular.

'So, are the five of us a weapon—to fight a weapon?' Aidan asked.

'God! I've really got a headache now,' said Augusta.

Twenty-six

'Where are you taking me?' Ryn asked, very disgruntled. 'And why on earth have I got to walk? Its bloody murder on my feathers, these trees are not gentle.'

'I told you, we have to get you well away from the castle. They'll have the monks and the forest rangers out searching for you now.'

'Shadra,' Ryn paused, 'it might have escaped your notice, but I am a Giant Albatross of the Wandering Albatross family. I am made to fly not walk!'

'Exactly, my avian friend! You take to the skies now and you'll be visible to every creature in the forest, including those we need to flee.'

'I see the logic in your argument, Shadra, but you seem to have forgotten something.'

'What is that?'

'I am making one hell of a lot of noise pushing through this undergrowth. Unless our pursuers are deaf they will hear me leagues away.'

'Oops!'

'What do you mean by that?' Ryn asked, blinking fast.

'I'd not thought of that,' and Shadra stopped in his tracks. 'Very well, you fly, I will follow.'

'And how are you going to follow? I will be way up there and you will be way down here. Or can elves fly?' he asked, unable to hide a smirk at the absurd notion of this little being aloft on the thermals flapping his arms like a madman.

Shadra, with hands on hips, stared up at his new friend. 'Look, if we are going to help each other there's no need to be facetious. Of course elves don't fly...I am going to have to run.'

'Run? At the speed I fly you will never keep up with me, little elf...run!' Ryn laughed uproariously. 'But I suppose I could give you a lift.'

'Wha-at! No thanks I'm quite happy running,' said Shadra shuddering.

'What's the matter? Afraid you'll get airsick?'

'No!' I just prefer to keep my feet on the ground and...what was that?' Shadra stopped speaking. He and Ryn heard a clatter and the sound of voices, in the distance.

'I do believe someone is looking for me, Shadra, and they are very near. You have no choice, climb on my back—now!' Ryn ordered, panicking.

'By the Shaman's blood, bird, don't you dare let me fall!' Shadra begged. The elf scrambled up and settled his legs in the crook of the bird's wings. Lying flat he gripped feathers in bunches making Ryn wince. He shut his eyes tight and moaned as the bird soared aloft into the darkening sky.

Ryn on the other hand yelled his pleasure, relishing the freedom of the almost cloudless sky. 'This is the life, Shadra,' he said flying higher and at the same time banking to turn west. There was no longer any pain in his wing; feathers had grown over the hole during the night.

Shadra screamed in terror. 'Slow down…slow down for pity's sake!'

'I can't go slow, little elf,' Ryn said, grinning behind his beak. 'If I do we'll fall out of the sky.'

'Don't you dare go slow…keep going,' Shadra said his teeth chattering with fright.

Ryn peered below at the endless greenery of the forest. 'I can see humans beneath us…look.' There was a line of men beating the undergrowth before them as they walked forward. It wouldn't have been long before they'd have come up with Ryn and Shadra.

'No, no, I must not look down. My mother always told me never to look down.'

'Why not?'

Shadra, his teeth clamped together making his jaws ache, his eyes screwed tightly shut, moaned as he gripped the bird's feathers even tighter.

'Well! Tell me, little elf.'

'Because I'm bloody well scared of heights!' Shadra shouted.

'Oh!'

Shadra opened his eyes and screamed again. 'Don't go that way; turn east and follow the river upstream!'

'But that's away from the sea,' Ryn said, puzzled.

'Yes! And well away from the white monks in the estuary!'

Ryn's heart turned over, he'd had enough of white-robed men to last him a lifetime. Obeying his new friend he banked and taking his bearings from the river flowing west beneath him, he flew eastwards towards the Scissor mountains in the far distance.

Ryn flew for hours landing only twice during the following night. The first time because the wind was buffeting Shadra into insensibility, the second for Shadra to get his bearings, he said he found it easier on the ground. Because he was a creature of the forest he needed to feel the earth beneath his feet to be able to read it.

Ryn was perplexed, neither had a notion of their final destination. Whether their ultimate goal was the vast mountain range ahead, neither knew for certain. They kept flying towards the snow-capped peaks hoping to recognize their objective even though the albatross desperately wanted to return to Aidan. The little wizard needed to be apprised of the unexpected reception his messenger had encountered at the castle. But he also realized it was his duty to ascertain the whereabouts of the prince and what had befallen him. Returning without answers was unhelpful, if Aidan was to make a decision on imprecise information it could well lead to injurious consequences.

He flew on eastwards with the river rolling elegantly beneath, a ribbon of silver in a vast landscape of every shade of green. Shadra had settled to the motion of the bird and eventually gained sufficient confidence to sit upright and acknowledge the odd osprey winging its way hither and thither. Bracing himself against the easterly wind he even managed to peer downwards – although not very often – at the terrain below. Trees as far as the eye could see, tall red silver firs, with their topmost branches waving in the breeze, and shorter alders, maples and cedars sheltering beneath the limbs of their taller companions, all seeming to embrace each other in the warm morning air.

Shadra loved the trees. Born and raised in the Great Forest he knew intimately its winding brooks and larger streams, its secret paths to hidden caves and secluded havens. His people had been originally nomadic, but they never overtly left the confines of this oldest of the world's forests, now. In long years past, they had roamed the open lands and had settled beside many of its rivers. But that had been in the halcyon days of dragons. His father still related the tales told him by his father of the great flying lizards and their escapades. The dragons had been friends and allies of the elves long before humans came along and spoiled it all. Now the elves hid in the Great Forest, the occasional ranger elf foraying unseen into the towns and cities of the humans. The dragons had long vanished from the eyes of everyone.

Shadra studied the Wandering Albatross of the Giant Albatross family between his legs – strange the bird always had to use the full title – and wondered if his elfish ancestors rode dragons? It seemed unlikely, forest elves were very small. But there were ancient stories of tall, human size elves – cousins of Shadra's – who had long disappeared in the annals of history. The great lizards were far larger than even this huge bird so their riders must have been correspondingly hefty; perhaps it was those cousins—if they were still alive. Melancholic, he tugged a feather in the albatross' neck.

'Ouch! Don't do that, it stings.'

'Don't be a baby! There's a clearing to our right with a stream running through it, let's land and have breakfast.'

'Will there be fish?'

'You and your fish, don't you albatrosses eat anything else?'

'At sea, little elf, not much vegetation grows,' he smiled, 'it gets kind of soggy.'

Shadra was becoming accustomed to his new friend's sarcastic sense of humour and chose to ignore him. 'How about all those islands you told me of, plants grow on those, don't they?'

Ryn landed with a sure step alongside a fast flowing stream of clear mountain water. The grass was high in this clearing evidence that very few visitors, if any, ever came here. Tall oaks and elms, birch trees and beech enclosed it; finches sang and fluttered from branch to twig, saffron spiced the air. Shadra looked up and saw a kestrel hovering overhead searching out its prey.

'I can see strange fish, Shadra. What are they?'

The elf strolled over to the albatross staring intently into the water. Kneeling down on the bank he peered below the surface until he espied movement amongst the rocks. 'Oh boy! We're in business…trout, lovely brown trout.'

'Are they nice to eat?'

'Oh yes, my big bird,' and Shadra salivated, 'gutted and boned and then baked whole with a knob of butter and a little wine they're out of this world!'

'Why go to all that bother? I'll just eat them as they are.'

'Have you tasted fish cooked in wine?' The elf asked, extracting his oven from the contents of his small bag, the purse again displaying a wondrous capacity.

'No, I've never tasted cooked food,' he paused, 'but, go on, I'll try anything…once.'

And two hours later, both bird and elf were sleeping the results away. Ryn had never partaken of anything as succulent, the taste had surprised him. He smiled as he fell asleep; this elf was having an undue influence on him.

In the early afternoon, they soared into the air again and landed in the foothills of the mountains just before dusk. They made camp in a little copse of larch trees in a wide, rocky ravine. The night was still pleasantly warm and the sky displayed a multitude of twinkling stars under a moon on the wane. The crevasse sheltered them from the cool wind blowing down out of the snow-capped peaks to the north and east.

'We are going to have to fly into those mountains, Ryn. Can you make it?' Shadra asked, frowning and staring intently upwards.

'I can fly anywhere, little elf. Why are you so worried and why there?'

'I am concerned because I feel that what we need is somewhere in those mountains.'

'I'm sorry, I didn't realize that we needed anything except a way home,' he said derisively.

'Well, my big feathery friend, we need each other, and as I'm being drawn to those peaks so must you be. Now let's eat and sleep. We have a big day tomorrow.'

Ryn puzzled over the elf's words. But being the bird he was he decided to follow his new friend, even though a disquieting tension was giving him a stomach ache.

There was a clatter on the stairs leading from the bedchambers above. Tragen and Cornelia concluded their quiet conversation on the sofa and awaited the arrival of the family. The three young wizards looked up from their pasteboards at the table where Aidan had been teaching both girls to alter the pictures on the royal cards. Unfortunately, Augusta's attempts to change the King of Hearts into the King of Clubs had realized a very odd picture indeed of a scowling Queen of Spades, the spitting image of the Portolan's cook.

'Don't you dare laugh,' Augusta told her friends, throwing her grimacing card to the table-top, frustrated.

Lodovico Portolan walked into the parlour accompanied by Thaddeus and followed by a red-eyed Alessa Barbat holding Janne's hand, the tall man almost dwarfing her.

'Oh, you three wonderful people, how can we ever thank you?' Mistress Barbat said hugging all three in turn.

'That's okay!' Aidan said, the absence of guilt making him grin.

'We have left orders for the banqueting table to be laid for a feast this evening,' said Portolan, smiling broadly. 'I wish to celebrate the homecoming of my son. All of you will join us, of course, and please remember in this house each of you will be a treasured guest, always.'

'What is that smell?' Thaddeus interrupted.

They all stared at the seneschal's son as he sniffed loudly and made a bee-line for the vase of roses on the sideboard. Thaddeus pushed his nose hard into the bunch and promptly exclaimed as he withdrew with a spot of blood oozing from his cheek. He put his hand to the small cut and, bringing it away, stared at the blood on his finger. 'What is that?'

Beatrix broke the silence. 'I see we have a lot of teaching to do here. Come, Thaddeus, if you don't mind Seneschal we'll take your son for a walk and introduce him to the world.'

Over the next week, Thaddeus experienced the world of colour in a way that he had never imagined. His mother had educated him the best she could, showing him the flora and fauna of the island in the wall of colours, even teaching him to read and write before he got lost in the Darkness. But that only covered two of his five senses – sight and hearing – she could not teach him the others.

After his first foray into his sense of smell he learned to be more circumspect and did not suffer serious physical injury. But with tasting and touch he learned the hard way. The boy who had spent all his life observing what should have been his from birth, was so utterly spellbound with the physical world he wanted to touch, smell and taste everything, and he learned to vomit…not all things were pleasant he found.

But he had an obsession which really irked Beatrix. He had an infernal fascination with beetles, the bigger the better. In fact he had a very strange affinity with all insects. He claimed he could comprehend their emotions. Beatrix stayed well away from him every time he picked up a "creepy-crawly" to study its antics in his hands.

Because of their shared experiences in the afterlife, a special closeness grew between them. The four were the same age and, despite being denied a normal childhood, Thaddeus speedily caught up with adolescence. He suffered the same trials and tribulations as the others. He liked late nights and couldn't understand his nurse waking him before noon. He never brushed his unruly blond curls unless he was nagged. They argued with each other and played games together, although Thaddeus did tend to shortness of breath when kicking an inflated sheep's bladder over the lawn. He learned to shout and to sing, and never felt self-conscious about either even though Augusta told him that both sounded the same.

And he learned to cry, he missed his mother terribly and, as with Beatrix, he grieved.

But he did indeed have magic. And he joined in the lessons whenever Aidan deigned to stay awake long enough to teach them the rudiments of the skill.

Aidan, no longer wondered why he'd passed on his gifts, he knew now it was because a god wanted them to defeat the Darkness. But all gods were trouble. Tragen had told him many stories of the wars waged in the afterlife, which quite often spilled over into this life. Innocent people always got hurt in their centuries long battles, and even when hostilities ended the gods always found another reason to quarrel and re-engage in warfare.

Aidan was glad he'd passed on his gifts, though. He often gazed at his friends when they weren't looking, he couldn't believe his good fortune, for a lone boy having friends was another kind of magic.

They all conversed with Anders and included their ghostly friend as much as possible in their activities. But Anders had other distractions, his own battles that he had to fight alone. He still found he needed to strive against the call of the Light its attraction overwhelming. He had to wrestle his natural inclinations; actually being on the outside of Paradise and looking in was sometimes too tempting, he had to turn his back to it many times. He'd already had a taste of what he was due and he wanted more.

Beatrix, because of her love for him, realized a small part of what he was going through and her mind began to set up its own defences against the hurt to follow.

Augusta also detected the change in Anders and was afraid to mention it to the others, hoping and praying that her friends would be prepared to let go when it was time for Anders to be finally called through the Light.

Aidan noticed nothing.

Cornelia remained at the house and spent most of her time in the company of the seneschal, when he was not working. And despite her disbelief she found that she and Lodovico Portolan were developing an affectionate relationship. Those times he was not free she spent with Alessa Barbat whose nursing abilities were more or less redundant now that Thaddeus could feed and wash himself. They talked for hours, Cornelia telling of her life at the Court of Mantovar, Alessa reciprocating with tales of Griffin before the feud, and of Bettina.

It was about ten days after the recovery of the seneschal's son that Leash had been required to take a message to the Grim. While he was there he made arrangements for the abduction of the youngsters from the woods behind the house. The fact that Aidan was an apprentice wizard troubled Leash not at all and he did not bother to inform the Montetors. Of course, he did not know of the growing ability in the others not that he'd have cared if he had known. Leash was exuberant; the Montetor had promised enough men to overpower the youngsters. But just in case Aidan was to use his powers, Leash intended staying in the background until the deed was completed.

Tragen left the house early that same morning to assist in searching Griffin Town and its surroundings for a small boy missing for the last couple of days. Why the seneschal bothered was a mystery to Leash, the boy was a nonentity, some dockyard scum. But it seemed that the seneschal, having found his own son, now wanted to ascertain the whereabouts of the dockworker's boy. Leash wasn't the least concerned—his demon was in the ascendency.

Repairs to the Grim were proceeding apace. New boards replacing those that had sprung, caulking, with its accompanying smell of tar, was progressing well and new rails were substituted for the broken. Trumper, the bo'sun, had discovered new canvas at the rear of the local chandlers and his men were busily sewing the cloths together to form the immense mainsail required by the huge ship.

But Locklear was worried; there was still no replacement for the mainmast or the mizzen, and no prospects of obtaining either on Griffin. He waited impatiently for news of Sanctity. He'd have to give his friend Tragen a nudge; neither could wait much longer to remind Portolan of his promise to aid them now that his son had been found.

Hugo Locklear stood on the quarterdeck watching the group of men huddling together on the jetty just along from the brow of the ship. Tragen, stooping down amongst them examined the small body that with the aid of his magic, although not his staff, had been discovered below the wharf. Janne, his hand on the hilt of his long sword, his very tall figure partially obstructing Hugo's view, stood over the wizard. Those of the crew on deck who could not be spared to aid in the search suddenly looked up as they heard keening. Tragen rose quickly with his arms around the shoulders of a short, powerfully-built, ginger-bearded man weeping and swaying in anguish. And as the man was ushered away by his friends, his boy's body was wrapped in a ship's blanket and carried after.

'A vampyrus, Hugo, that's what killed the boy,' said Tragen joining Locklear on the quarterdeck. 'A vampyrus! Unbelievable!'

'Here on Griffin...but how? I didn't think the island was big enough to hide the creature.' Hugo asked, shocked.

'It's not; they've never had a vampyrus here, so Marshal Janne informs me. Of course everyone knows of them and the authorities are always aware of the need to take precautions in case one arrives on a ship from an infected port.'

'Are you positive?'

'Yes, my friend. I have not encountered it for many years,' he scratched his beard. 'The last time I managed to come up with it the demon was actually in the act of feasting. It was in the town where I found Aidan. It was satisfying its Wanting on a young woman, there was nothing I could do for her...her head had been nearly ripped from her shoulders.' The vampyrus had also torn from her head her plait of long, black hair. Tragen closed his eyes remembering the lovely smell of lavender water in the tress. 'The demon had gorged itself at her neck as with this boy—a terrible, terrible way to die.' Tragen called for brandy. 'On that occasion, I had bad luck and the vampyrus escaped me. I have heard stories of it roaming the north over the years and I have searched many times for it, but I have always arrived too late,' he shook his head. 'It is a vile demon, Hugo, truly terrible.'

'You speak as if there is only one. Surely there are more?'

'No-one is really sure, it can move phenomenally fast and, of course, there is the tale of it transforming into a bat and flying away. Perhaps that is why there are believed to be more than one, it can feast in one town one day and appear in another town leagues away on the next,' the wizard tugged anxiously at his beard.

'Could we have brought it?'

'How can we? We have had no sign of such a devil onboard, although, of course, it is very difficult to identify. The demon infests a human being at will, jumping from one to another when its current host dies. Over time it comes to possess its new host completely, body and soul. But it still appears as a normal man or woman. It is a parasite, Hugo, an evil leech. No, Hugo, I cannot believe we brought it with us,' and the wizard downed his drink in one swallow.

'Yet, if you are correct and there is only one vampyrus then we must have carried it on the Grim,' Locklear said suddenly draining of colour, 'it cannot possibly have flown all this way, could it?'

'I have no idea, none at all. It seems unlikely but...'

'Lord Tragen,' Janne shouted from the brow, 'quickly, we must leave immediately,' his voice trembled with something that sounded like panic, as he beckoned the seneschal's coach along the jetty.

'There is no need to fear yet, Marcus, the vampyrus can last for months before the Wanting comes upon it again,' said Tragen, astonished at seeing such a huge man frightened. He hastened down on to the jetty to the security commander's side.

'You do not understand, I must inform Lodovico that we have a visitor,' and Janne nodded out to sea. On the horizon, sailing towards the harbour, was a barque with all sails flying.

'Who is it?' Tragen asked.

'Lodovico will tell you. Quick, make haste,' Janne ordered the driver of the coach when Tragen boarded. 'I will go on ahead,' and Janne leapt to his black destrier's back and dug in his heels.

That night, at dinner, the seneschal told them of Sanctity. 'It was populated centuries ago by a few fishermen and then about two hundred years ago, a small monastery dedicated to the Goddess Tarria was built there.' Aidan's ears pricked up on hearing the name of his personal God, the Goddess of healing and mercy. 'The monks never used to number very many, their life was hard, their work gruelling. They travelled the islands and were the physicians for all the people living here. But something happened about twenty years ago.' Portolan paused and studied the reactions of his captive audience.

'The exact circumstances I do not know, except that the monks stopped their roving and remain now, secluded on Sanctity and their numbers have increased many times over. The year following their self-imposed exile I paid my last visit,' he shuddered. 'I wish to all the Gods I had never gone.'

He sipped his wine, his face ashen with memories. 'My brother,' and he looked up at the Portolan's portrait hanging on the

336

wall of the banqueting room, 'was taken ill, desperately ill and we needed a physician if he was to live. As none were on Griffin, I left Bettina behind and sailed with him and his wife to Sanctity to obtain the necessary aid. Brother Dyfrig, the newly appointed abbot, God rot him, persuaded me that my brother should remain with them for a prolonged period of recuperation. Although I didn't much like him I trusted him, I had no reason not to; they had healed our people for years. I departed Sanctity leaving Ariana with Paul, at her request, and I assumed the mantle of regent in his absence praying for the day of his return. What a fool I was.'

Janne, listening, stared without blinking at the wall ahead of him. Alessa Barbat, chewing her bottom lip, brought a small spot of blood to her mouth; she ignored the meal in front of her, her gaze far in the past. Tragen and the others waited silently, growing more horrified as the tale unfolded.

Seneschal Portolan, breathing deeply to disperse the catch in his throat, continued to speak. 'The mad monk kept Paul and Ariana and he now holds them to ransom with the threat that if I attempt their rescue they will be killed,' he paused and stared at Tragen.

'That is why no ship can berth at Sanctity without prior approval. Any unexpected vessel that approaches the island will be deemed a rescue mission and the gallows standing on Sanctity's wharf will bear their bodies.' He stopped speaking and raised his mug to his lips, his hand trembling.

'What is the ransom?' Tragen asked softly.

Portolan nodded at Janne to continue the tale. 'My Lord Tragen, the payment is twelve lives, six from the Portolans and six from the Montetors,' staring at the shock on the visitor's faces, Janne continued. 'The Quota, as we call it, is surprisingly easy to fill on our part, I have little knowledge of how the Montetors comply although I suspect it is in the same manner. Our share comprises the felons and murderers always to be found in any busy seaport. And as the Quota needs to be delivered only once a year we…our Justice system, states that to be convicted of a capital offence carries the sentence of contributing to the Quota.'

'What happens to them there, Dada,' asked Thaddeus, appalled at what he was hearing.

'I do not know, Thaddeus, I can only surmise that it is death as we never see or hear from them again. But as they are convicted criminals and would be executed here for their crimes, anyway,' his voice hardened, 'I feel no guilt at using them to secure the safety of our family.'

Cornelia voiced the fear unspoken in the Portolan household for twenty years. 'Are they still alive, Lodovico, your brother and his wife?'

'I do not know. I have not seen either of them from that day, and I cannot go there without risking their lives. If they are not dead, then sighting my ship...' he closed his eyes briefly in pain. 'I would be responsible for bringing about their deaths. I would not be able to live with that.' He sighed as he stared at the woman who was gradually taking the place of his beloved Bettina. 'That is the quandary in which I find myself. If they are dead, the Gods forbid, then how do I find out?'

'Lodovico, perhaps that is why he is early, maybe Brother Dyfrig has come with bad news,' said Alessa Barbat.

'You mean that ship arriving carries this monk from Sanctity?' Tragen asked.

'Yes, he is two months early and I don't think the Montetors have got their Quota together yet,' said Janne. 'And if that's the case, Brother Dyfrig will take anyone he fancies.'

'Dear God, Marcus, he may take Thaddeus. Lodovico you have to get him away,' said Alessa frantically.

'Why are the Montetors involved in a Portolan kidnapping?' Cornelia asked.

'Because Ariana is the twin sister of Bazyli Montetor, and all that family blame me for her abduction. That is the reason for the deplorable unrest between us,' said Portolan. 'And what's more, the Montetors would delight in informing the monk of Thaddeus' return. Yes, we must get my son far away from here, as soon as possible.'

'Who do the monks worship now?' Aidan asked.

'A good question, my boy, I wish I knew. Is it important?' Lodovico asked.

'If Brother Dyfrig is the man of red in my visions, then it could be very important,' said Aidan, staring at his master.

'How long have we before he docks, Marcus?' Tragen asked.

'Tomorrow morning.'

Leash and the Montetors were hiding in the woods behind the house at dawn the next morning, their gaze fixed on the back door awaiting the emergence of their prey.

Leash smiled, speculating on what he thought the wizard's reaction would be. Firstly Tragen would fret at the boy's disappearance, perhaps disparage the boy at his tardiness, but the wizard would still search diligently. Achieving nothing but failure, Tragen would become frantic and turn the town inside out, in the process seriously upsetting the citizens and disrupting trade. And, if Leash was lucky, the good people of Griffin would turn on the wizard in their anger. But Tragen would continue to search even more desperately, his anguish making him careless of the feelings of others, until either the citizens forced him to stop or he came to the realization that his boy had gone for good. Perhaps it could even be arranged for the wizard to discover the boy's mangled body, for Leash would ensure it was mutilated.

Leash so wanted to see Tragen's grief, it was a physical need radiating from deep within his bowels, he hated the old man beyond measure. He wanted Tragen to suffer the same desolation that the wizard had inflicted on him, condemning him to eternal despair and loneliness.

The Montetor leader of this cohort was a man with the nickname Razor, who, unbeknown to Leash, was also Bazyli Montetor's right hand man, possibly his successor as leader of the clan.

Razor was Leash's contact from the docks. He was a short, swarthy man who had the unnerving habit of cleaning his fingernails with his razor-sharp dagger. He ruled his men with a rod of iron, discipline enforced not only by his prowess with the short, narrow blade of the misericorde the dagger favoured by Dolly, but also because Razor was a very violent man with a very short temper.

Bazyli had received word that morning of the monk's approach, almost before Janne had sighted the barque. He had impressed on Razor the need for success; he didn't want the abbot making up the numbers by taking any innocent Montetor. Bazyli wanted his full complement of prisoners on board the Montetor boat, ready for transferring to the monk's, within the next week.

As the house began to stir, the abductors settled down for a long wait. But, as luck would have it, a little later their prey appeared in the yard behind the house.

Leash peering through the branches of a gorse bush discovered the youngsters attired for a journey. He wondered where they were going as Janne led them all towards the stable where four horses were led out by grooms. Was this going to be more difficult than he'd planned? It seemed that the youngsters' usual routine had deviated this morning. The second helmsman of the Grim and the Montetors all waited silently.

'Left foot in the stirrup, Thaddeus, and always mount on the left,' Portolan said helping his son to mount his first horse. Thaddeus, decidedly nervous, heaved himself up and swung his right leg over the mare's back.

'It's…it's a bit high, isn't it.'

'Don't worry, Thaddeus, just do as I do. We won't be going very fast,' said Augusta.

'Don't forget the path, all four of you have seen it in my mind. I hope the mindmeld was clear?' The seneschal had earlier allowed the four youths to enter and read his mind, a very disconcerting procedure. 'You will reach the hunting lodge some time tomorrow afternoon. Marcus has supplied you with necessary food and blankets for an overnight camp, enough provisions to last a few weeks will be found at the lodge. I hope, though, you will not need to be absent for anywhere near that long.'

He then stared unblinking at each of them, his hard gaze unsettling as it was meant to. 'A word of warning and do not ignore it! Do not enter the catacombs you will see behind the lodge however curious you become. They are highly dangerous; many a person has entered never to be seen again. They are named the Devil's Keep and they are not called that without good reason!'

'Do not practise even the low spells while the monk is on Griffin,' added Tragen in the vain hope that he would be obeyed. 'Even though Lodovico has assured me the monk has no magic, I do not want to take a chance. I don't know if my staff will hide any of you from him while he is this close. If he does discover you the consequences may well be too intolerable to contemplate.'

'Take care, my son, I do not wish to lose you now that I have found you,' the seneschal said, patting his son's knee and then turning to look at the others, 'I do not wish to lose any of you.'

'Return when I mindmeld, Aidan, and not before—AND DO NOT USE MAGIC!' Tragen shouted again, as they rode off.

'Will they obey you?' Cornelia asked.

'I doubt it! But I can hope,' the wizard answered plaintively.

340

The riders moved out of the stable yard, leaving by the doorway set into the perimeter wall, and walked the horses towards the woods stretching away north. Their path took them through a guarded gate and up to the edge of the trees, here they turned and looked back, waved once, and broke into a trot. Skirting the low undergrowth, they headed for the foothills at the base of Mount Trespass, the higher of the two mountains that towered over Griffin Island.

That morning as the four youngsters set off, the barque with no name carrying Brother Dyfrig sailed into the harbour and docked in Griffin Town. Monks manned the ship and secured her to the wharf with the aid of Janne's militiamen.

The procedure followed a set pattern on each visit of this ship. It arrived once a year and when it appeared on the horizon, the usual harbour workforce disappeared like rabbits into a warren, leaving the wharf to Janne's men. A few people fled to relatives in the interior of the island. Others with no clear destination other than they did not want to remain in the town whilst the abbot was there, went into the hills and slept under makeshift shelters or even the stars, for the duration of his visit. However, those who would not leave their property barricaded themselves into fully provisioned cellars below their homes, refuges that were always prepared beforehand for occupancy of at least a week, the usual duration of the monk's visit. But now the monk had arrived early, the townsfolk were not ready and they panicked, grabbing what provisions they had to hand they fled.

Before the monk's barque had tied up, the town was completely devoid of life above ground, except for Janne's patrols. Squads of militiamen policed the town to foil those foolish enough to attempt looting, a crime that carried a sentence of transportation to Sanctity. The seneschal took his duties as regent responsible for the safety of his people and their property, very seriously.

On the Grim, Hopper apprised Locklear of the unusual security precautions in place in the town and that Janne had advised abandonment of the Grim until the monk departed.

'Never, the man must be insane if he thinks I will leave my ship,' said Locklear. 'Have Trumper bring the brow inboard, arm the men and have them standby but confine them to below decks. If these monks show any intention of boarding my ship, they will be met by Mantovar fighters. If pirates and brigands cannot take us then I am sure that a bunch of religious zealots will not succeed either.'

Brother Dyfrig, the Abbot of Sanctity for twenty years, appeared on the deck of his barque as the seneschal's coach drew up on the jetty. The abbot, his head newly shaved by his personal slave, stood at the head of the gangway. He was wearing a bright, spotlessly clean, white robe the cowl over his head. He paused with his foot on the plank and stared across at the dry-dock, inspecting what he could see of the Mantovarian warship. He noted its lack of masts and smiled. If they wished replacements they could not refuse his request, though the seneschal would have undoubtedly warned them. The monk was not too concerned, strategies were made to be altered and he loved a challenge, beating Griffin had become too easy.

He continued down the brow and settled himself in the coach, not deigning to glance at his escort, six horsemen following and six ahead with Janne leading. The coach set off immediately carrying its unwelcome visitor to the manor. Brother Dyfrig, feeling the hate flowing from Janne and his men, again smiled. The marshal's days would be numbered if he upset the monk, he could always add him to the Quota.

The enclosed coach, used for protection against misguided assassins – no-one knew what would happen to the hostages if Dyfrig was killed – rolled through the deserted town. The iron-rimmed, wooden wheels rattled over the cobblestones, a welcome breeze blowing through the open carriage windows.

Twenty-seven

Leash and Razor realized they now had a serious problem. However slow the youngsters rode, the pursuers would never be able to keep up with their quarry let alone catch them. Razor thought of cutting his losses, after all one recruit for the Quota was better than none at all. But he had six days; if he failed to seize these other four then recruits for the Quota could always be found elsewhere, even if they would be the port's layabouts. He tapped the point of his misericorde against his cheekbone, just below his right eye, another habit which unnerved his cohorts—he'd taken a few eyes with that knife, his favourite method of extracting information. He decided to follow; he would wait a few days more before making his final decision.

'Who is the second boy?' he turned to Leash his stare betraying his dislike.

'The seneschal's son, he has recovered from his illness,' answered Leash, returning the leader's stare without blinking. 'Does it matter?'

'I suppose not...he'll make an extra for the Quota, we'll have to hide him from the Portolans, of course,' he laughed, mirthlessly. 'We wouldn't want the seneschal taking revenge, now would we?' One or two of his men sniggered.

'Come,' Razor said, 'let us follow. We'll stay in the woods for as long as possible, I don't think we need worry about too much noise, they can't hear us at this distance. We'll close up at nightfall; the tracks they're leaving a blind man could follow. Do you know where they're going?' He grimaced when Leash shook his head.

'I thought there wasn't a forest on Griffin,' said Augusta, the four companions riding ever northwards, the trees on their left never ending.

'I asked the steward about that, he told me that was the case years ago,' said Aidan. 'This new forest was seeded to replace the depredations of the previous years. There used to be a very old forest on this land, the whole of Mount Trespass was covered in silver fir, larch, spruce and pine, but the Portolans sold the forest to the Montetors in the days before their feud. But he did tell me, as well, that centuries ago the original foresters of these islands disappeared.'

'What foresters?' Beatrix asked.

'There were other people living up here, the ones who are now buried in the catacombs. The steward went very secretive and wouldn't tell me anymore, he was afraid I think…he was very superstitious and muttered something about green devils,' said Aidan, easing his sore buttocks on the saddle, he hadn't ridden for some time.

'Hey, there's the river we have to make for over there,' said Thaddeus interrupting and pointing to his right. 'We have to follow that to its source, don't we?'

'It's bigger than I thought,' said Augusta, a little perturbed at the mention of green devils, she tended to be superstitious as well and wondered if the steward had a good reason for his secrecy. 'I didn't even realize there was a river until your father told us.'

'It disappears below the ground before it reaches the town and supplies fresh drinking water to all the wells in Griffin.' Thaddeus paused, and grinning, turned to Aidan. 'My father also mentioned that the river supplied the water to brew ales and spirits. You'll have to take me into Griffin Town when we return. I used to take a peek into taverns when I was at the wall of colours, I'd love to spend some time in one for real.'

'Men!' Beatrix and Augusta said together.

They made their way down to the river and followed in single-file the not much used dirt road running erratically alongside it. The morning was bright with clear blue skies, a cooling breeze blew over the river and Thaddeus stared entranced at the moving water, watching salmon swimming beneath the surface.

'Come on, Thaddeus,' said Aidan impatiently, as the boy seemed intent on delaying them, 'they're only fish.'

'I've never seen live fish before,' he said forlornly, and moved on.

'I'm sorry, Thaddeus,' Aidan said, kicking himself. He kept forgetting that his new friend had very little first-hand experience of this world.

'That One behind the Darkness has a lot to answer for,' said Augusta, threateningly, 'and I hope I'm there to see he gets what he deserves.' She didn't realize where that hope would lead her, if she'd known she would have bitten her tongue off and run the other way, not stopping until she'd found the deepest hole in the highest mountain in which to hide.

Sweet buckeye, black alder and box elder inundated the riverbank along with azaleas, periwinkles and bog myrtle all emitting a pleasing fragrance. At intervals tall reeds grew out from the banks, frogs and toads croaking everywhere. Thaddeus stopped frequently his head tilted to one side, wonderment lighting his face as he listened to their chorus, laughing occasionally at sight of the many grebes and bitterns and once, a lonely heron standing knee-deep in the water. Up ahead of them the woods grew down the slope and approached closer to the river, and the path leading through a profusion of cherry birch, eventually directed them into the undergrowth. Here foxgloves predominated along with an assortment of edible brown, fairy ring mushrooms and spongy yellow brain fungus, and here they first heard the noise.

'Sounds like something big pushing its way through the undergrowth,' said Aidan, twisting around to look behind them. His keen hearing, enhanced because of his long-time magical abilities, picked up the commotion earlier than the others.

'There's more than one,' said Beatrix, puzzled, 'Did the steward tell you of any large animals living in the forest?'

'No, he never said,' Aidan answered, 'but there must be wild boar and deer. Anders can you see anything?'

'No, I can barely see you under those trees, but I'm positive those are men I hear.'

'Can you make out what they're saying, Anders?' Beatrix asked.

'Aye,' and he laughed, *'their cursing worse than we ever did, Aidan!'*

'Are they?' Aidan replied with a glint in his eye. 'What are they saying?'

'Don't you even think about it!' Beatrix ordered.

'Would the monks be following us up here?' Augusta asked.

'I don't know,' said Aidan, her anxiety infectious. 'Keep an eye on them, Anders, if they get any nearer let us know.'

'Okay...I should be able to see them once they leave the trees.'

They rode on at a quicker pace, the path to the lodge veering away from the woods a little later.

Late afternoon found Ryn and Shadra resting alongside another of the many mountain streams, this one a lot colder they were now higher in the mountains, closer to the snow-line. They sheltered out of the wind in a ravine eating a freshly cooked fluffy omelette. Shadra had exceeded himself, in Ryn's opinion, by adding a pinch of garlic to a filling of cheese, tomatoes and wild mushrooms.

'Little elf,' he said licking his beak, 'you are one wondrous cook, I think I'll keep you with me for a while.'

'Thank you, I just wish you weren't such a messy eater. Why can't you use a knife and fork like normal people?'

Ryn looked at him disbelievingly. 'Elf, I am a bird...I do not have fingers or haven't you noticed?'

'You are magic—grow some.'

'Uh! How?'

'Easy, just stare at the end of your wings and push fingers from the bone.'

'You are a fool, Shadra. I cannot do that...look,' and Ryn followed the elf's instructions, and before his very eyes four fingers and an opposing thumb appeared from between his feathers at the tip of his wing. Ryn was dumbstruck!

'Right, clever boy! Now the other wing,' and as Ryn took no notice, shocked beyond belief, Shadra gave him a nudge. 'Go on...the other wing.'

And before he realized what he was doing, Ryn was flexing fingers on both wings and being taught by the elf how to pick up eating utensils.

'Enlightening, I must say!' A gruff voice said from the rocks behind them. 'A huge, magical bird accompanied by a very small, green elf. If my mother had told me I would ever see such a thing, I would have called her a liar.'

Ryn swivelled his neck to peer behind him, Shadra leapt to his feet and crouched holding his long knife before him.

'Excuse me, there is no need to fear me, I am quite alone,' and with that the owner of the voice appeared from behind a rock. A human, garbed in britches tucked into knee-high fur boots, a very dirty shirt and jerkin, and a heavy fur lined jacket complete with a large hood. Over his right shoulder was slung a longbow, a quiver empty of arrows secured to his belt. Hanging across his back was a lute, its long neck protruding well above the man's head.

'I smelled your food, and found the aroma overwhelming. Please forgive me for startling you, but you must admit discovering you two came as rather a shock. My name is Anselm,' and he held out his hand to Shadra.

The elf found the man's blue eyes and warm smile disarming, though still wary he lowered his knife. 'I am an elf of the Great Forest, Shadramintamablinski is my name, this is my friend,' releasing the human's hand he turned to the albatross, 'Ryn, a denizen of the Great Deep.'

'I am a Giant Albatross of the Wandering Albatross family, Anselm, and I am pleased to meet a friendly face out here. Do you live in the forest?' he asked, as he tentatively offered his fingers to be shaken by the stranger. He was very protective of his new appendages, but still curious about the strange feelings in his fingertips as he felt the gentle pressure of the man's hands.

'I find I do, for the moment…yes! I'm sorry, could I trouble you for a little bread. Unfortunately very good minstrels do not make very good hunters, and I have not eaten in a while.'

'Your manners are deplorable, elf. Give the man the rest of the omelette; can't you see he's starving?'

Anselm, at Shadra's invitation to sit, lowered his hood to reveal a shock of blond hair tied back in a ponytail, a habit of warriors, and devoured the egg dish in moments. He followed the food by gulping down the goblet of wine handed him, not wasting a drop. Shadra retrieved from his bottomless purse a cheese, an onion and a large loaf of bread and handed them to the hungry minstrel. And while he ate as if he hadn't seen food for weeks, Shadra poured more wine for all three. Both the elf and the bird sat back and awaited the cessation of eating before asking any further questions.

Anselm licked his lips, belched and rubbed his stomach in appreciation; he had eaten everything put in front of him. 'My friends, that was the finest meal I have eaten in many a long day, I thank you again.' And he lay back alongside the fire, pulled his hood up and put his head on a nearby tussock and promptly fell asleep.

Nonplussed, Ryn and Shadra stared at each other, not saying a word.

Anselm awoke at dusk to the noise of Ryn and Shadra arguing over the correct amount of chillies needed to cook smoked salmon enchiladas. A debate that was getting very heated when they noticed the minstrel had roused. Ryn and Shadra settled their dispute, agreeing to differ, while Anselm went off to answer a call of nature and to wash.

On his return, and while the food was cooking, Shadra spoke in no uncertain terms of his suspicions.

347

'Anselm, it is obvious to us that you are fleeing someone, or else you would not be out here in the back of beyond without provisions—and without arrows. Who is chasing you and where are you from?'

'Ah, yes!' he paused. 'You are quite right. I was pursuing my singing career in the castle at Mantovar, a few weeks back I had an unfortunate experience. My, that does smell delicious, Shadra, have you always been a decent cook?'

'I pride myself on my culinary abilities, please don't change the subject. Ryn gets very upset if people prevaricate.'

With that, the albatross attempted to look very stern but only succeeded in appearing comical as he screwed up his beak, his eyes popping slightly.

Taken aback at the bird's expression, Anselm continued. 'Well, I was sort of serenading this young wench in the castle...I hasten to add that it was at her request. Her husband took exception and I had to flee, not only the castle but the town also, he had lots of friends. Mind you, from what I gathered later, his wife had lots of admirers, so why he took exception to me I'll never know.'

'You mean that you ran...you are a coward?' Ryn asked, stretching his long neck in surprise.

'Bird, I prefer to call it a strategic withdrawal, the man was a foot taller than me and weighed fifteen stone more. I believe I made the correct decision...he did not deserve to die.'

'You would have killed him over a woman?' Ryn was extremely surprised. 'I will never understand humans.'

'And so you ended up here, leagues upon leagues away. A bit drastic to run this far, don't you think?' Shadra persisted.

'I am a minstrel and minstrels like to travel. I was headed in this direction and as I have never visited this part of the world, I did not change direction. God, that smells wonderful...I'm starving.'

'Umph!' said Ryn, disgust evident in his tone. 'Do you know what happened to the prince?'

'The Prince of Mantovar?'

'What other prince is there?' Shadra asked impatiently, he was not fussed on men who chased after married women and he didn't believe a word of what he'd just been told.

'When I left, there were a lot of monks in the castle. Far, far more than for a normal visit, there seemed to be a hundred at least, but that's a guess. You know with monks…see them in their robes and they all look the same.'

'I had words with one of them; he wore white and was bald. An evil man I will never forget him. Do you know of whom I speak?' Ryn asked.

'They are all bald and they all wear white, except for one, and he never leaves Sentinel. Was he tall and thin, a sneer always on his face?

'Yes, he had a very cruel voice, as well,' Ryn shuddered recalling the other voice within the mindmeld. 'He killed a man while I watched, there was nothing I could do, I'd been wounded,' he added, feeling guilty about flying away.

'The one you speak of is the abbot, he's the only one allowed to talk. I stayed well away from him, especially when the prince dismissed his old chancellor and appointed Cumbria in his stead.

'Do you think the prince had been coerced into making the appointment?' Shadra asked, frowning.

'Far be it from me to say. I was not privy to the politics of the decision. All I know is,' and he paused, 'the prince is very rarely seen now. But why do you ask? What possible events in the castle could interest an elf and an albatross?'

'But the prince is still in residence at the castle?' Ryn asked, ignoring the question.

Anselm shrugged his shoulders and sighed. 'I have no idea. I fled the castle some while ago, and you are the first I have spoken with since.'

In return for his supper, at which Ryn was forced to drink copious amounts of water to stop his beak turning red, the enchiladas had been very spicy, the minstrel offered to sing them a ballad of their choosing. Resting his back against a fallen silver birch, he took up his long-necked lute and strummed a few chords.

'What would you like, Shadra, perhaps an ode to good cooking, or,' looking across the fire at the albatross, and burping loud and clear, 'a ballad of strange friendships?'

Sleepily the elf replied from the shelter of his blanket roll placed beside the fire. 'I care not, you choose,' then changing his mind rapidly, he sat up. 'No! Do you know any of the old days…the happy days?'

'Ah, Master Albatross, when an elf talks of the happy days, he means the time of dragons.'

'Have you met many of my kinsmen?' Shadra asked surprised.

'One or two, now listen.' And plucking the strings of his lute, he launched into a song of dragons, big bad knights of old, and fighting elves assisting the guardians in their pledge to protect the flying lizards.

And before he fell asleep, long after Ryn and Anselm, the elf wondered how the minstrel had come upon other elves. His kindred in the Great Forest were secretive and did not have dealings with humans. If they had he should have known, but there again King Whistanrim might be keeping it from him, an even more disturbing thought. There was more to this minstrel being here than an irate husband.

The following morning, after a breakfast of oats in hot milk, smothered in honey, Ryn and Shadra prepared to say farewell to their companion.

'Please, you cannot mean this,' pleaded Anselm. 'I am lonely on my own and I need company to continue my journey into the mountains. Let me come with you and I will keep you both amused on the way.'

'I cannot carry an elf and a human, Anselm, I am sorry,' said Ryn.

'Then as you fly, I will follow on foot. Shadra can walk with me…elves like walking, don't they?'

'Most elves do, unfortunately for you I am a lazy elf and I have got used to peering down on the world as I travel,' said Shadra, wondering why on earth this human wanted their company unless, of course, he could not survive without them which was highly improbable. This man was well able to survive in the direst terrain.

Anselm stared at his two very unusual companions, and sighed. 'Do you know who live up there?' And he nodded towards the snowy peaks.

Shadra looked at the minstrel, waiting for him to divulge a little more information. 'Go on,' he said, standing with his hand on Ryn's back preparing to mount.

'Garda!'

Shadra stared at Ryn and Ryn stared back. Swivelling his head to stare at the minstrel, Ryn asked. 'And who or what are the Garda?'

'Tell him, Shadra, he might not believe me.'

'I am not sure,' said Shadra, unwilling to admit that he'd never heard of them.

'You are an elf who has never heard of the Garda?'

'I did not say that.'

'I hoped you would trust me,' Anselm said dejectedly. 'The Garda are guardians of a legend, but they are also extremely fierce warriors who usually kill strangers on sight.'

And then the elf suddenly faced up to a fact which utterly shocked him. For years and years, he didn't know how long, he had wandered the forest with not a care in the world as he did his king's bidding. But the last few years he had become aware of the mountains more and more. He found himself staring at them late at night, experiencing a calling, a strange attraction that this last year had finally overwhelmed him. He was obsessed with them, he had to reach the mountains, see what was there. Could it be the Garda that called him to those snowy peaks?

The coach rattled up the drive and halted at the foot of the steps. Standing, waiting before the high double doors were the seneschal dressed in his blue uniform, minus hat and Tragen wearing his green robe.

Brother Dyfrig, concealed within the coach, lowered his cowl and removing the cold talisman from around his neck he slipped it into a pocket. The monk fully intended rendering the wizard powerless at the first intimation of a threat. Looking through the small window in the coach door, his eyes flicked over the portly figure of the seneschal, dismissing him out of hand he knew him too well to be worried.

The wizard, though, was another matter entirely and he studied Tragen intently. Dyfrig tensed, he could feel Tragen's immense power even from this distance and wondered why his master wanted the wizard to retain his magic, surely their confrontation would be easier if Tragen was powerless. The abbot hoped it would not be necessary to use the charm too soon after their initial meeting. He didn't want the wizard to discover any loss of power too far in advance of their voyage; in fact Brother Dyfrig would prefer not to use it at all before returning to Sanctity.

Seneschal Portolan stood without moving, his arms to his side he waited for his enemy to alight. His mind though, was working overtime, questions tumbled through his head. Why was the monk early, his brother, his sister-in-law, were they still alive? Was Thaddeus safe? When was this nightmare of Sanctity ever going to end? It couldn't last much longer, being denied contact with the hostages for twenty years was a punishment beyond the pale. Perhaps he and Bazyli should come to an agreement and push for a conclusion?

Tragen also gave some thought to the monk's purpose in visiting at this time. He was confident that he had hidden Aidan; nonetheless, there was still a nagging doubt. Then there were the other three, they were new to magic and complete amateurs very often made detectable errors. He had complete faith in Aidan's ability to survive roaming the countryside. The boy had wandered far and wide in Mantovar for the last ten years with and without his mentor, and had learned to live rough off the land in desert and forest alike. But Aidan showed a deplorable and exasperating lack of responsibility by "playing" with magic. Hopefully that would be controlled by the sensible Beatrix, but Augusta also exhibited the same rashness, the princess and the wizard's apprentice, were very much alike. Could Beatrix exert restraints on both?

And there was the problem of Thaddeus. Nearly a full grown adult, he was totally inexperienced in the world. His innate courage reflected that of his parents but he had an otherworldly ignorance of danger, a naivety that was appealing to those that loved him, but could place him in serious peril with those that did not. Surviving within the Darkness for years and protecting his mother, did not furnish him with the necessary abilities to cope with the dangers inherent in the physical world.

Tragen smiled with undiluted admiration as he thought of the boy's mother. Bettina Portolan must have been a remarkable lady to fight off a demon at a woman's most vulnerable time—childbirth, and then to rear her son in the most peculiar of circumstances. Even without the behest of the Lady of the Light, Bettina would never have left Thaddeus. She was, perhaps, more courageous than any of them.

And then there was poor Anders taken before he could enjoy life as an adult, watching over them all, he should be at rest in Paradise—is probably yearning for the place.

The door opened and Brother Dyfrig stepped down from the coach with his cowl raised knowing this was more intimidating. His purpose was to unsettle the wizard from their first meeting.

'Abbot,' said the seneschal, without putting his hand forward to be shaken, 'this is an unexpected visit.'

'No welcome, Seneschal Portolan? You are discourteous in front of your guest.' The monk smirked beneath his cowl; he did like teasing this fat man. He turned his head and stared at Tragen, his inscrutable black eyes although shaded, just visible.

Tragen, returning the stare, attempted a blind mindmeld, hoping that the gentle contact would be undetectable. It was. The wizard was perturbed, the monk had a very effective shield in place, and his thoughts could not be discerned. How was this? The monk emitted no obvious signs of having magical abilities, his aura did not reveal any hidden expertise, and yet very strong magic was in use to hide the man's mind.

Portolan broke the silence. 'This is a very welcome and very honoured guest of mine,' his words intimating the fact that the monk was not. 'Lord Tragen, meet Brother Dyfrig, the Abbot of Sanctity.'

Tragen held his hand out to be shaken and as their fingers touched, the wizard felt a slight buzz of magic about the monk. 'I am pleased to meet you, Brother. I am afraid I do not know much of you,' he turned to the seneschal. 'Lodovico has been rather reticent,' he chuckled good-naturedly, but from the moment he touched the monk's fingers, Tragen was instantly on the alert, 'and I cannot help wondering the reason.' He had detected a magical artefact concealed on the monk.

'You are a wizard. I have not encountered many of your brethren, Lord Tragen.'

The monk entered the house without awaiting an invitation and turned left up the stairs. Striding through the banqueting hall he made himself comfortable in the parlour behind. Tragen and the seneschal had no option but to follow, the monk totally ignoring them.

Tragen frowned and glancing at Lodovico he could see him seething. The gross bad manners of this monk usurping his hospitality somehow shamed the seneschal.

Brother Dyfrig, lowering his cowl, drank the goblet of red wine that the steward had poured ready. This was clearly a rite. The monk, replacing the empty goblet on the side table, sat with his elbows on the arms of his chair. Clasping his hands together before his face, gently tapping his chin with both his index fingers, he stared silently into space and waited for the steward to replenish the vessel.

'Please sit, Lord Tragen, join me, I am afraid the wine is of a more mediocre taste than that I am used to, but it will suffice.'

Tragen bristled. 'I do not sit unless my host invites me, Brother Dyfrig, and I also do not insult his hospitality.'

'Very well, Lord Tragen, but you must realize that the seneschal and I have an understanding...he does what I tell him and I do what I want. But in this case, and as I have a favour to ask of you,' he waved a nonchalant arm, 'seat yourself, Seneschal.'

'Go ahead, Tragen, I do not sit with vipers,' fighting to keep control, Portolan moved to the window and leant against the sill, his words spoken so bitterly had created a desperate tension in the room.

'You are a passenger on that ship in dry-dock, Lord Tragen?' The monk asked contemptuously ignoring the seneschal's words.

'I am, Brother. May I enquire as to how you know?'

'I have my means. Tell me, you intend returning to Mantovar shortly?'

'You have good informants,' answered Tragen.

'I noticed that you have suffered extensive damage to the ship. How long will it take you to be ready for sea?'

'I do not know, only the captain can answer that.'

'Very well, send for him Seneschal and have him join us,' and the monk grimaced. 'Mind you, without the masts I cannot see you lasting long in rough seas, you'll need replacements, providing we reach agreement I'll see what can be done. We'll discuss further details when your captain arrives. Now, Seneschal, have you your Quota, I might as well take them with me when I leave,' he sneered.

Portolan ignored the query. 'How fares my brother and his wife?'

'They are well,' and the monk smiled again, the smile not reaching his eyes. 'Well? The Quota?'

'I have mine, yes,' then he made the ritual request. 'Can I come across and see them?'

'We will discuss that, also later. The Montetor has his?'

'I do not know,' answered Lodovico startled at the monk's reply.

'Send for him immediately. Now, I think I will retire to my room,' and he rose. Tragen and Portolan listened with bated breath to him climbing the stairs to the chambers above.'

'A truly obnoxious man,' stated Tragen.

'Yes, he is, and he is definitely up to something. I always receive a flat denial when I ask to see Paul and Ariana. I wonder why not this time?'

'Have you heard of him using magic, Lodovico?'

'Never, why do you ask?'

'He carries something magical about his person.'

'Thaddeus behave, that is disgusting,' said Beatrix, watching him playing with a beetle...an extremely ugly, brownish-yellow, click beetle running all over his hand.

Thaddeus looked up and laughed. 'They tickle! My mother taught me that not all insects are dirty and disgusting. Mind you she could never teach me how they feel—these beetles are friendly,' he said, sitting with his back against a rock in a clearing on the banks of the swiftly flowing river. All was silent except for the sorrowful chaffing of the chiffchaff and the gentle singing of the nightingale and, of course, the river thrumming along in the background drowning out the gurgling of a small stream.

'How do you know that?' Beatrix asked.

'It's a feeling I have. I even sense what my horse feels.'

'That's his speciality, ladies,' said Aidan, licking tomatoes off his fingers and then wiping them on his britches.

'Stop doing that, you pig, wash them in the stream,' said Augusta. 'And what do you mean "his speciality"?'

They had made camp for the night alongside a narrow brook that led into the main river, their blankets laid out on soft grass. The horses had been hobbled close by and were munching the sweet fodder. They were relaxing, weary after riding for most of the day.

Watching Thaddeus, Aidan had pondered on the boy's riding ability, picking it up so quickly was quite an accomplishment. The seneschal's son had gained the skill within an hour of mounting, and watching him now with the beetle explained it.

'Most wizards specialize...you know, become very good at a particular form of magic, better than other wizards. Mine is healing. It seems that Thaddeus can commune with animals by reading their emotions. The mare senses him almost as if they talk to each other,' he smiled at his very unusual friend. 'Not even I can do that.'

Augusta and Beatrix stared at Thaddeus, awestruck. Turning back to Aidan, Beatrix suddenly had an idea. 'What is my speciality, then?'

'I'm not sure, but I think it's something to do with your eyes.'

'My eyes?'

'Yes, you seem to have no trouble seeing in any light, even the dark. Am I right?'

'I have good night vision, yes. I hate the dark though, it terrifies me,' and she shuddered.

'And me, Aidan?' Augusta asked quickly.

'Ah! I have an inkling what yours is, Augusta. I noticed it when we walked through the seneschal's woods. You never had to bend your head and you never suffered a scratch, like the rest of us.'

'What does that mean?'

'You never had to duck to avoid low branches; you never had to push them out of your way either.'

'So?' Augusta replied, mystified.

'I think you can move objects from your path that most people would struggle even to lift, just by thinking and blowing them out of the way.' He looked at her pursed mouth, and looked away quickly; he had a yearning for those lips now that he had tasted them. Would she ever kiss him again? 'I know I couldn't shift them.'

Augusta, not noticing his reaction, glanced at the others. 'I don't know what you mean, I've never actually thought about moving anything.'

Aidan handed her a large pebble. 'Place that on your palm,' and she complied. 'Right, stretch your arm out and blow the stone, at the same time think of where you wish it to end up,' he said.

She looked at him and sighed. 'All right, I'll humour you,' and she blew at it matter-of-factly, and was stunned along with Beatrix and Thaddeus when the stone flew from her hand and landed in the river a full forty yards away.

Aidan laughed. 'Do you believe me now?'

Augusta stared at him, a regular cloud of butterflies churning in her stomach again. 'But that's only a small stone a…a fluke.'

'Try that branch over there,' and Aidan pointed at a large oak branch half embedded in the earth about a hundred yards away. Augusta started to rise and go towards it Aidan stopped her. 'Do it from here.'

She did, blowing and thinking no harder than before, the branch uprooted and tumbled end over end to land a further hundred yards away, startling a family of crows in a nearby tree. They flew off screeching while the horses whinnied and skittered in fright and they all stared in amazement.

'Bloody hell! With practise you should no longer need to blow, just thinking will be enough. Remember though that you will probably have to be in sight of the object you want to move and that the further

356

from it you are, the less chance of success. And that, Augusta, is very powerful magic, as is Thaddeus' so be careful with it, both of you,' warned Aidan.

'Oh, poor Leash,' Augusta said out of the blue, giggling.

'What?' Aidan asked puzzled.

'Don't you remember what happened to him? At the party on board when you and Anders got so drunk you were disgusting...'

'I am never disgusting in drink,' retorted Aidan.

'I remember...he was hit over the head by a belaying pin. What of it?' Beatrix asked.

'Well, it happened just after I'd wished that I could hit him with one like Dolly's mother tried to do to her husband. Nobber said that he'd seen the pin flying through the air!'

'He did to, and nobody believed him because he was drunk! Good, I don't like that man. Oh, drat it, I hope I discover what my special magic is before too long,' Beatrix moaned.

Leash and his surly companions emerged from the confines of the dense woods as dawn broke. They were tired and footsore having spent most of the night trying to catch up with their quarry. Instead, they had discovered that night is not the best of times to travel through a forest. They all suffered scratches and bruises, some minor, others more serious. One had turned both his ankles through stepping on treacherous rocks and stumbling over raised roots. Another, his arm now in a makeshift sling, had suffered a broken arm as a tree branch, bent forwards by the man in front, returned to its normal state, snapping his wrist. Both casualties had been ordered to help each other return home.

Razor was murderous. 'Does anyone have any idea where they're headed?'

'I've been up here a couple of times,' answered Pudge, a man in his sixties with a severely pock-marked face, who had suffered the smallpox when a young man. 'Ahead are the catacombs.'

'They are not likely to seek shelter in those—they'll have been warned,' retorted Razor.

'Aye, but on the slope below the catacombs is the Portolan's hunting lodge, which they'll gain this afternoon.'

'By Kaneshi's balls, I'd forgotten that! Okay, make camp. We'll move off at lunchtime, that way we'll reach the lodge in the early hours, we'll take them then.'

Leash sat on a nearby log disgruntled, nursing a grazed shin. He looked above to the sparsely wooded mountain ahead. Ignoring those around him, he searched for sign of the catacombs and failed. Razor's plan was as good as any, he thought, the youngsters would be sleeping fast when the hunters arrived at the lodge.

'What are the catacombs?' Leash asked of a man settling into his blanket alongside him.

'The Devil's Keep … no-one survives who enters there,' he replied.

'What kind of devil?'

'I haven't been in to find out,' he laughed mirthlessly, and then closed his eyes, weariness claiming him.

Twenty-eight

The hunting lodge was not your normal habitat built for the express purpose of sheltering hunters. It was a commandeered farm house, abandoned in the years of the forest's pillaging by the Montetors. The farmer, Josiah Croft, had never been able to survive on just his orchards and his kitchen garden; he'd needed the hunting in the forest as well. When that dried up he'd left to join his brother farming nearer the coast. But as the Portolans had sold the forest in the first place, they were partly to blame for the disappearance of the farmer's livelihood. And Josiah Croft hadn't bothered to seek compensation from the Portolan at the time for the simple reason he hadn't been on very good terms with Lodovico's father. But Lodovico did purchase the farm later at the going rate, which ensured the man's grudging loyalty.

The four sat their horses on the brow of the small hill looking down at the thatched-roof, two storey house. It seemed to have a life of its own squatting in a dingle in the foothills. The picturesque home was clean and peaceful, enhanced by the colour red painted on its exterior plaster—red to guard against the devil. Small windows nestling beneath the thatch's deep eaves appeared to be eyes peering from beneath its precision cut hairline, the small, dark, oak door at the front of the house its pursed mouth, closed now but still welcoming. Its nose was a plaque bearing the arms of the Portolan family. The front of the house, facing south, overlooked a small stone-wall enclosed flower garden, a rowan tree growing in its centre—again rowan to ward against the devil. On the east, was the large kitchen garden, surprisingly neat and tidy even though the seneschal had informed them that a caretaker visited only once a month to maintain the house and grounds and to replenish the stores. At the rear was a large, well-beaten yard with a pig pen built on to the house near its backdoor, and across the yard small stables.

Augusta and Beatrix fell in love with it immediately and, much to the boys' disgust, made sentimental comments and cooing noises, right up to the first step over the threshold. From then on and for perhaps an hour, the girls emitted small cries of delight at each new discovery, from copper pots and pans hanging in the dresser against the rear wall of the kitchen, to the ceiling of woven thatch visible in the bedchambers, of which there were three.

Supper that night was eaten sitting at a round table in the parlour. It consisted of a feast of boiled potatoes, peas and turnips accompanied by succulent smoked ham, a haunch of which was hanging in the inglenook of the open kitchen fire. All thought of mad monks was forgotten while they ate.

But later, on glancing out of the window in the rear bedchamber, a strange glow was visible higher up the mountain. The light was dim and flickering, hidden behind rocks. Discovering the entrance to the catacombs, the worries of the past days and weeks returned in a rush. Lower down the slope, below the entrance to the catacombs and a little further east, a waterfall rumbled. The source of the torrent was somewhere deep inside the mountain. This large cataract was the headspring of the river they had been following for just on two days.

Before they went to sleep that night, Aidan attempted to mindmeld with Tragen, and again failed. Thaddeus, Augusta and Beatrix all tried in turn and had the same negative result. They were not overly concerned as there could be many causes for this, including a predominance of certain rocks. Aidan had seen examples of the reddish-orange unakite which was sometimes used in jewellery to ward against wizards as it supposedly blocked the mindspeak. All four retired weary and replete, Anders having told them that their followers were still camped at the woods half a day behind. But sleep did not come easy that night, and the following morning found all four, bleary eyed and anxious, when they entered the kitchen.

'Aidan, there are men outside,' shouted Anders, peering intently at the wall of colours before him.

'What!'

'They are moving to surround the house, you'd better get out of there quick,' ordered Anders, beginning to panic. *'It's the men from the woods, they must have moved up through the night...I never saw them.'*

Augusta ran to the kitchen window and looked out. 'I can't see anyone from here,' she said, turning back to look at the others.

'Wait!' Thaddeus ran upstairs and peered around the drapes of the front bedchamber's window. Crawling on hands and knees up the slope leading to the flower garden wall were two men, obviously not on a peaceful errand as they were armed with bandoliers bearing assorted knives. Other men were creeping up on either side of the house one of whom was carrying a cutlass in his hand. All were

360

moving covertly and if those inside had not been warned, would have succeeded in reaching the house without anyone being aware.

Aidan ran through into the rear bedchamber and searched the grounds behind the house. He stared up at the long scrub and bracken covered slope towards the catacombs and espied no-one.

'Come on, Thaddeus. There's no-one out back, but it won't take them long. We have to move fast.'

'Are they the monk's men?' Thaddeus asked unable to hide his fear.

'I don't know. Run Augusta, Beattie, run up the hill as fast as you can go. And don't stop for anything,' Aidan ordered. He and Thaddeus followed the girls, slamming the door behind them, none having had time to retrieve any of their belongings.

The steep slope was riddled with broken rocks between the stubby dwarf birch, moss campion and upright chickweed. Gravel slipped beneath their pounding feet, and it wasn't long before Thaddeus was suffering a stitch in his side, his body not used to such exertion. Aidan seeing him struggle, slowed for him to catch up. Placing his hand on Thaddeus' side, he relieved the pain as both boys ran.

Razor hollered impatiently at his men. 'There's no need to crawl now, fools, they've seen you. Get up after them. By the Gods, who gave me these idiots?'

He glanced at Leash standing a little behind him on the brow above the house. All night they had spent coming up with their prey reaching the Lodge at first light. Splitting his eight men in three, two to approach from the south, three to creep up on either side, all had moved with practised stealth. Their quarry should have been taken easily. Why hadn't they?

Aidan, Thaddeus, Augusta and Beatrix were now in full flight running up the mountainside the catacombs immediately in their path, with the Montetor men gasping and cursing close behind. Razor and Leash watched as they were herded towards the Devil's Keep, no place to flee, no escape possible. Leash gloated. At last the boy was his, and he made his way around the brow of the hill to join the mad scramble.

Razor followed a moment later, there was something not quite right here, and he examined the slopes all around. Was there someone up there watching? But if so how had he told the youths? Razor shrugged, it was still going to be a good morning's work though, and Bazyli would be happy—five for the Montetor's Quota!

Razor chuckled and Leash turned his head to look at him. 'Don't worry, sailor, you will have your revenge, you will see the boy die,' he shouted after him, a strange glint in his eye.

Aidan and Thaddeus caught up with the girls as they arrived at the entrance to the catacombs, a large, dark gash opening into the depths of the mountain at the foot of a high cliff. On either side of the aperture stood a small statue, the features on both indistinguishable – worn away by weathering – but they must have been hewn from some sort of green rock, the colour still bright in patches. The level ground before it – littered with fallen boulders, bracken growing in profusion – was gained by a path between rock walls leaning inwards.

The Montetors finally came up on the fugitives and formed a semi-circle, pinning them against the gaping hole behind. They waved the dockworkers' favourite weapon in their hands, a belaying pin, as they stooped panting for air awaiting their leader. There was no escape.

'What do we do now, Aidan?' Augusta asked, nervously glancing behind at the dark cavern, large enough to walk into three abreast.

'Can't you blow them away, Augusta?' Thaddeus asked.

'No, Lord Tragen said not to use magic, the monk will detect us,' said Beatrix.

The men parted to allow Razor and Leash to walk through.

'Leash! What on earth are you doing here?' Aidan asked.

Leash smiled at the four youths in front of him, delighted, they were now in his power. 'Hello, brat, hello ladies, what a pleasure this is,' and he bowed mockingly.

'Who are you?' Razor asked Thaddeus.

'I am the seneschal's son. Who are you? Why do you threaten us?'

'Ah, my master is the Montetor and he requires recruits for his Quota, and Leash here, volunteered your three friends. But I'm sure you wouldn't like to leave your companions in a predicament, so you can stay with them. The five of you will come in very handy.'

'Five?' Leash asked frowning.

The old man clicked his fingers and to Leash's astonishment and before he could move, a noose was flung over his head and pulled tight around his neck. Two men pinioned his arms as others tied his wrists securely together.

'What are you doing?' Leash choked.

'Completing the deal,' Razor smiled crookedly. 'You wished to see the boy and the girls taken...you have. They are here before you, as you see they cannot escape. That is the first part of our deal; the second...you wished to see them die. You will, if the monk kills them before he slays you,' and he and his men laughed uproariously.

Leash raged.

'Please, don't struggle more Leash, we'll only choke you until you fall unconscious and then you'll miss us securing your enemies.'

'We are in trouble,' said Aidan as a vole ran over Thaddeus' foot.

'We can't be taken to Sanctity in chains, Aidan,' said Augusta. *'We'll never escape without using magic there.'*

'And if you do the monk will discover five wizards and not just the one,' added Anders fearfully, from his place at the wall of colours.

'The vole has just told me to take refuge in the catacombs,' said Thaddeus.

'You can't be serious?' Augusta asked, quaking. *'I mean the devil's supposed to rule in there...there'll be demons!'*

'The vole has said we'll be safe and he'll take us to friends.'

'Friends,' Beatrix said, incredulously, *'in there?'*

'We do not have a choice, ladies,' said Aidan.

Razor's men moved towards them, ropes and cudgels in hand, two men remaining with the tethered second helmsman of the Grim. Aidan darted into the catacombs followed by Thaddeus and the vole— and Augusta and Beatrix moaning with fright.

A short way inside the mouth of the huge cavern the high passageway led to their left into complete darkness, forcing them to stop after rounding the bend.

'Are they following?' Augusta asked, breathless and in agony from a stubbed toe.

Thaddeus stared behind and shook his head, then realizing he could not be seen he spoke in her general direction. 'No, they're not, but tell me who was that they have tied up?'

'He is a sailor off the Grim, we'll tell you about him later,' said Aidan. 'Wait here I want to creep back and see what they're doing.'

'No need, I can tell you,' mindmelded Anders. *'They've settled down outside waiting for you to come back out. They don't believe you'll go very far into the catacombs. Leash has been tied to a rock...I'm having some nasty thoughts about him, Aidan.'*

'So am I. But we have more pressing problems, now, like where the hell do we go from here,' he said aloud.

'Anders, how clearly can you see us?' Augusta asked.

'Well, you're a bit fuzzy, but I can see where you are all right. Why?'

'Can you see a way out of these catacombs?'

'Nope, they seem to go on forever. There are levels above you and many, many more below you. But you are right to worry—if you go very deep I'll lose you.'

'Great!' Aidan said disconcerted. 'And my bet is that if we walk any further into this passage we're going to end up very deep in this mountain aren't we?'

'Don't worry, I told you this vole will show us a safe passage to friends,' said Thaddeus.

'Friends? This place is called the Devil's Keep! I for one won't like making friends with a demon, and anyway I can't see in the dark. Can you?' Aidan retorted truculently, his nerves getting the better of him.

'Well, conjure a light,' Augusta snapped.

'I can't just like that!'

'Why not? You can make fire, so why not light?' Augusta asked.

'Because I need a little light, even a tiny spot, then I can make it grow brighter. Making light from complete darkness like this is very exhausting and very inefficient. I'd be able to light a little way in front, just enough to see your hand in front of your face, and that's all,' Aidan said exasperated.

'But you made fire from nothing,' she countered.

'No I didn't, I made fire from the heat in the air.'

'Where's Beattie?' Thaddeus asked suddenly.

It was then they realized that they hadn't heard her since they had entered the cavern. Thaddeus peered back around the corner and saw in the distance the entrance, there was no sign of her.

'She's not behind us. Anders can you see her?' Thaddeus asked.

'Yes, she's with you, a little farther in but there's something wrong.'

'Okay, stand still everyone,' said Aidan, and they listened as he chanted, low at first and increasing in intensity as it went on. And as the cadence reached a crescendo, a light appeared around Aidan. Not much of one, but still light enough to see the strain on his face and his arms stretched out before him. He set off further into the passage and in a moment, they found Beatrix.

She was in a terrible state, standing rigidly against the wall, her eyes shut tight, all colour drained from her face.

'Beattie, Beattie, what is it?' Augusta asked, clasping her friend in her arms.

'It's all right, Beattie, they aren't chasing us,' Thaddeus said worriedly.

Aidan continued his chant, afraid to stop in case they lost her again.

Augusta hugged her; squeezing her tight, she forced Beattie's head to rest on her shoulder. 'Come, Beattie, tell us please, you're frightening us.'

Beatrix shuddered and then sobbed. 'I can't help it…I'm petrified of the dark. I hate it…I always have. I'm sorry, I must go back, I can't stay in here,' and she fought against Augusta, trying desperately to free herself.

Thaddeus went to Augusta's aid and put his arms around them both. 'You'll be fine, Beattie, honest. We're here, we'll look after you.'

'You can't! I hate the dark and I hate creepy-crawlies…and there are thousands in here,' she screamed. Staring, her eyes bulging, she somehow got her hands free and sobbing bitterly she beat them against Augusta and Thaddeus. 'I must have light, I must have light,' she screamed hysterically, absolutely terrified. 'I must have…'

And she did.

It emanated from every pore in her body—a bright, white, shining light. Her terror had found her special magic. Her light radiated down the passageway illuminating every nook, cranny and rock for many feet until it found another corner up ahead.

'Bloody hell!' Aidan said, ceasing his chant, his own light fading fast. Augusta and Thaddeus let their arms drop and stared at Beatrix, mouths wide open.

Beatrix, bewildered at first, blinked her eyes in the sudden brightness and raising her arms she stared at them. The light poured from her, even from the pimple on the inside of her elbow that she had hidden for days. And if a smile could be more radiant than the light emitted, then Beattie's face lit up—a picture of absolute bliss.

'I hate breaking up this happy moment but the light can be seen by the Montetors outside. Beattie, I think you had better tone it down a bit before they gain courage and come to investigate.' Anders said equally amazed.

'Yes, and I think we had better move on, the vole is waiting at the corner,' said Thaddeus, finding his tongue and pointing ahead at the small rodent shaking its head, itself mesmerized by the sudden brightness.

That same morning Bazyli Montetor entered the home of his enemy, his one eye murderously settling on Marshal Janne who returned his look without blinking.

The only time Bazyli ever came to the manor was at the behest of the monk. He hated the abbot even more than he despised the contemptible fat man who had allowed his twin sister to be taken hostage.

He worshipped Ariana; she was the younger by ten minutes and had always mothered him. She was small and sweet, pretty and beguiling, she could twist him around her little finger, and often did. Ariana soothed his hurts, and held his hands when their father punished him for some petty misdemeanour, chastising him herself when it was more serious. And she loved to tease him over his choice of female companions. But that had been when he had two eyes and no scar. Now most of his female companions enjoyed his money and his power and did not look too closely at his face.

The sword thrust that had taken his eye and nearly his life had been delivered by the abbot at their first meeting when Bazyli reacted violently to the monk's demands for ransom. The monk had been fast—surprisingly fast in taking Bazyli's own blade from its scabbard and striking before Bazyli had even drawn breath. The monk had been the one to stop the bleeding thereby saving his life. The monk's master had needed Bazyli alive to ensure the ransom was collected and so had worked his healing through his underling. And Brother Dyfrig was happy, he loved humiliating the Montetor.

Bazyli had one obsession—to see his sister freed, but like Lodovico Portolan, he was hamstrung he didn't know how to accomplish the task without causing her death. So he stood in the hallway staring at the Portolan's compatriot and awaited the hateful summons to meet his tormentor once more.

The door opened again and admitted Hugo Locklear, very annoyed; this was not the time to leave his ship. Nevertheless, he had no alternative but to obey the summons of his friend and meeting the monk away from his home base of Sanctity was an unexpected opportunity to gain information. Locklear halted abruptly at sight of the terribly scarred man in the hall.

'Good morning, Captain, please allow me to introduce His Excellency, The Montetor. Excellency, this is Captain Locklear of the Grim,' Janne watched as both men appraised each other.

The Montetor and Locklear were much the same in height and physique, both shorter than Janne by at least half a dozen inches. One reared in the mountains and mines, and the other brought up on the sea, both their upbringings ensuring a toughness and strength in two extraordinary men. Bazyli and Locklear, both well used to command, took in at a glance the attributes of the other, wary they shook hands.

'Gentlemen, if you will follow me please, the monk will be informed of your arrival,' said Janne, leading the way to the family's parlour.

'Why is he early?' The Montetor asked a short while later, taking a mug of tea from Mistress Barbat and bowing his thanks. Bazyli, despite his appearance, only drank alcohol at mealtimes and never before noon. He glanced at Lady Cornelia and bowed his head and then turned to Tragen and studied him openly and unashamedly. 'You must be the wizard…welcome to my island.'

Tragen surprised, shook the proffered hand. 'I thought you and Lodovico shared Griffin, Excellency.'

'We do—for now,' and Bazyli looked for the first time since entering, at his host and asked again. 'Tell me, Seneschal, why is he early?'

Portolan, quite used to the abrupt manner of his brother's brother-in-law, indicated for them all to sit. 'It seems that he requires a favour from the Grim's captain.'

Locklear raised his eyebrows and stared at his friend. 'What favour…'

'Good morning, Captain Locklear,' said Brother Dyfrig suddenly appearing at the door. 'The wizard cannot answer you he knows not the nature of my request.'

The atmosphere, cold before his entrance, was now decidedly icy. Bazyli bristled as his hand went automatically to the hilt of his sword. Janne's hand had never moved far from his own.

'Ah! The handsome Montetor has arrived. Welcome to my humble abode. It is mine while I am here, is it not, Seneschal?' Receiving no reply, he went on. 'You have your Quota, Ironmaster?'

Bazyli ignored the monk's jibe. 'You are early, monk. How long before you leave? I wish to breathe fresh air again.'

The malice in his words did not faze Brother Dyfrig at all. Tragen and Locklear astonished at the Montetor's words, glanced at each other. There was no reaction at all from Lodovico Portolan or Marcus Janne. Mistress Barbat and Lady Cornelia sat with bated breath at the window.

The abbot chuckled, the humour not reaching his eyes. 'Your manners are abominable, one-eye; you have not greeted our other guest. Lady Cornelia I would ask you not to look above his neck it is a sight not fit for ladies.'

Cornelia, whose repugnance of the abbot now had no limits, stood, and moving closer, she smiled into Bazyli's eye. 'Excellency, beauty is only skin-deep, may I?' She lifted her hand and traced her finger down the terrible scar, amazing all who watched, and seriously displeasing Brother Dyfrig.

'The wound has healed somewhat ragged, but I know someone who could repair this,' Tragen started, surprised at her mentioning the possibility of another wizard. 'Unfortunately he is not with us at present, but I am sure I can persuade him to meet you.' Impishly she went on, her charm captivating another citizen of Griffin. 'He may not be able to do much about your eye, tidy it up a bit perhaps. But with a patch and unblemished skin, many women will find you intriguing.'

It was Mistress Barbat's turn to chuckle she couldn't help it. 'Can I persuade you to get an eye-patch, Marcus?'

'If, for no other reason, I am happy to be here to meet such a charming and lovely lady,' Bazyli raised Cornelia's hand and kissed her chubby fingers.

For the first time in years, jealousy gripped the seneschal. But then, as he looked at this very brave woman, an overwhelming sense of pride brought a glistening to the eyes of Lodovico Portolan.

'Enough!' Brother Dyfrig shouted his face purpling with rage. 'Your petty innuendoes are annoying. Montetor do you have your Quota ready?'

'When you leave they will accompany you.' Bazyli, making a decision he had mulled over for years, straightened and stared malevolently. 'But I warn you, enough is enough. I want my sister

368

returned this time or I will believe that you are unable. And if she is dead, monk, you will die very, very slowly, I promise.'

Silence that seemed to go on for ages greeted this threat; no-one doubted the Montetor.

'I am sorry, Bazyli,' said Lodovico Portolan coming to the same decision, 'but you will have to climb over me first, I am the one who will kill him. This is the last, monk, no more!'

Brother Dyfrig's composure broke for a second before resuming his sneering. 'Captain, I wish a favour, I need something transported to Mantovar and I do not have a ship large enough to make the journey with my cargo.' He turned his gaze from the looks of hate on both leaders' faces. 'In return I will allow you to find replacements for your masts. How long will it be before your ship is ready to put to sea?'

Locklear paused and looked at Tragen. 'A couple or three days.'

'Good, when you are ready, please carry the Montetor and the Seneschal to Sanctity. My work is at an end in these islands and I no longer need the Portolan and his wife.' And with that, Brother Dyfrig returned to his chambers above.

Later that afternoon, on the Grim, a conference was on the verge of breaking up in bitter acrimony. As the discussions needed to take place in utter secrecy, well away from Brother Dyfrig's prying eyes and ears, the captain's cabin had been chosen as the ideal venue. That the monk had a magical artefact on his person came as a shock to all and no-one was sure if it would enable the monk to overhear them speaking in the manor.

Following the threats of death from both clan leaders and the departure of the object of those threats to his quarters, a mutual understanding, though extremely fragile, had been reached by the Montetor and the seneschal for the first time in twenty years. Captain Locklear, grasping the opportunity, had invited them all on board his ship.

'You have both reached agreement on the outcome of this delivery of your last Quota,' said Tragen attempting conciliation, 'perhaps you can both now agree on a means to ensure the monk keeps his word.'

'It is true, this is the first time I have gone along with the Montetor,' said Lodovico, 'but that does not mean I trust his word.'

'And that feeling is mutual, seneschal,' spat Bazyli.

'Gentlemen, please, this attitude is not getting us anywhere,' interjected Cornelia. 'This is the only chance either of you have ever had of securing the release of these members of both your families. You owe it to them to work together. They are the ones who have suffered imprisonment for twenty years at the hands of this despicable monster—not you. So can we please have a debate without you both flying at each other?'

The discussion lasted until well into the afternoon with a semblance of a stratagem worked out before they all returned to the manor for dinner. As they sat at table without the monk – thankfully he always elected to eat in his room – Tragen again attempted a mindmeld to Aidan, and for the fourth or fifth time that day he failed. He was now extremely anxious.

The Montetor – having finally committed himself to a partnership with the seneschal – sent an aide to seek out Razor. If the youngsters had already been apprehended, on no account were they to be harmed, if they were still free then the chase was to be abandoned. Either way Leash was to be brought to the Grim for questioning.

Twenty-nine

Ryn looked up at peaks blanketed in snows that never thawed. It was going to be very cold up there, the wind very strong, he thought, preparing for flight. He flexed his wings and curled his new fingers tightly into his feathers to keep them warm.

'Where are you going?' Shadra asked.

'I go to think, my head is clearer when I am amongst the clouds, and there are many clouds over those peaks and at the moment many clouds in my head…the wind must blow them free.'

Anselm watched the huge bird soaring off into the blue sky. 'I'm sorry if I have frightened your friend.'

'Frightened him? Maybe you have, you certainly have me. He can be solitary on times though, it comes with spending most of his life airborne over empty oceans.'

Shadra gazed at the minstrel, wondering what he was keeping back. 'You have never met the Garda; you do not even know how they look. You know they are fierce warriors and do not like strangers and yet you seek them. This deposed chancellor must be quite a man to merit such a passionate loyalty that you place your life at risk for him on a mission that has every chance of failing. I find it truly astonishing.'

Anselm got to his feet and walked to the stream; his hands jammed in his jerkin, and stared at the organized turmoil at its junction with the fast flowing river. Silent for a while, he lifted his head and gazed up at Ryn riding the thermals overhead.

'I have served my masters for many years, ever since…' he turned and resumed his seat alongside the elf.

'Years ago I returned from a journey to the east, the other side of the Scissor Mountains, it was a longer absence from my family than usual for I caught the plague there. Although I recovered enough to journey home, unfortunately I was still highly infectious—I could not endanger my wife and child, so I never went near them. But I met a healer, a wonderful old wizard who was an advisor to the prince. The healing took weeks, but when I recovered I found that my wife had been killed—murdered,' he paused, a catch in his voice, 'my child missing.

'I attempted suicide. It was my mad wish to re-join my wife, to ensure she was safe in Paradise.'

'I am sorry my friend, you must have been truly devastated...grief can send us all temporarily insane,' said Shadra. 'Did you ever find your child?'

'No, by the time I was well enough to search all signs had disappeared. No, I failed miserably although I still keep looking as I travel. The wizard passed me over into the safekeeping of the chancellor and he placed me in the service of the prince. Both have always treated me honestly and fairly. Even now, when it seems that the prince has betrayed us, Chancellor Sevenoaks will not have a word said against him. He insists that he still has our interests at heart, and in time, we will discover the reason for his actions. Otherwise, why did the prince send me to tell the chancellor of his impending overthrow, and to warn him that his life was in danger? Why did he expressly command me to ensure that Sevenoaks escaped?'

He returned to his seat on a tree stump close to the fire. 'No, elf, I will not forsake him, or my liege lord. I was sent here to contact the Garda and seek their aid to defeat the monks and the evil one who controls them. And that is what I intend.'

'But the legend...the legend the Garda protect. You have absolutely no notion of what it is?'

'I have not. My chancellor said that I would have no problem in recognizing it, but on this occasion he felt that too much knowledge was dangerous...no-one can survive torture for long. I suppose he was right in that,' he grimaced, 'your bird was correct in his summation of my conduct, I am more of a coward than I like to acknowledge.' He stared at his hands, warming them before the fire. 'I have been close to being taken a few times now, and they still chase me. The monks never seem to tire—they're unnatural.'

'Ryn is not "my bird" as you say and you don't seem the coward to me. But that is how you were destitute when you came upon us?'

'Yes, I had to flee my last camp,' and Anselm chuckled, 'rather hastily although I did leave two monks no longer able to hunt me.' He shuddered. 'But the monks don't die naturally.'

'What do you mean?'

'I shot them with arrows, piercing their hearts...or where their hearts should have been. They should have dropped dead but they did not, they kept coming for me with the arrows swinging about in their chests. I couldn't believe it! It was only when they were almost upon me that I realized I would have to try something else.' Anselm halted,

372

his mind on his memories of the conflict as he stared at his hands in his lap.

'What did you do, Anselm?'

'I chopped off their heads!' He looked up at the little elf, his face ashen. 'They only died when I decapitated them.'

Ryn, riding the air currents above the camp, was perplexed. Ever since he had been given his voice, he had had problems.

Firstly, the storm had battered him almost senseless, and although the long flight had seemed to pass exceedingly swift, it had left him extremely weary at the end of it.

And then, of course, he had encountered the second problem— the abbot. What a despicable human being, killing that archer for failing to stop my escape. And then he recalled that evil voice mindmelding, it had totally unnerved him. That unknown voice scared him witless and he didn't know why—it was almost not human.

Ryn soared higher on a thermal, the current comforting. He flexed his new fingers in the warmish air; well it was warm compared to the currents blowing off the frozen north, he had often flown to that region—he enjoyed exploring. He loved his fingers and was very proud of them; it still amazed him that he was magic. He was the only bird in the whole world able to use a knife and fork!

This brought him to his next problem—the little elf! In the short time they had been together, he had grown very fond of Shadra. The elf had introduced him to a style of living that he had never encountered in all of his long life. Not just the elf's culinary expertise, but the companionship, trust and easy friendship they shared. Friendship was unknown in the avian world. The bond that held a flock of birds together when they migrated or flew the void was instinctual and, although mating for life was known among certain species in the bird world mutual affection across species was not. But in what was the elf getting him involved? Shadra was obsessed with reaching the peaks and he was passing that obsession on to Ryn.

His next problem was the minstrel who seemed to be fighting a war. Ryn had no experience of war. True he had the occasional spat with another bird, but full scale fighting between many? Never! The monks were intent on killing Anselm and would undoubtedly kill all those helping the chancellor's agent. So, should he and Shadra remain in Anselm's company?

And he had still not delivered his message to the prince—another problem. And there it was…gaining human speech had caused all his problems.

Could he give up the ability to speak? Would it solve anything if he did? He loved his voice, even if the elf did tell him to shut up on occasion. He grinned. No, he could never willingly surrender his voice.

He peered down at his friends, for the minstrel was now counted a friend, and he realized that he could not abandon Anselm to the mercies of the monks, either. He smiled. The minstrel had promised to teach him how to sing! And play the lute! He smiled down at the figures on the ground; they appeared as ants scrambling all over the hillside, all of them making for the river.

He almost stopped in mid-flight. How could Shadra and Anselm do that? They were safely down at the stream awaiting his return—he could see them. He panicked and dived towards his friends calling out as he did. But he was too late…the "ants" had surrounded them. Ryn pulled out of his plunge and returned to circle above the scene below.

He now had another problem—who in hell had just captured his friends?

'Well, I don't think we can stay here, those men aren't going to go away for a while,' said Aidan.

'Then we'd better follow the rat, perhaps we'll discover another way out of here,' Augusta said.

'It's not a rat…it's a harmless vole, and very pretty,' Thaddeus admonished. 'Come on, or we'll lose it.' They turned the corner following the rodent and found the floor sloping downwards to the head of a flight of steps.

Beattie had taken Anders' advice and toned down her light, but it was still sufficient to see twenty feet in front of them, and if they had looked, a fair way behind as well.

They plodded on down the dank, worn steps, the walls of the stairwell naked, grey rock glistening with moisture. The roof was a patchwork of roots sprouting through hairline cracks in the stone, some trailing to brush against their faces, Augusta just pursed her lips and the fronds flew from her. The steps, cut from the living rock, were buried in unstable detritus causing feet to slip and Beattie's light wavered as she encountered a mass of cobwebs hanging near her face.

374

She hurried past averting her gaze from the white spotted dew-drop spider fleeing the unexpected brightness...the arachnid fascinating Thaddeus.

The stairs ended eventually at the entrance to an old crypt. The burial chamber housed broken coffins, rotted and decayed to piles of dust on shelves on either side of the large, dank room, the floor littered here and there with human bones. The coffins were now home to several species of beetle and small scorpions, the skunk and the sexton beetles predominating. Thaddeus was in his element, he took every opportunity to study the huge variety of insect life, much to the continued disgust, and fear, of Beatrix.

The companions huddling close for comfort, and in Beattie's case in sheer terror, followed the vole through the room to leave by a further flight of steps, this far longer, leading far deeper. They trudged down these steps for over an hour until they reached the bottom and entered another chamber, even larger than the one above. The vole took them across and into a low tunnel which bore right, then left and continued to twist and turn, crossing junctions and bypassing side tunnels the floor continuing to slope ever downwards for many hours.

The air got mustier and their throats drier. Aidan told them to rub the damp walls and drink the moisture from their hands when needed, but the water tasted of the earth, roots and rotting animals. And they were starving, having been forced to leave the hunting lodge before breakfast hunger now gnawed at their bellies.

Aidan said he could smell bacon and eggs, but when he went on to speak of sausages, Augusta hit him and told him to shut it. 'That's it, I've had enough...I want decent drinking water, now, Aidan, or else!'

'But if there are demons down here, they might detect the magic,' Beatrix said, hoping for once that she'd be ignored, knowing exactly how Augusta felt.

'I don't care. If any turn up you can blind them while we run away. I need water, Aidan!' Augusta ordered, raising her voice.

'Don't shout or the devil may not need magic to detect us...your voice will draw it,' Thaddeus said peering around anxiously. 'Let's find somewhere to rest, first. And then Aidan can conjure up some water. God my mouth is dry...and I'm weary to my bones.'

'Oi! Don't I get a say in this?' Aidan asked.

'No! Come on, Beattie,' said Augusta putting her arm through hers; both girls walked ahead leaving Aidan and Thaddeus trailing behind. 'I've had enough of men for now…and Beattie should be the one who is tired, she's been burning up energy for hours, she needs a rest and so do my feet.'

Aidan gave in and followed. 'You keep a look-out, Anders…I don't want any demons following us.'

'How can I do that, I can't see you properly you're a blur, I can only hear you!'

'Dear God, then keep your ears open,' ordered Augusta.

The tunnel narrowed ahead and as they searched for a safe haven they completely lost track of time. The vole continued to lead them on past the side tunnels and eerie chambers, across junctions and around corners, the small animal not wavering in its purpose, the sameness of the passages giving rise to anxiety and increasing disorientation.

But they did find a small chamber with damp walls for Aidan to conjure fresh drinking water and for them all to rest. Within moments of satisfying her thirst, Beatrix was asleep, her head resting on Augusta's shoulder in complete darkness as her light faded.

'I wonder what voles taste like,' Aidan said, the prospect of eating rodents not appealing one bit.

'Don't you dare, Aidan, that vole may be our saviour yet,' said Thaddeus.

'Do you think we'll die down here…I mean, I'm completely lost,' asked Augusta, her voice shaking. 'God it's getting cold!'

'If there's any risk of us dying down here, we'll use magic to get us out. We'll deal with any demon we attract, then,' said Aidan. 'As for being cold, there's a very simple spell to warm you up and we won't need to teach Beattie either when she wakes, her light is sufficient to keep her warm.' And before anyone realized, they were all fast asleep.

Thaddeus heard the noise first; it woke him as if from a dream. It was a scrabbling and scratching that seemed to come from the other side of the tunnel wall. He woke the others and Beatrix rekindled her light.

'Anders, can you see anything? Aidan whispered nervously.

'No, everything's black, but I think you should move from there from the racket it appears to be getting closer to you.'

And with that all four rose and hurried off down the tunnel, listening all the while to the strange noises. But whatever was making it kept pace with them and without warning the vole speeded up and disappeared into the ground. They were left alone in a tunnel from which they had no hope of ever retracing their steps to daylight.

They wandered for hours more seeking a path that led upwards. But as soon as they found a likely passage, they'd eventually reach a crest and down the tunnel would go again.

But now they were seriously lost and hungry – desperately weary and sore – and they were very, very scared. Their hopes of finding escape declined the longer time past and yet the scratching kept apace on the other side of the wall. At first it was on the left and then somehow it crossed the tunnel and was heard from behind the wall on their right. With unspoken agreement, they turned away from the noise at every opportunity; they were now very deep underground.

'We're being herded,' said Beatrix.

'What…what do you mean?' Augusta asked anxiously.

'Whenever we walk in a particular direction for any length of time, and then go to turn a corner, that noise appears alongside us and we turn away. Something is directing our path,' she said.

'She's right,' said Thaddeus. 'And this tunnel has changed…it looks cleaner. The wall isn't very thick either and I can feel a life'form through it. Whatever it is its huge.'

'Does it mean to harm us?' Aidan asked.

Thaddeus looked at them all in turn as he chewed his bottom lip. 'It isn't sure what we are and is very wary. It's guiding us to a place of safety—safe for itself, not us.'

'So we'll meet it eventually?' Augusta asked, trembling.

'Umph…probably,' said Thaddeus, entering a large cavern, one of many that they had passed through in the last hours. This one was different though, Beattie's light did not stretch far enough to find the opposite wall.

'How long have we been wandering down here? I'm going to faint with hunger,' said Aidan, trying to put the thought of meeting their pursuer out of his mind.

'Is this the Devil's Keep?' Beatrix asked, gripping Aidan's arm tight and staring around the immense chamber.

'This bit? I don't know. Anders used to say that any object should be hidden at the centre of a labyrinth. So whatever is living in this maze we'll find somewhere towards the middle. Am I right, Anders?'

'In a normal labyrinth...yes. But is this a normal maze? You are nowhere near the centre, that's way below you and on the other side of the mountain.'

'Can you see us?' Thaddeus asked.

'The ground is hiding you. It's...I don't know...like thick soup. I can see you moving, but that's only because I've hardly taken my eyes off you. If I look away for any length of time I may not be able to find you again.'

'Can you tell us how long we've been down here?' Aidan asked.

'You know time runs differently in the afterlife, Aidan. But I think you've been down there nearly two days. It's approaching night-time again on the surface.'

'God, I've got to have some food before long, my stomach thinks my throat's been cut,' said Aidan, getting on Augusta's nerves, but before she could say anything Beatrix asked Anders the question that was on all their minds.

'Can you see enough of this place to guide us back?'

'No, it's too dark; the tunnels have merged into one black hole. I'm sorry Beattie.'

'Well if you can see us clomping around in here, can you see what's on the other side of the tunnel wall?' Aidan asked exasperated.

'I can't actually make you out, Aidan. All four of you are one big dark spot in another dark spot. But there's nothing on the other side of the wall—nothing at all. Just don't make any sudden movements, there's something very large in front of you on the other side of that cavern and it's watching every move you make.'

'You've chased my son and his friends into the catacombs?' The seneschal roared, swinging round from the starboard rail, frightened out of his wits. 'No-one survives who enters there—no-one. I should kill you now!'

It was the following day, the second of the wizards' sojourn in the catacombs, and the Montetor and Lodovico Portolan were on the Grim's quarterdeck with Tragen and Locklear. The meeting followed a crisis call from Bazyli to attend each other on the Grim without delay.

'We were at war,' snarled Bazyli. 'The Grim's seaman told me he wanted this boy Aidan caught and killed. I did not ask the reason,' he smiled crookedly. 'That is the way I fill my Quota—with strangers, otherwise I would have to incarcerate innocent clan members, and that

I will never do. The others with Aidan were just hangers-on, more strangers. I had no idea who they were and I didn't care!'

'You were going to add them to your Quota?' Tragen asked, shocked, struggling to keep his own temper under control, dismay beating an erratic rhythm in his head.

'Yes! I repeat...they were strangers, nothing to do with me. But when I realized what this boy Aidan meant to you, I sent for them to be brought safely here. But I was too late. They had already disappeared underground and there is nothing I can do about it except give you back your sailor.' He gestured at Leash trussed up and sitting in the middle of the well-deck at the foot of the broken mainmast, Razor and two others were standing guard over him with Trumper watching them.

'The ones who have been lost to whatever's in the catacombs have been ordinary people, haven't they?' Locklear asked.

'Aye...idiots searching for non-existent treasure! Why?' asked the seneschal.

'Ah,' said Tragen. 'I believe Hugo wishes to give us hope, Lodovico. Our children are far from ordinary.'

'Could four wizards survive, you think?' Portolan asked, his temper evaporating.

'They have a better chance than those without powers. They are four very potent wizards after all—their time in the afterlife tells us that. They are the only sorcerers I know of who have ever survived a journey into death and returned. And I do believe that Anders, will be aiding them.'

'What is this talk of wizards, man? I know of no wizards except Lord Tragen here...and what's this about death? Bazyli asked, his anger rising.

'Come, Bazyli, if Hugo will supply us with some of that excellent wine I purloined from my friend, Tragen, we have a story to tell that will amaze you. May we use your cabin, Hugo?' Lodovico Portolan asked, guiding his befuddled ally to the rear of the quarterdeck.

Thirty

They huddled together against the wall at Anders' warning, all of them afraid, none knowing what to expect.

'Douse your light, Beattie, maybe it can't see in the dark,' said Aidan, holding Augusta's and Beattie's hands very tightly.

Beatrix obeyed instantly, and Thaddeus said, only a little nervously as he shuffled in closer. 'Don't be daft! It lives down here, of course it can see in the dark.'

'Then what are we going to do?' The girls whispered, peering around in the pitch black scared out of their wits.

'Anders, can you tell us any more…like is it moving towards us?' Aidan asked.

'It's enormous and standing still.'

'Brilliant! That's a lot of help.'

'Shut up, Aidan. He's told us what he can see,' said Beatrix, frostily.

'Why not speak to it?'

'Oh yeah and what do we say? Hello master demon, sir, don't mind us we won't harm you,' said Aidan, very sarcastic.

'I'm glad to hear that, strangers,' said a voice from across the cavern. 'I also don't plan on hurting you, just yet.' And with that, a light blossomed in the roof and walls and Thaddeus grinned wide as his friends quailed.

The cavern was vast and roughly oval, the whole harbour of Griffin Town would have fitted into it. The roof was bare, black rock and the light came from lines of white quartz criss-crossing the rock face. There was a slight breeze, the air cool and only faintly musty. The vault, for such it appeared, had many openings and through the one nearest him, Aidan glimpsed coffins on shelves. These were unbroken, and he assumed that the other doorways led to similar burial chambers.

But they took in very little of their surroundings, their attention grabbed by the sight just along the cavern wall. Two hundred yards away lay the largest monster the four had ever seen. Fully a hundred feet from its head to the tip of its tail, the earthworm, for that it seemed to be, stared at them with sunken eyes the size of platters, its breath escaping through slit nostrils. It was twice as high as Thaddeus was tall and its pink skin was ridged around its girth, the rings running along the whole length of its body. But its most frightening feature

380

was its mouth. The orifice stretched from one side of its missing neck to the other and it had two rows of teeth in the upper and lower jaw, each tooth as long as Aidan's arm. It was terrifying, at least for Aidan, Augusta and Beatrix clinging desperately to each other.

Thaddeus, though, was unafraid. Returning its stare, he disentangled himself from his friends.

'Oh my, oh my, oh my, oh my…' he mumbled and then burst into peals of laughter.

'Aidan grab him, he's hysterical,' shouted Augusta.

'Oh no, Augusta, you have no idea what it is, do you? These creatures are absolutely amazing,' said Thaddeus.

'Is he right in the head?' Aidan asked.

'Shut up,' answered Beatrix. 'What is it, Thaddeus?' she asked, very apprehensive she stood alongside him staring at the monster.

'You understand who we are?' The strong voice asked, surprised.

'Yes,' and Thaddeus bowed low as his friends stared astounded.

'Bloody hell, Thaddeus, tell us will you?' Aidan ordered.

'Stop swearing, Aidan…it's not nice,' said Beatrix.

'It's only an animal for Gods' sake…isn't it?' Aidan retorted suddenly nervous, wondering if it was a demon.

'It isn't the monster that's speaking—that's the voice of its master,' said Thaddeus, his grin widening.

And from behind the worm's head stepped a man…his skin was green. He was about the same height and build as an ordinary human with eyes slightly enlarged. But these did not detract from his very attractive good looks, and at sight of him Augusta and Beatrix preened…Augusta running fingers through her hair and Beatrix furtively rubbing dirt from her hands.

Aidan stood his mouth agape. 'Who are you?' he asked gobsmacked.

'Surely it is my prerogative to enquire first as you are in my realm, human?'

'Our apologies,' and Thaddeus bowed again. 'My name, sir, is Thaddeus Portolan; I am the seneschal's son. These are my friends from Mantovar, the Princess Augusta, Beatrix, her companion, and this is Aidan, wizard's apprentice to Lord Tragen.'

The Green Man returned the bow. 'And I, young sirs and ladies, I am Leonid and this is Clarinda, my krynx,' and he waved at the giant earthworm.

'We are honoured to meet you, Leonid; your krynx is a truly fine animal. Are there many more of you, and them,' he nodded at the krynx, 'down here?' Thaddeus asked.

'Not as many as was,' Leonid said, cryptically. 'You all are wizards I see. Young magic, unusually powerful, not yet corrupted by the evil in your world. How come I find you in the catacombs?'

'It's a long story. We took refuge from criminals hunting us, very early yesterday morning,' said Thaddeus.

'Then you must need sustenance. Come, do not fear,' he said as Augusta, Beatrix and Aidan hesitated, 'Clarinda will not harm a soul unless I order it. I have sleeping accommodation and a store of provisions near here. You may eat and rest and tell me this long story so that I may decide your fate,' and Leonid beckoned them forward.

Aidan stared the worm in the eye wondering what it would do, if ordered.

Locklear stood in the waist of the Grim studying his second helmsman, trying to fathom the silent man's motive in wanting the youngsters killed.

Tragen, Portolan and Locklear had spent hours the previous evening relating the events of the last weeks, since the Grim had set forth from Drakka. Bazyli Montetor had remained silent throughout, leaving his questions until the end. The happenings in the afterlife intrigued him most, of course, especially the description of the Darkness and their suspicion that the Abbot of Sanctity was involved in its terror. It didn't take much to convince Bazyli of the monk's complicity, he'd believe anything bad of the mad monk.

The account had gone on into the early hours and Bazyli eventually departed the ship just before dawn intending to return before noon. He was not expecting to get much rest, he had a Quota to gather and thoughts of the Darkness would keep him awake—as would the hope that this time he'd bring his sister home.

Leash, chained to the stump of the mainmast all night, was seething at being deceived by the treacherous Montetors and impatient with himself for not considering the possibility. Leash eased the manacles on his wrists. He had plenty of experience with chains, suffering at the hands of a town's mayor in Mantovar, three years previously. The chains had not held him then and they would not hold him now. When he'd escaped that town, the mayor's head was on a gatepost for all to see.

Giving nothing away he returned Locklear's menacing stare, remaining silent when questioned. Ignoring Locklear he mulled over what he had overheard as the Montetors brought him down from the mountains. The monks were an enigma feeding his curiosity and he'd decided to go along with what they had planned, for the moment. He'd reassess the situation once they landed on Sanctity for the monks' ruthlessness appealed to him.

He was convinced now that the wizard had no recollection of the man he held prisoner, and that being the case, he was relatively safe. The only one who irked him was Dolly. The cook, not realizing how close he was to being killed, had spent most of the night leaning against the rails sharpening his knives and seeing how close to Leash's legs he could stick the blades without actually cutting him. Leash closed his eyes and took refuge in his safe dream.

Locklear returned to his cabin where Tragen was supping coffee. 'I can't get anything out of the man,' he said, taking up the cup poured for him. 'The man is inscrutable. I have absolutely no idea why he wanted Aidan dead.'

Tragen looked up and stared hard at his friend. 'Hugo, please sit down, I must voice a suspicion and I don't want you going off and killing the man, just yet.'

'Oh…and what would that be?'

'I think he murdered your nephew! He dropped that crate on the wrong lad. Anders' death was a mistake, but of course that doesn't excuse the man, it was still murder and for that alone he should remain in the Quota.'

Locklear stared at the mug in his hands, he should have realized. He raged at Anders' death thinking of several things he'd like to do to Leash, chief among them to hang, draw and quarter him. He didn't doubt Tragen's conclusion; it was the only scenario that made any sense of his nephew's death. Any fool would understand that allowing men to walk beneath a load crumbling on a hoist was extremely hazardous. Oh, yes, Leash wanted someone dead all right…the young wizard. It was no comfort knowing Anders was a mishap. Maybe he'd know the reason in time, if he didn't break first and kill him.

'The Grim is ready for sea, Tragen. Do you wish to tell the monk?'

'We'll wait for the Montetor and go up together. When do you intend moving the Grim out of dry-dock?'

'On this evening's high tide. Have you attempted mindmelding with Aidan this morning?'

'Yes,' and he shook his head, not needing to mention aloud his failure, and his worry.

Later that evening the huge ship eased out of the enclosed dock into the harbour, this time without the aid of Tragen's staff. Not that it was needed, high tide was enough to float the ship off the cradle and a veritable flotilla of small boats, all manned by Janne's militia, dragged her into open water. She tied up at the wharf, aft of the monks' ship in the early hours of the next morning.

Instead of delaying their departure and arousing the suspicions of the monk, Marcus Janne was entrusted with the task of rescuing the fugitives. To this end, the marshal mustered a large patrol to take up residence at the mouth of the catacombs and these men left immediately. Janne fully intended taking a search party down into the Devil's Keep.

Frantic with worry, Lady Cornelia needed no persuasion to remain on Griffin. She loved Augusta and Beatrix dearly, and Aidan had utterly captivated her. As for Thaddeus, every time she looked at him, he brought a lump to her throat. So much harm had been done the boy and yet there was not a malicious bone in his entire body. She was to spend the period until the Grim's return at the Portolan's hunting lodge with Alessa.

The middle of the morning arrived, warm and sultry, steam rising off the wharf from the early morning's rainstorm. With it came the coach bearing the Abbot of Sanctity.

Brother Dyfrig was apprehensive; he had not yet administered a drink that had been poisoned with his pendant. But he doubted he need carry out the task, maybe the nearer they approached the monastery the easier it would be for his master to influence the wizard directly. He boarded his ship and immediately gave orders to set sail. Glancing over at the occupants of the Grim standing on their quarterdeck watching him, he smiled, everything was going to plan.

He didn't even bother to check the Quota in the slave hold, the number would be correct. It would never dare be otherwise.

The Grim's crew were not happy; following in the wake of the monk's barque was not good for self-esteem, or their fear. The huge warship limping along behind the smaller sailing boat seemed to diminish the Grim's reputation and the crew felt slighted. Having spent the last few days berthed within sight of the oppressive barque and its menacingly silent crew, the Grim's seamen would have been delighted if she had sailed off on her own. But no, the Prince of Mantovar's flagship had to accompany the monks on an errand of mercy that no-one was under any illusion would be completed without violence.

When Locklear had informed the crew of the reason for Leash's imprisonment and punishment, there were men fully prepared to hang him from the yardarm there and then. But he had warned his men that the killing of Anders and the attempted slaying of Aidan would be dealt with in the proper manner. Leash would be transported to Sanctity for execution.

Hopper walked the quarterdeck, keeping a weather-eye on both the ship and his abnormally silent crew...and on the barque ahead. Talbot, at his usual post at the wheel, was training Bertram to replace Leash. Dolly, turning his nose up when someone suggested mackerel for dinner, prepared a very large pan of lamb and vegetable pottage, taking full advantage of the fresh food supplies obtained on Griffin.

And while Jason strummed his lute in the well-deck, attempting to lighten the unpleasant, dangerous mood of the men, the ironmaster and the seneschal kept themselves to themselves in their separate cabins in the passengers' quarters.

On the quarterdeck Tragen and Locklear, though, kept each other company, both men unable to look away from the barque gaining distance ahead, both worrying on what the future held.

Locklear contemplated his duty to his liege lord. His responsibility was plain—to protect his princess in her endeavours to battle the Darkness and if this placed the Grim in peril, so be it. But firstly, he and his crew had to rescue the hostages. Secondly, there was the problem of the masts, the Grim needed both the main and mizzen desperately to sail the oceans safely. If the outcome on Sanctity was in their favour and masts obtained then they could be home in a matter of weeks, but if not... Thirdly he had to return to Griffin and search for Augusta himself if Janne failed. Hopefully the prince had received

385

Tragen's message by this time and would have despatched ships to seek them out. Locklear grimaced, wondering what his liege lord would make of such an unusual messenger.

Tragen was brooding; he was desperately worried for Aidan. Again, he had failed to contact the boy and he could think of only two possibilities as to the cause. The first, and he hoped most likely, was that they were very deep underground and the rocks above them prove to be the obstruction. But this reason also gave cause for concern—if they were that deep, could they be lost? The Devil's Keep was the source of some hair-raising stories, most of which were patently old-wives tales. But the others, stories of demons and goblins, did they hold any truth? Tragen, unable to remain still, fretted as he walked back and forth across the quarterdeck using his staff as a walking stick, using it more out of habit than necessity; he didn't intend employing the staff's powers until Aidan was safe beside him.

Tragen grew more and more anxious. Chewing his bottom lip he thought of the others with Aidan. Three very inexperienced, very powerful wizards spelled danger to themselves and to those around them. They'd need to learn quickly before ignorance of their limitations led them into disaster. Tragen held no hope of Janne and his men rescuing them. The security commander was very able in his job but he had never yet encountered demons. How would he react when confronted by unnatural creatures? How would his men react?

The second possible cause of the wizard's inability to communicate with Aidan did not bear thinking about.

Surely, he thought, he'd know if his boy was dead?

Tragen speculated on their reception when they reached Sanctity. Without a doubt, the abbot would expect an armed response by the Grim if the hostages were not released. Could the monks fight, and if so, how many were they? There were four hundred men or more on the ship...were they enough? Could disaster be averted and the Grim return to Griffin with the hostages in time to rescue the youngsters? The old wizard shook his head, only time could answer.

Sitting in a chair in his cabin below decks, Lodovico Portolan also contemplated failure—and intolerable loss. He missed his son with an unbearable ache in his chest. To awaken the boy after fifteen years and then to lose him in a week or so was so desperately unfair. Fifteen years of constant and loving care bestowed on what he had thought – if he was truthful with himself – was a hopeless case. And then to be finally rewarded with his most earnest wish, was heartrending. He could not lose Thaddeus now…the Gods were not that cruel were they?

But now they were off to rescue the other members of his family from a merciless jailer. Could they gain the release of the two hostages imprisoned for twenty years? It was a truly desperate endeavour; the mad monk was not going to give them up easily. They were going to have to fight, wage a battle against the Gods knew how many. And if the conflict went on too long or Dyfrig realize he was losing the battle, would he kill Paul and Ariana just for spite?

And then something else occurred to him. There was an unpleasant accounting due—something that made him feel guilty and ashamed.

He stood from his chair and peered through the porthole at the low swell of the ocean. It had to be faced, of course, and it was the unlikely object of his romantic fervour, who gave him the courage to look inwardly and examine his true feelings.

Lady Cornelia had come into his life, out of the blue, her charisma totally captivating him. Her large form and her shining sincerity, her even larger charm and honesty had entranced him. What a last couple of weeks he had had, he thought. He had found his beloved son and, inexplicably, had discovered another woman to love and hopefully fill the void in his life that Bettina, his childhood sweetheart, had left. And what of the supernatural message Thaddeus had passed on from his mother? It was time to let go! And she liked Cornelia, so wasn't that tantamount to approval of a lasting relationship between them? He wondered if Cornelia wished to share her life with him. They seemed to have a lot in common, they laughed easily together, had the same outlook on life, the same sense of duty— and she was very fond of Thaddeus. He smiled at the thought of a marriage with her, he knew he'd be happy—and his heart flipped, he thought she might be as well.

This mission to Sanctity had to succeed; he needed to return and find Thaddeus as quickly as possible. Then, if he had the courage, he would ask the lady for her hand. And making that decision helped him to address the shameful fact that he'd always kept hidden from everyone, a despicable secret that he had to face before meeting his brother.

Lodovico liked ruling Griffin and had, until this moment, not wanted to give it up. But he also knew now that his life was to take a different path, he could relinquish the position and return it to its rightful governor.

And another thought came to mind, could he and Bazyli have reached an agreement before this? Need this imprisonment have lasted twenty long years?

Bazyli was also staring out of his porthole, scant feet from the seneschal, and had much the same thoughts. Could he and Portolan have demanded his sister's release earlier? Thinking on it, he concluded that circumstances had never been quite right before. This Grim had been the bargaining power, the turning point. The abbot needed the ship for some nefarious purpose. Was it to transport his vileness to Mantovar? If so, there were many, far more powerful men in that country to oppose the zealots. But that would not be his problem—he just wanted his sister home, he'd been lonely for far too long. And now that their father had died and he had become the clan leader, he needed her guidance and support even more.

But now he also had the horrendous task of normalizing relations between his people and the Portolans. Conciliation had to be found to ensure a lasting peace on Griffin. His thoughts were bleak, had he been in error to nurture the conflict with the Portolans? Blaming Lodovico for an act that was totally out of his control surely was wrong?

'Can't you shift this stuff, Tragen?' Bazyli asked.

'My staff could but I will not employ its powers, I will not risk Aidan's safety,' and the wizard stared emphatically at the sea of weed surrounding and trapping both ships.

The first day out and the unnamed barque had led them straight into a vast morass of seaweed. This morning, from nowhere, a vast area of brown sargassum had appeared and captured them. Its bulbous floats and saw-edged leaves stretching for leagues in every direction on the surface of the ocean, obliterating all signs of the blue water...the smell was abominable.

'This is what Anders must have seen,' said Locklear.

'I have never known the weed this far from shore before or act as this does. Has anyone knowledge of this?' Lodovico asked, peering down over the rail at the thick fibrous mass holding the Grim tight in its embrace.

The mate turned from making his own inspection and grimaced. 'I've never seen it but I've heard of it. There are stories of it marooning ships for weeks. It is native to the ocean many months sailing to the south of here; I've never heard of it this far north. It's called "bald man's hair" for the simple reason that men pull their hair from their head, frustrated, waiting for it to release them.'

'It is a natural phenomenon?' Bazyli asked.

'Aye, it is. Mind you there are folk tales of it being a tool of the Gods! Anders was right; it floats a little beneath the waves and waits for a likely victim before it rises to the surface. And the Grim being the biggest ship in the world would definitely be a prize worth catching.' Hopper sighed, 'there's nothing can be done. Patience is needed now, gentlemen. When the time comes, it will disappear and release us.'

'Aye, but patience is hard to come by these days,' said Locklear combing his beard with his fingers. 'Nevertheless, it is drifting slowly towards Sanctity; we'll reach our destination eventually.'

'What on earth is the monk doing?' Tragen asked, staring ahead at the barque stranded less than a league from them. The night before the barque had been several leagues ahead but it almost seemed now that the weed had delayed the monk on purpose until the Grim caught up. But the abbot was not prepared to linger. The monks had lowered a boat over the starboard side and men were now scrambling down nets onto the brown morass.

Locklear laughed. 'I do believe the fools are going to try and cut themselves free.'

The Grim's crew watched the activity for most of the morning as more boats were lowered to join the first. But as fast as each stem was cut, another thicker fibre appeared in its place. Frustrated, the abbot ceased at lunchtime.

And over the next few days, men did consider tearing out their hair, but as Nkosi was heard to say…who could possibly want to end up looking like the mad monk.

For the first time since going to sleep in the hunting lodge, Aidan and the others felt safe ensconced in a brightly lit chamber off the main cavern. Leonid had been as good as his word and supplied them with fresh drinking water, an assortment of cold vegetables and meats and to follow their main meal, a sumptuous assortment of fresh fruits including bananas, a fruit that neither Aidan nor Thaddeus had ever tasted before.

'Bloody hell, that's horrible,' Aidan said biting the banana.

389

'No, you silly boy, you're supposed to remove the skin first,' Augusta said laughing fit to burst.

'Oi! Who are you calling silly? Why didn't you tell me, if you're so clever?'

'There's no need to swear,' added Beatrix, 'it doesn't give Leonid a very favourable impression of us.'

Aidan snorted his disgust but took the advice. They needn't have worried, the green man respected their privacy while they ate and wandered off somewhere with Clarinda.

Beatrix sated with the best meal she'd felt she'd eaten for months relaxed now that she had no need to conjure a light and she stared at Thaddeus reclining on a cot.

'You know who he is, don't you?'

'Well, I know of them—the Green People! I never dreamt I'd meet any, though.' He smiled contentedly. 'My mother used to tell me stories to pass the time away. A lot of the tales were of the Green Man. Are you sure you've never heard of him?' he asked, not quite believing their denials. 'The Green Man is the guardian of mother earth and all that grow in it.' He continued impatiently when the only answer he got was blank looks. 'Mother Nature and all she nurtures! No plant grows and reaches maturity without being protected by the magic of the Green Man. They kill nothing that doesn't deserve to die and they'd never dream of hurting a soul!'

'We are safe? Then what did he mean by saying he would decide our fate later?' Aidan asked perplexed.

'I'm not sure what he means, all I know is, we'll come to no harm here.'

'No, just lose our freedom like all those other people that disappeared down here. Is that what he calls helping us? "Guardians of nature", well it sounds all very well and good, but this Green Man seems too sure of himself for my liking.' Aidan paced impatiently.

'Why were you so ecstatic when we first saw that monster, it scared me silly?' Augusta asked.

'My mother told me about the krynx. It's nothing but a giant, harmless earthworm with teeth.'

'Those teeth are massive or haven't you noticed,' said Aidan.

'The krynx is very docile, young strangers,' interrupted Leonid returning to the chamber, 'and we'd have been unable to survive in the caverns without them. The krynx is a large eater of rocks which it digests in its huge stomach at the same time adding several nutrients…it then defecates the rock as very rich loam. And that soil enables us to grow all sorts of food which is how we live down here.'

The Green Man sat on a vacant cot, his back against a wall, chewing a stalk of celery. He seemed perfectly normal, except for the pigmentation of his skin and his large eyes. Normal, that is, unless you were a female and took notice of his "smouldering" good looks, as Augusta thought of them.

'Why do you live down here, why not on the surface? Surely it would be easier to care for the earth and its fruits in sunshine,' asked Thaddeus.

'That is another long story that is not my task to divulge. Now that you have eaten, please take your rest, you are weary. There are enough cots here for many more than four, as you can see. Choose whichever and as you repose you can relate your long story so that I may make certain decisions regarding our future together.

'We must return to my father, Leonid, he will be desperately worried,' said Thaddeus.

'All in good time, if that is what is deemed necessary then we will comply. But first you have to convince me, and I in turn, persuade others. We have lived here for centuries, forgotten and undisturbed because of certain precautions we have implemented. It will take mighty arguments to place our concealment in danger.' Leonid settled himself more comfortably. 'I am waiting…start with who you are and whence you came.'

Thirty-one

'How far is this town, Leonid, we've been walking for hours?' Aidan asked he was footsore and getting hungry again. It was strange striding these tunnels. Although there was no visible means of initiating illumination, as they approached and then walked past, the quartz in the rocks glowed and emitted a light as bright as daylight, and after they had passed, the light dimmed until eventually it disappeared.

'Not far, now, young wizard,' and the Green Man smiled. 'Patience is a requirement to live here. Speed is never important, care and accuracy is.'

'Well that's Aidan out of it, for a start,' said Augusta, laughing. 'He's never had patience, mistakes are his forte, and he's never moved fast in his life, except when he's in trouble with Tragen!'

'Oi!' rejoined Aidan.

'Don't you two start quarrelling again, especially as we are guests,' ordered Beatrix, nudging Aidan painfully in his ribs.

'Oh!' Augusta halted so quickly Aidan bumped into her. They stood amazed at the sight before them, completely spellbound they walked out of a tunnel into another of the interminable caverns.

'Welcome to the outskirts of Bylani, my friends. You must continue to stay close to me, do not wander...until your story is told you will be regarded as trespassers. Trespassers usually cause damage.' Leonid said seriously.

They were all following behind Leonid with Clarinda leading, the worm's long body undulating along the floor. Her tremendously thick skin protecting her from any injury and, at the same time, abrading the surface of the floor until it was worn smooth. Relating their story the previous night they had felt it best to omit a large part of their history, only telling of the storm and their fear of Sanctity, its abbot and the Quota. Afterwards they had slept the peace of the innocent, knowing they were secure.

Leonid, on the other hand, did not sleep at all well it was obvious the wizards were concealing something. And people who hid things made him suspicious. He would have preferred to take them before the Elders with all knowledge revealed.

Nonetheless, the Elders needed to be informed immediately, these were not ordinary interlopers, treasure seekers from the upper world. Elder Zoran would want to question these four and he would not look kindly on delay. But Leonid was afraid. These were not normal wizards—not one was a wizard of nature as he was.

Were they the ones mentioned in the prophecy?

The cavern they entered was immense, the roof so high it could not be seen and a light as bright as sunshine on a summer's day shone down on the scene below. The walls across the cavern were not visible, not just because of the vastness of the place but also because of what lay before them. The walls were hidden by a veritable forest of teak and oak, pine and birch and pathways threading randomly between vast orchards...apple, pear, orange, cherry, too many to mention.

The fugitives stood at the top of a long slope of green turf, luxuriant in texture and vivid in colour, reminding Aidan a little of what the grass was like in Anders' Limbo. Their track led down into the woodland and wended on through the trees as far as the eye could see, other trails leading off from it at intervals along its length. In amongst the trees and along the many borders, Leonid's people toiled at a myriad of tasks, all with the express purpose of growing and harvesting trees. The wizards found it impossible to take it all in at once. They studied the houses built in clearings for the woodsmen and their families, each domicile having a small kitchen garden, pinewood smoke wafting through the air from cooking fires on hearths. And then Beatrix noticed other houses, empty yet fully maintained. There were a lot of them dispersed at intervals along the paths and in clearings within the forest.

They followed the main path through the woods, Thaddeus bringing up the rear grinning from ear to ear totally enraptured at the sight of so much Life. Their eyes never motionless the young wizards nearly forgot that they were still very, very deep beneath the surface of the island.

But Leonid's people returned the looks of the strangers as they walked by, some smiling sadly knowing these youngsters would never see their families again.

They walked through the woods and entered another series of tunnels. Each tunnel led them into another cavern, another world, another aspect of Life as amazing as the first. Aidan, though, was puzzled, the paths seemed to go on forever yet they walked them in a very short time.

One cavern held a fishing village alongside a river, this waterway Leonid explained was the source of the river that watered

Griffin Town. He did not explain how the watercourse flowed upwards to the surface. There were farms in others, green men, women and children hard at work in fields, home to cattle, sheep and a variety of other livestock. Unfortunately, it was also raining in this cavern, but the precipitation was warm and their clothes did not take long to dry. Leonid explained that the weather changed at regular intervals throughout the day, daytime and night-time regulated as if they all lived on the surface. Once again, he did not offer an explanation...or make mention of the many empty houses.

And then they entered the home cavern. Standing at the crest of another long slope, they examined the layout of the town of Bylani, the hub of the Green People's world and its administration centre.

Roughly circular rows of neat cottages and shops surrounded a large central building, the square before it holding a magnificent fountain, its form not evident at this distance. Dotted throughout the town were small parklands...and yet more empty houses.

Leonid halted and spoke to his companions. 'I must leave you with my wife,' and he indicated a large detached house in a well cultivated garden to the right of the road and on the edge of the town, 'while I see the Elders,' he added troubled.

'Why so worried, Leonid?' Thaddeus asked. 'No-one should ever be anxious here...Bylani is magical!'

'No visitor has ever been introduced to the council until they have become fully integrated. You will be the first; all others who have passed by the salamanders are absorbed into our lives first.'

'Salamanders? You have salamanders here?' Aidan asked excited. 'Where are they, I haven't seen any?'

'What are salamanders?' Thaddeus asked.

'Creatures of fire and light,' said Leonid. 'It is they who glow at all the openings in the mountain at night. It is they, who frighten away inquisitive people.'

'And keep you free of any disease,' added Aidan, his eyes glowing.

'You know of that?' asked Leonid. 'You have strange knowledge, my young friends,' and he led them to his home.

'Leonid? Why are there so many empty houses...there must be hundreds scattered everywhere?' Augusta asked.

'Perhaps the Elders will enlighten you, I dare not.'

Beatrix, trailing behind thought on the enforced exile of those people who had wandered into Bylani. Hadn't they lost something far more valuable than the treasure they sought—their freedom?

Leonid returned from the council hall looking weary and anxious. Kissing his wife, Jasmina, he joined his guests and his three young children at the dinner table.

Jasmina, tall and pretty, her long titian hair piled on top of her head in an untidy bun which kept falling out over her eyes as she worked, smiled easily and, at Leonid's greeting, sent spasms of jealousy racing through Augusta and Beatrix.

In his absence, Jasmina had directed them to the bathhouse in the yard and the four young wizards gratefully spent time scrubbing the catacombs off their bodies and dressing in clean shirts and britches.

Leonid smiled proudly at the non-stop chatter from his children. His elder son, Dom, was attempting to hold a conversation with Thaddeus over Prile's noisy questioning of Aidan. His daughter, Bella, the apple of his eye, sitting between Augusta and Beatrix stared from one to the other enthralled.

'Prile, cease your noise, let our guests eat,' he ruffled his son's dark hair as he joined them at the kitchen table. 'You need your haircut; you're beginning to look like your sister.' He looked round at the four young wizards. 'Please, continue with your dinner, my wife is an excellent cook and will be offended if you leave with food remaining on the table. When you have finished and rested awhile I will take you to meet the Elders.'

Convincing the leaders of his people that these youths were wizards had not been hard when Leonid divulged that Thaddeus had immediately recognized a krynx, for no human should know of the animal created by nature's magicians.

The Elders – desperate to meet the intruders – speculated on why there were only four, there had to be five. And if these were truly four of the five, where was the fifth and was the time now at hand? If this was the moment mentioned in the prophecy was the haven ready and were the people fully prepared? Zoran fleetingly considered the decision taken so many centuries before, to act in accordance with the directives propounded by his predecessor on his death bed. But it was a bit late to worry whether their judgment had been correct—they'd lived underground a millennium because of it.

'Please remember,' Leonid said, 'utmost respect must be shown the council if you wish to gain your freedom. Disrespect will only lead to your enforced exile and please understand, you must disclose all you know. The Elders will need to make far reaching decisions on what you divulge.'

Aidan stared at his host. It was obvious that the Green People had enormous magic, needed to control the nature of the land, how could they not realize the power of wizards of the mind? It would be easy to escape. But then it occurred to him that these people might have a similar ability to those tribesmen of the Drikander in southern Drakka—the skill to change the direction of paths and tunnels. If they did, it would be almost impossible to find their way to the surface. Is that why their journey into Bylani had seemed a long way to walk and yet didn't take very long?

Having no answers Aidan put it out of his mind hoping to learn something of it in the near future. He attempted to mindmeld with Tragen to seek his advice, and again failed…all day he had been unsuccessful, he was getting anxious.

Aidan, Augusta, Thaddeus and Beatrix followed Leonid along one of the arterial roads leading to the heart of the subterranean town. It was dusk on the surface and the light here in this vast cavern dimmed, keeping time with that above. People were at home relaxing, eating their evening meal, playing with, and in some cases, shouting at their children. But all stopped whatever they were doing to watch from their gardens or through their windows as the strangers passed along the main street.

Beatrix studied the town, Bylani seemed normal if you could ignore the fact that they were deep underground and that everywhere she looked was clean and tidy, abnormal in any town on the surface. And there were no unpleasant smells the drains very deep beneath her feet. There were shops, usually boarded up in Griffin Town at this time of night to deter thieves and vandals, but here were left unsecured. Yet she was intrigued, it seemed that for every house occupied there were five or six that were not.

They entered the central square and paused to examine the large fountain very similar – although vastly larger – to that in the garden of the Portolan's manor. This also depicted a family of Green People, but these were playing beneath a very strange-looking tree. A profusion of colours appeared and then disappeared running up and down its trunk and along the length of each of its branches. The diverse hues and shades formed lines and irregular patches which pulsed and gelled haphazardly to create new lines and shapes, the whole never constant. Its branches grew horizontally in a series of circles up the trunk, long branches at the bottom gradually reducing in size to very small ones at the top. Fresh drinking water cascaded from its tip.

'Come, my friends, we cannot keep the Elders waiting,' Leonid said anxiously when Beatrix hung back; she was strangely drawn to the tree.

The Council Hall was immense. Built of green speckled marble, it was one of the few buildings with its walls made entirely of stone; the walls of the houses were usually built of stone on the ground floor, the upper of timber. High double doors of black ebony opened off a veranda to reveal a vestibule, its walls lined with dark oak panels. The whole interior was illuminated by baskets of glowing quartz, some placed in niches along the walls, others suspended from the high ceiling. Leonid led Aidan, Thaddeus, Augusta and Beatrix across the polished mahogany parquet floor to another pair of double doors made of dark cherry inlaid with holly.

These opened into the central Moot Hall. The Hallmote was a long, wide and high ceilinged chamber, a raised dais at the far end of the room. On each side, and on several levels up the walls, were rows of benches empty now but capable of seating a couple of thousand, far more than the population of Bylani. On the dais and behind the long, polished teak table were five high straight-backed, brown leather chairs occupied by the leaders of the Green People.

Leonid had informed the visitors of the seating arrangement of the leaders as they walked from his home and impressed upon them that they were to remain silent until Zoran spoke. Elder Jerrod and Elder Thorin sat on Zoran's right and the women, Elders Varna and Gillray on his left. The youths reached the table and stood before it as Leonid bowed to the Elders and then moved away to stand on one side.

All was quiet as four young faces met five pairs of the strangest looking eyes they had ever seen. The five Elders had shrunk in size over the years. The skin of their faces – stretching tightly over sharp cheekbones and sagging at their necks – was almost translucent, giving them all a gaunt appearance and a similarity in looks that only came with great age. They gave the impression of having lived forever, their eyes very large almost protruding from beneath their foreheads. Beatrix frowned; the Elders were not ugly, just very strange.

Augusta was the first to fidget under the Elders' long and silent gaze. Being the only child of a ruling royal family she was unused to the disrespect of undergoing close scrutiny by a people who, to all intents and purposes, were her hosts, she their guest. She was not afraid of these people they did not instil fear in her, but she was wary and despite her rest she was irritable and still very tired. She had been walking for over two days and wanted to sit, her feet hurt, but good manners dictated that she should not until invited to. So she fidgeted.

She was followed closely by Thaddeus who was fascinated with everything in the large hall, from its carved wooden panelling to the hole in the corner of the room where he detected a mouse lurking. Smiling, he examined everyone and everything. He noticed the little things that would normally have been missed…from the neat darn in the elbow of Elder Zoran's black robe to the cobweb right up in the corner of the wall behind the head table. He searched for the spider and found it not far from Beattie's feet. He hoped she wouldn't notice.

Aidan, shuffling his feet at first because his legs were aching, stilled and examined Elder Zoran, his eyes seeming to stare through the old green man's face.

Elder Zoran looked down from the dais, examining each young wizard in turn, taking note that only one was not dancing around, she was standing quietly seeming at peace. From Leonid's description this one was Beatrix; Leonid had called her the quiet one, the one who had displayed the light. Zoran was intrigued, not many could withstand his assessment without showing any reaction. And the more he stared it seemed the quieter she became, the other girl, the princess, was more assured but appeared easily distracted. He studied Augusta intently for a moment as she grasped Aidan's hand.

Thaddeus, the taller of the two boys, was unfathomable at first, his gaze more distant and his eyes never still, he couldn't seem to stop smiling. Zoran studied him fixedly, and then he comprehended the reason the boy's eyes were different. They were innocent and full of wonder.

And then he examined Aidan. This boy moved him in some way he did not understand. Power poured from him, an immense, unusually potent magic. Never in his long life had he seen such raw magical energy totally uncorrupted. Zoran found it surprising in a boy of his age, power always corrupted to some extent. But there again, this boy's magic was not normal, did the boy know, he wondered? And then Aidan shocked him to the core—of course the boy knew.

398

'Elder Zoran,' Aidan said, breaking the silence. 'Have you no healers here?'

The other Elders at the table suddenly sat up straighter; shocked, they had remained silent waiting for their leader to open the interrogation. Leonid desperately put a finger to his lips to hush Aidan.

Thaddeus nudged him to silence him and Augusta grasped his hand tighter conveying her unease.

Beatrix stared at Zoran though, puzzled—what could Aidan see?

'Elder Zoran,' Aidan repeated quietly, his voice commanding everyone's attention. 'You are not well, sir, have you no healer competent to treat you?'

Zoran gazed at the young boy standing before him. Aidan with his shoulder length black hair brushed neatly for once at the insistence of Beatrix, his innocent face showing concern for a perfect stranger.

'We have salamanders but this is even beyond them. How do you know? How do you know I am ill, no-one else here has any idea?' Zoran sat rigidly in his seat, not a muscle moving. No-one except his personal healer knew of his headaches and loss of muscle use—his gradual decline into inevitable death.

Beatrix interposed. 'He is a healer, Elder. A very special healer,' she smiled radiantly and glanced at Aidan quickly before returning to Zoran. 'He can actually see your ailment, but there's no need for you to worry, he can help.'

'What!' Elder Thorin said, and he and the other Elders turned to Zoran. 'Is it true, Zoran? Are you ill?'

The senior Elder of the Green People knew now in his bones that no power of his or his people would ever be enough to overcome this young man and his friends. There was no way they'd be able to detain these four against their wishes and he became afraid. How were the Green People to ensure secrecy if these were not those of the prophecy? Bylani had to be maintained without interference if they were to fulfil their duty. Those in the upper world had probably forgotten their existence after all these years, and that was the way the Green People wanted it.

Zoran sighed. He had wanted to keep the fact of his illness secret until the last possible moment. He couldn't bear the thought of dying; he had so much left to do, so much more to give. He couldn't pass away without seeing the Green People's part in the prophecy completed. And there was his wife to consider.

'By the Gods, Zoran, is he the one?' Thorin asked, frightened out of his wits.

'The prophecy, Zoran…is he the first?' Jerrod asked, his hands trembling on the table in front of him.

'There should be five, Jerrod, five, please a moment if you will,' said Varna, the shock of her husband being ill bringing tears to her eyes. 'Why have you not told me, my dear?' She asked, clasping his hand tenderly to her face, her other hand stroking his sparse hair. She was terrified for Zoran, but also afraid of this youth. What else could he read in people?

If a Green Man could appear white, then Zoran was he. 'I'm sorry, my darling, I should have I know, but I kept hoping and denying it…and my death won't be for a while yet, my love,' he paused and smiled ruefully, knowing his words were lies. 'You'd think I'd have learned the lessons of false optimism long before now, wouldn't you?' His face ashen he turned to Aidan again.

'Who are you, young man?'

'Are you the first of the prophecy?' Gillray interrupted, she couldn't help herself panic was making her forget her place.

'Aidan, don't just stand there…say something,' Augusta said, her voice quivering, the wild reactions of the Elders seriously troubling her. She was again becoming frightened and this time thought she knew why—she didn't like talk of a prophecy especially one that so obviously scared her hosts.

'Aye, Aidan, hurry up, I don't want to spend the rest of my life down here,' said Thaddeus, again poking him in the side.

'Give him time, you two, can't you see he's in the Elder,' said Beatrix quieting her friends, unfortunately causing further consternation among the Elders.

'What do you mean, he's in the Elder?' Leonid asked, he'd never seen the council in such a state before, their hysteria almost tangible. He instinctively trusted Aidan but knew his leaders, for some reason, were very afraid. Had he done the right thing in bringing the wizards before them?

'Elder Zoran, you have a tumour that is choking your brain. If you wish, I can heal you of it.' He continued, staring at the astonished Elder. 'You have no need to fear me—only the tumour,' and he smiled his assurance.

Zoran, bemused and desperate, smiled nervously, and glancing at his wife he assented because he had no choice. But he still involuntarily shrank from Aidan's touch as the boy, walking around the table and coming up behind placed his hands over the back of the Green Man's head, covering the obscene growth buried deep within his brain stem. Zoran tensed and grasped his wife's hands tightly, staring at her as if it was his last moment, drinking her in he loved her so very much even after a thousand years.

'Relax, Elder, this is Aidan's special magic,' Beatrix chuckled, her eyes shining. 'I love watching him heal,' and it was her evidently good humoured sincerity, that calmed him.

Varna stared at her husband of centuries, willing Aidan's success with all of her might. She didn't want to live without Zoran and to that end had always planned to go with him when his time came. And that was the reason Zoran had not told her of his illness, he didn't want her to inflict harm upon herself. With tears in her eyes and bated breath, she held his hands to her face, her large eyes sinking into his.

Tears glistened in Gillray's eyes, watching her two friends still so obviously in love, each scared of losing the other. And then her heart beat faster when she saw relief growing in Zoran's face. The heat radiating from Aidan's hands brought tranquillity to the Elder and set the shrinking in progress of the vileness that was choking his nervous system. The Elder's head was coming alive for the first time in months, the deep ache perceptually disappearing, nerves unstitching, double vision clearing to leave him with normal sight.

Zoran stared at his wife, his look full of a seriousness that disturbed her. His life had been assured by the healing of this young wizard, he could feel it with every passing second, and that could only mean one thing.

'My dearest one, Elder Findar's time is nigh. I do believe this young man is the first of the prophecy.'

Aidan returned to stand alongside his friends. Augusta and Beatrix embraced him enthusiastically and Thaddeus moved towards him. 'Don't you dare hug me, Thaddeus,' said Aidan, closing his eyes as Thaddeus laughed and did just that…just to annoy him. 'Swine!'

'Aidan, stop swearing! We are guests. I'm sorry Elders, he just can't behave sometimes,' Beatrix, disgusted, lowered her eyes with shame.

'It matters not, young lady, after what he has done for my husband he can say whatever he wants,' said Varna, kissing Zoran.

'And don't you ever hide anything from me again, husband, or we will seriously quarrel,' she added, hugging him again impulsively.

'If he is the first what of these others, Zoran?' Gillray asked apprehensively, her befuddled brain realizing that this boy had just succeeded in creating a miracle before her very eyes.

Zoran ignored her for a moment, rubbing his head tentatively he recollected the heat emanating from the boy's hands, and he stared wonderingly at Aidan. 'I am truly healed?'

'Yes, Elder…well, at least the process has begun; the healing will still take time and you must not overexert yourself,' and then quickly changing the subject, 'now what's this bloody prophecy you're all talking about?'

'Aidan,' shouted Beatrix scandalized, 'don't swear!'

And as Zoran opened his mouth to thank him, Augusta interrupted. 'Please, don't thank him, Elder Zoran, or he'll go into a sulk…he doesn't like being thanked.'

'I don't sulk!'

'You do!'

'Shut it, you two,' ordered Beatrix, exasperated.

'You'll have to excuse them, Elder, they're always arguing,' said Thaddeus, staring around the Hall totally unconcerned, the mouse had left its hole and he was searching for it.

'Well, I hope it's a better prophecy than the last one I heard,' said Augusta.

'What was that?' Aidan asked, his eyes gleaming. 'I love prophecies, especially if they come true.'

'What, even the bad ones?' Thaddeus asked.

'I never listen to the bad ones!'

'How do you know if they're bad ones if you don't…oh, never mind,' said Beatrix, 'I give up!'

'It was years ago,' Augusta interrupted, giggling, 'do you remember, Beattie? You and I sneaked out of the castle and we met that seer in the carnival outside of town.'

'Oh, yes, she was beautiful, wasn't she? She had gorgeous long, black hair and the whitest…'

'All right, I don't think we need know what she looked like. What did she say?' Aidan asked impatiently. And despite the seriousness of the situation, even the Elders listened all agog.

'It was silly, really. We were supposed to help a son find his father and then...argh!' Augusta suddenly ceased her tale and stared at Beatrix, wide-eyed.

'Thaddeus!' The girls shouted together, astounded.

'What?' Thaddeus asked, perplexed, and then he realized what the girls meant. 'I suppose that's one prophecy that came true then.'

'But...I don't know, I'm not so sure now I think about it,' said Beatrix, 'Thaddeus always knew where his father was, didn't he? So he didn't need help to find him.'

'Yes, but his father didn't know where Thaddeus was, did he?' Augusta answered.

'Ladies, please, can we get on. I'm sorry Elders but they do prattle a lot,' said Aidan, disappointed, he'd hoped for a forecast with a little more life in it.

'We don't prattle!' Augusta retorted, getting her back up, 'I'm going to thump you in a minute, little wizard.'

'Shut it, you two,' ordered Beatrix.

'Aye, you're frightening the mouse,' said Thaddeus.

'Mouse, what mouse?' Beatrix suddenly screeched clutching her hands to her chest and shutting her eyes tight.

'Oh, it's gone now, you scared it, Beattie!' Thaddeus said, bending over and searching below the benches to one side of him.

Elder Zoran was utterly bemused. 'Before we proceed let us all relax, Leonid will you be so kind as to drag over a bench for our friends?'

'Speak of the prophecy, Zoran, perhaps these four can shed some understanding on that which has puzzled us all these years,' suggested Varna.

Zoran leaned against the back of his chair, massaging his eyes he sighed. 'The full story is long, my young friends. Leonid, you are not to mention this discussion outside these walls until given permission, only we here will know it all for now. Find yourself a seat,' and he added, 'Leonid, you did well in bringing these guests before us, your instincts were correct, as they have been many times in the past.'

Leonid, too wound up to smile his thanks for the unexpected compliment, sitting and hearing again the reason for the Green Man's exile below ground, was astonished anew now that he could fit a face to some of the tasks. The history of the Green People was long and involved, too much so to be related at this time and so Zoran felt it best to only give the bare bones of their tale—the part that concerned the four wizards.

'Nearly a thousand years ago, on his deathbed, my predecessor received a vision which he immediately passed on to me, at the same time ordering me to share it with the council on his demise.'

Aidan couldn't help it. 'A thousand years,' he was amazed, 'you are that old, Elder?'

Zoran nodded; he was too ancient now to take umbrage at being called old. 'Don't wizards live abnormally long lives?' He continued his narrative, all four young wizards amazed that anyone could be so advanced in years. And then they stared at each other as it sunk in that there was a possibility they may reach that age. But, of course, at fifteen years old every one over thirty was ancient, and at their young age death should never raise its ugly head. But there was Anders and their time in the afterlife—and the Darkness!

'The prophecy was spoken by a spirit not of this world. The spectre was a dazzlingly white figure, we believe a woman but we are not sure. She was very hurtful to the eyes.'

'Not her, again,' interrupted Aidan.

'Wha-at?' Zoran asked, taken aback at Aidan's vehemence.

'I'm sorry, Elder, but that woman seems to be haunting us, we'll tell you later. Please go on.'

'Elder Findar implored me to carry out to the letter every instruction in the prophecy. We were to wait for those mentioned, and then give all support necessary for those people to achieve success. For if they did not succeed…' and he paused, to emphasize his next words, 'if they did not succeed, then all life would be extinguished on earth.'

'Oh God! She's very melodramatic isn't she?' Augusta broke in, her tone one of disgust.

Zoran rose from his chair and coming around the table he sat on the bench alongside Leonid, baffled at their reaction.

'We have prepared a place of safety with the help of the krynxes, as asked for. That was the task set us, the reason we came below ground. We of the council felt it best that we keep the prophecy secret from all other races. And so we consulted with our own and made the decision to create the haven below this island. We travelled from afar, from the place you now call Mantovar and Drakka, and from all other corners of the world. We gathered together with friends already settled on this island and set up our new home here in this world of caverns.'

Zoran continued to speak as he met each person's eyes. 'We have waited…for almost a thousand years we have toiled. And in all that time, we have studied that in the prophecy we do not understand. All we are certain of is that when the ones spoken of appear, it will be at a time most perilous for us all. And,' he looked around at his colleagues, 'meeting you we believe the hour is here at last,' he paused. 'Elder Thorin be so kind as to speak the prophecy.'

Thorin cleared his throat, the panic he felt rising he thrust deep:

'The shadow's bane is nigh when young sorcerers defy
the design of the Dark One, to search all under the sun.

A haven must be found for all those who are bound
to flee the vile shadow, and ensure life will follow.

One sorcerer to heal the bane, a second to reassure its pain,
a third to show it the light, a fourth to aid its flight.

And one all-seeing, to guide, but not in this world does he bide.
When five strive together succeed the Dark One will never.'

'When thunder rolls and that which cannot toll, tolls in the
hands of Edele's enchanted, salvation will be established.

'That my friends, is the puzzle we have lived with all these years. Can you enlighten us? You are four; a fifth wizard is needed before you seek the bane. Who is Edele's enchanted? What is the shadow? Who is the Dark One and what does he search for? The haven is here, all around you, that is why there are so many unoccupied homes in Bylani, we have them ready. We will welcome any who seek shelter and wish to fight. But what do we fight?' Zoran stared at his guests as he finished speaking and his heart skipped a beat. There didn't seem to be as much confusion as he expected.

Instead there was abject fear.

He never took his eyes from the four wizards as he asked the most perplexing question of all—the answer to which had eluded them for a millennium.

'And what is the bane?'

Thirty-two

Janne escorted the ladies to the hunting lodge; he on his huge black destrier with the white blazon and the ladies in the seneschal's closed carriage drawn by the same four black horses, this time without red ribbons in their manes.

As the barque passed out of the harbour and before the Grim had slipped its berth, Janne and the coach were chasing after his men. Teams of fresh horses hobbled at the roadside by the earlier force, enabled the journey to be completed by the following morning. Janne, and the ladies both battered and bruised from the jouncing of the coach, arrived exhausted at the lodge and hastily partook of breakfast.

The patrol's captain, Jenson, made his report at the kitchen table informing Janne that all the men had volunteered to enter the catacombs. Janne grunted his thanks, he had expected nothing less.

'I will need no more than five fully armed to accompany me, Jenson. Ensure enough food for a week and as many faggots as each of us can carry…and chalk. We'll have to mark every turning we make to know our way back,' and over his subordinate's protestations he added. 'I'm sorry, Jenson, you will be needed here to care for the ladies and report to the seneschal if we don't return.' Janne looked at his companions, his glance lingering on Alessa Barbat. 'If we have not returned within the week, I do not expect to return at all.'

Alessa sucked in her breath sharply. 'You will return safely with Thaddeus and his friends. I feel it, just…' and she blinked tears away, 'take care, my love.'

That afternoon, after Janne had slept for a couple of hours, the security commander and his five militiamen entered the rift in the cliff face. Lamder, striper of the patrol, led the way followed immediately by Janne. "Fox" Lamder had earned his nickname by being an expert tracker, and it was his job to seek out any trail. He held his faggot out to the side, its light illuminating the easy trail left in the dust by the fugitives, and they turned the first corner. Conserving the faggots would be a priority and Janne made a mental decision to not only mark the junctions in the tunnel with chalk, but to also leave a small pile of stones to be felt for with fingers, if their supply of torches proved insufficient.

The four young wizards stared at each other, various degrees of fright and dismay on each face. Each had identified with a part of Findar's prophecy and didn't like what they'd heard.

'It is the bloody Gods playing with us!' Aidan said and such was the despair felt by them all that Beatrix never mentioned his cursing.

'I said she was melodramatic, didn't I,' Augusta said and cursed again, 'the bitch!'

'But why us, eh! Why us, Aidan? We've done nothing to deserve this!' Beatrix asked him, her voice unable to hide the terror she felt. 'Is this why you've passed your gifts on to us—because we are all players in some plan of the Gods?'

'But...but, if that's the case then it's my fault you're all involved!' Aidan said devastated at the thought.

'Oh, Aidan! Don't be silly, it's not your fault...the Gods are messing you about the same as us,' said Augusta, putting her arm about his waist and drawing him close.

'Dear God, but that also implies the trauma of my birth, my life with my mother in the Darkness, may well have been planned!' And at the horror of that undeniable conclusion Thaddeus suddenly spun away from them and made for the nearest wall, leaning his forehead against it to hide his tears.

Beatrix strode quickly over to him and putting her arm around him laid her head on his shoulder. Aidan and Augusta joined them both and all four clasped each other, seeking comfort in their friendship.

The Council of Elders watched them, not understanding a word of what they'd heard but understanding that the wizards' great despair had been caused by hearing the prophecy. They waited in silence until Aidan broke from his friends and returned to the bench, the others followed in unspoken agreement.

Thaddeus shuddered and through bleary eyes he caught Zoran's eye and broke the silence. 'The "shadow" we know of, we call it the Darkness. It is a weapon of dense fog, a black mist in which demons hide. In the confines of the fog, the demons search out the living. And all manner of torments are exacted on those helpless souls they ensnare.'

Thaddeus glanced at the other Elders through glistening eyes and continued. 'The Dark One is the God that wields the Darkness, and it is his minions that wander the mists herding the trapped souls into Purgatory. Those living that escape the fog will never be the same again—the horrors of the Darkness will be with them forever.' He paused and stared at the wall behind the Elders' heads, thinking of the dread terrors he had lived with for so long and the unspeakable inference he'd reached. Could he be wrong in his assumption? As he brought his gaze to bear on Elder Zoran again he knew without a doubt that he was right. 'A haven is crucial to all those who flee the Darkness.'

'By the Gods,' Varna said, 'Purgatory we know of, eternal damnation has the same name in all languages.'

'How do you know of this?' Jerrod asked his voice just above a whisper.

'Aidan and I have been there…in the Darkness so close to Purgatory that we encountered the God's herdsmen! We have experienced the horror of it and don't wish to know it again,' he looked across at the two girls, and attempted a smile. 'It's only because of Augusta, Beatrix, and Anders that we escaped.' Thaddeus stared into space, remembering the living nightmare he and his mother had suffered for years. It was unbelievable that the Gods could really have planned for them to suffer so.

'I don't understand, surely to be as near Purgatory as you say, then you must have died, and yet here you are?' Gillray asked.

'We are wizards. Tragen, my mentor, says that we are very unusual sorcerers. We are able to travel in the afterlife,' said Aidan.

'Dear God, I've never heard of wizards being able to die and then return to life!' Thorin said, stunned.

'We did not die, Elder, we travelled into Death and then returned to Life, there is a difference,' said Augusta dejected.

'Who is Anders?' Varna asked.

'A friend, who has passed over but has remained to help us,' answered Beatrix.

Zoran was astonished; in amongst all this talk of the Darkness and the Dark One, these youngsters could still grieve a friend, but what a curious form of words she used to express it. 'And Edele's enchanted?' Zoran asked.

'I don't know,' Beatrix asked.

'My mother's name was Edie, isn't that short for Edele?' Aidan asked. And for some unknown reason, the absurdity of what this implied seemed to suddenly lift their spirits.

'You're hardly an enchantment, Aidan,' Augusta chuckled.

'By the Gods, you're right there, Augusta,' and Thaddeus burst out laughing.

'I don't know, he can be very charming on times,' and Beatrix blushed when Aidan glanced at her, surprised.

'The bane, then, do you know what that is,' asked Zoran, these four puzzled him enormously. Were the Gods directing these four lives, if so, which Gods?

'I have no idea...a weapon to fight the Darkness?' Aidan shrugged his shoulders.

'The bane...it sounds as if it's something that lives,' said Thaddeus.

'Yes, we all agree on that,' said Varna, marvelling at the resilience of the young, from the depths of despair they had raised their manner to light-hearted jocularity, all because of a comment about a nickname.

'And unwell at present, otherwise you wouldn't need to heal it,' said Beatrix.

Zoran interrupted. 'From what you have all said, Aidan is the first...the healer, you Beatrix, are obviously the third...to show it the light. That's two...presumably the third and fourth are Thaddeus and Augusta, though we don't yet know where they fit in, but who is the fifth?'

'Oh, that's easy,' said Aidan, 'that's Anders, Beattie just told you of him. Although I don't know about him all-seeing, and if he's to guide us, I don't know if I'd trust his word, he's as blind as a bat sometimes...he nearly lost us down here. And he's definitely not of this world now.'

'Oi, peasant! You won't be of that world in a minute,' Anders said, making them jump.

'Anders, you can hear us?' Beatrix asked loudly.

'Of course I can...see you I cannot, you're too deep underground now.'

'See, I told you he'd lost us!' Aidan said.

'Oi, you would as well, it's like looking through mud...this wall is pitch black! So shut it!'

'Oh, please, don't you two start arguing now, we've had enough for today,' admonished Beatrix.

'Please my friends, you are losing us. You seem to be talking with someone we cannot hear or see. Explain,' asked Zoran.

'Oh, sorry, Elder, we're speaking with Anders…he's the fifth wizard. The prophecy stated that "not in this world does he bide", Aidan told you…he's watching over us from the afterlife,' said Beatrix.

'The afterlife? You mean you are communicating with the dead?' Zoran asked, incredulity making his eyes appear even larger.

'He helps us travel between worlds. We do not look on him as dead, Elder. He is still one of us,' said Augusta haughtily.

Gillray was utterly confused, the comings and goings, ups and downs, to-ing and fro-ing of these youngsters was giving her a serious headache. But she had no second thoughts, no doubts, she was convinced these were the ones spoken of in the prophecy and it was going to be the duty of the Council to aid them in any way possible.

'And you lot are a bit thick, you know. What are the other two tasks mentioned? To reassure and to aid the bane's flight. Well reassurance is usually spoken. I can't honestly see Augusta reassuring anyone or anything…no insult intended, Augusta. So, logically if Thaddeus is the one to reassure, then…'

'Then it has to be some sort of animal!' Thaddeus interjected, and turning to the Elders he enlightened them. 'My magic, as I've already told you, is interpreting the emotions of animals and, as Anders has just said, for me to reassure obviously means that I have to communicate with some animal. So, you are right, this bane has to be…I don't know, one of our furry friends or something, I suppose,' he finished lamely, scratching his head.

'Well done! See I told you a Portolan can have brains.'

'Oi, watch it!' Thaddeus said.

'Well I hope it's not a monstrous beetle,' Beatrix said with feeling, going cold at the thought.

'But that leaves me,' said Augusta. 'How am I going to help some animal to flee? And what predicament are we going to find it in that it should need to run away?'

'Your magic is all about moving objects isn't it, Augusta?' Varna asked.

'Yes, I can move things…big things.'

'How do you mean, move things? What exactly do you do?' Thorin asked, puzzled.

'Well, I can stare at something and make it go someplace else…to wherever I want it to go, I think. Mind you, I haven't fully tested it yet,' she answered, biting her bottom lip.

'So, let us see what we have discovered so far. The nature of the bane,' said Zoran, nonplussed, 'taken in order of the points as stated in the prophecy...is some kind of animal that is ailing and is afraid, hence it needs healing and reassurance. To be shown the light, it must at present be in the dark.'

'And the fleeing, what of that?' Augusta asked.

'What actually happens to the objects you have moved, Augusta? Think on it a moment...how do you make them move?' Zoran asked.

'Well, when Aidan gave me a stone, I sort of blew it, and it flew into the river. What has...flight...it doesn't mean flee as in run away. It means what it says! Fly! It's a bird!' She said, excited.

And Zoran smiled wryly. 'It could well be, but...a bird...it would need to be an extraordinary bird, one out of legend!'

'Why?' Leonid asked before he could stop himself. 'I'm sorry, Elder Zoran; I did not mean to interrupt.'

'That's all right, Leonid, you have every right to participate in this discussion. Why do I think a bird out of legend? I'll tell you. To tackle such a weapon as the Darkness would necessitate a creature of immense power and ability. This prophecy was spoken ten centuries ago, there was nothing around at that time that we know of that could possibly be the bane. There used to be dragons a few centuries before that...of course the prophecy may have been referring to them, they could well have been powerful enough. But the great lizards died out long before the spectre spoke to Findar. And there is nothing alive in this day, either, that we are aware of...your fifth sorcerer, Anders, all-seeing, to guide, maybe... This bird or animal is hidden from our sight, lost among the centuries. Anders must have the capabilities to help you find whatever it is!'

'Are you sure the dragons have become extinct?' Beatrix asked. 'Couldn't they have just disappeared?'

'From what we know of those years and what our history tells us of the turmoil of the previous centuries, we know that dragons lived alongside elves...they were partners in Life. Virtually inseparable they protected each other for the elves used to ride the giant lizards—coincidentally against demons. But there never were many dragons whereas there were very many elves. Centuries before Findar's prophecy and our decision to remove ourselves from the upper lands, the elves migrated into the Great Forest in Drakka and into the mountains further east. If they went anywhere else we have no way of

411

knowing. Over the centuries the Green People have lost all contact with the elf clans, the only ones who could possibly know the fate of dragons. One or two humans may know of elves, of course, there are so many of you in the world it's inconceivable that none know. No, my friends, I believe the dragons are long gone…the bane must be some other animal,' Elder Zoran suddenly rubbed the back of his neck, he'd just felt a tingling running part way down the top of his spine as if a nerve had re-awoken.

'Oh, no, Elder it's no other animal—the bane is a dragon! I know it,' Augusta said and she looked at the others with wonder. 'We have to find a dragon. If they fought demons once before we must need them to fight the demons again!'

'Sounds logical,' said Beatrix dubiously.

'Oh yeah, perhaps it does but where in hell are we going to find a…a dragon? You heard the man, they're long gone!' Aidan said derisively.

'Leave her be, Aidan, you don't know that she's wrong,' Beatrix said, coming to Augusta's rescue.

Well if we are all settled on a dragon, can someone tell me where in hell do I look in this wall for one?'

'Anders has no idea where to search,' said Beatrix aloud for the benefit of the Elders.

'Hang on a minute, could you be wrong? Couldn't it be another big bird like Ryn, for instance?' Anders asked.

'No, it couldn't be Ryn, he's an albatross, not a legend,' said Aidan. 'Besides Ryn doesn't fit the rest of the prophecy, you know…ill, in the dark…whatever. No, I think you may be right, Augusta, it's a dragon.'

'Who is Ryn?' Thorin asked.

'Oh, he's a giant albatross that Aidan gave a voice,' said Beatrix matter of fact, not realizing the effect of her words.

'By the Gods, my friends, you are truly amazing,' Zoran said. 'We will set scholars to search our archives immediately for all powerful creatures of legend. But if you are determined on dragons then I suggest you start by searching for the elves as they were the last ones on earth to know of them.'

'Oh boy…elves as well as dragons!' Aidan made a very contemptuous noise as he tapped his head. 'We must be nuts!'

'Aidan, behave,' Beatrix shouted, 'you're getting in one of your moods again!'

'I'm not!'

'You are, so shut it,' Augusta ordered with a no-nonsense glint in her eyes.

'And if we find a dragon, you lot, how do you propose we get it safely into the afterlife to fight the Darkness?' Thaddeus asked, completely bewildered.

But he never got an answer for then Anders told them of Tragen and the others setting sail for Sanctity. All hell broke loose when Aidan tried to run for the surface immediately.

'Oh, my stomach, Leonid,' moaned Augusta clasping her arms across her belly. 'This is worse than the seasickness. Have we got to go so fast?'

'It won't be for much longer,' he answered.

Leonid, sitting just behind the krynx's head, turned and watched his fellow passengers undergoing their first incredible ride strapped into saddles spaced at intervals along the length of Clarinda. An unbelievable experience as the saddles and their occupants rose and fell with the rapid undulations of the krynx's thick body flowing beneath them. It hastened along a path known only to itself and its master.

Arrangements had been expedited for the four wizards to return to the surface to seek a boat to follow the Grim. Leonid had offered the services of Clarinda as it could be ridden. The krynx was decidedly uncomfortable, though, until they adapted to the peculiar motion…and learned to bend their heads. Their initial journey to Bylani had taken them nearly two full days of wandering lost but now they had been assured that riding Clarinda, they would arrive on the surface in half that time.

Spending the previous night in the cavern in which they had first sheltered with Leonid, had given them all time to think…and to grow afraid again in the dark.

How on earth they were to find a dragon, a creature they knew nothing at all about except for stories heard in childhood, was anyone's guess. The only lead they had were elves—equally lost in the mists of time, but at least they had a starting point, the Great Forest. They just had to get home to Mantovar to begin the search. And even if they beat the odds and located a dragon, how the hell could they get it into Limbo to fight the Darkness. That is if the dragon knew how to fight it—just because it did thousands of years ago didn't mean that it knew what to do now!

Could they fulfil all the tasks of the prophecy? The first stipulation was horrendous…healing a dragon that had presumably been ill for the Gods alone knew how long, was an impossible task. For starters, after a thousand years its muscles would have atrophied and its bones become so brittle it could not be moved. As for Thaddeus talking to it and calming its fears, the mind boggled. And Beatrix showing it the light…okay, it was logical that a dragon would be hiding in a dark place, but if Beatrix showed it a light it would probably burn its eyes out. Aidan could not give sight to a blind dragon if it had no eyes.

Augusta was very apprehensive; perhaps more than any of them, she had no idea how to help a dragon to fly. How big would it be? Was it a baby or fully grown? Was it likely to burn them if it was afraid? Would she have to lift it into the air? The idea was so preposterous she nearly burst out laughing. The only thing that stopped her doing just that was the laughter would soon have changed to hysteria.

Anders also fretted. He stared at the wall of colours before his eyes, a wall consisting of moving shapes none of which had sharp outlines. Each shape, each colour, just floating and merging into the next, the wall pulsed with life sometimes fast, sometimes slow. But unless he knew roughly where the dragon was he had no chance of locating it, especially if it was deep underground. And did a dragon resemble the legends? He'd heard many stories of the creatures and the descriptions of dragons always varied with the telling. What size was it? If it was very big he'd have a better chance of finding it, perhaps, but what if it was small? And the differing tales also conflicted on whether the dragon was friendly or not, most stated the creatures had an evil temper and a staple diet of humans.

The wall was vast, stretching upwards and to each side, an endless panorama. Perhaps his mother's teaching of labyrinths would now become of inestimable value. His stomach plummeted at that thought…had his mother's teaching also been preordained? Had his murder? He felt like banging his head against the colours, but then he glanced to his right and saw the Darkness throbbing evilly at the foot of the slope and knew that however difficult the search would be, it was vital they succeed if they were to survive.

'There are men ahead,' Anders warned.

'Who? Is it the Montetor's men?' Aidan asked.

Leonid stared over his shoulder at Aidan knowing he was now speaking with the dead, a circumstance that he found totally incomprehensible and very frightening ...a feeling he shared with Lord Tragen, if he but knew it.

'It's Thaddeus' friend...you know the giant who always carries that sword that's as long as a lance.'

'Marcus!' Thaddeus exclaimed. 'Where is he? How far ahead are they?'

'Not far. I suggest you shout before Clarinda scares the britches off them.'

Janne was creeping along the tunnel wall, the patrol's light extinguished. He had been hearing strange slithering noises coming closer for the last ten minutes or so, but then a light had appeared around the next corner and the noise suddenly stopped. He and his men halted – bracing themselves against the wall ready to meet the demon – swords unsheathed and short stabbing spears thrust forward. They had followed the trail of the four youngsters for hours and had come to realize that the meandering tracks told of their quarry getting lost in the maze. Janne was desperately anxious; this place was not a safe one in which to go astray. And then he heard the unbelievable.

'Marcus! Marcus!' Thaddeus shouted. 'Don't be afraid, stay where you are, we're coming.'

'Thaddeus,' shouted Janne. 'Is that really you?' And the four young wizards turned the corner in front of him, Beatrix lighting the way. Relief was short lived though, amongst Janne's men when Clarinda rumbled into sight with a Green Man riding on top.

'Don't panic,' said Thaddeus, 'they're friends.'

Hours later, they reached the surface; Janne enlightening the youngsters as to the reason for the Grim's departure as they walked up through the mountain and out of the catacombs. Janne's men, following behind its immensely long tail, were unreservedly fascinated by the krynx. One man was heard to complain of dizziness as he watched a black spot on the skin of the worm waving up and down before his eyes.

It was on reaching the entrance to the catacombs that Leonid informed them that, at his suggestion, the council had agreed that a representative of the Green People should assist the wizards in their endeavours. Leonid had not only volunteered his krynx to convey

415

them to the surface but himself as the Green Man's emissary in the world above.

Tragen achieved contact with them a little before they exited the catacombs. Tremendously relieved he had replied to Aidan's mindmeld and answered the questions that Janne had been unable to.

The fact that the Montetors and the Portolans had joined forces came as no little surprise; though the four youngsters were very dubious…Razor had seriously scared them. Knowing that Leash was now a prisoner of the Abbot of Sanctity for the murder of Anders was welcome news. But facing the fact that his friend had been killed in his stead had come hard on Aidan, he now felt responsible. No amount of comforting from his friends in Life helped, but he was shocked into placing it at the back of his mind when Anders told him to "stop blubbing, I've a feeling that my murder was preordained as well".

Tragen, as old as the hills, was astonished that they had encountered the Green People. But when he heard the prophecy, unlike the others he reserved judgement on what the bane could be. Dragons seemed to be a bit outlandish, a nonsensical idea, although he seemed to remember that the huge lizards had once played a vital role in a Gods' war aeons ago. As for Edele's enchanted he had no idea. But the spectre that spoke the prophecy to Elder Findar…was she the same Lady in the Light as the youngsters assumed? If so, who was she—if she was a God, which one? There weren't many female Gods; the obvious one would have to be Tarria or her cousin Berra, the goddess of fortune perhaps. But there were others just as powerful, just as crazy. But Gods didn't speak to mortals, did they! They sent their minions to do their bidding.

But why wait a thousand years? And was the spectre still watching? Had plans made a millennium ago been delayed, interrupted in some manner? Were the plans of the Gods coming to fruition late or on time? But as Anders had already said—time ran strangely in the afterlife. Who was there to say a millennium really was a thousand years?

But what they really needed to know was the identity of the One behind the Darkness and what was his or her purpose. If they knew the answers to both those questions then perhaps a design for winning could be worked out.

But did they need a strategy? What if they had no control whatsoever over their futures? What if it was foreordained that they were fodder for the One—destined to die at the God's hands!

Frenzy was the only word to describe the greeting meted out by Cornelia and Alessa. And after fleeting explanations horses were speedily saddled and brought to the front of the lodge for the four wizards, along with Leonid and Janne, to race to Griffin Town.

Sanctity loomed on the horizon through a haze hanging above the ocean. Pushed up from the ocean floor in a subterranean cataclysm aeons ago, volcanic action had deposited ash and lava to form gentle slopes and a large island. Long dead, the cone had been covered in soil, seeds and insects carried there on the feet and wings of migrant birds. A veritable tropical growth of vegetation had attracted humans to harvest its rich resources.

Locklear was jubilant. On the western slope of the volcano, a forest of very tall teak trees was growing in abundance. The best timber in the world for making masts, Hugo explained.

On the eastern slope of the volcano monks had built a large monastery dedicated to Tarria, the Goddess of healing and mercy. They had been good people, overworked and easy of temperament…ripe for pillaging by an unscrupulous God's disciples.

Over the years, the monastery had grown ever larger. Originally it had been one long building housing the oratory and an open cloister running along its length with a room built on at one end to house the monks. Over the years the room had been converted into a long dormitory and another built at its other end, both set at right angles to the oratory; a refectory hall, kitchen and storerooms had been built across the other ends of the sleeping quarters resulting in one square building enclosing a courtyard, the cloister had been extended to run around its inner perimeter.

On the slopes above the monastery were the vineyards, growing grapes for their own home-brewed wines. There were newer structures lower down the slope, long and low, the whitewash peeling in strips off neglected walls. These housed a vast number of monks, several of whom were wandering slowly from doorway to doorway. On the western end of the island there were many farms, some with fields cultivating maize and others raising cattle and sheep.

On the waterfront, just back from the wharf, the buildings were newer again, also long and low, similar to the monks' dormitories. But there the resemblance ended. These buildings were black, barrack-like and surrounded by wooden stockades, barracoons built to house slaves. The wind blowing off shore over these pestilential structures brought the hideous smell of unwashed bodies and excrement.

'God it stinks! That is one trade that will end once the monk has sailed for Mantovar. There'll be no more slaves in the Griffin Isles,' said Lodovico, his hatred of the traffic well known.

Tragen wrinkled his nose in disgust. 'Why do they need slaves? I don't see much need for them, there's hardly any activity to require a high labour force. Farming and the timber industry won't call for many and as for the vineyard...'

'I asked the abbot that very question, a few years ago. The mad monk said a few were needed in the lumber trade, yes, but then he laughed and said the rest were a great aid in his religious services. I refused to even contemplate what he meant by that.'

The immense sea of weed had disappeared during the early hours of the morning, the day after the youngsters boarded their fishing boat at the wharf in Griffin Town, almost as if it had been waiting for the youngsters. Hopper, who had been on watch at the time, described its disappearance as a long low rustle, like the wind blowing through trees. The bald man's hair dropped beneath the waves leaving a vast sea of bubbles in its wake.

Free at last, Brother Dyfrig had set full sail and raced towards his home. Entering the lagoon at noon the following day, the barque berthed at the longer of the two jetties jutting out from the extensive wharf fronting the monastery buildings. The abbot wasted no time in disembarking at the site of the twin gallows, the only structure on the jetty, built for the express purpose of deterring any rescue attempt. He spent some moments staring at the Grim limping into the harbour. Smiling his satisfaction, he turned to an aide close by, whispered something and then strode off up the hill his robe flapping about his legs in the breeze. He skirted the dormitory at the southern end and disappeared into the oratory. Brother Dyfrig though, in his haste, had missed the small fishing boat on the horizon aft of the Mantovarian warship.

Thirty-three

Shadra stumbled along behind his big friend; both bound securely, arms behind their backs. Dragged along for days it seemed like, they had spent the last three nights bound and gagged in one cave after another somewhere in the mountains.

Ryn flew overhead frantically watching their progress. In desperation he had dived at the trolls with his claws stretched to their limits in an attempt to grasp his friends and lift them into the air. But each time he had been beaten off by the captors using clubs and spears.

The trolls stood a head taller than Anselm, their shoulders broad and muscular, their backs taut as iron and they stooped, their very long arms stretching below their knees. The thick black hair covering their bodies ensured they were impervious to the cold, their black eyes staring vacantly from brown, bulbous, weather-worn faces.

Anselm was dragged roughly to his feet as he fell to his knees for the umpteenth time on the narrow, rocky path running up the hillside just below the snow line. They headed for a small defile at the head of a gorge, the path disappearing over the crest. The minstrel moaned as fresh blood oozed from his battered knees, the abrasions visible through his torn britches, the cold turning his skin blue.

The elf, although used to rough terrain suffered even more, being small he was pulled along at a near running pace for most of the way. Exhaustion weakened him drastically and this coupled with the rarefied atmosphere this high in the mountains made his head spin. He brooded between bouts of dizziness. He tried to recall all he'd been told of trolls, to sift the truth from the fable. He knew they were not very intelligent; they acted mostly on instinct, although this band seemed more quick-witted than most. But trolls usually killed on sight unless they were hunting for sacrifices, and they did not differentiate between human and animal…or elf, when it came to offerings for their Gods. Shadra was very afraid now. Trolls sacrificed to Gods of Chaos, and the method, though various, was always slow and extremely painful. He wondered whether Anselm knew this.

The leading troll crested the ridge and disappeared over the rim into the valley below. From the heights, the troll village looked peaceful in the combe. The mud roundhouses set in a neat circle around a large, central fire pit. The whole village surrounded by a tightly knit, reinforced wattle fence, to protect against the wild black bear, the only animal known to alarm a troll.

Shadra stumbled on reaching the top of the ridge, vertigo causing further dizziness as he looked down the very steep track. The troll walking behind pushed him and this time Shadra could not recover his balance and he fell hard. He rolled a fair way down the hill banging his head on the rocks repeatedly as he did so, pain flared in his eyes and blood coursed down his face. A troll picked him up and threw him over his shoulder, carrying him the rest of the way.

It was a long way down to the valley floor, the path sheer and winding across the face of the mountain. Anselm inspected the village vainly trying to memorize the outlay of the place in case they had a chance of escape. He fell again just inside the gate and a female lifted him upright, took one quick glance at him and threw him towards the centre of the village.

He and Shadra were thrown into a sty, landing full stretch among the pigs. A troll woman untied their hands, pointing towards the trough where a pig was drinking she made it plain that was the only water they would get and the pigswill the only food. Anselm drew in deep breaths of the dung-laden air and almost vomited, the troll laughed as she left.

Anselm helped Shadra to sit, his back propped up against the wall near the water trough. Soaking his shirt sleeve in the dirty water, Anselm cleaned the blood from the elf's face. The cool water, soothing, brought the elf around and he smiled up at the minstrel.

'We appear to be in a fine mess, my friend,' he croaked and attempted humour. 'I don't believe these are the Garda.'

'I'm sorry, Shadra, I thought we were leagues from the trolls.' Sitting down alongside the elf, he looked up at the sky and watched the albatross circling overhead. 'I hope Ryn can think of something.'

Shadra fell unconscious, a little later, a result of the many blows to his head sustained in his falling down the mountain. Anselm held the little green elf on his lap much as a father would cuddle his hurt child. But the elf still clung to his bag like a barnacle to the hull of a ship; his fingers could not be prised from it. He was still alive…just, Anselm could hear his shallow breathing, see his chest rising and falling and feel the gentle flutter of the pulse in his neck. They had not eaten all day and had only sipped the dirty water in the trough against which they were resting. Anselm was frantic with worry.

It was dark and quiet apart from the gentle snuffling of the pigs settling down for the night; the trolls had gone to their beds, all except the guards around the perimeter of the settlement. From the low light given off by the fire in the centre of the village, and the moonlight in a clear sky, Anselm could see Ryn perched in a high redwood tree, well out of range of the trolls' spears.

The albatross had circled the village all day, keeping watch over his friends and he was panicking now. He had to rescue them somehow. But how was he to do it? He stretched his wings and flexed his fingers and wondered if he could use magic.

He had used magic to grow fingers, hadn't he? He had a voice…and tears running down either side of his beak. But he couldn't fight the trolls, he didn't know how to fight, and anyway there were too many, even now when it was night-time. The moonlight and the firelight showed every little dung heap in the pig pen, as well as every sow and piglet. And there were many of them, this was a rich tribe.

He watched as trolls ambled about the fire, taking food from a nearby table and dipping tankards into a large open vat on a rock almost within the embers of the fire. This was mead being kept warm, the sustaining drink in this part of the world. And that vat surely must contain the tribe's supply for the whole month, it was big enough. He glanced at a young, drunken troll as he accidentally rocked the vat, getting a cuff around the ears for being careless.

And then Ryn had a plan. He scanned the skies and saw in the distance a small cloud, just what he needed. He stared at it…and stared at it, and despite all his concentration, it did not come to him. He tried a different tack and in his despair, and because he concentrated even harder, the little cloud became a big cloud. And it continued to grow until it obscured the moon and the stars. The village below was now only lit by firelight and two or three lanterns hanging outside doorways.

Anselm had his head lowered sleeping over the cradled form of the elf. But Ryn needed to attract his attention and somehow make him understand that rescue was in the offing. Ryn could fly down over the pen but this would only serve to alarm the trolls and he didn't want them alerted. So he did the next best thing and threw a twig at the minstrel while the nearest troll was quaffing his mead. His aim was true; unfortunately, it bounced off Anselm's head. But it had the required effect; the minstrel watched Ryn's every move from then on.

When all was again quiet, he made his move; he needed to be fast as he didn't know how long the magic would last. He was afraid it would wear off and the clouds disperse before he completed his plan…and he was very nervous, never having done anything like this before.

Anselm suddenly tensed in the gloom as Ryn left his perch high in the tree and dived, not for the pen, but for the fire. The bird flew silently and as straight as an arrow at the vat of hot mead, using his talons he tipped it onto its side as he passed overhead. The resultant crash woke the nearby trolls and they watched in disbelief at their month's drink dousing the huge communal fire. Trolls rushed forward in the dark to retrieve the vat but the steam beat them back. There was pandemonium in the village, panicking trolls ran into frenzied trolls, both ending up crashing into the walls of the huts. Cries and screams rent the night air as the firestones continued to vaporize the mead, scalding all who ventured near.

Birds have excellent night-sight, albatrosses in particular due to spending long nights floating on the ocean, and Ryn was not in the least perturbed by the darkness, he continued his flight landing alongside his friends in the pig pen. The pigs frightened out of their normal torpor by a huge bird settling amongst them, squealed and ran about frantically, and breaking through the gate added even more to the hysteria in the village.

'Quick, Anselm, both of you get on my back,' ordered Ryn.

'You can't carry both of us…take Shadra, he's dying Ryn.'

Ryn felt a sudden lump in his chest. 'Then climb on quickly with him. We'll find help somewhere in these mountains.'

Anselm grinned and settled Shadra at the joint, forward of the bird's wings. 'Wait,' he said. Anselm ran to the gate and disappeared through returning a moment later with his lute and their weapons. Climbing up behind Shadra, Anselm smiled and gave a great whoop as Ryn lifted them into the air.

'I don't know how you have the strength, Ryn, but thanks be to all the Gods that you have,' shouted the minstrel, he clasped the unconscious elf safely in his arms.

Ryn grinned as best he could, his beak contorting into a most unusual shape as he screamed against the wind. 'It's magic, Anselm, my friend. IT'S MAGIC!'

Ryn was beyond exhaustion; he had carried his burden for most of the following day only snatching a temporary respite when desperately needed. But he could not carry his friends any longer. He discovered the hard way that magic did not last forever, and that a toll had to be paid for its use. He had called up magic to enhance his strength not realizing that the magic would also burn away his core energy.

Ryn's lack of stamina gave rise to unnatural panting which brought on panic attacks and he found it increasingly difficult to maintain height. Albatrosses flew vast distances by keeping their wings spread, locked in place to ride the thermals, that way they didn't have to expend energy on flapping their limbs like other birds. But now Ryn – to climb higher in the skies with the very heavy weight on his back – was forced to flap his wings almost continually thereby weakening him further. He couldn't last much longer and he flew lower to search out the terrain before he fell from the sky.

The cloud cover he had created over the troll village had brought on a blizzard, making it imperative that he find a safe haven. Anselm needed to light a fire and get something warm into Shadra still unconscious his health rapidly deteriorating despite being sheltered in Anselm's arms.

But the minstrel was also suffering greatly; he couldn't stop shivering and had nearly lost his grip on the albatross several times. His fingers ached with a desperate chill, for which he was grateful, for if there was no pain it was because frostbite had replaced it.

The albatross espied a cave below them and he alighted at its entrance. Weary beyond measure he sank to his belly on the ground unable to control the tremors racking his body.

The cave was barely large enough to afford shelter for Anselm and Shadra. But the snow drifting across the entrance gave them a ready-made windbreak and the minstrel laid the still comatose elf beneath the roof of the small grotto. Searching Shadra's bag, Anselm extracted the elf's small cooking stove and placed on it a kettle full of snow to heat for tea.

While Anselm was occupied with his ministrations, Ryn improved the windbreak as best he could to further shelter Shadra. He then flew through the blizzard to seek fuel to kindle a fire for the heat from the stove was nowhere near enough to save their lives.

Anselm, despite many attempts, failed to get Shadra to drink, the tea dribbling from the elf's mouth. Desperate, the minstrel used the remaining hot water to fill an empty pewter pot that he discovered in the elf's bag, along with a blanket. He placed the pot within the blanket and wrapped it around Shadra, hoping enough warmth would radiate through the elf's icy body to keep him alive.

The minstrel warmed his hands on the stove. His fingers pained excruciatingly as he flexed them, frostbite was already a certainty in his exposed face however much he rubbed at it. The open wounds on his legs – inflicted from falling on the path to the trolls' village – no longer bothered him he had very little sensation in the limbs cold had become his life. He stared at his fingertips wondering if he would ever play the lute again, singing was certainly out of the question his throat was burned from breathing the freezing air. He peered through the snow blowing almost horizontally across the mouth of the cave, rubbing his ears to stimulate the blood flow he shivered uncontrollably.

Ryn's new fingers were numb, hardly any feeling in them at all. He was clearing dead timber covered in snow, the cold permeating through to the bones in his wings. His muscles were freezing making it difficult to fly, the fuel he carried in his talons weighed him down forcing him to flap his tired wings, and he could hardly keep his eyes open. Gathering the fuel and toting it to the cave was painfully slow and there was something ailing in his chest, the pain almost unbearable. He knew now that he had carried his friends for longer than he should have…he had strained his heart.

But safety had to be reached; he had to get his friends as high into the mountains as possible in case the tribe still hunted them. All night they had fled the chasing trolls, for land beings they had been capable of extraordinary speed managing to keep the albatross in sight up until the middle of the morning. It was only then that Ryn had found himself outdistancing their hunters.

He wished he could have flown south or west into the warmth, but in both directions, the monk's soldiers continued searching for them. And it would have been impossible to hide a huge bird carrying two passengers. The only alternative had been to escape north or east, further into the snow-capped peaks. But they had not expected this terrible weather to close in as it had.

Ryn rested at the cave mouth when he had retrieved enough kindling to keep the small fire going for a while. He couldn't utilize his magic to keep the fire alight; he just didn't have the energy anymore so he used his bulk to further block off the adverse wind. The bird grew lethargic; he could feel his inner muscles stiffening and did not have the strength to move to keep warm. He knew the lack of physical activity would lead to him falling into a stupor and eventually die but he couldn't summon the energy enough even to care.

Shadra's breathing was very shallow and despite the warming pot in the blanket, the elf was getting colder, his coma deeper. Anselm lifted the elf on to his lap and nursed him, trying to get warmth into him by massaging his arms and legs.

But Anselm was also growing sluggish, his muscles freezing and his breathing laboured, rattling in his throat.

'You'd better leave us, Ryn,' said Anselm slowly, his teeth chattering loudly.

'Too late, my friend…too late, I am too tired.'

'Oh, Ryn, I'm so sorry.'

'Not your fault. I'm sorry the same fate awaits you and little Shadra,' he sighed. 'It's been a good life, though not long enough.' He tried to bend his fingers and, raising them before his face he found one missing. It had fallen away while he had been talking. Frostbite had killed it and he had not felt a thing. 'I liked my fingers, Anselm.'

'Aye, I wanted so much to teach you to play the lute…and to sing,' he croaked, the tears freezing on his cheeks. 'I very much wanted to live. I have failed my masters, the both of you and my family,' he sighed, closing his eyes to sleep.

'It wasn't your fault you failed, if anyone is to blame it is I…I conjured the storm!'

'That was an accident—to rescue us from the trolls. No, Ryn, you have no reason to reproach yourself,' Anselm said, slipping deeper into sleep.

'Sing…I wish I could sing…I have a beautiful voice,' he looked at Shadra in Anselm's arms. 'If I have to die, best it be with friends. Goodbye Anselm, goodbye little Shadra,' and then, looking inwards at his memories, 'I'm sorry I never delivered your message, Aidan, but I am no longer capable of even moving.' Ryn lowered his head and closed his small black eyes, all three very dignified as they prepared to meet their end.

'We must investigate, Xelnor, we've never seen such a sight before,' said Roidan.

'But it's only a very large bird,' Xelnor answered, staring suspiciously down the mountain at the place where Ryn had disappeared.

'Yes, but what if it has something to do with her?'

'Why would she be so obvious?'

'Well, that's the conundrum…is it a snare?' Roidan flexed his fingers, something he always did when puzzled.

'It may well be,' Xelnor answered worriedly. 'She'd love to capture one of us…especially you!'

'But the bird is patently ill, yet it carries kindling. What would a bird do with fire?'

'Attract us!'

Roidan stood silently with his friend Xelnor and studied the bird's antics as it flew slowly back and forth. Roidan knew there was a cave there, all be it a very small one. But it could shelter someone. He caught Xelnor's eyes and noted the anxiety in his face. 'I have to go, my friend. I have to satisfy my curiosity.'

'Then I will accompany you,' said Xelnor, full of doubt.

She watched them as they made their way down the slope of virgin snow, their white clothes and white skin insufficient camouflage…they could not hide from her.

She'd been taken unawares, though. If she'd realized earlier their intentions then she could have had them walk over her. They'd never have survived. But why were they risking their lives by moving in the full light of day down a hillside in search of the giant bird?

She was puzzled. Their whole purpose of being on the mountainside was to guard against her. She smiled…one of them was Roidan.

She slipped into the snow. Now she was totally invisible to her prey as she quickly followed beneath the freezing surface.

Thirty-four

At his first sight of the sea, the green man, standing on the wharf in Griffin Town wept unashamedly.

'I have so yearned to see the ocean, all my life I have heard stories of its vastness, its vibrancy but I have never been able to picture it as it is.'

'Do you like it?' Beatrix asked putting her arm through his.

'Oh, yes! I love everything about this world above Bylani, it's…it's so incredible; it breathes life into me as it should. And yet it is so totally different to what I expected…by the Gods I want my wife and children to see this. I want them to experience the sun and the moon and the real wind—and the sound, the smell, the taste of the sea,' he turned to Beatrix and smiled, his eyes alight through his tears. 'We have established a haven for those who will aid us fight the Darkness, let us pray that we are not too long in the caves, this is where I wish my family to live—we are meant to live up here.'

'Come on, Leonid,' and Beatrix led him into the boat, overcome with hope for all the Green People, and sadness at their fate. 'But be careful, not all things are pleasant in this world…seasickness for one.'

But what intrigued Leonid most of all was the sun. He had never seen its glow or felt the heat from the golden orb. But now, having been warned not to look directly at it, he settled back against the gunnel and savoured its life-giving quality and understood, for the first time, why Mother Nature was so revered among his people.

Janne had been an avid sailor and fisherman all his life, as most islanders were, and he was the proud owner of "Alessa" a small fishing boat he regularly took onto the waters around the island in his leisure hours. On these outings he was always accompanied by Alessa Barbat herself an expert with the rod, and before his recovery, by Thaddeus.

Though the boat was a little overcrowded, it was suitable for five people and there were now six, it had two distinct advantages. Firstly, with its sail hoisted it was extremely fast and flew through the water, cresting the waves as if it had a life of its own. Secondly, with its sail lowered and its mast unshipped, its broad bottomed hull could be rowed on to virtually any sandy shore.

Within a day they had sighted the Grim hardly moving within the seaweed, a day later they had caught up with her and the sargassum

427

disappeared. Tragen advised they stay well behind, hidden from the abbot until it was safe for them to board the warship. All six occupants and Anders from his vantage point at the wall of colours, watched as the Grim berthed against the jetty directly opposite the monk's barque.

'What do we do now?' Locklear asked, staring across the rail of his ship at the monks lining up on the jetty. The silent sentinels – dwarfed by the high gibbet behind them – faced the Grim, effectively dissuading anyone on the ship from disembarking.

'Not a very auspicious welcome, Hugo,' answered Tragen, pursing his lips he stepped to the side and studied the old monastery glistening in the sun some way away at the top of the gently sloping hill. He was troubled mightily; there was something strange in the air, the atmosphere smelled of something like brimstone yet the volcano showed no signs of life.

Searching for any small drift of smoke percolating through a fissure in the cone he noticed the whole island had an air of neglect. Why, he wondered, was it because the abbot intended leaving? Or was it the overpowering sense of despair?

'We wait,' said Bazyli Montetor his facial scar even uglier in the sunlight, his face drawn. Standing, his legs astride on the wooden deck, his hand never leaving the hilt of his sword, he glared hard at the silent, inhospitable monks. Lifting his gaze to the long, low monastery he wondered where his sister was incarcerated. He had a bad feeling in his gut. Because they were twins Ariana and he had always been very close and could usually feel the presence of each other even in the next room. Now there was nothing. He hoped it was because she was too far away. But this time there would be no leaving her behind—this time he was taking her home and the abbot would die.

'I suggest, Tragen, you tell Aidan and the others to hang back, wait until nightfall and then land outside of this harbour,' said Lodovico Portolan staring east along the wharf to the cliffs below the monastery. 'When they deem it safe to come ashore, tell them not to approach the Grim. I have a feeling we will be watched all night.' Studying the unnaturally motionless ecclesiastical guard, he was wound tight as a spring, ready to respond to any threat. And he like Bazyli searched for sign of the hostages.

'Well, if it's any comfort, it will be a fairly short night, tomorrow is Midsummer's Eve,' said Locklear, combing his beard with his fingers. He glanced at Hopper alert at the forward rail of the

428

quarterdeck and down at Trumper in the waist, both men prepared to go to war at the slightest provocation.

Sometime later, the occupants of the fishing boat, its sail lowered, sheltering from the sun beneath a stretched tarpaulin and lying a short distance from the entrance to the harbour, watched as a monk walked down the hill from the monastery. He strode unhurriedly along the jetty and approached the Grim's quarterdeck, his white robe billowing in the afternoon breeze, his bald pate reflecting the sun, he shouted his message.

He relayed the abbot's invitation to dinner for Tragen, the Montetor and the Seneschal, Captain Locklear was to accompany them. He also advised, for Tragen's benefit, that the wizard carry his staff, as the slope was treacherous in parts for an old man.

Tragen bristled; did the mad monk think he was in his dotage?

'What is happening?' Janne asked, watching as the brow of the Grim was lowered to the jetty.

'They have been invited up to the abbot's home for dinner, Marcus,' answered Augusta.

'And the abbot made a point of asking Tragen to take his staff,' said Aidan worriedly, 'surely he must realize how powerful a weapon it is—the abbot is up to something. By the Gods, I should be with him to watch his back.'

'Then I think it's time we found a landing site. I am inclined to agree with you, they are all in grave danger and there's nothing we can do about it out here,' said Janne. 'We'll move east and see what's at the other end of those cliffs.' He pointed to his right at a short stretch of land that had fallen into the sea, the waves pounding on the rocks at the base of the cliffs. At the top was a small open area leading up a grassed slope to a small copse just below the monastery. 'It's going to be a long stretch to row there; we dare not hoist the sail. We'll have to go out to sea a little not to be seen but if we time it right, we'll come ashore just before full dark.'

They unshipped the mast, a task that took moments, and took up the four oars and rowed eastwards, Beatrix sat in the stern at the tiller and Augusta in the prow, both girls scrutinizing the shore as they passed.

'Hey,' Augusta said, 'there's a cave in that cliff. Look, just in line with the monastery, a couple of feet above the waves. Couldn't we hide in there?'

'If you like the sweet aroma of a sewer, yes, we could,' laughed Aidan.

'Oh, that's what it is. Well, all right, there's a small cove just alongside it we could use that…it shouldn't be too smelly there.'

Janne peered intently at the spot she indicated, the light fading fast. 'I don't think we'll find better this night, turn for it,' he ordered.

A little while later, they rowed up onto the shore, and Janne and Leonid leapt out and tied the painter to a nearby rock outcropping.

'Come on then, come ashore,' Janne said as Leonid strode a little way across the white sand to the foot of an overgrown pathway leading up to the top of the cliffs.

'What ails you?' The green man asked, frowning he stared at the four youngsters hesitating to embark.

'I feel something,' said Beatrix looking at her friends. 'We feel something. There is an evil here—a great evil.'

'The Darkness is near,' said Thaddeus trembling. 'I could never mistake it.'

'We all feel it, Thaddeus,' said Augusta, clasping his hand to give comfort, her eyes unnaturally wide.

'Aye and we'll never find it while we sit in this boat. Let's move,' said Aidan stepping ashore, a stillness creeping over him for a moment, as a sense of impending doom took hold. He shook himself free of despair. 'We have to find Tragen and the others; they must be warned that the Darkness is near.'

Tragen, his staff in hand, entered the long, low, white building, a communal dormitory that had been clearly converted to house just the abbot. In front of his companions, he turned right and followed the messenger into a spacious living room. There, he was greeted by Brother Dyfrig acting the genial host, an unnaturally silent aide passing around goblets of red wine.

'Please be seated, gentlemen, and before you ask, the Portolan and his wife will not be joining us this evening. They are imprisoned on the other side of the island, I'm afraid…away from the rabble,' he smiled unctuously. 'But never fear they will arrive some time tomorrow.'

'That seems an excessive time, monk, why the delay?' Bazyli asked, relieved at discovering the reason for his inability to sense

Ariana, yet at the same time disappointed that he wouldn't see her this night.

'Your sister and her husband, handsome one,' he gloated as he ridiculed Bazyli again, 'are of an age when incarceration is not too kind to their disposition. Hold,' he said as Lodovico and Bazyli made to draw their swords, 'they are unharmed, but care must be exercised, they have become frail. Haste may damage my hostages before they are freed,' he again smirked. 'I ask you to join me in partaking of a decent wine and decent food ... you, Captain, are not invited. You are here so that I have no doubt you will keep to your side of the bargain and transport what I require to Mantovar. You will?'

Locklear nodded, his fists clenched he wanted to pound the monk.

'Good,' said the Abbot of Sanctity, 'you may now return to your ship. My aide will come to you sometime in the next day or so to make arrangements for you to enter the forest to select your masts. You cannot begin your search tomorrow as we celebrate a special festival culminating in a ceremony in the evening...your presence will not be required,'

Brother Dyfrig flicked his fingers at the monk standing at his shoulders indicating that he should escort Locklear from the room.

'Do not take this the wrong way, gentlemen, but you will remain as my guests until the ship is ready to sail. I will allow you access to your family sometime in the morning when they are settled into new accommodation, a place they will stay until we are ready to depart.'

He smiled at Hugo watching from the door. 'You may leave, Captain, our dinner is getting cold.'

Tragen nodded his goodbye to Hugo. 'There will be no tricks, Brother Abbot. I have not lived all these years to be taken in by a demented rogue,' he sat at the table and indicated for his friends to join him. It was going to be a long night.

It was also going to be a long night for those stepping from the fishing boat onto the milky sands, gleaming in the moonlight.

'We follow that, my friends,' said Janne, indicating an overgrown pathway meandering up the steep slope towards the small wood above. Another path, equally unused, made straight for the outflow of the sewer yards away on their left.

'Do you think the boat is safe here, Marcus?' Thaddeus asked, tapping the gunnel affectionately. 'I'd hate to lose it; I loved sailing in her with you and Alessa.'

Janne startled held his breath a moment. 'You remember being with us?'

'I used to watch us often, Marcus, you, me and Alessa out on the ocean,' he laughed quietly, trying to shake off his trepidation with innocent memories. 'We had fun, the three of us.'

Janne's eyes glistened, he had often wondered if he and Alessa were doing the correct thing in taking the unaware boy sailing. He shrugged off the tightness in his chest; he knew that he and Alessa were right in loving this boy.

'I will lead the way,' said Leonid explaining, 'my eyes have adapted to low light.'

Taking a last lingering look at the fishing boat, the four wizards followed the green man trudging up the steep path, Janne bringing up the rear, his sword unsheathed. Catching sight of it glinting in the moonlight Aidan stared for a moment at the naked blade, the horror of its purpose taking his breath, he halted.

'Put it away, Marcus,' he ordered.

'What?'

'Put the sword away, please. There will be no killing. We have enough magic between us to render any threat safe.'

'But Tragen has warned us not to use magic just in case the abbot can detect us,' said Beatrix.

'Nevertheless, there will be no killing!'

Janne looked at his companions, debating with himself whether he should obey the strange order, he was a soldier and his job was to kill, if necessary, to protect his charges. How on earth could he heed this young boy?

'We also do not kill needlessly,' said Leonid, holding up the dagger that he had been holding to his side, out of sight. 'But we must be prepared, Aidan, we do not know what we'll meet or how these monks will react.'

'There will be no killing; otherwise I will go on alone.'

'Very well, as you're so determined. I don't like this, but I will obey for now,' Janne said, replacing his long sword in its scabbard, Leonid following suit. They resumed the climb up the slope in silence, Janne flexing his empty fingers even more wary.

At the crest they found a short area of clear grassland before the woods. With their hearts in their mouths they crossed silently and entered the thicket of maritime pine trees. Leonid rested them all a moment for their eyes to adjust to the darkness within.

'There are no animals in here,' said Thaddeus, his voice sounding dreadful, his face unnaturally pale even in the reduced moonlight filtering through the long needle-like leaves on the branches above. 'No birds, very few insects…not even a moth.' He peered ahead at the monastery a hundred or so yards away through the trees. 'It seems that the wildlife disappears the closer we get to that place.'

Augusta, the nearest, hugged him. 'Let's go, Thaddeus, I don't like this place either. The sooner we are off this island the better I'll feel.'

They crept to the other end of the woods. Peering through the underbrush, six pairs of eyes stared across the hill towards the abbot's home. The ground before them was grass-covered to a low, grey-stone wall built across the hillside between them and the dormitory on the eastern side, at the north end they could just make out the refectory.

Tarria's monastery, once a haven of peace, had now been desecrated by disciples of an unknown, evil God. How she would hate the place this had become, Aidan thought, the keeping of slaves was abhorrent to her. To whom was the oratory now dedicated? Aidan shuddered; he knew of many Gods of Chaos, some more evil than others.

But the One behind the Darkness must be a paramount God. The lesser Gods would never have the skills to wield the power necessary to affect life on both sides of death.

Although there were many Gods who could exercise that sort of power, only three sprung immediately to mind being the most famous of them all. There was Kaneshi, the God of Disease and Despair, who sought to undo all the works of Tarria. Bindarune, the God of Desolation and Famine, one of Kaneshi's six brothers, though they hated each other. And then there was Tarria's brother, Maaluke, the God of Knowledge and Power, the God who wished to reign supreme but whose brethren could never allow him to succeed. Being King of the Gods would require obedience from the lesser Gods, which in turn would lead to order—a state anathema to all Gods of Chaos.

And then, of course, there were the Gods of Mischief, the ones who fomented discord among the others, one of whom was Kaneshi's own son who had tried to kill his father centuries before and had been exiled for it.

All were hideously powerful, their nature calling for them to be uncaring of all mortals. But the One behind the Darkness seemed to want complete destruction of all mortal life, an end that would surely bring on his own. Who would he rule if there was no-one left? Where would he replenish his powers? Without mankind to feed them, the Gods would diminish and enter Oblivion. The other Gods would have to stop him for their very survival.

And yet, Aidan mused, he and his four friends seemed to be intrinsic in a war between them…was it one of these three? If it was, then they might as well give up now there was no chance of surviving.

'Don't move any closer to the monastery, there are men in front of you,' warned Anders.

'Anders warns of men, Marcus,' said Thaddeus, his voice bringing Aidan from his musings.

'I see them,' and Leonid pointed, 'there, they are lying down this side of the wall, and I see poleaxes.'

'How many?' Janne asked, his hand instinctively finding the hilt of his sword, knowing though that no blade could beat a poleaxe unless he could get in very close. He was facing a weapon designed with a three-headed blade shaped into a hammerhead on one side, an axe blade on the other and a spear point at the top. And if they were of the modern type then the long shaft would be bound with hoops of iron to protect the wood from a sword cut. He would have to rely on his height and speed.

'I don't know but there are too many for us to handle. They have taken station all along the stretch in front of us…we cannot pass them unnoticed.'

'Damn!' said Janne. 'Let's move to the side of the refectory it may not be guarded there.

'It is, the place is completely surrounded,' Anders warned.

Just then one of the monks rose from his prone position and stood with his poleaxe by his side. He stared in front of him at the grove in which the wizards were hiding. They all froze, not moving a muscle, scarcely daring to breathe. The monk, as if at a signal, suddenly walked slowly forward his poleaxe held in both hands across his chest ready to be swung or thrust at an adversary.

'He's seen us,' whispered Augusta frantically.

'He can't have, we've been too well hidden,' said Marcus.

'Well something's caught his attention,' said Aidan. 'Wait a minute, I'll try and distract him,' and the wizard's apprentice attempted to mindmeld with the monk in an effort to send him somewhere else. 'Bloody hell, we're in trouble, and I mean lots of it. I can't mindmeld with him.'

'Why not? You told me wizards could mindmeld with anyone,' said Augusta, 'here, let me try.' Her exertions also failing she turned to Thaddeus, licking her lips she wondered how her next words were going to affect the seneschal's son. 'Thaddeus we couldn't mindmeld with your body here when your soul was in the Darkness, could we?'

'No…why?'

'She means Thaddeus my friend these monks are like you used to be…here and not here. In other words they have no souls in their bodies!' Aidan said.

'Hell, then how do we stop him?' Marcus asked, the trauma of Thaddeus' early days still causing nightmares.

'Augusta, you could try stopping him!' Aidan said, pensively.

'Force him to move, you mean?'

'Aye! Go on, give it a go,' Aidan urged her, 'but do it quick for God's sake, he'll be here before long.'

Augusta stared at the monk, and concentrating all her energy, she pushed her mind at him, wishing him back to his place in the wall. But nothing happened, he still kept walking forwards.

'I can't do it—my magic's failed, it's gone,' she stared at her friends bereft, the thought of losing her magical abilities devastating her.

'No, you haven't,' said Beatrix, quickly, 'we couldn't use magic with Thaddeus until we were touching his soul in Limbo.'

'She's right! I couldn't do anything with him until I was holding his hands in the Darkness. It wasn't until he returned to his body that our magic worked between us as normal. You'll never completely lose your magic now you've got it—it may hide from you for some reason, though, but never leave you for good,' said Aidan. And Augusta visibly relaxed, her confidence returning at his words.

'When you lot have finished your discussion…will you kindly think of something else, or I'm going to have to attack him! He's nearly upon us,' said Marcus, anxiously.

'Well, if my magic doesn't work on him, maybe it'll work on something else,' and with that, Augusta watched the monk raise his foot to cross over a high tussock in the hillside. So, smiling grimly, she raised the tussock beneath the monk's foot, leaving a large hole in the ground beneath it. She continued to raise the large clump of grass and earth, forcing the monk's foot upwards attempting to make him fall over. But the monk, with no change of expression on his face, eventually slid his foot sideways off the tussock. Unfortunately for the monk, his foot plunged into the gaping hole and he stumbled forwards, his leg snapping with an audible crack. Surprisingly the monk did not scream in pain, he stayed put, lying across the hole his leg twisted unnaturally beneath him.

Aidan paled, the monk might not be able to feel the pain, with his soul displaced the man could feel nothing, but that didn't lessen the extent of the injury. Aidan rose to go to his aid; he needed to heal the man.

'Quick, you lot, grab Aidan, the idiot's going to rescue the monk,' shouted Anders.

Beatrix, being the nearest, jumped up and knocked Aidan to the ground, falling on him she was soon joined by Marcus who held him still.

'Please! Let me go to him, he'll die otherwise,' pleaded Aidan.

'If what you say is true about his soul, wouldn't dying be a blessing for the man?' Marcus said, releasing his hold and allowing Aidan to sit up.

'But his soul will be trapped forever within the Darkness!'

'It is trapped now, Aidan, and the only way you and we can save him is by destroying the Darkness,' said Thaddeus.

Augusta grasped Aidan's hand and pulled him to his feet. 'Come on, let's go,' and she put her arm around his waist, 'we can do nothing here to help any of them.'

'Well said, Princess,' said Leonid, 'I agree…it's time to return to the beach.'

'Yes, and that means the sewer is the only way in,' whispered Beatrix. 'They won't have that guarded, will they?'

'Ugh!' said Augusta, hating the thought. 'All those rats,' and she shuddered.

'I hope there are rats,' said Thaddeus, despondently.

'I can't see any sentries, Beattie, but it is a tunnel and I can't see very far along it,' warned Anders.

'Come on; let's shift before any more of these monks get brave,' said Augusta.

Aidan hung his head, turning his back on the injured man. The only time he had ever done such a thing in his whole life.

He felt sick.

Locklear was in a foul mood arriving back onboard the Grim. He loathed leaving his friends at the abbot's home, especially when he saw the armed sentries move into place as he left.

'Hopper,' he ordered, 'I want every sailor and every marine armed to the hilt. I want this ship ready to sail at the drop of a hat, half the crew on duty at all times. Trumper,' he shouted and the bo'sun at the brow turned at the roar from Locklear, 'I want men aloft ready to unfurl the sails. Be ready to bring the brow inboard and station men to cast-off at a moment's notice. While you're about it, tell Dolly to douse his fire and order him to the quarterdeck with every knife he owns. I want that man with me if we have to foray ashore.'

Hopper lifted his eyebrows. 'Matters did not go to plan?'

'No! I smell treachery.' He walked to the rail and stared at the monks still lined up on the jetty facing his ship. 'Have you noticed their eyes, Hopper? Their eyes stare without moving, they do not even blink! Can they see anything? They don't seem to be in this world!'

Thirty-five

Tragen did not feel well. For a moment he wondered if he'd been poisoned but discounted that, he'd have detected it. He glanced at the others they seemed unaffected and they were all eating the same food and quaffing from the same wine jug. But there was definitely something wrong, he had never felt...what was the word he was seeking? Yes...empty. His stomach was aching and his head echoing. Yes, empty was definitely the feeling, he placed his knife and fork at the side of his plate, his appetite gone. He drank from his goblet again; at least the wine was very good the monk had an excellent vineyard even if it had been neglected this year. And then he felt guilty...was acknowledging that fact being traitorous to his friend?

Brother Dyfrig carried on eating, waiting for the inevitable. Before his guests' arrival, he had immersed the talisman in the jug of wine they were all drinking. His master had assured him that neither he nor anyone else would be affected in any way—he'd needed the reassurance, he'd be drinking the same wine. But suddenly he was afraid again. Had the immersion been too long? The wizard would lose all his magical powers almost immediately but would it be for good? Would they return in time—if not he'd join the other monks, a fate too horrible to contemplate.

The narcotic gel coating the cutlery used by the seneschal and the Montetor was undetectable to anyone's sight except the wizard's. But the wizard was otherwise occupied, totally immersed within himself. The two clan leaders would shortly fall into a deep sleep that would last until the following afternoon when they would awake with a raging headache...in the cages.

They were all fools, falling for the oldest trick in the world! Had they never been told that they should not imbibe food or drink offered by an enemy? Or were they relying on the wizard's powers too much? It would teach them a lesson although too late, after the rites of the next evening they would have no need to worry ever again. Never trust a wizard's powers of detecting poison, especially a powerless wizard. The abbot snorted to cover a laugh, he was enjoying himself!

A little later, concealed by the night, the unconscious Lodovico Portolan and Bazyli Montetor, and the un-minded, powerless Lord Tragen were carried through the oratory and down into the underground passageway behind the altar. There they were incarcerated in the dungeons at the cavern's north end.

'Ugh!' moaned Augusta for the fortieth or fiftieth time, 'this place really does stink. I smell abominable,' and she wrinkled her nose in disgust.

Returning to the cove Leonid had led them along the path through the rocks, the surf soaking them as they slipped and stumbled to the outfall.

The sewer had been hewn out of solid rock by hand, by men using chisels to enlarge an ancient pipe formed at the eruption of the volcano. At intervals the roof dipped very low and the party had to bend almost double, their noses just above the surface of the excrement. Gagging was endemic. But more often than not they could walk upright. Although the whole stretch of the sewer was narrow, allowing access for walking in single file only, occasionally two or three could walk abreast. But the atmosphere was horrendous, typhoid a living menace in every breath. And Thaddeus' fears were confirmed...there were no rats, the only movement that of the slow flowing sludge against their shins, the only sound their laboured breathing.

'Can you see us, Anders?' Beatrix asked.

'No, not now...I might be able to if you increased your light, but you dare not there may be guards at the other end.'

'I know...I'm scared the abbot may detect me as it is. It'll be a wonder if he hasn't already discovered Augusta's magic in the woods.'

'He might have for all we know,' said Augusta.

'I don't think we need worry, Tragen's staff is still far stronger than any magic we could ever use...it's still hiding us. Can you hear us all right, Anders?' Aidan asked.

'Aye...I'm answering you, aren't I?'

'Then keep your ears open more, if you can't see any sentries, you may be able to hear them instead.'

'I can't hear anything if you keep talking.'

'Shut up, you two, don't you dare start arguing again I'm frightened enough as it is,' moaned Beatrix.

'Leonid, have you any idea how far we've come. Surely we must have passed beneath the oratory by now?' Janne asked, trudging almost knee deep through the stream. 'And this flow seems too large for a mere monastery.'

'By my reckoning we passed below the monastery half an hour ago. We are now approaching the central fissure of the volcano; this sewer probably has its origins there.'

'Then we'd all best keep quiet, we don't wish another encounter with monks, especially in this foul place,' ordered Marcus.

'Agh!' Aidan shouted, floundering; Marcus' words had reawakened memories of the man he'd left behind unhealed and he lost his footing on something within the stream. 'I've stepped on...agh!' There was a loud splash as Aidan slipped and fell forward, instinctively flinging his arms out to save himself falling head first into the foulness. Nevertheless, it splattered his face and his lower body disappeared below the surface, he struggled up with the aid of Thaddeus. 'By the Gods, what's this?'

Beatrix came forward, the little light she was emitting now flooding around them all. They peered closely at what was in his hands. Thaddeus burst out laughing, the look of horror on Aidan's face bringing the first light moment they had enjoyed all day.

'Shite, Aidan, you are holding...'

'Enough, Thaddeus, we can see what he has. Throw it away, Aidan, don't just stand there,' said Beatrix absolutely disgusted when Augusta joined Thaddeus in laughing uproariously.

Aidan turned to his princess, now doubled up holding her sides, he held out a dirty hand to her. 'Come, Augusta, hold my hand as we walk,' and saying that he grabbed her and pulled her to him. And with his sludge splattered face inches from hers, he looked at her lips. 'Or do you want me to kiss you...this time?' He laughed quickly, suddenly embarrassed he released her.

'Let us keep silence now, we are too near the end for mirth,' warned Leonid.

They turned and followed him, Aidan cleaning his filthy hands on his stinking britches. Beatrix, walking in silence alongside her mistress, was shocked at what Aidan had suggested.

Augusta's emotions were in turmoil—she nearly had kissed him. She had wanted him to kiss her despite the slime on his face. She stared at Aidan's back as he plodded through the murky, vile-smelling, never-ending tunnel, wondering at her feelings for him. She was going to have to be very careful; her fondness for him was growing and she wasn't too sure where it would lead.

The dungeons on Sanctity were vast. A series of iron barred cages of differing sizes, erected in a series of natural caverns on either side of a corridor stretching far back into a very long tunnel running beneath the extinct volcano. The only entrance/exit was at the corridor's southern end, leading into the ceremonial chamber. An open sewer ran to one side of the central corridor with short runnels leading from each cage. There was very little light and what was available streamed through the door from the chamber and from the occasional torch placed in an iron bracket, these scattered at haphazard intervals along the passage.

The floors of the cages were of bare, cold rock, strewn with dirty, wet straw, the dampness of the covering a result of the cold, the vileness of the primitive ablutions, disease and utter despair.

Within the larger open grilled cages were imprisoned over two hundred men, women and children transferred over time from the barracoons on the wharf when replacements had been needed. These slaves had been drugged into submission. The narcotic's main aim, to keep the slaves under control as they chiselled at the edges of the great cleft in the floor to reveal the black rock emitting the freezing black fog and the stench of brimstone.

In a smaller cage near the door, the twelve members of the last Quota from Griffin were held, these had also been narcotized and all but one lay comatose on the filthy straw—Leash lay with his eyes open, watching.

Opposite Leash's cage were another two cells, the inner one held Lodovico Portolan and Bazyli Montetor, both fast asleep on the foul bedding. The other held Tragen, sitting with his back against the rock wall, still searching his emptiness.

The darkness was grossly oppressive. Light did not extend into the far reaches of the cages, and this lack seemed to enhance the dreadful sounds within…the heavy breathing of slaves either sleeping fast or lying in a stupor and young children whimpering in their nightmares. All of them waiting, knowing their dreadful fate.

Their slavery was about to end. There was to be no more digging, all the black rock within the basin had been exposed and its sublimation into freezing fog continued now unrestricted, although slow. They resigned themselves to becoming sacrificial offerings.

Brother Dyfrig stepped through the iron-barred gate into the passageway. Holding a nosegay to his face, the smell overpowering even for him, he strode to the cage holding the wizard. He smiled his satisfaction, Tragen was muttering quietly to himself, oblivious of all around him. The abbot stepped to the side and gazed in at the seneschal and the ironmaster, this time he chuckled out loud, he so hated these two.

All his life he had been frightened in one way or another. The son of a whore and an unknown courtier at the Emperor of Drakka's court, Dyfrig had fought himself free of the penury of the gutters. He had learned the hard way to survive, thieving becoming second nature, avoiding the authorities an art.

He had taken a place at the monastery on Sanctity to escape the retribution of a justice system that wanted to hang, draw and quarter him for the vile murders of seven whores and their various high-ranking customers. He had set fire to the whorehouse, in which he'd been reared as a child, with the express purpose of obliterating his mother from the face of the earth—he hadn't cared about the others inhabiting the house at the time.

Hiding here in Tarria's monastery had been a dark blessing in disguise. Two years into his sojourn he had needed to conceal himself temporarily from the prying eyes of his seniors…he had just stolen the purse of a rich supplicant at the monastery.

The great chamber and its terrible secret had been discovered by Tarria's disciples in the very early years of settling on Sanctity. But they had abandoned the cavern because of the dread feelings encountered from contact with the black mist dribbling slowly from the fissure running across the floor.

He had wandered into the partially excavated and long abandoned tunnel leading into the very heart of the volcano, twenty years ago. Here he discovered the crevice emitting its cloud of black vapour. An overpowering lust took control and he sat at its crumbling edge staring into its black depths. Later, he knew not when, he had felt an irresistible urge to plunge his hands into the mist. He did not remember exactly what happened next, but he had fallen asleep and dreamed of power—endless supremacy, a vision to satisfy his yearning for dominance over his fellows.

When he'd woken, his master was with him, appearing from whence Dyfrig did not know or care. But in later years Dyfrig had come to realize that he must have pulled his master from the fissure.

The black-robed man exuded enormous power from every pore in his body, and he made Dyfrig an offer he could not refuse. It wasn't long before Dyfrig was elected abbot at the sudden demise of his predecessor.

And from that day, Dyfrig worked diligently to achieve both his and his master's aims. But he still lived with unending fear.

He was mortally afraid of failing his master whose retribution was always horrific. And then he'd been frightened of the raw hatred exuded by these two clan leaders. But although he'd always been able to best the seneschal by using threats against the hostages, and humiliating the Montetor gave him a sense of satisfaction like no other, he'd always exercised extreme care when dealing with both Griffins. And it galled him beyond measure that they would not bow down to him, acknowledge he was the better.

He hated them for it. But now he never needed to fear them again for his master was about to ensure his servant's freedom from all fear.

Leash watched, afraid now.

His fear had started on the barque, imprisoned with the rest of the Quota below decks in the dark hold. The terror had not suited his demon and it stirred within him—its anxiety growing stronger.

But his guardian also grew stronger, she of his safe dream. He almost saw her many times, even though his demon fought against his recollections…for Leash could only come near her when he slept. He smiled, she always smelled of flowers—she said they were for him.

Leash could never forget, though, how he lost her.

Leash stared through slitted eyes at his long-time enemy imprisoned across from him, Tragen, still sitting upright against the wall almost comatose, his staff alongside him. Leash frowned, why did the old man not move or lift his head?

The wizard was obsessed with his feeling of emptiness, nothing else around him registered; he was looking inwards, the feelings engendered dragging him further into confusion. He did not know where he was, had no memory of being brought to the cages and had completely forgotten everyone.

Brother Dyfrig turned and looked in at his Quota. Leash, pretending sleep wanted to hide from the wizard, but at the same time needed to study the monk. This man who had succeeded in capturing Leash's enemy—overpowering the wizard when no-one else could, had to be very potent, but strangely Leash could not sense magic in the man. Only there was something here he could not fathom. It was in the very air he breathed, it scared the pants off him. But there was something else as well and it made his demon smile despite his trepidation—blood.

Brother Dyfrig, his examination of the Quota completed, beckoned to others standing silently at the gate and they followed him deeper into the passageway.

'There is a ladder in the wall,' said Leonid looking upwards at a trapdoor dripping moisture, another man's height above him.

They had arrived at the only purpose-built exit point they had discovered in the sewer. There could have been one farther along but all agreed, enough was enough, all were now suffering headaches.

Janne pushed past. 'I'll go first, Leonid you last. At the first sign of trouble...' and he stared at Aidan a moment, wondering if he'd take heed, 'at the first sign, promise me you'll all jump back down here and flee to the outfall.'

'I'll promise you this, Marcus. I will not kill and I will not use my magic unless you and any of my friends are in imminent danger of death. But I will seek my master he is in grave danger and he doesn't know it. I cannot contact him even with mindmeld for some reason, something has already happened to him. We four,' he didn't need to indicate his friends, 'can all feel the Darkness and know it is very close by. My master, the seneschal and the Montetor have never felt its presence and therefore do not know how near they are to damnation and...and the One. So please, let us climb out of this hell-hole and go and find them.' Aidan glowered through the grime on his face, determination in every muscle of his body.

And Leonid, the last to enter the abbot's prison, found all his new found friends surrounded by armed monks. Each had a short stabbing spear pressing against his or her throat and each had been taken too swiftly to even think of mindmelding a warning. They had exited the sewer at the deepest end of a very long passageway between rows of cages, the light at the other end showing them where the Abbot of Sanctity had entered from the chamber.

Brother Dyfrig, lowering his nosegay, was highly amused. 'Well what have we here, Marshal Janne? Could this lad possibly be the simpleton born to Portolan?' he smiled when the boy sneered, 'I do believe it is.'

He turned to Janne whose arms were pinned behind his back, a spear at his throat. 'Did you really think we would leave our underground entrance unguarded, smelly though it is?' he chuckled, mirthlessly, 'these others, who are they?'

444

'Just friends of Thaddeus,' Marcus said contemptuously, 'if you know what friends are!'

'Tut-tut, Janne, you must learn to show respect,' he nodded quickly and an armed monk hit Janne in the groin. Brother Dyfrig laughingly examined each captive in turn as Marcus doubled up in pain. Dismissing Aidan, Augusta and Beatrix as nonentities; he halted amazed in front of Leonid.

'My, my, a Green Man, would you believe it? And where have you been all these hundreds of years?'

'On Griffin Island,' answered Leonid, his expression divulging nothing of his fear.

'Where on Griffin Island?'

'Beneath it.'

Startled, Brother Dyfrig continued. 'Are there many more of you? Not that it matters,' he waved his hand dismissively, 'the dawn now rises on Midsummer's Eve, my master will welcome you all. Your added deaths will greatly please him.'

'You have a master, Brother Dyfrig, who is he?' Aidan asked, speculating on whether it was the man in red of his visions.

'Never mind, boy, you'll find out soon enough. Just pray that he slays you quickly. Throw them all in with the seneschal, the simpleton might as well spend his last hours on this earth with his father,' he ordered.

Walking off slowly he mulled over the appearance of a green man at this time. Could he be of any significance? There was definitely something about the Green People, though, and it niggled for a moment in the back of his mind. He mentally shrugged deciding not to trouble his master with the news just yet.

At first sight of the cell Thaddeus' heart nearly stopped on seeing his father prone on the floor of the cage. Rushing to the door he was shouting and attempting to pull it open before a monk had withdrawn the heavy bolt.

Heeding the uproar, Brother Dyfrig retraced his steps a little and watched the reunion, the distress on the boy's face and the rage in Janne's, giving him cause to gloat.

Thaddeus ran to the bodies and fell to the floor, cradling his father's head he looked up at the abbot. 'If you have killed him monk I will make sure you rot in hell!'

Brother Dyfrig surprised that the boy dared deliver such a threat, paled slightly. He knew all about hell. Recovering quickly, he looked at the others clustered around the supine forms of the two clan leaders.

'Do not worry, he is not dead yet. He is an invited guest at the celebration of Midsummer's Eve,' and Brother Dyfrig again laughed. 'My master wishes him to attend the ceremony alive and well so that all may enjoy his death—and yours, of course.'

'Who is your master?' Aidan asked again, staring intently at the mad monk, a very bad feeling growing in his stomach, his head pounding with growing tension, he could not read this monk's mind although he had a soul.

Brother Dyfrig suddenly unnerved laughed a little uncertainly and walked away without answering.

When all the monks had disappeared through the dungeon gate, slamming it loudly behind them, Aidan knelt and examined both men.

'They're all right they've been given a sleeping draught, they'll awake before long.'

'Aidan,' called Beatrix from behind him, peering into the murky cage next door, 'Aidan,' she repeated, very apprehensive. 'Look!'

'What?' he turned from the figures on the floor to look where she was staring. Tragen could just be seen in the dark, propped against the opposite wall, his eyes closed, his staff on the floor beside him.

'Master!' Aidan shouted frantically, and panicking he scrabbled from the floor and ran into the unseen bars between them, nearly knocking himself out. 'Master, what's wrong? Answer me,' in his frenzy, he was screaming and rubbing his forehead. 'What have they done to you?'

Leonid, coming up behind, calmed him. Placing his hands on his shoulders, he spoke quietly near Aidan's ear. 'My friend, he is alive, let us rouse the others to ascertain the reason for this malady. Come; help us wake them.'

Aidan roughly dried his eyes with a stinking dirty sleeve. 'Let me at them, Thaddeus.' Speaking more sharply than he intended, he burst into tears again. 'I'm sorry Thad, I'm sorry; I didn't mean to sound like that.'

'Oh, Aidan, Aidan...' Beatrix whispered desolately.

Within moments of Aidan touching their heads, both Lodovico and Bazyli were awake and sitting up.

'All I recollect is sitting down to dinner and all of us eating in silence,' said Lodovico, grasping his son and pulling him to the floor beside him, more concerned at the moment for Thaddeus. 'Thad, are you all right? How did you get here? How did he capture you?'

'We'll tell you later,' interrupted Aidan, impatient. 'There's nothing at all you can tell us about what's happened to him?'

'Nothing, I remember he ceased eating before the rest of us, but that's all I know,' said Bazyli, holding his head, despite Aidan's help, the appalling smell in the cage was giving him a raging headache. He stared up at Aidan, this boy the riddle he'd heard so much about and he looked from one to the other. If these were really four young wizards maybe the situation wasn't so bad after all. And then he noticed Aidan examining his scar.

'Remind me later, Excellency, I can get rid you of that,' healing distracting his hysteria, he traced his finger along Bazyli's scar from eye to mouth, only the second person ever allowed to do so.

Bazyli's mouth fell open in astonishment. 'You are the one Cornelia spoke of, the healer of wounds?'

'And other things,' said Augusta, 'he can't do it now for fear of detection. Waking you took small magic, getting rid of your scar may take somewhat more.'

'And we do not want the abbot to know we are wizards, yet,' whispered Beatrix.

'Augusta, I need you to bring Tragen near me, I have to place my hands on him. Can you do that? If you move him slowly, a little each time, you'll keep your power small. Will you try, please?' Aidan implored, barely controlling himself.

Leash sitting unnoticed had shuffled forward a little way to hear and observe more clearly. Wide awake and very alert, his exceptional hearing had picked up every word uttered by his enemies. He was puzzled, wondering if his hearing had misled him, all four of them wizards? Impossible, if that had been the case why hadn't they used magic at the catacombs. He smiled; the girl had also said that they did not want the abbot apprised yet. That was something to keep up his sleeve.

Watching Aidan and Augusta, Leash's demon was morbidly fascinated and deathly afraid. Wizards were the only living humans he needed to be wary of, the only ones who could hurt him for certain. But he needed to see what they were going to do next. And he stared hard, not taking his eyes from him he studied Aidan closely, and despite the demon something stirred in Leash's head—the boy reminded him of someone. But the memory was gone and suddenly its loss overpowered him. Leash curled up in a ball, bringing his head down to his knees. He fell on his side and lay against the wall as his demon and his guardian fought for control.

Thaddeus, sitting next to his father, watched Augusta, deep concentration etching heavy lines in her hard expression. He couldn't help noticing that her black hair was stinking dirty and sticking to her face, and he had the absurd notion that if Augusta could see herself in a mirror now, she'd probably scream at the state she was in. She was pretty though, through the grime on her face he could see what Aidan saw in her and butterflies stirred in his own gut.

Bazyli, a radiant smile on his face, was in a world of his own. Aidan's promise coming out of the blue had electrified him. And although Bazyli's eyes were on Tragen, his thoughts most definitely were not. His scar had been a terrible disability, blighting his life for so long now, that the thought of being without it was awe-inspiring. He rubbed it hard, unbeknownst to him pulling the corner of his mouth into an even crueller sneer. He stared over at the wizard's boy, his thoughts in turmoil; the boy's vow meant deliverance from loneliness. And if for no other reason he had to get the boy free somehow, he was not going to let him die.

Lodovico's feelings were also chaotic. Frightened silly for his son he watched his son's very powerful friends, and thought of Anders unbelievably in the afterlife watching over them all. He still found it difficult to believe that these three young strangers had brought him his heart's desire—and given love and friendship to his son. His heart bled at Aidan's abject despair and he made a silent vow. Thaddeus and his friends would escape even if it meant his own death.

Marcus standing against the bars at the front of the cage, also watched, his hand on his empty scabbard. He did not remember being disarmed and it shamed him. The first time in his life that he had been taken captive and the only time he had lost his weapons. He tried to shrug off the feeling that he was out of his depth, an emotion that was confirmed at the implausible sight before his eyes. Tragen was floating across the floor of his cell towards them. He smiled wryly, if these wizards could do something as outlandish as this then surely he must aid their escape, must ensure their survival whatever the cost to him personally.

Leonid, on the other hand, was fully conversant with magic although his people practised a different sort to this of Augusta's. The

Green People's skill harnessed the four elements of nature—earth, air, fire and water—he'd never seen magic of the mind as Augusta's was, but then, of course, he'd never known of Aidan's either—magic born of healing. He was utterly fascinated and tried to fathom exactly how she was creating it, but it was so alien to him he knew he'd have to study the magic for years before even comprehending a little of it. He glanced at Thaddeus and Beatrix as the two walked over and put their hands on the shoulders of their friends. Leonid wondered if Anders was also close by, another fact he couldn't understand. How could anyone speak with the dead? And then he thought back nearly a thousand years, wasn't the spectre who spoke the prophecy to Findar also dead? But one thing he knew for certain, these four had to get out of here, their mission was to fulfil Findar's prophecy, his to aid them in that. So for the first time in his life, Leonid turned his thoughts to using his magic to kill even if he killed himself in the process.

Augusta concentrated on Tragen. Very tense, she shuffled closer to Aidan, taking comfort from the pressure of his body against hers. But because of the disgusting conditions in which she found herself she couldn't seem to focus fully even though she felt the hands of Beatrix and Thaddeus on her. It was only when she sensed Anders near as well that she could centre her whole attention on the wizard.

Tragen, who had not moved a muscle since he had been placed in his cage, was still looking inward, the desolation possessing him to the exclusion of all else. He was seeking his loss, but being empty he did not know what he was looking for. Blissfully unaware of his surroundings, he did not flinch as he drifted across his cage. Ever so gently, sweat breaking out on her forehead and holding Aidan's grimy hands for support, she managed to levitate the wizard and float him, yard by yard, across his cage and lower him to the ground face to face with Aidan.

'Thank you, Augusta, you really are a wonderful wizard, you know,' he hugged her quickly.

Stretching his hands through the bars he held his master's head very gingerly, but moments later he gasped and withdrew sharply.

'What is it, Aidan?' Augusta asked.

'I don't understand, his mind seems to be searching...for his mind!'

'What do you mean?' Lodovico asked, getting to his feet.

'His mind is there but...he's all confused. Wait!'

Aidan replaced his hands on Tragen's head and poured heat into the man he loved as a father. Aidan felt utterly at peace with Tragen however much the older wizard exasperated him, even though he was more often than not being reprimanded by him. At the death of his mother, Aidan had been lost in the world. His mother had been the first to keep him safe. When she'd died he'd been set adrift not knowing how to control his power. Although healing was intrinsically good magic, everything in life had an opposite. His magic could also harm as he'd proved when he'd made Augusta's nose bleed. Tragen had rescued him from corruption.

Aidan strived until the sweat broke from every pore in his body, whatever had caused this in his master had been strong beyond anything Aidan had ever known.

And eventually Tragen felt him in his emptiness. The heat from Aidan's hands was the first outside influence to register in his head since dinner the previous evening. Tragen felt more and more of the heat until, distracted from searching inwards, he finally recognized his boy's healing.

'Aidan…is that you?' he moaned, raising his head, his eyes still closed.

'Master,' Aidan said, tears making runnels down his face. 'Master, it's me, open your eyes…look at me…please,' he begged.

'Oh, my boy, it really is you.'

The wizard struggling awake from his bewitched state, smiled forlornly at his son, his physical senses finally returning. He frowned, suddenly wrinkling his nose. 'God, Aidan, you stink,' and overcome with relief and affection the old man and the young boy clung to each other through the bars.

'What happened, Tragen, can you tell us?' asked the seneschal his senses confounded at what he'd just witnessed. 'The monk seems to have drugged us to make us sleep, and then thrown us all in here. He fully intends to kill us.'

'Where exactly are we?'

'We are imprisoned within Sanctity's crater,' answered Leonid.

'I'm sorry, my friends, I should have detected the poison, I usually can in an instant. The only reason I can give for my failure is that damned artefact the abbot has on his person. I…' his voice faltered, his face instantly drained of any colour and he stared bewildered at Aidan.

'What is it?' Aidan asked, puzzled. Tragen was trembling from head to toe. 'What's wrong, I can't feel any illness in you?'

Tragen, petrified with fright his eyes bulging, returned Aidan's stare. 'You...you cannot feel any illness in me? Can you feel any magic in me?'

'Master!' Aidan exclaimed, horrified. 'What's happened?'

'There is nothing in me—no magic, I have lost it all,' he rummaged around for his staff. Picking it up, he examined each and every rune, turning the stave repeatedly in his hands, frantic. 'Disappeared...gone...gone,' and he paused for a moment. 'The magic has been taken from me and from my staff, I...I am powerless!'

Shock spread tentacles like an octopus.

Thirty-six

Aidan's shock drove ice down his spine; he had never known anyone lose their magic. Suddenly a horrible thought rose to stick knives in his chest.

'Did I do it? Did I do it healing you?'

Tragen looked up, not understanding at first. 'What?'

'I healed you...did I take your magic the same time?'

'Oh no, it was not you, my boy,' he grasped Aidan's hands through the bars. 'No, whatever took my magic...it must have been taken last evening, probably at dinner.'

And unexpectedly, raucous, hysterical laughter erupted from across the passageway. Leash hearing every word and realizing that the hated staff had lost its powers, that it could no longer harm him, was ecstatic.

'At last it's dead, your staff is useless! You can't hurt me anymore, wizard...you can't,' he shouted, laughing long and loud.

'Why would Lord Tragen want to hurt you?' Bazyli asked. 'You are destined to die at the hands of the abbot; there's no need to harm you more.'

Leash, his face manic, ignored the Montetor and shouted to the guards standing just outside the entrance to the dungeon.

'Let me out, let me at the wizard! I want to kill him, I must!' And this time it was not his demon speaking, this was pure Leash, his hatred almost physical, pounding across the narrow passageway. Leash stretched his arms through the bars of his cage, his long fingers clawing for Tragen's neck, his eyes starting from his head.

Tragen, his anxiety momentarily thrust aside, instinctively shuffled backwards away from Leash's fingers although there was no way the sailor could reach him.

'Why do you want to kill me? Your sentence of death was ratified by Captain Locklear for the murder of Anders. It has nothing to do with me, although I believe your fate to be thoroughly deserved.'

'You don't recognize me, wizard, do you?' Leash panted almost out of his mind, his demon and his guardian buried deep within unable to surface through his incandescent rage. 'But I knew you straight away, oh yes! And that damned staff that ruined my life, condemned me to solitude and misery—gave me over to my demon!'

452

Leash slid down the bars to kneel on the filthy floor. Not taking his wild eyes from the wizard he spoke with a cool determination, the terror of the promise sending shivers down young backs.

'When we are taken from this cage, wizard, I will put my hands around your neck and you will pray that I kill you quickly!'

And Aidan, catching Leash's eye, recognized him for what he was—and felt his pain. 'You forget, Leash, that I am a wizard. I won't allow you to hurt my master.'

Leash returning Aidan's gaze became afraid again, the boy's eyes pierced his brain and he knew that he had discovered the nature of his infection. He had forgotten the boy could still use his powers to hurt him, perhaps kill—if he could be slain. Leash was not prepared to risk finding that out yet. He was not yet ready for death; he wanted to witness the killing of the old wizard first.

But he was unable to break eye contact with Aidan.

'Ask him about me,' said Anders, a silent listener to the altercation. Frustrated at his inability to help his friends he stared at the wall of colours attempting to make sense of the ever-changing dark shapes in the depth of the blackness before his eyes. Leash's bewildering words set him trembling.

'Why did you kill Anders, he had never harmed you?' Beatrix asked.

Leash tore his eyes from Aidan, her question quieting his hysteria. He moaned softly through tightly closed lips, his conscience stirred recalling the cabin boy's fate. He'd gazed disbelievingly as Anders disappeared below the surface of the water in the hold, his torso crushed beneath the weight of the broken crate, his plans coming to naught again.

And then the mania reappeared in his eyes.

'It was an accident. I followed both of them for ages below me in that hold...never took my eyes off them until I had to! I couldn't resist it. It was my best chance to hurt the wizard—kill his boy! It was going to be so easy,' and Leash shouted again, full of hate. 'I looked away from them for one second and they change places. I didn't mean to kill the cabin boy. I wanted to kill him!' He raged, spittle dripping down his chin, he pointed a shaking finger at Aidan.

A black slave watched from the next cage, his face a picture of astonishment...and sorrow.

The gate of the dungeon clanged open on rusty hinges and Brother Dyfrig strode in. Leash ceased his ranting and scurried to the back of his cage.

'What is this noise? Why are you in conflict with each other, surely you should all be making peace with your Gods?'

Brother Dyfrig stared in at the clan leaders through the bars of their cage, cold, gel-like moisture clinging in small droplets to the ironwork. 'Awake already, I am surprised, I must have a word with that slave; he can't have mixed enough of the powder in the solvent. I'd have him test the next lot himself but there's no longer a need for more. Still you are out of harm's way in there,' and he chuckled.

'Where is my sister, monk? Is she safe?' demanded Bazyli hating the abbot with an intensity only rivalled by that of the seneschal.

'Oh, my handsome one, you will be with her before long,' and he laughed again, 'although I do not suppose either of you will be safe.'

'What do you mean?' Lodovico Portolan asked, his sudden fear for his brother making his jowls tremble.

'You don't honestly believe that they are still alive, do you?' And seeing the look of horror and shock on their faces, he again chuckled. 'The Portolan and his wife were sacrificed on their first night with us. They are now happily…but perhaps that's the wrong word…unhappily residing with my God. He is enjoying them.'

Bazyli Montetor and Lodovico Portolan exploded, both making a rush for the abbot, the rusty bars bending slightly in their attempt to reach him, rage and the shocking revelation rendering them speechless.

The others looked on, profound disbelief on their faces as the full import of the abbot's words fell on them.

'I will leave you now, to contemplate your reunion with them at this evening's ceremony. I do hope you die as slowly as they, it was so…interesting!' and the abbot strode off laughing.

'My friends, I am so sorry…so very, very sorry,' said Tragen breaking the appalling silence.

Janne, shocked beyond belief, stared at his friend. 'I will kill him, Lodovico, the first chance I have, that man will die.'

'No!' shouted Aidan. 'You kill and you'll harm yourself and become like him.'

'What do you mean?' Leonid asked, standing behind Janne, utterly revolted at his captor's words.

'Listen to me, all of you,' said Aidan, and the desperation in his voice forced them to take heed. Bazyli, stepping away from the bars of the cage, turned and stared at him unseeingly through his grief, his scar shining livid in the low lantern light. Lodovico, his head bowed in abject desolation, dropped to the floor next to his son.

'Killing can satisfy your desires only if you are a killer. Leash is a killer, but he can't help it, it's not his fault.' Leash came forward in his cage at the words. 'You, Excellency,' he stared at Bazyli, 'are not, and neither are you, Seneschal. You both have the capacity for great love, and this already turns you away from needless slaughter.' Aidan turned to Augusta and Beatrix and held their hands tightly, 'I have already spoken of this to the others. Denying a soul, any soul, the right to life is wrong!'

The atmosphere of great terror in the miserably dingy dungeon seemed to add strength and an undeniable truth to his words. And his highly passionate feelings expressed with the earnestness of knowledge far beyond his years, went a long way to convincing them—but not completely. Their thoughts turning inwards as he continued, silence from across the passage indicating that the Quota and the re-awakening slaves were also hanging on his words.

'Life is a precious period of intensive learning. To complete its lessons you must live your allotted span before resting in Paradise and then returning later to learn more.'

'You mean that we live more than one life?' Lodovico asked, sceptical. Staring at the young wizard, he marvelled at the boy's grasp of matters ethereal, way beyond the knowledge of any philosopher in any Hall of Wisdom. But was he right?

And as if he read his mind, Leonid answered. 'Aye, Seneschal, in that he is correct. We of the Green People have always known it.'

'To have a better chance of returning and living another life, your soul must be whole and unharmed as much as possible. Each killing fades your spirit. You must care for your own soul's well-being, and the souls of others.' Aidan said no more, knowing if he did he'd lose them.

'But I've already killed, many times,' said Janne, troubled. 'Does that mean I am condemned?'

'Did you kill with hate in your heart?'

'I don't believe so…at least, not every time.'

'Then your soul will recover in Paradise, but you will not move forward to attain a higher level of existence until you have returned to re-learn the same lessons of this life.'

'What of the abbot, Aidan, will he come back?' Augusta asked.

'Brother Dyfrig is a man of pure hate, pure ambition, I think he's too far gone; there is no goodness left in him. He cannot recover, will never enter Paradise, he'll be unable to live another life.'

'And Leash, Aidan, what of him?' Beatrix asked as Leash listening intently, held his breath.

'Poor Leash is dreadfully ill...mentally and physically, although he fights it every desperate waking moment. He is a human that has been infected with the vampyrus demon.'

'What? But...' Beatrix astounded stared at Leash, totally lost for words.

Tragen looked up startled, his eyes roved between Aidan and Leash and he suddenly remembered where he'd first met the second helmsman of the Grim.

As the others stared across the passageway, Aidan continued with his diagnosis. 'He may recover in Paradise if he can get there, I don't know. The demon hasn't yet destroyed him completely—he continues to fight it. He may have enough integrity remaining to get through the Light it depends on how long he can continue fighting. I hope for his sake he never gives up. The vampyrus is eating away at him and if it wins all of his humanity will disappear. And Leash, God help him, will vanish forever from Life but won't be able to die until the vampyrus desires another body.'

Beatrix stared at Leash, the one who had killed the boy she loved. And at the terrible existence facing him was overcome with sorrow. How could she continue to hate and blame him for the actions of a demon he had no way of controlling? But she could only see Leash, not his demon. Forgiveness was not going to be easy.

Aidan continued to study the vampyrus, overwhelmed with grief for the man who was ceasing to be Leash. He'd realized what he was seeing when Leash had been screaming imprecations against Tragen. But it was a strange vision. Studying the real Leash he had somehow recognized the real man—he was familiar, a man from Aidan's past. But Aidan could not recall him. What he could see was the demon struggling to gain mastery within him and he mourned because he did not know how to banish it.

But there was someone else behind Leash's eyes—and just a trace of an aroma. He shook his head, it couldn't be he was imagining things; it was totally out of place. But it smelled of lavender.

Aidan averted his eyes, again feeling as bereft as he had on the mountainside above when he'd abandoned the monk with the broken leg. He sighed and turned to his master to seek his advice...and staggered. Releasing the girls' hands, he grasped the wizard's through the bars.

'Oh, Master! Oh, no...no...no!' Aidan cupped Tragen's face in his hands, he gulped, his words sounding strangled.

'Oh, my boy...is it true, this premonition I have?' Tragen asked, desperately.

'Oh, Master!' And Aidan, his face whiter than white, clasped his mentor's hands to his face. 'Don't be afraid, Master, but I...' Aidan stopped, tears streaming down his face as he frantically brushed the hair from Tragen's eyes.

Tragen trembling deeply stroked Aidan's cheeks, drying the boy's tears with his fingers. 'Please, my boy, do not weep,' the wizard agonizingly attempted comfort where none could be given. 'My Aidan, you have brought so much pleasure and love into my life, I...'

'Oh, Master, first Anders and now you, how will I bear it?'

'As you told Anders, so you can tell me. Will I be safe?'

'Aye, but...'

'Hush, my boy, hush now.'

'What's going on? What do you mean, Tragen? I have had enough of riddles,' said Bazyli, frowning.

'My son—he sees my impending death!'

Augusta and Beatrix gasped and reached for each other, neither wanting to believe their ears.

Aidan spoke again, though his voice shook. 'Anders...Anders are you there?'

'Aye, Aidan.'

'You look out for him...let no harm come to him,' and then he begged, 'please?'

'You know I will,' Anders had once wondered if ghosts could cry; now he knew as tears ran down his face.

'I don't understand, how can you be so sure?' Lodovico asked.

'I have always been able to see death, Seneschal,' he said quietly, still grasping his father's hands, for he would always regard Tragen as such. 'You may ask how I know so much of the afterlife…but I don't remember not knowing, perhaps my mother taught it to me. She did have a little lore.'

'Your mother, you have not mentioned her in years,' said Tragen, his concern for his boy taking the place of his black despair. 'Who knows, perhaps I'll meet her in Paradise! Tell me more of her, what was she like?'

Without warning an overwhelming need to remember her, to speak of her, gripped Aidan, the smell of lavender on Leash bringing her back. And for the first time in years he recalled her face instantly, her smooth skin, hazel eyes, and white teeth behind full red lips, always smiling. Her smell and her touch quickly followed and he beamed, lost in the pleasure of her.

'What can I tell you?'

Aidan quieted and, keeping his eyes closed, settled on the floor with his knees against the bars, one arm in Augusta's, his other hand gripping Tragen's tightly. He thought back to his early childhood in Miskim Town.

'She was very, very pretty, and had the whitest teeth of anyone I ever met.'

Tragen smiled, whose mother was not pretty? But then, as his boy continued to speak, Tragen felt a stabbing in his heart.

'She was small and very thin, skinny I suppose. I remember that because I used to complain about her bony shoulder sticking in me every time she turned over in bed,' and he laughed at the memory. 'She used to hug me a lot, comb her fingers through my hair and kiss me…she was always kissing me…and holding me. And I remember the smell of lavender, she used it all the time—lavender water, she said it helped her sleep and that my father loved it. She used to throw it over me when she bathed me, and I'd pull her hair.'

Leash for some reason, held his breath, listening to every word, every nuance, not moving a muscle.

'She had lovely hair, so very long, it used to cover my face whenever she wrapped me in the blanket before putting me to bed,' he chuckled again, the memories coming thick and fast, he had loved his mother very much, still did, of course. 'Other times she wore her hair in a braided rope, she used to pretend to whip me with it. It was very long, it hung below her waist…I used to spend hours brushing it.'

Aidan halted, suddenly realizing that Tragen was very tense. 'What is it, what's wrong? Let me speak of life with you; my time with you has been the best.'

458

Tragen shuddered; very pale he remembered everything of the incident, recalled everything of that tragic afternoon. 'What was the colour of her hair?'

'As black as jet, like mine...and very shiny. Why?'

'And it was about a year before I found you that she died?'

'Aye, Master. The mayor buried her; she had been murdered by a marauder.'

'Yes, Aidan, by the Gods,' and Tragen put his hands over his face, his fingers kneading a sudden blinding headache. 'She was slain by the same marauder who killed a little boy in Griffin Town a couple of nights ago...the same...the same one who killed Anders! All these years, I never realized that poor woman was your mother. She was killed by the vampyrus!'

Leash sat rigid before the bars of his cage, shocked to his very core. He couldn't believe it, didn't want to believe it. He moved closer to the front of the cage and pressed his face up against the bars, he stared intently at Aidan...the face, the eyes...again he struggled to remember, and again he keened quietly.

'You lie, boy,' he spat vehemently, 'she never had children. She would have told me...she would never have kept you from me.'

He turned and glared at Tragen. 'You remember me now, wizard, don't you?' He sniggered and then licking his lips he screamed at his enemy. 'I remember her well, I cannot ever forget her she was so...so...' he left it in the air unable to finish, tears streaming down his face. 'There was no need to stop me,' he wept, the tears flowing unashamedly down his cheeks, 'I was only feasting. I had to; she knew that, the Wanting was on me...she understood it had to be satisfied. I was nearly finished when you came along and ruined it all. You and that damned staff. You couldn't even shoot straight,' and he screamed again. 'I will kill you, wizard, kill you,' and then he looked at Aidan. 'And you...' he said maniacally, 'you lie! You were never her son! I am glad that I killed your friend. Do you hear, boy? Listen to me—it made me happy!'

Aidan stared at him, understanding for the first time, a killing rage understanding hate, but not Leash's words. Why did he think he'd lied? But the emotion was fleeting and he took his eyes from Leash and stared at his mentor silently.

Augusta rose and stood facing the vampyrus while along the passageway from Leash the small black man continued to watch and listen intently.

'Look at me Leash,' Augusta said.

And when the vampyrus turned his face to her, he became very afraid again. Augusta having the ability to affect all movement exercised it now, ruthlessly. Holding Leash upright with the power of her mind, she brought him to stand against the bars. Unable to speak or break away, he showed his terror in his bulging eyes. And everyone watched, disbelieving the scene they witnessed, equally unable to move as Augusta proceeded to carry out her retribution. Forcing the sailor to stand rigidly, she caused Leash's head to turn on his neck until his chin rested on his right shoulder. He screamed in agony when Augusta continued to turn his head, her clear intention to break his neck.

Tears ran down her face. 'My Lord Tragen may have lost his powers, Leash, I have not. You have killed my friend Anders and you have tried to kill us all. I am the Prince of Mantovar's daughter and, as such, I have the power of life and death over my father's subjects, and...'

'No, Augusta,' said Aidan, coming up behind her and putting his arms around her waist, pressing his tear-stained face into the crook of her neck. 'No, Augusta, do not harm your soul for a man who cannot help being what he is. It is the vampyrus within him that we must destroy—not Leash.'

'Oh, Aidan,' she closed her eyes for a moment, knowing that she would listen to him, whatever he said. 'What are we going to do? Why us? We are too young for all this. Why are the Gods meddling with our lives?' She swivelled in his arms and putting her arms around his neck, they hugged as if their world was coming to an end and weeping with him, they kissed each other. This time Aidan savoured the taste of her lips properly, and it brought him a kind of peace.

Leash, released from the killing stare, scrambled to the back of the cage, whimpering in his madness. His insanity, his infection, was no longer hidden and the others in the cage scrambled as far away as possible.

The black slave continued to watch, as silent as the grave.

Later that morning, when all was quiet, Aidan moved to sit in front of Bazyli Montetor. Despite the warnings of Tragen against doing it, and while the others watched entranced their terror almost forgotten for a moment, he used his magic not caring anymore if he was discovered.

460

Aidan healed the Montetor's face; the scar which ran from his eye to the corner of his mouth disappeared, leaving flesh unblemished.

'There, Excellency, if you are to meet your God this night you may now smile in a proper fashion.'

Bazyli Montetor sat motionless and silent for quite a while before daring to peer at his reflection in a bowl of water.

'Tragen, what is so special about Midsummer's Eve that this monk and his master make so much of it?' Marcus asked.

'It is one of the nights when the divide between life and death becomes so narrow that it can be breached. If you have the power the spirits of the dead will be able to walk in life!'

'Why would they want to?' Leonid asked.

Tragen, not knowing the answer, stared at the four youngsters on which so much depended.

'Aidan, all of you and Anders if he can hear me, listen to me. You five are the wizards spoken of in Elder Findar's prophecy, so…so your safety is paramount. The abbot and his master intend invoking unbelievable power tonight. To do this he needs our deaths. It is imperative that you survive to find the shadow's bane, the dragon, and continue the fight to defeat the One behind the Darkness. You have no option or all is lost, there will be no place left for those who wish to be re-born, to live again to continue the lessons of Life. You agree, Aidan?'

'It seems that way.'

'Yes…but heed me closely, it is definitely the way of things. I have been thinking these past days of the self-same question Augusta just asked. We all know without a shadow of a doubt that you are instruments in a great plan. Your destinies have been mapped out since Elder Findar spoke of the prophecy to Elder Zoran.'

He paused and stared at the numbed faces before him. Tragen was putting in words what they all knew, and it didn't help.

'Therefore, we five, Lodovico, Bazyli, Marcus, Leonid, with me, must endeavour to gain your release. We must strive to ensure that you escape to the Grim and have Captain Locklear sail to Griffin, and on. And escape you have got to, you must flee at the first possible moment and…I mean this, you are not to stop to rescue us. I suspect it will take all of our skills and abilities to distract the abbot and whoever his master proves to be. To try and save me would be pointless anyway, as you know it is here I will die. You must hide your magic for as long as possible unless it is necessary to aid your escape. If we must…if we must all die to save your lives, then we will that is our duty. You are not to fight these monks unless you have to. Do not deny us our duty…any of you. Your duty is to flee. Do you understand?'

'I understand that I am a puppet, Milord, a plaything of the Gods. And I do not like it. One way or another I will make the Gods realize that I am my own person. I will act as I think fit, not as they want me to. If I have a destiny,' and Beatrix looked at her friends, 'and my friends have theirs, then I will control my own fate, as will they. I will defy all the Gods, if needs be. My life is mine…I am my own mistress.'

'And I am with you. I did not seek life to live as others dictate,' said Thaddeus, standing with her, taking her hand in his.

Aidan and Augusta stood beside their friends, all four united to fight the Darkness—and the interfering Gods.

'And Anders is with us,' added Augusta.

Bazyli Montetor looked up from his reflection in the bowl of water, rubbing his non-existent scar, fascinated with its aftermath. He contemplated the young wizards' words and gazed at Tragen.

'Somehow,' he grimaced, 'I feel sorry for the Gods. They had better watch their backs, I think their plans are not going to go the way they want,' he paused. 'I believe these youngsters are going to give them a run for their money.'

'Talking of escape, why don't we aid their escape now instead of waiting until we enter the chamber?' Marcus Janne asked staring along the passageway to the entrance. 'I cannot see any monks about and it wouldn't take long to re-enter the sewer. It should be easy enough for them to open these cages.'

There are monks in the sewer keeping watch,' said Anders.

'I thought you couldn't see,' said Aidan.

'As time goes on I improve.'

'What is Anders saying,' Tragen asked.

'He warns of monks in the sewer. But I will not go. I won't leave you to die alone, so don't try and persuade me otherwise.'

'Aidan, my boy, your first duty now is to seek the bane, not protect me. It will be easy enough to disable the monks,' Tragen implored.

'Not as easy as you think, we…' Beatrix stopped when Tragen shouted, beginning to lose his temper, desperate to get them away.

'Why not? There are simple enough spells to confuse them, to stop them seeing you…you do not have to harm them.'

'It's not so much the monks they have to worry about, Milord. He sees us,' said Leonid interrupting.

'I don't understand…who is he?'

'I think he's the abbot's master. He watches us through the soulless ones. I have been studying them and I have seen an unnatural gleam in their eyes. One or two of my people are able to use the same technique.'

'It doesn't matter anyway, I will not leave my father here, or anyone else,' Thaddeus said, nodding his head indicating the slaves and the Quota. 'For whatever crimes these felons have committed, they do not deserve a death such as this. And the slaves,' he shuddered, 'I could never abandon them. No, I will not go.'

In the silence his words had provoked, the Montetor looked down at his spread fingers.

'Thaddeus, I have something to say to you and I call on these to witness my words,' he looked around at the curious faces turning to him. 'My twin sister was married to your father's brother and, until you were born, she was my only living relative. Now that she is no longer with us,' and his voice cracked, saying the words aloud seemed to give his loss a finality he didn't like. 'Now that she has gone, you are the only one left of my family, however distant the relationship might be. My clan know this, but have always thought you a simpleton. They have told me in no uncertain terms that after my death they will not accept a boy with no soul as their leader,' and he smiled, a new smile which did not twist his mouth into a sneer.

'But you are no longer a simpleton! We have found your soul, Thaddeus, and the little I've seen of it over these last days, you have a soul to treasure—a heart of courage and a dignity that puts many a man to shame. You are a young man any father would be proud to acknowledge. What I am getting at, Thaddeus, is this…you are also my heir.'

Thaddeus stunned, looked at his grinning father for support.

'Take this.' And the Montetor took from his middle finger the hefty gold signet ring bearing the likeness of the Griffin. 'As my heir, you will wear this, and all our clan will acknowledge you as their leader for they will understand that I have named you before my death. Lodovico, it seems that our two clans will become one when we relinquish our leadership. The Isles of Griffin will have a king at last. And I believe our people could not be in braver and better hands.'

And as Thaddeus Portolan placed the ornate ring on the middle finger of his left hand it seemed to him that for a moment it vibrated as it settled below the lowest knuckle. The ring emitted a comfort that pierced his soul, a soothing of his anxiety resulting in a wholeness of spirit that he'd never felt before—it was as if the ring had found its home. Thaddeus sensed completeness, a unity between him and the ancient artefact. And he stared at it in wonderment not understanding its purpose but knowing whatever it was it had been waiting for him.

Thirty-seven

'You had better name him now clan leader...a king without a name is no ruler.'

'What! Who said that?' Aidan asked, peering across the passageway, the voice had come from among the slaves, startling them all.

Augusta joined Aidan at the bars of their cage. 'There, he's the one who spoke.'

She indicated the small black man standing watching at the bars of his cage. He was about five feet tall, had short tightly curled black hair, an emaciated body and eyes that told of unbearable pain though he returned Augusta's look with a steady gaze.

Bazyli Montetor stared at him. 'What do you mean?'

'In my country, one acknowledged by his people to be the heir, is always re-named, the new name denoting the qualities of leadership that he will always manifest.'

'Who are you?' Aidan asked, frowning.

'Forgive me, young Master Wizard,' and the black man bowed from his waist. 'I am Mazumbai of the Brakwanna.'

'Brakwanna? On the Dark Continent? Didn't your country export brimstone and nitre to us about twenty years ago?' Lodovico asked curiously.

'So we did. You have a good memory, clan leader.'

'Not really, but I do recall using such minerals from your land in fertilizer for our re-forestation projects.'

'And such was our downfall. The abbot learned of that and brought his monks to Brakwanna to harvest slaves.'

'By the Gods, I had no idea,' exclaimed the seneschal.

'How long have you been here, Mazumbai?' Beatrix asked.

'Many years have we toiled to excavate the obscenity in the abbot's chamber, young Wizard of the Light, though it seems now that we will not be here much longer,' he smiled bitterly.

'What do you mean?' Augusta asked nervously.

'You will see, Wizard of War.'

'War?'

'Oh, yes...you are the warrior!'

Augusta paled...the idea of killing had become abhorrent to her after listening to Aidan. She started to ask another question but was interrupted by Thaddeus. 'Who is Mazumbai?'

'I am chief of the Brakwanna, Wizard of Understanding, and we are grateful for your sentiments. But if needs be you may forget us, there is nothing you can do to aid us for our fate is cast and it seems that you have a mission greater than any.'

'Hang on a minute, Thaddeus. Mazumbai you are calling us all wizard of this, wizard of that—light, war, understanding. How do you know this?' Aidan asked.

'I have certain knowledge of the auras of people; I can see what you all are by the colours you emit.'

'Then what can you see of Aidan?' Augusta asked, grasping the bars in front of her.

'Aidan?' Mazumbai stared at the boy who had passed on his gifts. 'Aidan is the Master Wizard of Life and Death!'

'I don't understand, Mazumbai,' Aidan said.

'You will.'

'And the Abbot of Sanctity...what do you see of him?' Leonid asked quietly from his place on the floor.

'The Abbot of Sanctity is a victim of his own ambition, his evil aim is unattainable and before long he will realize this, Wizard of the Elements. And you are perfectly correct in your assumption—his master does peer through the eyes of the silent ones.

'Are you going to name your heir, clan leaders? It is his rightful due.' Mazumbai gazed at Lodovico and Bazyli; raising his eyebrows, his look demanding an answer.

Tragen, the silent onlooker from the next cage, interrupted softly. 'There is only one name and title that could possibly apply to Thaddeus, my friends.'

They all looked at him; he was smiling, his eyes gleaming merrily his sombre mood lifting momentarily.

'What is that, Lord Tragen?' Thaddeus asked.

'What has the courage of a lion and the wisdom of the eagle? Who wishes to spread his wings and lay down his life to protect his people and his friends?'

They waited for him to continue until Lodovico Portolan could wait no longer. 'Yes, Tragen,' his voice aching with pride, 'oh, yes, my friend, there is only one name! What do you say, Bazyli?'

'Prince Griffin!' Bazyli intoned, softly.

'Hail, Prince Griffin of the Isles of Griffin, Wizard of Understanding,' and Mazumbai bowed to Thaddeus.

466

Thaddeus was speechless for once, he automatically returned the obeisance and as he straightened, Aidan spoke, bringing them all back to earth.

'Now all we've got to do is get him out of here to make sure he becomes King Griffin.'

'What can you tell us of the chamber out there, Mazumbai?' Beatrix asked.

'Ah, Wizard of Light, what I know can only give rise to greater despair. Perhaps it is better if I remain silent.'

'No,' Aidan broke in, 'if it's what I think it is then we need to prepare ourselves.' He stared at the little black man and asked what he feared to know. 'What do you know of the man wearing red?'

'I have seen a figure in black on several occasions…each time I wished I hadn't…' he shuddered, 'his robe ends up red!'

'Who is he?' asked Thaddeus.

'The one you refer to is a man no longer—though he is the abbot's master, the one who performs the particular sacrifices.'

'Particular sacrifices? You imply there are others?' Lodovico asked.

'The common ceremonies in which we are the sacrifices are performed by the abbot.'

'Dear God, what do you mean "common ceremonies"?' Bazyli Montetor asked. 'How are you sacrificed?'

'I will say this for now…and only this. There are two methods of sacrifice, in both the victim dies. One method takes some time to bring on death, the other…takes longer!' With that, Mazumbai turned and disappeared into the pitying crowd of his countrymen.

Later, Mazumbai watched from his place at the back wall. His heart cried out for these people, he had seen so many arrive scared and bewildered, and watched as they were tortured to death in the most horrific manner.

But the nightmare of his, and his people's, existence was also about to end despite his countrymen having slowed their work in recent months in an attempt to delay the inevitable.

The Qembana was completed.

Countless numbers of slaves had died over the years through exhaustion and acute depression whilst excavating the monstrosity. Hundreds more had been sacrificed deliberately to the black fog. But the worst profanity had been carried out at regular intervals throughout the year to those men and women of the Quota, one of whom was always locked in the cage suspended above it.

He had felt so helpless standing to the side, staring upwards at each victim. He hadn't needed to look, of course, he could have closed his eyes the black-robed one would never have noticed being too intent on his work. But Mazumbai had a conscience and a self-imposed duty. He would not leave the tortured one to die alone without some semblance of support. So he stared into the eyes of the victim as he was being tortured, and he held that victim's gaze with his own until the light left their eyes. And Mazumbai hoped that each victim received a modicum of solace in knowing that someone prayed for his soul. The only succour he could give.

Mazumbai was a solitary man although he was chief of his tribe. He was a wise man of renown throughout the Dark Continent. He lived with his thoughts as he studied life around him. He was the owner, or rather had been the Keeper of several arcane scrolls some telling of the history of his people, others relating to that of their neighbours. And he had studied them avidly, so much so that to retain his sanity in this hell on earth, each evening he recited one treatise from memory.

He had been obliged to marry when he inherited the chieftainship and Serrana had been all the wife a man could desire. Loving and caring, she had borne him two sons and a daughter; the boys long dead now—in the Qembana.

He very rarely looked into the past nowadays it was too painful, he had learned to live for the day. The memories of the monks landing on the beach in front of their village, the foolish welcome showered on them by Mazumbai's people who thought they'd come to trade for nitre. The anxiety he'd felt at reading the abbot's unhealthy aura.

And then the terrible betrayal—slavery.

Mazumbai sighed, if his gift of mindmeld had failed him that long ago morning, then his wife and daughter would also have been taken. Instead they had escaped into the interior.

Many times Mazumbai had berated himself for not reading the abbot's mind earlier. It was not until that last fateful morning, when he glimpsed the abbot step unconcernedly over a silent one who had just fallen from the yardarm to the deck of the unnamed barque, that he began to have doubts. But it had been too late for the people of his home village, and for those villages within two or three leagues of it.

Most had been brought to Sanctity. But he had managed to send out warnings to the rest of his people in other villages of Brakwanna. He prayed daily that his wife had managed to get his daughter to his younger brother's home farther down the coast.

Mazumbai looked across the passageway and sorrowed. All captives in that cage passed over from this world in a most horrendous manner. And then his heart fluttered momentarily, all the victims over the years had been ordinary people—these were wizards. And recalling the earlier conversation he'd overheard, only one wizard was known to the abbot, the unpowered one. There were others, two young men, two young women, and a green man and, if he'd heard correctly possibly another one close by who were not known to the mad monk! Could there possibly be hope for his people? He watched and he waited…and he prayed as he'd never prayed before.

The rest of the afternoon dragged. Few moved, their thoughts taking all their energy. Others walked the short length of the cages, back and forth, back and forth, unable to stay still but all equally absorbed in their thoughts.

Tragen sat next to the bars of his cage, close to him sat Aidan with Augusta's head on his shoulder. Beatrix and Thaddeus sat arm in arm alongside Lodovico, Bazyli with them. Marcus Janne stood at the bars watching the gate through which the abbot had disappeared, in the very dim light he could just make out a pile of hammers and chisels discarded to one side of the chamber. Leonid sat in a corner, his head down.

Across the passageway, the Quota all avoided Leash as best they could. Leash remained unmoving, his back against the wall, he spent the time muttering to himself the demon again in the ascendency.

Alone with their thoughts, only taking comfort from the nearness of each other the rest dwelled on what fate held in store.

Death…death was before their eyes, everywhere they looked.

Augusta and Beatrix glanced at each other both with the same thought uppermost—they were too young to die. Had Mazumbai really meant it when he said that one method of dying took a long time, the other even longer?

Thaddeus knowing the Darkness like the back of his hand, trembled, he was petrified at the thought of being trapped as a dead soul within its confines. This time he knew there'd be no escape.

Aidan could see nothing but Tragen's death, his grieving beginning before the dreaded event. He had never ever thought of life without the wizard. Tragen was old, always had been old and therefore indestructible. He'd always be there! Aidan shuddered. Whoever had taken his master's magic had to be powerful beyond belief and that one could only be the abbot's master, no-one else. Could magic be used to beat the man, if he was a man…hadn't Mazumbai hinted that he wasn't? They certainly couldn't use magic to fight the monks without souls, at least not directly; the monk on the hilltop had shown them that. It was possible that their magic could only be used against one—the abbot. Whatever horror was beyond the gates of the dungeons was undoubtedly unspeakable, the manner of their forthcoming deaths equally so. He knew though that the site of his first visions was in there, in that chamber along with the man in red. Aidan was terrified.

A little before sundown Bazyli Montetor broke the silence with a request totally unexpected and which showed the desperate courage of the man.

'Aidan,' receiving no response he called again, the boy was far away, lost in the depths of his misery. 'Aidan, my young friend, I need you to do something before the mad monk comes to take us away.'

'What?'

'Brother Dyfrig always humiliates me whenever he sees me…always. He delights in seeing my scar. And that's the problem. He will look at me this evening and not see the cicatrix and will realize there is another wizard here. We dare not let him discover you. I…I want you to give me back the scar.'

'Oh, no, Excellency…no, you can't,' said Beatrix horrified.

Tragen stared at the Montetor for long moments; smiling sadly he turned to Aidan. 'He is right, my boy, the abbot would guess immediately.'

'But…'

'No buts, Aidan, we must keep you hidden. Put the scar back on my face exactly as it was before, but I thank you, it was wonderful to have one afternoon without the blemish,' and Bazyli stared straight in Aidan's eyes. 'It will not be for long anyway—my death is inevitable!'

Aidan wrinkled his brow and stared at Bazyli strangely. 'You are wrong, you know, Excellency. I can see my Lord Tragen's death but I can't see yours. Now I wonder why that is,' and he looked at his friends in turn. 'I can't see death in any of you!'

'That doesn't mean we are not going to die tonight, though, does it? You may see our deaths later,' Thaddeus said, staring at the boy who'd saved his life once before. 'I'm right, aren't I?'

Augusta and Beatrix waited with bated breath; Aidan was very slow in answering.

'I suppose,' he said, deflated. 'All right, Excellency, but I don't have to make it permanent. I can make it appear illusory.'

'What do you mean?' Bazyli asked.

'The only one to see your scar will be the abbot!'

'Good, Aidan, very good,' said Tragen chuckling.

'And before the abbot dies, we will show him that he has been deceived,' said Lodovico. 'I, for one, will want to laugh at him as he has laughed at you all these years, my friend.'

And when Aidan chanted and stroked Bazyli's face, the scar did appear, but no-one saw it.

When the iron gate of the dungeon opened that evening, torchlight crept in, along with a long line of silent monks. A cohort of soulless men wearing white, their cowls raised, walked to the rear of the dungeon and returned dragging a heavy chain. This they laid out on the ground along the length of the passageway, its leading end in front of the door to the slaves' cage.

The men, women and children of Brakwanna, enslaved by Brother Dyfrig all rose as one and thrust Mazumbai, despite his protestations, to the rear of the cage.

'You cannot do this to me,' Mazumbai raged. 'I must lead you into death; I must be the first to die!'

'No, Mazumbai,' a woman's voice called out. 'You are our chief! You have cared for us all these years. In here you have always put yourself in the forefront of danger, protecting us as much as you were able from the evil of these monks. No more! I, Mantawi, wife of your dead nephew Mulumba, will go first. We will protect you now!'

'But don't you understand? Nkimba, Nkoross, you will be punishing me even more! I cannot watch my people die before me…please!'

'Mazumbai,' another voice said—this one an older voice—a frail sounding man with breathing problems. 'If I am to die with courage, I will need to look you in the eye as I go. Please, my chief, help me…help me to die as a man should, without weeping!'

'Akumamba, you are the bravest man I know,' and Mazumbai, his heart full with love and pride for his fellow Brakwannans, gazed at them through glistening eyes. 'My people, I will make you this solemn vow. I will never look away from you, my eyes will lock with yours as you fall—and I will die with each of you!'

Augusta and Beatrix sobbed as each slave was brought from their cage. Tragen, Lodovico Portolan, Bazyli Montetor, Marcus Janne and Leonid of the Green People stood with respect, frustrated and helpless in the face of such a display of bravery by a people who had suffered terribly at the hands of the mad monks.

Aidan and Thaddeus stared at the column shuffling past, aware somehow that these people were about to enter the Darkness. Completely helpless, the two young wizards stood by, dazed, desperately seeking a plan but having no ideas.

The slaves shambled out slowly. And as each stepped forward an iron link was fixed to an ankle by the silent monks and the very long line of slaves, mostly men, a few older children and desperately emaciated women, were led out into the chamber.

It took over an hour before Mazumbai was shackled to the chain.

Towards midnight the Abbot of Sanctity appeared wearing his usual spotless white robe the cowl around his shoulders, his head and face newly shaved. He halted briefly at the cage holding the Quota and studied the abject terror on the faces of those inside. Cringing with fear they tried not to return his gaze but most failed and those saw their fate mirrored in his gloating eyes. He turned and walked across to gaze balefully in at the Griffin captives, jubilant, he could see defeat in their eyes even behind their defiant expressions. The abbot no longer feared his most hated enemies and smirked as he examined the Montetor's scar for the last time.

He glanced across at Tragen standing at the adjacent wall and thinking back to his last visit to the dungeon wondered how the talisman-induced delirium had lifted in the man so soon. It hadn't registered then that the wizard, although still powerless, was cognizant of all around him and the abbot broke into a cold sweat. Would his master realize that the spell had not lasted as long as it should have? Should he warn him?

472

Brother Dyfrig turned his back on Tragen and, biting his lip, he signalled for the Quota's cage door to be opened. The felons rose to their feet as one and rushed for the back wall, in their terror they crowded Leash, one or two hoping for a quick death at his hands. But Leash kept his eyes on the abbot as each of his companions was dragged into the passageway. The prisoners stood or slumped in various degrees of distress, some whimpering, one or two almost comatose, a couple struggling violently with their captors. All these men had committed murder at some time in the past and most were regarded hard men by their peers. But the horror flowing in waves from the abbot and his monks unmanned them entirely.

Using the simple expedient of slipping two nooses over the heads of each prisoner, the terror-stricken men, eyes bulging, ceased their struggles. The ends of the ropes were held by monks and in this manner they were led individually through the gate into the chamber, the nooses choking them if they faltered.

Leash was the last of the Quota to leave the cage and Brother Dyfrig delayed him for a moment for the big second helmsman of the Grim was again muttering incoherently, spittle dribbling from his mouth.

Fascinated, the abbot laughed. 'Well, such a big man afraid to die! Are all the men like this in Mantovar, wizard?'

'He is infected by a demon,' interrupted Janne in disgust.

The abbot's eyes widened. A demon—maybe his master would have a different use for such a one. He certainly couldn't be killed in the normal manner. If the human was to die, a new host would have to be found for the demon or it would find its own. Brother Dyfrig shuddered; it could quite easily jump into him and he didn't fancy playing host, especially when he'd achieved his ambition. The abbot decided to stay well clear of him.

'Take him, but do not tether him with the others,' he ordered. He watched them leave and when they shuffled through the iron barred gate to follow the slaves into the chamber he turned back and looked at Tragen now standing in the centre of his cage.

'We will take the wizard next,' and everyone watched helplessly as the nooses were placed about Tragen's neck. 'My master will want a quiet word with Lord Tragen before the rest of you join him for the ultimate ceremony. I will accompany him,' and he sniggered, 'to introduce him,' and he held out his arm in mockery as if to usher a friend into the next room. 'My dear Lord Tragen you have

473

forgotten your staff, I would never dream of parting you from your companion, please pick it up,' and the abbot turned to his cohorts. 'You,' and he pointed at those monks waiting with him, 'secure these others and bring them in together at my signal.'

Half an hour of unutterable suspense passed before they were given the word, and with nooses around their necks, a monk either side, Lodovico Portolan led the way.

Aidan, squinting at moving from the dungeon gloom into the bright light shed by the many candles in sconces around the walls, recognized the chamber at once. Halting abruptly at the gate alongside the pile of discarded tools, he stared at the location of his first visions and panic stabbed painfully in his chest. His mind recalled the man in red laughing up at someone he was torturing. He now knew for certain that the red colouring was not the original colour of the monk's robe.

He was too afraid to look up at the cage he knew was there, or around for the man in red and, keeping his eyes lowered, he broke into a fevered sweat every muscle in his body trembling. Is this the way they were going to die…tortured in a cage? A low moan broke from his lips for barely a moment before both nooses around his neck were pulled taut. Choking off the sound of his voice, his two warders jerked him forward nearly bringing him to his knees.

Marcus Janne, walking just ahead of Aidan, hearing his stifled cries halted and tried to reach him to give support. There was chaos for minutes; it was not an easy task for his two captors to drag a heavily muscled, seven foot tall man. Two others joined their colleagues, and it took the combined strength of all four captors to regain mastery over him.

But Bazyli Montetor studying the incident, perceived something that had gone unnoticed by the others. These monks were not as strong as they looked and were definitely slower than normal.

Augusta and Beatrix were petrified; they had only experienced the use of nooses on one previous occasion when they had defied the emperor's orders and witnessed an execution by hanging. Augusta, for months after, had been unable to free her mind of the sight of the man's dancing legs and his swollen tongue protruding from his mouth. Augusta and Beatrix all but swooned as they were led deeper into the cavern.

Thaddeus was horrified. In all the years of his exile in the afterlife, his mother had never taught him how to deal with the

474

helplessness he now felt, and seeing his father trussed in a similar manner, made his terror worse. He shuffled forward in a daze, his mind in full retreat as he felt the Darkness very nearby.

Lodovico Portolan raged he couldn't stomach the mortal threat to his son. Regardless of his own danger, he ranted imprecations, pure hate in his voice and fathomless malice in his eyes.

Leonid was another not actually overcome with fear. Managing to control his horror he stared around the cavern studying all within his sight. But even he was dismayed at the numbers imprisoning them and he failed to discover any possible means of escape.

Around the cavern, the tiered seats were all occupied by silent, zombie-like men; others stood around the walls and filled the aisles. There must have been upwards of four perhaps five hundred hooded monks all staring towards the hub of the chamber.

Lodovico led them to the left, around the back of the mass of slaves standing silently between the dungeons and the cloud of black fog in the centre of the chamber. And as they came around the flank into sight of the dais, their eyes were drawn immediately to the dense, pulsating smog in front of Chief Mazumbai.

Aidan, Thaddeus, Augusta and Beatrix caught their breath, inhaling sharply; they knew now the source of the dread feeling they had suffered ever since landing on the island. Their eyes inevitably fixed on the violent activity of the miasma contained within the perimeter of the rock basin. It bubbled as if in a boiling cauldron, but instead of heat, cold radiated from the cloud shards of ice puncturing their brains, the abominable stench forcing them to breathe shallowly to avoid vomiting. The young wizards did not need to tell the others of what the stone basin held, the sickness in their faces told all.

'How is it here, Aidan, dear God, how?' Anders asked, trembling at the wall of colours that had just changed to a darkness darker than black.

'I wish I knew. Bloody hell, I don't want to go near that!' Aidan answered sweat dripping from him.

Lifting his eyes from the vaporous mass he stared across the black, loathsome smelling cloud and saw the Brakwanna slaves standing crowded together along the opposite bank. Still chained together, Mazumbai was at the front returning his look, his face grey. At the rear of the slaves Aidan glimpsed the top bars of the dungeons and turning quickly he glanced behind him, and there saw an open door, the foot of a stairway just visible inside.

475

At the foot of the dais, guarded closely, were eleven men of the Quota cowering in abject terror. The twelfth member, Leash, no longer muttering, was kneeling on the hard stone floor to one side. His eyes, starting from his head, were glued to the two-foot high, black stone pyramid sitting atop the granite altar, its two horns looking like antlers protruding at its apex.

The wizards' party were brought to stand on the edge of the grey rock basin facing the slaves, Beatrix and Augusta standing between Aidan and Thaddeus, Bazyli and Lodovico nearest the altar, and Leonid and Marcus at the farthest end.

Only now were their eyes inextricably drawn upwards.

And the horror of the sight gave rise to desperate anguish and drew a high-pitched, strident keening. A tone of such desolation issued from the throat of Aidan that it unnerved everyone who heard it.

Still clutching his staff, Tragen was held immobile from head to toe. His face glistening with perspiration, he was imprisoned in the cage suspended from the ceiling directly above the centre of the churning black cloud. His long white hair, and long even whiter beard, tousled and tangled together almost obscuring his face, his colourless grey eyes staring at Aidan desperately.

'Remember what I said…remember your purpose,' and he smiled his encouragement through his own terror. 'I am so very proud of you, my boy, never forget that.' Then his eyes grew steely and he stared at the others. 'Keep to your purpose whatever you see, whatever happens keep to your purpose. Do not disappoint me! Do not let me die in vain!'

'Weep all of you, weep! My master wishes you to despair,' rejoiced Brother Dyfrig, speaking hysterically as he stood at the foot of the dais his arms outstretched. 'At last, my time has come, I attain my ambition—immortality will be bestowed on me with the wizard's death! I will live forever to serve my God! Look around you, all present will witness the greatness and the power of my God. Your souls will join those others who have gone before you to succour him. You will live forever in his safekeeping…and he will enjoy your torment for as long as he wishes.' Brother Dyfrig stared over their heads, bringing his hands together his eyes on the open door behind them.

'I am sorry, my friends, but take what consolation you can…the wizard's death will be swifter than yours,' mindmelded Mazumbai. And such was the horror and loss of hope suffered by the young

wizards that they never realized that the chief of the Brakwanna had spoken in their minds.

But Anders was aware. *'How can he mindmeld, Beattie?'*

She shrugged her shoulders, not caring; she couldn't take her eyes from the tall stately gentleman she used to be in awe of. Now she wished she had the courage to take his place, but knew she'd break if anyone suggested it.

Augusta, though, heeding Anders' words, also wondered if she'd heard correctly. *'Chief Mazumbai, was that really you mindmelding?'* Augusta asked, testing his ability.

'Yes, warrior wizard. Along with perception of auras I have the ability to speak silently.

'Then what did you mean when you said he would die quickly...will we die slowly, then?'

'I said his death will be swifter than yours. I'm sorry; his death will be full of unbearable pain and will last some time. But yours...your deaths will be far slower and far more horrendous, I'm afraid. Try to take courage and strength from each other, for my friends, you will sorely need it.'

Thaddeus, not knowing how, found his voice and spoke, his voice ringing through the ceremonial chamber. 'You are a fool, Abbot; listen to your own words. Look around at your monks; heed their blank stares, they have all lost their minds, yes…their very souls. They "live forever in your God's safekeeping". Gaze in their eyes, Abbot, what do you see? They are neither alive nor dead, are they? They have been granted immortality before you—you halfwit. This is the eternity that awaits you, cretin!'

Brother Dyfrig convulsed, shock rippling through him, suddenly realizing the truth in the boy's words he stared at Thaddeus, terror making him speechless. Why had he never thought of it? He knew his master was cruel, had seen ample evidence over the years. His master had broken many promises and laughed at doing so, he could never be trusted. Dyfrig trembled uncontrollably, falling to the floor he vomited. The undeniable truth of the boy's words had opened his mind to dryness, to obscene, appalling failure—to a future far too hideous to contemplate.

'Do not listen to him,' a cold voice of horror said from just inside the open doorway behind the wizards. 'You are my faithful ally, you will not be as these. Close your ears they seek to sow discord between us.'

Thaddeus and Aidan screamed together. 'DOWN! All of you, down on your knees—DO NOT LOOK AT HIM.'

'DO NOT MEET HIS EYES! He is a Herdsman of the One come to take our souls into Purgatory!' shouted Thaddeus, panicking, the sick feeling of the Darkness engulfing him. 'Whatever he says…whatever he does. DO NOT MEET HIS EYES!'

Thirty-eight

They all, wizards, clan leaders, friends and slaves obeyed Thaddeus and Aidan without a second thought, and fell to their knees bowing their heads as if in supplication to the herdsman. Terrified, icy sweat pouring from their brows, they stared at the base of the mist now mere feet from their faces.

Augusta stared unblinking at chisel marks in the banks of the grey rock, the floor of black stone beneath the miasma not registering in her brain.

And Beatrix now knew what Mazumbai meant when he said that the abbot's master was no man.

Lodovico Portolan, having heard so much about the devil creature succumbed to an overwhelming urge to see what he looked like. He started to raise his head but Bazyli Montetor stopped him.

'No, Lodovico, for the love of your God, obey your son!' And they both stared at the hem of the black robe, petrified to hear the next words.

The herdsman, very tall and lean, dressed in a black robe its cowl pulled over the top of his head almost to his mouth, strode slowly and soundlessly to the dais and stepped up to the altar. Turning, he gazed down at the Abbot of Sanctity.

'You have done well, my servant, and your ambition will be granted on the deaths of these present,' the voice held the terrible hiss of the snake.

And Aidan remembered and heard the voice of his visions.

'The storm my God conjured still blows, and it has brought us a harvest beyond our most earnest wishes. The tempest will remain in place forever to ensnare other prey for our friends elsewhere. Look at the wizard, Abbot, his staff is the most powerful we have ever encountered. But even its power could not hide from the One. Its power, along with the deaths of all these here will be more than sufficient for our God's needs. He will succeed!'

He turned away from the distraught monk and staring up at Tragen, totally helpless in his cage, the herdsman held out his hand to Brother Dyfrig on his knees quaking in terror. 'Return the pendant; I will give him back his magic.'

Brother Dyfrig's hand shook uncontrollably as he retrieved the small, black, two-horned pyramid from his pocket and dropped it, trancelike, into the herdsman's outstretched palm.

And the demon within Leash convulsed when he recognized the artefact. The vampyrus retracted into the very depths of Leash's psyche to hide—relinquishing control of its mesmerized host.

The horror hissed his boasting. 'Wizard, allow me to introduce myself, I am Zorzecai the Collector.'

And at the name Tragen's brow creased in puzzlement he had heard the name before, long ago, and tried to remember where. But his fear wouldn't let him.

The herdsman bowed mockingly. 'It was so…so easy to entice you here,' he sniggered. 'When I encountered you in my God's storm I knew my plans would at last be achieved, for you had not realized I could observe you through your staff.' His shallow breath coming in short bursts, it chuckled hoarsely. 'I could see and hear everything you did, wizard! And there was you thinking I wanted a spoilt little girl for ransom! Later you committed another error thinking it was you I was after.

'You are a fool, wizard. It was your staff I wanted! Your staff…so powerful, unbelievably so, its capture has ensured my God's triumph!

'But I was curious; a staff so magical in the hands of a mortal, surely the man must also wield vast power. So I decided to test you. Your failure surprised me enormously and set back my plans for a while, for in failing I had no alternative but to bring you here.

'I allowed you to turn the ship without you suspecting a thing. Your shield charm was never powerful enough on its own. When I saw the puny strength in the spell, I laughed and aided you…and you nearly succumbed, but for some reason you escaped me! So I tested you again, and again you fell short.

'You could not see the visions I sent you of me at work in my chamber!'

Aidan startled; his nightmares had really been meant as a test for Tragen? He couldn't understand it, how then had he intercepted them? But another question was answered, the reason no other wizard had been detected. It was the staff that drew the demon—Aidan and his friends had none! But the herdsman had also erred. He had not realized that another wizard had rescued Tragen. And Aidan had felt Zorzecai yet the demon did not know.

'If you had seen the visions you would have invoked even more power from your staff in an endeavour to protect yourself. For it is certain that if you had seen me at work you would have found the sight irresistible and would have sought its origin. I'd have been able to milk all the power from your staff without the need of you here. But being not as powerful as I had assumed, my visions went to waste…a pity! I should have realized only a wizard capable of the most extraordinary power would see them.'

Aidan stared up at his master, frowning, wondering at the meaning of this. Surely the herdsman didn't mean to imply that the apprentice was more powerful than the teacher!

The herdsman continued, not realizing the bewilderment he had created amongst the friends.

'Because of your lack of ability, wizard, I could not allow you to drown, your ship to sink as it should have. It would have saved me so much time and effort if you had died then. But I needed your staff here to drain it…and you to invoke its power so that I could. The first I have, the second I will have before long.

'So I fooled you! I gradually reduced the power of the storm the nearer you came to me to give the impression you were fleeing to safety, and like the idiots all mortals have become since my day, you fell for it. My final act, to dismast the ship, ensured you ended up on Sanctity the only island with suitable replacements.'

Its sibilant snigger sent a cold shiver up the backs of all those listening. 'So my delayed plans will now succeed on a most auspicious day. You are here helpless within that cage and your staff's energy concentrated in that small space should be all I need to open the Qembana…the Gateway to Purgatory!'

Zorzecai paused as if to get his breath. 'You see this, wizard,' and he held up the pendant on its chain. 'This is what deprived you of your powers…it now holds them in thrall until I release them.'

The herdsman held it up at arm's length before Tragen's eyes allowing it to sway gently, teasing the wizard.

Tragen followed the arc it travelled, his eyes displaying raw, naked hunger for his magic. And as the bell swung in the skeletal fingers of the demon, it attracted the eye of everyone, yet it did not sound. But only one human had the enhanced eyesight to realize its pyramidal shape was similar to that resting on the end of the altar. The pendant drew in all light around it and it glowed brightly.

'Here, wizard, I return your puny power,' and the herdsman twirled the bell at the end of its chain.

And as it gained speed it seemed to blur and lose substance until eventually it spun so fast that, when released, it disappeared in an eye-aching, bright flash of white light into the chest of Tragen and out of his back.

Beatrix, the flash not troubling her at all, continued to watch the amulet and she swore afterwards that it had disappeared into the black rock beneath the fog. The others had long given up staring at it before that happened, the light dazzling even behind their closed eyelids.

And as the last vestiges of the amulet disappeared into the afterlife, the magical power that Tragen had lived with all his life returned to him in a bright argent blaze. Silver enveloped the wizard from head to toe. Tragen spasmed, every muscle in his body tensed and twitched. A moment later, he relaxed and breathed an enormous sigh of relief as he felt the magic course through his body and come alive in the runes of his staff.

'Why, Herdsman? Why have you returned to me the means to fight you?'

'Fight me?' Zorzecai hissed not taking his eyes from Tragen. 'You do not understand the nature of your imprisonment! You do not have the power to reach through the cage, let alone touch me. My God protects me from all those who wield magic.'

And it was those words that finally drove the last trace of hope from all those listening. Utter despair spread rapidly. Despite discovering on the slopes below the monastery that the silent ones did not succumb to magic, there had always been a glimmer of hope that perhaps the abbot and his master might be vulnerable.

But who could fight a God?

Seven wizards allied against the Darkness and all helpless— useless! The Gods' centuries' old plans for the youths had come to naught. Desolation ruled now. They were going to die and be ensnared in the Darkness and there was no escaping it.

The herdsman's ranting eventually broke into their defeatist thoughts and they listened with a wretchedness that could not grow any deeper.

'I return your powers, without them you cannot invoke the magic within your staff. And please, do not say that you will not,' his hiss impossibly sounding like a smile, 'you will be unable to avoid doing it,' and he laughed again. 'The power in the staff will be mine to use through you.'

'Never! Never, demon…never will I allow my staff to work for you!'

The herdsman continued to laugh obscenely and he ignored Tragen's protestations and turned away. Taking his time he looked around the chamber studying those within. He wondered why the name of Zorzecai was unknown to the wizard, mortals were so ignorant, they forgot easily. He gazed down at the abbot...especially this one. *Perhaps he realizes now, at the end, that I needed someone to retain his soul only to facilitate communication with the outside world.*

He stared across at Mazumbai and his countrymen, their faces lowered. 'When I give the word, Abbot, you may commence walking those into the mist.'

Pointing at Leash, standing to one side separate from the rest of the prisoners, the herdsman frowned. 'Why is that man not amongst the rest?'

'Master, please, I beg you...' implored the abbot, all dignity gone, scared witless, falling to the floor and cringing at the black-garbed demon's feet. 'Master, I have served you well, please do not take my soul into the Darkness. Do not punish me! I will do anything you wish, Master!'

'Answer me!'

The abbot swallowed his mouth suddenly as dry as the deserts of the south. 'Master, he is different to the others, he is host to a demon.'

The vampyrus within Leash didn't so much as blink an eyelid; it was too terrified to move even a hair on the back of Leash's hand.

For the vampyrus knew the identity and the real purpose of the One behind the Darkness.

It was aware now of the mistake it had made in not fleeing the Grim. But Leash had been stronger than the vampyrus realized and it had been cajoled into going along with the insane desire of its host to see the old wizard die. But now, here in this ceremonial chamber in the heart of a volcano, the vampyrus was mortally afraid—if this Collector realized who he was! Somehow it had to hoodwink this being of almost unimaginable power yet it had no idea how. But the vampyrus was lucky; Zorzecai was in a hurry his God's plans were about to succeed.

'A demon? A lesser incubus, of course...it must be a mediocrity to have allowed mortals to take it prisoner,' Zorzecai said disparagingly.

He clicked his fingers and the soulless guards pulled the Griffin captives to their feet. But they remained with heads lowered, heeding

Thaddeus' advice. Bazyli, Lodovico, Aidan, Augusta, Beatrix, Thaddeus and Marcus, silently withstood the demon's scrutiny. Unable to hide their trembling they were also unable to keep defeat from their faces.

And then Zorzecai the Collector discovered Leonid and he rounded on Dyfrig in a rage.

'You fool, Abbot, you stupid, stupid cretin!'

And Brother Dyfrig crumpled even more at the scorn and rage in his master's voice. Still on his knees grovelling, he clutched his hands in supplication, begging for his life.

'Please, I've carried out your orders…every time, please I'll do whatever you want…don't punish me, Master. Tell me…what have I done?'

'You have brought a Green Man into the presence of the One,' he raved. 'Do you not realize that the Green People are poison? All plans go awry in their presence! Take him away,' screamed the herdsman at the two monks holding Leonid's nooses. 'Throw him back in the cages until I decide what to do with him.'

Astonishment on their faces, Janne and the others watched as Leonid was dragged away, past the slaves, presumably to die another day.

'Abbot,' the herdsman shouted burning with rage, 'I have had enough of your imbecility…enough! I have kept you alive too long! You have served your purpose. Go and join my God!'

He stepped from the dais and grabbed the abbot around the neck and, with Brother Dyfrig shrieking, the herdsman threw him into the black, freezing mist. And all watched as the abbot's body froze solid, a white rime forming and encasing him from head to toe. He floated within the fog for moments, completely aware but unable to move, the abbot stared terrified out at those watching. Zorzecai lifted a dagger from the altar and touched it to the two-horned pyramid at its end. Instantly an ear-splitting, unearthly knell sounded throughout the chamber and Brother Dyfrig's frozen body shattered into a thousand and more pieces and dropped to the black stone at his feet. And then, at the moment of his disintegration, the fog reacted violently and gusted in huge black bubbles. The agitation lasting for several seconds until it settled as a little more of the black rock sublimated into dense smog—and an unearthly sound of torment rose and sliced into the brains of all those listening.

Augusta and Beatrix, whimpering, stretched for each other. The Darkness was closer!

'What are you, Herdsman?' Tragen asked, utter disbelief on his face.

'Me, wizard?' he chuckled hoarsely, 'I am your nemesis!' And then he gave the word for the true horror to begin.

Zorzecai lowered his cowl to expose features that resembled a cadaver that had been immersed in water for months. He was completely bald, his skin an unhealthy puffed-up white. Wrinkled from the top of his head to his neck, the skin looked as if it was too big for his skull. His mouth was large, his lips even larger over rotted teeth. His nose was snub and his nostrils spread like the snout of a pig and his ears were long, the lobes drooping well below the level of his mouth.

But it was the demon's eyes that drew their gaze. And as much as Thaddeus and Aidan fought against it, they also looked. His eyes were a deep red, the only colour in his face. And seeing those pupil-less orbs they knew they could not disobey him whatever he ordered—they were lost!

The Quota was the first to supply a victim. A small, dark man of indeterminate age with rings through his nose and tattoos across his cheekbones was lifted bodily by his two captors, stripped of his shirt, and placed screaming on the sacrificial altar to lie in the depression cut into the slab. The herdsman, placing one hand on his victim's head, stilled the man's struggles and he held up the long dagger with which he had just tapped the pyramid.

The black-garbed disciple of an evil God made the first slow incision across the man's abdomen.

The man screamed long and terrible, his eyes starting from his head he automatically brought up his knees to hold the flesh closed in his belly. The herdsman broke each of the man's thighs with a practised blow with the edge of his hand. And as the man screamed again, his shattered legs dropped and the blood gushed from his stomach. Spurting vertically into the air it eventually fell and splattered the herdsman, drenching his robe. The remainder of his blood flowed along the channel and poured from beneath the two-horned pyramid. It fell into the miasma and hit the surface of the black rock at its base, freezing instantly in the bubbling, hissing cloud. Decay permeated the chamber, the smell one that Thaddeus and Aidan knew well.

485

The prisoners, including the sad-eyed Brakwannans, as much as they wished to look away, found their eyes irresistibly drawn towards the terrible sight. They were compelled to watch as the torturer, taking his time, ritually disembowelled the man.

Aidan panicked, nearly wetting himself he understood now that this was truly the red man of his visions. He stared up at the demon standing on the dais, his hands in the body of his victim. He groaned. His friends were going to suffer this same terrible fate. How could he kneel here and witness Augusta and Beatrix stretched out on the slab with their entrails exposed? Aidan was at the edge of insanity—and knew it.

Staring at the first man of the Quota, Aidan felt the terrible agony of the victim's pain, physically and mentally. He stared at the sailor writhing on the slab as his intestines were withdrawn from his abdomen, the herdsman's clear intent to inflict as much pain as possible.

The young wizard's apprentice could no more stop himself taking action, than he could live without breathing. Forgetting his master's warnings on using magic, he instinctively took the man's hurt from him—and into himself. But as he did so, the pain knifed through him with a suddenness that took his breath. It started in his abdomen and lanced both ways, down his legs and up into his brain. He could neither speak nor breathe, his eyes bleeding in their sockets the blood slowly dripping down his face.

Aidan had once before taken someone's pain from a gut wound in an effort to heal...unable to think around the pain he had failed miserably. But the distress suffered by this man was indescribable; Aidan felt as if his own entrails were being pulled from his body. He fell to his knees, folding his arms over his stomach holding himself together, praying the man would not take too long to die.

The victim ceased his screaming and lay stunned and demented, his organs held up before his eyes. A sight so inconceivable his mind could not register the fact of it.

His silence, as he lay dying painlessly, was not thought unusual by Zorzecai. He automatically assumed the man had no more strength to scream. Throwing the entrails on the man's chest, he indicated for the removal of the body, and the first of the Quota was thrown, still alive, into the mist to follow Brother Dyfrig. And as the man entered the fog his frozen body floated momentarily until the herdsman again touched the dagger to the pyramid. At the sound of the death knell the cacophony increased.

And as the man crumbled in smithereens Aidan recovered, gasping, he stood.

The herdsman stood away from the altar. Awaiting his next victim he studied the black swirling mist, his head on one side listening to the raucous sounds. The demon looked up and studied the impotent wizard trapped in the cage like a wild bird.

'I have chosen you to die last, wizard. I want you to witness the agonizing death of your friends, your loved ones. They are all going to suffer the same as this one…these insignificant, short-lived mortals. Later you will feel and hear their pain and watch as your friends go out of their minds.' Rubbing his hands in the depression on the altar, covering his hands in the blood, he held them aloft and laughed. 'This blood, their life's essence, will slake my God's thirst while their pain feeds his hunger! And you, wizard…you will use your magic to free him!'

And Tragen's magic did flare in a desperate attempt to conceal that used by Aidan. He could not blame the boy for not obeying; in fact, he would have been greatly surprised if Aidan had done nothing. As Mazumbai had intoned earlier, Aidan truly was the Wizard of Life and Death.

'Why, Zorzecai? Why this barbarity?' Tragen asked, desperately hoping to distract the demon from Aidan.

And the herdsman hissed joyfully as another victim was placed on the altar. 'Have you not been listening, old man? My God requires the pain of mortals, it rouses him; the everlasting agony is his lifeblood,' he looked up at Tragen. 'The more pain, the stronger he becomes, the easier he finds it to control the Darkness and his minions within it. And before long the pain will arouse the magic in your staff to a degree you have never felt before.'

Tragen sighed, he had no option. 'Cease your torture and I will give you all the magic you need.'

'Wizard…wizard you still do not understand. You cannot bargain when you have nothing to offer. I do not require your acceptance! You cannot halt the power in your staff, now it has begun it is my God's to use as he wishes.'

It was on the third victim, a man whose tattoos covered his entire body, that the fiend realized something was wrong. As he plunged the knife into the terrified man's abdomen, the blood spurting as before into the channel and at the same time over him, he uttered no sound.

Aidan in desperation used the only means he could think of to avoid having to absorb the pain himself. He'd had no option; he'd never have been able to survive another victim. He killed the pain sensors in the man's brain. He removed all sensation from the victim as he was placed on the altar.

Zorzecai, puzzled at the lack of reaction in the man, looked up at Tragen swinging very slowly in the cage. 'Wizard, what is happening...you can't be doing this?'

'I am taking his pain.'

'I repeat...you cannot, that cage is made to halt the passage through of all magic in either direction until my God requires its power. So it cannot be you,' and Tragen's heart plummeted when the demon continued. 'Can there possibly be another wizard here?' He turned and glanced perfunctorily at those behind him. 'Whoever you are, I will discover you,' warned the herdsman.

The miasma's increasing activity swelled to a deafening crescendo of harsh rumbling as the black rock absorbed the maimed bodies, and changed to black smog.

But the blood flowing into the nauseating tangle, gave off a smell and an airborne residue that was sweet and cloying, acrid and harsh. No-one could avoid tasting the blood—including Leash.

Leash was frantic, the smell of the blood, the taste, the very essence of the wholesale slaughter acted upon his demon drawing it up inexorably from its hiding place and bringing on the Wanting with an intensity he had never felt before.

And for the first time in its existence the vampyrus fought against the need to feast. It could not allow the wielder of the Lobos talismans to discover him.

But even in his inner conflict, Leash found it strange that as soon as the first victim was sacrificed he could smell lavender. He couldn't understand it, wondered if he was imagining it; there were no flowers in this hellhole. But the odour gave rise to memories...his memories of his happy times for he loved the aroma of newly crushed lavender. For the merest moment his eyes glistened. He searched around in his confusion and discovered the fragrance was emanating from Aidan. Leash's stomach ached, he moaned. The boy could never be hers!

He struggled against the ropes around his neck, the monks choking him into submission. He keened through the constriction. Howling, as he had never done before, he distracted the herdsman. Zorzecai glanced at Leash, and as his eyes passed over Aidan, he saw the intense concentration on the boy's face, the blood dripping from the boy's eyes and he knew he had found the other wizard.

Was this the boy? He seemed so puny, he couldn't possibly be. And yet...Zorzecai looked for the boy's staff. Not finding one he studied the boy again. It matters not, whoever he is, he's going to die. If he is the one he'll be known.

The demon smiled, blood dripping down his head and face, his black robe now the colour red. Looking up at Tragen, he ordered the cage to be lowered until the wizard's feet hung just inches above the surface of the dense black cloud. Bending down in front of the altar, Zorzecai retrieved from the floor a blood-encrusted iron bar, one end sharpened into a very fine point. Brandishing this in front of the cage he laughed at the knowing look on Tragen's face. He rested the point of the spear on the cage directly in front of Tragen's left eye.

'You boy, you are a wizard with this one. Do you wish me to mutilate him slowly before he dies?'

The herdsman's venomous hiss spread like ice through Aidan's bones.

Thirty-nine

Aidan staggered to his feet, his initial nightmares returning with a vengeance, he'd already seen what this spear could do to a victim. He couldn't allow it to inflict the same damage on his father's face.

'No, Aidan, don't listen to him,' begged Tragen frantically. 'Remember what I said, remember your mission.' And the magic in the staff thrummed and glowed brighter, attempting escape from the cage. But as the energy thrust against the mesh, it rebounded, causing an even greater iridescence. The magic began to feed on itself. And Tragen despaired…he could not halt the flow.

'Master, my father, listen to me. I can't allow this demon to torment these prisoners. I can't remain silent and witness the same for you and my friends! If magic cannot pass through the cage how am I to heal you?' his voice broke. 'Master, I love you, I cannot let him hurt you. Earlier, you said you would die for me. Can I do any less for you?'

'No, Aidan, it's not meant to be. I love you, my boy, but I am going to die anyway, you know that you've seen it, you…' Tragen's voice was drowned out by the herdsman's.

'Take my knife, boy,' ordered Zorzecai, 'and lie on the stone. My God will require all your blood and all your pain…as he requires the magic in this one's staff. Do it now or the spear will enter his eye and I shall continue to mutilate him until you obey.'

He watched Tragen striving to break free of the cage. 'Keep struggling wizard. Struggle all you like, as much as you like,' and he laughed again, 'all you do is increase the flow of power in your staff.'

He turned and watched Aidan come to a decision. 'Do not think of using your magic, boy, you have it right…magic cannot harm me, or aid this old man.'

And Aidan believed it, accepted every word the herdsman uttered. Zorzecai would torture Tragen with no second thoughts and it would be his fault. He had to obey.

As if in a trance he moved towards the altar and lay on the blood smattered slab, knowing that his life's essence would have to join with that already spilt so that his beloved mentor would not be subjected to the terrible torture he'd seen in his visions. And it was the memories of his visions that he saw before his eyes now. The man screaming in the cage would be Tragen, the man below him, the torturer Zorzecai. And the red robe would be the herdsman's black robe drenched in the lifeblood of his adoptive father. And Aidan understood implicitly the only way to halt the persecution of Tragen was to do what the herdsman wanted.

He held the devil's knife in both hands above his abdomen— blade pointing downwards.

He didn't hear the panicked screams of his friends. He couldn't think straight anymore, he'd let go, surrendered to the inevitable. The horror of the past hour had overwhelmed him, his thoughts no longer made sense. So he thought no more. He forgot his words to everyone earlier that day. Placed at the back of his mind the consequences of committing suicide and did not recall that it would be a waste of time, that he would be unable to pass over. He blanked out his friends, even Anders watching terrified at the wall of colours, calling to him. He blocked his mind to all mindmelding.

The obsession was everything…to stop Tragen being tortured, help him pass over safely. And then he needed to be with his master in the afterlife, to protect him there in the Darkness as Anders had protected his mother. He prepared himself for the demon's word, ready to plunge the knife deep.

He'd had enough.

He'd given up on Life.

But his friends had not given up on him.

Augusta, despite the tightening of the nooses around her neck, concentrated all her magic on taking the knife from Aidan's hands, but to no avail. Aidan's magic was different to hers and far more powerful, but she persevered she didn't know what else to do.

Bazyli Montetor was the nearest to the altar and roaring at the top of his voice he managed to drag his captors to the foot of the dais before others came to restrain him.

Lodovico Portolan, for the first time in his life succumbed to the strength of others. The monks pulled him over onto his back and he was almost strangled by the ropes around his neck.

Thaddeus added his screaming voice to the pandemonium. Calling Aidan's name, begging him not to carry out the foul act, he followed his father in being dragged to the floor.

Marcus Janne, bellowing his rage, almost reached the blood drenched herdsman before he was felled from behind by another monk using his pikestaff as a cudgel. His head bleeding, Janne helplessly watched Aidan, his anguish total.

Tragen was frantic. Unable to halt the magic in his staff, he seemed to disappear within the cage. The magic was now rebounding chaotically within the confines of his prison, the flashes of blinding fluorescence taking his sight, the booming of the collisions deafening him. He no longer had any sense of what was happening on the outside. The cage see-sawed wildly but the two monks holding him suspended over the Qembana moved not one iota.

'When I give the word, boy, plunge the knife in deep and slash it across,' ordered the herdsman, turning his back on everyone to watch Tragen's magic feeding on itself. 'Good…very good, that is what my God wishes, wizard! You cannot halt the power in your staff now, it will rage as never before.'

And Beatrix railed as never before. And as her fear for Aidan increased so did the light pouring from her body. It burned as bright as the light in Tragen's cage and once again Zorzecai was distracted. He turned and studied her, marvelling at another wizard within his grasp. Surely there could be no doubt, more than enough power was now at hand to open the Gateway. Her light blinded him to all else around, it was Zorzecai's turn to be bewitched. It wasn't magic that held him. It was the ultimate fascination that a creature of the dark held for pure, unblemished light. He couldn't take his eyes off her.

The light also distracted Augusta and, in pure desperation, she mindmelded a plea to the Brakwanna. *Mazumbai, we can't let this demon win without fighting back, please…help us!'*

'How, warrior wizard, what can we do? We are chained ready to follow the abbot into the mist.'

Augusta, the warrior wizard, named as such by the small black man speaking silently to her, did not want the life it signified. She did not want to kill; she wanted to believe Aidan's exhortations not to harm another's soul even if part of her felt they were naïve beliefs. But she couldn't deny her upbringing. All the years of watching her father's soldiers train…her own skills with the sword which all royal children had to acquire, being female no excuse, all now dictated her moves. Whether she liked it or not she was the warrior wizard.

Concentrating on the chain, she ran her mind along the full length of it and opened every single bolt. The manacles fell from each slave's ankle.

'Take care…the monks cannot be killed by ordinary means their souls have already passed over. You must either disable them or

throw them into the fog!' Augusta warned, blocking out the horror of her words.

Mazumbai, recovering quickly from his astonishment, shouted to his freed countrymen. 'Now...for Brakwanna, our dead and our friends, throw the monks into the Qembana!'

And all hell broke loose as two hundred emaciated men, women and children attacked over five hundred fit, strong monks.

At first, surprise was on the side of the small slaves. And because they were so much shorter and lighter than their opponents and vastly more desperate, the Brakwannans moved faster. The men following Mulumba, Akumamba and Nkoross, nipping in, under and around the taller monks fought in teams of twos and threes, the children and women led by Mantawi and Nkimba, grouping together in gangs of even greater numbers.

And the initial attack was successful primarily because the taller, stronger monks were totally unprepared for the assault. They knew how to fight but it seemed that the signals from the brain received by each limb took a lot longer than was normal to create the stroke intended. By the time a monk's nerves had passed a message to the necessary muscle to tell it to lift his arm or kick with his leg the purpose of the retaliatory action had become superfluous.

There was no planning in the battle no formal charge or counter-charge, it was a melee, a totally chaotic riot, a great number of isolated clashes. Brakwannans clung to their adversaries like limpets. Once an engagement had commenced it continued until either was hurt too badly to continue the struggle or he or she passed into the smog and froze. Monks were borne to the ground, their heads hammered repeatedly on the stone flags of the floor, concussion or skull fractures rendering them incapable of continuing the fight.

Brakwannans dragged monks to the edge of the Qembana and pushed the white-robed men into the mist, or in their frenzy and pursuit of revenge still clinging to their opponent, slave and monk both fell into the miasma. The slave to watch through eyes in frozen bodies, not dead yet as the Lobos talisman had not been sounded for the dagger was in Aidan's hands. The soulless monk already dead disintegrated immediately his body turning the black rock to smog.

Between the Qembana and the dungeons bitter fighting took place—blindly, with great anger and a desperate bravery. But time, numbers and physical strength found in the monks' favour.

The first and second ranks of the monks' defence crumpled under the onslaught. But in due course the slaves came up against the vast bulk of the remaining monks and they could move forward no longer. The small gaps opened in the lines by Mulumba and Nkoross filled with reinforcements from the tiers of seats around the walls and from those standing in the aisles. The monks ultimately, almost by accident it seemed, formed an impenetrable wall between the slaves, the Qembana and Aidan on the altar.

And the fighting slowed as exhaustion swiftly set in. The adrenalin peaked quickly in the slaves' starved bodies and dissipated just as fast.

The Brakwannans had no weapons. Hands and feet were used by Mantawi and Nkimba to gouge unprotected eyes and pummel faces and bodies. Those monks who were unarmed used pure brawn, grabbing and squeezing and tearing until necks or limbs broke. But there were other hooded figures with poleaxes and spears and these wrought terrible mutilations.

The initial onslaught could not last. The forward surge of the slaves, slowed by lack of strength, petered out eventually until both sides were fighting toe to toe neither gaining ground.

A little later it was the turn of the larger, stronger monks to force the Brakwannans to retreat towards the dungeons.

But the slaves were bent on revenge. They had existed for years in squalor, starving, forced to watch loved ones die sometimes by their own hands as their spirit broke, others becoming the obscene sacrifices of the abbot. Having nothing to lose but their lives which were forfeit anyway, they exerted themselves way beyond their physical capabilities, each success begging another. But strive as they might, they were still not strong enough to beat their foe alone.

The monks with an odd unearthly glint in their eyes retaliated with an alien dedication, fighting silently, never giving in even when hurt. They picked up the smaller Brakwannans in arms twice as thick as the slaves' thighs and threw them over the heads of other slaves to land on stone floors, their bones crumbling before they even came to rest. Monks stepped over and on the bodies of the fallen not bothering to distinguish between white robes or dirty britches, showing an utter callousness for whoever was in the way. Wounded or dead they were trod on, ground into the floor.

Augusta, her heart pounding, used her magic and lifted the discarded pile of tools at the dungeon entrance and dropped the

494

weapons among the slaves. The hammers and chisels and sundry metal baskets were grabbed gratefully and urgently by the Brakwannans. The monks, some dragging their broken limbs, were again driven back to the basin's edge.

But, despite being totally outnumbered as more of the monks left their seats around the chamber to aid their silent comrades, the slaves chanted their battle songs bludgeoned heads and limbs, scratched at eyes, stamped on those who fell. They were reaping recompense for all their countrymen dead at the hands of the unfeeling, soulless, silent monks and their mad leaders.

A cohort of slaves led by the old Akumamba, who seemed to have been born again such was his fervour, succeeded in breaking through the wall of monks and turning to their sides attacked the monks from the centre. They pushed their white-robed enemy into the pulsating black cloud and created a wider rift, splitting the body of the monks in two. But the slaves were terribly weak. At the edge of the mist slave and monk continued to disappear together into the Qembana.

But as they battled they received assistance from an unexpected quarter. Thaddeus, ceasing his abortive mindmelding to attract the attention of Aidan, discovered the presence of rodents scurrying frantically beneath the surface of the stone-slabbed floor. Attracted by the overwhelming lure of blood and guts the rats had overcome their initial fear of the chamber. Thaddeus called them to him, and he directed them at the monks, and there were hundreds. Mazumbai forced to rest, his stamina all but gone, watched as a black horde of the long-tailed rodents attacked and overpowered his opponent. But it took at least five minutes to subdue the big monk, dismally slow considering there were hundreds more white robes waiting to join the battle.

But the rats gave new heart to the Brakwannans and the small black men rose again. Now, slaves and rodents fought side by side. The slaves swinging hammers smashed faces; those with chisels stabbed and tore at flesh. And the rats swarmed over the unnaturally silent men, nipping at bare flesh, clawing at eyes, ears and mouths with tiny, devilishly sharp teeth.

And while the slaves and rats battled the monks on one side of the basin, so did the wizards and the prisoners on the other side. Augusta severed the nooses freeing them from all constraints. The clan leaders along with Janne and the remaining members of the Quota fought with a ferocity equalling those of the slaves.

Janne launched a furious attack on those around him and pushed his way forward slowly through the horde of white robes towards the herdsman.

Bazyli Montetor and Lodovico Portolan drifted away from Marcus and fought desperately to get to the altar, their aim to rescue Aidan thwarted by a phalanx of monks bearing poleaxes. But the zombie-like enemy were dismally slow. It took little effort to dodge the thrusts of the weapons, but wrenching the long poles from the monks' strong hands took time they did not have.

Thaddeus fought with the rats, directing them to where the most vicious fighting was taking place. It didn't strike him until later that somehow his magic had changed, he was now directing the emotions of the animals, no longer just reading them.

Augusta, her normal feelings buried deep, used dead bodies to hamper the monks; lifting the cadavers with her magic she used them as missiles.

Beattie's whole awareness, though, was riveted on Zorzecai and despite the dreadful clamour around her she continued to engage the attention of the herdsman, mesmerizing him with her light.

But the sheer numbers were again defeating them. As one monk went down three more took his place, and Bazyli, Lodovico and Marcus were overwhelmed in turn and borne to the ground. The wizards, their magic powerless against the monks, were next and they wept with frustration as they capitulated to their far stronger opponents.

And all the while the herdsman laughed. Zorzecai was in raptures, protected by his God from magic and by his monks from physical harm. Although his fascination for the light held his eyes on Beatrix, his awareness of the battle was unimpaired.

The resultant pain and agony on both sides nurtured his God; the bodies fed the black rock and changed it rapidly to smog and the agitation within the black miasma surged. It was of no concern to him whether it was slave, prisoner or monk that died, as long as someone died in agony. His plan's success was very close now, a few minutes more that's all.

And all the while, Aidan lay on the slab, holding the dagger in place awaiting the demon's order to stab downwards into his abdomen, oblivious to all. And Tragen, trapped within his staff's magic remained insensible to all outside his cage.

But what no-one had perceived was the reaction of Leash. He couldn't take his eyes from Aidan. The smell of lavender was even greater now that the boy was nearer him. But this time the aroma was not only emanating from the young wizard, it seemed to be oozing from the pores of Leash as well.

Leash studied Aidan's face, his black hair, his large brown eyes brimming with misery. And it was that wretchedness that he recognized. He'd seen that look before, that and the shape of the boy's jaw-line, his mouth…her jaw-line…her mouth!

There was such a deluge of noise that no-one noticed the manic howling of the Wanting had ceased. For Leash, his demon and the lady had made their decision.

Leash now allowed the sickly sweet smell of blood to wash over him, engulf him. He allowed the vampyrus to take complete control—he needed its strength. He stared ahead of him, his senses reeling, his purpose plain, his motive uncertain.

Leash submerged his psyche in his demon's senses and prepared to make his move. All he could smell was blood; all he could taste was blood, all he could see was blood. He bathed in it. But the blood before his eyes was on the red robe in front of him—the blood-soaked raiment worn by Zorzecai the Collector.

And Leash's body changed, his fingernails turned black and grew irregularly long. His skin twitched, rapid ripples running through his abnormally strengthened facial muscles, the white sclera in his eyes pulsing red around the pitch-black, oval irises. His hair hung lank, sweat dripping from the ends to join the perspiration oozing from every pore on his body.

Leash sucked in his breath and using his enormous strength, he grasped the ropes both sides of his neck and yanked violently. The two monks swung together so speedily and unexpectedly that their bald heads collided…but only Leash heard the crunch as both skulls crushed liked chicken's eggs.

He swiftly removed the ropes from his neck.

And Leash lunged for the blood on the herdsman.

Zorzecai, his back to the vampyrus, was still captivated by the pure light created by Beatrix though his attention was on the battle. He was satisfied that no-one would escape. The slaves were all but overcome, isolated pockets of resistance here and there, the Griffin prisoners restrained once more and no threat. He cherished the carnage, more fodder for his God! He smiled; the presence of a Green Man had, after all, not interfered in any way with his plans.

He turned his full attention once more on the girl, Beattie's luminosity had reached a purity he had never encountered before; she could not be seen within the radiance, he marvelled at her strength.

Zorzecai, the Herdsman of Purgatory, Collector for his God, had no chance.

Leash reached out, the Wanting totally possessing him. His fingers curled around the neck of Zorzecai and Leash tore the herdsman's head from his shoulders. And as the head fell, to roll into the fog in front of Beatrix, Leash plunged his mouth into the gaping neck wound and feasted on the hot blood spurting from Zorzecai's jugular.

And as the herdsman dropped dead, so did every monk in the chamber, their atypical animation tied irrevocably to that of the life of the demon herdsman. Slaves about to die at the hands of the monks were suddenly reprieved as their opponents dropped before their eyes. The Griffin prisoners, shaking off their shackles, scrambled free of their captors.

And Aidan screamed.

The herdsman's death had not only released the strictures on the prisoners, and curtailed the battle with the Brakwannans; the monks holding Tragen's cage suspended above the cloud of smog had also dropped lifeless to the banks of the Qembana.

Aidan continued to scream as the cage slowly fell, the magic within emitting a light so bright it was too unbearable to watch. The cage disappeared within the dense black cloud taking Tragen with it.

The survivors looked on in helpless disbelief. Aidan, the knife wrenched from his hands by Bazyli, leapt from the altar on the dais and lunged towards the mist, his desperate leap into the Qembana halted by Janne.

Time seemed to stop; everyone stared at the smog rumbling wildly, the noise now so violent it was hurting their ears. And as they stared they could make out the frozen bodies of the slaves floating, trapped in the black vapour, their eyes sparkling with terror awaiting their death.

'Keep that dagger away from that thing…that pyramid on the altar,' screamed Lodovico, desperately. 'Do not let it sound!' he turned and sought out Augusta slumped wearily on the ground.

'Augusta, can you save them, can you draw them from the gateway?'

'What?'

'The slaves frozen in the fog…can you drag them out? We may be able to save them!' Lodovico implored desperately. 'They are not dead yet. If you can bring them out of the fog before that thing sounds by some other means, they may survive.'

Augusta at last understood through her exhaustion and she stood a little way from the edge of what was undoubtedly the gateway to hell and beckoned to each figure within the mist. Mazumbai and his people held them as their bodies thawed and laid them on the ground to recover…some inevitably yielded to their injuries but their souls flew free of the Darkness. Aidan watched as they passed over, safe finally from the depredations of Zorzecai.

'Augusta, find Tragen, bring him out…please,' begged Aidan frantically.

'Oh, Aidan…she cannot,' said Beattie, her light dimming, her despair choking her. 'I'm sorry, Aidan, but he's gone.'

'What do you mean? He fell into the fog we all saw him! If Augusta can bring the Brakwannans out, she can do the same for Tragen.'

'I'm sorry, Aidan, but Tragen is no longer in the mist. I watched his light disappear into the rock. I don't know where he is.'

Aidan looked from one to the other, from Beatrix to Augusta, and suddenly his face crumpled and he turned away. Completely devastated he roamed among the injured, healing where he could.

Thaddeus followed wherever he went, never taking his eyes from him, afraid in case his friend made a run for the violently pulsating fog. He returned to the rats their free will as he roved and they scurried away to disappear beneath the floor of the cavern.

Augusta, panting heavily, fell wearily to the floor.

Anders, fell to his knees at the wall of colours sweat pouring from him, but as he gasped with relief he was distracted by something he couldn't quite understand.

Lodovico Portolan stood and surveyed the carnage around him, still unable to understand how they had managed to fight free. Chief Mazumbai, cradling a broken arm, walked across to him. They stared at each other silently, each recognizing a brave and powerful ally.

'How, Mazumbai…how are we still alive?'

'Wizards, my friend…wizards…and a vampyrus!'

And then they noticed there was still one sound that could be heard over all, the repulsive slurping of the deformed Leash, his head almost buried in the neck of the decapitated demon. Ignoring everyone, he sated the Wanting on the herdsman's body, it would be a while before he remembered his reason for killing Zorzecai.

Leonid, the Green Man, released from the dungeons when his guards fell dead, stood to one side shocked to his very core. Although he'd already contemplated it himself, death wantonly inflicted was against the very nature of the Green People. Leonid stared into the violently pulsating Qembana along with Bazyli Montetor and Marcus Janne, all three wondering at their miraculous survival, equally stunned at the demise of the wizard.

'Come, my friends,' Mazumbai said, calling to a few of the Brakwannans walking around inspecting the bodies of their slain, hunting for loved ones, assisting the injured. 'Let us leave this evil place,' he turned to Lodovico and grasped his arm. 'My friend, I and my countrymen will be delighted to see daylight again after spending all these years in the bowels of this volcano.'

'I presume the quickest way is up the stairs through that door, am I correct?' Portolan asked.

'We have watched that doorway, dreamed of walking up those steps for so long now, I am almost afraid to go through it.'

'Mazumbai, we will forever be in your debt,' said Lodovico Portolan unable to smile, the terrible strain having etched deep lines in his grey face.

'Brakwanna will always count Griffin as friend—we have seen the ultimate evil and survived together,' intoned Mazumbai turning to gather in what was left of his people.

'Come Thaddeus, it is all over. Come, all of you, let us leave this hell-hole to the demons,' said Lodovico, standing over his son.

Turning their backs on the churning, black miasma, they walked slowly towards the open doorway and freedom. Halfway there silence descended like a thunderclap on the black smog.

They all spun around and discovered that the herdsman had won.

A terrible rumble erupted from the Qembana. The black fog slowly expanded and overran the edges of the basin. The Darkness had breached the divide. It was leaking into Life, into this world and along with it came the demented noises of the tormented souls trapped within it.

The Gateway to Purgatory was wide open.

And they ran, slaves, prisoners, wizards all, stricken with terror they ran towards the door through which the herdsman had entered the chamber, leaving Leash behind still gorging.

'Augusta,' Thaddeus shouted, 'bring the roof down over the dungeon, we have to seal the Darkness inside!'

With a tremendous roar, the rocks above the entrance to the cages came crashing down, the dust billowing up, obscuring that end of the chamber. And when they all exited, Augusta did the same with the lintel over the door, not caring that Leash remained inside.

Bazyli called a halt at the head of the long stairway, everyone gasping, stooping to catch their breath and at the same time covering their mouths to keep the dust from their lungs. Augusta had reached the end of her tether, she had conjured an enormous amount of magic over the last hour and it had exacted its toll on the warrior wizard. When everyone had recovered their breath, with Marcus Janne carrying Augusta in his arms and Aidan, Beatrix and Thaddeus helping each other, they stumbled along the long passageway leading up into the oratory.

Of the two hundred slaves that had been discovered in the dungeons, only ninety-five led by Chief Mazumbai, with Akumamba, Mantawi, Mulumba and Nkimba, sadly Nkoross had died, walked or were carried out into fresh air and freedom. Lodovico Portolan, Bazyli Montetor, Marcus Janne and Leonid, the four wizards, Aidan, Thaddeus, Augusta and Beatrix, all sat on the rocks at the side of the footpath leading down to the Grim tied up at the jetty.

Racing up the hillside from the harbour, came Captain Hugo Locklear, with Dolly alongside him, a knife in each hand. These two were far in the van of the rest of the crew running up the slope.

Locklear had ordered the rescue party to disembark when the monks standing on the jetty, fell dead.

Forty

The next hours were hectic and yet proceeded with a dreamlike quality for Aidan. The insanity of the last few hours and days was deep seated in his psyche. The loss of his master numbed his senses to such an extent that he sleepwalked through the rest of the night.

Injured Brakwannans and the half a dozen felons, surviving remnants of the Quota, were helped aboard the Grim by the bemused crew, followed by the exhausted and traumatized passengers. Only Aidan's instincts kept him going the rounds healing each and every injured victim…healing others always gave him ease.

But, of course, the numbers that needed his ministrations finally came to an end, leaving him with time to think. And that did the damage…thinking…and lying down on his bed. For his guilt devastated him so deeply that he cut himself off from everyone.

Hugo Locklear, already grieving for Anders, now had to grieve for his best friend Tragen. He coped by organizing a search for replacement masts, keeping busy stopped him thinking of the terrible manner of his friend's death.

Augusta, Beatrix and Thaddeus who had all slept for only a few hours were now watching over Aidan deeply asleep in his bunk.

Anders speaking from his place in Limbo was frightened. *'The Darkness is drifting into the wall of colours and I can see shapes within it. What are we going to do? We just can't sit here.'*

'When the replacement masts are on board we'll transport them to Griffin to carry out repairs and then have a formal council of war, I suppose,' said Thaddeus glumly.

'By the Gods, I'm glad we're out of there,' said Augusta, putting in words their enormous relief at their unexpected release from the indescribable horrors…and from imminent death. 'Poor Tragen, I shall miss him dreadfully,' she said miserably.

'Poor Aidan,' said Beatrix, holding the boy's hand tight.

'And all those Brakwannans who died fighting to the end,' said Thaddeus.

'Yes, now they've escaped they'll be able to get home from Griffin,' said Beatrix.

'I wish you'd all escaped, Beattie,' said Anders equally miserable. *Tragen was taken by the Darkness…his soul is trapped,'* and his voice suddenly cracked. *'How do I tell Aidan?'*

'There is something else I have not told any of you,' said Beatrix, forlornly. 'This gift of light that I have means that no light blinds me. At the end…at the end I saw Tragen using his staff to try and break free as the cage fell through the floor. Don't you understand?' she asked as they stared at her, not comprehending. 'Every time Tragen has used his staff lately, it has sent Aidan into the Darkness! We have to rouse him. He has to fight whatever it is sends him there!'

'Aidan is going to come here anyway! Zorzecai's body may still be in the chamber but his soul is here in the Darkness,' and with his voice sounding as if he was being strangled, Anders added. *'He still has Tragen!'*

It was at that moment they felt the Grim lurch and leave the jetty, and Leonid came running into the cabin.

'The Darkness, we can see it…it is leaking from the sewer outfall,' he stared at them, his green face turning grey.

'We flee!'

Leash was fortunate. He watched from the corner of his eye as the wizards and their friends escaped unable to leave the body of the herdsman until the Wanting was sated. Lifting his head from the neck of Zorzecai, his face dripping blood, he recalled the wizards coming up through the sewer.

Racing from the smog billowing into the chamber, he hurriedly removed rocks from the fall at the dungeon gate. It didn't take him long; satisfying the Wanting had restored not only his mind but his strength as well. Escaping into the passageway through the dungeons, leaving a hole in the rockfall, he climbed down into the sewer before the Darkness could trap him.

Reaching the outfall, he discovered Janne's fishing boat, and now he was safely ensconced on board, lying on the bottom boards between the thwarts fast asleep dreaming his safe dream knowing that she was happy with him. They had found each other again over the demon's protestations.

His body returned to normal, the boat drifted out to sea, northwards of the Grim.

His tongue was swollen, it filled his mouth, and his lips cracked, impossibly dry. With eyes gummed tight shut and his hearing muffled, he strained to make sense of his surroundings. Cocooned in warmth, he felt gloriously safe. And then he felt a strange tickling in his mouth and throat. He frowned trying to identify the hot sweet drink someone was trickling into his mouth. He couldn't, and didn't much care. He swallowed reflexively and coughed once. Drinking more, he licked his lips, feeling the cracks in the skin already healing.

Resting a moment, he listened to the sound of his heart beating rhythmically in his chest, felt the blood pounding through his veins. And then he listened to his breathing…shallow, but getting stronger by the minute. He squirmed in the blanket feeling the texture of the wool against his cheek, and he turned his head into the small breeze wafting across his face. His hearing improved dramatically, his ears no longer blocked. And he smiled, identifying Anselm's voice. But who was that with him, the one with the sing-song tones?

Anselm wiped a warm damp cloth across Shadra's eyes to remove the stickiness, and the small green forest elf opened them for the first time in days and peered up at the human who was still cradling him. And he smiled again, Anselm grinning joyously in return. Shadra looked towards the entrance of what he now saw was a cave and found his other friend, too big to come closer. Ryn, tears in his eyes, twisted his beak into what he deemed to be a wonderful smile, welcoming Shadra back to the living.

And then the sing-song voice spoke from somewhere near Shadra's feet, and the small elf looked in that direction, but the owner of the voice he could not see at first.

'Welcome, cousin. We have not had the pleasure of the company of a schrat for many, many years.'

Shadra wrinkled his brow. 'That is an ancient name, not even my grandfather was ever called a schrat…forest elves we have been named for centuries. Who are you?'

And then, from behind Anselm, appeared a tall figure with pointy ears, the same stature as a human—a pale skinned elf.

And Shadra smiled ecstatically. 'You are liosalfar…you are the guardians of the legend!'

'I am Roidan, liosalfar yes. Legend? I'm afraid I know naught of what you speak,' the pale skinned elf spoke quietly hiding extreme shock. How had this little one known of what they guarded?

'Come, Roidan, I feel the Cragga near. We have been here days too long we must get them to Alfhime…now!' Xelnor said, unable to keep the fear from his voice.

THE END

504

Lightning Source UK Ltd.
Milton Keynes UK
UKOW05f1140121113

220882UK00002B/355/P